Harry Turtledove (signature)

HARRY TURTLEDOVE

THIS SPECIAL SIGNED EDITION
IS LIMITED TO 1000 NUMBERED COPIES.

THIS IS COPY 664 .

THE BEST OF
HARRY
TURTLEDOVE

THE BEST OF
HARRY
TURTLEDOVE

SUBTERRANEAN PRESS 2021

First Edition

ISBN
978-1-64524-022-8

Subterranean Press
PO Box 190106
Burton, MI 48519

subterraneanpress.com

Manufactured in the United States of America

Table of CONTENTS

THE VISITOR FROM THE
EAST

Oh, hell," Bill Williamson said when the alarm clock assassinated a particularly juicy dirty dream. Cussing at it didn't make it shut up. Resigned that the dream was dead—he'd never be so limber in real life—the Governor of the state of Jefferson hit the top of the clock with a massive fist. He got the OFF button and didn't break the clock, though not from lack of effort.

Yawning, he sat up in bed. "So early?" his wife muttered.

"Sorry, Louise," Bill said. "But I've got the get to the coast to greet the visitor, and Yreka ain't exactly coastal."

He lumbered into the bathroom and did what needed doing in there, then pulled a pair of shorts up over the thick, reddish hair on his legs. His wallet sat in one pocket; his keys clinked in the other. Out he went, to grab some breakfast before he hit the road.

Ceilings in the Governor's Mansion were thirteen feet tall. Doorways were ten feet high. Bill, at nine-two, didn't need to worry about ducking or bashing his head every time he went through one. Charlie "Bigfoot" Lewis, the second Governor of Jefferson—and the one who built the mansion during Coolidge prosperity—had been a sasquatch himself, and ran it up on a scale that suited his own comfort. Too big for humans, he'd figured, was easier to deal with than too small for his own folk. Bill blessed him for that.

"Here you go, Governor," the steward said when he walked into the dining room. "Coffee's hot, and breakfast'll be up in a minute."

"Thanks, Ray." Bill drank coffee by the quart mug. He was halfway down his first cup when Ray brought him eight fried eggs, a pound of bacon, and a dozen slices of wheat toast. As he plowed through the food, he hoped he wouldn't get hungry while he was driving.

The Stars and Stripes and the state flag of Jefferson flew in front of the mansion. Jefferson's banner was green, with the state seal centered on the field: a gold pan with two X's that symbolized the double-crosses northern California and southern Oregon had got from Sacramento and Salem till they formed their own state in 1919. After World War I, self-determination was all the rage in Europe, and they'd run with it here, too. That neither Sacramento nor Salem was exactly sorry to see the seceders go hadn't hurt.

Below the flagpole sat the Governor's car: a 1974 Cadillac Eldorado he fondly called "The Mighty Mo." The Detroit behemoth wasn't quite the size of a battleship, but it came close. It was five years old now, getting long in the tooth, but he kept it anyway. Since the Arab oil crisis, cars had shrunk like wool washed hot. For someone Bill's size, they'd gone from dubious to impossible. The Mighty Mo got next to no mileage, of course, and gas was six bits a gallon. Bill didn't care. If the state wouldn't pay, he would.

He slid into the left rear seat: the driver's seat, with a long, long shaft for the steering wheel. The ignition was on the column, not on the dash. *A good thing, too*, he thought, starting the car.

Like the Governor's Mansion, the Capitol had gone up before the Depression hit. Wings and colonnades and gilded dome showed off

Jefferson's wealth, or maybe delusions of grandeur. The government office building next door? A square WPA block, as ugly as it was functional. The miracle was that it had got built at all.

Barbara Rasmussen waited in front of the office building. The Governor's publicist was highly functional, too, but far from ugly: a shapely blonde with big blue eyes. To use Jimmy Carter's immortal and immoral phrase, Bill had looked on her with lust in his heart a time or two. He was married, but he wasn't blind. Sasquatches and little people had been getting it on since long before blondes came to Jefferson—not all the time, but every so often. Some stories said one of Bill's great-grandmothers was a little person. He didn't know if that was true, or care.

Barbara got into the right—and only—front seat. "Morning, Governor," she said. "Early enough for you?"

"Oh, pretty much," he answered, miming a yawn. She laughed. He sometimes wondered if she was interested in a roll in the hay with him. Some little women (not at all in the Louisa May Alcott sense of the words) hopefully looked for sasquatch men to be big all over. They were seldom disappointed in that. Other ways? Men were men and women were women, big or small. Sometimes they clicked, sometimes they didn't.

None of which mattered right now. His size thirty-two right foot swung from brake to gas. Away the Mighty Mo went. He drove south on Jefferson State Highway 3 to the 299, then west toward the coast. What Jefferson called state highways would have been narrow, twisty, no-account two-lane blacktop roads anywhere else. That was partly because the state hadn't really bounced back after Hoover's name became a swear word, partly because the terrain was so rugged.

From Yreka to Eureka was just over 200 miles: three hours on an uncrowded freeway, assuming there was any such animal. Setting out just after six, Bill pulled into Eureka just before eleven. The overturned logging truck sure didn't help. The ship he was supposed to meet was due in at eleven-thirty. That cut it closer than he liked.

His back crunched when he unfolded himself from the Eldorado. A car that big wasn't meant for those roads, but he didn't fit into anything smaller. "Hey, Gov!" somebody called. Bill waved a broad-palmed hand. Sasquatch or little person, no pol could ignore constituents.

A few reporters and a couple of camera crews waited at the base of the pier where the *Heiwa Maru* would dock. Its arrival would be news here and in Yreka and Redding and Ashland and Port Orford and the rest of Jefferson. Maybe one of these birds was an AP stringer, in which case the story might go farther. But the gentlemen of the Fourth Estate just stood idly, some smoking cigarettes. "What's happening?" Bill called.

"Not a damn thing," a Eureka newspaperman answered. "Harbormaster says the ship's running an hour late." He sounded disgusted.

Bill was delighted. "In that case, we've got time for lunch. C'mon, Barbara. Let's hit Freaky Willie's."

The diner was only a block from the harbor. BIGGEST SHAKES IN TOWN, a sign painted on the window bragged, next to a picture of a sasquatch doing a swan dive into a strawberry milkshake. Bill didn't think he'd want to try that. He'd never get the goo out of his pelt afterwards. But the food was good and abundant and cheap, all of which mattered even if he was on state business and putting it on the taxpayer's tab.

He inhaled three Ginormous Burgers and half a farm's worth of fries, along with two of those big shakes (chocolate). Barbara ate, well, rather less.

Another citizen greeted him as he came out. Bill's hand didn't quite engulf the other man's when they shook. Haystack Thornton was a little man, but a big little man, close to seven feet tall and wide in proportion. He might have been part sasquatch himself. His bushy russet beard rose high on his cheeks, while his hairline came down almost to his eyebrows.

He wore bib overalls and a Pendleton underneath; Eureka had to be twenty-five degrees cooler than Yreka.

"Just wanted to tell you thanks for all you've done and for all you haven't done, Governor," he said. "Me and my friends appreciate it, believe me."

"No worries, man," Bill said. Haystack Thornton and his friends were the leading growers of some highly unofficial crops around Eureka. Jefferson looked the other way, and wouldn't help the Feds when they didn't. *Do your own thing* had been a way of life here long before the hippies found it. Besides, Bill thought smoking marijuana was more fun than drinking beer, though nothing was wrong with beer, either.

Thornton ambled into Freaky Willie's. Bill and Barbara went back to the harbor. Sure enough, the *Heiwa Maru*—Japanese for *Peace Ship*—had come into Humboldt Bay. A pavilion of saffron cloth stood on the deck before the bridge. *Good thing it's August,* Bill thought. *I wouldn't want to cross the Pacific under canvas in January.*

Snorting tugs nudged the *Heiwa Maru* into place. Lines snaked out from the ship. Longshoremen secured them to bollards. Down came the gangplank. Bill, Barbara, and the reporters and cameramen strode down the pier to meet the ship and its important passenger.

"Permission to come aboard?" the Governor called to the Japanese skipper at the far end of the gangplank.

"Permission granted," the man said in good English. He added, "Have no fear, sir. It will bear your weight."

"I expected it would." Onto the *Heiwa Maru* Bill went. The skipper bowed. Bill bowed back. As he straightened, a Japanese sailor snapped a photo of him.

Bill walked toward the pavilion. The saffron cloth on one side folded back and the Yeti Lama came out to greet him. "Hello, Governor Williamson," the holy man said, his English more hesitant than the skipper's. He wore a loincloth and cape of scarlet silk to show his rank. Two other yetis, both in saffron loincloths and capes, followed him. So did two saffron-robed human monks. The big folk never could have used ordinary cabins.

The Yeti Lama was someone Bill could look up to—literally. He overtopped the Governor by six inches. Anyone seeing them side by side could tell they were of the same kind but different races. In little-people terms, they might have been Mongol and Swede. The yeti's pelt was browner than the sasquatch's; he had broader cheekbones and lower brow ridges.

"Welcome, your Holiness," Bill said. "Welcome to America. Welcome to Jefferson."

"I thank you so much." The Yeti Lama bowed and held his hands in front of himself with palms pressed together. Bill imitated the gesture. The newcomer looked to be in his mid-forties, near the Governor's age. Along with many pious members of his folk, he'd fled into exile when the Chinese invaded his mountainous Tibetan homeland twenty years before.

One reason more reporters weren't here was that Washington and Beijing had been thick as thieves since Nixon went to China. To the State Department, the Yeti Lama was just another tourist. Bill had all sorts of reasons for feeling otherwise.

A newshound who worked for a paper in Redding called, "Your Holiness, can you tell us why you came to Jefferson in particular?"

"Oh, yes. It is my pleasure." The Yeti Lama's English wasn't perfect, but he used what he had. "Jefferson in all the world is where I most feel a sense of, ah, communing—"

"Of community, you mean, sir?" Bill said helpfully.

The Yeti Lama smiled. His teeth were large and broad. One bore a gold crown. "I thank you. Yes, that is the word. A sense of community. You have in Jefferson mountains, and I of course grew up in mountains. Yours are small, but that is a trifle."

"We think they're pretty good-sized." Bill waved east, toward the Klamath Mountains serrating the horizon.

"I hear many have trees all the way up to top." The Yeti Lama smiled again, mischievously now. "Next to the Himalayas, that makes them foothills. Is right word, foothills?"

"Foothills is the word, yeah. You've got me there," Bill allowed.

"But this is not important," the Yeti Lama said. "It is only land. People on land, they are what matters. You here in America, you here in Jefferson especially, you set example for the world. Here you have small folk and large, living together in happiness and harmony. Here you have one of a large race, chosen peacefully, freely, by large and small to lead all. Not like this in land I come from. Chinese call us *xueren*—snowmen." His heavy features twisted in sorrow, or perhaps anger. "They treat us abominable—ah, abominably."

"I'm not even Jefferson's first sasquatch Governor, either," Bill said. State pride counted. The less said about earlier times, when this land was squabbled over by Russia and Spain, then split between California and Oregon, the better. But little people with guns hadn't hunted sasquatches for the fun of it in more than a hundred years. That was progress, any way you looked at it. Sasquatches had guns of their own now, too.

And, when you thought about what China was doing to yetis and Tibetans alike, Jefferson had to look like heaven on earth by comparison. No wonder the Yeti Lama wanted to call here.

Barbara said, "Can we all get together for pictures to show this harmony?" She turned to the *Heiwa Maru*'s skipper. "Captain, please join us with some of your men. Everyone gets along in Jefferson."

"That's right," Bill said. "Next month I'm going up to Port Orford to visit a businessman there. He moved to Jefferson from Japan more than fifteen years ago."

The captain spoke in Japanese. He and three sailors joined the Yeti Lama, his retinue, the sasquatch Governor, and the blond publicist.

Barbara was taller than any of the crewmen from the *Heiwa Maru* or the human Buddhist monks, but even she barely came up to Bill's chest.

Well, that was the point of this exercise, wasn't it? Sure it was. Big people and little people could all get along together. Different kinds of big people could, too. And so could different kinds of little people, even if their countries had fought a ferocious war only half a lifetime earlier.

The skipper's wrinkles and bald spot said he was old enough to have fought for Japan against the USA. But, again, even if he had, so what? He was here in Jefferson in charge of the *Peace Ship*. He'd brought the Yeti Lama, one of the greatest peace symbols in the whole world (except perhaps China). That was what counted.

"Smile, everybody!" a cameraman called. Everybody did.

PEACE IS
BETTER

Here we go again, Barbara," Bill Williamson said. "Ready to roll?"

Barbara Rasmussen nodded. From the left rear seat of the Mighty Mo, the sasquatch Governor of Jefferson watched his publicist's blond curls bob up and down above the back of the right front seat. "I sure am," she said. PR people never lacked for enthusiasm. That sometimes made them scary, but they needed it.

"Then we'll do it." Bill stepped on the gas. He stood nine feet two in his stocking feet, though he was much too hairy ever to have put on stockings. The back seat of a car as humongous as his '74 Caddy with the extra-long steering column let him drive for himself, which he enjoyed.

Yreka had been a state capital for sixty years now, but it was still a sleepy little place. Anyway, the government office building lay only a couple of blocks from the onramps to the I-5: Jefferson's backbone and, when you got right down to it, the whole Pacific Coast's.

He put pedal to the metal as soon as he swung onto the northbound Interstate. He didn't worry about fifty-five, or about saving gas. Even at fifty-five, the Mighty Mo's mileage was a joke. The Eldorado's engine was only a little smaller than a World War II fighter's. The beast weighed as much as a Messerschmitt-109, too, especially with him in it.

Fifteen minutes out of Yreka, he and Barbara rolled through Hilt, which was two gas stations and a Burger King. A moment later, Barbara said, "The old border between California and Oregon was somewhere right around here."

"Sure was." As if on cue, they passed a road sign that said WELCOME TO JACKSON COUNTY. Bill went on, "That was Oregon. Siskiyou, where we were, used to be in California. We don't miss Sacramento—"

"Or Salem," Barbara put in.

"Or Salem," Bill agreed. "And they don't miss us."

Another hour put them at Wolf Creek, where they got off the Interstate and onto Jefferson State Highway 71. No one ever called it that, though, not even to make Highway 71 Revisited jokes. "Here we are," Barbara said as they headed toward the ocean, "on the Gable Memorial Highway."

Now Bill was the one who nodded his big, shaggy head. Unless in the rear-view mirror, Barbara couldn't see that, so he said, "You betcha. If ever a politician delivered for his home town, Gilbert Gable was the guy. Without him, Port Orford wouldn't be much bigger than Hilt back there."

If not for Gilbert Gable, who became Governor of Jefferson in 1934, miles of the road across the mountains to Port Orford probably would still remain unpaved. If not for Gilbert Gable, the railroad probably wouldn't have gone through. If not for Gilbert Gable, the big breakwater that turned Port Orford into a proper port probably would never have been built. If not for Gable and FDR and the WPA and the CCC and the other half-forgotten thickets of Depression-era initials...

He died in the saddle, three days before Pearl Harbor. The papers called it acute indigestion. Bill had heard from Yreka old-timers that he drank like a fish. Drunk or sober, what he did lived after him. The highway and the railroad and the breakwater let Port Orford play its part in shipping men and weapons across the Pacific to fight Japan.

Thinking about that, Bill chuckled. "If not for Gilbert Gable," he said, "chances are we wouldn't be doing this photo op at the Port Orford Datsun dealership."

"Well, no," Barbara said. "If not for Gilbert Gable, chances are that Datsun dealership wouldn't be there. But it's a good photo op—and Mr. Fujita will be so proud to have you recognize him for all he's done."

"This is Jefferson. Everybody gets along here," Bill said. "That's what I told the Yeti Lama a month ago, and it's the truth. Even if we have to work at it sometimes, it is."

"He knew that before you told him. He wouldn't have wanted to visit Jefferson if he didn't." Barbara paused a moment, then went on in a smaller voice: "He's impressive, isn't he?"

"Yeah." Bill nodded again. He hadn't wanted to admit, even to himself, just how much the holy yeti exiled from Tibet had impressed him. "Me, I sold houses, I got a law degree, I went into politics. I shake hands, I slap backs, I twist arms, I make speeches. I've got a knack for it, like."

"You do a lot of good. I wouldn't want to work for you if you didn't."

"Thanks," Bill said, more because she sounded as if she meant it than for her words themselves. "But the Yeti Lama... When he says something, he *means* it. He means it all the way down. He's not a politician, talking to hear himself talk. You have to take him seriously. I don't know that I ever met anybody like that before."

"*Gravitas,*" Barbara said.

"Huh?"

"*Gravitas,*" she repeated. "It's a Latin word that means what you just said. I learned it a few years ago, watching the Nixon impeachment hearings. Barbara Jordan has it, too, and I'm not saying so because we've got the same name."

"No, you're not. And you're right. She does," Bill said.

On they went. A lot of the cars they shared the road with were little Japanese machines: Datsuns and Toyotas, Hondas and Mazdas. Their sales had boomed since gas went through the roof after the first oil embargo. To Bill, they all seemed the size of roller skates. If he hit one with the Mighty Mo, he could bring it home on his fender like a moose—if he noticed the accident at all.

Also on the road heading for Port Orford were smoke-spewing eighteen-wheelers hauling this, that, and the other thing to the harbor for export. More big trucks heading east carried what came into Port Orford, as well as lumber from the nearby mountainsides and fish and crabs pulled out of the Pacific. Gilbert Gable would have been proud had he lived to see it.

Once they came out of the mountains, the land fell swiftly toward the sea. The Mighty Mo's temperature gauge dropped, too. Bill watched it with relief. The massive car had been working hard. The Gable Memorial Highway joined U.S. 101 a mile or so north of Port Orford. Bill drove south on the 101 almost to the breakwater-protected harbor. He turned left on Seventh and went a couple of blocks to Jackson.

At the corner there, an enormous American flag flew on a tall aluminum pole topped by a gilded eagle. An equally huge flag of Jefferson, pine-green with the gold-pan state seal in the middle, waved beneath it. They fluttered over the land of the free, the home of the brave, and an auto dealership whose sign proclaimed it FUJITA DATSUN OF PORT ORFORD in big red neon letters.

"We're here," Bill announced, pulling onto the lot. A local TV news van had already parked there. The cameraman was checking something on his equipment. The reporter, his hair sprayed so the breeze couldn't get playful, gabbed with a couple of newspapermen Bill recognized. He asked, "What time you got, Barbara?"

His publicist was left-handed, so she wore her watch on her right wrist. She raised it to her face to read the tiny women's-style dial. "It's a quarter to twelve, Governor," she answered.

"Good. Thanks. We aren't late." Bill parked two spaces from the news van. Not showing up on time here would have been embarrassing but not unforgivable. He'd really worried when he went to Eureka to meet the Yeti Lama. He'd made it—and the *Heiwa Maru,* the holy yeti's ship, came into port an hour late. Well, it let him and Barbara grab lunch.

He got out of the car and stretched. The Mighty Mo was as comfortable for a sasquatch as any car was likely to be, but standing up felt good just the same. He smiled at the shiny new Datsuns on the lot, mileage proudly painted on their windshields. He might have been able to drive some of the bigger ones from the trunk. A sleek little 280ZX? Not even that way—not a chance.

The hairsprayed reporter waved to him. "How's it going, Governor?"

"Not bad, Stu," Bill answered easily. "Always good to get out and let the people take a look at me."

"I guess it is," Stu said. "And there's a lot of you to look at." In a different tone of voice, that would have pissed Bill off. But the TV guy didn't mean anything by it. He was just talking to hear himself talk. Bill let it slide.

A car salesman walked up. He might have come straight from Central Casting. Hair sprayed even stiffer than Stu's. Porn-actor mustache. Loud wide tie straight out of 1973. Gold Qiana shirt. Plaid jacket made from what looked like the hide of a particularly ugly furnished-apartment sofa. Polyester pants with white belt. White shoes. There he stood, a gladhanding cliché.

"Welcome to Fujita Datsun, Governor Williamson. Welcome to Port Orford. I'm Dave Jenkins." He stuck out his hand. As Bill carefully shook it, Jenkins went on, "Shall I tell Nobuo you're here?"

Like many of his kind, he had a gift for the obvious. But Bill had the politician's gift for putting up with such people. "That would be good," he said, and left it right there.

Dave Jenkins hurried away. He came back a deferential pace and a half behind the dealership's founder and owner. Nobuo Fujita was in his late sixties, short and skinny. His close-cropped gray hair receded at the temples. He wore a charcoal-gray suit, a white shirt, and a sober navy tie.

He looked more like a dentist than someone who sold cars. A dentist, though, wasn't likely to be carrying a sheathed samurai sword. Well, neither were most automobile dealers.

"Thank you for coming, Governor," he said in fluent but accented English. "You do this simple businessman too much honor."

Bill paused a moment to make sure the reporters and cameramen were in place. Seeing they were, he answered, "I don't think so, sir. After all, this is the tenth anniversary of the opening of Fujita Datsun. And you first visited Port Orford a lot longer ago than 1969."

"Oh, yes. That is true." Fujita's smile seemed embarrassed, even rueful. "It was thirty-seven years ago this month: September 9, 1942. I was warrant flying officer in Japanese Navy. The submarine *I-25* surfaces off coast of Jefferson at six in morning, just as it gets light. We have in watertight container on deck a Yokosuka E14Y1—a small floatplane. We assemble pieces from container. We fuel. We put on two 77-kilo incendiaries—big load on small plane. I am pilot. I get in with Petty Officer Shoji Okuda. We take off, fly east to America."

"And you came to Port Orford," Bill said.

Nobuo Fujita nodded, looking back across the years. "I came to Port Orford, yes," he said. "I saw harbor. I saw town. I dropped my bombs. I flew away as fast as I could. Antiaircraft guns started shooting. I was lucky. Only one small hole in left wing before I am out of range. I flew back to submarine. It picked up Okuda and me and plane and got away."

"I remember that. I was seven or eight then," the Governor said. "You set a ship on fire and burned down a warehouse. Everybody started hopping around like fleas on a hot griddle."

"It was small thing, nuisance thing," Fujita answered with a shrug. "On twenty-ninth of September, *I-25* came back. We took off again with more incendiaries. This time, orders were to start forest fire. I dropped bombs in Siskiyou National Forest, flew back, and escaped again."

"It must have been wet. No fires that time," Bill said. "No one here even knew about the second raid till you told us."

The old Japanese man shrugged once more. "It was war. You try what you can. But after war was over, I felt sad—Port Orford beautiful town. In 1962, I ask American embassy in Tokyo if I could see it in peace without being treated as war criminal. They graciously say yes."

"I should hope so!" Bill exclaimed. "Plenty of Americans who bombed Japan and Germany have visited those places." He thought of Hyman Apfelbaum, the Attorney General of Jefferson. He'd flown thirty-one missions over Europe in 1944. After the war, he toured Germany, getting by with his Yiddish. He got by so well, a local asked him if he'd been there before. He told the man no, that seeming preferable to *Only in a B-17*.

Nobuo Fujita shrugged yet again. "You won. We lost," he said bleakly. But then his smile returned. "When I came, everyone was so kind." He hefted the samurai sword. While the reporters scribbled shorthand in their notebooks, the TV cameraman swung in for a closeup. Fujita went on, "This was in my family four hundred years. I gave it to mayor of Port Orford to show I was sorry to attack town."

"But now you have it back again," Bill said.

"Now I have it back again, yes," Fujita said. "I worked for Nissan—parent company of Datsun cars. I learned English. When they told me they wanted dealership in Port Orford, I remembered friendly people and lovely country. I came in 1969. When I got here, kind mayor returned sword to me. I will be here for rest of my life. I am U.S. citizen since year before last."

"That's wonderful, Mr. Fujita. That's an American story. That's a *Jefferson* story," Bill said, looking into the TV camera. "You bombed Port

Orford a long time ago, but now everybody here's glad to have you for a neighbor. A month ago, the Yeti Lama told me he wanted to see Jefferson because this is where everyone gets along, regardless of race or size."

"Yeti Lama very holy personage," Nobuo Fujita murmured.

"He was right," Bill said. "I'm nine feet-something, you're five feet-something, but so what? Once our countries were at war, but so what? Now we're at peace. And we'll stay that way, too, because peace is better."

"Peace is better," Fujita agreed. Bill Williamson draped a large, companionable arm over his shoulder. The still photographers snapped away.

TYPECASTING

Governor Bill Williamson of the state of Jefferson sat on the bed, waiting. He was ready to go. He had his shorts on, his wallet in one pocket, his keys in the other. That was as dressed-up, and as dressed, as he ever got. Several clean pairs of shorts sat in a small suitcase by the bed. Being a sasquatch made dressing and packing easier, one of the few advantages it had in a world dominated by little people.

Or he thought it made dressing up easier, anyhow. He looked at the bathroom door, which remained resolutely closed. He looked at the clock on the nightstand. What he saw made him mutter to himself. He looked at the bathroom door again. Still closed.

His patience slipped, which was dangerous for a politician and even more so for a husband. "Come on, Louise!" he called—bellowed, if you want to get right down to it. "We need to hit the road."

"I'll be out in a minute," she said.

It was one of the longer minutes Bill had ever known. Impatient or not, he'd been married too long to say so. What he did say, when she came out in shorts much like his but a brighter blue and a matching top that covered and supported her breasts, was, "Whatever you did, it worked." They'd had their silver anniversary the summer before. As husband and as politician, he knew how to keep people sweet.

Or he did most of the time, anyhow. All Louise said was, "Hrmp." She didn't like being noodged—a useful word Bill had picked up from Hyman Apfelbaum, Jefferson's attorney general.

Getting up from the bed, he went over and hugged his wife. At nine feet two, he was almost two feet taller than she was; sasquatch genders differed in size more than little people did. "You'll knock 'em dead in Ashland, kiddo," he said.

"Save the soft soap for the head of the Appropriations Committee, okay?" she said tartly. But she couldn't help smiling, and after a moment she relaxed in his arms and squeezed him back.

"Mike and I lie to each other all the time. It's part of the game. I don't play those games with you," Bill said, which was largely true. Politics and marriage had different rules. Anyone who thought otherwise wouldn't stay married, or in politics, long.

Louise picked up her own suitcase. It was bigger than Bill's, but not a lot. "I'm ready. Let's go," she said. "It'll be great to see Nicole."

"It sure will," Bill agreed. Their older daughter was a senior drama major at Jefferson State Ashland. Bill had no idea what kind of job she thought she'd get after she graduated, but he didn't need to worry about that for another few months, anyhow.

Out the bedroom door he and Louise went. The doorways in the Governor's Mansion were ten feet high; rooms had thirteen-foot ceilings. When Jefferson split off from Oregon and California right after the end of World War I, the first governor lived in a rented house. The new state's treasury flush with Coolidge-era prosperity, the second governor built the mansion and the state Capitol. Charlie "Bigfoot" Lewis was a sasquatch himself, and had his architect run them up on a scale that suited him. His working assumption was that little people could deal with too big more easily than sasquatches could with too small. Bill blessed him every time he didn't have to duck or bang his head.

The chief steward waited for them at the front door. Opening it, he said, "Enjoy your vacation, Governor, Mrs. Williamson. Give your daughter my best. She'll be in...*The Tempest,* isn't that right?"

"That *is* right, Ray," Bill said, pleased the man had remembered. "I'll tell her hello for you."

Old Glory and Jefferson's state flag flew on a tall pole in front of the mansion. Jefferson's banner was pine green, with the state's seal centered on the field: a gold pan marked with two X's. They stood for the double-crosses Jefferson had endured from Salem and Sacramento till its people finally got a bellyful and formed their own state.

After the War to End War, self-determination was all the rage in Europe. People in what had been southern Oregon and northern California grabbed it, too, grabbed it and ran with it. That neither Salem nor Sacramento was exactly broken-hearted to see them go didn't hurt, either.

Bill's car waited in the driveway by the flagpole. He fondly called the bronze 1974 Cadillac the Mighty Mo. It wasn't quite the size of a battleship, but it came close. That was the last model year when Detroit could build for size without worrying about mileage. Then the first oil embargo hit, gas prices zoomed like a moon rocket, and cars got small faster than unpreshrunk jeans in a hot dryer.

The Mighty Mo was six years old now. It was getting elderly—cars aged faster than dogs. Bill aimed to keep it running as long as he could. He didn't know of anything newer that could replace it. It guzzled gas the way a wino gulped muscatel, but what could you do? Economy and sasquatch size didn't go together.

Bill dug out his keys and opened the trunk. It was big enough to hold a squad of little-people Marines. His suitcase and Louise's vanished into its depths as if they had never been. The cavernous trunk seemed to say *Is that all?* Since that *was* all, Bill slammed the lid.

Then he opened the right front door and slid the right front seat as far forward as it would go. The Mighty Mo's right front seat moved on a special track that let it slide forward a long, long way. Bill slammed the right front door and opened the right rear door. He waved Louise into the car. With the seat all the way forward, she didn't fit badly. He closed the door. She locked it.

He walked around to the left rear door and got in himself. There was no left front seat. The Mighty Mo had an extra-long steering column so he or someone else his size could drive it. He stuck the key in the ignition and turned it. The enormous engine under that prairie of a hood rumbled to life.

"Ready to go?" he asked.

"Would I be sitting here next to you if I wasn't?" Louise answered reasonably.

"Okay." Bill put the Eldorado in gear, swung his size-thirty-two right foot from the brake to the accelerator, and headed for the north-bound onramp to the I-5.

Yreka had been the state capital for longer than he'd been alive, but it still wasn't what anyone would call a big city. The Governor's Mansion lay only a few blocks from the Interstate. The Mighty Mo rolled past the Capitol and the state government office building next door to it.

The Capitol was splendidly neoclassical, with colonnades and a gilded dome. The office building was a Depression-era WPA special, square and ugly and functional. The wonder was that it had gone up at all. Gilbert Gable, who was governor then, did all he could for his home town of Port Orford and as little as he could get away with for Yreka.

Bill waited in the left-turn lane till he got a green arrow. Then his foot mashed the gas pedal again. The Cadillac zoomed forward. It was twice as heavy as a nice, economical compact car, but it had twice the motor, too. At least twice.

More and more of the cars that share the Interstate with it were compacts, Datsuns and Toyotas and Hondas and Pintos and Vegas and Gremlins. They were a lot cheaper to run than the dinosaur-burning monster he piloted. He wouldn't have minded having one himself, if only he could have driven it from anywhere forward of the trunk.

Hardly anyone on I-5 took the federally mandated speed limit of fifty-five seriously. Bill sure didn't. The Mighty Mo's mileage was atrocious even at the double nickel. If it got a little worse at seventy or seventy-five, so what? He got where he was going sooner.

Signs on roadside fenceposts and barns shouted for Ted Kennedy and Jimmy Carter and Ronald Reagan. The Jefferson primary was coming in a couple of weeks. Reagan already had the GOP nomination pretty much in his back pocket. Bill figured the ex-governor from one state south would have breezed here any which way. Jefferson's Republicans averaged just to the right of Attila the Hun. Its Democrats, by contrast, were tree-huggers and left-over hippies. That made Kennedy the odds-on favorite.

From Yreka to Ashland was a little less than forty miles. The Mighty Mo had just passed from Siskiyou County to Jackson County—from what had been California to what used to be Oregon—when Louise said, "I don't think Nicole's happy about her part."

"No?" Bill said. "She ought to be. She ought to be happy she's got a part at all. The Ashland Shakespeare Festival gets to be a bigger deal every year. It draws more and more out-of-state tourists. It makes Ashland money. It makes Jefferson money. Sitting where I do, I can't help liking that."

His wife sighed. "I know, I know. She's not happy anyhow."

"She ought to be," Bill repeated. "The festival gets more professional every year, too. They don't usually let the Drama Department at Jefferson State put on a show any more. It's not like it was in 1935—not even close."

Jefferson State Ashland had started life as the Southern Oregon Normal School. It became the Ashland Normal School when Ashland and Oregon parted company, and went right on training teachers. One day in the mid-1930s, an instructor there named Angus Bowmer noticed that the roofless old building which had once housed Chautauqua lectures would do very nicely as an Elizabethan-style stage. Bowmer had always wanted to perform and to teach drama; he was training teachers because it was the Depression and you grabbed any job you could find and clung to it like a limpet.

The first few festivals were sort of like Ren Faires with plays. They included things like archery contests, bowling greens, and dances. Some of the actors were locals, others outsiders who odd-jobbed it while they performed. Nobody got paid, not at first.

It wasn't like that any more. The festival had grown and grown. It went on without its founder, who'd retired in 1970 and died a year ago. It had its own campus now, not far from the state university, with three theaters, and ran from spring to fall. Jefferson State drama students still pitched in, but more often behind the scenes now than on stage.

Louise Williamson clucked, as if disappointed in Bill. "I understand all that," she said—yes, she was unhappy with him. "It's more complicated than you're making it out to be, though."

Or else Nicole's taken arms against a sea of troubles that aren't there, Bill thought, remembering *Hamlet* from his own high school and college English classes. Twenty-one-year-olds were good at that. They saw how many things were wrong with the world, and saw it very clearly. They didn't see that fixing all those many things was usually harder than it looked. Bill hadn't at twenty-one, either.

Ashland was a town of about 15,000: a college town and, this past generation, a Shakespeare town, too. Hotels and restaurants and shops catered to the outsiders who came to watch the plays. The locals who didn't cater to tourists raised pears and apples and grain on the fertile soil of the Rogue River Valley.

They had reservations at the Columbia Hotel on Main Street, just a couple of blocks from the festival campus. The Columbia was right next to the Varsity Theater, but that ran movies, not live drama. At the moment, the marquee plugged *Mad Max* and *Gilda Live,* which struck Bill as one of the odder pairings he'd run across lately.

One of the entrances into the hotel was tall enough for him to use without ducking very much, either. He didn't have to walk through the lobby all hunched over, either. He'd been in the Jefferson State Senate when the Equal Accommodations Act finally passed in the early 1970s. If you ran a business in Jefferson, you had to do so in a way that let sasquatches—or yetis, or other oversized visitors—have access to it without turning into quasi-Quasimodos. Not all of it had to fit their needs, but some did.

Businessmen had fought the law all the way to the Jefferson Supreme Court. They'd lost. They'd lost in federal district court, too, and at the federal appeals level. If they took it to the U.S. Supreme Court, Bill expected them to lose there, too. Size was a civil-rights issue, dammit, just as much as race or gender.

The little man behind the registration desk smiled up at him and Louise. "Hello, Governor. Hello, Mrs. Williamson. Welcome to the Columbia," he said.

"Thanks." Bill wondered whether ordinary sasquatches got the same kind of treatment he did. Remembering the days when he'd been on the road all the time selling real estate, he had his doubts. But he had the trappings and recognizability of rank now. He would till he lost an election. People would go on recognizing him even then. He wasn't exactly inconspicuous.

He and Louise went through the rituals of checking in. He presented his American Express card. This trip was on his nickel, not Jefferson's. "You'll be in the Governor's Suite—that's room 111," the desk clerk said. "Would you like me to ring for someone to take your bags?"

"No, that's okay. Don't bother." Bill always declined such "favors." He was so much bigger and stronger than anyone the desk clerk would call, having a flunky carry luggage for him seemed more an embarrassment than a service.

"Here you go, then." The clerk handed him two keys. He gave Louise one. The clerk pointed. "It's down that hallway and to your left."

"Thanks." Bill already knew that; he'd stayed at the Columbia on the campaign trail. But he appreciated the way the clerk worked to treat him like anyone else. Everybody got along in Jefferson, or at least tried. No one here gaped at him like a movie special effect, the way little men and women back East did when he traveled for a governors' conference. (Some of the people who gaped most were other governors.)

The year before, the Yeti Lama, exiled since Mao's soldiers overran Tibet and the Himalayas in 1959, had visited Jefferson. He wanted to see for himself how people of many races and sizes could lived together without murdering one another over differences in religion and politics and hairiness.

People here didn't murder one another over such differences... these days. Bill hadn't gone into detail about his state's unfortunate past for the holy traveler. Well, damn few places didn't have unfortunate pasts. Too many places, the Yeti Lama's homeland among them, had unfortunate presents.

The door to Bill's room suited a person of his size. The Columbia dated back to 1910; this was the Governor's Suite because Bigfoot Lewis had stayed here back in the day. They didn't need the Equal Accommodations Act to get with the program. Bill hardly minded bending a little to put the key in the lock. Sasquatches weren't the only people who used the suite. You had to give to get.

Louise set down her bag and sat on the bed. She pulled a piece of paper from her purse. "Nicole's number at the dorm," she said. "I'm going to call her, let her know we're here."

"She'll be glad to find out," Bill said. "Mom and Dad are in town! No more dorm food for a while!"

"It's not too awful, from what she says. And the meal plan…could be worse, anyhow," his wife replied. Naturally, sasquatches ate more than little people. Just as naturally, university dorms expected them to pay more, too. Louise dialed the room phone. Actually, it was a modern one with buttons, and easier for her to use. She wasn't that much bigger than little people; in a pinch, she could manage with a real dial. Bill had always needed a pen or pencil to deal with one of those. From force of habit, he still used one most of the time even on the push-button models.

This one was quite loud. From halfway across the room, he heard two rings and then a "Hello?" he thought was his daughter's.

Sure enough, Louise said, "Hello, dear. We're in Ashland, at the Columbia. Can you meet us at Gepetto's at noon for lunch? You know—the place on Main, a couple of blocks down from the hotel." She paused, listening. This time, Bill couldn't make out what Nicole said. But Louise nodded. "See you then. 'Bye." She hung up.

"Noon, huh?" Bill said. "Well, fine. And then I'll hear the grand and gruesome story of why she isn't happy with her part?"

His wife nodded again. "That's right."

"Oh, boy. I can hardly wait," Bill said. Louise rolled her eyes. *I know I can fib better than that*, he thought. *If I couldn't, they never would have elected me to the State Senate, let alone governor.*

He and Louise got to Gepetto's ten minutes early. For Bill, that counted as right on time. He had a working politician's horror of being late. It was as pleasant a morning here as it had been down in Yreka. They waited outside for their daughter to walk over from campus.

Standing there soaking up the springtime sun, Bill people-watched. In a college town, he remembered John Donne. *No man is an island, entire of itself,* Donne wrote. *Any man's death diminishes me, because I am involved in mankind.*

Bill wanted to believe that, just as the old-time Englishman had. A pol who'd once sold houses and lots was, and needed to be, a gregarious soul. But Bill felt isolated in ways John Donne never could have imagined. Even in Jefferson, sasquatches were a tiny minority. Most people didn't see them every day. Yes, staring was rude, but the sidelong glances he got instead might have been worse.

Then he smiled. He couldn't help himself. Here came a pair of his own kind, walking down Main Street holding hands. They were both close to Nicole's age. The boy wore an outsized baseball cap with JSA on the front, so they were college kids. They didn't give a damn about feeling isolated, or anything else except each other. They walked past him and Louise without even noticing them.

They were lucky. They didn't know how lucky they were, which was another way of saying they were young. Still smiling, Bill glanced down at the top of his wife's head. Twenty-odd years ago now, he'd felt that way about her. He still did, even if experience tempered romance now. Louise would know what he was thinking. She would have had her own dark moments down through the years. Man or woman, big or little, you couldn't very well reach middle age without them.

She suddenly waved. "There's Nicole!" she said. Sure enough, up Main Street from the direction of campus walked their firstborn. Being no more than an inch taller than Louise, she didn't stand out that much from the little people around her. Jefferson's settlers mostly came from northwestern Europe, and ran tall for their kind. Some of them also had a trace, or sometimes more than a trace, of sasquatch blood. For that matter,

Bill thought—though he wasn't sure—one of his great-grandmothers was a little person. Whether that story was true didn't matter to him one way or the other.

Nicole waved back. She hurried toward them. Her last few steps were a trot. She hugged Louise and then Bill. "Sometimes I forget there are people as big as you, Daddy," she said.

"Here I am, such as I am," Bill said. "Sometimes I forget there are people bigger than I am. I was looking up to the Yeti Lama every which way last summer. He's the only really holy person I ever met—and he's six inches taller than me." Maybe that had to do with the great-grandmother he'd never met. Maybe yetis averaged taller than their North American cousins. Or maybe the Yeti Lama was just a great big fellow and Bill not so much.

His daughter pointed toward Gepetto's front door. "Let's eat," she said. "They do pretty good burgers, and their wontons are great."

"Works for me. I bet I could eat one ton of them all by myself." Bill pronounced the weight so it sounded like the Chinese dish. Louise and Nicole both groaned. They knew that, tall as he was, he had a low taste for puns. He had to work hard not to let it out where it could alarm his constituents.

"Governor Williamson!" exclaimed the middle-aged woman at a lectern who seated people. "You'll want a table set up for big people, won't you?"

"Yes, please, if you have one," he said.

"We sure do. Right this way." She scooped up menus and led them to a table and chairs that suited their size. No trouble with the Equal Accommodations Act here—and Bill wouldn't need to worry about where to put his knees.

The waitress who took their orders was short even by little-people standards. Bill needed a moment to notice that; all little people, even basketball players, seemed short to him. He saw she was cute right away.

Living in the wider culture his whole life made him as much aware of attractive little-people females as his own kind. He was happy with Louise, so he'd never done anything more than notice. The waitress's head hair almost matched his own russet pelt, which was interesting and uncommon among her kind.

When the food came, they spent a while giving the hamburgers and wontons and fries and shakes the attention they deserved. After a while, happily replete, Bill asked, "How's the play coming along?"

Louise shot him a warning glance. Like most such, it arrived too late. Nicole's face clouded over. "Pretty bad," she said. "You know I'm one of the best at the school."

"Uh-huh." Bill nodded. He did know that. Quietly and without any fuss, he'd made it a point to find out. He also knew it would do his daughter less good than she hoped once she left the friendly confines of Jefferson State Ashland. He ate a few more French fries. Then he said, "So?"

"So we're doing *The Tempest,* right?" Nicole spoke to him as if sure he was none too bright: the tone that always did so much to endear the rising generation to its elders. "So I was hoping they'd cast me for Miranda. But the director isn't a JSA guy. The Shakespeare Festival brought him in—he's from *Pittsburgh,* for crying out loud." She stopped, too disgusted to go on.

"So what part *did* he give you?" Bill asked, fearing he knew the answer before he heard it. And he did.

"Caliban!" His daughter spat out the name with so much venom, several little people's heads whipped around. In a slightly—but only slightly—softer voice, she went on, "Talk about stereotyping! My God!" She made as if to clap her hands to her head. But her fingers were greasy, so she didn't.

"You see what I mean," Louise said.

Bill nodded unhappily. "Who's playing Miranda, then?" he asked.

"Jackie van Herpen," Nicole replied.

"She any good?"

His daughter turned her right thumb toward the floor. Vespasian couldn't have done it with more imperial hauteur. She said, "I suppose she's pretty, if you like brainless blondes."

Some men, little and big, did. Quite a few, in fact. Bill found another question: "Is the guy from, uh, Pittsburgh sleeping with her?"

For the first time since naming Shakespeare's mooncalf, Nicole smiled. "I don't *think* so," she said. "He's gay as gay can be."

"Okay. Good, even." Most of the time, Bill didn't care who went to bed with whom, or why. But if the director was balling his Miranda, no way in hell he'd change his mind about casting. Since he wasn't, he might—possibly—listen to reason (which, to Bill, meant doing what he wanted). "What's his name, and how do I get hold of him?"

"He's Reggie Pesky, and he's at the Angus Bowmer Theatre, the small one—that's where we'll perform." Nicole suddenly looked anxious. "Maybe you should call over there and meet him somewhere else. Out of his territory."

Bill nodded thoughtfully. "That makes sense, but I'll do it anyway." Nicole stuck out her tongue at him. He went on, "Remember, just because we talk, there's no guarantee of anything. All I can do is try."

"I know, Dad." Nicole sounded confident, though, and why not? Wasn't her father nine feet tall (and then some)? Wasn't he governor of Jefferson? Didn't all that mean he could do anything?

As a matter of fact, no, Bill thought. Nine feet tall or not, he was only human. And a recalcitrant legislature had taught him a governor could only do so much. Of course, Reggie Pesky was a theatre guy, not a politician. He might not grok that. If he didn't, Bill had no intention of enlightening him.

———

Sitting in a sasquatch-sized chair in the Columbia's lobby, Bill pretended to read the *Ashland Daily Tidings*. In fact, he barely noticed the words on the newsprint. He'd spent the afternoon at a different kind of reading. He hadn't dug into Shakespeare since English Lit in college. He wondered why not. The old boy knew a trick or three, sure as hell.

Reggie Pesky walked in at six o'clock sharp, on time to the minute, which made Bill think well of him. He recognized the little man at once from Nicole's description: longish yellow hair, blue eyes, very pale skin, broad cheekbones, snappy clothes. Bill would have bet dollars to dimes the director hadn't been born with the moniker he used these days. By his looks, something on the order of Riszard Paweskowicz seemed more likely.

But that had nothing to do with the price of beer. Bill stood up. He wanted to intimidate a bit, or more than a bit. Pesky was fair-sized for a little man; he stood close to six feet. That put his eyes on a level somewhere near Bill's diaphragm.

"Hello, Mr. Pesky. Thanks for coming by." Bill's voice, deeper than deep, was another polite weapon. He held out his hand. The way it engulfed the director's was one more.

"I'm delighted to meet you, Governor Williamson. Your daughter is very…impressive. You're even more so." Reggie Pesky stared at his hand as if delighted to get it back again.

Bill didn't think Nicole was wrong about which way he swung. "Call me Bill," he said. "I'm just trying to get along, same as anybody else."

"Then I'm Reggie, of course," Pesky said.

"Shall we get something to eat? The restaurant's pretty decent—I've stayed here before," Bill said. His wife and daughter would have dinner somewhere else. Bill wanted to talk to the director with his governor hat on, not his daddy hat.

In they went. As at Gepetto's, a couple of tables were large enough to let sasquatches eat comfortably. A busboy brought Pesky a tall chair so he could sit at one with Bill, the way a child would have got a booster seat at a regular table. The expression on the little man's face was a caution.

Reggie Pesky ordered a Bombay Sapphire and tonic, Bill a triple scotch. He liked beer better, but he needed half a gallon for a buzz. Pesky raised a pale eyebrow. "Your bar tab must be hell," he said sympathetically.

"Now that you mention it, yes," Bill agreed. "My grocery bill, too. Being big ain't all it's cracked up to be."

The director hoisted his eyebrow again, in a slightly different way this time. Bill thought he knew what that meant. Gay sasquatches from Jefferson had joined their little brethren in the move to San Francisco. Their…attributes were in great demand among a certain set there. A rather smaller set of little women admired straight sasquatches for similar reasons.

When the drinks came, Bill and Pesky clinked glasses. Bill savored his smoky single malt. "I'm so glad I came to Jefferson," Pesky said. "This is the first chance I've had to work with sasquatches. Yunz are remarkable people."

"Yunz?" Bill wondered if he'd heard right.

"Did I just say that?" The director looked astonished at himself. He seemed to play a tape back in his head, because he sighed. "Good God, I guess I did. It's…Pittsburgh for *y'all,* is what it is. They call people who talk that way *yunzers.* My folks sure as hell did—do—but I thought I outgrew it years and years ago." He laughed and sipped his drink. "Shows what I know, doesn't it?"

"We're more like other people than we're different," Bill said.

"Well, I tell people the same thing, and most of the time it's true," Pesky replied. He, no doubt, wasn't talking about his size or how hairy he was. Bill nodded anyway. Reggie Pesky went on, "Sometimes it isn't, though. Sometimes the differences matter."

Before Bill needed to answer that, the waitress came up and said brightly, "Would you gentlemen care for another drink? And are you ready to order, or do you need another few minutes?"

Bill looked a question at the director. Pesky bobbed his head up and down. "I'd like another drink, yeah," Bill said. "And I'll have the sasquatch-sized prime rib, rare." Reggie Pesky ordered a fresh gin and tonic and broiled salmon.

"Thank you." The waitress beamed at them. "I'll bring the drink right away, and I'll have your dinners for you as soon as they're up." Bill watched her backside work when she hurried away. Pesky forgot about her as soon as she wasn't standing there any more. Sure enough, there were differences, and then there were differences.

The drinks came as fast as promised. Reggie Pesky smiled when Bill sipped from his. "I'd fall over if I had two that size," he said.

"There are little men who drink more than I do," Bill said. "Some of the old-timers in Yreka… They start putting it away right after breakfast, and they quit when they go to bed. You never see 'em falling-down drunk, though. They just go along like that, full of antifreeze—"

"Till their liver conks out," Pesky put in.

"Uh-huh. Or till lung cancer or emphysema gets 'em, 'cause they mostly smoke like chimneys, too."

Pesky grinned crookedly. "We're cheerful, aren't we?"

"Oh, at least," Bill said, which made the little man chuckle. The governor added, "And here's the chow."

Up strode the waitress, a large tray on her left shoulder. With the deftness of long practice, she supported the tray with her left hand while using her right to set plates on the table. "There you go," she said. "Do you need anything else right now?"

"Don't think so," Bill said. She lowered the tray and hustled off to whatever she had to do next.

Reggie Pesky eyed Bill's slab of prime rib with undisguised admiration. "They got all of that from one cow?" he said.

"Looks like it." Bill cut off a bite, dipped it in the *au jus,* chewed, swallowed, and smiled. "A cow that died happy, too."

About halfway through dinner, Pesky paused and said, "I just wanted to let you know what a pleasure it is working with your daughter, Governor."

Bill had heard that tone of voice before. It was the tone of a man who knew which side his bread was buttered on. Bill said, "That's part of the reason I invited you to dinner tonight."

"I thought it might be," the director said. No, he was no dope. Well, he wouldn't have the slot he had if he were. He continued, "She understudies Miranda very well. I've been impressed. I know I said that before, but she has talent."

"Thanks." Bill picked his words with care: "If she's so good, why didn't she get the part?"

Reggie Pesky looked at his drink and seemed disappointed to find it empty. "A couple of reasons," he said after a moment, also plainly thinking about what came out of his mouth. "Probably the most important is that here in Jefferson I have a chance I probably never would anywhere else—the chance to do *The Tempest* with a Caliban who doesn't need makeup."

"What makes you say that? Caliban's not a sasquatch. Shakespeare never heard of sasquatches. We hadn't run into white people yet," Bill said. "Caliban's a cross between a woman and a devil. He can look like anything you want him to. Saying he looks like a sasquatch, isn't that the worst kind of typecasting?"

Pesky blinked. "I never dreamt you—or Nicole—would take it like that. It's not how I meant it."

The alarming thing was, Bill believed him. "You know, I think you could get away with that kind of casting in Boston or Philadelphia, maybe even New York." He made a point of not mentioning Pittsburgh. After a bite from one of his baked potatoes, he continued, "This is Ashland, though. Little people here are used to sasquatches. They see them all the time. They take them for granted, as much as they do with, say, black people or Vietnamese." He exaggerated, but by less than he would have anywhere else in the country.

"Mm." Reggie Pesky also did some eating. If he needed time to think, Bill would give it to him. Pesky blotted his lips with his napkin. He was very neat, very precise. "There is also a certain difficulty with suspension of disbelief, you know."

And with that they came down to it, as Bill had guessed they would. "I've got two things to say, Mr. Pesky." So much for first names. "The first one is, it's called *acting*. You must have seen the movie with Olivier playing Othello."

"Oh, sure." The director nodded.

"Does he look like a Moor to you?"

"He looks like Olivier with shoe polish on his face."

Bill laughed. "Okay, we're on the same page. Is it a good performance?"

"If you like chewing the scenery the way the Brits did a generation ago, maybe." Pesky realized he couldn't stop there. He grudged a nod. "Yes, it's a good performance."

"All right. The other thing is, you don't believe Nicole can make people believe she's Prospero's daughter?"

"It's...a stretch," Pesky said.

"Says you. The thing is, Prospero may honest to God be the kid's three-times-great-grandfather."

"Run that by me again?" the director said.

"There's a family story that says one of my great-grandmothers—Nicole's great-great—was a little woman. I don't know that that's true, but I don't know that it's not, either. A lot of sasquatches here in Jefferson have little people in the woodpile, and the other way around. And I have no idea who great-granny's father was. Maybe it *was* Prospero, if his revels weren't then ended."

"A lot of people, I'd think they were making that up to bullshit me," Pesky said. "I believe you. Don't know why, but I do."

Life's too short for bullshit. Bill believed that. He didn't think Pesky would believe *him*. And, just because he disliked bullshit, that didn't mean he didn't use it now and again. It was an indispensable lubricant in the working politician's toolbox.

He tried a different tack instead: "How good is the girl you've got doing Miranda now?" He knew what Nicole thought of Jackie van Herpen. He also knew his kid might not be completely objective.

"She's okay." Pesky might or might not be praising with faint damn. After glancing around to make sure no one but Bill could hear, he went on, "Miranda should be pretty, and Jackie's what they call a double-breasted mattress-thrasher. Most of the guys in the audience will notice."

The *they* and the *most* distanced him from the people he was talking about. Bill felt even more distanced himself. To little people, and especially to little people who weren't used to them, sasquatches' size and hairiness and heavy features were off-putting, to say the least. Nicole was a fine-looking girl…if you had the eyes to see it. A gay little man from Pittsburgh wasn't likely to.

"This is Jefferson, you know," he said, going as far as he thought he could in that direction without getting offensive. "Audiences here don't look at things the way they do where they haven't grown up with us."

Maybe he went too far anyway. "Mr. Williamson, if you were a sasquatch who sold shoes or drove a truck, you'd never have the nerve to rattle my cage about casting," Reggie Pesky said. "Because you're governor, you think you can throw your weight around, the same way you would if you were a—what do you say?—a little man. Some things *don't* change, do they?" He put a twenty on the table. "Even at hotel prices, this'll cover mine and the tip. See you." He slid off the tall chair and walked away.

Bill scowled after him. Little people made the same jokes about sasquatches as they did about gorillas. They didn't make them where sasquatches could hear—not more than once—but he knew about them. *Where does the 500-pound sasquatch sit? Anywhere he wants to.* Bill nodded to himself. Five hundred pounds was just about what he tipped the scales at. He had a lot of weight to throw around.

Jerry Turner had succeeded Angus Bowmer as producing director for the Ashland Shakespeare Festival in 1971. He wasn't a native, but he'd started performing at Ashland in 1957. He'd taught drama down at Jefferson State Arcata till he took the slot here. If anybody who wasn't born in Jefferson got how things here worked, he was the man.

If anyone did. All Bill could do was find out—and play a little politics while he was at it.

He guessed Turner was five or ten years older than he was himself. The producing director had a cramped office in the festival's administration building near the Bowmer Theatre. It seemed all the more cramped with Bill in it. "Are you all right, Governor?" Turner asked with what sounded like real concern. "We can talk outside if you'd rather."

"Don't worry about it. You were kind enough to get a chair that fits my big old behind, and to see me early in the morning," Bill said. The ceiling here was just about tall enough, but he felt as if the walls were closing in on him. From long practice, he shoved that out of his mind. Sasquatches dealt with claustrophobia all the time. In a world with a few of them and swarms of little people, they had to.

"When the Governor says he wants to see me, he can see me," Turner answered. "I suspect I have some idea of what this is about."

"Do you?" Bill said, unsurprised. "Reggie Pesky talked to you?"

"He called last night, yes," Turner said. "He was...a little bent out of shape."

"He doesn't quite see what Jefferson is like," Bill said. "Or that's how it looks to me, anyhow. You've got a sasquatch in your troupe? What'll she play? Caliban! Talk about typecasting! Talk about stereotypes! C'mon—you've been here a long time now. Is that what you want the Ashland Shakespeare Festival to stand for? It's not what this state's all about."

Jerry Turner steepled his fingers as he thought. As befit someone who ran things, he didn't shoot from the lip. "It bothers me, too," he said at last. "But when I invite someone to come here and work with our people, I'm reluctant to second-guess him. Otherwise, it turns into my play, not his—and next year I'll have trouble finding anyone who wants to work with me."

"I understand that," Bill said. "But when somebody plainly hasn't got a clue—"

"Can you give me an example of what you mean?" Turner interrupted. "No offense, but I do want to make sure you're not just a parent bitching about the part his kid got."

Bill *was* a parent bitching about the part his kid got, but he hoped he wasn't just that kind of parent. "I sure can," he said. "Last night, he told me he was glad Nicole was in the troupe because she could play Caliban without any makeup."

Turner's mouth puckered as if he'd bitten into an unripe persimmon. "Oh, dear," he said.

"Uh-huh." Bill nodded. "If that's not clueless, I don't know what is. He looks at a sasquatch, and all he sees is a funny-looking critter. He doesn't see an actor. He doesn't see how there can be an actor under the fuzz, if you know what I mean."

"That kind of thing won't make the reviewers happy. Not in Jefferson. Not in Ashland," Turner said fretfully. Bill smiled, but only inside, where it didn't show. He'd hit the producing director where he lived. Turner went on, "The festival grows out of what the state is. If we're about anything, we're about giving people chances because of what they can do, not because of what they look like."

"Feels the same way to me." Bill had come to see Jerry Turner with a carrot as well as a stick. He said, "The Ashland Shakespeare Festival's brought Jefferson credit for a long time. Even before the war, the state WPA Guide talks about it."

"Yes, I know—and it calls Angus Bowmer Angus Bowman," Turner said with a grin. "He used to laugh about it and say, 'Fame is getting your name spelled wrong in the history books.'"

"I like that," Bill said. "So anyway, I was thinking maybe it's time to change the name of what goes on here from the Ashland Shakespeare Festival to the Jefferson Shakespeare Festival, and to put in a little state money to help things grow and move along."

"No strings attached?" Turner asked.

"How do you mean?"

"A couple of years ago, the National Endowment for the Arts offered us a $50,000 grant, but we had to sign a pledge that we wouldn't do anything obscene. We said thanks but no thanks."

"Jerry, I don't give a damn what you do with the money, as long as you don't frighten the horses," Bill said.

The producing director didn't ask how much money the Governor was talking about. That was good. It showed a certain amount of trust. And Bill knew too well that some primitives in the legislature threw nickels around as if they were manhole covers. But he was pretty sure he could get this through. Hardly anyone in Jefferson wasn't proud of the Ashland Shakespeare Festival.

What Turner did say was, "Well, I'll talk with Reggie about reconsidering. *He* may frighten the horses when I do, but I'll make it work."

"Thanks. Thanks very much." Something else occurred to Bill: "I hope you can get the programs fixed in time for opening night."

"We won't print new ones. That would cost way too much," Turner replied. "We'll do inserts instead. But they'll look good, promise. We got ourselves a Wang word processor last year. It's crazy—it's a computer that sets type. I don't know what we'd do without it."

"I've seen 'em. State government's starting to use 'em, too," Bill said. "They're amazing, all right. Who knows what they'll come up with next?"

"Yeah." Jerry Turner nodded. "Who knows?"

The usher smiled up and up at Bill and Louise. One of the nice things about handing out programs before a play was the interesting people you met. "Hello, Governor. Hello, Mrs. Williamson," he said. "The sasquatches' box is on your left, down at the front. I hope you enjoy the show."

"I'm sure we will," Louise said, beating her husband to the punch.

Bill opened his program and looked through it as he and Louise walked to their seats. Sure enough, the insert did look good. It was on the same coated stock as the rest of the booklet, and the typeface matched, too. They could do wild things these days, all right.

He took a step down to the sasquatches' box. The floor there was lower than in the rest of the Angus Bowmer Theatre, so big people could get down close without blocking the view of the little folks behind them. Another couple was already in the box. Bill didn't know them, but they looked familiar. A moment later, he realized why. They were the college kids who'd walked by when he and Louise were waiting for Nicole outside Gepetto's.

They realized who he was at about the same time. Both of them bobbed their heads at him—the guy wasn't wearing his JSA cap now. He said, "That's your daughter in the show, right?"

"Yup." Bill beamed.

"How cool is that?" the girl said.

"Do you know Nicole?" Bill asked. Sure enough, they did. He'd figured they would. Sasquatches stuck out from the crowd of little people. The two couples chatted till the house lights dimmed.

The Tempest's opening scene, out on the ocean, was all *Sturm und Drang*—literally. Kettledrums supplied the thunder, as they would have in Shakespeare's day. Lasers blazing through dry-ice smoke did duty for stormclouds and lightning. Reggie Pesky knew more staging tricks than were dreamt of in the Bard's philosophy. As their ship foundered, the men in it took to the boats.

Act One, Scene Two was set in front of Prospero's cell on the island where the main action took place. Bill tensed when the young little man playing Prospero—decked out in a gray wig and a pretty good fake gray beard—and his own daughter as Miranda entered. A couple of murmurs rose from the audience, but no angry shouts and (he thanked heaven) no laughter. Much of the crowd would be from Jefferson, used to sasquatches and used to suspending disbelief for them if a performance rated it. The out-of-staters seemed willing to roll with things for a while, anyhow.

"'If by your art, my dearest father, you have/ Put the wild waters in this roar, allay them…'" Nicole went on with Miranda's first speech. She had the words down, and the feelings behind them. Her voice was deeper than a little woman's, but she didn't sound like a little man, either. She sounded like—herself.

That scene filled the rest of the first act. Ariel's tight-fitting costume was covered with thin diffraction-grating disks that gave off rainbows whenever the girl playing the spirit moved. Caliban looked more like a lumpy alien from the *Star Wars* cantina than a sasquatch. Bill hadn't pictured the semi-human that way, but the makeup didn't set his teeth on edge.

Bill's other anxious moment came in the last act, when Miranda exclaimed, "'Oh, wonder!/ How many goodly creatures are there here!/ How beauteous mankind is! Oh, brave new world,/ That has such people in 't!'"

By then, though, Nicole had done well enough so the audience took her for granted in the role. More than that, she couldn't hope. Well, she could hope—it didn't hurt. Whether she hoped or not, though, Bill didn't expect the Royal Shakespeare Company to call any time soon. Good as she was, Nicole wasn't *that* good. Stratford-on-Avon wasn't Jefferson, either.

He blistered his palms when the cast came out to take their bows. His daughter got as big a hand as he thought she deserved. He felt about to burst with pride.

In spite of the Equal Accommodations Act, when Bill went backstage he had to walk carefully to keep from bumping his head on the ceiling. Nicole's dressing room barely held three sasquatches. "I did it!" she kept saying. "Oh, my God! I really did it!"

"You sure did," Bill said. "You were great, too." That might have stretched things a bit, but people who told the truth, the whole truth, and nothing but the truth to their nearest and dearest soon found themselves not so near and not so dear.

After a bit, Louise tugged at his arm. "We shouldn't hang around," she said. "We can talk more later. She still has stuff to do."

"I suppose so," Bill answered grumpily, knowing she was right. When he opened the dressing-room door to go out, he almost ran into— ran over—Reggie Pesky coming in.

"Hello, Governor," the director said with a sour smile. "I was hoping you'd come back. I have a couple of things I want to tell you."

"Go ahead. I'm listening," Bill said.

"The first one is, that worked better than I thought it would. Your daughter did a nice job, and the audience bought it."

"Okay, that's one. What's the other?"

"Fuck you. Just…fuck you."

Bill could have driven him into the ground like a nail. People would have talked if he did, though. "Don't worry about it, man," he said after a beat. "I love you, too."

"Are you ready, Governor?" his publicist asked. A blonde with a nice shape, Barbara Rasmussen was almost too decorative for the work she did.

Bill took his place behind the massive gubernatorial desk. Once Bigfoot Lewis's, it had sat in storage for years and years, till in their wisdom the people of Jefferson chose another sasquatch to lead them. He made sure the bill on the desk was the one he was supposed to be signing. He also made sure the pen he'd sign it with wrote.

The bill was the right one. The pen did have the write stuff. The Governor nodded. "We're good to go. You can let 'em in."

Barbara opened the door to the Governor's study. Reporters and still photographers came in. TV cameramen took their places at cameras already set up and waiting for them. Barbara turned a rheostat. The lights above the desk got brighter—and hotter. Bill started to sweat.

"Governor Williamson will make a brief statement," Barbara said, telling the press corps what they already knew. "Then he'll sign the bill, and then he'll take a few questions."

As soon as the red lights under the camera lenses went on, Bill smiled at them and said, "Hello folks. We all know the Ashland Shakespeare Festival has helped put Jefferson on the map since the Depression was at its worst. I'm proud that our state has America's first Elizabethan theatre. And, under the new producing director, Jerry Turner, the festival has grown in size and scope. It draws coverage from around the world, and it draws lots of visitors to Jefferson.

"Because of all that, the legislature and I have agreed it's high time our state recognizes how important the festival is. The bill I'm going to sign today changes its name from the Ashland Shakespeare Festival to the *Jefferson* Shakespeare Festival. And, to show we're putting our money where our mouth is, the bill authorizes an annual state grant of $75,000 to the festival to support it and help it expand even more."

He'd wanted to give the festival $150,000 a year. He'd expected the tightwads in the Capitol to haggle him down to a flat hundred grand. They proved even tighter than he'd figured on, though. One of the things politics was was the art of taking what you could get. Otherwise, you ended up with nothing.

Bill ceremoniously picked up the pen and signed three copies of the bill as the TV cameras followed his every move and the still photographers flashed and clicked away. Then he waved to the reporters, inviting the questions Barbara had promised.

"What kind of strings go with the money?" asked the man from the *Port Orford Post*.

"Well, Pete, the usual financial kind, to make sure the people in Ashland only spend the grant on things that have to do with the festival. Jerry Turner won't head for the closest Bentley dealership with the check." Bill got a few chuckles. He went on, "Of course, if I thought he'd do anything like that I wouldn't have proposed the bill in the first place. And there are no artistic strings attached."

"None?" Pete said.

"None," Bill echoed. "This is Jefferson. This isn't a place where we give with one hand and take away with the other. This isn't a place where we tell people how to do things. This is a place where we let them do things. If you don't like what they do, you don't have to go. We got to be a state by doing our own things here. We've been doing it ever since, long before the hippies latched on to the phrase."

"Did your daughter being in a Shakespeare play have anything to do with this grant?" the reporter from the *Ashland Daily Tidings* asked.

"Maybe a little something, Annie." Not usually someone given to understatements, Bill paused a moment to admire that one. Then he continued, "She certainly helped put Ashland on my radar, and the festival deserves all the help we can give it."

"Her casting changed at the last minute," Annie said. "Did *that* have anything to do with what you just signed?"

Bill shrugged his wide, wide shoulders. "I have no artistic control over the festival. I don't want any, either. I'd just foul it up. I will say I'm a proud papa like any other proud papa."

If any or any other people wanted to push it, they could raise a stink. Reggie Pesky would likely be glad to lend a helping hand. But no one seemed eager. It was a feel-good bill. It was a feel-good story. Why mess with it?

A few more harmless questions followed. Then the reporters and photographers hurried out of the study to get their stories and pictures in. Bill leaned back in his swivel chair. It creaked.

"That went fine," Barbara remarked.

"Yeah, I think so, too," Bill said. "And all's well that ends well." He winked.

JUNIOR AND ME

Listen, you yellow-bellied son of a green-yolked egg, this is how it happened. And if you don't like it, well, we can just step outside and Junior and me'll chew your snout off for you.

This here was down in the Red River bottoms, sixteen—no, seventeen—years ago now. I was down on my luck. I guess you could say so. The dancing girl in Dodge I'd got sweet on, she laughed in my face. She was after somebody who'd keep her in the style she wanted to get used to. She had somebody in mind, too, and it wasn't me.

I could have killed him. Not, I wanted to kill him. I *could* have killed him, easy as you please. He was fresh out of the shell, practically— a kid from the East who kept books at the bank and for the grocery store. He didn't know what she was, any more'n he knew about knives and eight-shooters. All he knew was, he liked the curve of her haunches.

If I did kill him, I might've done him a favor. Caught up in her web, he'd have had a demon of a time biting free. He wouldn't be the same afterwards, neither. You never are.

But Sssue—that was her name, Sssue—wouldn't've given me a tumble even with him gone, not the way I was then. I had trouble buying my own firewater, let alone anything a dancing girl with big dreams might want. If he got dead, Sssue would've latched on to the next fella like him she ran across.

I had sense enough to see that, even if it took longer'n it should have. Soon as I did, I got out of Dodge. No, I didn't know where I was going. North, south, east, west? I didn't care, long as I got the hells out of there. I headed south on account of…on account of I did.

That's how I ended up going toward the Red River country. Dumb luck, and I still wonder sometimes if it was good or bad. But I didn't know about any of that. All I knew was, I needed to get gone.

You've seen how, when you get a tenth of a daytenth outside of a town, the air starts smelling sweet again? You get away from the stinks of all the people and critters packed too tight together. You get away from sour smoke and stirred-up dust and everything else. The world starts tasting the way it must have right after the gods hatched it. You get used to the way a town smells, but you don't hardly ever get to where you like it.

I was free. I told myself I was, anyways. I just about made myself believe it. Whether it was true or not, it made the feathers on my crest come up for a spell.

Of course, lots of times free means free to starve. Yeah, I didn't owe a soul any silver, much less gold. A good thing, too, 'cause I didn't have hardly any silver, much less gold. Sssue had it straight when she saw I wasn't rich and likely never would be.

Little birds hopped in the grass to either side of the trail. They cocked their heads as I ambled past. Some of them flew away, just to stay on the safe side. Things like me ate things like them when we got the chance. Somewhere down deep in their little birdbrains, they knew it.

I started panting. It was warm and sticky, the way it gets when you're heading south from Dodge. When I came to a stream, three or four turtles jumped off rocks and into the water. Like the birds, they didn't trust me. Like the birds, they had their reasons.

Before I crossed, I gave that stream my own once-over. The turtles that splashed away were little, no bigger'n my hand with the claws all spread. But you don't want to find a snapper with your foot while you're wading, not if you care to keep that foot in one piece.

"Ahhh!" I hissed in pleasure when I came up on the far bank. The water drying on my scales cooled me off for a little while. It felt mighty fine.

A line of great shadows swept across the plain, sliding straight toward me. One passed plumb over me. I didn't like that, not even a little, and made a sign with my thumb and first finger to turn aside the dark omen. People say you're liable to die soon if a huzzard's shadow catches you. Huzzards eat carrion, so you can see why folks talk that way. I didn't exactly believe it, but I didn't exactly *not* believe it, neither.

One of the huzzards let out that croak they make. Hearing it didn't make me feel any easier. I scowled after their flight line. On they glided, not caring about me at all. Why should they? A huzzard's wings are wide as five or six people lying snout to foot. We're big enough for them to notice, but there's not enough meat on one of us for a flight to get excited about.

So they soared on, and I kept on. I crossed another creek. This time, I kept a closer eye on the turtles. But they kept an eye on me, too. I didn't get to grab one. Pretty soon, I'd start feeling the empty in my belly. Thinking about that made me imagine I felt it before I really did.

I was panting hard when it got to midday. The sun was hot, and my shadow puddled under me like it was trying to hide. I wouldn't've minded lying up for a spell, but I couldn't find anywhere to do it.

A bit later, I heard a clatter behind me. When I turned around, the southbound stage was gaining on me. Four overworked drosaws hauled the coach full of folks who didn't care to use their own hind legs to get where they were going. I might've taken it myself if I could've paid the fare.

The drosaws rolled their eyes when they got close. They can smell that things like me eat things like them. That's why hardly anybody rides 'em, you know. They just won't put up with it. The harnessing keeps 'em far enough away from the coach to get too worked up about it. Most of the time, it does.

Got me a surprise when the coach stopped alongside me. The driver leaned my way and said, "Ha! Thought that was you, Rekek. Had enough of Dodge, have you?"

"Oh, you might say so, Havv," I answered. "But what's it to you?" If he wanted to laugh at me because of Sssue, I was gonna climb up there and bite chunks off him. *That'd* fill my belly, all right.

But he didn't. He said, "You see I don't got nobody riding blunderbuss for me. Gafk, he came down sick this mornin'. You want to ride along in case we run into trouble, you can do that. You'll get his wages till we come to Newtown."

"Which Newtown?" I asked. I must've gone through a dozen places by that name, some of 'em tinpot, others good-sized.

"On the Red River," Havv said. "You know that's the route we run."

When I thought about it, I did. I didn't want to do much thinking, though. I didn't much want to wash up in that Newtown, either. Not that anybody there wanted me dead or anything, but it wasn't where I'd aimed for.

But so what? Riding instead of walking, more silver in my pouch afterwards? "I'm your man," I said, and scrambled up alongside him. Folks always said I was a natural-hatched fool. I reckon they knew what they were talking about. Now I do. I was proud of myself then. Yeah, a fool.

———

The blunderbuss Havv handed me had more range and more oomph than an eight-shooter, but not a whole hells of a lot. It'd faze the little raptors or the natives, maybe even the middle raptors. A ranno'd laugh at it. If a ranno came after the stage, we'd've all jumped out and run for it. You do that, you hope the ranno goes for the drosaws, not the people. You hope it doesn't have smaller killers skulking along behind, too. Otherwise, the huzzards will circle down and take care of the raptors' leavings.

We didn't see any rannos that day. Hardly any raptors, either, little or middle. The big hornfaces and the drosaws' wild cousins, they've been hunted in those parts till they're right scarce. You'd almost reckon you was back East.

Almost, but not quite. We didn't get to Cycadia till most of a day-tenth after sundown. One of the drosaws got itself a limp, and Havv had to slow down so it could keep the pace. The passengers grumbled. They cussed up a storm, to tell the truth.

Havv listened for a while. Then he lost his temper, or made like he did. "I'm doin' the best I can, dad gum it!" he hollered. "You can shut up in there, or you can git out an' walk!"

Nobody got out. Havv's mouth dropped open. The nictitating membrane slid across his left eye, the one toward me. He had the whip on the passengers, same as he did on the drosaws, and he enjoyed it.

He handed me some smoked meat. I gnawed on it. It needed some gnawing. He passed me a flask. I took a good knock. That went down a sight easier'n the meat.

Before the sunlight died altogether, he struck a match against a square of slate and got a paraffin lantern going. The light it threw was thin and orange. "Hard to make like it's daylight," I said.

"You do what you can, is all," Havv said, and he wasn't wrong.

I hate the dark. Everybody does. Bad things happen then. The nasty, hairy critters sneak out from wherever they hide and make trouble. Or if they don't, you keep expecting they will, and that's just as bad.

Something howled, out beyond the lantern's small circle. The hairy critters don't see so real good; they make noise to warn others they're around. The drosaws didn't like it a bit, not even the half-lame one.

For all their snorting and honking, though, they kept plugging along. One of them let go of the trace with its hand for a spell, but the length of wood was lashed to its forearm, too, so that didn't do it any good. It got a grip again and soldiered on.

When the dark really slammed down, I said to Havv, "Give me one of your matches, will you?"

"Here you go." He handed me a match and the slate. "What you want it for?"

I struck it, then took the last cigar out of my pouch and stuck it in my jaws. It was so dark even with the lamp, the match's flare near blinded me for a bit. I puffed, got the cigar going, and sucked in smoke. It eased the nighttime jitters a bit. If I coughed, then I coughed, is all.

I thought so, anyways. Havv said, "Nasty habit you got there, Rekek. Stinks—and it's bad for your wind, too."

"How about you let me fuss over all that?" I said.

He clucked like a broody hen, tear my tail off if he didn't. "I'd've known you'd went native, like, I would've let you keep walking back there."

Yeah, the natives've been smoking burnweed forever and a day. It's always grown here, far as anybody knows. But I never saw anything wrong with it, really. I like the smell, no matter how Havv grumbled. I like the way it relaxes you. And they say burnweed'll kill you if you use it long enough, but how long is that? Chances are something else'll get you first.

Something out of the prairie wanted to get us. Out at the edge of the lanternlight, out where I couldn't see much but a shape skulking along on all fours—horrible!—two eyes glowed green, not red like people's eyes and raptors' and drosaws'. I always did think that was unnatural. Way it seemed to me was, the nasty fur thing wanted to make a run at a drosaw, likely the lame one, who was on that side. But it didn't have the size or the nerve. It yowled and disappeared into the black, one more ghost I hoped I never saw again.

"Reckon it's gone?" Havv wasn't griping about the cigar anymore.

"Hope so," I said. "If it'd hung around much longer, I was gonna let fly with the old blunderbuss."

"If you didn't do it on your own, I'd've told you to. I hate them things."

"Who doesn't? They make the feathers stand up all down my backbone and my tail," I said. "Whatever god hatched 'em from the World Egg must've been havin' herself a bad day."

Havv looked at me. "A World Egger, are you? Me, I've always leaned towards Out of the Sky."

We knocked the gods back and forth like smashpins till the drosaws finally hauled us into Cycadia. The town has a spring that never fails. Explorers and trappers and hornface herders liked that. The cycads growing all around the spring gave the place its name. It's smaller than Dodge, but it's more peaceful. Not a bad town at all.

People stumbled out of the stage and staggered toward the hotel. They'd been cooped up as long as anybody could stand. Havv and me, we got the drosaws to the stable and made sure they were seen to. Then we made for the hotel our own selves.

Naturally, it was full up by the time we walked in. The old lady behind the counter said she'd push tables together in the dining room and find us blankets, but she'd have to charge us for a regular room. I hefted the blunderbuss. Havv took out his eight-shooter and looked at it. Didn't point it anywhere near the old lady. Made her thoughtful just the same.

All of a sudden, price came down by half. "I'll see what's in the kitchen, too," she said. "On the house." So we got a place to sleep and fried chicken—pretty good even if it had gone cold—for cheap. Havv shelled out for everything, and got hisself a receipt from the old lady. Sooner or later, the stage company'd pay him back.

"Later, I bet," he said as we wrapped ourselves up in the blankets and tried to get comfy on the tabletops. "They're so tight, they don't even shit."

"That's how you get to run a company," I said, not that I knew the first thing about it.

Not far from us, a lantern burned low. Nobody likes true dark. True dark still belongs to the little hairy things. Some rustles and scrabbles said they might come out in spite of the lantern. I was too worn to care. I closed my eyes. Unless a varmint walked over me, I aimed to sleep till sunup.

And what I aimed at, I hit.

———

Havv got even with the passengers for snaffling all the rooms ahead of us. He banged on their doors as soon as the sun woke him and me, most of a daytenth before we were supposed to head out of Cycadia. Some of 'em cussed him, but he didn't care a bit. They had to be awake to cuss him, and awake was how he got 'em.

The stablehands gave us a fresh drosaw team. Some papers for Havv to sign, on account of ours that hurt its foot—they couldn't use that one for a replacement till it healed up. He signed. Why not? He was doing it for the company.

Some of the passengers were still sore at him when they got on. Some were sore at me, too. Did I help with the door-banging? Oh, maybe a bit. I didn't fancy sleeping on tables, neither. All that grumpy rolled off us like water off your scales. Nothing much they could do about it 'cept haul their own baggage while they walked.

Off we rolled. The drosaws started kicking up dust right away. I hissed and snorted. My nictitating membranes did what they could, flicking bits of grit out of my eyes. Say what you will, dust is better than mud. Slogging through mud up to your cloaca? If you've ever done it— and who hasn't?—you know how awful that is.

Flies buzzed around. The drosaws' hides twitched. They didn't have feathers to flick bugs away. Mine started working double time. Scales are tough, sure, but some of those bloodsuckers have mouths that'll punch through iron thick as your thumbclaw. Sure feels that way when they punch into you, anyhow.

We kept on south across the plains. A small herd of wild hornfaces grazed off in the distance. We left them alone, and we were lucky enough that they did the same with us. They were more worried about some middle raptors prowling around. They started to go into a horn circle to stand 'em off. You always wonder how they know to do that. Not like they could learn it in school or anything.

More huzzards spiraled overhead. These were way higher up than the ones I'd seen the day before. The white of their underwings looked small against the blue. Any time a huzzard's wings seem small, you know it's a long ways off.

They slid across the sky toward the hornfaces and the raptors. Huzzards aren't stupid. Matter of fact, they're pretty damn smart, especially when it comes to vittles. They saw there might be some dead meat left over for 'em in a little while.

We went on rolling along. Every so often, a drosaw or two would pause to graze a bit, pulling up some trailside grass and grinding it in that battery of teeth they have. Long as they didn't linger, Havv let 'em do it. He knew you get more out of critters in good shape than from peaked beasts you whipped along till they dropped.

Farther south we went, warmer and muggier the weather got. More and more cycads and palms sprouted alongside streams. Thunderheads started piling up. Havv's tongue flicked in and out—he didn't like that one bit better'n I did.

"Rain, rain, go away," I said. Yeah, if there's anything worse than plowing through mud in a heavy stage on narrow wheels, fry me if I know what it might be.

The huzzards liked the weather fine. They ride the winds around those clouds like you wouldn't believe. I swear by the gods, when they get winds like that they reckon they're overgrown buzzbirds. You'd pay money to watch 'em, but I didn't have to. They were just up there for free.

"Ain't that somethin', Havv?" I pointed up to them cavorting.

"Somethin'. Yeah." But he didn't hardly look. He paid attention to the trail and to the drosaws and to whatever spots ahead might be dangerous. That was as much as he had room for inside himself. What I'm telling you is, he made a damn fine driver, old Havv did.

Sharp as his brainclaws were, though, I spotted trouble first. I mean, the huzzards did. One heartbeat, they were flinging themselves around in the sky the way they had been, gallivanting all around for the sport of it. The next, they all started winging off to the east fast as they could go—and huzzards go pretty good, let me tell you.

They don't spook like that on a whim. They don't go after food that hard, either—not like they have to chase it. No, something they saw wasn't right. I clicked the blunderbuss to half-cock, just in case. "Maybe you should get your eight-shooter handy, Havv," I said. "Something wrong off to westward."

He'd been minding the drosaws, the way a driver should. But his pupils went from slits to big black circles when he saw the huzzards flying off. "Shove a stick up my cloaca if you ain't right," he said, and shifted the reins to his right hand so he could shoot with his left.

He tried to get more speed from the team without picking up the whip. He didn't have three hands, any more than anyone else does. Even with the whip, I don't reckon he could've done enough. Robbers or natives were going to do what they could any which way.

I worried about the natives more than robbers. Robbers'd take what they wanted and then leave us alone unless our fightback riled 'em too much. Natives wouldn't leave us anything. They were after what we had, and they were after our meat. They hate us even more than they fear us.

Look at it through their eyes and you can't hardly blame 'em. Over the past few hundred years, we've pushed 'em back from the coast almost all the way to the Rockies. They had bronze and crossbows when we got here, but not iron and gunpowder. They fought again and again. They lost again and again. And they sickened and died like nobody's business. That thinned out big tracts of land.

They ain't like us—the natives, I mean. Oh, some of 'em know our lingo, even if they talk funny. And some of 'em raise their tails in salute to our gods. But they ain't really like people. Shorter, squatter, feathers in funny places, hides brown instead of green.

Everybody knows that. Not everybody knows or believes they can't breed with real people, any more than rannos can with raptors. They smell wrong, so you don't want to cross tails with their womenfolk to begin with. No matter what you hear, they don't want anything to do with ours, neither. "I'd sooner screw a drosaw," one of 'em told me once, and I didn't even bite him, on account of I felt the same way about his.

And they're sneaky. By the Eggshell, they're sneaky! They've learned they can't lick us straight up, but they don't fight straight up. I looked in the direction the huzzards came from, but I didn't spy anything out of the way. If I hadn't had a thing or three to do with natives before, I would've wondered if I was imagining things.

———

I didn't spy anything out of the way—and then I did. Four or five natives popped up out of nowhere all sudden-like and rushed the stage. I know—not out of nowhere. The gods-damned rotten eggs must've been there all along. They must've been, but I didn't spot 'em. And I have me some practice spottin' 'em, too. I'd be gnawed bones if I didn't.

Havv let out a holler: "You passengers with pistols, now's the time to use 'em! Try not to shoot each other, hear?"

Just then, a crossbow bolt hissed by in front of my snout, too fast for my eyes to cross. That took *that* native out of the brawl for a bit. A crossbow'll kill you as dead as an eight-shooter will, but you can't load it up again near as quick.

One of the natives had an old musket he'd begged or bought or stolen from somebody who should've known better than to let him get his scaly fingers on it. He stopped to fire, but he didn't shoot straight. He stayed stopped, too; a muzzle-loader's almost as much fun to ready for another shot as a crossbow is. I knew that too well—my blunderbuss worked the same way. I'd likely have one shot, and I'd need to make it count.

Havv started banging away then, and so did two passengers. The drosaws went crazy. They don't know what shooting's all about, but they know they don't like it. Then one of them crumpled up with a crossbow bold in the short ribs. If the natives got one more, the team wouldn't be worth turds. They knew it as well as I did, too.

"Oh, gods!" Havv bawled. "Here's more on the other side of us!" He fired that way, once, twice.

The natives on my side were just about to the stage. If they couldn't shoot us, they'd tear us to pieces with their teeth and claws. I gave 'em the blunderbuss. I hate flintlocks, I purely do. Click, hiss, then *bang!* half a heartbeat later. If you're lucky. If you don't misfire.

I got my *bang!* I wouldn't be spinning this yarn if I didn't. Kick damn near busted my shoulder. You don't hardly aim a blunderbuss. You put in a charge and fill the barrel half full of shot or junk or whatever you've got. The muzzle flares, to make sure the stuff goes every which way when it flies out.

I knocked over two. One took a lot of the charge square in the chest—wasn't much left of it from the middle up. The other thrashed for a bit before he lay still, but lay still he did. That's about as much as you can hope for from a blunderbuss.

And fry me if Havv didn't reach out with another blunderbuss as soon as I let fly with the first. How? I don't know how, consarn it. Maybe he really did have three hands. I pointed the piece at the natives. They took off running like middle raptors—which they ain't so far from, you ask me. A passenger winged one with a pistol shot. Only made the stinker run faster.

"Hoped they'd lowtail it," Havv said. "That one ain't loaded."

"Remind me I never should ought to game with you," I said. His bluff paid off, though, so I couldn't cuss him the way I wanted to. The natives on his side of the stage had had themselves a bellyful, too, and ran away like their pals. We were safe. Compared to how we'd been a little while before, anyways.

While Havv got the team under control, I borrowed his eight-shooter and went back to make sure the native who hadn't got all chewed up wasn't playing mammal and getting ready to do something nasty and sneaky. You got to check every single time.

But this one was a goner. Some junk had gone in through an eye. The thrashing? Didn't matter a copper's worth.

Something moved by the other carcass, though. The feathers on my back twitched. That native, he should've been *dead*. Wasn't enough of him left to be alive, not any more. But his leg kept twitching irregardless.

No, not *his* leg. Hers. When the natives raid, sometimes they all raid. If a gal's got a hatchling, she'll tie it to her leg to keep it out of mischief and go with the rest.

A shot rang out behind me—Havv, putting the wounded drosaw out of its pain. I wondered if I should smash in the little fella's head. I didn't feel bad about killing his mama. She would've done the same to me, and given the hatchling my liver to eat. She would've had some herself, too. But slaughter someone just out of the egg? Call me thin-shelled, but I couldn't stomach it.

"Let me have a chunk of that drosaw meat," I said.

"You don't want to eat none of her, Rekek. Nasty stuff," Havv said.

"Not for me. For Junior here." I held up the hatchling. I named him, too, though I didn't know it yet.

Havv hissed. "Don't keep that little monster! Good gods, bite off its head and get things over with." A couple of passengers peering out the window shouted the same thing, only louder and filthier.

Well, that just made me mad. You don't want to rile me—I reckon you found that out your ownself, didn't you? I kind of aimed the second blunderbuss at the stage. Stupid passengers didn't know it wasn't loaded. They shut up right smart. You bet they did.

"I'll hang on to him a while, see what he turns into," I told Havv. "If he tries biting my tail off or starts stealing or whatever the hells, I'll cut him loose. If he don't…I got no hatchlings of my own that I know about."

"You're crazier'n a hornface that's been eating locoweed," Havv said, but he cut me a nice chunk of drosaw kidney. I fed it to the baby native. Junior gulped it straight down. I gave him more. He ate that, too. Then he licked my hand. When I bent down over him, he sniffed my snout. Then he licked it, same as with my hand. Then he bared his little needle teeth to show he was happy.

Our hatchlings act the same way. They got to know who'll feed 'em, and it ain't like they can talk or understand straight out of the egg. To Junior, I was his new mama. He was so little, he'd never recollect the one who laid his egg.

Anyways, that's how I came by him, and he's been with me ever since. Yeah, he talks a bit mushy. He can't help it. But he's a better person than most ordinary folks I know, and we get on fine. If you want to say one more stupid thing about it, we gods-damned well *will* take you outside and teach you manners. Ain't that right, Junior?

See? He said, "Right." You followed him good, didn't you? *Didn't* you, stranger? Yeah, I figured you did.

BONEHUNTERS

Junior and me, we got up into the Black Hills country and the Badlands not far away. Yes, thank you, I know that's not the kind of place where you want to end up. What do you mean, how come I'm looking at you like you're some kind of natural-hatched fool? How else am I supposed to look at somebody who's a natural-hatched fool?

Tell you what you can do, though. You can buy me a drink, and you can buy one for Junior, too. That'll go some ways to makin' amends. Or you can try the two of us out in the alley and see how you fancy that. Maybe you'll have more sense after we bite some chunks out of you so it can get in.

Ah, thank you kindly. Much obliged. See? You ain't a great big fool, anyways.

What d'you mean, do I know Junior's a native? He's my hatchling. I'd cursed well better know. No, I didn't spawn him. We can't breed with the natives. Anybody who tells you we can is a gods-damned liar. Junior's my hatchling anyway. He's been with me since he was tiny. Neither one of us'd know what to do without the other now.

Have I got that straight, Junior, or am I wrong? There! You see, stranger? He feels the same way I do, and as long as he does it's no consarned concern o' yours a-tall.

What d'you mean, he talks all mushy? You ain't been out West real long, have you? He can't help the way he sounds. It comes from the way his mouth is shaped. You can't make proper native noises, neither.

You wouldn't care to? This here's the West, pal. You may need to one fine day, and sooner than you reckon, too. You just never can tell.

And I'd be farther along in my story if you didn't keep bangin' your teeth. You want I should tell it or not? Oh, you do? Well, then, I will— long as you keep your biter shut, I will.

We were by the Black Hills, like I told you. This was in the days when there was still a native kingdom there. No, Junior's not from them parts. We met up years and years ago, a good bit farther south. You got to understand, this was before they found there was gold in them thar hills. Nobody cared about the natives running things there, on account of nobody reckoned the land was worth anything.

Ever see the Badlands? They look the way your hide does after you get over rinderpest, all bumpy and wavy and slaggy. I heard one fella say they look like what would've happened if the gods beat some of the white of the World Egg into peaks and let 'em get hard out there. I mostly don't hold with that kind of language my ownself, but it does get the notion across.

Or it would, except the Black Hills, they're home to different gods. You'll have seen the stereoscopes if you ain't never been there yourself, am I right? Sure I am. Them great big heads, all sharp teeth and eyeballs, carved into the mountainside… Shingto and Fferso and Incol and Oosev, those're their names. You better learn 'em, too, before you go into that country.

It's impressive work. It'd be impressive for us, and we've got iron and steel and gunpowder. The natives, they used bronze and stones and lots of people and lots of time. Nobody knows how long ago they made 'em. Nobody knows how long it took, neither. The natives don't remember, and we ain't found out.

No, Junior and me, we didn't go up there just to see the sights. You travel for the sake o' sightseein', you got to be rich. Do I look rich to you? Does Junior? Didn't think so. We were there for whatever work we could find, hunting or herding or playing guide for hornface hunters after a trophy.

Wasn't my first trip there. I'd been in those parts years before. I knew my way around pretty good—for a fella whose scales are green, anyways. The natives, what they can do, you wouldn't believe it if you didn't see it for yourself.

It's like they were hatched there or somethin', you say? Oh, you're a regular cutup, you are. They gods-damned well *were* hatched there. No, don't get your feathers all ruffled. You don't make any more stupid jokes, and I won't sit on 'em. How's that for a bargain?

Suit you? All right, then. I'll go on with my yarnin'…

━━━━━━━━━

It was a daytenth before sundown when Junior and me, we came within hailing distance of Fort Ironclaw. Folks who've never been anyway near Fort Ironclaw call it the Gateway to the Black Hills. Anybody who's ever seen it—soldier or traveler, don't matter a pinfeather—calls it that horrible shithole plumb in the middle of nowhere.

Which it is. Soldiers don't get sent to Fort Ironclaw on account of they've won a promotion. They get sent there to work off their sins from somewhere else.

Somebody in the fort winded a horn while we were still a long ways off. I couldn't spy anyone on the stockade yet. Hells, I could hardly see the gods-damned stockade. The sentry, he must've had hisself a spyglass with some juice in the tube.

We kept walking. Heads popped up on the stockade when I got close enough to make 'em out. You may have been a busted egg to get exiled to Fort Ironclaw, but you don't dare stay sleepy once you wash up there. The natives would've liked nothing better than to swarm over the fort, and everybody in there knew it.

One of the sergeants bellowed at us through a big leather loud-hailer: "Who comes?"

I didn't have a loud-hailer. What kind of use'd I have for one? I cupped my hands in front of my snout and hollered back: "Rekek and Junior. Don't you recognize us, Snegor? I sure know your voice."

"Keep on comin'. We won't shoot you yet," Snegor said, as full of himself as any sergeant ever hatched.

"They're itchy about me," Junior said quietly. You can follow him fine once you get used to how he talks. Wasn't anybody ever gonna be more used to it than me.

"You hush. Long as you're with me, everything's jake," I told him. He's a native, of course. Anybody can see that, and hear it. But, like I say, he's been with me since he was fresh out of the egg. No matter that his hides's brown and he's got feathers in funny places. No matter that he talks a little strange. He makes better people than most ordinary folks I know.

If you don't know him, though, he just looks like a native. At the edge of the Badlands, that's plenty to make soldiers hop and scratch.

We were inside easy rifle range when Sergeant Snegor picked up the loud-hailer again. By then, I could spot the soldier with the spyglass. Reckon he could count my feathers, and Junior's, if he was so inclined.

"You are who you say you are," Snegor allowed. He sounded as if admitting it pained him, but admit it he did. Somebody else up there said something to him; I couldn't make out what. Snegor went on, "Feel like hiring out for some guiding?"

"Mebbe," I answered. You never want to sound eager, especially when you are. Lean times lately. "Might depend on who wants to pay me to do it. Will depend on where he wants me to guide him to."

"His name's Otnil. He's a perfesser, from one o' them fancy schools back East," Snegor said. "He's after old bones, if you can believe it. Anybody wants to know what I think, he's crazy as a bedtick, but who the hells wants to know what I think?"

He was shouting this, y'understand, through that big old loud-hailer of his. I could hear him. Junior could hear him. If any natives were close by in the Badlands, they could hear him. And for sure everybody inside Fort Ironclaw could hear him, including Professor Otnil. Well, Snegor never was the brightest candle in the chandelier.

"I'll talk with him. See what he wants. See what he pays," I said. I'd heard of these bonehunters before, but I'd never met up with one. They get as excited about the old skulls and teeth and things that weather out of the sides of bluffs and creekbeds as regular folks would over gold and silver. Maybe *crazy as a bedtick* wasn't so far wrong after all.

By then, Junior and me had come up to the ditch around the fort. It was dry; you don't get a whole bunch of rain in those parts. But it was deep, and it was full of pikes pointing straight up. Natives attacking the fort couldn't jump down in there and commence to undermining the stockade.

I sat back on my tail and looked up at Snegor. "Well? You gonna let us in so's we can palaver with your perfesser?"

"Oh. Right." Yeah, Snegor was dim. He started bawling orders. The drawbridge creaked down. Inside the fort, a squad of riflemen stood ready in case a swarm of riled-up natives tried following Junior and me. But it was just the two of us. Our toeclaws clicked on the sun-faded planks when we walked over the bridge. Soon as we got inside, more soldiers started hauling it up again.

Of course the flag flew over the fort. Soon as we got inside, Junior and me, we both set our left hands on our snouts for a heartbeat or two to show our respect. Wasn't any breeze to speak of; the red and green stripes hung limp against the pole. But that flag flew everywhere from sea to salty sea, except for a few little places where the natives still hung on. It deserved respect, by the gods.

I looked at things that way, anyhow. If Junior felt any different, he kept his trap shut about it.

Sergeant Snegor took me to Lieutenant Diffi. Diffi also knew me; he took me to Captain Jawj. Jawj kinda hissed when he saw me. He knew me, too; he did that with everybody. He hated the whole gods-damned world, Jawj did. He'd been a colonel in charge of a couple of brigades in the big war back East. When the war ended, so did his fancy rank. He was lucky to wind up in charge of a dusty little fort at the edge of the Badlands instead o' counting cannon balls and coils of rope somewhere.

He understood that as well as anybody could. Only he didn't reckon it was the good kind of luck.

"You'll show crazy Otnil where the bones are at?" He sounded sour as an esrog. He mostly did. A lot of officers, if that happened to them, they'd drink and drink and never stop. Not Jawj. He never touched the stuff. I got to say, stayin' sober didn't improve him none.

"That's right, Longfeather," I said. Longfeather was what the natives called him in their language. His crest really did stand up when he was in a temper, and he was most of the time. I went on, "I will if he pays me decent, anyways, and if he treats Junior good."

Jawj looked at Junior like he was measuring him for a pyre. He had no use for natives, Jawj. Junior could see that. He looked back at Jawj the same way. Junior don't back away from nobody; it ain't in him.

Jawj snarled something under his breath. He gestured to Lieutenant Diffi. "Take him to the crazy huzzard," he said. "Take 'em both. Get 'em the hells out of my sight."

"I'll do it, Captain." Diffi saluted. Being a soldier means taking guff no freeman'd ever put up with if the fella dealing it out didn't outrank him. I don't know what a lieutenant's pay is. Not as much as Diffi deserved—you can bet on that.

He took us to the officers' quarters. That's where they'd stashed Otnil and the rest of the diggers. One of the junior smart boys looked up from the dice game they had going and said, "He isn't here. He's over in the stables, checkin' on that drosaw with the sore arm."

"Over to the stables, then," Diffi said, and over to the stables we went.

Along the way, I asked him, "This here Otnil—he's a drosaw doc, too?"

"He fancies that he is," Diffi answered, and bit down on whatever he was going to say after that.

Stables smell funny, like drosaws and like drosaw shit, which smells a bit like the critters it comes out of but more like moldy, rotten grass and leaves. Not near so sharp a stink as from what comes out of my cloaca. But people eat meat, mostly. Our droppings smell like what raptors and rannos leave behind. I am glad we use flags instead of piles of poop to mark our territory, I will say.

First time I set eyes on him, Otnil was poking and prodding at a cut on a drosaw's arm. The duckbill didn't like it much. They're skittish around people; they can smell that we eat 'em. If this one lashed out with its tail, it could send Otnil into the planks of the stall wall, or maybe through 'em.

The perfesser wasn't tall or strong, but he had hisself a big, round head. Folks who say they can tell what you are by the bumps on your skull would've had a tough time with him, on account of he had no bumps to speak of. A lot of brains, though, leastways if you went by what was wrapped around 'em.

"Professor Otnil?...Professor Otnil?" Diffi sounded more respectful than he did talking with Captain Jawj. Otnil went on poking at the drosaw till he finally noticed somebody was trying to get through to him. When he did, Diffi went on, "Professor, this here is Rekek. He knows his way around these parts, Rekek does. If you're after bones, he can point you at 'em."

Otnil focused on me. It was almost like being looked at through a magnifying glass, he stared so hard. "Pleased to make your acquaintance, Master Rekek," he said, and held out his left hand. It had drosaw blood and maybe pus on it, but I ain't fussy. I clasped with him. He had a fair grip for a little fella, he did. Then he dipped his head toward Junior and asked, "Who's your colleague?"

A lot of ordinary people, they pretend not to notice natives unless they can't help it. I liked Otnil better on account of he wasn't like that. "This here's Junior. He's my stepson. Been with me near as long as he's been out of the egg," I said, and I bet I sounded as proud as if he was my own spawn.

"Rekek Junior, I am pleased to meet you, too," Otnil said, and crack my shell if he didn't clasp with him same as he did with me. I didn't know then that Otnil made a point of getting on with the natives. *They aren't our kind*, he'd say, *but that doesn't make them knaves or hatchlings.* He's right, too. If only more people believed it.

"Pleased to meet you, Professor," Junior said. I raised him to be polite.

The perfesser had no trouble with how he talked; he must've heard the like often enough before to get used to it. He asked, "How much do you know about the paleontological past of this part of the country?"

"About the what?" Junior and me, we said it in chorus, like. You asked me, I would've guessed Otnil stole a word from some native language nobody talks any more. I would've been wrong, but I didn't know that then.

"About its ancient past, as revealed in fossils and other traces," Otnil said grandly. He had a way of talking, all right, the perfesser did.

"I can find you old bones, where they weather out of bluffs and banks and things," I said. "This is about the first time I ever heard they was worth even as much as a crap on the ocean, though."

"Is it? *Is* it?" The perfesser swung my way. When he stared at me, his pupils went from slits to circles so big and black that they filled up his eyeballs and swallowed all the yellow there. I set myself, on account of I was afeared he'd jump on me and commence to chawing. But he didn't—quite. In a low, deadly voice, he asked me, "You haven't been hanging around with that scoundrel of a Trinka, have you?"

"Don't reckon I ever met or even heard of anybody by that name," I answered. Junior dipped his head to show he hadn't, either. "Who is the nasty little son of a mammal, anyways?"

Well, I made Otnil laugh, gods damn me if I didn't. I didn't know then how hard that was. He answered, "Trinka fancies himself a paleontologist, too, the ignorant, arrogant...son of a mammal's a good name for him, Rekek. He's so sneaky, he'd grow hair if only he could. He and his band of bone thieves prowl around spots where I've been digging, looking to steal what they can and describe it in print before I'm able to. But he doesn't know as much as he thinks he does, and you can count on that."

Wonder what Trinka'd say about you, I thought, but I had too much sense to come out with it. Instead, I said, "What do you know?" That's safe enough most any time.

Not in that stable. Straightaway, Otnil answered, "I know for a fact that he mounted an ancient plessy skull at the end of the creature's tail instead of on its neck. I know because I saw him do it with my own two eyes."

"How about that?" I tried for another safe play. Still plessies in the ocean to this day. They look like snakes that swallowed a giant dinner plate and then grew paddles on it. People hunt 'em same as they hunt mossies, for the fine oil and meat they yield. But they're dangerous critters. Sometimes folks kill them, and sometimes they kill folks.

"So you see he is a blowhard, an ignoramus, a fraud who does not deserve to come within miles of important fossils," Otnil said.

I wondered what Trinka'd say about that, too. But Trinka wouldn't be paying the freight for Junior and me. Otnil would. Which reminded me… "What kind of wages you aim to give us, Professor?"

He named a number. It wasn't a great big number. Otnil, he had money. He just didn't fancy parting with it. I must've looked unhappy, 'cause he said, "And a bonus for every fossiliferous site you and Junior lead us to. If you find me fine fossils, I shall be generous. By the World Egg, I shall!"

Junior and me, we were Eggers, too. But Eggers can cheat just like anybody else. I oughta know. Still, I believed Otnil here. He sounded as crazy as a feller who falls tail over snout for some chorus girl with a fine rump and fancy feathers.

"Reckon we got ourselves a deal," I said. "Only what's that long word you used mean? Fossiliferous?" No, I wasn't sure I was sayin' it right.

"It means 'fossil-bearing,'" he answered. "Take me where my associates and I can do some proper excavating."

"The best places I know, they're on native land. Will the king and his people be all right with you comin' in?" I asked. The natives don't like what you do, they'll try their best to kill you and eat you. They ain't cannibals; they never eat their own kind. They like the taste of us, though, when they can get it. We've made the price of that meat pretty gods-damned expensive."

Professor Otnil waved my worries off to one side. "Don't you fret," he said. "I don't steal from natives, I don't cheat them or rob them, and I'm not after gold. King Red Cloud knows that about me. He's let me know he'll let me work on his land."

Our mouths don't work for native words any better than theirs do for our lingo. Mostly, we just translate their names into regular talk, the way the perfesser did. Sometimes they sound funny, but at least you can wrap your tongue and teeth around 'em.

"Here's hoping you're right," I said. "Junior and me'll be puttin' our necks on the block along with yours." We clasped hands again. The deal was done. I hoped I wouldn't be too sorry it was.

———————

The perfesser, the other fellas who knew about fossils, the drivers, the diggers, and Junior and me, we all left Fort Ironclaw two mornings after I got there. Sergeant Snegor was cheerful as ever when he gave his men the order to let down the drawbridge. "Hope the natives don't throw you and your bright boys back at us in chunks," he told Professor Otnil.

The natives don't make many cannon. They don't work iron, and copper's harder to come by and costs way more. Plenty of traders'll sell 'em rifles—you'll always find folk who put silver ahead of their own kind—but not artillery. Still and all, they do know how to build catapults, ones that'll trouble even forts for a few shots. So they could fling us back that way if they decided to go to war.

Snegor didn't faze Otnil so much as a claw paring. The perfesser, he kinda looked at him and said, "If you were half as funny as you think you are, you'd be twice as funny as you really are." Snegor ain't the hottest pepper in the sauce; reckon I said that already. He needed a few heartbeats to work out what Otnil was drivin' at. Once he finally got it, didn't his tail lash back and forth! Oh, you bet it did! He was that mad, Snegor was.

Down thumped the drawbridge. Over we went. When it started getting raised again, Snegor hollered through the noise of rattling chains: "I hope they eat you up bones and all, every last one of you!"

Then Lieutenant Diffi started giving him hells. It just wasn't Snegor's day, not even a little bit.

Junior nudged me and said, low, "Hope he doesn't turn the soldiers against us if we do need help."

"You and me both," I told him. You'll hear folks say natives aren't as smart as we are. Most of the fools who come out with that never set eyes on a native in their lives, and'd turn tail and run if they ever did. The rest are nasty rogues, raptors that sleep in beds and tell lies for all the world as though they was people. Sure as sure, Junior understood how things worked.

Fort Ironclaw shrank behind us till a swell of ground swallowed it. A raven let out a froggy croak. They're right clever birds. If they had thumbs and fingers 'stead of beaks, they'd start cheating each other like one more set of people.

Much higher up, huzzards wheeled in the sky. They didn't care about us, not while we were alive and moving. If the natives did kill us and their feast had leftovers, the huzzards'd come down and clean up. Meanwhile, they circled. They had to be a good ways up, on account of they looked small. A huzzard's wingspan is as wide as a drosaw is long—say, five or six people lying nose to tailtip with each other.

People say it ain't good luck if a huzzard's shadow slides over you. I've had it happen a few times. I'm still here. But I ain't exactly handsome and I ain't exactly rich, so people may know what they're talking about after all. Or they may not. With people, you never can tell.

Sometimes you can't even tell if they *are* people. *Something* was moving on a ridgeline ahead of us and off to one side. I could make that out, but only just barely. Might've been some of Red Cloud's natives, keeping a sly eye on us whilst we moved into their country. Or it might've been a pack of droms or other middle raptors, sizing us up to see whether we were prey or something too scary to mess with.

If they were raptors, I hoped they decided not to bother with us. We'd drive 'em off, but some of us'd wind up hurt or dead. Supposing they were natives, we'd wind up dead soon as Red Cloud said the word. So would some of them, but fat lot of good that'd do us. And the soldiers would make 'em sorrier yet, which also wouldn't help us none. It was hot, and getting hotter. I started to pant. I wasn't the only one, either. We had a couple of water barrels along, but they were for drinking, not for splashing over our hides to cool us down. Water's hard to come by in the Badlands. Only a few good drinking and watering holes that don't go dry. Most streams do in summertime. 'Course, when a thunderboomer blows in, you get too much water all at once. You can drown in what was just a gully a tenth of a daytenth earlier.

After a bit, Professor Otnil pointed over to that ridgeline. Things had been so quiet over there, I'd almost decided that was a raptor pack and they didn't care to take us on.

Shows what I know. Puffs of smoke were going up into the sky: big ones, little ones, then big ones again. "It's the natives' fire code," Otnil said. "They're telling Red Cloud we're in their country."

"Reckon you're right," I said. "Can you read what it says?"

"I've never studied that." By the way Otnil said it, he felt he was admitting a lack in himself. "How about you or Junior?"

"I can't. I don't expect Junior can. He pretty much knows what I've learned him." But I asked him anyway. He's grown up a lot lately, and he picks things up on his own. He tossed his head to show he didn't savvy either, though.

"All right." Plain as the snout in front of my eyes, Professor Otnil didn't reckon it was. After a bit, he asked me, "How far is the fort from the first fossiliferous outcropping, Master Rekek?"

"Just Rekek is fine, thanks," I said. They talk fancier back East than we mostly do out here. "If the natives don't give us trouble, if the wagons don't bust a wheel or an axle, we should get there a daytenth or so before sundown."

"All right," Otnil said again.

He sounded happier this time, so I asked him a question of my own: "What gets you and your pals here so all-fired excited about bones old enough to turn to rock?"

The feathers in his crest stood straight up. I must've surprised him good—maybe he'd reckoned I already knew. Maybe he reckoned everybody knew, and got all hot and bothered same way he did. He said, "Why, to trace how the extinct animals of the vanished past developed into those we know today. If we're very lucky, to find some specimens that help us trace the evolution of the natives of this continent from the raptors that were their ancestors—raptors not far removed on the tree of life from those that were our own forebears."

That there was a mighty big egg of thought to lay all at once. I figured I'd better nibble at it a little bit at a time. "'Evolved'?" I said. "That's a word I've heard a time or two, but hang me if I know just what it means."

His crest feathers popped up again. "Have you never read or even heard of Dinwass' great book, *A Rationale for the Development and Change of Living Forms through Time*?"

"Perfesser, you got to bear with me. I ain't no scholard. Ain't nothin' but an ordinary son of an egg, gettin' by as best I can."

"I suppose so." Otnil's sigh wasn't just that he was disappointed in me. He was disappointed in the gods for letting dullards like me scramble out of the shell to begin with.

Then he started talking—and talking, and talking. I got mebbe one word in three. If I followed him straight—don't count on it, on account of I still ain't sure—it went like this. The critters that were better suited to living where and how they were living had more hatchlings that lived, and those hatchlings had more hatchlings, too, and on and on till what had been good enough wasn't anymore and the looks of critters changed.

"Where are the gods in all this?" I asked when Otnil slowed down to take a breath. Let me tell you, I had to wait a spell.

"Why, wherever you want them to be," he answered. "You are an Egger, I believe, as I am?"

"That's right." I dipped my head. So did Junior, who was listening to the perfesser an' me going back and forth.

"Well, can you not imagine the gods cracking the Great Egg and then standing aside to let it grow as it would?…to let it grow as they'd willed beforehand, if you like that better?" Otnil said. "Those who believe life and light came Down from the Sky may believe they came down in the Beginning, and then developed as they did—or as the gods willed. There is no fight between faith on the one claw and evolution and natural selection on the other. None!"

The perfesser, he sounded certain sure. Whether he was or not, I can't begin to tell you, and I won't try. I asked, "But wouldn't your old evolution and—what did you call it?—natural selection, that's the moniker you used, work just as well with no gods at all to start off?"

"Some people will say that." Now Professor Otnil talked slow. I could hear how careful he was, picking his words. "I do not happen to be one of them. The discoveries of science have nothing to do with whether the gods and what people feel about them are real."

"No, huh?" I wanted to think he was right about that. I wanted to, from my snout all the way back to my tailtip. It wasn't so easy, though. I kept my big mouth shut about that. You don't go out of your way to squabble with the fella who's payin' you, not unless you're a natural-hatched idjit you don't.

———

We didn't get to the bluff with the bones till the sun was less than half a daytenth from setting. You never go as fast as you hope you will. Otnil, he'd been out bonehunting often enough to know that as well as I did. He didn't get riled at me, the way I was kind of afeared he might.

"Yes," he said, sweeping up and down the bluffside with a spyglass. "Oh, yes." I've seen gents watchin' dancing girls who didn't sound so excited. Hells, I've been one o' them gents.

A middle raptor skittered away from us. In a brawl, likely it could've torn any one of us to bits. But it had the wit to see it couldn't kill us all, not by its lonesome it couldn't.

"Is that a rock it's got in its fist?" I asked the perfesser.

He swung the spyglass toward the critter. "I do believe it is," he said. "It comes from a line related to that which led to the natives here. No surprise it can use primitive tools."

"They go after drosaws or hornfaces with rocks and sticks, the critters get a surprise, I bet. Only they don't laugh for long," I said, and I kinda retooled the thought I'd had about ravens: "Hells, give them raptors a little time and they'll start cheating their way through quarrels 'stead o' bitin'."

Professor Otnil dipped his head. "It could happen, though the natives and we ourselves have already filled that niche pretty well."

"Niche?" I'd heard that word before, too, but not the way he used it. "You mean like a space dug out of a wall where you can set a lamp or a pretty?"

"A space on the tree of life that's already filled," Otnil said. "On the plains here, rannos fill the large-carnivore niche, while huzzards are the large scavengers. Do you follow?"

"Reckon so," I answered. Junior's eyes went all big with thought. We were nothing but a couple of ordinary fellas, him and me. Otnil treated us like we could come with his ideas if he gave us half a chance, though. And you know what? When he treated us like that, we *could,* at least partways.

He and a couple of the younger brainy folks with him, they went over to the bluffside and started scouting it. One of them bent down and scratched at the crumbling rock. He held something in the soft-scaled palm of his hand.

Some of the other folks were unloading digging tools and camp gear and whatnot from the wagons. Junior and me, we lent a hand. Wouldn't've felt right, standing around while they worked. One of them patted Junior on the shoulder in place of saying thanks. Junior, he hopped up in the air—he was *that* happy about getting treated like anybody else.

That same fellow who'd patted him called over to the one who'd found whatever the devils he'd found: "What you got there?"

"Chunk of mammal jaw from the days when there are a few modern forms," answered the scraper. "Looks to be a gnawing beast."

"Mammals." If I sounded disgusted, it was only because I was. Thinking about mammals disgusts just about everybody. They're little; the biggest ones aren't even the size of a lesser raptor, and most of 'em are a lot smaller than that. They come out at night and gnaw things and steal things and creep over you when you're asleep. *Creep* is right; like lizards and salamanders, they go on four legs, not two. And they don't have feathers. They're all covered in nasty fur instead. Beady little eyes. Twitchy little noses. Horrible!

"They tell us how the world developed and changed, same as our own ancestral forms do," the young educated fellow by me said. "For a while, it was touch and go whether their kind or ours would fill the large-creature niches in the world."

I tried to imagine a world full of big, four-legged critters, all covered with matted, smelly hair. The gravel in my gizzard ground, let me tell you. I'd never've dreamt of anything so all-fired revolting on my own. What good are smart fellas if all they do is give you more reasons not to sleep at night?

"Bring the digging tools!" Otnil yelled from the bluffside. They had shovels and picks like you'd expect, but they also had trowels and scrapers and little tiny pointy tools like the ones dentists use when your tooth goes bad and the new one hasn't grown in yet, and even little brushes. The brushes were made from mammal hair, so that is something the horrid little sneakers are good for, anyways.

But with the sun just about ready to disappear under that jagged Badlands horizon, Otnil and his friends came back before they did a whole bunch of digging. We went on setting up camp.

The perfesser, he walked over to me and said, "Looks like you'll get your bonus, Rekek. Didn't get to excavate as much as I would have liked, but this is plainly a rich area."

"Glad it makes you happy," I said, on account of *Glad I'll get my claws on some extra silver* is rude.

We ate dried meat plain and dried meat stewed and dried meat soaked and fried in hornface fat and dried meat every other way the cook knew how to fix it. We'd have to do some hunting pretty soon if we wanted anything better. For the first night, we ate what we'd brought. Everybody gabbled about the fossils, all excited, till people started winding down. Then we wrapped ourselves in padded leather blankets, got as close to the fires as we cared to, and fell asleep.

And when we woke up next morning, there were natives all around us. They must have snuck up during the darkness, sly as mammals. We had watchers out, but we might as well not have bothered. They were better at that stuff than we were.

If they wanted to kill us and eat us, they could. There were enough of 'em, our guns wouldn't stop 'em. Captain Jawj might make 'em sorry later, but how much good would that do us now? Not enough, I reckoned. Not near enough.

———

Some of the natives had crossbows. Some had old-fashioned muskets or blunderbusses. Quite a few carried rifles as good as the ones the soldiers in Fort Ironclaw used. Yeah, they could have done for us, all right.

"Phew!" one of the drivers said. "We might not've heard 'em skulking around, but shouldn't we have smelled 'em?"

Natives do have a different odor. A lot of people don't care for it. Me, I was used to it, from spending so long with Junior. Junior didn't mind me, either, but a lot of natives don't care for the way *we* smell. That's why we don't jump on their women, or they on ours. Who wants to screw something that smells more like a wild animal than a person?

Professor Otnil stood up so the natives could see him and recognize him. "I come in peace!" he said loudly, holding out his hands to show he held no weapon. "I come with King Red Cloud's permission. I come not to steal, but to increase knowledge of the world."

He used our language. We make as much a mess of their tongues as they do with ours. But, just because their mouths are different from ours, their earholes aren't. A lot of them have learned to understand what we say just fine.

One of the natives raised his left hand. That could have been the signal for the lot of them to swarm down on us. It could have been, but it wasn't. When I noticed the brownskin had a couple-three gold bracelets on his arms and a fat gold collar round his neck, I realized who he was pretty likely to be.

Otnil raised his left hand the same way. He had no bracelets or bangles, just one o' them newfangled smallclocks on a drosaw-leather strap. But he spoke as one equal to another: "Welcome, King Red Cloud!"

"Welcome to my land," Red Cloud answered. He didn't talk our lingo even as well as Junior did. Along with his native's mouth, he had an accent from his own language, where Junior'd learned our words from the time he was big enough to use any at all. But you could make out what Red Cloud said, and when you get right down to it who needs more than that?

"It *is* your land," Otnil agreed. "Will you come down and break your fast with my men and me?"

"I do that," the king said. Then he spoke in his own language. Some of his warriors shouted at him. He shouted back. I got the drift—*What are you doing arguing with me?*—without understanding a word.

We couldn't hope to feed all the fighters, not without runnin' out o' grub ourselves. He seen that, Red Cloud did. He brought a few a his big wheels with him, and left the rest to shift for themselves. He spotted Junior right away—natural enough. He said something to him in his talk.

Junior spread his hands to show he didn't follow. In the only language he really knew, he answered, "I speak this tongue. No others well."

Red Cloud's feathers jumped in surprise. "How does this happen, when you are not a greenskin?" he asked in our lingo.

"Here is my stepfather, from when I was tiny." Junior curled his tail around mine. "I have learned from his mouth."

That made the native king give me a long, measuring stare. "Tell me your name," he said. "Tell me how you came by a hatchling of ours."

"I'm Rekek, your Kingship." I told him the story. Junior already knew it; no harm in that. Junior's mother would've killed me and eaten me if she didn't get shot herself. I finished, "I brung him up best way I know how."

"You could have killed him," Red Cloud said. "No one would have thought you wrong. But you let him live. You helped him live."

I kinda shrugged. "He was little and helpless. He didn't do me no harm. I didn't want to do him none, neither."

The king must've translated for his chieftains. They all looked my way. One of them held a hand over his eyes for a heartbeat. I understood. It meant the same as when we dip our heads deeper than usual: a sort of salute. I did dip my head to him. Junior looked proud of me. That felt good.

After breakfast, Red Cloud asked Otnil what kind of bones he'd found. Sounding embarrassed, the perfesser said, "We only just began yesterday. But I can show you this." He had the half a mammal jaw in a little pasteboard box, wrapped in cloth so it wouldn't break any more than it was already.

Red Cloud held it up close to his snout for a good look. "Something like a rat," he judged, and Otnil dipped his head in agreement. The native went on, "This is more rock than bone, though. How does that happen? I have seen it before, but I do not understand it."

Otnil talked about fossils, and went right on talkin'. I learned a good bit myself. I didn't know how bone turned into rock, neither. But I commenced to get bored. Red Cloud didn't. He was ready to listen as long as Otnil was ready to talk.

Finally, Otnil said, "If you want to come and see where we're working and what we dig up there, we'd be pleased to have you along."

Speak for yourself, I thought. Then I decided that, if it was a choice between Red Cloud watching and Red Cloud fighting, watching seemed the better bet.

He must have felt the same way, on account of he said, "I will do that for a while, yes." He didn't need long to notice Junior and me weren't heading out to the dig. He included us in. Otnil didn't say boo. We turned into bonehunters for the day.

"Maybe we'll even find something," Junior said while we tramped over to the bluff.

"Never can tell," I answered. Anybody might spot bones there—there were that many of 'em. I'd noticed 'em before, going through the Badlands.

Which came back to claw me, because Red Cloud asked, "How did you pass through this land before?" When I didn't say anything right away, he kind of laughed and said, "On my honor, no harm to you for your answer."

"Wasn't anything much, really," I said. "Junior and me, we was just takin' a little shortcut across the edge of your kingdom." I've hatched plenty of lies bigger'n that one. Hells, it even had some truth in it, though I didn't tell all there was to tell about the rotten eggs on our trail then.

When we got to the bluff, the real fossil fellas showed what they could do. They saw old-time bones where Red Cloud and Junior and me, we just saw pebbles. Otnil took half a daytenth chipping a chunk of skull out of the rock around it—the matrix, that was the word he used.

Red Cloud held the bones and gave 'em the once-over. "Something like a middle raptor, only not just like that," he said.

"No, not just like that," Otnil agreed. "This form has been extinct for many, many years. From the shape of the back of the braincase, it may be part of the line that leads to your folk."

"What do you mean? Shingto and Fferso and Incol and Oosev, they made us from thunder and tornadoes," Red Cloud said. "Other gods, or it could be demons, who did not know so well what they were about, they made your kind."

Junior chuckled, all soft-like, when he heard that. I thought it was pretty blamed funny, too. *So there* ran through my head. Otnil didn't stir a feather. "All religions tell different stories," he said. "Nature gives true answers—if we ask the right questions and if we understand what we find."

"How do you know what is true? How do you judge?" Red Cloud was no one's fool.

"The same as you do with anything else." Otnil did him the courtesy of taking him serious. "You fit each new piece in with what you already know. Do your hatchlings play with puzzles?"

"They do," Red Cloud said.

"Well, think of the past as the biggest puzzle anyone can imagine. We fit pieces together as well as we can. We know there will always be more pieces missing than ones we find. We know we will sometimes make mistakes and put a piece where it shouldn't really go. Sometimes other bones later show us how we've done it wrong. Sometimes mistakes stay in place a long time. Science isn't perfect. It can't be. We aren't perfect. But it's a better thinking tool than any other we've found."

The native king, he pondered that for a bit. Then he said, "This science, it is what gives you spyglasses and rifles and steam engines and the like, yes?"

"That's right." Otnil dipped his head.

"Then it is worth having." Red Cloud spoke in his own language to the native tallfeathers who'd come with him. Maybe not all of them followed our lingo real well. Some of the brownskins seemed as interested as the king. Others looked bored. Then Red Cloud came back to talk we could understand: "One day, we shall do science for ourselves and know as much as you do."

"Maybe you will. I hope you do." Otnil really meant it, I reckon. He did everything he knew how to do to give natives a fair shake. He did a lot more'n most folks, for sure.

Some of the fellas he worked with were making sure that busted chunk of bone they found didn't get busted any worse. They wrapped it in wet burlap and plaster. When the plaster dried, it'd be like the armor clubtails have to give rannos a tough time killing 'em.

Otnil didn't expect to turn Red Cloud into a bone collector himself. The king stayed around a little longer. Then he said, "May your work go well," and took himself and his nobles back to the fighters. They all decamped and headed back to whatever they had that needed doin' when they weren't bothering bonehunters.

I felt happier after that. I know they could come back and stir up the hells any time they chose, but they weren't there and panting to do it, anyways.

Otnil and his pals showed Junior and me how to put on the burlap and plaster, so we wouldn't be all useless while they worked— just mostly useless. And they tried to show us how to spot at a glance whether something small on the bluffside was a bit of bone sticking out or just a gods-damned rock. Junior was better at it than me. Well, his eyes were younger.

If I'd had the money and the time and the smarts, I wouldn't've half minded bonehunting fulltime myself. Since I didn't, I was glad Otnil did, and even gladder he paid me some little part of what I reckoned I was worth.

———

So the perfesser'd pay me more of what I thought I ought to get, I went out scouting for more bluffs and banks with bones coming out of 'em. Sometimes I'd travel with Junior, sometimes by my lonesome. I saw natives every now and then. Well, why not? It was their country.

They saw me, too. You bet they did. Odds are they saw me before I saw them most of the time. Ain't nobody like the natives for doin' a sneak and popping out where you had no notion they was around. Like how they showed up around the camp, for instance.

Reckon they could've killed me an' roasted me a time or three if they'd had a mind to. They didn't have a mind to, though, proof of which is, I'm here leanin' back on my tail all nice an' easy an' tellin' you this story. They knew Otnil and his friends were in good with Red Cloud. They might not've liked me for maggots, but if I was all right with their king they wouldn't drygulch me for the fun of it.

Did I feel safer when Junior was with me? Maybe a bit; for sure not a lot. Junior might've had scales and feathers that matched theirs, but he was gods-damned near as foreign in the Badlands as I was.

He knew it, too. It itched him considerable. "I don't reckon I'll ever have a place where I fit in right," he said one afternoon.

I didn't care to hear him talking that way. "Of course you do. Of course you will," I said. "You always got a place with me."

He dipped his head, but he answered, "It ain't big enough." I just kept quiet. I didn't know what I could say to that.

I was out by myself one day, heading down towards an undercut creek-bank, when something moved off in the distance. Faster'n I know how to tell you, I was behind a sagebrush with my eight-shooter in my hand. I figured it for a middle raptor—it was about my size. Not a native; a native wouldn't have let me see him that way.

Come to that, I was surprised a middle raptor would. I eased up a couple of fingers' breadth higher for a better peek. Try as I would not to, I let out a startled hiss. I purely couldn't help it. Last thing I expected to see there was another fella like me.

And when I say like me, I mean just like me. He had hisself a pistol in a holster, and he had a short-handled spade slung over his back. If he wasn't another bonehunter, you can call me a mammal's hatchling. (Only mammals don't have hatchlings. The little varmints come straight out of their mothers' cloacas without even a shell around 'em. Can you imagine anything more revoltin'?)

He was poking the ground here with a fingerclaw and prodding at it with his shovel. He'd pick up a rock and chuck it away when he saw it was only a rock. Sure as hells, after them fossils.

I hadn't hardly given that Trinka fella any thought a-tall, not once I signed on with Otnil. I figured the perfesser, he had hisself a tick bitin' at him between his scales, and Trinka wasn't really anybody to worry about. Now it seemed like maybe I was wrong.

That other bonehunter, he didn't have the faintest notion I was anywhere around. The sagebrush hid me pretty good, I will say. No, he didn't reckon there were any other people for days and days around him. He would've been more careful if he'd worried. He couldn't hardly've been any *less* careful.

Finally, he got close enough so I could've gods-damned near spit on him, never mind plugging him with the pistol. I clicked back the eight-shooter's hammer. That little noise drilled into his earholes, all right. You hear it once, you don't ever mistake it for anything else.

He jumped so hard, I thought he was gonna shed his tail like a lizard. He started to grab for his own equalizer, then realized that wasn't such a hot idea when I had the drop on him. His left hand jerked away from the grip like it'd all of a sudden gone red-hot.

"Who—who in blazes are you?" he asked, tryin' to sound tough instead o' scared. He didn't have much luck.

"Mebbe you should tell me who *you* are, friend," I said. "I'm here by Red Cloud's leave. Bet you can't say the same."

All the feathers along his back, maybe even the down on his armbones, they flattened out. That's how much I scared him. But he kept putting a bold snout on things. "Likely tell," he said. "Way I hear it is, the natives don't let anybody onto their land."

"Then you hear it wrong," I said. "Who the hells are you, anyways?"

"My names Sterba," he said. "I work with Professor Trinka. He's the grandest bonehunter in the whole wide world, Trinka is."

"He's the fella who mounted the plessy with its head wrong way to?" I said.

"He never did!" Sterba hissed, but the way he did it made you know he knew he was lying.

"Professor Otnil says he did. I believe him. You go on back and tell Master Backwards Head he better clear out of Red Cloud's kingdom, or else he won't live to regret it."

"We've got clearance from Fort Ironclaw to dig here," Sterba said. "You can't run us off that easy."

He rocked me back some when he threw the fort at me. A lot of folks reckon they can push natives around any old way they please. Down through the years, a lot of folks have. It's harder now, though. The natives, they've got better at pushing back.

"Fort has no say-so in the Badlands," I told Sterba, hoping I was right. "You better let Trinka know it, or he's liable to start hisself a nasty little war over bones a huzzard wouldn't touch."

"I'll tell him," Sterba said. "He's not what you'd call good at listening, though. Not Trinka!"

That made Trinka sound like Otnil. Did you have to be crazy to be a bonehunter? Mebbe not, but I bet it helped. "Git!" I said. He got. I would've banged a shot off to one side if he hadn't. Saved myself a bullet and some powder.

———

Otnil, he was spittin' mad by the time I finished spinning him my yarn. "Trinka! That stinking, scavenging mammal's hatchling!" he shouted. "He's out to steal my specimens! He's out to steal my publication rights!

He's nothing but a thief, and you know what thieves deserve! I'll turn Red Cloud loose on him. By the gods, Rekek, and by the Egg they hatched, I may even sit in at the feast afterwards!"

You can say a thing like that and sound like you're joking. You can, but Otnil didn't. He sounded like he wanted to use a little twig to pick bits of Trinka and Sterba and the rest of those bonehunters out from between his teeth.

"What are you going to do about it?" I asked. "You really gonna tell Red Cloud and his fighters about 'em?"

He snapped his teeth, he was so steamed. "I'm tempted. I truly am. It would serve Trinka right for poaching on me. I'd like to poach him, I would—poach him like an egg!" He spat again.

"But—" I kept trying to calm him down. I didn't have much luck. I was just a stupid guide. He didn't have to listen to me. Big shots never have to listen to folks like me. Not needing to listen to folks like me is part of what makes 'em big shots. Then I said, "Slaughtering 'em'll just land Red Cloud and his natives in trouble."

That got into his earholes. He didn't want it to, but it did. "You have something there," he said in a voice sour as vinegar. "The soldiers want an excuse to fight them and push them out, never mind that they've been pushed too far already. That Jawj back at Fort Ironclaw hates them worse than he hates raptors or rannos. He hates them the way I hate Trinka and his crew of robbers."

"How come Trinka sticks in your gizzard so much, Pefesser?" I said. "Just on account of the head he stuck on the wrong end of the critter? Don't seem reason enough, you ask me."

"Oh, there's more," Otnil said grimly. "Specimens I had on a railroad siding waiting to get shipped home wound up going to *his* college instead. Who paid off the shipping agent to change the invoices? Who else but him? And so he got to publish them first. I curse his name on account of it!"

One of his junior diggers came running up then. "Professor!" he said. "Professor, Red Cloud's here. Says he's got to talk to you right away!"

"Of course I'll talk to him," Otnil said, and then, to me, "I'll bet you anything you care to stake that he knows Trinka and his thieving crew are sneaking around on his land."

"No bet." I spoke up quick, since the very same thing was goin' through my own head.

Red Cloud came up to the fire all by his lonesome. This was his country, not ours; he reckoned he didn't need to have guards in it. Oh, sometimes he brought them along to make people thoughtful, you might say. But he didn't *need* them, not on his own lands.

I never dreamt anybody could have as much dignity as he showed that night. I don't mean any native. I mean anybody. Not all natives are dignified, any more'n all of us are. Look at Junior. Dignified? Nah, he's as much like me as anyone's ever likely to be, poor old egg. Not his fault—I'm the one who raised him, so I get the blame.

"The smell of other greenskins spreads across our land," Red Cloud said to Otnil.

"I just heard about this myself," the perfesser said. "Rekek here brought me the word. He ran across one of those other bonehunters himself this afternoon."

Red Cloud's head swung my way. His eyes surveyed me like he had tripods and spyglasses all set up. He didn't just look me over, either. He looked inside me. You wouldn't want Red Cloud eyeing you if you had a bad conscience, not even a little you wouldn't. But then he dipped his head. I'd passed the test. I have me a few things I'm less proud of. Yeah, just a few.

"You are the one who fostered a True Person," he said, like he was reminding himself. We aren't quite people to the natives. Well, too much of the time they aren't to us, either. Red Cloud, he went on, "Tell me what passed between you and the thief who wants to rob us of the bones of our ancestors."

He'd listened when Professor Otnil told him about how critters—how life—changed through time, all right. And that one bone we found *might've* come from his umpty-great-grandsire, or at least from his umpty-great-uncle. I set out what had happened with me and Sterba for him, same as I had for the perfesser.

When I got done, Red Cloud didn't say anything for a little bit. He just stood there leanin' back on his tail, thinkin' hard. Then his head swung toward Otnil. "Speak to me of this Sterba, of this Trinka."

I got to give Otnil credit. He could've cussed 'em up one side and down the other. He could've, but he didn't. He told how they were doing the same kind of work he was, only not so well. And he finished, "Before I looked for ancient bones on your land, King Red Cloud, I asked you if I might. Trinka and his followers don't care whether you mind or not. They aim to get bones any way they can. I have seen that before." And he told the native king how Trinka and his pals made those bones on the railroad siding all of a sudden end up where he could study 'em 'stead o' Otnil, who'd found 'em to begin with.

Red Cloud listened. He thought some more. You couldn't guess what was goin' through his noggin. Not the kind o' fella you'd care to gamble against, not even a little bit.

Finally his mouth opened so wide, you could count all of his teeth. He had hisself a hells of a set, too. He said, "I will show this Trinka what coming on my land without my leaves costs." His eyes swung toward me. "You, Rekek, you and your fosterling will come, too. The stupid officer at Fort Ironclaw will believe what you tell him. I am a native. Never will he hear a word I say."

I reckoned that was part of why he wanted me along, but only part. He liked me better'n he liked a lot of folks with green scales just on account of I'd raised Junior from the egg, or near enough. Maybe he even trusted me a little, the way he trusted Otnil: as much as he *could* trust somebody with green scales. That was funny, if you like, since I was the leastest, the lowliest, the ignorantest greenskin in the camp.

Red Cloud, he didn't care nothin' about that. He cared about me and Junior. That carried the weight for him.

Professor Otnil said, "I will come with you, too, if you think it will help. I wouldn't mind seeing Trinka off your land, not in the slightest."

But the native king tossed his head. "No. Let it be Rekek and his son of my kind. I will come for them tomorrow at dawn with my fighters." He didn't let Otnil try and argue. He just turned tail and walked away. Otnil stared after him. Have to tell you, so did I.

———

"What's he gonna have us do?" Junior asked me while we were both waiting for the new day to bust out of its eggshell.

"Be witnesses, like," I said, and then, "I think." Have to say I wasn't what you'd call sure myself. "But if it's anything that would fuss your gizzard, don't do it, that's all."

"What if he tries to make me?"

"Tell him no. He'll let you get by with it." I thought I was right. I hoped like anything I was, for Junior's sake and for mine.

Otnil had sentries out, the way he always did. A native came through 'em for Junior and me, and they never noticed. He wasn't there; then he was. They have the knack, I got to tell you. But he pointed at himself and then out into the night. It was still dark enough for mammals to prowl around, but you knew it wouldn't be for long. Sure enough, dawn was on the way.

We went out right past a sentry. He looked stupid-surprised, seeing us come out of the murk that way, but he kinda waved when we walked by.

I could see tolerable good by the time the native got us to Red Cloud. I could see how many fighters the king had with him, too, and the rifles and such they had with 'em. If Trinka's expedition was anything like Otnil's, it wouldn't stand a chance. Red Cloud, he maybe could've took Fort Ironclaw with that many fighters. But he never would've won the war that came afterwards, and he had sense enough to know it.

He even had a bunch of half-tamed drosaws along. The handlers kept 'em on long leads, not that it did 'em a whole bunch of good. The smell of meat-eaters made 'em all spooky. If you're a drosaw, you know a person—brownskin or greenskin, don't matter—eats things like you. We smell like raptors. By what Otnil says, we *are* raptors, raptors with brains.

"Good," Red Cloud said when he set eyes on Junior and me. "Now we go. Now we make this Trinka thing sorry it came to sneak and steal in places where it does not belong."

People—ordinary greenskins, I mean—will sometimes talk about natives like they're nothin' but raptors without brains. Vermin, in other words, near as bad as mammals. Hells, I did it myself back before I started fostering Junior. And here was Red Cloud goin' on about Trinka like *he* was just a critter. It made you think. We're every bit as strange to them as they are to us.

Off we went. Red Cloud and his band, they knew where Trinka was denning, all right. All Junior and me had to do was keep up and try not to make too big a racket while we were about it. The natives hardly said anything when we were on the move. Didn't matter to me one way or the other, I didn't know a word of their palaver.

The eastern sky went from no-color gray to salmon and fire and gold to morning. Birds commenced to chirp. Up on top of a tall bluff you'd need to be a spider to climb, a huzzard sentry looked around, making sure everything was safe. It saw us farther down and ducked away. They know a bunch of us can mean trouble. The big scavengers wouldn't start flying till we were safely gone.

A little raptor—one of the kind that's maybe half as tall as a person—spied us, too. It lit out fast as it could go, nose low, tail stretched out behind it. It held its arms out to either side. It couldn't fly or anything, but it had more in the way of feathers on those arms than most do. Maybe it got some glide from them.

Red Cloud pushed as hard as he could. I'm in pretty fair shape, but I know I started panting real soon. Junior, too, and he ain't even half my age. Then, from up ahead, somebody let out a shout: "By the Holy Eggshell, it's all the natives in the gods-damned world!"

It wasn't, of course, but it was a lot of natives—plenty to take care of a band of bonehunters. Now that they'd been spotted, Red Cloud strode forward. Unlike most of his fighters, he talked our lingo about as well as a brownskin could. "Go back," he told the sentry. "Tell Trinka and the one called Sterba to come here straightaway. No harm will find them if they hurry. But if they choose to fight or flee, they will bring doom down on all your heads. Go!"

I could hear him, but I was still a ways behind. I made out a little flicker of movement that had to be Trinka's watcher hightailin' it back to the camp. I didn't know how far away the camp was, but I reckon Red Cloud did. He knew how long he intended to wait, too.

He didn't have to wait that long. One of his people brought Junior and me right on up to him. We didn't even have time to lean back on our tails before two greenskins came up at a right good clip. "King," I said to Red Cloud, "the skinnier one, that's Sterba."

"I thank you," he said. "The other one, then, is Trinka?"

"Professor Otnil could tell you," I answered. "Sorry, but I can't. I never set eyes on him before."

"It will be as it is," Red Cloud said with a kind of shrug.

It was Trinka, all right. He was the kind of feller who was used to running things. You could tell right away just by looking. And he was as mad as though a hornet'd stung him in the cloaca, where it hurts worst.

He ran straight on up to Red Cloud and shouted into his face: "What is the meaning of this outrage?"

Red Cloud, he didn't answer in words, not right away he didn't. He raised his left hand a couple o' digits instead. All of a sudden, maybe a hundred rifles and muskets and blunderbusses was aimed at Trinka. One peep and he'd be all chopped up for stew. He took a step back. I reckon he couldn't hardly help hisself.

Once he got Trinka's attention, like, Red Cloud said, "This land's not your land. This land is my land. From the Badlands bluffs here to the Black Hills carvings, this land was made for me and mine. You have no business hunting bones on it without asking me first if you might. The wise man Otnil has my let. You do not. You never will."

Trinka did have feathers on his spine. They all stood up straight to show how mad he was. He called Otnil every name in the book, and some the book hadn't even heard of yet. He looked like he wanted to call Red Cloud every name in the book, too, but he didn't quite try that. A bunch of gun muzzles lookin' at you will give you some sense no matter how riled you get.

Finally, he said, "The government soldiers at Fort Ironclaw said I could excavate on these lands. I have a paper from them that proves it."

"They are not my fighters. This is not their land. That is not my government," Red Cloud said. "If they come on my land without my consent, I will fight them all."

"You'll lose," Trinka said in a hard, flat voice.

Red Cloud only shrugged again. "Better to die fighting to be free than to roll over and be a slave." Plenty of greenskins would've said the same thing, but with Red Cloud, you knew he wasn't just talking to hear himself talk. He went on, "Take me to your camp. Take us all to your camp. We will see these bones you have stolen."

"I haven't stolen a gods-damned thing," Trinka said hotly. "These bones are important to science." He didn't quite tack on *you stupid savage,* but he might as well have.

"Take us to your camp," Red Cloud repeated.

"I will." Trinka was still ticked off. "You can see for yourself. We aren't taking anything that's worth anything to you off your land. No gold, no silver, no jewels, nothing like that. Just old bones. Aren't I right, Sterba?"

"Sure are, boss," the other bonehunter said. He'd spotted me by then. He'd spotted Junior next to me, too. I wondered what he made of that, but not enough to care to the extent of a fart in a tornado.

By how long it took Trinka's sentry to get back to their camp and fetch him and Sterba, I could cipher out about how far away it was. When we got there, Trinka's fellas looked about half ready to fight. They thought twice about that when they saw how much muscle Red Cloud had behind him, though, let me tell you.

The natives fanned out and surrounded the campsite. Trinka said, "No worries, boys. The big chief here, he's just making sure we aren't taking out anything that matters to the natives."

"Show me these bones you have," Red Cloud said.

"I'll be glad to do that." Trinka sounded like somebody who reckoned he had a handle on things. He showed Red Cloud bones wrapped in burlap and plaster—same way of keeping 'em safe Otnil used. Others were in crates. Trinka offered Red Cloud a prybar. "Open whichever ones you please. You'll see they're the same kinds of things we've got out in the open here."

Red Cloud did jimmy one or two. Sure enough, they held fossil bones. He dipped his head. One of Trinka's assistants nailed the crates shut again. Trinka looked as happy as an eggstealer in a hornface nest.

Then Red Cloud said something to his fighters in their own language. Some of the natives kept Trinka and his bonehunters covered. Others started loading bones—the ones that were just out there and the ones in crates—onto the backs of the drosaws they'd brought along. The drosaws grunted and hooted and squirmed like they always do. They purely hate workin', drosaws. I've known people like that, too.

When Trinka saw what the brownskins were up to... Well, if he was gunpowder, he woulda blown up. "What do you think you're doing?" he screamed. "What? Tell me, gods damn it!"

"We will take these bones to the wise greenskin named Otnil," Red Cloud answered, calm as you please.

"What?" This time, Trinka bellowed like a ranno in rutting season. "You can't do that!"

The native king gestured. Quick as you can flick your nictitating membrane across your eye, Trinka was staring down all them gun barrels again. "You do not tell me what I cannot do on my land," Red Cloud said. "Do you understand me?"

"But it's robbery, nothing else but!" Trinka had nerve, or maybe he was just so riled he didn't care any more. "You're taking away the bones my helpers and I worked hard to dig out and preserve. You're handing them to my...rival." I'm pretty sure he wanted to say *enemy,* but he saw that'd only make things worse.

"They are not your bones. You stole them from our land," the native answered in a voice as stony as the gods carved into the Black Hills, and never mind the way he talked our lingo. "I could have you put them back and cover them over again, but I know your kind. You would only return to steal them once more. So I will give them to the wise greenskin Otnil. He is here with my consent. Let him have the benefit from them and show the world what they mean. And I will do you one more favor."

"If it's anything like robbing me of all my work, don't bother," Trinka hissed.

He got lucky. Red Cloud didn't care to listen to him. "You will want this one," the native king said. "I will let you and your bonehunters leave my land alive and unharmed instead of cutting you all up and throwing you in the stewpot. And tell the officer Jawj at Fort Ironclaw that he may not say who comes and goes here."

Trinka and his crew were out of there and heading back to the fort inside of another daytenth. The natives kept all their rifles and ammunition, too. Well, almost all—they let Trinka's gang hang on to a couple of rifles so they could fight off a ranno or raptors or whatever other critters they ran into along the way. Even a herd of hornfaces could mean trouble if the big males got spooked.

Then Red Cloud turned back to Junior and me. "Well, Rekek, you and your fosterling have seen what I did here. By the lights of your folk, is it fair? Is it just?"

"I'm not a judge or anything," I said. "You got to know that, your Kingship. I'm about as ordinary a feller as ever made it out of the eggshell."

"You are not." Red Cloud tossed his head. "Few greenskins would have brought up one of ours as if it were his own. You did, though, and I see the bonds of affection and duty between the two of you."

I kinda eyed Junior. He was kinda eyein' me, too. The way the king talked, I reckon it embarrassed the both of us.

By the time we got back to Otnil's camp, most of the native fighters, they'd gone on their merry way. Red Cloud didn't need 'em any more. He had no squabble with Otnil. He went all the way to the camp hisself, along with the brownskins herding the drosaws that way.

Otnil and his bonehunters hadn't gone out to dig. They were all back lollygagging around by their tents, shooting dice or reading or just sitting back on their tails. A couple of 'em, the go-getters, were chipping bones out of the rock that coffined them.

When Otnil spied the dust the drosaws kicked up (not the natives; you'll never know natives are close by unless they want you to), he came running out to meet us. He had nerve, Otnil did. "What's all this?" he called to Red Cloud when he saw the crates that all the drosaws were hauling. "What have you got there?"

"Egg from my own nest, I bring you what is rightfully yours," Red Cloud answered. Junior and me, we looked at each other again, this time on account of we were both so surprised. Maybe half the natives leading the drosaws—the half who could follow our kind of talk—acted just as startled as we were.

Egg from my own nest is a big thing, maybe even bigger with the brownskins than it is with us. Junior was an egg from my own nest, you might say. You can be friends with a fella for thirty years and never once call him that. Sometimes you don't treat folks who are eggs from your own nest by actual hatching as well as you treat someone you freely give the name to.

Otnil understood that as well as I did. He leaned forward so his tail came way off the ground, sowing Red Cloud proper respect. "Your Majesty, you do me too much honor," he said.

Red Cloud tossed his head. "I think not. You deal with us as fairly as though we are of your own kind. We can do no less for you. And so I present to you the bones Trinka and those with him stole from my land. I know these things are important to you, so you should have them. Let the world know we respect knowledge and we respect honesty."

"You...took all the bones Trinka excavated away from him?" Otnil sounded like he couldn't believe what just came in through his earholes.

"It is so," Red Cloud said gravely.

And when Otnil really got that it *was* so, he laughed and laughed and laughed. By the Great Eggshell, *how* he laughed! When he cut loose, it wasn't halfway. I never seen nobody laugh like that before, and I ain't never seen nobody laugh like that since, neither. I was half afeared he'd kill hisself. More than half afeared.

After a good long while, he got where he could finally talk again. "Oh, my!" he said. "I will describe and publish every single bone from your gift, Red Cloud, I promise you that. And I will give you credit for passing the bones on to me. I also promise that."

"No need," the native king said. "They belong by right to you, not to the thief, Trinka."

"You are gracious," Otnil told him. "But I want the whole world to know you gave me the bones. I want it to know Trinka tried to take them from you without your leave. I want to shame him—do you understand? I want everyone to laugh at him when he comes to bonehunters' gatherings, and I want everyone to think his papers must be foolish just because he wrote them."

Red Cloud didn't say anything for a few heartbeats. Then he turned to the natives who were taking the plastery bones and the crates off the drosaws. He talked to them in their language. Of course I didn't follow one single word of it, but by the way he kept pointing at Otnil I got the notion he was translating what the perfesser'd said. And by the way the other natives looked at Otnil, they were more impressed with him than they expected to be with anybody from our kind of people.

Then Red Cloud, he went back to talkin' so's I could understand: "I did not know greenskins also played the game of revenge. By the way you talk, you play it well. These bones will let you make this Trinka mammal look the proper idiot, then?"

"King Red Cloud, they will. You may rely on it," Otnil said. He bowed low again, same way as he had before. This time, you can boil me in a natives' pot if Red Cloud didn't bow back—not quite so deep, but almost. *That* got the other natives' notice, too, let me tell you it did.

Once all the drosaws were unloaded, the natives made ready to go back to where they lived. Before they took off, though, Red Cloud came over to Junior and me. Junior looked like him, but acted like me. He'd been with me since he was little enough for me to hold in one hand. How could he act any other way, no matter what he looked like?

"It is well with you? Truly well?" Red Cloud asked him.

"As well as it can be when I look like one thing and act like another," Junior said. "Rekek tries hard to keep that from being any more trouble than it has to be."

"Good." The native kinda touched my arm, just for a heartbeat. Then he looked back to Junior. "I would invite you to join us here, but I fear you would fit no better."

Junior dipped his head. "Afraid you're right, your Kingship. Out in the big world, I look wrong but act right. Here, I'd look right but act wrong. I'm not yolk or white. I just have to get along as best I can." He took half a step closer to me. "Got me some fine help."

"I also think you do," Red Cloud said, and he walked away.

Not far off, Otnil was chuckling over the bones he'd got from the natives like they were eggs he'd laid his very own self. I don't expect a mother hen could've been prouder of what she had in her nest. But I'll tell you somethin', yes I will. Standin' there with Junior, I reckoned I had me a hells of a lot more to be proud of than the perfesser ever would.

THE QUEST FOR THE GREAT GRAY
MOSSY

Call me Milvil. It is not my name, but it will serve. And let me begin my tale with my tail, and the rest of me, in a boat bound for Faraway Island. The wind, at our backs, filled the sail and made the canvas thrum. So also my thoughts thrummed with excitement and the hope of gain, for from Faraway Town I purposed putting to sea to hunt and try the great monsters that dwell subaqueously.

When I turned my head into the wind to survey the other passengers, a tiny bit of grit—or maybe it was smoke from an old fellow's pipe—made my eye sting. My nictitating membrane flicked across it, wiping away whatever the trouble was. Would that all my woes might so easily be swept away!

I wondered who among those aboard the neat little cutter with me might also intend to go over the wide sea in a greater ship. I at once dismissed the old chap with the pipe. His snout was wattled with fat; the feathers on his head and down his spine hung pale and limp with age. Seeing him, in fact, induced in me a strange kind of terror, as if he were a vision of what cruel time would one day work on me if by some strange chance the line of my existence should stretch as long as his.

No, not for him plying an oar in a swift mossy boat. Not for him standing in the bow, fingerclaws digging into the hardwood shaft of a harpoon ere letting fly. He might be one who profited from oil and meat, but never would he earn them in terror and exultation.

Not would the three females, who might have been sailcloth weavers or might equally have danced for the entertainment of seafarers. They would not put to sea. Ships full of hunters are better off without the confusion and quarrels rutting hatches.

But there were also a couple of young fools like myself who might have aimed to test their luck that way. How many such burst from the egg every day? Enough to keep the mossy ships never short of crews, enough to carry blunderbusses and muskets and fight the brownskins in the distant West, enough to hunt drosaws and hornfaces and even savage rannos on the plains there, enough for every sort of savage stupidity under the sun. By the gods, I should know.

A lovely bit of steering let us glide into Faraway Town's neat little harbor. There's not another harbor in the world that smells like Faraway Town's. Oil, meat, curing hides… Gulls and ramphies circled over the moored ships, screeching, on the hunt for scraps or even for fish if they had to stoop so low. Some perched on the spars. You'll never see fatter terries or birds than you will at Faraway Town. There's so much to eat there, people don't even begrudge them their thievery—or not so very much, anyhow.

When I disembarked, I made for the finer lodging houses, the ones set farther back from the water, to escape as best I could at least some small portion of that pungent, persistent aroma. One landlord after another turned me away. "We're so full up, we couldn't squeeze in even a mammal," a fat fellow with a patch covering an empty eye-socket told me.

My guess was that he'd put to sea once too often, and come back to Faraway Island after his mutilation. Be that as it may, I didn't care to have him liken me to a nasty, hairy little nighttime skulker. "I dare say you will already guest a great plenty of them," I said, and took myself elsewhere.

"Now see here! What's that supposed to mean?" he called after me, but he was talking only to the tip of my tail.

I worked my way through the better establishments, pausing once for fried cod and once for a beaker or two of something refreshing. By then, the sun was sinking toward the horizon. As twilight began to deepen, I found myself back by the seaside. The smell was still there, but by then, through familiarity, I began to notice it rather less. At any rate, I told myself I began to notice it rather less.

By the look of it, there were mammals aplenty prowling at the dive that called itself the Plessy's Flipper. By then, I'd gone through the better places in Faraway Town. Unless I cared to sleep in the street like someone who'd downed a great many beakers indeed, I could not afford to turn up my snout at whatever shelter I might find.

"Aye, I can give you a place to doss," said the chap who also served the drinks and immolated the meat and fish and shellfish. "I can if you don't mind taking only half a bed, anyhow."

"Half a bite's better than empty," I said, and so the bargain was made.

He handed me a little oil lamp whose wick, once lit, smelled as vile as if its essential fuel had been rendered from the fat carcass of some mammal whose habits were even fouler than those of most of that foul breed. The faint, flickering flame was all that lit my way up the stairs and along a winding corridor until at last I found the room with the verdigrised brass number 27 on the door.

I wondered whether the key he'd also reluctantly doled out would fit in the lock, which seemed as much suffused in antiquity as the numbers near it. Rather to my surprise, it did, and with a loud click the door came open.

Another lamp, even more odoriferous than the one I held, guttered towards extinction on a stand beside the bed. Anyone who can whilst sleeping in an establishment like the Plessy's Flipper will make a light to keep creeping mammals and other crawling vermin from scuttling over him in darkness. There are places where one would not have to worry about such things, but that inn, alas!, was not among them.

Someone wrapped in all the blankets suddenly ceased snoring; the click of the lock must have awakened him. He stuck out his head and peered curiously in my direction. My own curiosity was likewise excited. His scales were the pale green—almost yellow—of the folk who hatch in the various southern islands of the Peaceful Ocean.

"Sorry to disturb you," I told him. "The landlord sold me half your bed for the night."

"Ah. Him do that?" My to-be-bedfellow spoke our language poorly at best. He did, however, seem friendly. "Well, you come on, then. Me have name Geekgeek. What you have name? Not like to sleep by someone me not know name to."

I told him what to call me. With the rude simplicity of the savage, he seemed satisfied: so satisfied, indeed, that with my requesting it he divested himself of half the bedclothes and vouchsafed them to me. As it was growing chilly—Faraway Island, full of fogs and mists, is seldom warm during daylight, much less by night—I was glad enough to have the covers, even if they smelled powerfully of Geekgeek, and perhaps also of some indefinite but large number of previous occupants of the bed.

As I was lying down, Geekgeek asked me, "You go on mossy ship?"

"I was looking to, yes," I said. "I've never done it before. I've been to sea, on ordinary traders, but never like that."

I could not have told him why I sought this adventure, either, had he asked me, which he did not. I fled no failed love affair. I had none to flee; no one on earth cared whether I lived or died or wished I would do one or the other. I was not particularly greedy for adventure. If I sought anything at all, I sought to be settled instead of gliding hither and yon like a huzzard on the breeze. Settle, you say, on a ship that cruises all the world's oceans at its skipper's whim or lore, on a voyage that may last four months or four years? But yes: on such a ship someone will always set you your tasks, leaving you with scarcely a shred of time in which you must think for yourself. Sure enough, if I was after anything, that would have been it.

Geekgeek cared not a copper for whatever made me do whatever I did. "Me harpoon man," he said. "Not have no mossy ship without harpoon mans, no. You come with I, they take you, too, sure sure."

After I spoke, I saw the lamplight glittering from the steel heads of the tools of his trade. I should have spied them sooner, but we all should do a great many things at which we fail. "My thanks," I told him. "Likely I will."

"Good. Now us sleep." He turned his back at me, so that his tail brushed my legs. And sleep he did: the sleep of barbarism, of savagery, of innocence, the sleep I would have thought surely extinct in this modern, bustling age. After a long while, I slept as well. My slumber was light, fitful, suitable to the present day. But it was what the gods gave me, and I endeavored to make the most of it. At any rate, I knew little more till the rising sun drove the mammals back to their hiding places and woke Geekgeek and me.

———

After we broke our fast, Geekgeek slung his harpoons on his back and repaired to the harbor. I followed in his wake, swept along by his purpose when I had so little of my own. The mossy stink was still there, but I minded it less, having continued to accustom myself to it. Thus habit simplifies life for us all.

"Which ship do you have in mind?" I asked the harpoon man.

He waved to the nearest one, which was even then taking on barrels of salt meat and water. Its name—*Queepahd*—was written in letters of gold (well, letters of gilt or possibly polished brass) on the stern, above the skipper's cabin. "Us try here first," he said. "Them no want, us go till them somewhere yes want."

By the way he said it, he was ready to work his way through every mossy ship tied up at the quays till he found one where his services were desired. He might have been a South Sea savage, but he showed more persistence and ambition than many an individual who is called civilized.

As for me, I still drifted on his current of resolve like a leaf fallen in a river and floating downstream. With no purpose to my name, I was more than content to borrow his. "Why not?" I said, and followed him along the tarry planking.

"Come aboard?" he called, and the first mate, seeing those fangèd harpoons, waved him forward at once. I continued to follow as we walked along the gangplank, and no one said me nay.

The mate, whose name was Stabbak, hired Geekgeek at once. That he was a barbarian from distant, heathen lands fazed Stabbak not a whit. The reverse, if anything. "Some of the best harpoon men come from the strangest places," the mate remarked. "With you, we'll have Ootag, who escaped from slavery, and Tashteg, a brownskin from somewhere in the West."

He waited to see how Geekgeek would take that. The natives of this continent are not of our kind. They know less than we; we push them harder year by year. Not reckoning them truly people, some want nothing to do with them. What would have passed had Geekgeek been one such, I cannot say. But he merely shrugged and remarked, "Him can stand I, me can stand he."

"Good enough," the mate said, and then, at last, deigned to notice me. When he observed, "This will be your first time on a mossy ship," it was not a question.

"True enough." I admitted what I could scarcely deny. "I have been to sea before, though."

"That helps you less than you might think," Stabbak replied. "Well, tell me about yourself and what you may be able to do." To the best of my ability, I did. He scratched behind his earhole with a fingerclaw in a way that suggested my best was none too good. "I'd better take you back and let Captain Baja decide about you."

"However you please, of course," I replied. If I did not suit the *Queepahd*'s skipper, I would bid Geekgeek godsspeed and try my fortune on the next mossy ship, and, if need be, on the ones after that. On the way to the skipper's cabin I met in passing Shtup and Frask, the second and third mates. One was old; the other, short. Past that, they left little initial impression on me.

Stabbak tapped softly on the door that gave the captain's cabin more privacy than most enjoy aboard any ship. Hearing nothing, he tapped again, hardly louder than before. This time, a harsh, rusty voice came through the oaken planking: "Enter."

The mate opened the door and ducked inside. As I had followed Geekgeek aboard the ship, so I followed Stabbak into the cabin. He said, "Your pardon, sir, but here's one who'd sail with us. He's been to sea before, he says, but on a mossy ship he's still an unhatched egg. I thought I'd best get your view before taking him on."

"Thou'rt care itself, Stabbak," said Baja, turning to survey me. As he moved, his tail scraped against the deck beneath it. This tail was made from highly polished mossy bone, and attached to the stump of his gods-given appendage by a cunning arrangement of drosaw-leather straps. It was, I suppose, better than no tail at all, but not nearly so good as the one of which he'd been robbed by some catastrophe, I knew not what.

That artificial tail was the most remarkable thing about him, but not by any great stretch. He was the most weathered old salt I'd ever seen; his green-scaled hide was nearly as leathery as the straps sustaining his tail.

Even his feathers were sad and draggled, showing the effect of sun and rain and storm. A great scar seamed his jaw, and just missed his left eye. That and its corresponder on the other side were two of the piercingest I'd ever encountered. Not to put too fine a point on it, at first glance he terrified me, a sentiment which increased on further acquaintance rather than dissipating.

"A seaman, art thou?" quoth he, and hurled questions nautical at me one after another, as if they were so many harpoons with which he aimed to pin down the truth. I answered as best I could. He scratched at himself with a sharp-clawed forefinger, then continued, "Well, thou know'st somewhat. 'Twill serve thee less well than thou think'st. For the true query is, When the mossy rises from the sea with toothy maw all agape, wilt thou hold steady or give way to fear?"

"I hope I'll be steady. I'll try to be steady," I said. "Before the egg of fate hatches, though, how may anyone know?"

Stabbak's hiss showed he thought I'd thrown away my chance to ship aboard the *Queepahd*. But the banked fires in Captain Baja's terrible eyes glowed a bit brighter. "Thou'rt honest, at any rate," he said. "And thou'rt friends with a harpoon man."

I looked at him in surprise. So did the first mate. Neither of us had mentioned that I boarded the ship with Geekgeek and his spears. Baja was in his cabin all the while. He could not have known—except he did. This was the first time he startled me that way, but it would not be the last.

"Go along, go along," Baja said. "Stabbak'll see to thy papers. I care little for such foolishness. But friendship is a line that binds together those who share it. With thy friend at the bow of thy mossy boat searing the monsters from the vasty deep, thou'lt betray him not, for fear of severing the sacred line."

And so it was decided. Had I slept elsewhere at the Plessy's Flipper, or found a room in some other hostel altogether, this would be a different story. Different in which ways? Reader, I cannot tell you. We may have the potentiality to live many lives, but we knowingly realized only one of them. Thus I tell the only tale I—*this* I—can tell.

———————

A light but fair breeze let us escape the harbor at Faraway Town. We sailed north until we could round Great Point—the lighthouse there is most impressive—and then spread all sail to hasten south across the Ocean of Storms to the watery territory in which mossies best thrived.

Day followed day, each a little warmer, each a little milder, than the one before. The sun stood higher in the sky each noon when Captain Baja shot it with the sextant to fix its position and note that in his log. The *Queepahd* might as well have been an ordinary trading ship, for we were not yet on the hunt. I could scarcely have asked for a more delicate introduction into my strange new world.

Masts and spars and lines and sails… I had their measure. Scrambling about up there fazed me no more than it did any of the others who went aloft to keep the ship headed as the skipper decided it should be. No one without a head for heights will ever put to sea, except as passenger.

As we got farther south, flying fish began leaping from the water. Some would wind up on deck. They are tasty raw, and even tastier roasted or fried. The cook's spices improved the blandest of victuals, and got to prove as much over and over again with dried and salted drosaw and hornface flesh. Next to that bill of fare, the odd flying fish was a bit of excitement on the tongue.

I did not go aloft every shift. There was also plenty to do on deck and belowdecks, and Captain Baja made it all too clear how little he thought of idleness amongst the crew. Thus I was holystoning dirt mostly imaginary from the deck timbers when someone high above sang out, "Turtle! King turtle off the port bow!"

As it happened, I was working on the port side, not far from the rail. I gave over holystoning; the skipper's view to the contrary notwithstanding, one does not live by labor alone. I had heard of these monsters of the deep, but set eyes on only a couple of them, and those but fleetingly. I wanted a proper look, if one was to be had.

King turtles are both smaller and scarcer than mossies or plessies. Not many go out to hunt them, and mossy ships will not lower boats to pursue them, reckoning them not worth the trouble. Nevertheless, they are not to be despised. A big one, like this fellow snapping up jellyfish now, will be longer than two people from nose to tailtip, and will weigh, I suppose, as much as twelve or fifteen. I got a good look at the monster's ribbed blue-green carapace, and at its great head. As I watched, its mighty maw opened to swallow down a stinging galleon. If it felt the stings from the jellyfish, they troubled it not, but perhaps added piquancy to its repast, much as the cook's peppers did with ours.

Just for a moment, the king turtle's little squinting eyes met mine. What long, slow thoughts ran through its brain? What did it make of the thing of wood and canvas that glided through its world? Did it reckon the *Queepahd* strange and abnormous, a thing of ill omen, or did it with animal resignation take the ship for granted? These were all questions easier asked than answered.

And then another question was asked of me, in a rough voice I recognized at once: "Why'rt thou not working as thou shouldst? She who laid thine egg is not here. She will not holystone for thee."

My mouth started to fall open, but I arrested the motion ere it was well begun. I could not show the skipper my teeth; he had the right to order me about, and to correct me if he found me wanting. All save the captain aboard ship are slaves—voluntary slaves, it may be, but slaves just the same.

And so I said, as meekly as I might, "I pray your pardon, sir. I sought but a quick glimpse of the king turtle we're sailing past."

Mollify him I did not; I might have known I wouldn't. "Faugh!" he said: not a word but a sound of pure disgust. "If thou'dst scan the sea with some purpose, scan for the Great Gray Mossy, the one who robbed me of the trusty tail I was hatched with."

Turning abruptly, he stumped away before I could give him any of the myriad questions suddenly all abubble in my head. Mossies are commonly green, but that was the smallest thing I wondered about. Wonder I would have to keep on doing. Captain Baja's artificial tail thumped against the timbers until I could hear it no more, the sound it made being drowned out by the holystone's harsh, monotonous scraping.

I thought of seeking more about the skipper's Great Gray Mossy from Stabbak, but in the end fought shy of that. I could not be certain the mate would not inform Baja of my untoward curiosity, a consummation devoutly not to be wished. Thus, I sought out Geekgeek instead. A harpoon man would know the things that were in the sea: might even know them better than the skipper would. And a harpoon man, unlike the first mate, would feel no temptation to bear tales.

Yet I was balked of my questioning for some little while, as I found Geekgeek busy at his devotions. He was propitiating a little black idol of carven wood with dried meat and blood. "Have to keep Yojo happy or me lose my luck," he said, indicating the statuette with a thumbclaw.

"Yojo?" I echoed foolishly.

"One of the gods of my people. Most stay home, but him travel with I, look over I as me look out for he."

"Where did you get the blood?"

Geekgeek shrugged. "Kill a rat, me did."

"Oh," I said on a falling note. Of course mammals *will* get aboard any ship ever built. Many skippers let a couple of small raptors roam free to keep them down, but no hunting, not even the most diligent, will ever root them out altogether. Like ticks and mosquitoes, mammals are an unfortunate part of life.

I reckon myself a loyal, if not an overly pious, follower of the creed of the World Egg. Though I do not follow it, the belief that life instead came Down from the Sky fails to offend me. Geekgeek's ritual, by contrast, seemed a relic of outworn paganism, one almost forgotten in this modern, busy day and age. I waited with such patience as I could muster whilst he propitiated his precious and surely nonexistent Yojo.

At last, the rude little ceremony was complete. Geekgeek began to pay heed once more to things other than his much-traveled godlet. I asked him a question: "May I ask you a question?"

"Ask," he said with a grand gesture. Then he tempered that by adding, "Maybe me answer. Maybe no."

"Even if you do not, I shall be no worse off," I said. "What can you tell me of the Great Gray Mossy"—I spoke the name as Captain Baja had, with majuscules audible—"that took off the skipper's tail?"

"Bad fish, that one. Terrible bad fish," Geekgeek said.

Any naturalist will tell you mossies are not fish, no more than plessies are. They may swim in the sea, but they have no gills and breathe air. Their blood is warm, not fishy-cold. They do not spawn, rather giving birth to live young. Geekgeek cared nothing for naturalists' fine distinctions. In his simple view of the world, anything that lived in the water had to be a fish.

After a moment, he continued, "Old bad fish. Big bad fish. Many hunt Great Gray Mossy. Him still live. Them say him charge boats. Them say him charge ships, even. Years ago, him sink one, eat half the mossy hunters. Like you say, him take captain's tail." His toothy jaws opened and shut to show what he meant by *take*.

"But Baja yet survives," I said.

Geekgeek dipped his head in agreement. "Them rescue he after Great Gray Mossy wreck his boat. Blacksmith sear tailstump with hot iron"—this punctuated by a hiss, as of hot metal cauterizing flesh—"so him no bleed out. Him swear big revenge oath. Big, big oath."

Skippers, being themselves little gods whilst aboard ship, can go a long way down the path of eccentricity without anyone's having the temerity to remark on it. It had already struck me that Captain Baja luxuriated in this license. Now, having heard what the harpoon man divulged to me, I could not help asking, "Does he have all his oars in the water? Or is he more dangerous to the *Queepahd* than any mossy, no matter how great or gray, is ever likely to be?"

"Baja, him number one ship handler." Geekgeek did not try to misunderstand me, for which I felt myself indebted to him. "Him number one mossy hunter. Him number one mossy killer. Number one, you hear? Him go against Great Gray Mossy again, not know number one good enough." He tapped his curious South Sea idol with a fingerclaw. "So me feed Yojo. A god are happy with you, chances better. Maybe not good, but better."

"But will not Yojo be grateful to you and not to the skipper?" I asked.

"Me tell he who me feed he for," the savage harpoon man replied. "Him listen, me bet."

Normally, I should have had no truck with such heathen superstitions. But nothing aboard a mossy ship is normal, not when compared to the life a landsman leads. And, I was coming to see, precious little having to do with Captain Baja was normal, not even when compared to life aboard your common mossy ship.

Had I walked along some other gangplank, I might have been happier than I now was. Having walked along the one I chose, I was in Baja's power until the cruise ended, whether in six months or three or four years. A skipper may be a little god, but plenty big enough to rule a little world like that of the *Queepahd*.

Not long after I had my colloquy with Geekgeek and Yojo—heaven forfend I should omit Yojo from the colloquy—one of the watchers on the foremast cried, "Plessy! Plessy to starboard!"

I was in the rigging myself then, halfway up the mainmast, and, if I turned my eye in the direction the lookout indicated, Captain Baja was most unlikely to criticize. In fact, he stood at the wheel, so he could ensure that his ship followed the exact path of his implacable, inexorable will.

The plessy was one of the long-necked kind, not the thicker variety that puts one more in mind of mossies. Its head thrust up more than my length above the salty sea and twisted this way and that. Plessies hunt that way; I've seen their toothy maws snatch flying fish out of the air, and seabirds, and once even a terry I should have thought too large to go down such a narrow throat. But in thinking that I should have been mistaken, for the big flyer vanished, never to be seen again.

And thrusting its head so far up into the air also let the plessy see farther than it could have otherwise. No sooner had it seen the *Queepahd* than we aboard the *Queepahd* saw it no more, for it dove deep. Under the sea, its sculling paddles would swiftly take it away from what it perceived to be mortal peril.

At the wheel, Captain Baja lifted one fist from the polished wood to make claws at the plessy. "Thou coward! Thou fool!" he shouted after it in his rough, hard voice. "I sought thee not! I'd not dirty my ship's harpoons with thy blood. Thou stupid creature, this is a mossy ship. I'm after nobler prey than thy kind!"

As I believe I have mentioned ere now, ships do put to sea to slay plessies. A person not familiar with those who go to sea in ships for the purpose of greasing our wheels, lighting our cities, and feeding our hatchlings could never distinguish between the one sort of vessel and the other. No more could the plessy. As far as it was concerned, any kind of ship meant danger; it impartially fled all.

"That's a rare fine rant from the skipper," said one of my comrades aloft, with obvious delight in Baja's mighty pride and scorn.

Those roused different feelings in me. I could not help thinking that, no matter how mighty a man might be, was he mighty enough to measure himself against the sea? What was Baja next to the Ocean of Storms on which we sailed? Why, less than a biting tick when compared to the drosaw whose blood it sucked.

Yet bold tick Baja, knowing himself to be so minuscule, nonetheless persisted in his war on mossies in general and on the Great Gray Mossy in especial. He would have boiled the ocean, were that in his power, to rid the world of what he hated most. It was folly, but was it not grand folly?

Then again, is not even the grandest of follies folly still?

———————

Two or three of our sailors had not crossed the Equator until doing so on our voyage. As is the custom, they were hatched from the egg anew. They were besmeared with yolk—not the freshest of yolk, either—and had other indignities visited on them as well. Most of the filthy, menial work fell to them over the next few days.

The mate on the trading ship aboard which I was hatched anew had been harsher to his first-time crossers than Stabbak was on the *Queepahd*. But then Stabbak was a genuinely good-natured soul, and very much needed to be such to mitigate Captain Baja's holystoned harshness. On my old ship, the skipper was honey-sweet, whilst the mate did his level best to make life intolerable anyway.

South and east we cruised. We spied plessies, and even a plessy ship or two, though the ships that hunted the creatures were not near enough to the ones we spied for our intelligence of those long-gone beasts to do them any good.

The plessy ships' skippers had likewise seen mossies now and then, but not recently enough to help us in our quest. They disdained mossies as we disdained plessies, regarding ours as a trade conducted without due regard for life, limb, or tail. They did not say as much in so many words, not after seeing what sort of tail our skipper sported, but they meant it nonetheless.

(I think they were wise to have chosen circumspection. Had one of their skippers been rash enough to have twitted Captain Baja about his abridgement, I do believe he would have served out cutlasses to his crew and led the boarding party himself. And the offending plessy ship's deck would have run with blood that did not stream from its quarry. Say what you would about Baja, but he required being taken seriously.)

Since we did not have to turn pirate, then, in due course we rounded the Cape of Good Hope. By that time it would have been autumn back on Faraway Island, but in traveling as we had we'd turned the seasons upside down. The weather was not much different, but got better instead of worse. If only one could travel fast enough, one might enjoy summer the year around. Or, in a mossy ship, be too busy to enjoy it.

Once we were well into the Southern Ocean, where mossies might be found and hunted in this season, Captain Baja took a mallet and two sturdy nails from the ship's blacksmith. Summoning the crewfolk to foregather by the mainmast, he held up a goldpiece and let the sun glint from the snout of the famous dead individual immortalized on its obverse.

"Do ye see this, lads? Do ye?" he called.

See it we did, and loudly attested to the fact.

"Good," the skipper rasped. Taking one of the nails, he spiked the coin to the pine of the mainmast. "It goes to whoever first spies the first mossy we catch and kill on this cruise. Is that all right by you?"

"Better than all right!" Tashteg shouted in his mushy voice—being of distinct species, brownskins can't properly form all the sounds in our language, any more than we can properly shape all those in theirs. However odd he sounded, though, no one was left in any doubt as to what he said. Geekgeek and Ootag gave forth with cheers, nor were Tashteg's fellow harpoon men the only ones to do so. I confess a whoop of glee—or, if you would rather, a whoop of greed—escaped my own teeth.

But Captain Baja had not yet finished. He took from a pouch on his belt another goldpiece, a great fat lump of the precious metal, all stamped to perfection and worth ten times the first one; worth, to be honest, many times the concatenated wealth of most of the crewfolk.

"By the gods and by the Great Egg from which the world hatched at the beginning of days, my rogues, do ye see *this*?" Baja cried.

For a moment, a moment that stretched and stretched, he got no response at all. Staring at so grand and gaudy a goldpiece paralyzed us all, as the sea serpent's venom is said to paralyze whatever it bites, leaving the victim ready to be engulfed. But then we all hissed and snarled as if we were so many middle raptors, not properly men at all. What a horn-face's meaty carcass might do for hungry animals, gold does for—or, I might say, does to—hungry people.

"This," Baja said, "*this* to the huzzard-eyed rogue who spots for me the Great Gray Mossy, to be paid after we lower and harpoon and try the monster!" He nailed the second coin to the mast, well above the first. With a fierce laugh, he added, "I've spiked it well, I have. No thief will walk off with it in the middle of the night!"

I would not have wanted to try that, not when it ran the risk of having the skipper—who seemed to sleep very little—catch me in the act. What would he do to me, or to any other foolish, luckless would-be thief? If he only fed the miscreant to the ever-hungry sharks, the fellow might well count himself lucky.

———

There are terries that dive headlong into the sea after fish or squid or ammonites that they spy from great heights. They are, generally speaking, terries of the tropics, relying on the bright, nearly vertical sun to illuminate their meals for them.

And there are other terries, more widely spread in respect to latitude, that glide low above the ocean's surface and scoop up unwary little fish with great, underslung lower jaws. Skimmers earn a more reliable, steadier living than hellsdivers, even if every now and then a plessy will snatch one out of the air and abruptly turn it from eater to eaten.

Sailors, now, sailors admire hellsdivers for their boldness and enterprise. But sailors on mossy ships know skimmers are the terries more likely to guide them to their prey. For skimmers skim where the fishes swim thickest, and where they have the highest hope of reward. Mossies likewise gather in such places, for in those places their may fill their gigantic stomachs with the least labor. Laziness is not a trait known on dry land alone.

And so, when one bright, hot, humid morning we spied skimmers flocking almost like gulls, there was a singular rush to go aloft, as if everyone aboard the *Queepahd* were suddenly stricken with incurable gold fever. Where there were skimmers, there would be fish; where there were fish, there would be mossies; where there were mossies, there would be gold, whether of the smaller minting or the greater.

Or so we fondly believed. Skimmers we saw in great profusion, and fish so many that we watched them springing from the sea in their fear. Yet of mossies that first day full of skimmers we spied none. It was enough to drive one mad, assuming anyone's service in a mossy ship not to be prior evidence of lunacy.

"Where is them?" Geekgeek sounded angry at the monsters of the depths for not queuing up to be slaughtered. "Where them hiding?"

Of all the things in the world, or in the watery portions thereof which they inhabited, hiding was among the last I should have expected from mossies. They lorded it over the ocean; even the greatest thick-bodied plessies and murdertooth sharks commonly chose to swim away from them, not toward them with a view to combat. Only we in our wooden ships challenge them for supremacy of the sea; and, as Captain Baja's artificial tail attested, even now the fight is far from one-sided.

Slyly, I asked Geekgeek, "Cannot your little wooden idol, your Yojo, order the mossies to make themselves known to us?"

He tossed his head to show it was a thing impossible. "Him little god. You see he. *Little*. How him make to do things, mossies? Him have trouble plenty give *I* luck, and me smaller, lots smaller, than mossies."

With that I had to be contented, or rather discontented. Where was the logic in assuming that, because the god's image was small, the god himself had to be likewise? Where was the logic in assuming that small size meant small power? Where? Inside Geekgeek's skull, that was where. And that skull proved thick as a bonkhead's, and impervious to penetration by rational thought.

No help for it, then, but to wait until mossies manifested themselves of their own accord. If they did so soon, Geekgeek might graciously allow Yojo to take credit for the apparition. If not, he would generously forgive the small god for failing to accomplish that which lay beyond the reach of his small divinity.

Three days went by. No sign of mossies saw we. Perhaps Yojo was talking, or he was pursuing, or he was in a journey, or peradventure he slept. Everyone in the *Queepahd* grew irritable; we were one and all annoyed with the word and with one another, from the cook's helper, a half-grown lad named Fredugg, of the same ofttimes-serile race as Ootag without even feathers yet on his arms, to Captain Baja himself.

Those who had the duty at the mossy ship's stern whispered of strange noises emanating from the skipper's cabin. I wondered whether Baja was in his own way communing with Yojo, or with some private daimon all his own. He called himself an Egger, as I did, but I was sure orthodoxy mattered nothing to him when measured against the pursuit and extermination of the Great Gray Mossy.

Stabbak seemed worried. Of all aboard the mossy ship, he had to be the least blind to and the most concerned with the skipper's savage obsession. It thrust all our lives into danger. Baja might not care about that, but the good first mate did. Perhaps even worse, from Stabbak's perspective, was that the skipper's obsession thrust the owners' profits into danger. Baja might play at killing other mossies, but he cared about killing only one. If he could carve what is known as scrimshander work into one of the Great Gray Mossy's teeth torn from its dead jaw, every other such creature might go hang for all he cared.

Worse—from the mate's view of things, at any rate—was his own inferior position in the grand scheme of things. Stabbak could not order the skipper to desist from his impetuous folly. Baja would have clapped him in irons for making a mutiny had he attempted any such thing, if in his fury he did not slay him on the spot. No maritime court in the world, I feel sure, would have condemned the skipper for such a killing. On the contrary; Stabbak would have been weighed in the balances and found wanting. A mossy ship's skipper—any ship's skipper—is, as I have said, a small god, but a god natheless.

Stabbak grasped all this perfectly well. He was a good mate, maybe even a mate better than Baja was a skipper. He would suggest; he would implore; he would importune; command, he could not, nor did he ever seek to do so. If his suggestions and importunations fell upon plugged earholes, as they assuredly did, he could but go on with the ship's business in the best way he knew how to manage it.

Which he did. And he worried every heartbeat whilst doing it. The skipper had spiked gold to the mainmast to show what the Great Gray Mossy meant to him. About Stabbak's worries he cared not a counterfeit copper. The first mate doubtless knew as much, and doubtless worried even more as a result. He was, as I say, a most excellent mate.

Then one hot, muggy morning, half a daytenth before the sun reached its daily zenith, a sailor sang out in high excitement from even higher in the foremast's rigging: "Spout! By the Eggshell, it's a spout! Mossy off the starboard bow!"

———

Like plessies, mossies blow out vapor and water when they come to the surface for a sip of the fresh air their continued existence requires. A long-necked plessy will commonly thrust its head well out of the sea, leaving no doubt as to what it is. A thick-bodied plessy may be distinguished from the mossy it resembles at a distance by the shape and size of its spout. Those with any experience of both will never mistake the one for the other.

The first mate began to hurry aft to let Captain Baja know what had chanced if by some misfortune his aging earholes had not caught the cry from aloft. But a slam of the cabin door and the rattle of the skipper's artificial tail on timber told Stabbak and everyone else aboard the *Queepahd* that Baja was alert to all that passed on his ship. Soon he appeared on deck, nor was he alone, for five of the lean, all but demonic folk who roam the deserts south of the Middle Sea accompanied him.

I think we were all less astonished than we might have been without those reports of odd sounds coming from his cabin at odd daytenths. Not unastonished, mind, but less astonished. By then, I believe, nothing the skipper did could have astonished us very much. His having a secret boat crew all his own did not stand tall amongst the ranks of possible surprises.

For that was what those scrawny raptors of the desert—I do them no insult, that being but their own name for themselves—plainly were. The largest, leanest, and most villainous of them carried a harpoon even more deadly-looking than any I'd seen clutched in Geekgeek's scaly fist. The others, broader in the shoulders and thicker in the arms, must have done their share of rowing and more.

"Stabbak, thou'lt stay aboard and tend to the ship," Baja declared. "Faidal here and his gang of thieves and I, we'll go after the mossy in your boat."

"But, Captain—" The mate would not protest a lawful order, but wanted to with every fiber of his being. This was his courage, his spine, being questioned, or so he could not help seeing it.

The skipper understood why the mate's tail quivered. "Thou'rt a man, Stabbak. Thou'rt a fine man, and I know it. Also I know thou'rt a young man, with wife and hatchlings back in Faraway Town. Should anyone's luck be out, let it be mine. But I expect to slay, not be slain, for the gods will assuredly take me not till I've had my try at vengeance against the Great Gray Mossy."

To that the good mate could offer no response save acquiescence. He dipped his head and mumbled, "As you say, sir, so shall it be."

Ootag, his harpoon man, who had once been a slave, might have had somewhat to say to Stabbak on the question of unquestioning obedience. Since Stabbak would not put to sea, neither would Ootag. He looked unhappy that he would not be rowed into peril of his life. So he looked, and so, no doubt, he felt. This willingness to hazard all for the sake of others' approval is a curious business. And I had my own smaller share of it, else I should not have taken ship aboard the *Queepahd*, much less rowed in Shtup's boat to take Geekgeek out where he could harpoon the mossy.

"We'll do our job, by the gods," quoth the second mate. "We won't let those funny foreign sons of sour yolks get ahead of us, either, will we, boys?" As we raised a cheer, Shtup seemed suddenly to recall something of importance. He dipped his head to Geekgeek. "Meaning no offense to you, I'm sure."

Geekgeek waved aside the apology, if such it was. "Us here. Mossy there. Us go kill he," he said, as single-minded in his purpose as the most modern captain of manufacturing.

Down went the boats, into the warm sea. Down scrambled the crews after them: harpoon men, rowers, and, at the rudders, the second and third mates and the skipper himself. Baja's unlimber, artificial tail made his scramble more awkward than most, but he accomplished it. Faidal and his fellow desert demons traveled down the ship's flank as easily if they were so many geckos with sticky toes.

The three boats pulled away from the mossy ship. "Give it all you have, lads," Shtup said; to him, everyone on the ship save Baja would have seemed a lad. "Pull! Pull, curse you! We'll not let the other boats beat us, not either one of 'em!"

Pull I did, along with my fellows at the oars. Facing the stern, I had to trust to Shtup and Geekgeek, who could see where they were going, not merely where they'd been. The *Queepahd* shrank behind us, as hatchlinghood does when time moves us away from it. Then I had not worried about how I was directed; I had to hope now that Shtup knew how best to guide boat to target and that Geekgeek could do what wanted doing when the instant came.

I could glance to either side. We stood neither much ahead of nor much behind Frask's boat and the skipper's. Those lean desert raiders could row, but so could we all. And so we did, as if possessed.

"Ah, the mossy's spied us," Shtup said. "Now we find out what he does."

Mossies have not intelligence in the sense that people do. They build no cities; they make no laws. Yet neither are they foolish creatures of the fishy kind. Aboard ship, I had listened to a great deal of talk about this crucial moment, the one wherein the mossy first sets eyes on the little boats full of folk who will slay him if they can.

Four things are possible, experienced crewmen averred. The naïve mossy, the one never before hunted, may simply wait to find out what these curious creatures are. This sort is easy to harpoon. Or the creature may flee, at a speed oars cannot match. Or it may dive, in which case the steersman turns prophet, as it were, divining where it will surface again after a stay in the depths of half a daytenth or more.

Or, if the hunters' luck be out, the mossy may charge their boats, toothy jaws agape, tail ready to smash and break. Some mossies that charge have been oft pursued, and understand aggression is the better part of valor. Others, say those in a position to know, are simply possessed of an evil temperament, as some people are.

This mossy dove. "Oh, the stinking rotten egg!" Shtup said. "Now we'll be out here gods know how long, and we may never get another glimpse of him."

Geekgeek pointed back toward the *Queepahd*. "That way, me think." No less than steersmen, harpoon men fancy they can think themselves inside a mossy's long, narrow, savage skull. Being savage himself, Geekgeek might have enjoyed some advantage in that regard.

"I don't know." Shtup seemed less than sure of himself.

Frask's boat was making off in exactly the opposite direction. As for Baja, his desert demons were resting on their oars, as if believing the mossy would seek air again from the very point whence he departed.

"That way," Geekgeek repeated.

"Well, we'll try it." The second mate hissed laughter. "If it doesn't work out, I'll blame you." This sally sailed straight over the crest of feathers atop the harpoon man's head. Shtup went on, "Half speed, rowers! We have the time to get in place, I reckon." We turned in as small a circle as the rudder allowed, and the mossy ship's wooden walls began to rise before us. At length, Shtup asked, "Will this do, your Excellency?"

"Little more," Geekgeek responded, and on a little more we went.

I would have bet that the skipper's boat would prove closest to the mossy's surfacing point. Both Baja and Faidal seemed to own all but occult powers of insight into the way the monsters of the deep swam and even thought. I said nothing; I was the least experienced, most ignorant fellow in our boat, and had wit enough to understand as much.

And it is as well that I did not open my jaws, for when the mossy rose to breathe once more, it breached no farther from us than a couple of huzzards' wingspans. Shtup stared at Geekgeek. "You can call them, sure enough," the mate said.

"Smelled right," Geekgeek answered smugly, which might have meant anything or nothing.

To us at the oars, Shtup said, "Softly, lads, softly, and we'll be on him before he ever dreams we're there."

I rowed soft as ever I could, wishing I might look back over my shoulder to see how close we were getting and what the mossy was up to while we neared it. But I was a mere gear in the vast machinery of slaughter. Such knowledge being inessential to my function, I was denied it. Shtup used hand signals to slow us further, and worked the rudder in accordance with Geekgeek's guidance; though I could not see the harpoon man at the boat's bow, I felt his every move and shift.

And I felt him lean back and then forward, casting the harpoon at the mossy with all the strength in his well-thewed left arm. A great groaning hiss broke from the mossy's mouth as it swam along the surface as fast as it could go, dragging us along behind on what they call a Faraway sled ride.

The rope, coiled in the tub with utmost care so it would not twist and catch harpoon man or rower in a deadly embrace, hissed from its storage place, so fast that Sthup exclaimed, "By the gods, Geekgeek, wet it before it catches fire!" But Geekgeek, being not without practice in such matters, had already knelt and dipped a long-handled pot into the sea so he could use the salt water to cool the line as it unwound.

For a while, all we could do was let the mossy tow us and pray to whatever gods we owned that it would not turn round on us instead (I added a small petition to Geekgeek's Yojo, which, though it might not help, would surely do no harm).

Baja's boat, and Frask's, both followed us to lend what aid they might. For the moment, they could do naught; the mossy, in its pain and rage, swam faster than any boat might go. Then Geekgeek exclaimed, "Him dive!"

"He won't stay down long," Shtup predicted. "He'll have to breathe again soon, same as anybody who's run a long way with a spear in his gizzard. When he comes up, we'll find out just how bad hurt he is."

True to the second mate's prognostication, the mossy soon rose and spouted. Geekgeek sounded disappointed as he said, "Same blow like usual."

I did not fully grasp the significance of that, being on my first hunt on my first cruise in a mossy ship. Shtup, who fancied hearing himself talk, spelled out the harpoon man's meaning for him, saying, "He'll blow blood out his snout soon enough, I reckon."

Up from behind us came Baja's boat, which had taken a considerable lead on Frask's. At the bow, Faidal waved a question to Shtup, who returned a silent gesture of agreement or permission. Baja, at the rudder, dipped his head slightly, acknowledging the assent. The desert demons rowed the skipper's boat past ours and up to the mossy, which had greatly slacked its pace as the wound took a toll on it.

Faidal undid the line from his harpoon before casting it at the mossy. Geekgeek's line still secured the creature. The mossy jerked and leaped as if lightning-stricken when the spear went home, then tried to tear off as it had when our harpoon man hit it.

But, doubly tormented by barbed iron in its vitals, it lacked the vim for another wild jaunt across the water. Its speed soon flagged and, as Shtup had foretold, it spouted red rather than white. Soon it lay on the surface, two flippers upturned, twitching its life away.

Baja took a long lance with a pennon on the butt end and thrust it into the aquatic monster so it stood straight up. Those aboard the

Queepahd could spot the pennon from farther than they could see the mossy, and in spotting it they would realize the pursuit had succeeded and they might bring up the ship to commence converting the creature to its essential oils and other worthwhile parts.

"Bravely done, boys, bravely," Shtup said. "I'm proud of you all. Geekgeek, don't reckon you could've hit him any better."

The savage held out his left arm as if it were not part of him but rather some independent entity with powers of its own. And he spoke of it in the same wise, replying, "Him do good, yes."

Looking behind me, I could see the *Queepahd* approaching, her sails full of wind. Sailors on the deck and in the rigging cheered our prowess. At the wheel, Stabbak dipped his head in salute to the skipper. By the way Baja accepted the gesture of respect, he reckoned it no less than his due.

With the rest of those who'd gone out on the mossy boats, I scrambled up from them to the ship once more. Small and cramped as the *Queepahd* commonly seemed, it might have been a continent by comparison to the boats. No sooner was I arrived than I helped hoist the boats aboard and aided in securing the enormous floating corpse of the mossy to the ship's starboard flank.

Even as we were making it fast with hooks and chains and lines, sharks drawn by the delicious scent of blood in the water gathered for the feast we had set out before them. Baja grumbled at the wastage, though he understood perfectly well that it was an inevitable accompaniment to what mossy ships did.

"They run from live mossies," Frask said, "but when their betters slay them they aren't ashamed to take their place at the table. Huzzards of the sea, that's all they are."

In turn, Geekgeek, Tashteg, Ootag, and Faidal went to work with spears and saws to sever the mossy's head from its body so it might be brought up on deck for the special treatment it required. This was a hard labor, and a dangerous one. They stood on the corpse to dismember it. A wave might crush one of them between the dead mossy and the ship's timbers. Or that same wave, or its mischievous brother, might playfully swipe them into the ocean. The sharks gorging themselves on mossy meat would not disdain fresh harpoon man should they find it on the menu.

When Geekgeek came back on deck, all tired and bloody, after a long shift of carving the carcass, I told him, "By the gods and the Eggshell, whatever they pay you, it is not a sufficiency."

He shrugged. "Want to spear shark for I. Shark great big good eating. Feed Yojo shark liver, too, you bet."

"He's welcome to my share," I said. I have heard that, in large quantities, shark liver will poison you. Not finding liver of any sort appetizing, I cannot speak to the truth of this.

In due course, as has befallen both kings and those who fought kings, the mossy's head and body parted company. Much hard work on capstans and much profanity led to the great head—it was a third the length of the whole animal, and nearly as heavy as the rest put together—being hauled up on deck. Seawater-diluted blood spread over the planking; in my mind, I envisioned long dreary daytenths with the holystone, restoring shipshape cleanliness once more.

One of the tools a mossy ship carries is a combined axe blade and pick mounted on a stout staff, stouter than that which holds a harpoon head. Yes, something so medieval as a halberd still has a place in our modern, hurrying world, not for discomfiting warriors armored in plate but for splitting mossy skulls that scoffed at any less imposing implements of persuasion.

Ootag, the largest and burliest of the harpoon men, took up the halberd. He leaned so far back on his tail that I thought he must surely topple over, but used his enormous strength to come forward once more and swing his skull-cleaver in a glittering arc through the mild, moist subtropical air. It smashed against the very midpoint of the mossy's head with a sound like that of a butcher's shop, though greatly magnified.

The stalwart skull rebuffed it like a dainty votary of the Great Egg spurning the town drunkard. Unfazed as the drunkard cut by the votary, Ootag delivered another blow, and yet another. At the third, a rending crunch proclaimed that the escaped slave had at last set at liberty the valuable contents of the mossy's braincase.

Once the breach was effected, subtlety replaced brute force. Spreaders widened the gap between the thick hard bones on one side and those on the other, so that the sun shone in on the mossy's brain.

A mossy may easily weigh as much as five hundred people. Its brain, though larger than a person's, is not proportionally larger. Mossies with the brains of five hundred people would contrive to hunt us on land rather than being themselves hunted in the water. The scarcity and difficulty in obtaining mossy brains add to the value of those that are obtained. For, after fermentation in the cask, as it were, nothing will help turn hides to leather like the organ which guided the living mossy in it progress through the sea. Other brains may suffice for lesser leathers, but only the mossy's will produce the very best.

Once the brain was properly casked and carried below to commence its curing process, Ootag handed his halberd to an ordinary sailor for cleaning and took a rather smaller weapon—an ordinary knife—from the sheath on his belt. He used it to slice off a choice gobbet of the meat between the mossy's hide and skull and pop it into his mouth without visiting upon it fire or even salt.

"Ah!" he said with a deep hiss of satisfaction. "Nothing's better!"

This proposition struck me as dubious, but others with more knowledge of such matters seemed to agree with him. After allowing him the first morsel, they swarmed over the severed head, each after his favorite bit of flesh. Some carved chunks from the top of the mossy's head, as Ootag had; others chose theirs from near the neck, still others from the mossy's tongue. It was the rudest of feasts, one our barbarous ancestors would have fully appreciated.

So I thought, at least, until pangs of hunger prompted me to join it. We were at least marginally more civilized than the raptors, for we did not bite and claw each other as we fed ourselves. Then again, there was such a great plenty of meat to go around as to make quarrels over who claimed which portion simply preposterous.

I hacked off a great slice of mossy tongue, popped it into my mouth, chewed briefly, and gulped it down. It was sweet, it was mild, it was tender—as with flying fish, it was *not* the timberlike smoked and salted drosaw and hornface flesh upon which we had all been so long subsisting. As Ootag said, nothing could have gone down better. Perhaps unfamiliarity enhanced flavor and texture, but you could not have told me so whilst I consumed it. As soon as it was done, I cut myself another slab, from as close to the first as I could get.

After satisfying hunger, some of the sailors began worrying the mossy's teeth from their sockets with knives and pliers, for scrimshander work or to sell to landlubbers once the *Queepahd* came home to Faraway Island once more. Here, however, Stabbak took a hand. "Half the teeth to the crew, half to the ship," he said. "You all know the bargain as well as I do—and as well as Captain Baja does. The ship *will* have its half. What's over and above that will be yours. Forty-four for the ship, the rest for you."

Mossies commonly have eighty-eight teeth, sometimes a few more, sometimes a few less. But eighty-eight is the number on which the two moieties are based.

Sometimes it so happens that the smaller and poorer fangs go the the ship, the larger and finer to the sailors. Aboard less happy ships, the converse may come to pass. On the *Queepahd,* I was given to understand, the division would be as even and exact as ingenuity, sharp eyes, and a good set of scales could make it. In this regard, the skipper was a god and the first mate a prophet of scrupulosity.

I would have expected nothing less from Captain Baja. He might have been mad; indeed, there can be no doubt he *was* mad in his pursuit of the Great Gray Mossy. He owned as much himself; on days when the wind was southerly he knew a hawk from a huzzard. But no single speck of dishonesty tarnished his madness.

———

Once the head and its valuable contents were eaten and otherwise disposed of, we hoisted the remainder of the carcass aboard for skinning and rendering into essential oil and for the search for gray amber. The meat from the head that the sailors had not devoured was already bubbling in the cauldron of the tryworks, which sat and smoked like some dark deity's altar betwixt mainmast and foremast. Fire is always a great fear aboard ship despite water all around; stout and sturdy brickwork shielded our timbers from the furnace's flames and heat.

Nothing, though, could shield our snouts from the stenches the tryworks sent forth. We might go belowdecks or high as we pleased in the rigging without escaping the reek of baking flesh, charring flesh, and bubbling oil. We inhaled mossy with every inspiration, and thought we should go on smelling it until our expiration.

Stabbak seemed contented enough and to spare. "That's the odor of money, boys!" he would say to anyone who would listen. "That's what the owners back on Faraway Island want to smell! And we all get our share! Every single drop of oil we render makes us money!"

"Mossy, him still stink," quoth Geekgeek, and most of us found ourselves in his corner rather than the mate's. The mossy even fueled its own destruction; chunks of flesh from which all oil had been cooked away went into the furnace smoking beneath the cauldron to keep it hot and enable the rendering of yet more oil from yet more flesh.

Once all the oleaginous meat had been flensed away from them, the strips sliced spirally from the mossy's scaly hide got special treatment of their own. They were tanned—no, not in mossy brains, for this would be leather of the roughest, of the toughest, kind—and set aside to cure. As needed, strips or squares would be cut from them and used to effect shipboard repairs. Whatever the *Queepahd* had left at her eventual (her most extremely eventual) return to Faraway Town would be sold, the proceeds, such as they might prove to be, adding to the profit the ship brought her owners and those of us who labored aboard her or, if worse came to worst, mitigating whatever losses she might suffer.

And mossy oil went from the tryworks into the barrels that would also be sold once we came to port again. Mossy oil helps light the world, and helps grease it as well, also greasing commerce as it leaves the mossy, leaves the mossy ship, and becomes a corpuscle in the bloodstream of trade. Few who fill their lamps or lubricate their lathes pause to consider how the oil they pour with lavish hand is won. I seldom did myself before my chance association with Geekgeek took me on to Baja's vessel.

The skipper seemed strangely indifferent to the liquid gold pouring from cauldron to barrel. The mossy we had slain was not the mossy whose blood he thirsted after. Somewhere in the broad blue ocean, the Great Gray Mossy still swam; still slaughtered sharks and plessies, king turtles and tunnies, great squid and ammonites; still *lived*. To Captain Baja, that was affront grandiose and unpardonable.

Yet he was not altogether uninterested in the proceedings—in the *breaking down* of the great sea beast, as mossy sailors are wont to call it. "Have a care when ye slice the guts, lads!" he said, not once but several times. "Have a care, aye! For remember, if there's gray amber to be found in there, it's worth even more, weight for weight, than the finest fermented mossy brains. If it's there to be found, find it you must, and whoever does will win handsome reward, I vow."

This gray amber is a product of sickness in mossies, not of health. It accretes like soft, slimy nacre round squids' beaks and bits of ammonite shell that fail to digest as they should. Whilst fresh, it reeks powerfully of what you would expect to find in a mossy's gut, which fouls the water on passing out through the creature's cloaca.

Yet dung remains dung for ever. Gray amber, once washed and heated and otherwise treated, becomes, by some near-mystical transmutation I cannot claim to comprehend, the basis of many of the finest fragrances and perfumes ever concocted.

This mossy had fed well before Geekgeek harpooned it. Its gut was full of dung, through which the sailors had to guddle in search of the precious commodity they sought. Breaking down a mossy is never work for those whose hands must be clean at all times and under all circumstances. Going after the gray amber may be the worst of it. As sailors will, they laughed and chaffed one another and played with bits of excrement as if it were a hatchling's toy.

Basins of seawater and strong soap adapted to use on the ocean let them wash their scales and feathers after the search was done (incidentally, they found none of what the skipper had hoped for).

Standing by watching them splash one another with salt water and soapsuds as they had before with dung, Stabbak murmured, "They can clean their outsides well enough, but what of their souls?" After a moment, he added, "I might have told Baja the quest for gray amber would lay no eggs. The mossy was too healthy; only beasts sick from clogged guts produced what he wanted. Is he as daft in his hunt for the Great Gray Mossy? Of course he is, but he has caught all of us in the net of his obsession there."

He fell silent then. He might have noticed my listening to his mutterings, or he might simply have said all he had to say. I could not very well ask him; no one on shipboard wants the name of snoop stuck to his hide. I did not know then, and I do not know now, after so much has gone by and so many extraordinary things have happened. Myself an invention of the gods, whatever that may mean, I am inventing on my own here.

———————

Since rounding the Cape of Good Hope, the *Queepahd* had roamed the oceans all solitary, without companions but for those that fly above the water or swim in it. Yet mossy ships and plessy ships do meet upon the sea now and again, as I have said. Vast though it is, they often travel similar watery tracks. When they encounter one another, especially when one is inbound whilst the other heads out, they will exchange letters and papers and magazines—anything to ease the tedium of existence in our floating coffins.

And they will exchange news, news of what has happened back home and on the sea. When we encountered another vessel, Captain Baja would always hail it with, "Hast spied the Great Gray Mossy in these waters?"

The other skipper would always tell him he had not, so monotonously that, were it not for Baja's absent caudal appendage and the testimony of others who confirmed the creature's existence in the material world, I should have began to wonder whether the Great Gray Mossy was naught but a figment of our lord and master's unwholesome imagination.

Once a chance acquaintance had denied knowledge of the object of Baja's obsession, matters would proceed as they did between any two ships passing in the daytime. If there followed a note of melancholy on our side of the exchange, we could pray our new and brief comrades would little note nor long remember it.

Once I happened to eavesdrop on the harpoon men hashing out how things stood. Geekgeek made no attempt to disguise his views. "Captain, him heap big crazy," he said.

"Have to be crazy to do what he does, what we do," said Tashteg, and I thought the brownskin had got to the yolk of things at once.

Ootag laughed at both of them. "What difference does it make?" he said. "As long as we go home to Faraway Town with mossy brains, with oil in the barrels, with meat smoked and salted, Captain Baja can be as crazy as he likes," he declared.

"Him too crazy, him get ship sinked," Geekgeek said. "Him maybeso crazy enough, do just that."

Until then, Faidal had kept silent, so silent I had not been aware the skipper's desert demon was even present. But he let out a soft, deadly hiss, of the kind one might expect to burst from the throat of a castanet viper. "You know not what you speak of, none of you," he said softly.

"What you know?" Geekgeek demanded. "What you *think* you know?" I do believe Faidal frightened him some, as Faidal frightened everyone save perhaps Captain Baja. But he gave a good, game try of not showing it.

"Can you not see the gods hold the captain in the hollow of their hand?" Faidal said. I doubt I was the only one to wonder which gods he meant. Not clarifying that, he continued, "How can a mossy harm someone who will perish only from a hempen necklace?"

"Who told you? Your lying gods?" Tashteg, at least, did not reckon Faidal's to be his own as well.

"Sometimes it is given to one to know such things," Faidal said, which could have signified anything under the sky and above the sea.

He might have added more, but Shtup came along just then and spoke as officiously as it is ever given to second mates to speak: "Come on, you lazy mammals' hatchlings, you! If you can't be busy, at least look busy, so you don't shame the ship!" The harpoon men broke up their gathering and went off each his own way, intent, I am sure, on looking busy. Shtup strutted around the corner and spotted me. I endeavored to look busy, but did not succeed sufficiently so as to satisfy him. He ground his gizzard stones by shouting at me as he had at the men who flung the darts of iron.

Two days later, we descried another sail on the northeastern horizon. With a favorable wind, we sailed towards it with all canvas set. The strange ship also seemed desirous of meeting us, for it tacked to help narrow the distance. Someone high aloft with a spyglass called down to the deck, saying, "That's the *Flowerbud,* skipper!"

"I know that ship. She's also out of Faraway Town," said Captain Baja, whose clawed fists clutched the wheel. "Captain Kain is an able fellow—no one has ever dared claim otherwise. But his luck is not in. It has not been in for some years now. I wonder whether it will ever run his way again."

He summoned Stabbak to take control of the *Queepahd* whilst he himself went forward to hail the *Flowerbud* and enquire after the Great Gray Mossy. But Captain Kain raised a leathern loud-hailer to his snout and called out to us first: "Ahoy, the *Queepahd!* Have you seen any sign of a wayward mossy boat, or of any sailors clinging to the wreckage of such a boat?"

"We have not," Baja shouted back through our ship's loud-hailer, though his unaided voice was so loud and brassy that he scarcely needed the artificial aid. On hearing the reply, Captain Kain at once slumped as if harpooned in the vitals. Baja went on, "This is a boat from thine own vessel, I would guess?"

"It is," Kain said in a dead voice, "and carried my eldest hatchling till the cursed Great Gray Mossy stove it in and either slew or set adrift the whole crew."

Captain Baja could have stood no stiffer and straighter had lightning flashed down from the cloudless heavens to electrify him. Even the tip of his artificial tail seemed suddenly to quiver with his excitement. You may tell me it was a dead thing, a thing of polished, cleverly jointed mossy bone with leather strapping to hold it to the living part of him, and incapable of any such motion. You may tell me whatever you please. I shall tell you what I saw.

"Thou'rt certain sure 'twas the Great Gray Mossy and none other?" the skipper demanded.

"As certain as I stand here talking to you," the skipper of the *Flowerbud* replied. "Can you help me search for my poor lost hatchling or any of the others who were in the boat with him? I fear for them all— that monster knows no mercy."

"Tell me where the mishap occurred," Baja said.

Captain Kain pointed back in the direction from which he had come. "That way, a bit more than a day's sail."

"Then that is where we shall make for; that is where we shall search." Baja turned to call to Stabbak at the wheel: "Steer us northeast by north! Crowd on all sail, lad, as much as we have. We'll pickle the Great Gray Mossy's brains and boil him down for oil. And I shall feast on his tongue and his tasty cheek meat."

"But the currents would bring the boat back this way!" protested the skipper of the *Flowerbud.*

"Kain, I wish thee good fortune; gods know thou'rt deserving of it," Captain Baja said. "If they be kind, thou'lt find thy hatchling. Do as thou must, and I shall do likewise. My quarrel's not with thee; 'tis with the monster that assailed thy boat. I shall avenge thee as I avenge myself."

Kain stared across the water at him even as the *Queepahd* spread more canvas and began to leave the *Flowerbud* behind. "You're daft!" he cried out. "Daft as a barking mammal!"

Baja dipped his head in what might have been mere acknowledgment or agreement. "Thy servant, sir," he said. "I wish thee no ill. Pray do not make me regret I wish thee no ill. We all go where and as the gods' winds blow us."

"The gods' winds have blown you into madness, if your yolk wasn't addled before you ever hatched!" Captain Kain said furiously. Had the

Flowerbud been a sloop of war rather than a mossy ship, surely he would have given the *Queepahd* a broadside.

That he could not do, nor aught else unless he wanted to board us and fight it out with harpoons and shortswords and whatever pistols might be on board the two vessels. I do believe he was sore tempted, but he desisted.

"I grieve for thy hatchling, but he is not mine. Thou hast thy quest, I mine own," our skipper answered, to the eye or earhole not a bit put out. The *Queepahd* sailed in one direction, the *Flowerbud* in the other. They speak of ships that pass in the night, but these, that passed in broad daylight, were never so far apart as when they came closest together.

———

Back at the wheel once more, with Stabbak relegated to some menial task, Baja tapped a fingerclaw against the great gold coin he had spiked to the mainmast. He'd used the carpenter's claw hammer to free the smaller one so he might present it to the sailor who'd fist spied the mossy that went through our tryworks.

Tap! Tap! Though the goldpiece made no music while so rudely nailed in place, still any contact with it seemed to own a magnetism that drew our notice as a lodestone draws iron—as, it was once said, lodestones on some distant shore drew the nails from sailing ships so they fell to pieces and drowned their crews. I could not help but wonder whether Baja himself was likewise falling to pieces. Perchance he wondered the same himself, but, if he did, he did not care. The Great Gray Mossy swam somewhere not far ahead. He cared for nothing but that.

Tapping again, he said, "Do ye hear it, lads? Well? Do ye? That's the sound of gold! That's the sound of victory! It goes to the first to spy the Great Gray Mossy, as I told ye aforetimes. Be on watch! Don't let your nictitating membranes flick across your eyeballs, lest ye miss summat ye should have seen. The chase has been long, but it's not got far to go now!"

Faidal came up to him and waited respectfully to be noticed. The desert devil did not care to distract the skipper whilst he had the helm. In due course, Captain Baja dipped his head to the harpoon man. They spoke together, too low to be overheard for a little while. Then the skipper, nettled, tossed his head and bared his teeth. All submission—at least the shell of him was all submission—Faidal bent nearly double and crept away.

And yet I could see the skipper's hands all aquiver on the wheel as he conned the ship toward the Great Gray Mossy, or toward where Captain Kain swore it swam. Which of Baja and Faidal was master and which slave still lay in the realm of the undetermined, for all that Baja might have come out on top in this particular encounter.

Also still in the realm of the undetermined lay whether the skipper pursued the sea beast out of love or out of hatred. For Baja and the Great Gray Mossy were very much alike when it came to the boundless determination of each to prevail regardless of the magnitude of the forces aligned against him. For Baja to purpose killing with his own lance the Great Gray Mossy was like some tiny, miserable, skulking mammal to purpose killing Baja. The difference in size and power between hunter and hunted was in both case unmeasurably great.

And yet the Great Gray Mossy struggled against not just Baja but every mossy ship, every skipper, every sailor on the sea: in effect, against every soul in this great land of ours. One against thousands, if not against millions! War with the world! When looked upon in that fashion, the Great Gray Mossy's fight seemed as crazed and as futile as Baja's campaign against it did when viewed from another perspective.

Yet we sailors dwelt but little upon such transcendental concerns. Every one of us spent aloft all the time he could, the better to see farther and quicker. The lure of gold sent folk flying across the continent like huzzards after carrion when the precious metal was found near the shore of the Peaceful Ocean two years gone by. So the lure of that great goldpiece got every one of us itchy and excited.

How many had died when their hopes of riches in the unexplored West sank on reality's jagged rocks? No more than my comrades in the *Queepahd* did I ask myself such questions. No more than they did I wonder what fate had in store for me. The sooner we staked our claim, the better off we would be. We were all certain of it.

Well, almost all of us were certain of it. Stabbak made so bold as to approach Captain Baja that night, when the skipper held the wheel for another shift. "Sir, would you not do better to give over?" the first mate asked. "Would we not be better off filling our hull with barrels of oil and meat and pickling brains from lesser mossies than pursuing this profitless quest?"

"I will do what I must do until the egg of my great vengeance hatches," Baja replied. "And answer me this, sirrah—when is it the mate's duty to tell the skipper how to steer the ship?" One fingerclaw of his ominously tapped the wheel then.

"It is the mate's duty to speak when the captain steers the ship astray," Stabbak answered bravely. "O Captain—my Captain!—I know you have a wife and hatchlings back in Faraway Town, just as I do. Do you aim to leave her a widow, bringing them up on whatever scraps you've left behind?"

"I have not left scraps. I have provided a sufficiency, and more than a sufficiency." Pride rang in Baja's voice. "An thou hast not, 'tis thy lookout alone. As for my wife, she knew what she was marrying when we pledged each other before the gods. She'd scorn me if I shed this skin now!"

"Give me leave to doubt, sir," Stabbak said. "Surely she'd sooner have you than not have you, if you take my meaning."

"Not if what she has falls short of what she wed," the skipper replied. Stabbak must have known he would fail before he spoke. Yet speak he did anyhow, so as to be certain he left no stone unturned in his effort to soften the skipper and unruffle his feathers. Baja pointed imperiously toward the bow. "Go tend to thy duties."

"Captain, I am tending to them now," Stabbak said in a low voice. But he went. What else could he do? He was but the mate, lesser in rank than the skipper he served. And he was lesser in his self than Baja, too; he had none of Baja's mad, driving assuredness. He would have been first to agree to that, though he would have argued he was better off without it.

Better or worse, it did not matter. He tried; he failed. And Baja and the *Queepahd* sailed on toward their appointed end.

"Mossy spout off the starboard bow!" The shout came from high above me whilst I was holystoning the deck. What I felt when I heard the cook's helper's high, thin cry was nothing but jealousy that blazed like a forest fire. Orders kept me at a menial duty away from the shrouds when good fortune dipped its snout to the lucky little fellow in the rigging.

Had I known the price of the great goldpiece he hoped to claim... Well, who can say what I would have done? A great many questions are easier asked than answered.

Captain Baja asked a question, loudly: "*A* mossy or *the* mossy, Fredugg?"

"By the gods, skipper, I do think it is *the* mossy!" Down floated Fredugg's answer, even more impassioned than before. "Never have I seen on of such great size or of this color."

"Thou should have the gold, after the beast is slain." Baja raised the call all mossy hunters live for, crying, "Lower all boats! Shtup and Frask, your crews will go. So too will mine own. Stabbak, as before, take charge of the ship whilst I go to win my revenge. Then shalt thou have the better hope of sailing home safe to thy wife and hatchlings small."

"I am not afraid to put to sea in a boat, sir," the first mate said stiffly.

"I said naught of fear. But thou hast spoken of thy family, which was in my mind even before thou didst, as thou may'st recollect. See? I hear thee, yet thou'rt not content," Baja said. "Such is life. But thou shalt do my bidding here."

Stabbak might have argued further. I knew not; I was scrambling down the *Queepahd's* wooden flank and into Shtup's boat. Geekgeek took his place at the bow a feather before I seized my oar. "Now pull your hearts out, my dears, my lovelies! Pull your tails off, my beauties!" Shtup shouted. "The skipper may reckon he'll scuttle the Great Gray Horror, but I want the critter chalked up to our account. What say you, my darlings?"

We all cheered as we commenced the long pull out to the mossy. Frask was likewise exhorting his crew to great effort. Captain Baja said never a word to his desert demons. But he stood at the bow in their boat, in the harpoon man's spot, consigning to Faidal the handling of the rudder.

Faidal owned as much pride as anyone who ever came from an egg. I reckoned he would make the skipper pay when the time came. But that would be later. We were affixed in the moment, as a scorpion from vanished time may be affixed forever in golden amber.

The three boats flew over the blue water. Try as any crew would, none could gain the least superiority over the other two. Ahead—not so far ahead now—the Great Gray Mossy spouted once more. So Shtup said, at any rate; all I could see was the *Queepahd* receding behind us. It did not in fact recede so very much, for Stabbak sent the mossy ship after the boats. If by chance he and the sailors still aboard might lend us any aid, lend they would.

Never have I known a sweeter, kindlier fellow than Stabbak. Oh, how dear it cost him!

"Great Gray Mossy! Great green harpoon man! Me kill he!" Geekgeek's shout rang out across the ocean. He sounded excited, almost gay.

"Great brown harpoon man!" Tashteg shouted back. They brandished their harpoons at each other in mock ferocity, laughing all the while. It was a game. It was a sport...until, all at once, it was no more.

With Shtup whooping us on, we outdid Frask's boat and even the desert devils who rowed the skipper toward his fate. "Be ready, you rowdy savage!" the second mate called to Geekgeek. "Be ready and cast hard. Gods, I reckon this here's the biggest, meanest mossy I ever seen!"

We stroked up alongside the sea beast, which continued disporting itself on the surface as if unacquainted with the word *fear*. I glimpsed a mountainous gray flank and a tail blithely stroking from side to side. Then the boat bobbed as Geekgeek flung the harpoon with all his strength.

"Hit!" Shtup screamed. "Oh, gods love you, a hit!" Rope smoked out of its tub. The mossy streaked away. But the Faraway sled ride on which it took us did not drag us far away at all. Only a few heartbeats after the mossy began its run, the line of a sudden went slack. The second mate let out a cry of horror. "Back oars and swing to starboard, hard as you can! The monster's heading straight at us!"

Usually, a wounded mossy will flee. The Great Gray Mossy was no usual creature. Geekgeek grabbed another harpoon to fend it off. Too late, too late! Its huge jaws closed on him and on the rower right in front of me. How I escaped I shall never know. But those of us who still lived were pitched into the ocean. I held my oar and seized a plank from the riven boat. They kept me from drowning straightaway.

Up sped the boat with Captain Baja in the bow. "Take thy just deserts, foul fiend!" Baja shouted, as if the Great Gray Mossy could understand. Then he cast his harpoon. As Geekgeek's had, it struck home.

The mossy again fled for little while. Line hissed from the tub and paid out after the beast. We always make sure to coil the hemp with the greatest of care, lest any kink spell disaster. But we are all only imperfect creatures, not the gods themselves. A kink there was, one that had escaped everyone's notice. The line seized the skipper round the throat and resistlessly threw him into the sea.

The mossy meanwhile turned back, as it had with us. Faidal, his prophecy fulfilled, cut the line to give the skipper what chance he could, but how could anyone hope to swim well, or at all, without a true tail and with a false one dragging him down toward doom? Then the desert demon seized another harpoon from the floor of the boat and rushed to the bow to defend it as best he could, as Geekgeek had before him. Never let it be said he lacked for bravery.

But also never let it be said bravery alone will defeat all foes. Faidal might as well have stood against the volcano or the hurricane. He had scant time for his cast, which gashed the Great Gray Mossy's snout but then bounced almost harmlessly away instead of sinking deep into the sea monster's flesh. Faidal was stooping to snatch up yet another spear when the mossy's jaws closed on him. A shriek, and most of him was gone forever. One of the sailors went into the sea as the creature destroyed the boat. The rest either sank or were devoured. Then the Great Gray Mossy dove again.

I peered down into the limpid water, fearing the last thing I should ever see was that pair of massive jaws opening wide to take me in. The Great Gray Mossy, though, was a beast of deep and subtle cunning. It knew wrecked boats posed it no threat, and likewise knew the harpoon man at the bow of an intact mossy boat was the source of danger for it. And so it rose from the depths directly *under* the boat carrying Tashteg, Frask, and their rowers, hurling it into the air and spinning it about like a hatchling's toy. Then the mossy beat the water with its tail, flailing the helpless mariners until they had no hope of survival.

And still the Great Gray Mossy had not finished its war upon the land-dwelling tormentors who went down to the sea in ships to pursue it. Rather than swimming away in triumph, the beast swam straight at the *Queepahd* fast as a speeding locomotive, and struck the vessel with no less force than a runaway locomotive would have possessed. After breaking a great hole in the mossy ship's side, it drew back and finally departed the scene. Water jetted over the gunwales as frantic sailors worked the pumps for every copper they were worth, but I saw from the outset it was hopeless. More poured in than could possibly be ejected. The *Queepahd*'s deck sank toward the surface of the ocean. Then the ship turned turtle, which surely doomed all those yet aboard.

It may be that Geekgeek's dart, or Captain Baja's, at length put paid to the Great Gray Mossy once for all. No report of the monster has come to my earhole since the sinking of the *Queepahd*, at any rate. But then, I know not what, if anything, that may prove, for I have not gone to sea in a mossy ship since that dreadful day. The gods will take me in their own good time come what may, and mix me into the new and perfect Eggshell they are forming, so that I may be rehatched perfect in my own self. I have no desire to meet them ere I must, and hunting mossies is not calculated to foster longevity in those who practice it again and again, or even once.

Indeed, I thought my doom had met me there, in those warm blue waters so far away from Faraway Island. I alone, though, survived to tell the tale. Some of my shipmates the Great Gray Mossy slew directly, with teeth or pounding flukes. Others drowned, aboard the *Queepahd* or after being cast from her boats. Still others, flotsam like me, were taken by sharks or plessies. I saw dorsal fins and fanged heads on long necks, and heard more than one mortal shriek, but none of the sea's lesser terrors chose to dine on me.

This would not have lasted much longer; sharks were circling the wood to which I clung when a sail came into sight on the southwestern horizon. I thought at first I must be dreaming it, but no! It was real. The *Flowerbud*, searching yet for Captain Kain's lost hatchling, had doubled back upon her course.

One of the sailors aloft in her rigging spied my feeble thrashings. I was a disappointment to them when they hauled me up on deck, they hoping I would prove to be someone else. But the skipper was gracious, saying he was glad to have saved someone even if not the someone he most longed for. And so I came back to civilized lands once more, and set these things down as best I recall them. The writing was for me a cleansing; may the reading be for you the same.

VILCABAMBA

The President of the United States looked out of an Oval Office window at Grand Junction, Colorado. The Oval Office was square, but the President's workplace kept its traditional name. Harris Moffatt III sighed and bent to his paperwork again. Even in Grand Junction, that never disappeared.

Washington, D.C., remained the de jure capital of the United States. Harris Moffatt III had never been there. Neither had his father, President Harris Moffatt II. His grandfather, President Harris Moffatt I, got out of Washington one jump ahead of the Krolp. That the USA was still any kind of going concern came from his ever-so-narrow escape.

Harris Moffatt III was also Prime Minister of Canada, or of that small and mountainous chunk of Canada the Krolp didn't control. The two countries had amalgamated early on, the better to resist the invading aliens. That, of course, was before they realized how far out of their weight they were fighting.

When the enormous ships were first detected, between Mars' orbit and Earth's, every nation radioed messages of welcome and greeting. The Krolp ignored them all. The enormous ships landed. There were still videos—Harris Moffatt III had them on his computer—of human delegations greeting the aliens with bouquets and bands playing joyful music. At last! Contact with another intelligent race! Proof we weren't alone in the universe!

"Better if we were," the President muttered. When the Krolp came out, they came out shooting. Some of those fifty-year-old videos broke off quite abruptly. And "shooting" was the understatement of the millennium. Their weapons made ours seem like kids' slingshots against machine guns.

Seeing how the Krolp wanted things to go, half a dozen militaries launched H-bomb-tipped missiles at the great ships. They couldn't live through that, could they? As a matter of fact, they could. Most of the missiles got shot down. Most of the ones that did land on target didn't go off. And the handful that did harmed the Krolpish ships not a bit and the rampaging, plundering aliens running around loose very little.

They weren't invulnerable. Humans *could* kill them. Unless somebody got amazingly lucky, the usual cost was about two armored divisions and all their matériel for one Krolp. Back in the old days, the United States was the richest county in the world. All the pre-Krolp books said so. Not even it could spend men and equipment on that scale.

Back before the Krolp came, a fellow named Clarke had written *Any technology sufficiently advanced is indistinguishable from magic.* Harris Moffatt III didn't know about that. What the Krolp did wasn't magic. The best scientists in the USA—the best ones left alive, anyhow—had been studying captured or stolen Krolpish gadgets for half a century now. Their conclusion was that the aliens manipulated gravity and the strong and weak forces as thoroughly as humans exploited electromagnetism.

Humans could use Krolpish devices and weapons. They could even use them against the invaders, for as long as they kept working. What humans couldn't do was make more such devices themselves. The machines weren't there. Neither was the theory. And neither was the engineering to turn theory into practice.

And so Harris Moffatt III ruled an attenuated state between the Rockies and the Wasatch Range. He understood too well that he ruled here not least because the Krolp hadn't yet taken the trouble to overrun this rump USA (and Canada).

From everything he'd heard, the United States still was the richest country in the world. The richest human-ruled country, anyhow. And if that wasn't a telling measure of mankind's futility in the face of the aliens, Harris Moffatt III was damned if he could figure out what would be.

———

His appointments secretary stuck his head into the Oval Office. "Excuse me, Mr. President, but Grelch wants to see you."

"Tell him I'll be with him in a few minutes, Jack," Moffatt said. "I really do need to study this appropriations bill." Calling the economy in the independent USA rotten would have praised it too much. So would calling it hand-to-mouth. Robbing Peter to pay Paul came closest, except Paul mostly got an IOU instead.

Jack Pagliarone turned to pass the news on to Grelch—but Grelch didn't wait to hear it. The Krolp shoved past the appointments secretary and into the office. "I see you, Moffatt," he said—loudly—in his own language.

"I see you, Grelch," Harris Moffatt III answered—resignedly—also in Krolpish. There was a lot of Grelch to see. He was big as a horse: bigger, because he was a tiger-striped centauroid with a head like a vampire jack-o'-lantern. He had sharp, jagged jaw edges—they weren't exactly teeth, but they might as well have been—and enormous eyes that glowed like a cat's. He smelled more like limburger cheese than anything else.

"I have some things to tell you, Moffatt," he declared. No titles of respect: the Krolp had them for one another, but rarely wasted them on humans.

"I listen," the President said, more resignedly yet, wondering what Grelch would want this time. He was bound to want something, and he'd make trouble if he didn't get whatever it was.

Not for the first time, Harris Moffatt III wondered what Grelch had done to force him to flee to Grand Junction. A dozen or so alien renegades lived here. Humans had learned a lot from them, and from their predecessors. But they were deadly dangerous. They were Krolp, and had Krolpish defenses and Krolpish weapons. And they were almost all of them sons of bitches even by Krolpish standards. No alien who hadn't done something something awful to his own kind would have to stoop so low as to live with humans.

"I need snarfar, Moffatt. You've got to get me snarfar," Grelch said.

"I can do that, Grelch." The President tried to hide his relief. Some Krolp chewed snarfar. It gave them a buzz, the way nicotine or maybe cocaine did for humans. Harris Moffatt III didn't know the details; snarfar poisoned people. He did know the aliens turned mean—well, meaner—when they couldn't get the stuff.

But he *could* get it. They grew it in the flatlands of the Midwest— what had formerly been wheat and corn country. He still had connections in the lands his grandfather once governed. People and things informally slid over the border all the time. He'd arranged to bring in snarfar before. He'd known he would have to do it again, for one Krolp or another, before too long.

"You better do that, Moffatt. By the stars, you better," Grelch snarled. He turned—which, with that four-legged carcass, needed some room—and stomped out of the Oval Office. The ripe reek that came off his hide lingered in the air.

The President sighed. "That's always so much fun."

"Yes, sir," Jack Pagliarone said sympathetically. Even a renegade Krolp, an alien who'd put himself beyond the pale of his own kind, was convinced down to the bottom of whatever he used for a soul that he was better than any mere human ever born. All the evidence of fifty years of conquest and occupation said he had a point, too.

"If we didn't need to pick their brains…" Harris Moffatt III sighed again. Humanity needed nothing more.

"By the stars, Mr. President, if the first big uprising had worked—" Jack sadly shook his head.

Back when Harris Moffatt III was a boy, Americans, Russians, and Chinese all rebelled against the centauroids at once. They rocked the Krolp, no doubt about it. They killed forty or fifty of them, some with stolen arms, others with poison. But close didn't count. The Krolp crushed mankind again, more thoroughly this time.

Jack had spoken English with the President. Humans in the free USA mostly did. Even humans in Krolp-occupied America did when they talked among themselves. But the appointments secretary said *By the stars* anyhow.

Well, Harris Moffatt III sometimes said *By the stars* himself. More and more humans these days believed what the Krolp believed and tried to imitate the conquerors any way they could. Weren't the Krolp stronger? Didn't that prove they were wiser, too? Plenty of people thought so.

The President had when he was younger. Like his father before him, like Harris Moffatt IV now, he'd spent several years in St. Louis, the center from which the Krolp ruled most of the USA. He'd gone to what was called, with unusual politeness, a finishing school. In point of fact, he'd been a hostage for his father's good behavior, as his older son was hostage now for his.

He'd learned Krolpish—learned it more thoroughly, that is, because he'd already started lessons in Grand Junction. He'd learned the Krolp creed, too. He'd kept company with the pampered sons and daughters of the men and women who helped the centauroids run the occupied USA. Some of them were descendants of people who'd served in the American government with Harris Moffatt I. They were all much more Krolpified than he was. They thought him a hick from the sticks, and weren't shy about telling him so.

By the time he finished finishing school, he was much more Krolpified himself than he had been when he got there. He was so much more Krolpified, in fact, that he didn't want to go back to the independent United States. His own people had come to look like hicks to him.

He hoped he'd got over that. He hoped Harris Moffatt IV would get over it when the kid came home. You had to hope. If you didn't hope, you'd give up. And where would free humans be then?

Come to that, where were free humans now? In places like Grand Junction, Colorado, that was where. Happy day!

———————

One of the men with whom the President went to finishing school was the grandson of an important official in the DEA. No one in the United States these days, free or occupied, worried about enforcing human drug laws. No one had time for that kind of nonsense. But Ommat—he even had a Krolpish name—knew how to get his hands on snarfar, and how to slip it discreetly over the border. Grelch got his chew. He didn't bother Harris Moffatt III for a while.

As far as Moffatt was concerned, that was all to the good. He had other things to worry about. The Krolp in St. Louis announced that they were going to send an embassy to Grand Junction. Not that they wanted to send one, but that they were going to. Asking permission of humans wasn't a Krolpish habit.

The U.S. Army still had a few tanks that ran. It had plenty of machine guns. And it had several dozen Krolpish weapons, which cut through a tank's armor as if it weren't there. As soon as one of those weapons hit it, it wasn't.

Several suits of Krolpish body armor had fallen into American hands, too. The only trouble was, humans had no way to adapt those to their own shape. Nothing people knew how to do would cut or weld the transparent stuff. The tools... The science... The engineering...

Harris Moffatt III received the envoy and his retinue with a mixture of human and Krolpish ceremonial. The Stars and Stripes and the Maple Leaf flew behind him. He wore a polyester suit and tie and shirt from the days before the invaders came. Bugs and moths ignored polyester. They sure didn't ignore wool or linen, the independent USA's usual fabrics.

A star shone over the President's left shoulder. That sort of display was standard among the Krolp. With them, as far as human observers and savants could tell, it was a real star, even if a tiny one. And it hung in the air with no means of support at all, visible or otherwise. The Krolp routinely did things that drove human physicists to drink.

Humans...imitated and improvised. *This* star was made from LEDs surrounding a battery pack. It hung from invisibly fine wires. It wasn't as good as one of the originals, but it showed Harris Moffatt III claimed sovereign status. (Its weakness might say he didn't deserve it, but he refused to dwell on that.)

A star followed the Krolp envoy, too. His name, Moffatt had been given to understand, was Prilk. His star was brighter than the human-made simulacrum, but did not float so high. He was a representative, not a sovereign.

Prilk's overlord wasn't the Krolpish governor of North America. He was the ruler of the Krolp, back on their home planet. He wasn't exactly a king or a president or an ayatollah. Not being a Krolp, Harris Moffatt III didn't understand exactly what he was. He was the boss: Moffatt understood that much. Krolp here could petition him. So could humans. Letters took months to reach the homeworld. Decisions took... as long as they took. Answers took more months to come back. Once in a blue moon, those answers made things better for people, not worse. It wasn't likely, but it did happen.

Prilk's guards kept a wary eye on the American soldiers carrying Krolpish hand weapons. Those were dangerous to them and to the envoy, unlike almost any merely human arms. Reading Krolpish body language and expressions was a guessing game for people. Harris Moffatt III's guess was that the centauroids thought humans had no business getting their hands on real weapons. Well, too bad.

The envoy surprised Moffatt: he said, "I see you, Mr. President," in slow, labored English.

"And I see you, Ambassador Prilk," the President replied, also in English. He hadn't expected to use his own language at all in this confab. He smiled broadly.

Then the envoy went back to his own harsh tongue: "I see you, Moffatt." In Krolpish, he didn't waste time with any polite titles. That he'd done it in English was remarkable enough.

"I see you, Envoy Prilk," Harris Moffatt III answered, in Krolpish this time. He might not grant special honorifics to any of the renegades who were such uncomfortable guests here, but he had to give the ruler's representative his due. The Krolp often acted as if humans offended them by existing, and especially by refusing to become Krolpified. They only got worse when they discovered real reasons for affront.

"Good," Prilk said, continuing in his own language. Chances were he didn't truly speak English at all: he'd memorized a phrase or two to impress the natives. And impress them he had. Now he could get down to business. He could, and he did: "We want something from you, Moffatt."

"You can't have the renegades. They're under my protection," the President said. They were what Prilk was most likely to want, as far as he could see. The Krolp didn't like it when free humans learned from them, although their finishing schools and other academies taught people in the broad occupied zones quite a bit.

Prilk waved his hands. They looked funny by human standards: they had four fingers in the middle and a thumb on each side. The thumbs had nails. The fingers had claws. Even a weaponless and unarmored Krolp was no bargain. "I do not care about the renegades, Moffatt. We do not care about the renegades. If we cared about the renegades, you would never seen them. Believe it. It is true."

Maybe so, maybe not. The Krolp weren't immune to bullshit: one more hard lesson out of so many the past fifty years had taught mankind. But if Prilk said the renegades weren't the issue now, they weren't. *They probably aren't*, Harris Moffatt III amended to himself. Prilk might find a way to come back to them later.

Warily, the President asked, "Well, what do you want, then?"

Prilk waved his hands again, this time purposefully. A map appeared in the air between the envoy and Harris Moffatt III. It was, naturally, a Krolpish map, with the place names written in the Krolpish language. That hardly mattered. Moffatt read Krolpish as well as speaking it. And the aliens had borrowed most of the place names from English. Why not? That was easier than making up their own.

Long before the Krolp landed, Americans had borrowed a lot of place names from the Native Americans who'd lived in these parts before them. Much good that did the Native Americans, most of whom were swiftly dispossessed. And much good the English toponyms on a Krolpish map did the USA, too.

"You see this place here?" Prilk pointed. A small patch of northeastern Utah glowed red on the map. How? Harris Moffatt III didn't know, any more than he knew how the map appeared when Prilk waved. Krolpish technology was that far ahead of anything humanity can do. Or—shit—maybe it *was* magic. Harris Moffatt III sure couldn't prove it wasn't.

"I see that place there," Moffatt said. "What about it? I see it is in the territory that belongs to the free United States. I see that it is in territory that belongs to me. Not to you. Not to Vrank." Vrank was Prilk's immediate superior, the Krolpish governor of North America. The President took a deep breath. "Not to your ruler, back on your planet, either."

There. He'd made it as plain as he could. Too plain, maybe. As far as the Krolp were concerned, anything they could get their weird hands on belonged to them. But that glowing patch lay right in the middle of what was left of the USA. Harris Moffatt III had to do whatever he could to hang on to it. If he didn't, what point to being President?

Prilk opened his jack-o'-lantern mouth wide. It looked like a threat display—*I will eat you.* As a matter of fact, it was. "You say this to me, Moffatt?" he growled.

"I say this to you, Envoy Prilk," Moffatt answered, as steadily as he could. "Flarglar agreed that this land belonged to humans. Belonged to the USA. Belonged to my father." Flarglar had been Vrank's next-but-one predecessor. U.S. archives still held a copy of the treaty.

How much good would showing it to Prilk do? The envoy waved once more, dismissively. "Flarglar is not here any more. Neither is your father."

Flarglar, sure enough, had been recalled to the homeworld in disgrace. A drunken Krolpish renegade (the Krolp, damn them, loved whiskey as well as snarfar) had killed Harris Moffatt II. He'd died for it. Not much was left of West Yellowstone, Montana, these days, but that renegade was by God dead.

"The agreement is here. Your ruler did not reject it. It is still good," Harris Moffatt III said, with more confidence than he felt.

"We did not know everything when we made that stupid agreement. We have been here longer now. We know more," Prilk said. "There is silver under this land, silver and some gold. We want it."

Winter ran through the President of the United States. The Krolp took human works of art, in exactly the same way as human conquerors looted the folk they overwhelmed. And the Krolp took minerals in a way that was like nothing on Earth—which was putting things mildly.

They thought Earth was a treasure trove. It was more tectonically active than most of the planets they knew, which meant it kept recycling its riches instead of locking most of them away beyond even Krolpish reach. And the reach of the Krolp went far beyond anything humanity could match. Twenty miles down? Fifty miles? A hundred? The Krolp didn't care. Controlling the forces they did, they could go that deep with ease.

Of course, they made kind of a mess in the process. Harris Moffatt III knew people had strip-mined whole mountains. The Krolp strip-mined whole countries. Not much worth living on was left of Spain. The Krolp had found a big deposit of mercury under there, and they'd gone after it, and they'd got it. The environment? They worried about the environment on the homeworld. Not here. No, not here.

If they went after silver under northeastern Utah, they'd trash most of what was left of the free USA. What point to being President of an uninhabitable country? "That silver is ours," Moffatt said. "You cannot have it."

"I give you some advice, Moffatt," Prilk answered. "Do not say 'cannot' to someone who is stronger than you."

"That silver is ours. It is not yours," the President insisted.

This time, vast scorn informed the Krolp's gesture. "You cannot get this silver. You did not even know it was there. You will never get at it. We can. We will. For us, it is easy."

"Stealing is easy," Moffatt said bitterly.

"Not stealing. Taking." Plainly, a difference existed in Prilk's mind.

"It is ours. If you take it, that goes against the treaty. I will appeal to your ruler." Harris Moffatt III played one of the few cards he had. He was only too aware it was liable to be the three of diamonds. That could be worth something if it filled a flush. Most of the time, it was just the goddamn three of diamonds.

"Let me show you this, Moffatt." Prilk could snap two fingers on the same hand at the same time. When he did, the map in the air between him and the President disappeared. He waved again. A document—an appallingly official Krolpish document—sprang into being in its place. Vrank had already told the ruler the silver was there. The ruler told Vrank to go ahead and get it.

"I can still appeal. I have learned my rights," Moffatt said. His three of diamonds wouldn't fill a flush this time. His main right was to do as he was told.

"You will lose." Prilk didn't even sound regretful. He just sounded certain, the way he would if he talked about sunrise tomorrow.

The President still had one more card. "If you come after what is not yours, I can fight. The United States can fight."

Krolpish laughter sounded a lot like human farting. "Well, you can try. Remember how much good fighting has done you up till now," Prilk said.

"We are still free, here in this part of the United States. Most humans are not," Harris Moffatt III said.

"You are free because you have not been worth bothering about. Now you have again something we want. Give it and you may yet stay free."

"Free in a place where we cannot live," Moffatt said. "What kind of freedom is that? Better to fight."

"You will lose. Then we will take what we want anyway," Prilk warned.

"We have a saying—'Live free or die,'" the President said.

"I do not know about living free. If you fight, dying can be arranged. I promise you that." This time, it wasn't so much that Prilk sounded matter-of-fact. He sounded as if the prospect delighted him.

"I must consult with my officers," Moffatt said.

"I will give you a day. It is more than you deserve, but Governor Vrank wants as little trouble with you as he can arrange," Prilk said.

"A day," Moffatt agreed. "In the meantime, you are our guest. We will treat you as well as we can."

"Oh, joy." Prilk sounded as thrilled as a human explorer offered a big bowl of stewed grubs by some tribe in the back of beyond. That was probably just how he felt. Well, too goddamn bad for him.

Grelch and Willig—another Krolpish renegade—sat in with Harris Moffatt III's Secretary of Defense and Secretary of Alien Affairs. The latter's predecessors had been Secretaries of State. The new title reflected the new dispensation.

The renegades could judge Krolpish likelihoods better than people could. Grelch's tail lashed rhythmically: back and forth, back and forth. He'd had a good chew of snarfar, then. It might cloud his wits—but then, as the President knew, Grelch didn't have much in the way of wits to begin with. He was a ruffian, a soldier, a deserter. He would never be welcome in polite company.

But he knew all kinds of things humans had never learned. That made him valuable, if not exactly welcome.

"If we fight, we're screwed," the Secretary of Alien Affairs said.

"If we don't fight, we're screwed, too," the Secretary of Defense said.

Harris Moffatt III let out yet another sigh, a deep one. Once upon a time, somebody'd told him two things that contradicted each other couldn't both be true at the same time. He'd believed the poor, silly son of a bitch, too. He didn't any more.

The Krolp had found something here they wanted. They were going to take it. If humans didn't care for that, tough luck for humans. The President turned toward the alien renegades. "How can we keep them from digging?" he asked.

Grelch looked at Willig. Willig looked back at Grelch. Reading Krolpish expressions might be guesswork for humans, but Harris Moffatt III had more practice at it than most people in the free USA. He didn't like what he thought he read.

"Forget it," Grelch said.

"Run north," Willig agreed. "Maybe it won't be *so* bad." As if conferring a great boon, he added, "We'll come with you."

"Of course you will," the President said harshly. "Your own folk sure don't want you around."

"You insult us?" Grelch's rumble sounded ominous. Snarfar usually calmed a Krolp, but it could also enrage. It was a lot like booze—except it wasn't. Grelch hadn't carried any weapons into the meeting, but that might not matter. If a renegade killed *another* President of the United States...

Harris Moffatt III drew a Krolpish hand weapon. If he fired it, it wouldn't just steam-clean Grelch. It would take out a big part of the building, maybe enough to make the rest fall down. Even so... "The truth is not an insult," he said. "If your own people did want you around, you wouldn't be here with us."

He waited. Plenty of Krolp wouldn't listen to anything from humans, even the truth—especially not the truth. Grelch was right on the edge of being one of them. His tail twitched faster, with a sort of boogie-woogie beat. Moffatt relaxed fractionally. That was a good sign. Most of the time, anyhow.

"All right," the renegade said at last. "We are losers. So are you, Moffatt. All you humans, you are losers."

"Now you have lost," Willig added. "You can't fight a stand-up fight against my folk."

The President already knew that. He couldn't very well not know it. Humans had tried again and again, and got smashed again and again. They'd learned a lot from the Krolp these past fifty years. They'd stolen a lot, too. They could annoy the aliens. They could harass them. It didn't come within miles—it didn't come within light-years—of being enough.

But there were ways to make war that didn't involve stand-up fights. Before that drunken Krolp murdered him, Harris Moffatt II made sure

Harris Moffatt III soaked up some pre-invasion history. Names rang inside his head. Vietnam… Iraq… Afghanistan…

"We do not want to fight a stand-up fight," he said. "Or not a stand-up fight and nothing else, anyhow. But we've got…connections… in the rest of America. Can we cause your folk enough trouble to make them change their minds?"

He smiled at the Secretary of Defense. That worthy's second cousin held a prominent post in the centauroids' administration. They kept in touch with each other through some highly unofficial channels. The Secretary of Defense's cousin didn't love the cheesy-smelling aliens he worked for. There were humans who worked for him who didn't love the Krolp, either.

Multiply such cases by a hundred or a thousand. If all those humans raised hands against the invaders or simply stopped doing their jobs or started doing them wrong… It would screw up the Krolp, without a doubt.

Would it screw them up enough? Doubt. Big doubt.

Grelch and Willig eyed each other. "Maybe," Willig said, in tones that meant he didn't believe it for a minute.

"If we do that and if we fight to keep what is ours…?" Harris Moffatt III said.

One more glance between the two Krolp. This time, Grelch was the one who said, "Maybe." He also didn't believe it.

Of course, Krolp never believed humans could do anything. Half a century of occupation gave them solid reason not to believe it, too. Every once in a while, they did get an unpleasant surprise. That they'd got a few was the main reason the free United States remained the land of the free and the home of the brave.

Of the stubborn, anyhow.

Harris Moffatt III took a deep breath. "Well, we're going to try it," he said.

Willig and Grelch walked out. That pretty much ended the meeting. They had scant hope, or maybe none. Harris Moffatt III had scant hope, too, but not none. Not quite. Muttering under his breath, the Secretary of Defense also left. His men would have to try to stop the invaders. When the irresistible force met the movable object…

The Secretary of Alien Affairs lingered. "I was poking around in the library at Mesa State the other day," he remarked, with luck not apropos of nothing.

"Okay," the President said. The college library held mostly human knowledge. Education in things Krolpish hadn't trickled through the system even now. The chaos of the past half-century had a lot to do with that. Educators' slowness had even more. Moffatt went on, "You found something interesting?"

"Might be. Might be just depressing," the Secretary of Alien Affairs replied.

"That's what I need, all right," Moffatt said. "And you're going to tell me about it, aren't you?"

"Unless you don't want me to, sir."

"Oh, go ahead," the President said. "It can't possibly make me feel worse than I do when I think about telling Prilk no."

"You could still tell him yes," the Secretary of Alien Affairs said.

"That doesn't do me any good, either," Harris Moffatt III said, shaking his head. "So go on. Say your say. Depress me some more."

"Er… Yes, Mr. President. You probably know the Spaniards conquered the Incas in Peru six hundred years ago."

"Sure." Now Moffatt nodded. He remembered that from studying history, too. And Peru—or the mountainous, inaccessible parts of Peru—still maintained a precarious freedom from the Krolp. Moffatt had exchanged a few messages with *el Presidente*. That was as much as either one of them could hope to do. "What about it?"

"The Incas never knew what hit 'em. They were just starting to use bronze. They didn't even write. The Spaniards had guns. They had armor.

They had swords. They rode horses. They... Well, to make a long story short, they had three thousand years on the Incas. The Native Americans fought like hell, and it didn't do 'em one goddamn bit of good."

Harris Moffatt III felt an unpleasant *frisson*. Given his circumstances, how could he not? "What goes around comes around. Is that what you're saying?"

"Not exactly, Mr. President," the Secretary of Alien Affairs said, which wasn't exactly reassuring to Moffatt. His advisor went on, "The Incas who didn't give up built a new town called Vilcabamba, in the jungle on the east side of the Andes. Their ruler—*the* Inca—lived there, and his court, and stuff like that. And they tried to...to adapt to what had happened to them."

"What do you mean, adapt?" Moffatt asked.

"They learned whatever they could. They stole horses and swords. Some of them became Christians—mostly to keep the Spaniards off their backs, I think, but also because their own gods weren't doing them much good. But other ways, too, littler ways. Some of the houses there had tile roofs instead of the thatch they'd always used before."

"Huh," the President said uneasily, remembering the LED display that aped a real Krolpish minisun. He asked the obvious question: "What happened to them?"

"They hung on for about forty years. They had trouble with their renegades, too," the Secretary of Alien Affairs said. "Then the Spaniards finally got sick of their nuisance raids and overran them."

"We've lasted longer than they did, anyhow," Harris Moffatt III said. "We've just got to keep on doing it, that's all."

"Yes, Mr. President," the Secretary of State replied. What else was he supposed to say?

———

Prilk and his guards waited impassively in the square. "Well, Moffatt, what is it going to be?"

"You can't mine silver on our land," Moffatt said. "You would ruin our whole country"—*what's left of our whole country*—"if you did."

"We are going to mine that silver," the Krolpish envoy said, his voice flat and hard. "You cannot stop us from doing it. Because you cannot stop us, you cannot say in truth that the land is yours."

"If your folk comes onto our land without our leave, you will see what we can do," Harris Moffatt III said. His son was already on his way back to the free USA from St. Louis. He hoped.

Prilk let out flatulent Krolpish laughter. "I foul myself in fear," he said.

A sarcastic Krolp was the very last thing the President needed. "You will see," he repeated. "Tell Governor Vrank the land is ours, the silver is ours, and he may not have it."

Prilk leaned his torso forward, toward the President. As with humans, that meant earnestness among the Krolp. "Moffatt, you had better think again. You have no hope of winning."

"We have no hope if you trash our country, either," Moffatt said, which was nothing but the truth.

"But we would not interfere with you if you did not act like a fool," Prilk said.

"If I did what you told me to do, you mean," Moffatt replied. "And you would interfere with the United States. You would interfere badly. That interferes with me."

"You will be sorry," Prilk warned.

"I am already sorry. Everyone on Earth is sorry. We are sorry you ever found us," the President said.

"Which has nothing to do with how many claws are on a franggel's foot," Prilk said.

Harris Moffatt III had never seen a franggel. Come to that, neither had Prilk. The Krolp had hunted them to extinction hundreds of years before.

They lingered on in proverbs, though. The President had heard this one many times before. *Nothing to do with the price of beer,* an English-speaking human probably would have said. But he'd heard about a franggel's foot even in English. Krolpish phrases, Krolpish ideas, gained. Human notions retreated. Pretty soon, they'd have nowhere to retreat *to.*

Vilcabamba.

The President hadn't imagined he'd remember the name of the place, not while the Secretary of Alien Affairs was yakking about it. He also hadn't imagined he would sympathize with the poor befuddled Inca holdouts who tried to hang on to their old way of life there. If the Krolp started strip-mining in Utah, the old American way of life, or what was left of it, was gone forever.

"Envoy Prilk, we will fight to stop you," he repeated, his voice firmer than it had been a few minutes earlier.

"Moffatt, we will eat your brains, if you have any." Prilk turned and walked away. His guards formed up around him. If the humans wanted to start fighting now, they were ready. Here, though, human and Krolpish customs coincided. The envoy was suffered to leave in peace. Trouble would start soon, but not yet. Not quite yet.

———

The free Unites States had to keep the Krolp away from the place in northeastern Utah under which they'd found silver. If the aliens started mining, they would turn too much of what was left of the country into a place not worth inhabiting. But the free USA also needed to show the Krolp that fighting a war for the silver would be more expensive than it was worth.

If we can, Harris Moffatt III thought gloomily. *If we can.*

He'd already got out of Grand Junction by then. He'd pulled north to Craig, Colorado, just in case. He sat in front of a microphone that led to an AM sending unit. AM radio had been almost extinct even on Earth when the Krolp came. To the striped centauroids, it was as one with hand axes and bows and arrows. That made it as secure a communications system as humanity had left. Smoke signals were primitive, too, but as long as the Native Americans could read them and the U.S. Cavalry couldn't...

"Execute Plan Seventeen," Moffatt said into the mike. "I repeat—execute Plan Seventeen."

In the room next to his, an engineer flicked a switch, then lifted his thumb in the air. The order had gone out, and now the radio was off again. The cavalry could learn what smoke signals meant, and the Krolp—or the human traitors who served them—might monitor the AM band. You never could tell.

Moffatt's mouth twisted. Oh, yes, you could. Whatever the aliens did drove more nails into the coffin of human freedom. It wasn't even always intended to, but it did.

They didn't attack the instant Prilk left the free USA. The President had feared they might. That would have complicated things for the United States—complicated them even worse than they were already. But, although Moffatt had feared a sudden assault, he hadn't really expected one. The Krolp were so arrogant, they had trouble believing human beings still dared to tell them no and mean it.

He wished he could launch thermonuclear-tipped missiles at all the increasingly Krolpified cities in the occupied United States. In point of fact, he *could*; it wasn't as if he didn't have them. The only trouble was, they wouldn't do much good. The Krolp would swat them out of the air with contemptuous ease.

No, you couldn't stand toe-to-toe with the centauroids and slug. First they'd stand on your toes. Then they'd stand on you.

Well, the Native Americans couldn't slug things out with the U.S. Cavalry. They still drove it crazy for a hell of a long time. They also lost in the end, something Harris Moffatt III didn't care to dwell upon.

He and his Department of Defense experts monitored as many Krolpish channels as they could. They had to rely on bought and stolen devices; they could no more make the communicators the aliens used than Geronimo could have manufactured a telegraph clicker. But the aliens weren't very good at keeping things secret from humans. They didn't think they needed to bother, and most of the time they were right.

A major brought Moffatt a report: "The subgovernor of the South Central Region has been taken ill. He's in a Krolpish hospital. They're trying to figure out what's wrong with him."

"I hope it's nothing trivial," Moffatt said.

"Me, too, Mr. President." The major grinned. He wore one broad red stripe on each of his collar tabs to show his rank. That was a human adaptation of the Krolpish system. Once upon a time, the USA had used rank badges of its own. Harris Moffatt III happened to know that. What they were, he couldn't have said. He'd never seen them. A few antiquarians might know, if the free United States still boasted antiquarians.

More reports floated into the free USA. Krolp administrators and their human flunkies came down with exotic illnesses or sudden cases of loss of life. A Krolpish flyer—which bore about the same relationship to a 797 airliner as the airliner did to a paper plane—slammed into the ground, killing several aliens and injuring several more. (Most survived unharmed. The Krolp built tough.) Bridges and overpasses mysteriously—or not so mysteriously—collapsed.

We can hurt you, the free USA was saying, as loud as it could. *We can cause you more trouble than you thought we could.*

So far, so good. Pretty soon, though, the Krolp would have some things of their own to say. Moffatt didn't care to listen to them. As far as the Krolp were concerned, that meant less than nothing.

The free USA was as ready as it could be. Soldiers guarded the passes through which the centauroids were likeliest to come. The ground was mined, sometimes with nuclear explosives. The blasts wouldn't bother the Krolp much. The avalanches they were positioned to set off would do more…everyone hoped.

Winning wasn't in the cards. The President knew as much. Fifty years of bitter experience had taught him as much—him and the rest of the handful of surviving independent human leaders. Living, and living free, to fight another day was as much as he could hope for.

He got reports that Krolpish forces were advancing on both the Rockies and the Wasatch Range. That didn't sound good. Neither did the fact that one of those reports cut off all at once, as if the human sending it got interrupted. Fatally interrupted? Moffatt didn't know. It gave him one extra thing to worry about, as if he needed any more.

And Grelch disappeared. Even Craig, Colorado, didn't feel safe enough to suit the renegade. He had no confidence that the free USA could hold the line against his own people.

"Don't worry about it, Mr. President," the Secretary of Defense said. "The Krolp always underestimate us. We never would have been able to hang on this long if they didn't."

"I know," Moffatt said, wishing the Cabinet official hadn't tacked on that last sentence. In the hierarchy of wishes, though, that was only a sprat. As always, the big fish was wishing the Krolp had never found Earth. *Yes, and wish for the Moon while you're at it,* the President thought. Had they found anything on it they wanted, the Krolp would have strip-mined the Moon, too.

Two days later, the centauroids started hitting back. That was the day after the assassination attempt against Governor Vrank failed. It took out several of his guards and quite a few merely human minions, but Vrank survived. And he was not happy, any more than a cat the mice had tried to bell.

Perhaps because the Governor of North America wasn't happy, his soldiers slammed headlong into the free USA's defenses. The Krolp killed far more humans than they lost themselves. They always did. But they didn't get very far, not with that first thrust. If humans spent enough blood and laid enough traps beforehand, they could slow down the alien invaders.

They could. For a while. The idea was to make the mining scheme unprofitable for the Krolp. That was the human idea, anyhow. But the Krolp had ideas of their own. One of those ideas was not to let the backward natives get uppity and start thinking they could push their betters around.

Quite suddenly, Grand Junction ceased to exist. That wasn't an H-bomb, though it might as well have been. But Harris Moffatt III hadn't just slipped away from Grand Junction himself. He'd feared the Krolp would strike his capital. People started slipping out as soon as he told Prilk he would fight. Most of them were safe. So were most of the data stored in Grand Junction, and even some of the factories that had been there.

Craig was unlikely to last long, either. Moffatt and his advisors moved farther north still, up into an even smaller town. As long as you had radio, where you were didn't matter too much.

That all made good military sense. So did stopping the enemy when he came at you. Surprising the Krolp once hadn't been too hard. Neither had disrupting them behind their lines. But disrupting them wasn't the same as killing them all, and killing them all what what the free USA really needed. The centauroids shook off the disruption. They weren't so easily surprised the second time they attacked.

And the American defenses crumbled. Human-made arms never did much against the Krolp. Captured, stolen, or bought alien hand weapons performed like—well, like hand weapons against the full weight of Krolpish military might. As well turn a .357 magnum on a tank. You could, sure, but how much good would it do you?

"We need to be able to make those gadgets for ourselves!" Harris Moffatt III raged, as his father and grandfather had before him.

"Yes, Mr. President," the Secretary of Alien Affairs said. No doubt *his* predecessors had told the two previous Presidents the same thing.

Perhaps unlike his predecessors, he added, "The Incas needed to be able to make muskets and swords and armor to fight the Spaniards, too. The only trouble was, they couldn't. They didn't know how."

The President knew only too well that humans couldn't make Krolpish weapons. The principles were beyond them. Even if the principles hadn't been, the manufacturing techniques were.

By the third day of the second attack, it wasn't much of a war any more. It was a rout. American troops in the mountains surrendered as fast as they could—when the Krolp let them. The centauroids made examples of some of the troops. That wasn't pretty, either. They were as far ahead of mankind in torture technology as they were in everything else.

To add insult to injury, they started smashing northeastern Utah to smithereens as soon as they got there. They might have been saying that human resistance wasn't even worth noticing. As a matter of fact, that was just what they were saying, both to themselves and to what was left of mankind.

———

Harris Moffatt III got over the former border between the USA and Canada about twenty minutes before the Krolp caught up with him. His fuel cell-powered car was limited to paved roads. Nothing seemed to limit the Krolp. One second, he was rolling north, trying to figure out some way to keep resisting. The next, the Krolpish equivalent of an armored car appeared as if out of nowhere on the highway in front of him. The weapon it carried could smash a city without breaking a sweat; its armor laughed at nukes. For good measure, more Krolp vehicles came up from either side.

Brakes screeched as Moffatt's wife Jessica, who was driving, stopped before the car ran into that first one. A voice filled the passenger compartment: "Give up, Moffatt!" If God spoke Krolpish and were really pissed off, He might sound like that.

The President had already made up his mind what he would do if and when the Krolp caught him. "You've got the wrong guy," he said. "My name's Ed Vaughn, and I raise chickens." He had some excellent false papers to prove it, too.

Not that they did him any good. *Man proposes; the Krolp dispose,* the saying went. Flatulent Krolpish laughter filled the car. "Don't waste time lying, Moffatt!" the voice roared. "We know your smell! We know your coil!" He supposed they meant his DNA. Whatever they meant, they had him, all right.

Dully, hopelessly, he got out of the car. A Krolp emerged from the armored fighting vehicle. "Here I am," Moffatt said. "Can you get it over with fast, anyhow?"

"We do not kill you, Moffatt. The ruler does not want you killed. You are a worthless native, yes, but still you were a ruler, too. You were," the Krolp repeated. "No more. Now your stupid United States are out of business."

That was, if anything, an understatement. "Well, if you aren't going to kill me, what will you do with me?" the President—no, the ex-President asked.

The Krolp gestured toward his vehicle with a massively lethal hand weapon. "Get in, you and your female. You will find out."

They took him to St. Louis. They squeezed everything he knew about the free USA out of him. They didn't need torture for that. Knowing when a prisoner—even a lowly human prisoner—was telling the truth was child's play for them.

One of them told him, "If you ever fuck with us again, even a little bit, we will blow your head apart from the inside out. It will seem to take a very long time, and it will hurt more than you can imagine. Do you understand? Do you believe?"

"Yes," Moffatt said. The Krolp could do things like that. It was the kind of thing they would do, too.

And so he and Jessica settled into exile life. Even the humans whose families had served the alien invaders since their ships came down gave him a certain amount of respect for what he had been. When the wind blew from the west, it sometimes dropped gray, gritty dust on St. Louis. Harris Moffatt III didn't know that that came from the Krolpish strip-mining operations in Utah, but he couldn't think of anywhere else it was likely to come from.

Once in a while, he remembered the Secretary of Alien Affairs talking about Vilcabamba. Those old Incas might have sympathized. But, really, that wouldn't have done them or him a hell of a lot of good.

THE
MAMMYTH

The mammyth is out there. Unless, of course, it's not. First there is a mammyth. Then there is no mammyth. Then there is. Unless there isn't.

How do you find a legendary, maybe mythical, creature? You may seek it with thimbles—and seek it with care. You may hunt it with forks and hope. You may threaten its life with a… Oh, wait. That's liable to be something else, but there's no need to get snarky about it.

There's a high priest's throne whose panels are supposed to be carved from mammoth ivory. You can see pictures of it in Fallmereyer's famous tome, *Geistkunstgeschichtliche Wissenschaft*. They say you can, anyhow. But you know what they say is worth.

And they also say that somebody went through every single copy of *Geistkunstgeschichtliche Wissenschaft* with a razor and cut out the illo of the mammyth-ivory priestly throne panels, so you can't see it. Some of them say it was Fallmereyer himself. Since *Geistkunstgeschichtliche Wissenschaft* had a print run of nine copies (eleven with a tail wind), it's not impossible. One more time, though, you know what they say it worth.

There's an Emperor who paraded down the main thoroughfare of his very imperial capital wearing a robe woven from mammyth wool. There's supposed to have been such an Emperor parading down such a thoroughfare in such a robe, at any rate. Such a robe! There's also a nasty little boy who said rude things about the robe the Emperor was or wasn't wearing. Or there's supposed to have been such a little boy who said such rude things. Such a boy!

I could go on. I could go on and on, in fact. After all, I'm getting paid by the word. But we need an Adventure. A Quest! If we don't find one pretty damn soon, you'll go read some other story, and then where will I be? That's right, and without a paddle, too.

So here's Tundra Dawn, seeking the mammyth with all her strength. She wants ivory. She wants wool. She wants glory. She wants to be able to shuck off her chainmail shirt, which is *the* questing fashion accessory this year but which proves fashion and comfort don't go hand-in-hand even in jurisdictions where that's legal.

Tundra Dawn isn't alone on her Adventurous Quest. No story's heroine is worth the paper she'll eventually be printed on without sidekicks. Tundra Dawn has a couple of them. Lucky her. She has Cleveland, for instance. No, not Cleveland the city with the inflammable river. Cleveland the sidekick. He's fuzzy and blue and excitable and not too bright. But he helps the plot along sometimes. If he feels like it. Which is about as much as you can hope for from a sidekick.

And she has Tremendous Ptarmigan—or sometimes he spells it Ptremendous Tarmigan. TP/PT (he calls himself a translettered avian) is, or may be, worth his weight in drumsticks when it comes to hunting mammyths. In fact, he insists he has one for his best friend. That nobody else has ever seen that mammyth doesn't bother him a bit.

"They're very shy, you know, mammyths," he says. "They don't let just anybody set eyes on them."

"One of them had better let me set eyes on it, and pretty darn quick, too," Tundra Dawn declares. "This here is only a short story. I don't have time to mess around the way I would in a novel, or even a novella."

"Short stories are good things," Cleveland says. "You cannot have a monster at the end of a book if there is no book."

"Maybe there will be a monster at the end of the story," Tundra Dawn says.

"Oh, no! There had better not be! Then it would be a scary story, and it is supposed to be a funny story." Cleveland is better at getting excited over nothing than any other three more or less people you can think of.

"It's a good thing you told 'em the story's supposed to be funny," Tundra Dawn says. "They might not figure it out otherwise."

"Everything will turn out fine." Tremendous Ptarmigan is a great believer in happy endings. He has other annoying characteristics, too, like a high, thin, kinda squeaky voice. But, because he is so Tremendous, he can see a long way. He points ahead. "Looks like we're coming to a town."

"Low bridge! Everybody down!" Cleveland sings out. He knows all kinds of useless things, and commonly turns them loose at the worst possible moment.

There is a bridge over a straight channel of water in front of the canal. Ghosts moan and whuffle their sheets above the eerie canal. Once Tundra Dawn and her sidekicks have got past it, she sees what a big place they've found. "It's not just a town," she says. "It's a city!"

"It's not just a city," Cleveland exclaims. "It's a metropolis!"

This is not one of the useless things Cleveland knows. There's a sign not far past the bridge: WELCOME TO METROPOLIS! Cleveland isn't wrong all the time—just often enough to be completely undependable.

What, you may well ask, is a metropolis, or even Metropolis, doing in the middle of the tundra? This particular one is kind of sitting there waiting for the adventurers to arrive and get on with things. So they do.

Being a metropolis, Metropolis is the capital of the local kingdom. "What," says a gate guard, in tones of darkest suspicion, "is your purpose in entering our fair city?"

"We're looking for—" Cleveland can open his mouth wide enough to fall right in.

Tundra Dawn stomps on his foot. He yips and does an amazing dance. Tundra Dawn says, "We want to talk to the King, man." She sounds like someone who has wandered into a burger joint with a late-night case of the munchies.

"Right." The gate guard is anything but impressed. He must have heard the routine before. But he stands aside. "Go on in, then. Quickest way to get to the palace is with the subway—the Metro, we call it." His meager chest swells with civic pride.

"Why do you call it that?" Ptremendous Tarmigan isn't the shiniest ornament on the tree, or even on the ptree.

"Beats me." Neither is the gate guard.

There's a Metro station just inside the gate. That's handy. It saves steps, and exposition. A stairway goes down, down, down to the permafrost layer. Tundra Dawn and her sidekicks approach the ticket seller, a short, squat, bearded bloke with a bad case of stocking cap who twitches every so often.

"Who's he?" TP/PT does have that gift for missing the obvious.

"He's the Metrognome," Tundra Dawn explains.

"He certainly tics like one," Cleveland says.

On getting paid, the Metrognome stylishly turns the turnstile. Tundra Dawn and Cleveland and Tremendous Ptarmigan go on to the subway car. It's pulled by a team of four large, broad-shouldered, metamorphic-looking individuals. "Stop!" One of them holds out an enormous, mineralized paw. "Pay troll!"

"Nobody told us this was a troll road," Tundra Dawn says.

"Is," the troll assures her.

"We already paid the fellow back there!" Cleveland squawks.

"No pay," the troll says, "no go."

"Here." Angrily, Tundra Dawn forks over again. "I still think you're full of schist."

"Complain all you want, meat lady," the troll answers. "Long as you pay, I don't care. I got me a big apatite to feed."

"Meat lady!" The pupils in Tundra Dawn's eyes roll round and round under their clear plastic outsides, she is so mad. Not only is the troll a bigot, he is a stupid bigot. *Must have rocks in his head,* she thinks, which is not altogether tolerant, either. But if he doesn't know foam rubber and terry cloth when he sees them… *It's his loss, is what it is,* goes through Tundra Dawn's noodle.

Cleveland, of like construction, is quivering with rage of his own. But quiver is all he does. Even he is not usually foolish enough to piss off a troll. Things that piss kidney stones are better left unpissed. Ptremendous Tarmigan? Even his friends have trouble telling what TP/PT is thinking, or if he is thinking. He is dumb as rocks in his own right, although not constructed of same, and his beaky face ain't what you'd call expressive.

How can foam rubber and terry cloth come to life and have adventures? Because this is a fantasy story, that's how. They could come to life if this were a skiffy story, too, but then I'd have to bore you with a bunch of bullshit explanation. See how lucky you are to miss all that?

The trolls haul the subway car down the long, cold tunnel. People and other forms of allegedly intelligent life get on and off. "Avenue J!" the lead troll bawls, and then "Lois Lane!" and then, after a while, "Avenue Q!"

"Stop that, Cleveland," Tundra Dawn whispers. "This is a family story."

"I can't help it. I feel like double-clicking," Cleveland whispers back.

They leave Avenue Q behind. Cleveland finally does stop that. After what seems like forever but is really just a long time, the troll roars, "The palace! You wanna play the palace, this is where you get off!"

"I already got off," Cleveland says to no one in particular.

"Someone should beat that troll with a big shtick," Tremendous Ptarmigan says as he and Cleveland and Tundra Dawn get down from the subway car.

No one guards the way out. "Where's the Metrognome here?" Tundra Dawn wonders.

"Probably at the Mets game," Cleveland doesn't quite explain.

Up the stairs they trudge, and themselves in the very heart of Metropolis find. Into the palace they walk. Very palatial it is, yes. Escorted straight to the King they are. Backward run sentences until reels the mind.

If getting escorted straight to the King doesn't prove this is a fantasy story, I don't know what would. In skiffy, you pretend hardest to be realistic when you're most un-. In fantasy, you can roll with it. Sometimes. So roll with it. Please?

The King—his name is Wolcott, which is why he likes getting called *King* a lot—looks them over. "What are you doing in my throne room?" he asks. This is not the kind of fantasy where everybody, or even anybody, knows everything. It is more the kind of fantasy where nobody knows anything.

You see? It is more realistic than you thought.

"We're hunting the mammyth." This time, Cleveland comes out with it before Tundra Dawn can trample his toes.

"In my throne room?" King Wolcott says. "I don't know everything there is to know about mammyths" (told you so—*if* he's a reliable narrator) "but I never heard that they were very common in palaces. Isn't that more what the tundra's for?"

Wistfully, Tundra Dawn says, "If they were very common anywhere, we wouldn't have to hunt them so hard."

"Well, why are you hunting them?" the King asks.

"It's a Quest," Cleveland says.

"An Adventure," Ptremendous Tarmigan adds.

"It's a whole 'nother story," Tundra Dawn says. And, since it is, I don't have to tell it here. I can get on with the silly one I'm in the middle of.

TP/PT raises an arm—a wing—a whatever the hell. "Excuse me, your Kinginess, but where to you keep your big birds' room?"

"Go out there." King Wolcott points to a doorway. "Turn left, then right, then left again. You can't miss it."

He and Tundra Dawn and Cleveland yatter away for the next half hour. Tundra Dawn presumes that Tremendous Ptarmigan damn well can miss it—damn well has missed it—after all. But when Ptremendous Tarmigan comes back, he does seem relieved. He seems happy, too. TP/PT seems happy most of the time. Tundra Dawn guesses it has a good deal to do with the seeds he eats.

At last, when the spectacle of a muppetoid heroine in chainmail and her clunky sidekicks commences to pall, the King asks, "How can I help you in your quest?" By which he means *How can I get you the devil out of here?*, but it sounds much nicer the way he says it.

They dicker for a while, which, unlike some of the bits here, is less obscene than it sounds. King Wolcott decides that some horses and some food are a small price to pay for washing these adventurers right outa his hair and sending them on their way. He even throws in a little cash. He watches them ride away into what would be the sunset, only the sun doesn't set on the tundra at this time of year.

And that washes him right outa this story and sends him on his way. Well, almost, because a couple of days later Tremendous Ptarmigan says, "I had a nice chat with the mammyth at the King's palace."

"Is that what took you so long?" Cleveland said. "I thought you fell in."

Tundra Dawn reins in. She sends Ptremendous Tarmigan as exasperated a look as she can manage with eyes from a craft-shop discount table. "Um, you do remember we're searching for a mammyth? Hunting a mammyth, even?" By the hopeless way she says it, she has no confidence that TP/PT ever remembers anything.

But Tremendous Ptarmigan nods brightly. "Oh, sure," he says.

Tundra Dawn holds on to her patience with both hands. With sidekicks like hers, she has considerable practice. Morosely, she considers it. Then she asks, "Why didn't you tell us that before it was, like, too late to do anything about it?"

"You heard the King," Ptremendous Tarmigan answers. "He said mammyths weren't very common in palaces."

After considering her practice some more, Tundra Dawn says, "They don't need to be very common. There just needs to be one of them, so we can hunt it."

"What did you and this mammyth, if there was a mammyth, talk about?" Cleveland asks. Then he sneezes. Even in tundra summer, baby, it's cold outside.

"Don't snuffle up at me," TP/PT says. "We chatted about all kinds of things. He says to watch out for the one from fit the eighth. I don't know what that means, though."

"The Baker could tell you," Cleveland says.

"What Baker?" asks Tremendous Ptarmigan.

"*The* Baker," Cleveland says. They go on confusing each other, and Tundra Dawn, for some little while.

Then our chain-mailed (but not chain-stored) heroine cocks her head to one side and says, "I hear music."

"But there's no one there." Cleveland comes in right on cue.

"It's, like, a bell," Tundra Dawn says, which is not the next line, but which is, like, what it is.

There may not be anyone there, but Ptremendous Ptarmigan points to motion in the distance. "Look!" he exclaims. "It's a herd of cheeseheads!"

Cheeseheads they are, ambling across the frozen tundra in search of tailgates and other Arcana of the Sacred Pigskin. Instead of by an ordinary bellwether, they, like some other faithful, are led by a lamb. Like an ordinary bellwether, the lamb wears a bell around its neck. Unlike an ordinary bellwether's, the lamb's bell is held on by a pink satin ribbon with a fancy bow.

Tundra Dawn spurs her horse forward, careless for the moment of worries about animal cruelty (what she will do if and when hunting the mammyth segues into killing the mammyth is something she resolutely refuses to dwell on). The horse jumps high over the lamb's bell-bedizened neck. After her touchdown, she waves her sidekicks forward. They too perform the lamb-bow leap.

Cleveland wrinkles his nose. With the kind of nose he has, this isn't easy. With the kind of nose he has, this shouldn't even be possible. But I'm the narrator, and I'm here to tell you he does it. In fact, I repeat myself, slowly: Cleveland…wrinkles…his…nose. Okay? Wrapped your visualizer around it yet? Sweet! Then we'll go on.

"What smells nasty?" Cleveland asked.

"I don't smell anything," Ptremendous Tarmigan says.

"Of course you don't, you translettered avian, you," Cleveland says. "The only avians, translettered or not, with a good sense of smell are vultures."

"Sounds discriminatory to me," TP/PT says. "And elitist. Everyone should be able to smell as good as everyone else."

"If you want to smell good, try taking a bath," Cleveland says. "If you want to smell well, try not being an avian."

Tremendous Ptarmigan gets mad and puffs out his feathers to look, um, ptremendouser. Before the bickering can get really bitchy, Tundra Dawn says, "Boys, boys." She's defused, and defuzzed, these squabbles before. She goes on, "I think you're smelling the cheeseheads, Cleveland. They're Roqueforts."

"Rogue farts?" Cleveland nods. "They sure are!"

"I used to watch *The Roquefort Files* sometimes," the Tarmigan says. "I didn't smell anything bad then."

Tundra Dawn sighs. Good sidekicks are hard to come by. And stinking cheeseheads are a fact of life on the frozen tundra. "Faa-aar-vv!" they bleat mournfully. "Faa-aar-vv!"

"Come on," Tundra Dawn says. "We'll ride away from them. Then we won't smell them so much."

Away they ride. The smell does get…not so bad, anyhow. Cleveland keeps complaining about it anyhow. TP/PT keeps complaining about Cleveland's complaining. Instead of resolutely not dwelling on killing the mammyth, Tundra Dawn resolutely doesn't dwell on killing the two of them.

It may be summer on the tundra, but it is the tundra. There is still snow on the ground, at least where the story needs there to be some. In a patch of snow that Tundra Dawn and Cleveland and Tremendous Ptarmigan conveniently happen to ride past, there is a hole as if someone has pushed down with the bottom of a big, round wastebasket. Or it would look like that if big, round wastebaskets came equipped with stubby toes.

"Is that a footprint?" Nothing gets by Cleveland. Nothing gets through to him, but nothing gets by him.

"It *is* a footprint," TP/PT says. "And do you know what?"

"No. What?" Cleveland says.

"It looks… It looks like it could be a mammyth's footprint."

Tundra Dawn rides on to the next convenient patch of snow. "Here is another footprint," she says. "If we follow the mammyth's toes, we will go in the same direction it is going. Pretty soon, we will catch up with it."

"You are so smart, Tundra Dawn! I never would have thought of that," Cleveland says. The good news for Tundra Dawn is that even half-assed sidekicks like hers give you egoboo. The bad news is, she totally believes he never would have thought of it.

They follow the tracks. And they follow the tracks. And they follow the tracks some more. They come to the edge of the cold, cold sea.

Walking along the muddy beach are a Walrus and a Carpenter. The Walrus is fat. The Carpenter is skin and bones. In spite of the season, the Walrus and the Carpenter are carrolling together.

Tremendous Ptarmigan waves to the pair. "How are you doing, Paul?"

The Walrus waves a flipper back. "Not bad. How about you, Ptremendous?"

"I'm fine. I'm looking for a mammyth right now," the Tarmigan answers. "Oh, and have you seen Dave?"

"Dave? Dave's not here," the Carpenter says quickly.

He's only just begun, but the Walrus interrupts him by pointing with that flipper. "Might be a mammyth over that way. Don't know what else you'd call it," he says.

"C'mon, sidekicks!" Tundra Dawn hollers. "We're heading for the dénouement!"

"For the who?" TP/PT asks as they ride away.

"Not for the who. For the what," Cleveland says.

"For which what?"

"For the end."

They ride up a small rise and down the other side. They ride up another one. Tundra Dawn spots something moving on the far side. "Is that—?" she asks Tremendous Ptarmigan, who may have seen one before. "Could that be—?"

"Yes, I think it's—" Ptremendous starts.

Then they softly and silently vanish away. Tundra Dawn's armor clatters about her, or about where she has been—an epic ending granted a mock-epic heroine. For the mammyth, even if it doesn't quite scan, *is* a Boojum, you see.

THE EIGHTH-GRADE HISTORY CLASS
VISITS THE HEBREW HOME FOR THE
AGING

A sunbeam slipped between the slats of the Venetian blinds. Anne Berkowitz opened one eye. The clock on the nightstand by the bed had digits big and bright enough to let her read them without her glasses—6:47. She muttered and rolled away from the sneaky sunbeam. She didn't want to get up so early.

But she was awake. And she was having trouble breathing—not bad trouble, but the kind she had almost every morning after she'd stayed too flat for too long. She reached for the nasal cannula and put it in place. Clear plastic tubing connected it to the green-painted oxygen tank that sat on a wheeled cart by the other side of the bed.

Wrinkled skin hung loose on her arm as she reached out to turn the valve at the top of the tank. She'd never been fat, not once in her eighty-four years. She'd hardly ever been as skinny as she was now, though. If she kept going this way, pretty soon there'd be nothing left of her.

She nodded to herself as oxygen softly hissed through the tubing. Pretty soon there *would* be nothing left of her. The doctors said she had maybe a year left, maybe two, three at the outside. She worried about it less than she would have dreamt possible even ten years before. As long as it didn't hurt too much, she was about ready to die.

The oxygen made her feel stronger. The trouble wasn't her lungs. It was the narrowing of the big artery that came out of her heart. Aortic stenosis, the docs called it, which was the same thing in Greek. An operation—a graft—could fix it, but they said she had not a chance in a thousand of waking up again after they put her under. So here she was, watching her clock wind down.

After a couple of minutes, she reached out and turned the valve on the tank the other way. The oxygen shut off. Anne sat up. Once she got vertical, she was okay, or as okay as she could be these days.

She put on her glasses. The room came into sharper focus. The room… Her mouth twisted. The Hebrew Home for the Aging insisted it was an apartment. They could call it whatever they pleased. It still looked like a room to her.

A TV on a stand. A computer on a stand. A bookcase. Novels. History. Poetry. Genealogy. A black-and-white photo of her husband, looking handsome and *Mad Men*-y in a suit with narrow lapels and a skinny tie. Sheldon had been gone for almost twenty years now, and not a day went by when she didn't miss him.

Color photos of her son the CPA and of her son the ophthalmologist. Color photos of her grandsons and granddaughters, and a new one of her baby great-granddaughter. Not least among her reasons for keeping the computer was that so many other photos of Elizabeth were on Facebook.

The room—the apartment, if you insisted—also boasted a minifridge and a hot plate. Anne could cook there, after a fashion. She could, but she seldom did. Meals were social times at the Home for the Aging.

She walked into the little bathroom. The tub had a gap in the side so unsteady seniors wouldn't have to step over it—and so the water couldn't get more than two inches deep. She'd heard there were some bathrooms with real tubs, but she'd never seen one.

Morning meds first, though. Anne's mouth quirked. When you got to her age and state of decrepitude, you were what you took. She opened the medicine cabinet. Brown and green plastic pill bottles crowded the shelves, swamping things like toothbrush and deodorant. She took a blood-pressure pill, a stomach-acid suppressor, a vasodilator, a pill to steady her heartbeat, one to hold osteoporosis at bay, and a couple of old-fashioned aspirins for her arthritis, which wasn't *too* bad. They all sat on her tongue while she filled a glass with water. Even if it wasn't long and sticky, it could hold more at once than a chameleon's.

She brushed her teeth. They were in better shape than the rest of her—most of them were implants. Then she closed the cabinet. As she always did, she marveled at the little old lady who peered back at her from the mirror. How did that happen? How did time get to be so cruel?

Her eyes. She still knew her eyes. Even behind the lenses of her glasses, they were dark and bright and knowing. And her narrow chin hadn't changed so much, even if she had a turkey wattle under it now. The rest? Wrinkles gullied cheeks and forehead. Her nose was a thrusting beak. Ears as big as Golda Meir's. Thin, baby-fine hair, white, white, white.

Nothing she could do about any of it, either. Oh, she could dye her hair. She had for a while, when Sheldon was still alive. But she'd been younger then herself. It hadn't looked so phony as it would now.

After a shower, she started to put on a long-sleeved T-shirt and a pair of heather-gray sweatpants. They were easy, they were comfortable, and what else mattered?

Most of the time, nothing. This morning, Anne caught herself. The kids would be coming today. She'd almost forgotten. She didn't care about looking nice for anybody here, but for them she did. The T-shirt and sweats went back on the shelf in the closet.

She chose a silk blouse with a floral print and dark blue polyester pants instead. She'd still look like a little old lady, but so what? She *was* a little old lady. These were the kind of clothes the kids' grannies put on when they came over to visit.

Her Nikes had Velcro fastenings, not laces. Tying shoelaces wasn't easy any more. She opened the door, closed it behind her, and walked down the hall to the stairway.

A young Filipino aide smiled at her. "Good morning, Mrs. Berkowitz!" the woman said in accented English.

"Hello, Maria." Anne's voice held a vanishing trace of accent, too. If you listened, you could hear it in the vowels and in the slight guttural flavor she gave the *r*.

She walked down a flight of stairs, holding on to the banister and feeling brave. Going up, she'd take the elevator—that was hard work. But down was okay, as long as you watched where you put your feet.

A garden stretched between her residence block and the dining hall. The same warm, bright San Fernando Valley sunshine that had woken her poured down on it. A scrub jay in a pale-leaved olive tree screeched at her: *"Jeep! Jeep! Jeep!"* Anne smiled. The bird figured the garden belonged to it.

She ambled along the smooth concrete path. A hummingbird flashed past her on its mad dash from one flower to the next. Its whole head glowed magenta. Anne admired hummingbirds for their beauty and for their take-no-prisoners attitude. She'd never seen one till she came to America.

Another Filipino attendant wheeled an old man up the path toward her. The man in the wheelchair stared at the orange and yellow flowers as if they were new to him. For all practical purposes, they were. Far gone in Alzheimer's, he had no idea he'd been here last week, and the week before that, and…

"Morning, Ninoy," Anne said to the attendant as she walked by.

"Morning, ma'am," he answered. "Nice day, isn't it?"

"It is, yes." But Anne frowned once her back was to him and he couldn't see her do it. The Hebrew Home for the Aging's Alzheimer's wing was in a severely modern three-story building near the dining hall. She thanked heaven she'd be dead before she had to go in there. Forgetting whom you'd loved, forgetting who you were, forgetting even how to use the toilet... She frowned again, and shook her head. Yes, truly ending was better than a living death like that.

She had oatmeal for breakfast, and canned fruit, and a cup of real coffee, not the decaf she usually drank. Her doctor would cluck when she told him she'd done it. But he was only in his forties, younger than her boys. What did he know? It wasn't good for her? *Nu?* So what? She was dying by inches anyhow.

After eating and chatting for a little while with a couple of other residents who still had their marbles, she went over to the visitors' center. Nothing there had sharp edges or corners. Most of the chairs were at a height convenient for old folks to use without too much bending.

Two big aquariums dominated the main room's decor. One held freshwater fish; the other, more colorful saltwater. A woman with Alzheimer's gaped at the saltwater tank. An attendant stood close by, waiting, watching. When the woman's attention flagged, the attendant gently led her toward the dining hall.

Anne watched the fish herself for a little while. Then she sat down in one of those inviting chairs. No more than half a minute after she had, one of the Hebrew Home for the Aging's community-outreach workers stuck her head into the visitors' center and looked around.

"Here I am, Lucy." Anne waved.

"Oh, good! Glad to see you, Mrs. Berkowitz." Relief glowed on the outreach worker's sharp features. She hurried over.

Dryly, Anne said, "I do try to hit my marks." She knew the Hollywood patter. Movie stars had fascinated her even when she was a girl. And, like so many Angelenos, she'd taken a shot at scriptwriting back in the day. She'd never had one of her own produced, but she'd done uncredited doctoring on a couple that did get made.

"Sure, sure." Lucy nodded. "And I want to tell you again how wonderful, how impactful, I think it is that you've agreed to do this. For today's middle-school kids to get the chance to talk with a Holocaust survivor and hear what it was like from someone who went through it… That's just marvelous!"

"I was lucky," Anne Berkowitz said: nothing less than the truth. She tried not to show what she thought of *impactful*. Like many who'd learned English as a foreign language, she had a strong feel for when it was spoken well and when badly.

"They need to understand what people are capable for doing to other people when, when…" Lucy gestured vaguely.

"When everything goes off the rails," Anne finished for her. She couldn't blame this middle-aged woman who hadn't gone through it for not getting why and how the Nazis could have done what they did. She had, and she didn't get it, either. Which wouldn't have stopped the Nazis, of course, or even slowed them down.

The community-outreach worker took her phone from her purse to check the time. "They'll be here at half past eight—it's a first-period class," she said, and pointed over to a little meeting room where Anne could talk with the children. "Will you need anything special?"

"If you could get me a water bottle, that would be nice."

"I'll take care of it." Lucy hurried back toward the dining hall.

Anne stood up and walked into the meeting room. She didn't hurry—she didn't think she could hurry any more—but she got there. The room held a chair like the one she'd just escaped and a couple of dozen ordinary folding chairs for the kids. Sitting on one of those for longer than a minute or two would have paralyzed Anne's butt. The eighth-graders probably wouldn't mind at all.

Lucy came back with the water bottle. She'd brought a big one, which was good. "You're all ready," she said.

"Almost," Anne said. "Could you open it for me, please?" As with tying shoes, her hands weren't what they had been once upon a time.

"Sure." Lucy took care of it with ease. She was young enough and healthy enough to do such things without even thinking about them. Anne had been. She wasn't any more.

A clamor outside said the schoolkids were here. "Keep it down, *please!*" their teacher said, amusement and despair warring in his voice. Mr. Hauser had taught history at Junipero Middle School since it was a junior high in the 1970s. He still wore his hair long, the way he must have back then, but it was gray now. Despite the hair, he had the unflustered calm of someone who'd dealt with middle-schoolers his whole adult life. He also knew his history. Anne had talked with him on the phone and in person setting this up.

Lucy hustled out of the meeting room to bring in the class. The kids wore uniforms: white or dark blue polo shirts, khakis, dark tartan skirts right to the knee. Mr. Hauser also wore khakis, and an old blue blazer to go with them. He came up and shook Anne's hand. "Thank you so much for taking the time to talk with us this morning, Mrs. Berkowitz," he said, pitching his voice both to her and to the students.

"I'm glad to do it. It's something different," Anne replied. Most days were pills and oxygen and meals and TV and books. Days doing nothing, days waiting to die. The different days stood out, when there were any.

The students stared at her. They fidgeted on the chairs—not because the chairs were so uncomfortable, Anne judged, but because thirteen- and fourteen-year-olds couldn't *not* fidget. There were about twenty of them: white, Hispanic, Asian, one plainly from India or Pakistan, one African-American. Junipero was a Catholic school, but Anne would have bet a couple of the white kids were Jewish. A good education was where you found it.

Mr. Hauser turned and spoke to them: "We've been studying about World War Two. You remember how, in 1940, Germany invaded Denmark and Norway, and then conquered the Low Countries and France and seemed to be about to win the war. Well, when that happened, Mrs. Berkowitz was living in Amsterdam, the capital of Holland. How old were you then, Mrs. Berkowitz?"

"I was ten—it happened just before my eleventh birthday," she said. "I wasn't Mrs. Berkowitz then, of course. I wasn't Missus anybody. I was only a girl named Anne."

Some of the kids took notes. Some didn't, but listened anyway. And some looked as if they wished they were running around in the sweet spring air outside. Well, that was about par for the course.

"You weren't born in Amsterdam, though, were you?" Mr. Hauser asked.

She shook her head. "No. My father and mother and Margot—my older sister—moved to Holland from Germany in 1933. I stayed with my grandmother in Germany a little longer, and I went to Amsterdam in early 1934."

"Why did your family move?" the teacher asked.

"Because my father could see how hard Hitler was making things for the Jews. He was a very smart man, my father," Anne said. "He got a job at a company that made jam, and then at one that turned out spices. Some of my other relatives saw trouble coming, too. Two of my uncles came to America."

"They got far enough away from the Nazis to be safe, didn't they?" Mr. Hauser said. "But your family didn't. What were things like for Jews after the Germans invaded Holland?"

"They were bad, and they kept getting worse and worse. The Germans and the Dutch Nazis made more and more laws and rules against us."

"There were Dutch Nazis?" a boy exclaimed, his voice right on the edge of being a man's.

Sadly, Anne nodded. "Yes, there were some. Most of the Dutch people hated Hitler and *really* hated Seyss-Inquart, the Austrian who ran Holland for him. Without help from people like that, my family never would have made it through the war. But there was a fat fool called Anton Mussert, who led the Dutch Nazi Party and helped the Germans rule Holland. Some people did follow him, either because they truly believed or because they thought that was the side their bread was buttered on."

"What kind of laws did the Germans make?" Mr. Hauser tried to keep things simple.

"We had to wear yellow stars on our clothes, with *Jood* on them. That's *Jew* in Dutch," Anne said. "We couldn't use trams. We had to give up our bicycles. We weren't allowed to ride in cars. We had to shop late in the afternoon, when there was next to nothing left to buy. We couldn't even visit Christians in their houses or apartments. We couldn't go out at all from eight at night to six in the morning. We had to go to only Jewish schools and Jewish barbers and Jewish beauty parlors. We couldn't use public swimming pools or tennis courts or sports fields or—well, anything."

"Why did they do that?" a pretty Asian girl asked.

Before Anne could answer, the boy who'd been amazed about Dutch Nazis said, "Is that when they, like, tattooed numbers on the Jews' arms?"

"Jordan..." By the way Mr. Hauser said the name, Jordan had a habit of breaking in whenever he felt like it.

Not quite smiling, Anne explained, "They only tattooed numbers on you when you went into a camp. If you went in, you probably wouldn't come out again. We knew that by 1942. Even that early, the BBC said Jews were being gassed. So that summer, when the SS sent my father a call-up notice, he didn't go. We hid instead, in some rooms above and in back of the place where Father worked."

"Your family, you mean?" the Asian girl asked. She must have decided she wouldn't get a sensible answer about why the Nazis tormented the Jews. Anne knew *she* didn't have one, not after all these years.

"My family, and a man my father worked with, Hermann van Pels, and his wife and son—Peter was almost sixteen when we went into hiding, about the same age as Margot. And a couple of months later we decided we could fit in one more person. Fritz Pfeffer was a dentist. We were all German Jews who'd gone to Holland and then found out that wasn't far enough."

"How big were these rooms?" the Asian girl wondered.

"Not big enough." The heat with which Anne snapped out the words surprised even her. "Before Dr. Pfeffer moved in, Margot and I had slept together in one room. After that, she moved in with Mother and Father, and I got to share that room with the dentist."

"Eww!" The kids made gross-out noises. Some of them probably had dirty suspicions. They were a lot less naïve about the facts of life than she'd been at the same age. Fritz Pfeffer hadn't been that kind of nuisance, anyway. Plenty of other kinds, yes, God knows, but not that one.

As if plucking the thought from her mind, Mr. Hauser smiled with only one side of his mouth and said, "And you all got along like one big, happy family, right?"

"No!" Anne said, so sharply that everybody laughed—everybody but her. She went on, "By the time the war ended, I never wanted to see any of those people again as long as I lived. My own mother was a cold fish. Auguste van Pels—that was Hermann's wife—was an airhead. A ditz."

The students laughed again. Anne didn't. She hadn't had those words to describe Mrs. van Pels back then. She couldn't find any that fit better, though.

And she was just getting started. "Dr. Pfeffer was in love with Dr. Pfeffer. He hoarded food. And he complained I made too much noise and shushed me all the time, even when I just rolled over in bed."

"Why didn't you, like, do something to him?" Yes, that was Jordan. Who else would it be?

"I wanted to," Anne answered honestly. Some of the kids snapped her picture with smartphones. She went on, "I thought about the different things I could do. But I didn't do any of them. We were stuck there with each other for as long as the war lasted. We couldn't go anywhere, not unless we wanted to get caught. We had to try to get along."

"You've said some hard things about the people who were in there with you—even about your own mom," Mr. Hauser said. "What did they think of you?"

"They thought I was stuck-up. They thought I was snippy. They thought I was too smart for my own good," Anne answered, not without pride.

"Were they right?" a kid asked.

"Of course they were. We were all right about each other. That's what made getting along so hard," Anne said.

"What did you do about food?" the pretty Asian girl asked. "Did you have piles and piles of canned things hidden with you, so you wouldn't need to worry about it?"

She wasn't just pretty, Anne Berkowitz realized—she was smart, too. She knew which questions to ask. She wasn't altogether unlike Anne herself at the same age, in other words. "We had some things stored away like that," the old woman said, "but we tried to save those for emergencies. We had money saved up, too. The people who were helping us used it to get ration books for us, and they used the coupons from them to buy us food. They bought food on the black market, too, for themselves and for us."

"Can you explain that, please?" Mr. Hauser said.

"You couldn't get much food with your ration coupons, and you couldn't get any good food with them," Anne said. "The Germans stole food from Holland. They stole it from all the places they took over. They wanted it for themselves, and especially for their soldiers. So the Dutch people held on to as much as they could. That was against the Nazis' rules, and getting that black-market food cost a lot of money. But almost everyone did it. You couldn't live without it."

"What if the Nazis caught you doing it?" As usual, Jordan didn't bother raising his hand. "What did they do to you?"

"They arrested you. Even if you weren't Jewish, you didn't want to wind up in a German jail, or in a camp." Anne paused, remembering. "It would have been right at the start of spring in 1944 when the people we'd been buying things from got arrested. We had to get by on what we could use our ration books for—potatoes and kale."

"What's kale?" three kids asked at the same time.

"It's more like cabbage than anything else," Anne told them. "This was old, stale kale, and it smelled so bad I had to put a hanky splashed with cologne up to my nose when I ate it. The potatoes were like that, too. We used to try to figure out which ones had measles and which ones had smallpox and which ones had cancer. Those were the kinds of jokes we made."

"Did things get better after that?" Mr. Hauser asked.

"A little bit, for a while," Anne said. "But the last winter of the war, the winter of 1944–45, was terrible. Not just for us—for everybody in Holland. They still call that the Hunger Winter. Nobody had anything then. People starved. There was no wood for coffins to bury the dead. People ate tulip bulbs, even. The bread—when there was bread—was gray and disgusting. Everyone knew the Germans had lost. Even they knew. But Holland was off to the side of the way the Americans and English and Canadians were going, so Seyss-Inquart and the Nazis hung on and on."

"Did you use up all your cans by the time the Hunger Winter was over?" the Asian girl asked.

"Long before then. We were *so* skinny when Amsterdam finally got liberated. I wondered if we'd live to see it."

"Was being hungry all the time the worst thing about hiding out for so long?" Mr. Hauser asked.

Anne Berkowitz sent him a hooded look. That was the first dumb question he'd asked. Maybe he didn't really understand after all. Or maybe he was asking for his students' benefit. After a moment, she decided to give him the benefit of the doubt. She shook her head. "No. Remember, we were cooped up with each other for almost three years. That was worse. And we never went outside in all that time. That was worse, too. When the Germans in Holland finally quit, we were as white as ghosts. Everyone knew we'd been in hiding till we got some sun. Oh, Lord, fresh air was wonderful!" She smiled, recalling how marvelous it had been.

"Anything else?" the teacher asked. Anne relaxed. The way he put the question showed he knew what he was doing, all right.

She gave it to him: "The worst thing, I think, the very worst thing, was being afraid all the time. So many ways to be afraid. English bombers came over Amsterdam at night. The Americans flew over in the daytime. Most of the time, they'd go on to Germany, but sometimes they'd drop bombs on us. The Germans in Amsterdam would shoot big antiaircraft guns at them, too, and sometimes knock them down. The noise was terrible. It scared all of us—Mrs. van Pels most of all."

"What would have have done if a bomb hit the building where you were at?" irrepressible Jordan asked.

No doubt at all, though, that that was a dumb question. "We would have died," Anne said bleakly. Jordan opened his mouth. Then he closed it again—the most sensible thing he could have done.

The Asian girl said, "You were most scared of getting caught, weren't you?"

"Yes!" Anne's head bobbed up and down. She'd feared none of the kids would have any idea what she was talking about. Who was she? Just an old lady they'd never met before. But the Asian girl got it, whether the others did or not.

Mr. Hauser saw the same thing. "Good question, Vicki," he said, so Anne finally had a name for her. "While Mrs. Berkowitz was hiding in Amsterdam, Jean-Paul Sartre—who went through the German occupation in Paris—wrote *Hell is other people*. Maybe he wasn't talking about this, but maybe he was."

Some of the kids, Vicki among them, nodded thoughtfully. So did Anne Berkowitz. She'd heard the line before—who hadn't?—but she'd never applied it to her own predicament till now. She wondered why not. It fit only too well. To hide what she was feeling, she sipped from the water bottle.

"Can you tell us a little about that fear?" Mr. Hauser said.

She sipped again before she answered. "To start with, not everybody who worked at the spice plant knew we were hiding there. And the people who came in to buy things didn't know, of course. So we had to stay as quiet as we could during business hours. We'd sit on beds and chairs and try not to move unless we had to. We couldn't flush the toilet. Sometimes we couldn't even use the toilet—an empty can or a bottle would be a chamber pot. So that was bad. And when we did have to walk around, we never knew whether the noise would give us away."

"Wow," one of the eighth-graders said, more to herself than to anyone else.

"That wasn't all," Anne said. "We had burglars—more than once. Spices had to do with food, and people got hungrier and hungrier. And I suppose they hoped the office downstairs had money in it, or things they could steal and use to get money or food. The longer the war went on, the more people in Amsterdam stole. It was the only way to get what you needed."

"Did you hear them breaking in?" Mr. Hauser asked.

"Yes. We ran into them once or twice, too. We would go downstairs at night, when we were the only people there. Sometimes we would put spices into packets. Or we would listen to the BBC on the radio. It was the only way to get news that wasn't full of German lies."

"You could get in trouble for that, too, couldn't you?" the teacher said.

"Oh, yes," Anne agreed. "For us it was no worry—being a Jew in hiding was a worse crime than listening to the BBC. But people who weren't Jews did it, too. When the burglars broke in, though… They must have been as scared as we were. Almost, anyhow. They weren't looking for anybody, and we didn't want to see anybody we didn't know. We'd shiver for days afterwards."

"How come?" a girl asked.

Holding her patience, Anne explained, "Because even a burglar could turn us in to the Nazis. He'd probably get a reward if he did. If he knew we were Jews, or if he just guessed…" Her voice trailed away. She drank more water.

"Were your rooms hidden well?" Mr. Hauser asked.

"You couldn't tell they were there just by looking," Anne answered. "There was a bookcase built in front of the doorway on the second-floor landing. It was attached with hooks. But it wouldn't keep anybody out who really wanted to come in. That was what we were most afraid of—a fat SS sergeant or a bunch of Dutch Nazis who would have packed us off to Auschwitz." Her mouth narrowed. "If that had happened, I wouldn't be sitting here now talking to you."

"But it didn't," Mr. Hauser said. "You all made it through till the Germans surrendered."

"That's right." Anne Berkowitz looked across almost seventy years. "Those were strange times. The Germans in Holland started letting in food a few days before they gave up. They could see it was over. And then, after the surrender, they kept order and handed out the food for a little while, till the Canadians came in."

"How did they get away with that?" Jordan demanded.

"They were there. They still had guns. They were organized, too, so the Allies used them," Anne told him. "They even shot a couple of deserters the Canadians handed back to them—this was after the surrender. It kicked up a big stink, and they didn't get any more deserters back after that."

She looked across the years again. The Canadians marching into Amsterdam had been so ruddy, so fit, so splendid—so different from the shabby, scrawny, hangdog Dutchmen who'd gone through defeat and five years of occupation. They'd been delicious, was what they'd been. No wonder she lost her cherry that summer, and it wasn't as if she were the only one: not even close.

Well, that was something the middle-schoolers didn't need to hear.

She might have lost it to Peter van Pels while they hid together. She'd had a crush on him for a while. Margot had liked him, too, which made things...interesting in their cramped, smelly little refuge. But Peter'd stayed almost a perfect gentleman. No, people then hadn't taken things that had to do with sex for granted. Was that better or worse than the way things worked these days? Anne didn't know. It wasn't the same. She knew that.

"What happened to the rest of the Jews in Holland?" Mr. Hauser asked. "How many of them were there?"

"There were about 140,000 Jews in Holland when the war started—110,000 who'd lived there for a long time and the rest refugees like my family," Anne Berkowitz answered. "Three-quarters of them died. We were lucky—*very* lucky."

"I guess you were," the teacher said. "How did you come to America? Can you talk a little bit about your life after you got here?"

"Sure. Like I told you, two of my uncles were already here. One of them was a citizen after the war. He helped arrange things so I could come. My father and mother moved to Switzerland. My sister stayed in Amsterdam and ended up marrying a Dutchman. We'd all seen too much of each other during the war. After it was over, we broke apart."

"And you learned English. You learned it just about perfectly," Mr. Hauser said.

"I was already studying it while we were hiding. I wasn't very good, but I had a start. I soaked up Dutch like a sponge because I was so little when I went to Holland. I used to tease my parents—it came harder for them. And English came harder for me: I was older by then. I know people can still tell I wasn't born here."

"Lots of people who live here weren't," Mr. Hauser said. By the way three or four of his students nodded, they hadn't been.

"True," Anne said. "Anyway, I came here, and pretty soon I married Mr. Berkowitz. He'd been a gunner in a B-24 during the war. We wondered if I ever heard his plane flying over Amsterdam. I could have—who knows? He ran an advertising business. I helped him out with it here and there. Some of the songs and slogans people heard on radio and TV were mine, but we never said so. You didn't always admit things like that in those days."

"It's different now. Women have more of a chance to be independent," Mr. Hauser said.

"Oh, yes, and it's good that they do. But they didn't back when I was raising a family." Anne held up a hand. "I'm not complaining. I've had a good life. Sheldon and I loved each other a lot as long as he lived. I watched my children grow up and do well, and my grandchildren, and now I've got a baby great-granddaughter."

"Aww," a couple of girls said.

"And I lived by myself and took care of myself till about a year and a half ago, when I finally got too frail. And now"—Anne shrugged—"I'm here."

"We're glad you're here. We're glad you're here all kinds of ways. And we're so glad you were kind enough to take the time to talk with us this morning," Mr. Hauser said. "Aren't we, kids?" The children clapped. A couple of them whooped. It wasn't the kind of noise the Hebrew Home for the Aging usually heard. Anne Berkowitz liked it anyhow.

Vicki came up to her and held up a phone. "May I take your picture, please?"

"Go ahead," Anne said. The others had snapped away without asking.

"Sweet." Vicki took the photo. She turned the phone around and showed it to Anne.

"Looks like me," Anne admitted.

"I'm gonna put it up on my Facebook page and talk about all the things you told us," Vicki said. "That was awesome!"

"Facebook…" Anne smiled in reminiscence. "We had nothing like that back then, of course. But I used to keep a diary when I was all cooped up. About a year before the end of the war, one of the Dutch Cabinet ministers in London said on the radio that they were going to collect papers like that so they could have a record of what things were like while we were occupied. I went back and polished mine up and wrote more about some things."

"So you gave it to them?" Vicki's eyes glowed. "You're part of history now, and everything? How cool is that?"

A little sheepishly, Anne shook her head. "While the war was still going on, I intended to. But almost the first thing I did after we could come out was, I threw it in the trash."

"Why?" the Asian girl exclaimed.

"Because I hated those times so much, all I wanted to do was forget them," Anne Berkowitz replied. "I thought getting rid of the diary would help me do that—and some of the things in there were pretty personal. I didn't want other people seeing them."

"Too bad!" Vicki said, and then, after a short pause for thought, "Did throwing it out help you forget?"

"Maybe a little," Anne said after thought of her own. "Not a lot. Less than I hoped. When you go through something like that, it sticks with you whether you want it to or not."

"I guess." Vicki'd never needed to worry about such things. She was lucky, and, luckily, had no idea how lucky she was.

From the doorway to the little meeting room, Mr. Hauser called her name. "Quit bothering Mrs. Berkowitz," he added. "The bus is waiting to take us back to school."

"She's not bothering me at all," Anne said, but Vicki scooted away.

Lucy walked up to Anne. "I think that went very well," the outreach worker said. "I'm sure the children learned a lot."

"I hope so," Anne said.

"I know I did," Lucy told her. "So scary!" She gave a theatrical shiver.

To her, though, it was scary like a movie. It wasn't real. It had been real to Anne, so real she'd wanted to make it go away as soon as she could. As she'd said to Vicki, though, some ghosts weren't so easy to exorcise.

Lucy wanted to talk some more, but one of the privileges of being old was not listening when you didn't feel like it. Anne walked out of the meeting room, out of the visitors' center. She blinked a couple of times as her eyes adjusted to the change from fluorescents to bright California sun.

She started back to her room. She wouldn't get there very fast—even before she came to the Home for the Aging, one of her grandsons had taken to calling her Flash—but she'd get there.

Or maybe she wouldn't, not right away. There was a bench by the garden path where the olive tree gave some shade. She sat down on it and looked at the flowers swaying in the soft breeze. A lizard skittered across the concrete and vanished under a shrub.

No, tossing out the diary hadn't helped that much. She could still remember some of what she'd written in it, better than she could remember most of what happened week before last. She'd wanted to be the best writer in the world. If she'd stuck with Dutch, she still thought she could have done well enough to make some money, anyhow.

In English, it hadn't quite happened. She'd taken too long to feel at home in the new language. The quiet help she'd given Sheldon, the brushes with Hollywood... She shrugged. She'd had more, more of almost everything from adventure to love, than most people ever got.

A hummingbird hovered above the path. After a moment, it decided it couldn't get any nectar from the flowers on her blouse. It zoomed away. She smiled and watched it disappear.

SHTETL DAYS

Jakub Shlayfer opened the door and walked outside to go to work. Before he could shut it again, his wife called after him: *"Alevai it should be a good day! We really need the gelt!"*

"Alevai, Bertha. *Omayn,"* Jakub agreed. The door was already shut by then, but what difference did that make? It wasn't as if he didn't know they were poor. His lean frame, the rough edge on the brim of his broad, black hat, his threadbare long, black coat, and the many patches on his boot soles all told the same story.

But then, how many Jews in Wawolnice weren't poor? The only one Jakub could think of was Shmuel Grynszpan, the undertaker. *His* business was as solid and certain as the laws of God. Everybody else's? Groszy and zlotych always came in too slowly and went out too fast.

He stumped down the unpaved street, skirting puddles. Not all the boot patches were everything they might have been. He didn't want to get his feet wet. He could have complained to Mottel Cohen, but what was the use? Mottel did what Mottel could do. And it wasn't as if

Wawolnice had—or needed—two cobblers. If you listened to Mottel's kvetching, the village didn't need one cobbler often enough.

The watery spring morning promised more than the day was likely to deliver. The sun was out, but clouds to the west warned it was liable to rain some more. Well, it wouldn't snow again till fall. That was something. Jakub skidded on mud and almost fell. It might be something, but it wasn't enough.

Two-story houses with steep, wood-shingled roofs crowded the street from both sides and caused it to it twist here and turn there. They made it hard for the sun to get down to the street and dry up the mud. More Jews came out of the houses to go to their jobs. The men dressed pretty much like Jakub. Some of the younger ones wore cloth caps instead of broad-brimmed hats. Chasidim, by contrast, had fancy shtreimels, with the brims made from mink.

A leaning fence made Jakub go out toward the middle of the narrow street. Most of the graying planks went up and down. For eight or ten feet, though, boards running from side to side patched a break. They were as ugly as the patches on his boots. A hooded crow perched on the fence jeered at Jakub.

He had to push in tight to the fence because an old couple from the country were pushing a handcart toward him, and making heavy going of it. The crow flew away. Wicker baskets in the handcart were piled high with their fiery horseradish, milder red radishes, onions, leeks, and kale.

"Maybe you'll see my wife today, Moishe," Jakub called.

"Here's hoping," the old man said. His white beard spilled in waves halfway down his chest. He wore a brimless fur cap that looked something like an upside-down chamber pot.

Chamber pots... The air was thick with them. Shmuel Grynszpan had piped water in his house, as his wife never tired of boasting. Not many other Jews—and precious few Poles—in Wawolnice did. They said—whoever *they* were—you stopped noticing how a village stank once you'd lived in it for a little while. As he often did, Jakub wished *they* knew what they were talking about.

Signs above the tavern, the dry-goods store, the tailor's shop, Jakub's own sorry little business, and the handful of others Wawolnice boasted were in both Polish and Yiddish. Two different alphabets running two different ways… If that didn't say everything that needed saying about how Jews and Poles got along—or didn't get along—Jakub couldn't imagine what would.

He used a fat iron key to open the lock to his front door. The hinges creaked when it pulled it toward him. *Have to oil that,* he thought. Somewhere in his shop, he had a copper oilcan. If he could find it, if he remembered to look for it… If he didn't, neither the world nor even the door was likely to come to an end.

He was a grinder. Anything that was dull, he could sharpen: knives, scissors, straight razors (for the Poles—almost all the Jewish men wore beards), plowshares, harvester blades. He was a locksmith. He repaired clocks—and anything else with complicated gearing. He made umbrellas out of wire and scrap cloth, and fixed the ones he'd made before. He sold patent medicines, and brewed them up from this and that in the dark, musty back room. He would turn his hand to almost anything that might make a zloty.

Lots of things might make a zloty. Hardly anything, outside of Grynszpan's business, reliably did. Wawolnice wasn't big enough to need a full-time grinder or locksmith or repairman or umbrella maker or medicine mixer. Even doing all of them at once, Jakub didn't bring home enough to keep Bertha happy.

Of course, he could have brought home more than the undertaker made and still not kept his wife happy. Some people weren't happy unless they were unhappy. There was a paradox worthy of the Talmud—unless you knew Bertha.

Across the way, the little boys in Alter Kaczyne's *kheder* began chanting the *alef-bays*. While Alter worked with them, their older brothers and cousins would wrestle with Hebrew vocabulary and grammar on their own. Or maybe the *melamed*'s father would lend a hand. Chaim Kaczyne coughed all the time and didn't move around very well any more, but his wits were still clear.

Jakub went to work on a clock a Polish woman had brought in. His hands were quick and clever. Scars seamed them; you couldn't be a grinder without things slipping once in a while. And dirt and grease had permanent homes under his nails and in the creases on top of his fingers. But hands were to work with, and work with them he did.

"Here we are," he muttered: a broken tooth on one of the gears. He rummaged through a couple of drawers to see if he had one that matched. And sure enough! The replacement went into the clock. He didn't throw out the damaged one. He rarely threw anything out. He'd braze on a new tooth and use the gear in some less demanding place.

The woman came in not long after he finished the clock. She wore her blond hair in a short bob; her skirt rose halfway to her knees. You'd never catch a Jewish woman in Wawolnice in anything so scandalously short. She nodded to find the clock ticking again. They haggled a little over the price. Jakub had warned her it would go up if he had to put in a new gear. She didn't want to remember. She was shaking her head when she smacked coins down on the counter and walked out.

He eyed—not to put too fine a point on it, he leered at—her shapely calves as her legs twinkled away. He was a man, after all. He was drawn to smooth flesh the way a butterfly was drawn to flowers. No wonder the women of his folk covered themselves from head to foot. No wonder Jewish wives wore *sheitels* and headscarves. They didn't want to put themselves on display like that. But the Poles were different. The Poles didn't care.

So what? The Poles were *goyim*.

He sharpened one of his own knives, a tiny, precise blade. He often did that when he had nothing else going on. He owned far and away the sharpest knives in the village. He would have been happier if they were duller, so long as it was because he stayed too busy to work on them.

A kid carrying a basket of bagels stuck his head in the door. Jakub spent a few groszy to buy one. The boy hurried away, short pants showing off his skinny legs. He didn't have a police license to peddle, so he was always on the dodge.

"*Barukh atah Adonai, eloyahynu melekh ha-olam, ha-motzi lekhem min ha-aretz,*" Jakub murmured. *Blessed art Thou, O Lord our God, King of the Universe, Who makest bread to come forth from the earth.* Only after the prayer did he eat the bagel.

Yiddish. Polish. Hebrew. Aramaic. He had them all. No one who knew Yiddish didn't also know German. A man who spoke Polish could, at need, make a stab at Czech or Ruthenian or Russian. All the *Yehudim* in Wawolnice were scholars, even if they didn't always think of themselves so.

Back to sharpening his own knives. It had the feel of another slow day. Few days here were anything else. The ones that were, commonly weren't good days.

After a while, the front door creaked open again. Jakub jumped to his feet in surprise and respect. "Reb Eliezer!" he exclaimed. "What can I do for you today?" Rabbis, after all, had knives and scissors that needed sharpening just like other men's.

But Eliezer said, "We were talking about serpents the other day." He had a long, pale, somber face, with rusty curls sticking out from under his hatbrim, a wispy copper beard streaked with gray, and cat-green eyes.

"Oh, yes. Of course." Jakub nodded. They *had* been speaking of serpents, and all sorts of other Talmudic *pilpul*, in the village's *bet ha-midrash* attached to the little *shul*. The smell of the books in the tall case there, the aging leather of their bindings, the paper on which they were printed, even the dust that shrouded the seldom-used volumes, was part and parcel of life in Wawolnice.

So… No business—no money-making business—now. Bertha would not be pleased to see this. She would loudly not be pleased to see it, as a matter of fact. But she would also be secretly proud because the rabbi chose her husband, a grinder of no particular prominence, with whom to split doctrinal hairs.

"Obviously," Reb Eliezer said in portentous tones, "the serpent is unclean for Jews to eat or to handle after it is dead. It falls under the ban of Leviticus 11:29, 11:30, and 11:42."

"Well, that may be so, but I'm not so sure," Jakub answered, pausing to light a stubby, twisted cigar. He offered one to Reb Eliezer, who accepted with a murmur of thanks. After blowing out harsh smoke, the grinder went on, "I don't think those verses are talking about serpents at all."

Eliezer's gingery eyebrows leaped. "How can you say such a thing?" he demanded, wagging a forefinger under Jakub's beaky nose. "Verse 42 says, 'Whatsoever goeth upon the belly, and whatsoever goeth upon all four, or whatsoever hath more feet among all creeping things that creep upon the earth, them ye shall not eat; for they are an abomination.'" Like Jakub, he could go from Yiddish to Biblical Hebrew while hardly seeming to notice he was switching languages.

Jakub shrugged a stolid shrug. "I don't hear anything there that talks about serpents. Things that go on all fours, things with lots of legs. I don't want to eat a what-do-you-call-it—a centipede, I mean. Who would? Even a *goy* wouldn't want to eat a centipede… I don't think." He shrugged again, as if to say no Jew counted on anything that had to do with *goyim*.

"'Whatsoever goeth upon the belly…among all the creeping things that creep upon the earth,'" Reb Eliezer repeated. "And this same phrase also appears in the twenty-ninth verse, which says, 'These also shall be unclean unto you among the creeping things that creep upon the earth;—'"

"'—the weasel, and the mouse, and the tortoise after his kind.'" Jakub took up the quotation, and went on into the next verse: "'And the ferret, and the chameleon, and the lizard, and the snail, and the mole.' I don't see a word in there about serpents." He blew out another stream of smoke, not quite at the rabbi.

Eliezer affected not to notice. "Since when is a serpent not a creeping thing that goeth upon its belly? Will you tell me it doesn't?"

"It doesn't *now,*" Jakub admitted.

"It did maybe yesterday?" Eliezer suggested sarcastically.

"Not yesterday. Not the day before yesterday, either," Jakub said. "But when the Lord, blessed be His name, made the serpent, He made it to speak and to walk on its hind legs like a man. What else does that? Maybe He made it in His own image."

"But God told the serpent, 'Thou art cursed above all cattle, and above every beast in the field: upon thy belly shalt thou go, and dust shalt thou eat all the days of thy life.'"

"So He changed it a little. So what?" Jakub said. Reb Eliezer's eyebrow jumped again at *a little,* but he held his peace. The grinder went on, "Besides, the serpent is to blame for mankind's fall. Shouldn't we pay him back by cooking him in a stew?"

"Maybe we should, maybe we shouldn't. But that argument isn't Scriptural," the rabbi said stiffly.

"Well, what if it isn't? How about this…?" Jakub went off on another tangent from the Torah.

They fenced with ideas and quotations through another cigar apiece. At last, Reb Eliezer threw his pale hands in the air and exclaimed, "In spite of the plain words of Leviticus, you come up with a hundred reasons why the accursed serpent ought to be as kosher as a cow!"

"Oh, not a hundred reasons. Maybe a dozen." Jakub was a precise man, as befitted a trade where a slip could cost a finger. But he also had his own kind of pride: "Give me enough time, and I suppose I could come up with a hundred."

A sort of a smile lifted one corner of Reb Eliezer's mouth. "Then perhaps now you begin to see why Rabbi Jokhanan of Palestine, of blessed memory, said hundreds of years ago that no man who could not do what you are doing had the skill he needed to open a capital case."

As it so often did, seemingly preposterous Talmudic *pilpul* came back to the way Jews were supposed to live their lives. "I should hope so," Jakub answered. "You have to begin a capital case with the reasons for acquitting whoever is on trial. If you can't find those reasons, someone else had better handle the case."

"I agree with you." The rabbi wagged his forefinger at Jakub once more. "You won't hear me tell you that very often."

"Gevalt! I should hope not!" Jakub said in mock horror.

Reb Eliezer's eyes twinkled. "And so I had better go," he continued, as if the grinder hadn't spoken. "The Lord bless you and keep you."

"And you, Reb," Jakub replied. Eliezer dipped his head. He walked out of the shop and down the street. A man came in wanting liniment for a horse. Jakub compounded some. It made his business smell of camphor and turpentine the rest of the day. It also put a couple of more zlotych in his pocket. Bertha would be…less displeased.

Shadows stretched across Wawolnice. Light began leaking out of the sky. The rain had held off, anyhow. People headed home from their work. Jakub was rarely one of the first to call it a day. Before long, though, the light coming in through the dusty front windows got too dim to use. Time to quit, all right.

He closed up and locked the door. He'd done some tinkering with the lock. He didn't think anybody not a locksmith could quietly pick it. Enough brute force, on the other hand… Jews in Poland understood all they needed to about brute force, and about who had enough of it. Jakub Shlayfer's mobile mouth twisted. Polish Jews didn't, never had, and never would.

He walked home through the gathering gloom. "Stinking Yid!" The *shrei* in Polish pursued him. His shoulders wanted to sag under its weight, and the weight of a million more like it. He didn't, he wouldn't, let them.

If the *mamzrim* saw they'd hurt you, they won. As long as a rock didn't follow, he was all right. And if one did, he could duck or dodge. He hoped.

No rocks tonight. Candles and kerosene lamps sent dim but warm glows out into the darkness. If you looked at the papers, electricity would come to the village soon. Then again, if you looked at the papers and believed everything you read in them, you were too dumb to live.

Bertha met him at the door. *Sheitel,* headscarf over it, long black dress… She still looked good to him. She greeted him with, "So what were you and Reb Eliezer going on about today?"

"Serpents," Jakub answered.

"Pilpul." His wife's sigh said she'd hoped for better, even if she hadn't expected it. "I don't suppose he had any paying business."

"He didn't, no," the grinder admitted. "But Barlicki's wife came in for her clock. I had to swap out a gear, so I charged her more. I told her before that I would, but she still didn't like it."

"And God forbid you should make Barlicki's wife unhappy." Bertha knew he thought the Polish woman was pretty, then. How long would she go on giving him a hard time about that? The next couple of days ought to be interesting. Not necessarily enjoyable, but interesting.

He did what he could to show Bertha he appreciated her. Nostrils twitching, he said, "What smells so good?"

"Soup with chicken feet," she replied, sounding slightly softened. "Cabbage, carrots, onions, mangel-wurzel…"

Mangel-wurzel was what you used when you couldn't afford turnips. Chicken feet were what you put in soup when you wanted it to taste like meat but you couldn't afford much of the genuine article. You could gnaw on them, worrying off a little skin or some of the tendons that would have led to the drumsticks. You wouldn't rise up from the table happy, but you might rise up happier.

He stepped past her and into the small, crowded front room, with its rammed-earth flood and battered, shabby furniture. The little brass mezuzah still hung on the doorframe outside. He rarely gave it a conscious thought. Most of the time he only noticed it when it wasn't there, so to speak. Stealing mezuzahs was one way Polish kids found to aggravate their Jewish neighbors. Not only that, but they might get a couple of groszy for the brass.

Bertha closed the front door behind him and let the bar fall into its bracket. The sound of the stout plank thudding into place seemed very final, as if it put a full stop to the day. And so—again, in a manner of speaking—it did.

———

Jakub walked over to the closet door. That the cramped space had room for a closet seemed something not far from miraculous. He wasn't inclined to complain, though. Oh, no—on the contrary. Neither was Bertha, who came up smiling to stand beside him as he opened the door.

Then they walked into the closet. They could do that now. The day was over. Jakub shoved coats and dresses out of the way. They smelled of wool and old sweat. Bertha flicked a switch as she closed the closet door. A ceiling light came on.

"Thanks, sweetie," Jakub said. "That helps."

In back of the clothes stood another door, this one painted battleship gray. In German, large, neatly stenciled black letters on the hidden doorway warned AUTHORIZED PERSONNEL ONLY. Being an authorized person, Jakub hit the numbers that opened that door. It showed a concrete stairway leading down. The walls to the descending corridor were also pale gray. Blue-tinged light from fluorescent tubes in ceiling fixtures streamed into the closet.

Jakub started down the stairs. Bertha was an authorized person, too. She followed him, pausing only to close the hidden door behind them.

A click announced it had locked automatically, as it was designed to do. The grinder and his wife left Wawolnice behind.

Men and women in grimy Jewish costumes and about an equal number dressed as Poles from the time between the War of Humiliation and the triumphant War of Retribution ambled along an underground hallway. They chatted and chattered and laughed, as people who've worked together for a long time will at the end of a day.

Arrows on the walls guided them toward their next destination. Explaining the arrows were large words beside them: TO THE SHOWERS. The explanation was about as necessary as a second head, but Germans had a habit of overdesigning things.

Veit Harlan shook himself like a dog that had just scrambled out of a muddy creek. That was how he felt, too. Like any actor worth his salt, he immersed himself in the roles he played. When the curtain came down on another day, he always needed a little while to remember he wasn't Jakub Shlayfer, a hungry Jew in a Polish village that had vanished from the map more than a hundred years ago.

He wasn't the only one, either. He would have been amazed if he had been. People heading for the showers to clean up after their latest shift in Wawolnice went right on throwing around the front vowels and extra-harsh gutturals of Yiddish. Only little by little did they start using honest German again.

When they did. The fellow who played Reb Eliezer—his real name was Ferdinand Marian—and a pimply *yeshiva-bukher* (well, the pimply performer impersonating a young *yeshiva-bukher*) went right on with whatever disputation Eliezer had found after leaving Jakub's shop. They went right on throwing Hebrew and Aramaic around, too. And the reb and the kid with zits both kept up a virtuoso display of finger-wagging.

"They'd better watch that," Veit murmured to the woman who had been Bertha a moment before.

"I know." She nodded. She was really Kristina Söderbaum. They were married to each other out in the *Reich* as well as in the village. The people who ran Wawolnice used real couples whenever they could. They claimed it made the performances more convincing. If that meant Veit got to work alongside his wife, he wouldn't complain.

The guy who played Alter the *melamed* caught up to Veit and Kristi from behind. In the wider world, he was Wolf Albach-Retty. "Hey, Veit. Did you see the gal who flashed her tits at me this morning?" he exclaimed.

"No! I wish I would have," Harlan answered. His wife planted an elbow in his ribs. Ignoring her, he went on, "When did that happen?"

"It was early—not long after the village opened up," Wolf said.

"Too bad. I was working on that clock for a lot of the morning. I guess I didn't pick the right time to look up."

"A bunch of the kids did. Boy, they paid even less attention to me than usual after that," Albach-Retty said. Veit laughed. The *melamed* rolled his eyes. "It's funny for you. It's funny for the damn broad, too. But I'm the guy who had to deal with it. When I was *potching* the little bastards, I was *potching* 'em good." He mimed swatting a backside.

"Nothing they haven't got from you before," Veit said, which was also true. Everything the villagers did in Wawolnice was real. They pretended the curious people who came to gawk at them weren't there. But how were you supposed to pretend a nice set of tits wasn't there (and Veit would have bet it was a nice set—otherwise the woman wouldn't have shown them off)?

"Worse than usual, I tell you." Wolf leaned toward self-pity.

"You'll live. So will they," Veit said. "If they don't like it, let 'em file a complaint with the SPCA." Kristi giggled, which was what he'd hoped for. After a moment, Wolf Albach-Retty laughed, too. That was a bonus.

The corridor to the showers split, one arrow marked MEN, the other WOMEN. Veit stripped off the heavy, baggy, dark, sweaty outfit of a Wawolnice Jew with a sigh of relief. He chucked it into a cubbyhole and scratched. The village wasn't a hundred percent realistic. They did spray it to keep down the bugs. You weren't supposed to pick up fleas or lice or bedbugs, even if you were portraying a lousy, flea-bitten kike.

Theory was wonderful. Veit had found himself buggy as new software more than once coming off a shift. So had Kristi. So had just about all the other performers. It was a hazard of the trade, like a director who happened to be an oaf.

He didn't discover any uninvited guests tonight. Hot water and strong soap wiped away the stinks from Wawolnice. He took showering with a bunch of other men completely for granted. He'd started as a *Pimpf* in the *Hitler Jugend*, he'd kept it up through the Labor Service and his two-year hitch in the *Wehrmacht*, and now he was doing it some more. So what? Skin was skin, and he didn't get a charge out of guys.

Reb Eliezer and the *yeshiva-bukher* were still arguing about the Talmud in the shower. They were both circumcised. Quite a few of the men playing Jews were. Prizing realism as it did, the Reenactors' Guild gave you a raise if you were willing to have the operation. Veit kept all his original equipment. He didn't need the cash that badly, and Kristina liked him fine the way he was.

He grabbed a cotton towel, dried himself off, and tossed the towel into a very full bin. A bath attendant in coveralls—a scared, scrawny Slavic *Untermensch* from beyond the Urals—wheeled the bin away and brought out an empty one. Veit noticed him hardly more than he did the tourists who came to stare at Wawolnice and see what Eastern Europe had been like before the *Grossdeutsches Reich* cleaned things up.

You were trained not to notice tourists. You were trained to pretend they weren't there, and not to react when they did stuff (though Veit had never had anybody flash tits at him). It was different with the bath attendant. Did you notice a stool if you didn't intend to sit down on it? More like that.

Veit spun the combination dial on his locker. He put on his own clothes: khaki cotton slacks, a pale green polo shirt, and a darker green cardigan sweater. Synthetic socks and track shoes finished the outfit. It was much lighter, much softer, and much more comfortable than his performing costume.

He had to twiddle his thumbs for a couple of minutes before Kristi came down the corridor from her side of the changing area. Women always took longer getting ready. Being only a man, he had no idea why. But he would have bet the ancient Greeks told the same jokes about it as modern Aryans did.

She was worth the wait. Her knee-length light blue skirt showed off her legs. Veit wasn't the least bit sorry the *Reich* still frowned on pants for women. Her top clung to her in a way that would have made the real Jews on whom those of Wawolnice were based *plotz*. And the *sheitel* she had on now was attractively styled and an almost perfect match for the mane of wavy, honey-blond hair she'd sacrificed to take the role of Bertha Shlayfer.

"Let's go home," she said, and yawned. She shook her head. "Sorry. It's been a long day."

"For me, too," Veit agreed. "And it doesn't get any easier."

"It never gets any easier," Kristi said.

"I know, but that isn't what I meant. Didn't you see the schedule? They've got a pogrom listed for week after next."

"*Oy!*" Kristi burst out. Once you got used to Yiddish, plain German could seem flavorless beside it. And Veit felt like going *Oy!* himself. Pogroms were a pain, even if the tourists got off on them. Sure, the powers that be brought in drugged convicts for the people playing Poles to stomp and burn, but reenactors playing Jews always ended up getting hurt, too. Accidents happened. And, when you were living your role, sometimes you just got carried away and didn't care who stood in front of you when you threw a rock or swung a club.

"Nothing we can do about it but put on a good show." He pointed down the corridor toward the employee parking lot. "Come on. Like you said, let's go home."

The corridor spat performers out right next to the gift shop. Another sign reading AUTHORIZED PERSONNEL ONLY and a prominently displayed surveillance camera discouraged anyone else from moving against the stream. A ragged apple orchard screened the gift shop and the parking lot off from Wawolnice proper. That was good, as far as Veit was concerned. The gift shop was about paperbacks of *The Protocols of the Elders of Zion* and plastic Jew noses and rubber Jew lips. Once upon a time, no doubt, the village had been about the same kinds of things. It wasn't any more, or it wasn't exactly and wasn't all the time. As things have a way of doing, Wawolnice had taken on a life of its own.

Veit opened the passenger-side door for his wife. Kristi murmured a word of thanks as she slid into the Audi. He went around and got in himself. The electric engine silently came to life. The car didn't have the range of a gas auto, but more charging stations went up every day. Though petroleum might be running low, plenty of nuclear power plants off in the East made sure the *Reich* had plenty of electricity. If they belched radioactive waste into the environment every once in a while, well, that was the local Ivans' worry.

He drove out of the lot, up the ramp, and onto the *Autobahn,* heading east toward their flat in Lublin. A garish, brilliantly lit billboard appeared in his rear-view mirror. The big letters were backwards, but he knew what they said: COME SEE THE JEW VILLAGE! ADMISSION ONLY 15 REICHSMARKS! The sinister, hook-nosed figure in black on the billboard was straight out of a cartoon. It only faintly resembled the hard-working reenactors who populated Wawolnice.

"I hate that stupid sign," Veit said, as he did at least twice a week. "Makes us look like a bunch of jerks."

"It's like a book cover," Kristina answered, as she did whenever he pissed and moaned about the billboard. "It draws people in. Then they can see what we're really about."

"It draws assholes in," Veit said morosely. "They hold their noses at the smells and they laugh at our clothes and they show off their titties and think it's funny."

"You weren't complaining when Wolf told you about that," his wife pointed out. "Except that you didn't see it, I mean."

"Yeah, well…" He took one hand off the wheel for a moment to make a vague gesture of appeasement.

Lublin was about half an hour away at the *Autobahn*'s *Mach schnell!* speeds. It was clean and bright and orderly, like any town in the *Grossdeutsches Reich* these days. It had belonged to Poland, of course, before the War of Retribution. It had been a provincial capital, in fact. But that was a long time ago now. These days, Poles were almost as much an anachronism as Jews. The Germans had reshaped Lublin in their own image. They looked around and saw that it was good.

"Want to stop somewhere for dinner?" Veit asked as he pulled off the highway and drove into the city.

"Not really. I am tired," Kristi said. "We've got leftovers back at the flat. If that's all right with you."

"Whatever you want," he said.

They could have afforded a bigger apartment, but what would the point have been? They poured most of their time and most of their energy into the village. If you weren't going to do that, you didn't belong at Wawolnice. They used the flat as a place to relax and to sleep. How fancy did you need to be for that?

Kristina warmed up some rolls in the oven. A few minutes later, she put sweet-and-sour cabbage stuffed with veal sausage and rice into the microwave. Veit's contribution to supper was pouring out two tumblers of Greek white wine. "Oh, thank you," his wife said. "I could use one tonight."

"Me, too." Veit went on in Hebrew: *"Barukh atah Adonai, elohaynu melekh ha-olam, bo're p'ri ha-gafen."* Blessed art Thou, O Lord our God, King of the universe, who bringest forth the fruit of the vine.

"Practice," Kristi said as they clinked the big, heavy glasses.

"Aber natürlich," Veit agreed. "If you don't use a language, you'll lose it." He assumed the flat had microphones. He'd never heard of one that didn't. How much attention the *Sicherheitsdienst* paid…well, who could guess? Then again, who wanted to find out the hard way? If you started praying in the dead language of a proscribed *Volk*, better to let any possible SD ear know you had a reason.

The microwave buzzed. Kristina took out the glass tray, then retrieved the rolls. Veit poured more wine. His wife put food on the table. He blessed the bread and the main course, as he had the wine. They ate. He made his portion disappear amazingly fast.

"Do you want more?" Kristi asked. "There is some."

He thought about it, then shook his head. "No, that's all right. But I was hungry."

She was doing the dishes when the phone rang. Veit picked it up. *"Bitte?"* He listened for a little while, then said, "Hang on a second." Putting his palm on the mouthpiece, he spoke over the rush of water in the sink: "It's your kid sister. She wants to know if we feel like going out and having a few drinks."

She raised an eyebrow as she turned off the faucet. He shrugged back. She reached for the phone. He handed it to her. "Ilse?" she said. "Listen, thanks for asking, but I think we'll pass… Yes, I know we said that the last time, too, but we're really beat tonight. And there's a pogrom coming up soon, and we'll have to get ready for that. They're always *meshuggeh*… It means crazy, is what it means, and they are… Yes, next time for sure. So long." She hung up.

"So what will we do?" Veit asked.

"I'm going to finish the dishes," his wife said virtuously. "Then? I don't know. TV, maybe. And some more wine."

"Sounds exciting." Veit picked up the corkscrew. They'd just about killed this bottle. He'd have to summon reinforcements.

They plopped down on the sofa. TV was TV, which is to say, dull. The comedies were stupid. When a story about a cat up a tree led the news, you knew there was no news. The local footballers were down 3–1 with twenty minutes to play.

And so it wasn't at all by accident that Veit's hand happened to fall on Kristina's knee. She made as if to swat him, but her eyes sparkled. Instead of pulling away, he slid the hand up under her skirt. She swung toward him. "Who says it won't be exciting tonight?" she asked.

Getting ready for the pogrom kept everyone hopping. The reenactors who played Wawolnice's Jews and Poles had to go on doing everything they normally did. You couldn't disappoint the paying customers, and the routine of village life had an attraction of its own once you got used to it. And they had to ready the place so it would go through chaos and come out the other side with as little damage as possible.

A couple of buildings would burn down. They'd get rebuilt later, during nights. Along with everyone else, Veit and Kristi made sure the hidden sprinkler systems in the houses and shops nearby were in good working order, and that anything sprinklers might damage was replaced by a waterproof substitute.

Veit also moved the Torah from the Ark in the *shul*. A blank substitute scroll would burn, along with a couple of drugged and conditioned convicts who would try to rescue it. The Poles would made a bonfire of the books in the *bet ha-midrash*—only not out of the real books, only of convincing fakes.

People slept in their village living quarters, or on cots in the underground changing areas. Hardly anyone had time to go home. They wore their costumes all the time, even though the laundry did tend to them more often than would have been strictly authentic.

Eyeing a bandage on his finger—a knife he was sharpening had got him, a hazard of his village trade—Veit Harlan grumbled, "I'm Jakub a lot more than I'm me these days."

"You aren't the only one," Kristina said. His wife was also eligible for a wound badge. She'd grated her knuckle along with some potatoes that went into a *kugel*.

"We'll get to relax a little after the pogrom," Veit said. "And it'll bring in the crowds. Somebody told me he heard a tourist say they were advertising it on the radio."

"'Come see the Jews get what's coming to them—again!'" Kristi did a fine impersonation of an excitable radio announcer. It would have been a fine impersonation, anyhow, if not for the irony that dripped from her voice.

"Hey," Veit said—half sympathy, half warning.

"I know," she answered. Her tone *had* been too raw. "I'm just tired."

"Oh, sure. Me, too. Everybody is," Veit said. "Well, day after tomorrow and then it's over—till the next time."

"Till the next time," Kristi said.

"Yeah. Till then," Veit echoed. That wasn't exactly agreement. Then again, it wasn't exactly disagreement. Wawolnice moved in strange and mysterious way. The *Reichs* Commissariat for the Strengthening of the German Populace knew in broad outline what it wanted to have happen in the village. After all, National Socialism had been closely studying the Jewish enemy since long before the War of Retribution. Without such study, the Commissariat would never have been able to re-create such a precise copy of a *shtetl*. Details were up to the reenactors, though. They didn't have scripts. They improvised every day.

The pogrom broke out in the market square. That made sense. A Polish woman screeched that a Jew selling old clothes—old clothes specially manufactured for the village and lovingly aged—was cheating her. Rocks started flying. Jews started running. Whooping, drunken Poles overturned carts, spilling clothes and vegetables and rags and leather goods and what-have-you on the muddy ground. Others swooped down to steal what they could.

When the *melamed* and the boys from the *kheder* fled, Veit figured Jakub had better get out, too. A rock crashing through his shop's front window reinforced the message. This part of Wawolnice wasn't supposed to burn. All those elaborate fire-squelching systems should make sure of that. But anything you could make, you could also screw up. And so he scuttled out the front door, one hand clapped to his black hat so he shouldn't, God forbid, go bareheaded even for an instant.

Schoolchildren, plump burghers on holiday, and tourists from places like Japan and Brazil photographed the insanity. You had to go on pretending they weren't there. A pack of Poles were stomping a man in Jewish costume to death. One of the convict's hands opened and closed convulsively as they did him in. He bleated out the last words that had been imposed on him: *"Sh'ma, Yisroayl, Adonai elohaynu, adonai ekhod!"* *Hear, O Israel, the Lord our God, the Lord is one!*

Another performer playing a Pole swung a plank at Veit. Had that connected, he never would have had a chance to gabble out his last prayer. But the reenactor missed—on purpose, Veit devoutly hoped. Still holding on to his hat, he ran down the street.

"Stinking Yid!" the performer roared in Polish. Veit just ran faster. Jews didn't fight back, after all. Then he ran into bad luck—or rather, it ran into him. A flying rock caught him in the ribs.

"Oof!" he said, and then, *"Vey iz mir!"* When he breathed, he breathed knives. Something in there was broken. He had to keep running. If the Poles caught him, they wouldn't beat him to death, but they'd beat him up. They couldn't do anything else—realism came first. Oh, they might pull punches and go easy on kicks where they could, but they'd still hurt him. Hell, they'd already hurt him, even without meaning to.

Or they might not pull anything. Just as the reenactors in Jewish roles took pride in playing them to the hilt, so did the people playing Poles. If they were supposed to thump on Jews, they might go ahead and thump on any old Jew they could grab, and then have a drink or three to celebrate afterwards.

A woman screamed. The shriek sounded alarmingly sincere, even by Wawolnice standards. Veit hoped things weren't getting out of hand there. The less the senior inspectors from Lublin or even Berlin interfered with the way the village ran, the better for everybody here. "Jews" and "Poles" both took that as an article of faith.

Veit ducked into one of the buildings where Jews lived in one another's laps. As long as nobody could see him from outside... A woman in there gaped at him. "What are you doing here?" she asked—still in Yiddish, still in character.

"I got hurt. They banged on my teakettle once too often," he answered, also sticking to his role. He grabbed at his side. Would he have to start coughing up blood to convince people? He was afraid he might be able to do it.

What kind of horrible grimace stretched across his face? Or had he gone as pale as that village miracle, a clean shirt? The woman didn't argue with him any more (for a Wawolnice Jew, that came perilously close to falling out of one's part). She threw open her closet door. "Go on. Disappear, already."

"God bless you and keep you. I wish my ribs would disappear." He ducked inside. She closed the outer door after him. He fumbled till he found the light switch. Then he went to the inner door, identical to the one in his own crowded home. He was an authorized person, all right.

On the far side of that door lay the modern underpinnings to the early twentieth-century Polish village.

Now he didn't have to run for his life. Slowly and painfully, he walked down the concrete stairs and along a passageway to the first-aid center. He had to wait to be seen. He wasn't the only villager who'd got hurt. Sure as hell, pogroms were always a mess.

A medical tech prodded his ribcage. *"Gevalt!"* Veit exclaimed.

"You don't have to go on making like a Jew down here," the tech said condescendingly. Veit hurt too much to argue with him. The neatly uniformed Aryan felt him some more and listened to his chest with a stethoscope, then delivered his verdict: "You've got a busted slat or two, all right. Doesn't seem to be any lung damage, though. I'll give you some pain pills. Even with 'em, you'll be sore as hell on and off the next six weeks."

"Aren't you even going to bandage me up?" Veit asked.

"Nope. We don't do that any more, not in ordinary cases. The lung heals better unconstricted. Step off to one side now for your pills and your paperwork."

"Right," Veit said tightly. The tech might as well have been an auto mechanic. Now that he'd checked Veit's struts and figured out what his trouble was, he moved on to the next dented chassis. And Veit moved on to pharmacy and bureaucracy.

A woman who would have been attractive if she hadn't seemed so bored handed him a plastic vial full of fat green pills. He gulped one down, dry, then started signing the papers she shoved at him. That got a rise out of her: she went from bored to irked in one fell swoop. "What are those chicken scratches?" she demanded.

"Huh?" He looked down at the forms and saw he'd been scribbling *Jakub Shlayfer* in backwards-running Yiddish script on each signature line. He couldn't even blame the dope; it hadn't kicked in yet. Maybe pain would do for an excuse. Or maybe least said, soonest mended. He muttered "Sorry" and started substituting the name he'd been born with.

"That's more like it." The woman sniffed loudly. "Some of you people don't know the difference between who you are and who you play any more."

"You've got to be kidding." Veit wrote his own name once again. "Nobody wants to break *my* ribs on account of who I am. That only happens when I put on this stuff." His wave encompassed his *shtetl* finery.

"Remember that, then. Better to be Aryan. Easier, too."

Veit didn't feel like arguing. He did feel woozy—the pain pill started hitting hard and fast. "Easier is right," he said, and turned to leave the infirmary. The broken rib stabbed him again. He let out a hiss any snake, *treyf* or kosher, would have been proud of. The medical tech had been right, dammit. Even with a pill, he was sore as hell.

———

"We have to be *meshuggeh* to keep doing this," Kristina said as she piloted their car back toward Lublin at the end of the day.

"Right now, I won't argue with you." Veit wasn't inclined to argue about anything, not right now. Changing into ordinary German clothes had hurt more than he'd believed anything could. The prescription said *Take one tablet at a time every four to six hours, as needed for pain.* One tablet was sending a boy to do a man's job, and a half-witted boy at that. He'd taken two. He still hurt—and now he had the brains of a half-witted boy himself. No wonder his wife sat behind the Audi's wheel.

She flashed her lights at some *Dummkopf* puttering along on the *Autobahn* at eighty kilometers an hour. The jerk did eventually move over and let her by. Veit was too stoned for even that to annoy him, which meant he was very stoned indeed.

Kristi sighed as she zoomed past the old, flatulent VW. "But we'll be back at the same old stand tomorrow," she said, daring him to deny it.

"What would you rather do instead?" he asked. She sent him a reproachful side glance instead of an answer. Wawolnice offered more chances for honest performing than almost anywhere else in the *Reich*. Television was pap. The movies, too. The stage was mostly pap: pap and revivals.

Besides, they'd been at the village for so long now, most of the people they'd worked with anywhere else had forgotten they existed. Wawolnice was a world unto itself. Most of the kids in the *kheder* really were the children of performers who played Jews in the village. Were they getting in on the ground floor, or were they trapped? How much of a difference was there?

Veit didn't feel too bad as long as he held still. With the pills in him, he felt pretty damn good, as a matter of fact. Whenever he moved or coughed, though, all the pain pills in the world couldn't hope to block the message his ribs sent. He dreaded sneezing. That would probably feel as if he were being torn in two—which might not be so far wrong.

Moving slowly and carefully, he made it up to the apartment with his wife. He started to flop down onto the sofa in front of the TV, but thought better of it in the nick of time. Lowering himself slowly and gently was a much better plan. Then he found a football match. Watching other people run and jump and kick seemed smarter than trying to do any of that himself.

"Want a drink?" Kristi asked.

One of the warning labels on the pill bottle cautioned against driving or running machinery while taking the drugs, and advised that alcohol could make things worse. "Oh, Lord, yes!" Veit exclaimed.

She brought him a glass of slivovitz. She had one for herself, too. He recited the blessing over fruit. He wasn't too drug-addled to remember it. The plum brandy went down in a stream of sweet fire. "Anesthetic," Kristi said.

"Well, sure," Veit agreed. He made a point of getting good and anesthetized, too.

No matter how anesthetized he was, though, he couldn't lie on his stomach. It hurt too much. He didn't like going to bed on his back, but he didn't have much choice. Kristi turned out the light, then cautiously straddled him. Thanks to the stupid pain pills, that was no damn good, either. No matter how dopey he was, he took a long, long time to fall asleep.

———

They went back to Wawolnice the next morning. Cleanup crews had labored through the night. If you didn't live there, you wouldn't have known a pogrom had raged the day before. Just as well, too, because no pogrom was laid on for today. You couldn't run them too often. No matter how exciting they were, they were too wearing on everybody—although the Ministry of Justice never ran short on prisoners to be disposed of in interesting ways.

Putting on his ordinary clothes at the apartment had made Veit flinch. He'd swallowed a pain pill beforehand, but just the same... And changing into his Jew's outfit under Wawolnice hurt even more. No wonder: the left side of his ribcage was all over black-and-blue.

"That looks nasty," Reb Eliezer said sympathetically, pointing. "Are you coming to *shul* this morning?"

"*Fraygst nokh?*" Veit replied in Jakub's Yiddish. *Do you need to ask?* "Today I would even if it weren't my turn to help make the *minyan.*"

A couple of *yeshiva-bykher* were already poring over the Talmud when he got to the cramped little synagogue. The real books were back in place, then. The men who made up the ten required for services ranged in age from a couple just past their *bar-mitzvahs* to the *melamed's* thin, white-bearded father. If the old man's cough was only a performer's art, he deserved an award for it.

They all put on their *tefillin,* wrapping the straps of one on their left arms and wearing the other so the enclosed text from the Torah was between their eyes. Phylacteries was the secular name for *tefillin*. It had to do with the idea of guarding. Veit's aching ribs said he hadn't been guarded any too well the day before. Wrapped in his *tallis*, he stood there and went through the morning service's prayers with the rest of the men.

And he had a prayer of his own to add: the *Birkhas ha-gomel*, said after surviving danger. *"Barukh atah Adonai, eloheinu melekh ha-olam, ha-gomel lahavayim tovos sheg'malani kol tov."* Blessed art Thou, O lord, *our God, king of the universe, Who bestowest good things on the unworthy, and hast bestowed upon me every goodness.*

"Omayn," the rest of the *minyan* chorused. Their following response meant *May He Who has bestowed upon you every goodness continue to bestow every goodness upon you. Selah.*

At the send of the services, the *melamed*'s father poured out little shots of *shnaps* for everybody. He smacked his lips as he downed his. So did Veit. The two kids choked and coughed getting their shots down. Their elders smiled tolerantly. It wouldn't be long before the youngsters knocked back whiskey as easily and with as much enjoyment as everyone else.

One by one, the men went off to their work on the village. Reb Eliezer set a hand on Veit's arm as he was about to leave the *shul*. "I'm glad you remembered the *Birkhas ha-gomel*," the rabbi said quietly.

Veit raised an eyebrow. "What's not to remember? Only someone who isn't *frum* would forget such a thing. And, thank God, all the Jews in Wawolnice *are* pious." He stayed in character no matter how much it hurt. Right this minute, thanks to his ribs, it hurt quite a bit.

Eliezer's cat-green stare bored into him. To whom did the rabbi report? What did he say when he did? A Jew in a Polish village wouldn't have needed to worry about such things. A performer who was a Jew in a Polish village during working hours? You never could tell what somebody like that needed to worry about.

"Thank God," Reb Eliezer said now. He patted Veit on the back: gently, so as not to afflict him with any new pain. Then he walked over to the two men studying the Talmud and sat down next to one of them.

Part of Veit wanted to join the disputation, too. But the services were over. He had work waiting at the shop: not so much work as his wife would have liked, but work nonetheless. Eliezer did look up and nod to him as he slipped out of the *shul*. Then the rabbi went back to the other world, the higher world, of the Law and the two millennia of commentary on it and argument about it.

The day was dark, cloudy, gloomy. A horse-drawn wagon brought barrels of beer to the tavern. A skinny dog gnawed at something in the gutter. A Jewish woman in *sheitel* and headscarf nodded to Veit. He nodded back and slowly walked to his shop. He couldn't walk any other way, not today and not for a while.

A tall, plump, ruddy man in *Lederhosen* snapped his picture. As usual, Veit pretended the tourist didn't exist. When you thought about it, this was a strange business. Because it was, Veit did his best *not* to think about it most of the time.

Every now and then, though, you couldn't help wondering. During and after its victories in the War of Retribution, the *Reich* did just what the first *Führer* promised he would do: it wiped Jewry off the face of the earth. And, ever since destroying Jewry (no, even while getting on with the job), the Aryan victors studied and examined their victims in as much detail as the dead Jews had studied and examined Torah and Talmud. The Germans hadn't had two thousand years to split hairs about their researches, but they'd had more than a hundred now. Plenty of time for a whole bunch of *pilpul* to build up. And it had. It had.

Without that concentrated, minute study, a place like Wawolnice wouldn't just have been impossible. It would have been unimaginable. But the authorities wanted the world to see what a horrible thing it was that they'd disposed of. And so twenty-first-century Aryans lived the life of early twentieth-century Jews and Poles for the edification of…fat tourists in *Lederhosen*.

Repairmen had installed a new front window at the shop. Remarkably, they'd also sprayed it, or painted it, or whatever the hell they'd done, with enough dust and grime and general *shmutz* to make it look as if it had been there the past twenty years, and gone unwashed in all that time. Wawolnice was tended with, well, Germanic thoroughness. A clean window would have looked out of place, and so in went a dirty one.

As Veit opened up, the voices of the children chanting their lessons floated through the morning air. He'd been an adult when he came to the village. Would the boys grow up to become the next generation's tavern-keeper and rabbi and ragpicker…and maybe grinder and jack-of-all-trades? He wouldn't have been a bit surprised. The *Reich* built things to last. Chances were Wawolnice would still be here to instruct the curious about downfallen Judaism a generation from now, a century from now, five hundred years from now…

You learned in school that Hitler had said he intended his *Reich* to last for a thousand years. You also learned that the first *Führer* commonly meant what he said. But then, you had to be pretty stupid to need to learn that in school. Hitler's works were still all around, just as Augustus Caesar's must have been throughout the Roman Empire in the second century A.D.

Something on the floor sparkled. Veit bent and picked up a tiny shard of glass the cleaners had missed. He was almost relieved to chuck it into his battered tin wastebasket. Except for the lancinating pain in his side, it was almost the only physical sign he could find that the pogrom really had happened.

He settled onto his stool, shifting once or twice to find the position where his ribs hurt least. The chanted lessons came through the closed door, but only faintly. The kid who went around with the basket of bagels—no *kheder* for him, even though it was cheap—came by. Veit bought one. The kid scurried away. Veit smiled as he bit into the chewy roll. Damned if he didn't feel more at home in Yiddish than in ordinary German these days.

In came Itzhik the *shokhet*. "How's the world treating you these days?" Veit asked. Yes, this rasping, guttural jargon seemed natural in his mouth. And why not—*fur vos nit?*—when he used it so much?

"As well as it is, Jakub, thank the Lord," the ritual slaughterer answered. He often visited the grinder's shop. His knives had to be sharp. Any visible nick on the edge, and the animals he killed were *treyf*. He had to slay at a single stroke, too. All in all, what he did was as merciful as killing could be, just as Torah and Talmud prescribed. He went on, "And you? And your wife?"

"Bertha's fine. My ribs…could be better. They'll get that way—eventually," Veit said. *"Nu, what have you got for me today?"*

Itzhik carried his short knife, the one he used for despatching chickens and the occasional duck, wrapped in a cloth. "This needs to be perfect," he said. "Can't have the ladies running to Reb Eliezer with their dead birds, complaining I didn't kill them properly."

"That wouldn't be good," Veit agreed. He inspected the blade. The edge seemed fine to him. He said so.

"Well, sharpen it some more anyway," Itzhik answered.

Veit might have known he would say that. Veit, in fact, had known Itzhik would say that; he would have bet money on it. "You're a scrupulous man," he remarked as he set to work.

The *shokhet* shrugged. "If, *eppes*, you aren't scrupulous doing what I do, better you should do something else."

Which was also true of a lot of other things. After watching sparks fly from the steel blade, Veit carefully inspected the edge. The last thing he wanted was to put in a tiny nick that hadn't been there before. At length, he handed back the slaughtering knife. But, as he did, he said, "You'll want to check it for yourself."

"Oh, sure." Itzhik carried it over to the window—the window that might have stood there forgotten since the beginning of time but was in fact brand new. He held the knife in the best light he could find and bent close to examine the edge. He took longer looking it over than Veit had. When the verdict came, it was a reluctant nod, but a nod it was. "You haven't got a *shayla* on your *puppik,* anyway," he admitted.

"Thank you so much," Veit said with a snort. A *shayla* was a mark of disease that left meat unfit for consumption by Jews. His *puppik*—his gizzard—probably had a bruise on it right this minute, but no *shaylas.*

"So what do I owe you?" Itzhik asked.

"A zloty will do," Veit said. The *shokhet* set the coin on the counter. After one more nod, he walked out into the street.

Those chickens will never know what hit them, Veit thought, not without pride. The knife had been sharp when Itzhik handed it to him, and sharper after he got through with it. No one would be able to say its work went against Jewish rules for slaughtering.

Jewish rules held sway here, in Wawolnice's Jewish quarter. Out in the wider world, things were different. The *Reich* let the performers playing Poles here execute—no, encouraged them to execute—those convicts dressed as *shtetl* Jews by stoning them and beating them to death. Assume the convicts (or some of them, anyhow) deserved to die for their crimes. Did they deserve to die like that?

As Veit's recent argument with Reb Eliezer here in the shop showed, Jewish practice leaned over backward to keep from putting people to death, even when the letter of the law said they had it coming. He'd learned in his own Talmudic studies that an ancient Sanhedrin that executed even one man in seventy years went down in history as a bloody Sanhedrin.

Again, the modern world was a little different. Yes, just a little. The *Reich* believed in *Schrechlichkeit*—frightfulness—as a legal principle. If you scared the living shit out of somebody, maybe he wouldn't do what he would have done otherwise. And so the *Reich* didn't just do frightful things to people it caught and condemned. It bragged that it did such things to them.

Along with the quiz shows and football matches and historical melodramas and shows full of singers and dancers that littered the TV landscape, there were always televised hangings of partisans from Siberia or Canada or Peru. Sometimes, for variety's sake, the TV would show a Slav who'd presumed to sleep with his German mistress getting his head chopped off. Sometimes she would go to the block right after him, or even at his side.

All those executions, all those contorted faces and twisting bodies, all those fountains of blood, had been a normal part of the TV landscape for longer than Veit had been alive. He'd watched a few. Hell, everybody'd watched a few. He didn't turn them on because they turned him on, the way some people did. He'd always figured that put him on the right side of the fence.

Maybe it did—no, of course it did—when you looked at things from the *Reich*'s perspective. Which he did, and which everyone did, because, in the world as it was, what other perspective could there be? None, none whatsoever, not in the world as it was.

But Wawolnice wasn't part of the world as it was. Wawolnice was an artificial piece of the world as it had been before National Socialist Germany went and set it to rights. Performing here as a Jew, living here as a Jew, gave Veit an angle from which to view the wider world he could have got nowhere else.

And if the wider world turned out to be an uglier place than he'd imagined, than he could have imagined, before he came to Wawolnice, what did that say?

He'd been wrestling with the question ever since it first occurred to him. He was ashamed to remember how long that had taken. He wasn't the only one, either. To some of the reenactors who portrayed Jews, it was just another gig. They'd put it on their résumés and then go off and do something else, maybe on the legitimate stage, maybe not. Down in Romania, there was a Gypsy encampment that reproduced another way of life the National Socialist victory had eliminated.

For others here, things were different. You had to be careful what you said and where you said it, but that was true all over the *Reich,* which amounted to all over the world. Adding another layer of caution to the everyday one you grew up with probably—no, certainly—wouldn't hurt.

No sooner had that thought crossed his mind than the shop door swung open. In strode…not another village Jew, not a village Pole with something to fix that he trusted to Jakub's clever hands rather than to one of his countrymen, not even a tourist curious about what the inside of one of these hole-in-the-wall shops looked like. No. In came a man wearing the uniform of an SS *Hauptsturmführer:* the equivalent of a *Wehrmacht* captain.

Veit blinked, not sure what he was supposed to do. The Wawolnice in which he lived and worked—in which he performed—lay buried in a past before the War of Retribution. A Wawolnice Jew seeing an SS *Hauptsturmführer* would not automatically reduced to the blind panic that uniform induced in Jews during the war and for as long afterwards as there were still Jews. A modern Aryan still might be reduced to that kind of panic, though, or to something not far from it.

If a modern Aryan was reduced to that kind of panic, he would be smart to try not to show it. Veit let the *Hauptsturmführer* take the lead. The officer wasted no time doing so, barking, "You are the performer Veit Harlan, otherwise called Jakub Shlayfer the Jew?"

"That's right. What's this all about?" Veit answered in Yiddish.

The SS man's mouth twisted, as if at a bad smell. "Speak proper German, not this barbarous, disgusting dialect."

"Please excuse me, sir, but our instructions are to stay in character at all times when in public in the village," Veit said meekly, but still in the *mamaloshen*. He'd thought Yiddish was a barbarous dialect when he started learning it, too. The more natural it became, the less sure of that he got. You could say things in German you couldn't begin to in Yiddish. But the reverse, he'd been surprised to discover, also held true. Yiddish might be a jaunty beggar of a language, but a language it was.

All of which cut no ice with the *Hauptsturmführer*. He laid a sheet of paper on the counter. "Here is a directive from your project leader, releasing you from those instructions so you may be properly questioned."

Veit picked up the paper and read it. It was what the SS man said it was. *"Zu befehl, Herr Hauptsturmführer!"* he said, clicking his heels.

"That's more like it," the SS officer said smugly. Veit counted himself lucky that the fellow didn't notice obedience laid on with a trowel.

Making sure to treat his vowels the way an ordinary German would—in this shop, remembering wasn't easy; Veit felt as if he were using a foreign language, not his own—the reenactor said, "Sir, you still haven't told me what this is about."

"I would have, if you hadn't wasted my time." Nothing was going to be—nothing could possibly be—the *Hauptsturmführer*'s fault. He leaned toward Veit. No doubt he intended to intimidate, and he succeeded. "So tell me, Jew, what your rabbi meant by congratulating you on your prayer this morning."

He couldn't have practiced that sneer on authentic Jews. Authentic Jews were gone: gone from Germany, gone from Eastern Europe, gone from France and England, gone from North America, gone from Argentina, gone from Palestine, gone from South Africa, gone even from Shanghai and Harbin. Gone. *Spurlos verschwunden*—vanished without a trace. Off the map, literally and metaphorically. But he must have seen a lot of movies and TV shows and plays (Jews made favorite enemies, of course), because he had it down pat.

First things first, then. Veit pulled his wallet from an inside pocket on his coat and took out his identity card. He thrust it at the SS man. "*Herr Hauptsturmführer*, I am not a Jew. This proves my Aryan blood. I am a performer, paid to portray a Jew."

Grudgingly, the officer inspected the card. Grudgingly, he handed it back. "All right. You are not a Jew," he said, more grudgingly yet. "Answer my questions anyhow."

"You would do better asking him." Veit pressed his tiny advantage.

"Don't worry. Someone else is taking care of that." The officer stuck out his chin, which wasn't so strong as he might have wished. "Meanwhile, I'm asking you."

"All right. You have to understand, I'm only guessing, though. I think he meant I played my role well. I got hurt when the village staged a pogrom yesterday—a broken rib."

"Yes, I've seen the medical report," the SS man said impatiently. "Go on."

"A real Jew, a pious Jew, would have given the prayer of thanksgiving for coming through danger at the next *minyan* he was part of. I play a pious Jew, so I did what a pious Jew would do. The actor who plays the rabbi"—Veit came down hard on that—"must have thought it was a nice touch, and he was kind enough to tell me so. Please excuse me, but you're wasting your time trying to make anything more out of it."

"Time spent protecting the *Reich*'s security is never wasted." The *Hauptsturmführer* might have been quoting the Torah. He certainly was quoting his own Holy Writ. He stabbed a forefinger at Veit. "Besides, look at the village. This is a new day. The pogrom never happened."

"*Herr Hauptsturmführer*, they've fixed up the village overnight. My ribs still hurt," Veit said reasonably. He reached into a coat pocket again.

This time, he took out the plastic vial of pain pills. He displayed them in the palm of his hand.

The SS man snatched them away and examined the label. "Oh, yeah. This shit. They gave me some of this after they yanked my wisdom teeth. I was flying, man." As if embarrassed that the human being under the uniform had peeped out for a moment, he slammed the vial down on the counter.

Veit tucked the pills away. He tried to take advantage of the officer's slip, if that was what it was: "So you see how it goes, sir. I was just playing my role, just doing my job. If I have to act like a dirty Jew, I should act like the best dirty Jew I can, shouldn't I?"

"Dirty is right." The *Hauptsturmführer* jerked a thumb at the window behind him. "When's the last time somebody washed that?"

"I don't know, sir," Veit answered, which might have been technically true. He wasn't flying—his latest pill was wearing off—but he knew he might burst into hysterical laughter if he told the SS man that window had gone into place during the night to replace one smashed in the pogrom.

"Disgusting. And to think those pigdogs actually got off on living like this." The SS man shook his head in disbelief. "Fucking disgusting. So you remember you're playing a fucking part, you hear?"

"I always remember," Veit said, and that was nothing but the truth.

"You'd better." The *Hauptsturmführer* lumbered out of the shop. He slammed the door behind him. For a moment, Veit feared the glaziers would have another window to replace, but the pane held.

He wasn't due for the next pill for another hour, but he took one anyhow, and washed it down with a slug of plum brandy from a small bottle he kept in a drawer on his side of the counter. The warnings on the vial might say you shouldn't do that, but the warnings on the vial hadn't been written with visits from SS men in mind.

He wondered how Reb Eliezer's interrogation had gone. As they'd needed to, they'd picked a clever fellow to play the village rabbi. But the

SS specialized in scaring you so much, you forgot you had any brains. And if they were questioning Eliezer, maybe he didn't report to anybody after all. Maybe. All Eliezer had to do was stick to the truth here and everything would be fine... Veit hoped.

He also wondered if the rabbi would come over here to talk about what had happened. There, Veit hoped not. The *Hauptsturmführer* had proved that the *shul* was thoroughly bugged. No great surprise, that, but now it was confirmed. And if they'd just grilled one Jakub Shlayfer, grinder, the walls to his shop were bound to have ears, too. Would Reb Eliezer be clever enough to realize as much?

Eliezer must have been, because he didn't show up. Before long, the potent pill and the slivovitz made Veit not care so much. He got less work done than he might have. On the other hand, they didn't haul him off to a *Vernichtungslager*, either, so he couldn't count the day a dead loss.

———

"I'm tired," Kristi said as they walked across the parking lot to their car.

"Me, too." Veit moved carefully, like an old man. The rib still bit him every few steps.

"Want me to drive again, then?" his wife asked. She'd thrown out a hint, but he'd tossed it right back.

"Please, if you don't mind too much."

"It's all right," she said.

Veit translated that as *I mind, but not too much*. He waited till they were pulling onto the *Autobahn* before saying, "Let's stop somewhere in Lublin for supper."

"I've got those chicken legs defrosting at home," Kristi said doubtfully.

"Chuck 'em in the fridge when we get back," Veit said. "We'll have 'em tomorrow."

"Suits me." She sounded happy. "I didn't feel much like cooking tonight anyway."

"I could tell." That was one reason Veit had suggested eating out. It wasn't the only one. He hadn't told her anything about what had happened during the day. You had to assume the SS could hear anything that went on in Wawolnice. You also had to figure they could bug an Audi. But you had to hope they couldn't keep tabs on everything that went on in every eatery in Lublin.

"That looks like a good place," he said, pointing, as they went through town.

"But—" she began. He held a vertical finger in front of his lips, as if to say, *Yes, something is up.* No dope, Kristi got it right away. "Well, we'll give it a try, then," she said, and eased the car into a tight parking space at least as smoothly as Veit could have done it.

When they walked into the Boar's Head, the maître d' blinked at Veit's flowing beard. They weren't the style in the real world. But Veit talked like a rational fellow, and slipped him ten Reichsmarks besides. No zlotych here. They were village play money. Poland's currency was as dead as the country. The Reichsmark ruled the world no less than the *Reich* did. And ten of them were plenty to secure a good table.

Veit and Kristi ordered beer. The place was lively and noisy. People chattered. A band oompahed in the background. It was still early, but couples already spun on the dance floor. After the seidels came, Veit talked about the *Hauptsturmführer*'s visit in a low voice.

Her eyes widened in sympathy—and in alarm. "But that's so stupid!" she burst out.

"Tell me about it," Veit said. "I think I finally got through to him that it was all part of a day's work. I sure hope I did."

"Alevai omayn!" Kristi said. That was a slip of sorts, because it wasn't German, but you had to believe you could get away with a couple of words every now and then if you were in a safe place or a public place:

often one and the same. And the Yiddish phrase meant exactly what Veit was thinking.

"Are you ready to order yet?" The waitress was young and cute and perky. And she was well trained. Veit's whiskers didn't faze her one bit.

"I sure am." He pointed to the menu. "I want the ham steak, with the red-cabbage sauerkraut and the creamed potatoes."

"Yes, sir." She wrote it down. "And you, ma'am?"

"How is the clam-and-crayfish stew?" Kristi asked.

"Oh, it's very good!" The waitress beamed. "Everybody likes it. Last week, someone who used to live in Lublin drove down from Warsaw just to have some."

"Well, I'll try it, then."

When the food came, they stopped talking and attended to it. Once his plate was bare—which didn't take long—Veit blotted his lips on his napkin and said, "I haven't had ham that good in quite a while." He hadn't eaten any ham in quite a while, but he didn't mention that.

"The girl was right about the stew, too," his wife said. "I don't know that I'd come all the way from Warsaw to order it, but it's delicious."

Busboys whisked away the dirty dishes. The waitress brought the check. Veit gave her his charge card. She took it away to print out the bill. He scrawled his signature on the restaurant copy and put the customer copy and the car back in his wallet.

He and Kristi walked out to the car. On the way, she remarked, "Protective coloration." Probably no microphones out here—and it there were, a phrase like that could mean almost anything.

"*Jawohl,*" Veit agreed in no-doubt-about-it German. Now they'd put a couple of aggressively *treyf* meals in the computerized data system. Let some SS data analyst poring over their records go and call them Jews—or even think of them as Jews—after that!

Again, Veit got in on the passenger side. "You just want me to keep chauffeuring you around," Kristi teased.

"I want my ribs to shut up and leave me alone," Veit answered. "And if you do the same, I won't complain about that, either." She stuck out her tongue at him while she started the Audi. They were both laughing as she pulled out into traffic and headed home.

———

As the medical technician had warned, getting over a broken rib took about six weeks. The tech hadn't warned it would seem like forever. He also hadn't warned what would happen if you caught a cold before the rib finished knitting. Veit did. It was easy to do in a place like Wawolnice, where a stream of strangers brought their germs with them. Sure as hell, he thought he was ripping himself to pieces every time he sneezed.

But that too passed. At the time, Veit thought it passed like a kidney stone, but even Kristina was tired of his kvetching by then, so he did his best to keep his big mouth shut. It wasn't as if he had nothing to be happy about. The SS didn't call on him any more, for instance. He and his wife went back to the Boar's Head again. One *treyf* dinner after an interrogation might let analysts draw conclusions they wouldn't draw from more than one. And the food there *was* good.

He was pretty much his old self again by the time summer passed into fall and the High Holy Days—forgotten by everyone in the world save a few dedicated scholars…and the villagers and tourists at Wawolnice—came round again. He prayed in the *shul* on Rosh Hashanah, wishing everyone *L'shanah tovah*—a Happy New Year. That that New Year's Day was celebrated only in the village didn't bother him or any of the other performers playing Jews. It was the New Year for them, and they made the most of it with honey cakes and raisins and sweet kugels and other such poor people's treats.

A week and a half later came Yom Kippur, the Day of Atonement, the most solemn day of the Jewish calendar. By that extinct usage, the daylong fast began the night before at sundown. Veit and his wife were driving home from Wawolnice when the sun went down behind them. He sat behind the wheel; he'd been doing most of the driving again for some time.

When they got to their flat, Kristi turned on the oven. She left it on for forty-five minutes. Then she turned it off again. She and Veit sat at the table and talked as they would have over supper, but there was no food on the plates. After a while, Kristi washed them anyhow. Neither a mike nor utility data would show anything out of the ordinary.

How close to the ancient laws did you have to stick? In this day and age, how close to the ancient laws could you possibly stick? How careful did you have to be to make sure the authorities didn't notice you were sticking to those laws? Veit and Kristi had played games with the oven and the dishwashing water before. In light of the call the SS *Hauptsturmführer* had paid on Veit earlier in the year (last year now, by Jewish reckoning), you couldn't be too careful—and you couldn't stick too close to the old laws.

So you did what you could, and you didn't worry about what you couldn't help. That seemed to fit in with the way things in Wawolnice generally worked.

At *shul* the next morning, Kristi sat with the women while Veit took his place among the men. How many of the assembled reenactors were fasting except when public performance of these rituals required it? Veit didn't know; it wasn't a safe question, and wouldn't have been good manners even if it were. But he was as sure as made no difference that Kristi and he weren't the only ones.

After the service ended, he asked his village friends and neighbors to forgive him for whatever he'd done to offend them over the past year. You had to apologize sincerely, not just go through the motions. And you were supposed to accept such apologies with equal sincerity. His fellow villagers were saying they were sorry to him and to one another, too.

Such self-abasement was altogether alien to the spirit of the *Reich*. Good National Socialists never dreamt they could do anything regrettable. *Übermenschen*, after all, didn't look back—or need to.

And yet, the heartfelt apologies of an earlier Yom Kippur were some of the first things that had made Veit wonder whether what people here in Wawolnice had wasn't a better way to live than much of what went on in the wider world. He'd come here glad to have steady work. He hadn't bargained for anything more. He hadn't bargained for it, but he'd found it.

You needed to ignore the funny clothes. You needed to forget about the dirt and the crowding and the poverty. Those were all incidentals. When it came to living with other people, when it came to finding an anchor for your own life... He nodded once, to himself. This was better. Even if you couldn't talk about it much, maybe especially because you couldn't, this was better. It had taken a while for Veit to realize it, but he liked the way he lived in the village when he was Jakub Shlayfer better than he liked how he lived away from it when he was only himself.

———

People who worked together naturally got together when they weren't working, too. Not even the ever-wary SS could make too much of that. There was always the risk that some of the people you hung with reported to the blackshirts, but everyone in the *Reich* ran that risk. You took the precautions you thought you needed and you got on with your life.

One weekend not long after the high Holy Days, Wawolnice closed down for maintenance more thorough than repair crews could manage overnight or behind the scenes. Autumn was on the way. By the calendar, autumn had arrived. But it wasn't pouring or freezing or otherwise nasty, though no doubt it would be before long. A bunch of the reenactors who played Jews seized the moment for a Sunday picnic outside of Lublin.

The grass on the meadow was still green: proof it hadn't started freezing yet. Women packed baskets groaning with food. Men tended to other essentials: beer, slivovitz, *shnaps,* and the like.

One of Kristi's cousins was just back from a hunting trip to the Carpathians. Her contribution to the spread was a saddle of venison. Her cousin was no *shokhet,* of course, but some things were too good to pass up. So she reasoned, anyhow, and Veit didn't try to argue with her.

"Let's see anybody match this," she declared.

"Not likely." Veit had splurged on a couple of liters of fancy vodka, stuff so smooth you'd hardly notice you weren't drinking water…till you fell over.

He waited for clouds to roll in and rain to spoil things, but it didn't happen. A little dawn mist had cleared out by midmorning, when the performers started gathering. It wasn't a hot day, but it wasn't bad. If shadows stretched farther across the grass than they would have during high summer, well, it wasn't high summer anymore.

Kids scampered here, there, and everywhere, squealing in German and Yiddish. Not all of them really noticed any difference between the two languages except in the way they were written. Lots of reenactors exclaimed over the venison. Kristi beamed with pride as Reb Eliezer said "I didn't expect that" and patted his belly in anticipation. If he wasn't going to get fussy about dietary rules today…

They might have been any picnicking group, but for one detail. A car going down the narrow road stopped. The driver rolled down his window and called, "Hey, what's with all the face fuzz?" He rubbed his own smooth chin and laughed.

"We're the Great Lublin Beard-Growers' Fraternity," Eliezer answered with a perfectly straight face.

All of a sudden, the Aryan in the VW wasn't laughing any more. The official-sounding title impressed him; official-sounding titles had a way of doing that in the *Reich.* *"Ach, so.* The Beard-Growers'

Fraternity," he echoed. "That's splendid!" He put the car in gear and drove away, satisfied.

"Things would be easier if we *were* the Greater Lublin Beard-Growers' Fraternity," Veit remarked.

"Some ways," Reb Eliezer said with a sweet, sad smile. "Not others, perhaps."

Alter the *melamed*—otherwise Wolf Albach-Retty—said, "There really are clubs for men who grow fancy whiskers. They have contests. Sometimes the winners get their pictures in the papers."

"Our whiskers are just incidental." Veit stroked his beard. "We raise *tsuris* instead."

Wolf hoisted an eyebrow. Yes, he made a good *melamed*. Yes, he was as much a believer as anyone here except Reb Eliezer. (Like Paul on the road to Damascus—well, maybe not *just* like that—some years before, Eliezer had been the first to see how a role could take on an inner reality the Nazi functionaries who'd brought Wawolnice into being had never imagined.) All that said, everyone here except Wolf himself knew he was a ham.

If the SS swooped down on this gathering, what would they find? A bunch of men with beards, along with wives, girlfriends, children, and a few dogs running around barking and generally making idiots of themselves. A hell of a lot of food. No ham, no pig's trotters, no pickled eels, no crayfish or mussels. No meat cooked in cream sauce or anything like that. Even more dishes than you'd normally need for all the chow.

Plenty to hang everybody here, in other words, or to earn people a bullet in the back of the neck. Suspicious security personnel could make all the case they needed from what was and what wasn't at the picnic. And if they weren't suspicious, why would they raid?

Someone here might also be wearing a microphone or carrying a concealed video camera. Being a Jew hadn't stopped Judas from betraying

Jesus. Even the so-called German Christians, whose worship rendered more unto the *Reich* than unto God, learned about Judas.

But what could you do? You had to take some chances or you couldn't live. Well, you could, but you'd have to stay by yourself in your flat and never come out. Some days, that looked pretty good to Veit. Some days, but not today.

Reb Eliezer did what he could to cover himself. He waved his hands in the air to draw people's notice. Then he said, "It's good we could all get together today." He was speaking Yiddish; he said *haynt* for *today,* not the German *heute.* He went on, "We need to stay in our roles as much as we can. We live them as much as we can. So if we do some things our friends and neighbors outside Wawolnice might find odd, it's only so we keep them in mind even when we aren't up in front of strangers."

Several men and women nodded. Kids and dogs, predictably, paid no attention. What Eliezer said might save the reenactors' bacon (*Not that we've got any bacon here, either,* Veit thought) if the SS was keeping an eye on things without worrying too much. If the blackshirts were looking for sedition, they'd know bullshit when they heard it.

"All right, then." Eliezer went on to pronounce a *brokhe,* a blessing, that no one—not even the most vicious SS officer, a Rottweiler in human shape—could have found fault with: "Let's eat!"

Women with meat dishes had gathered here, those with dairy dishes over there, and those with *parve* food—vegetable dishes that could be eaten with either—at a spot in between them. Veit took some sour tomatoes and some cold noodles and some green beans in a sauce made with olive oil and garlic (not exactly a specialty of Polish Jews in the old days, but tasty even so), and then headed over to get some of the venison on which his wife had worked so hard. Kristi would let him hear about it if he didn't take a slice.

He had to wait his turn, though. By the time he got over to her, a line had already formed. She beamed with pride as she carved and served. Only somebody else's roast grouse gave her any competition for pride of place. Veit managed to snag a drumstick from one of the birds, too. He sat down on the grass and started filling his face…after the appropriate blessings, of course.

After a while, Reb Eliezer came over and squatted beside him. Eliezer seemed a man in perpetual motion. He'd already talked with half the people at the picnic, and he'd get to the rest before it finished. "Having a good time?" he asked.

Veit grinned and waved at his plate. "I'd have to be dead not to. I don't know how I'm going to fit into my clothes."

"That's a good time," Eliezer said, nodding. "I wonder what the Poles are doing with their holiday."

He meant the Aryans playing Poles in Wawolnice, of course. The real Poles, those who were left alive, worked in mines and on farms and in brothels and other places where bodies mattered more than brains. Veit stayed in character to answer, "They should grow like onions: with their heads in the ground."

Eliezer smiled that sad smile of his. "And they call us filthy kikes and Christ-killers and have extra fun when there's a pogrom on the schedule." Veit rubbed his ribcage. Eliezer nodded again. "Yes, like that."

"Still twinges once in a while," Veit said.

"Hating Jews is easy," Eliezer said, and it was Veit's turn to nod. The other man went on, "Hating anybody who isn't just like you is easy. Look how you sounded about them. Look how the Propaganda Ministry sounds all the time."

"Hey!" Veit said. "That's not fair."

"Well, maybe yes, maybe no," Reb Eliezer allowed. "But the way it looks to me is, if we're going to live like *Yehudim*, like the *Yehudim* that used to be, like proper *Yehudim*, sooner or later we'll have to do it all the time."

"What?" Now Veit was genuinely alarmed. "We won't last twenty minutes if we do, and you know it."

"I didn't meant that. Using *tefillin?* Putting on the *tallis?* No, it wouldn't work." Eliezer smiled once more, but then quickly sobered. "I meant that we need to live, to think, to feel the way we do while we're in Wawolnice when we're out in the big world, too. We need to be witnesses to what the *Reich* is doing. Somebody has to, and who better than us?" That smile flashed across his face again, if only for a moment. "Do you know what *martyr* means in ancient Greek? It means *witness,* that's what."

Veit had sometimes wondered if the rabbi was the SS plant in the village. He'd decided it didn't matter. If Eliezer was, he could destroy them all any time he chose. But now Veit found himself able to ask a question that would have been bad manners inside Wawolnice: "What did you do before you came to the village that taught you ancient Greek?" As far as he knew, Eliezer—Ferdinand Marian—hadn't been an actor. Veit had never seen him on stage or in a TV show or film.

"Me?" The older man quirked an eyebrow. "I thought everyone had heard about me. No?… I guess not. I was a German Christian minister."

"Oh," Veit said. It didn't quite come out *Oy!,* but it might as well have. He managed something a little better on his next try: "Well, no wonder you learned Greek, then."

"No wonder at all. And Hebrew, and Aramaic. I was well trained for the part, all right. I just didn't know ahead of time that I would like it better than what had been my real life."

"I don't think any of us figured on that," Veit said slowly.

"I don't, either," Reb Eliezer replied. "But if that doesn't tell you things aren't the way they ought to be out here, what would?" His two-armed waved encompassed *out here:* the world beyond Wawolnice, the world-bestriding *Reich.*

"What do we do?" Veit shook his head; that was the wrong question. Again, another try: "What *can* we do?"

Eliezer set a hand on his shoulder. "The best we can, Jakub. Always, the best we can." He ambled off to talk to somebody else.

Someone had brought along a soccer ball. In spite of full bellies, a pickup game started. It would have caused heart failure in World Cup circles. The pitch was bumpy and unmown. Only sweaters thrown down on the ground marked the corners and the goal mouths. Touchlines and bylines were as much a matter of argument as anything in the Talmud.

Nobody cared. People ran and yelled and knocked one another ass over teakettle. Some of the fouls would have got professionals sent off. The players just laughed about them. Plenty of liquid restoratives were at hand by the edge of the pitch. When the match ended, both sides loudly proclaimed victory.

By then, the sun was sliding down the sky toward the horizon. Clouds had started building up. With regret, everyone decided it was time to go home. Leftovers and dirty china and silverware went into ice chests and baskets. Nobody seemed to worry about supper at all.

Veit caught up with Reb Eliezer. "Thanks for not calling Kristina's venison *treyf*," he said quietly.

Eliezer spread his hands. "It wasn't that kind of gathering, or I didn't think it was. I didn't say anything about the grouse, either. Like I told you before, you do what you can do. Anyone who felt differently didn't have to eat it. No finger-pointing. No fits. Just—no game."

"Makes sense." Veit hesitated, then blurted the question that had been on his mind most of the day: "What do you suppose the old-time Jews, the real Jews, would have made of us?"

"I often wonder about that," Eliezer said, which surprised Veit not at all. The older man went on, "You remember what Rabbi Hillel told the *goy* who stood on one foot and asked him to define Jewish doctrine before the other foot came down?"

"Oh, sure," Veit answered; that was a bit of Talmudic *pilpul* everybody—well, everybody in Wawolnice who cared about the Talmud—knew. "He said that you shouldn't do to other people whatever was offensive to you. As far as he was concerned, the rest was just commentary."

"The Talmud says that *goy* ended up converting, too," Eliezer added. Veit nodded; he also remembered that. Eliezer said, "Well, if the *Reich* had followed Hillel's teaching, there would still be real Jews, and they wouldn't have needed to invent us. Since they did… We're doing as well as we can on the main thing—we're human beings, after all—and maybe not too bad on the commentary. Or do you think I'm wrong?"

"No. That's about how I had it pegged, too." Veit turned away, then stopped short. "I'll see you tomorrow in Wawolnice."

"Tomorrow in Wawolnice," Eliezer said. "Next year in Jerusalem."

"Alevai omayn," Veit answered, and was astonished by how much he meant it.

———

They wouldn't have needed to invent us. For some reason, that fragment of a sentence stuck in Veit's mind. He knew Voltaire's *If God did not exist, it would be necessary to invent him.* Before coming to Wawolnice, he'd been in a couple of plays involving the Frenchman. Frederick the Great had been one of Hitler's heroes, which had made the Prussian king's friends and associates glow by reflected light in the eyes of German dramatists ever since.

If a whole *Volk* had nobody who could look at them from the outside, would they have to find—or make—someone? There, Veit wasn't so sure. Like any actor's, his mind was a jackdaw's nest of other men's words. He knew the story about the dying bandit chief and the priest who urged him to forgive his enemies. *Father, I have none,* the old ruffian wheezed. *I've killed them all.*

Here stood the *Reich,* triumphant. Its retribution had spread across the globe. It hadn't quite killed all its enemies. No: it had enslaved some of them instead. But no one cared what a slave thought. No one even cared if a slave thought, so long as he didn't think of trouble.

Here stood Wawolnice. It had come into being as a monument to the *Reich*'s pride. *Look at what we did. Look at what we had to get rid of,* it had declared, reproducing with typical, fanatical attention to detail what once had been. And such attention to detail had, all unintended, more or less brought back into being what had been destroyed. It was almost Hegelian.

After talking with Kristina, Veit decided to have the little operation that would mark him as one of the men who truly belonged in Wawolnice. He got it done the evening before the village shut down for another maintenance day. "You should be able to go back to work day after tomorrow," the doctor told him. "You'll be sore, but it won't be anything the pills can't handle."

"Yes, I know about those." Of itself, Veit's hand made that rib-feeling gesture.

"All right, then." The other man uncapped a syringe. "This is the local anesthetic. You may not want to watch while I give it to you."

"You bet I don't." Veit looked up at the acoustic tiles on the treatment room's ceiling. The shot didn't hurt much—less than he'd expected. Still, it wasn't something you wanted to think about; no, indeed.

Chuckling, the doctor said, "Since you're playing one of those miserable, money-grubbing kikes, of course you'll be happy about the raise you're getting for going all out."

"As long as my eel still goes up after this, that's the only raise I care about right now," Veit answered. The doctor laughed again and went to work.

Bandaging up afterwards took longer than the actual procedure. As Veit was carefully pulling up his pants, the doctor said, "Take your first pill in about an hour. That way, it'll be working when the local wears off."

"That would be good," Veit agreed. He got one more laugh from the man in the white coat. No doubt everything seemed funnier when you were on the other end of the scalpel.

He didn't have Kristi drive home; he did it himself, with his legs splayed wide. He couldn't feel anything—the anesthetic was still going strong—but he did even so. He dutifully swallowed the pill at the appointed time. Things started hurting anyway: hurting like hell, not to put too fine a point on it. Veit gulped another pill. It was too soon after the first, but he did it all the same.

Two pain pills were better than one, but not enough. He still hurt. The pills did make his head feel like a balloon attached to his body on a long string. What happened from his neck down was still there, but only distantly connected to the part of him that noticed.

He ate whatever Kristi put on the table. Afterwards, he remembered eating, but not what he'd eaten.

He wandered out into the front room and sat down in front of the TV. He might do that any evening to unwind from a long day of being a Jew, but this felt different. The screen in front of him swallowed all of his consciousness that didn't sting.

Which was odd, because the channel he'd chosen more or less at random was showing a string of ancient movies: movies from before the War of Retribution, movies in black and white. Normally, Veit had no patience for that. He lived in a black-and-white world in Wawolnice. When he watched the television, he wanted something brighter, something more interesting.

Tonight, though, with the two pain pills pumping through him, he just didn't care. The TV was on. He'd watch it. He didn't have to think while he stared at the pictures. Something called *Bringing up Baby* was running. It was funny even though it was dubbed. It was funny even though he was drugged.

When it ended and commercials came on, they seemed jarringly out of place. They were gaudy. They were noisy. Veit couldn't wait for them to end and the next old film to start.

It finally did. *Frankenstein* was about as from from *Bringing up Baby* as you could get and still be called a movie. Some of the antique special effects seemed unintentionally comic to a modern man, even if the modern man was doped to the eyebrows. But Veit ended up impressed in spite of himself. As with the comedy, no wonder people still showed this one more than a hundred years after it was made.

He took one more green pill after the movie and staggered off to bed. He slept like a log, assuming logs take care to sleep on their backs.

When he woke up the next morning, he wasn't as sore as he'd thought he would be. And he'd rolled over onto his side during the night and hadn't perished, or even screamed. He did take another pill, but he didn't break any Olympic sprint records running to the kitchen to get it.

"You poor thing," Kristi said. "Your poor thing."

"I'll live." Veit decided he might even mean it. Once he soaked up some coffee and then some breakfast—and once that pill kicked in— he might even want to mean it.

Caffeine, food, and opiate did indeed work wonders. His wife nodded approvingly. "You don't have that glazed look you did last night."

"Who, me?" Veit hadn't been sure he could manage indignation, but he did.

Not that it helped. "Yes, you," Kristi retorted. "You don't sit there gaping at the TV for three hours straight with drool running down your chin when you're in your right mind."

"But it was good." No sooner had Veit said it than he wondered whether he would have thought so if he hadn't been zonked. Kristina's raised eyebrow announced louder than words that she wondered exactly the same thing.

Maybe he wouldn't have enjoyed the silliness in *Bringing up Baby* so much if he'd been fully in the boring old Aristotelian world. But *Frankenstein* wasn't silly—not even slightly. Taking pieces from the dead, putting them together, and reanimating them... No, nothing even the least bit silly about that.

As a matter of fact… His jaw dropped. *"Der Herr Gott im Himmel,"* he whispered, and then, *"Vey iz mir!"*

"What is it?" Kristi asked.

"Wawolnice," Veit said.

"Well, what about it?" his wife said.

But he shook his head. "You weren't watching the movie last night." He didn't know what she had been doing. Anything that hadn't been right in front of him or right next to him simply wasn't there. She'd stuck her head into the front room once or twice—probably to make sure he could sit up straight—but she hadn't watched.

And you needed to have. Because what was Wawolnice but a Frankenstein village of Jews? It wasn't meant to have come to life on its own, but it had, it had. So far, the outsiders hadn't noticed. No mob of peasants with torches and pitchforks had swarmed in to destroy it—only performers playing Poles, who were every bit as artificial.

How long could they go on? Could they possibly spread? Reb Eliezer thought so. Veit wasn't nearly as sure. But Eliezer might be right. He might. One more time, *alevai omayn.*

ZIGEUNER

Hauptsturmführer Joseph Stieglitz looked up into the gloomy gray late-October sky. Drizzle speckled the lenses of the SS officer's steel-framed spectacles. It wasn't really raining, but it also wasn't really not raining. Muttering, he pulled a handkerchief from the right front pocket of his *Feldgrau* trousers and got his glasses as clean as he could.

He peered across the town square, then nodded to himself. Yes, the *Kübelwagens* and the trucks were ready. Everything here in Zalaegerszeg seemed peaceful enough. Yes, the town lay in Hungary, but on the west side of the Platten-See (on Magyar maps, it was Lake Balaton). Off in the eastern part of the country, the *Wehrmacht* and the *Waffen*-SS and the Hungarian *Honvéd* were fighting thunderous panzer battles to try to halt or at least slow the onrushing Red Army.

Better not to dwell on that too much. Better to hope the Germans could use their now-shorter supply lines to advantage. Better to hope the *Honvéd* would fight hard now that it was defending its homeland. Better to hope Ferenc Szalasi and his Arrow Cross Fascists would make the *Honvéd* fight harder than Admiral Horthy had. Horthy the trimmer, Horthy the traitor, Horthy who'd tried to fix up a separate peace with

261

Russia till the *Führer* got wind of it and overthrew him before he could make it stick.

Because if you did dwell on that, if you looked at where the Red Army was and at how far it had come since the start of summer, what could you do but realize the war was lost? Like almost all German officers in the autumn of 1944, Joseph Stieglitz made the effort of will he needed not to realize that.

He walked across the square toward the transport he'd laid on. The hobnailed soles of his jackboots clicked on the cobbles. The drizzle was turning the stones slippery; he planted his feet with care so he wouldn't take a tumble. As long as he kept his head down, the patent-leather brim of his cap protected his glasses well enough.

Some of the men in the *Kübelwagens* wore German *Feldgrau* like Stieglitz. Others were in Hungarian khaki. Despite the brown *Stahlhelms* on their heads, they were militiamen, not real soldiers; their Arrow Cross armbands showed as much. The truck drivers were also Hungarians. *Hauptsturmführer* Stieglitz shrugged. For this operation, he probably wouldn't need anything more.

His driver was an *Unterscharführer* named Klaus Pirckheimer. The junior noncom waved as Stieglitz came up. "We're all ready, sir," he said. "Let's go clean those bastards out."

"Sounds good to me." Stieglitz slid into the right front bucket seat.

Pirckheimer started the engine. As he did so, the bells of the Catholic church on the square chimed the hour: ten in the morning. The *Hauptsturmführer* had gone into the church to admire its eighteenth-century frescoes. Though no Catholic himself, he appreciated fine art wherever he found it. He was, and worked at being, a man of *Kultur*.

The road leading south had been blacktopped, but not recently. Some of the potholes the *Kübelwagen* hit seemed big enough to swallow the utility vehicle. But it kept going. It didn't have four-wheel drive like an American jeep, but was surprisingly nimble even traveling cross-country.

"Don't miss the turnoff, Klaus," Stieglitz said. "We want the right-hand fork, remember."

"Zu Befehl, mein Herr!" Somehow, in Pirckheimer's mouth, a simple *Yes, sir!* sounded more like *Why don't you shut up and leave me alone?*

He did find the fork—just in time, with a hard right turn, to keep from driving past it. The rest of the column followed his lead. No sign marked the road's branching. Maybe there had been one before the war drew near, and the local authorities took it down to give invaders a harder time navigating. More likely, the turnoff never was important enough to mark.

A couple of kilometers past the turnoff, maybe ten kilometers out of Zalaegerszeg, lay the village of Nagylengyel. Though it too boasted a Catholic church, it couldn't have held more than three or four hundred people. Two grannies were selling beans and grapes at a little roadside market. An old man hawked sausages on a folding table and had a half-grown pig on a rope tied to one of the table legs. Business looked slow.

"We're getting close, hey, *Herr Hauptsturmführer?*" Pirckheimer said.

"Well, I hope so," Joseph Stieglitz replied. "The *Zigeuner* encampment was reported to be three kilometers south of Nagylengyel. SS headquarters in Szombathely got the word a couple of days ago. They didn't waste any of their precious time telling *me* about it till last night, of course."

"Of course," the driver agreed. Stieglitz was an officer, but officers and enlisted men united in sneering at the headquarters oafs who didn't bother to let them know what was going on. Pirckheimer went on, "Gotta be better than even money the rats have found a new hole between then and now."

"If they have, we'll find them," Stieglitz said, shrugging. "If we don't find them today, we'll find them tomorrow. If we don't find them tomorrow, somebody else will next week."

"And then they'll get what's coming to the, the stinking *Untermenschen*," Pirckheimer said.

"*Ja,*" the *Hauptsturmführer* agreed, though he preferred not to think about that too much. His job was rounding up the *Zigeuner* and arranging for them to be transported. What happened after they got where they were going to... That was none of his business. The fewer questions you asked about such things, the less you officially knew, the better off you were. But there had been almost a million *Zigeuner* in Europe when the war started. If any were left when fighting finally stopped, it wouldn't be for lack of effort.

———

The *Kübelwagen* rounded one more corner. Klaus Pirckheimer let out a happy little yip. "They *are* still here! Too dumb even to run, looks like."

Another *Zigeuner* encampment, as filthy and disorderly as all the rest. Six or eight wagons that looked as if they'd been designed and possibly built in the seventeenth century sat on the grass by the side of the road. The donkeys that pulled them when they were on the move grazed one here, one there, one somewhere else. The sorry beasts were scrawny and tiny: hardly bigger than large dogs. To give comparison, a couple of big, toothy, plainly mean dogs prowled among them and started barking as the vehicles neared.

A motley assortment of tents sheltered the *Zigeuner* from the elements. By the faded paintings on its canvas, one had come from a traveling circus a long time ago. Another... The *Hauptsturmführer*'s mouth twisted. It was assembled from no doubt stolen German shelter halves. *Zigeuner* produced next to nothing for themselves, but they were first-rate thieves.

"Pull past them and stop," Stieglitz said.

"I'll do it, sir," his driver replied, and did. The other *Kübelwagens* and the trucks halted behind the first.

SS men and Arrow Cross militiamen hopped out of the vehicles. The Germans carried Schmeissers or captured Russian PPDs. The submachine guns weren't worth much out past a couple of hundred meters, but they made dandy intimidators at close range. The Hungarians had Mausers and pistols.

Stieglitz himself wore a Walther P-38 on his belt, but didn't unholster it yet. Instead, he cupped both hands in front of his mouth and bellowed, *"Alle Zigeuner raus!"* For good measure, he added, *"Sofort!"* Right away!

Out they came: swarthy, sharp-nosed, feral-looking men and women in shabby clothes, some of the women's outfits ornamented with incongruously bright embroidery. They all wore the brown triangle, point down, required of their kind; they didn't break the law in such small ways.

A skinny, gray-mustached fellow who looked like a pimp down on his luck spoke to the others in the gibberish the *Zigeuner* used among themselves. Their dark, frightened eyes went back and forth from Stieglitz to him.

The leader of the pack, the *Hauptsturmführer* thought. He pointed at the man. *"Du! Sprichst du Deutsch?"* He used the familiar pronoun, as he would have with children or servants or anyone else with whom he didn't have to bother staying polite.

Only a string of that incomprehensible lingo came back at him. Stieglitz rolled his eyes. He could have just taken out the pistol and pointed with it. That probably would have worked. But the *Zigeuner* might have panicked if he gave orders with the barrel of a gun. They were liable to have a shotgun or two in the tents or in their wagons. If a hothead grabbed one, he might hurt somebody before he could be disposed of.

So Stieglitz turned to the Hungarian lieutenant who headed up the militiamen. *"Sprechen Sie Deutsch?"* With the Hungarian, who was on his side, he used the formal pronoun.

But the man spread his hands and shook his head. He answered in Hungarian. That did the *Hauptsturmführer* as little good as the nonsense the *Zigeuner* spouted.

He eyed the rest of the Hungarians. The armed militiamen were all young, like their officer. One of the truck drivers, though, had graying hair and the beginnings of a wattle under his chin. He was bound to to be close to fifty. Stieglitz walked over to him. "How about you?" he asked. "Do *you* speak German?"

"Military German," the said. Stieglitz nodded; that was what he'd hoped for. German had been the language of command in the Austro-Hungarian army during the last war. Basic words got drilled into soldiers of all nationalities. Then the Magyar unbent enough to go on: "Maybe more than military German. We had a division from the Kaiser's army on our left for a while in the Carpathians, and we got friendly with them. I think it was the one your *Führer* served in."

"Ach, so." Joseph Stieglitz nodded. "It could be." He knew the *Führer* had fought against the Russians in World War I. Everybody knew that. It was where he'd acquired his rancorous hatred for the *Zigeuner*. They'd stolen horses and boots and telegraph wire from his outfit, and cost it casualties it wouldn't have taken if they hadn't prowled around. Now he was taking his revenge on them, as he had on so many others.

Which Austro-Hungarian division had served on the German unit's flank, Stieglitz couldn't have said. That didn't much matter, though.

"Translate for me, will you?" he said to the truck driver. "They may act like they don't speak German, but I don't think they can pretend they don't know any Hungarian."

"I'll do it, *Herr* Major," the driver replied. He could read German shoulder straps, anyway. Stieglitz's SS rank was equivalent to major in the *Wehrmacht*.

"Danke schön," Stieglitz said. "Tell them we're going to put them in the trucks and transport them up to Zalaegerszeg."

He waited for the veteran to translate that. As soon as the man did, the old villain who led this band of *Zigeuner* let loose with his own torrent of Hungarian. "He says, What will you do with us there?" the truck driver reported.

Stieglitz suspected the chieftain said some other things as well, but that would do for now. "We'll put you on a train with others of their folk," the *Hauptsturmführer* said. "We'll take you to resettlement camps in Poland, far away from the fighting. You'll be well housed there, and well fed."

The driver duly translated. The chieftain said, "But we like it where we are now just fine. We don't want to be resettled."

"It's a matter of military necessity," Stieglitz said, trying not to meet the *Zigeuner*'s dark and piercing gaze. He told the old bandit what his superiors instructed him to say whenever he rounded up a band of these subhumans. Maybe it was true; maybe it wasn't. Poking into that wasn't good for your career. If you poked too hard, it wasn't good for your own safety.

"Why is it military necessity for us to get shipped away and not for the Hungarians?" the chieftain asked after he got that turned into a language he could follow.

"Because the Hungarians are allies of the *Reich*," Stieglitz answered. "We trust their loyalty." *We do now, with Horthy out and Szalasi in. Szalasi has no more use for* Zigeuner *than the* Führer *does.*

"It doesn't matter whether we're loyal or not," the old man insisted. "We want nothing to do with this cursed war." He spewed out more of his own jargon. The rest of the *Zigeuner* bobbed their heads up and down in unison to show they wanted nothing to do with it, either.

"I'm sorry, but it's not as simple as you make it out to be. That's why I have my orders, and why I'll carry them out." Joseph Stieglitz let the truck driver translate that, then continued, "Besides, it's for your own safety. Some *Zigeuner* bands have stolen from German supplies. Some have spied and scouted for the Red Army. You can guess what happened to them after that."

"We would never do any such wicked things! By the Mother of God, I swear it!" The chieftain made the sign of the cross. After he told his chicken thieves and slatterns and brats why he did it, they crossed themselves, too.

The SS officer was not a Christian. The SS discouraged religious observances of any kind. He strongly doubted the *Zigeuner* were Christians, either. They were for themselves, first, last, and always. *Cockroaches and rats with—almost—human faces,* he thought, curling his lip in distaste.

"Look, tell him I didn't come here to argue with him," he said to the Hungarian truck driver. "Tell him I came here to relocate his band. I'll do that peacefully if I can. If I can't, I'll do it anyway. He won't like that so much. Make sure he understands how much he won't like it."

"Yes, sir. I'll do it, sir." The driver could have sounded no more obedient if he were a German. By the way he pointed at the submachine guns and rifles the SS men and Arrow Cross militiamen carried, he was making the point with gestures as well as with his jabbering.

Stieglitz watched the air leak out of the *Zigeuner* chieftain as he weighed his chances and found them bad. He deflated still more when he tried to choose between bad and worse. He didn't realize even yet that none of his choices was merely bad; they were all worse. The *Hauptsturmführer* didn't aim to enlighten him on that score. Soon enough, he'd find out for himself.

His lined, tanned face a mask of bitterness, he said something in his own lingo. A couple of the younger *Zigeuner* men started to gabble out protests. As the truck driver had before him, the chieftain pointed to the weapons the Germans and Hungarians held at the ready. He spoke again. Stieglitz didn't need to know what the words meant to get the drift. *What can we do? They'll murder us right here if we give them grief.*

He was right. The young bucks in the band could see it, too. They might not like it, but they could see it. They subsided.

Wearily, the mustachioed villain switched back to Magyar. "He says he and his people will go to the train with you, sir," the truck driver told Stieglitz. "He says he relies on your honor as a German officer that everything will work out the way you told him it would."

"Mein Ehre heisst Treue." Joseph Stieglitz quoted the SS motto—*my honor is loyalty.* And it was. He was loyal unto death to the *Führer.* He was just as loyal to the *Reichsführer*-SS, the commander-in-chief of the Black Corps. To an unwashed old *Zigeuner?* That might be a different story.

By the look in the old man's eye, he suspected it was. *Untermensch* or not, he was nobody's fool. But when all your cards were bad, how many brains you had didn't win you even a pfennig.

"Tell him to tell his followers"—Stieglitz wouldn't call them people—"they can go back to the wagons and tents and take whatever they can carry in their hands. Tell them to get into the trucks then. And make sure you tell them that if anyone tries to jump out of a truck and run, it's the last stupid mistake he'll ever make."

"I'll take care of it, sir." The Hungarian turned that into his own language. The *Zigeuner* chieftain translated the translation. How long had this band lived in Hungary? Generations, by the look of things. Were there still some of these petty bandits who knew no Magyar? Evidently there were, though Stieglitz had trouble believing it. He shook his head. They were aliens. They didn't belong here. They didn't belong anywhere. The *Führer* was dead right about that. He usually was right.

"Come on," Stieglitz said sharply. "Let's get moving. We've wasted enough time here already." He noticed a couple of the Arrow Cross militiamen nodding before the driver translated. So they followed more German than they let on, did they? Somehow, the *Hauptsturmführer* found himself unsurprised. Hungary was like that. It remained Germany's ally, but nothing could make the Magyars enthusiastic about the struggle against subhumans and Bolshevism.

———

The *Zigeuner* went off to snag their movable property. They came back with coats and trousers and blankets and pots and pans. Stieglitz suspected they'd taken the chance to stash rings and chains and coins and bills where they wouldn't be so easy to find. He also suspected that would do them less good than they hoped.

One little girl cradled an ugly puppy in her arms. By the smiles she gave it, it wasn't ugly in her eyes. The Arrow Cross lieutenant sent Stieglitz a questioning glance. Stieglitz shrugged an answer. If carrying the dog kept the girl quiet, she was welcome to it as far as he was concerned.

The chieftain walked over to Stieglitz and the truck driver. His shirt looked lumpy. What all had he stashed under there? "Please, your Excellency," he said, "but what about our donkeys? What about our watchdogs?"

"I'm sorry, but they have to stay," Stieglitz replied. "The people in Nagylengyel will tend to them, I'm sure."

The people in Nagylengyel would shoot the dogs (Stieglitz was glad his men hadn't had to shoot any themselves) and either work the donkeys to death or butcher them for their meat. By the old *Zigeuner's* narrowed eyes and tight lips, he knew it as well as Stieglitz did. But he also knew he couldn't do anything about it. He turned his head to the side before spitting on the grass. "It will be as it must be," he said. "Everything will be as it must be."

That was true. It couldn't very well help being true. Stieglitz figured the scrawny *Zigeuner* couldn't tell the truth any other way.

"Everyone have everything you can take?" the *Hauptsturmführer* asked loudly. Also loudly, the truck driver turned his words into Hungarian. Stieglitz went on, "All right—into the trucks, then. We'll take you back to Zalaegerszeg."

Into the backs of the Opels they went. Men helped women climb up and hoisted children in. No one raised a fuss. Part of that was the *Zigeuner*'s hopelessness of resisting the firepower the SS men and Arrow Cross militiamen had. And part of it, Joseph Stieglitz judged, was the fatalism of their kind, a fatalism spawned in ancient days far beyond the borders of Europe.

Stieglitz went back to the men he led. "We'll put *Kübelwagens* between trucks on the way up to Zalaegerszeg," he told them. "If anybody tries to jump out and run for it, you'll finish off the damn fool, right?" He waited for the driver to render that into Hungarian for the benefit of the Arrow Cross militiamen, then continued, "You fellows behind the wheel, look into your rear-view mirrors every now and then. If the *Zigeuner* try to overpower a driver and hijack the truck, they won't get away with it."

As he got into his *Kübelwagen*'s front passenger seat, Klaus Pirckheimer hopped in on the other side. "Been easy so far, *Herr Hauptsturmführer*," Pirckheimer said as he fired up the sturdy little utility vehicle. "Let's hope it stays that way."

"Yes," Stieglitz agreed laconically. "Let's."

And it did stay easy all the way back to Zalaegerszeg. No *Zigeuner* sprang out and tried to dash for the roadside bushes. The *Untermenschen* didn't try coshing the Hungarian truck drivers. They didn't send any of their prettier women to seduce the drivers away from their duty, either. *Fatalism*, Stieglitz thought again.

Yes, everything was fine as long as the convoy stayed on the road. It all went sideways when the trucks and *Kübelwagens* came into town and made for the railroad station to unload the *Zigeuner* onto the waiting train. But traffic around the station had gone to the devil.

Another train, this one completely unexpected (at least as far as Joseph Stieglitz was concerned), had come into Zalaegerszeg while he was out on the roundup. The new arrival was full of *Wehrmacht* troops bound for eastern Hungary and the fight against the Red Army. But the driver of the train that would haul the *Zigeuner* up into Poland had refused to clear the track to let the German soldiers head for the front.

That left the major in charge of the held-up regiment hopping mad. Seeing they weren't going anywhere right away, some of his men had got off to rubberneck or grab something to eat or a glass of beer. The major took out his fury on Stieglitz. "I'll be hours herding everybody back into place!" he shouted. "Some of these bastards will find a way to get left behind, too—see if they don't. *Gott im Himmel!* How are we supposed to win the war if we can't get to where we need to be when we need to be there?"

"I'm very sorry, my dear fellow." Stieglitz's tone gave his words the lie. "I must remind you, though, that SS transports have priority over all other rail traffic. That includes troop movements. So the train driver's done the right thing. We might have made other arrangements if anybody in Szombathely telephoned or wired to tell us you were on the way. But no one did. And so…" He shrugged.

The *Wehrmacht* major exhaled angrily. "We're fighting the Russians, you know."

"We're fighting the *Zigeuner,* too. I presume you *have* read the *Führer's* book and all he has to say about them?" Stieglitz's voice, silky with menace, presumed no such thing. But *he'd* gone all the way through the hefty volume—gone through it two or three times, in fact. He knew exactly what it said about enemies of the *Reich.*

"They're less likely to shoot us or blow us up than the Red Army is." But the *Wehrmacht* officer knew he was fighting a losing battle here. He threw his hands in the air. "All right. All *right,* dammit! Would your most gracious Majesty please be kind enough to let me know when my men can proceed to their little tea party with the Ivans?"

Had Joseph Stieglitz been a vindictive man, he could have made the younger major pay for that. But he wasn't. He was just a fellow trying to do the job his superiors had given him. "I'm not trying to hold you up," he said—fighting the Russians, after all, was its own punishment. "We're all in the same struggle, you know."

"Yes, and the way things are going right now, we're all losing it." The *Wehrmacht* major had to be either a fine soldier or a hell of a lucky man. No ordinary jerk could have won the rank he had without learning how to put a governor on his tongue. Shaking his head, he clumped away.

Stieglitz let him go. It wasn't that he was wrong, only that he was impolitic. The *Hauptsturmführer* went back to his own command. "Let's get them onto the train," he said. "The sooner they're on, the sooner they're gone, the sooner the soldiers can head east."

The *Wehrmacht* major seemed eager to get into the fight against the Red Army. How many of the troops he led shared his eagerness? Not so very many, not if Stieglitz was any judge. German soldiers commonly wanted to avoid the Eastern Front, not to go there. But, these days, not so many got what they wanted. And the Eastern Front was coming to them.

Pretty soon, we won't be fighting the Russians in Hungary and Poland. We'll be fighting them in Germany. As he always did when that thought floated to the surface of his mind, Stieglitz shoved it under again. However many times he tried to drown it, though, it kept popping up.

The transport train sat waiting, a thin plume of steam and smoke rising from the stack. All the cars behind the locomotive and its tender were cattle cars. Some already had their doors barred and secured. Others were ready for more *Zigeuner*.

When the band Stieglitz had rounded up came out of the trucks, their chieftain took a long look at the train. Arrow Cross militiamen opened one of the cattle cars and grinned in mocking invitation as they waved the *Zigeuner* towards it. Instead of climbing in, the chieftain ambled over to Stieglitz. "So much for your honor," he said in pretty good German.

That didn't altogether astonish the *Hauptsturmführer*. "We all do what we're required to do," he said.

"Yes, I know." With immense dignity, the old man walked to the cattle car and climbed in. The rest of the band followed him. As they had with the trucks, men helped women and children board. The dark little girl with the puppy hesitated for a moment in front of the cattle car. Then she put the dog down on the gravel. It didn't want to leave. She drew back her leg and kicked it in the ribs. It ran off, yipping in pain and shock. The girl clambered into the car without help from anyone.

She'd made the right choice. If the dog went with her, it had no future at all. Now someone in Zalaegerszeg might give it a home. Or if nobody did, it might eke out a living by guile and theft, the way the *Zigeuner* had for so many centuries.

Not for much longer, though, Stieglitz thought. The *Führer* had ordered Europe purified of *Zigeuner* and Bolsheviks and homosexuals and other such riffraff. The Bolsheviks had an unfortunate tendency to shoot back. The others, though… The others were sand in the tide of history, and the tide was going out.

As soon as the last short-pants boy went into the cattle car, the *Hauptsturmführer* gestured sharply at the Arrow Cross militiamen standing in front of the door. They slid it shut. The bar slammed down into the steel **L** that secured it. Chains and padlocks made sure no one would defeat it from the inside.

Stieglitz walked up to the locomotive. The engine driver was swigging from a bottle of slivovitz or vodka. When he spotted Stieglitz, he quickly made the bottle disappear. Stieglitz wouldn't have called him on it. He'd seen the like plenty of times. Some people needed numbing before they could do what they were required to do.

"They're here. They're loaded and secured. You can take them away," Stieglitz said.

"*Zu Befehl, mein Herr.*" The engine driver didn't sound thick. When you had enough practice, you didn't get sloppy drunk the way someone new to the sauce would. You didn't show it. You soaked up the hooch and went on about your business.

The whistle screamed, once, twice, three times. The world needed to know the train was leaving the station. Smoke belched from the locomotive's stack. The drive wheels began to turn, ponderously slow at first but then faster and faster. Away went the train. Away went the *Zigeuner*. Except through tiny space between the planks of the cattle car, they wouldn't see daylight again till they got to Poland. After they got there, they probably wouldn't see it for long.

With the cork that had plugged his way east gone, the *Wehrmacht* major started chivvying his men back to the troop train. No, they weren't so eager to go as he was to get them going. Junior officers and noncoms gave the regimental CO what help they could.

So did the chaplains. In their purple-piped frock coats, they stood out from the soldiers. They weren't supposed to carry weapons, but the Lutheran minister wore a holstered pistol on his hip. The world was a rougher, crueler place than the striped-pants gentlemen who made rules like that could imagine.

When one of the chaplains turned and happened to catch his eye, Stieglitz waved to him. He would have had trouble saying why. Maybe the way the little *Zigeuner* girl put down her puppy was still on his mind. Maybe it was that the chaplain followed the faith the *Hauptsturmführer*'d been raised in. Maybe it was all of that. Or maybe not. Maybe it was just a spur-of-the-moment thing.

Whatever it was, the *Feldrabbiner* walked up to Stieglitz. Where his Catholic and Protestant counterparts wore two different versions of the cross on a chain around their necks, he had a Star of David. Another one replaced a cross on his officer's cap. Unique among German servicemen, he was allowed to have a beard.

"Something I can do for you?" he asked, his voice friendly, his accent Bavarian.

"I don't even know." Joseph Stieglitz wished he'd kept his damn hand at his side. "Those *Zigeuner*—" he started, and then broke off. He didn't know what he wanted to say. He didn't know if he wanted to say anything.

"That's a hard business, all right." The *Feldrabbiner* studied him with shrewd eyes. "You'll tell me if I'm wrong, but I'd say you also come from a family of Germans of the Mosaic faith."

That *also* invited Stieglitz back into something he'd invited himself out of long before he joined the SS. It was nothing he much wanted to return to. Nevertheless, he couldn't bring himself to lie. "Well, what if I am?" he said harshly.

"If you are, *Herr Hauptsturmführer*, I suggest you do what I do every day," the *Feldrabbiner* said. "Count your blessings."

"Excuse me?" Stieglitz said, in lieu of something like *That's fine for a clergyman, but not for an SS officer.*

The *Feldrabbiner* understood him whether he said it out loud or not. "Count your blessings," the man repeated. "Some Englishman is supposed to have said, 'There but for the grace of God go I.' I often think that when I see *Zigeuner* getting on those trains."

Stieglitz wished he hadn't waved to the *Feldrabbiner*. "I'm afraid I don't follow you," he said, and began to turn away.

But the man with the frock coat and the Star of David didn't let him escape so easily. "When you're a Jew, when you remember you're a Jew, you also have to remember such things can happen to you, too."

"Oh, *Quatsch!*" Stieglitz said.

"It isn't rubbish," the *Feldrabbiner* insisted. "Plenty of people don't like us. Let's not mince words. Plenty of people hate us. If the *Führer* hadn't seen what the *Zigeuner* were like when he fought in the east during the last war, if he hadn't already despised the Russians and seen how they mistreated the Jews in the Austro-Hungarian provinces they over-ran… *Herr Hauptsturmführer,* you might have boarded that train yourself instead of putting them on it."

"You are a man of the cloth. I make allowances for that. But if you say one more word along those lines, I will give you to the *Sicherheitsdienst,*" Stieglitz said, his voice colder than any blizzard on the Eatern Front. "I am a good German, and whatever religion my grandparents held has nothing to do with it. I follow the *Führer's* orders the way any other good German would. Since you wear the uniform, *mein Herr,* you had better do the same."

If he hadn't put the fear of God in the *Feldrabbiner,* he had put the fear of the SD in him. That would do. The man gulped. He licked his lips. "I mean nothing by it, of course," he said quickly. "Just, uh, think-ing on how things might have been." He showed far more alarm than the wicked old *Zigeuner* chieftain had.

"Of course." Stieglitz freighted the words with all the scorn he could. When he turned this time, the *Feldrabbiner* didn't bother him. He walked away, grubbing in his pocket for a pack of cigarettes.

BEDFELLOWS

There are photographers. There are strobing flashes. They know ahead of time there will be. They leave their rented limo and walk across the Boston Common toward the State House hand in hand, heads held high. They're in love, and they want to tell the world about it.

W is tall, in a conservative—compassionate, oh yes, but conservative—gray suit with television-blue shirt and maroon necktie. O is taller, and his turban lends him a few extra inches besides. His *shalwar kamiz* is of all-natural fabrics. He's trimmed his beard for the occasion—just a little, but you can tell.

"How did you meet?" a reporter calls to the two of them.

They both smile. O's eyes twinkle. If that's not mascara, he has the longest eyelashes in the world. Their hands squeeze—W's right, O's left. "Oh, we've been chasing each other for years," W says coyly. Joy fills his drawl.

"It is so. *Inshallah*, we shall be together forever," O says. "Truly God is great, to let us find such happiness."

News vans clog Beacon Street. Cops need to clear a path through the reporters so W and O can cross. A TV guy looking for an angle asks one of Boston's finest, "What do you think of all this?"

"Me?" The policeman shrugs. "I don't see how it's my business one way or the other. The court says they've got the right to do it, so that's what the law is. Long as they stay inside the law, nothing else matters."

"Uh, thank you." The TV guy sounds disappointed. He wants controversy, fireworks. That's what TV news is all about. Acceptance? One word—boring.

The State House. Good visuals. Gilded dome. Corinthian colonnade. The happy couple going up the stairs and inside.

More reporters in there. More camerapersons, too. O raises a hand against the bright television lights. More flashes go off, one after another. "Boy, you'd think we're in the middle of a nucular war or something," W says. He always pronounces it *nucular*.

"Nuclear," O says gently. "It's *nuclear.*" You can tell he's been trying to get W to do it right for a long time. Every couple needs a little something to squabble about. It takes the strain off, it really does.

"Can we get a picture of you two in front of the Sacred Cod?" a photographer asks.

"I don't mind." W is as genial as they come.

But O frowns. "Sacred Cod? It sounds like a graven image. No, I think not." He shakes his head. "It would not play well in Riyadh or Kandahar."

"Aw, c'mon, Sam, be a sport." W has a nickname for everybody, even his nearest and dearest. And he really does like to oblige.

But O digs in his heels. "I do not care to do this. It is not why we came here. I know why we came here." He bends down and whispers in W's ear. W laughs—giggles, almost. Of course, maybe O's beard tickles, trimmed or not.

W gives the reporters kind of a sheepish smile. "Sorry, friends. That's one photo op you're not gonna get. Now which way to the judge's office?"

"Chambers. The judge's chambers," O says. You wonder which one was brought up speaking English.

"Whatever." W doesn't care how he talks. "Which way?" There's a big old sign with an arrow—➜—showing the way. He doesn't notice till one of the reporters points to it.

He and O start down the hall. A reporter calls after them: "What do you see in each other?"

They stop. They turn so they're face to face. They gaze into each other's eyes. Now they have both hands clasped together. Anyone can tell it's love. "We need each other," W says. Even if he doesn't talk real well, he gets the message across.

"My infidel," O says fondly.

"My little terrorist." W's eyes glow.

You've seen couples who say the same thing at the same time? They do it here. "Without him," they both say, each pointing to the other, "I'm nothing." O strokes W's cheek. W swats O on the butt. They're grinning when they go into the judge's chambers.

———

The justice of the peace looks at the two of them over the top of her glasses. How many times has she done that, with how many couples? "You have your license. I can't stop you. But I do want to ask you if you're sure about what you're doing," she says. "Marriage is a big step. You shouldn't enter into it lightly."

"We're sure, ma'am," W says.

"Oh, yes," O says. "*Oh*, yes."

"Well, you sound like you mean it. That's good," she says. "You're making a commitment to each other for the rest of your lives. You're promising to be there for each other in sickness and in health, in good times and in bad."

"We understand," O says.

"I should say we do." W nods like a bobblehead, up and down, up and down. "We already look out for each other. Why, if it wasn't for Sam here, my poll numbers would be underwater."

O beams down at him. "My friends need infidels to hate, and W makes hating them so easy. Take Abu Ghraib, for instance. You'd think he did it just for me."

"Nope. Wasn't like that at all." Now W's head goes side to side, side to side, as if it's on a spring. "We both had fun there. We share lots of things." He grins at O. "See? I told you I'd bring you to justice."

O laughs. "All right." The corners of the justice of the peace's mouth twitch up in spite of themselves. She doesn't meet devotion like this every day. "Let's proceed to the ceremony, then." She reads the carefully nondenominational words. At last, she gets to the nitty-gritty. "Do you take each other to have and to hold, to love and to cherish, as long as you both shall live?"

"I do." W and O answer together. Proudly.

"Then by the authority vested in my by the Commonwealth of Massachusetts, I now pronounce you man and, uh, man." Even though they're legal, the judge is still new at same-sex marriages. Who isn't? But she recovers well: "You may kiss each other."

They do. In here, it's nothing but a little peck on the lips. They wink at each other. They know what the cameras outside are waiting for.

———

An explosion, a fusillade of flashes when they come out into the hallway. You can see W's mouth shaping *nucular* again, but you can't hear him— too many people yelling questions at once. You can see O tolerantly nodding, too. He knows W's not about to change.

A guy with a great big voice makes himself heard through the din: "Is it official?"

"It sure is," W says.

"Have you kissed each other yet?" somebody else asks—a woman.

"Well, yeah," W answers. The reporters make disappointed noises. W and O wink at each other again. Sometimes they're like a couple of little kids—they seem to think they've invented what they share. "We could do it again, if you want us to," W says.

The roar of approval startles even him and O. O grabs him, bends him back movie-style, and plants a big kiss right on his mouth. W's arms tighten around O's neck. The kiss goes on and on. Another zillion flashes freeze it in thin slices so the whole world can see.

Everything has to end. At last, the kiss does. "Wow!" a reporter says. "Is that hotter than Madonna and Britney or what?"

"Than who?" O doesn't get out much.

W does. "You betcha," he says. If his grin gets any wider, the top of his head will fall off. Is that a bulge in those conservative gray pants? Sure looks like one.

"Where will you honeymoon?" another reporter calls.

"In the mountains," O says.

"At the ranch," W says at the same time.

Not quite in synch there. They look at each other. They pantomime comic shrugs. They'll work it out.

Still hand in hand, they leave the State House. "Massachusetts is a very nice place," O says. "Very...tolerant."

"Well, if they put up with me here, they'll put up with anybody," W says, and gets a laugh.

———

"Gotta take you to meet the folks," W says as they start back toward the limo.

O raises an eyebrow. "That should be...interesting."

"Well, yeah." W sounds kind of sheepish. His folks are very, very straight. Then out of nowhere he grins all over his face. "We can do it like that movie, that waddayacallit I showed you." He snaps his fingers. *"La Cage aux Folles,* that's it." You think W has trouble with English, you should hear him try French. Or maybe you shouldn't. It's pretty bad.

"You *are* joking?" There's an ominous ring in O's voice.

"No, no!" W's practically jumping up and down. He's got it all figured out. He may not be right, but by God he's sure. "We'll put you in a bertha, that's what we'll do!"

"A what?" O says.

"Come on, Sam. *You* know. You ought to. You've seen 'em close up, right? One of those robe things that doesn't show anything but your eyes."

"A *burka?"*

"That's what I said, isn't it?" W thinks it is, anyway.

"The *burka* is for women," O says in icy tones. Then he smiles thinly—very thinly. "Oh, I see." He draws himself up to his full height, straight as a rocket-propelled grenade launcher. A cat couldn't show more affronted dignity, or even as much. "No."

And W laughs fit to bust. He howls. He slaps his knee. "Gotcha! I gotcha, Sam! Can't tell me I didn't, not this time. I had you going good." He pokes O in the ribs with a pointy elbow.

"You were joking?" O looks at him. "You *were* joking," he admits. He laughs, too, ruefully. "Yes, you got me. This time you got me."

W gives him a hug. You can't stay mad at W, no matter how much you want to. He just won't let you. "I'm glad I've got you, too," he says.

And O melts. He can't help it. "I'm glad I've got you, too—you troublemaker," he says. They both laugh. O goes on, "But maybe we could meet your parents another time?"

"After the honeymoon?" W says.

"Wherever it is," O says.

"I love you," says W. "You made me what I am today."

"And you me." O kisses W, and they walk off across the Common with their arms around each other's waists.

NEWS FROM THE
FRONT

December 7, 1941—Austin Daily Tribune
U.S. AT WAR

December 8, 1941—Washington Post
PRESIDENT ASKS FOR WAR DECLARATION!
Claims Date of Attack Will "Live in Infamy"

December 8, 1941—Chicago Tribune
CONGRESS DECLARES WAR ON JAPAN!
Declaration Is Not Unanimous

December 9, 1941—New York Times editorial
ROOSEVELT'S WAR

Plainly, President Franklin D. Roosevelt has brought this war on himself and on the United States. On July 25 of this year, he froze Japanese assets in the United States. On the following day, he ordered the military forces of the Philippine Islands incorporated into our own—a clear act of aggression. And on August 1, he embargoed export of high-octane gasoline and crude oil to Japan, a nation with limited energy resources of its own. Is it any wonder that a proud people might be expected to respond with force to these outrageous provocations? Are we not in large measure to blame for what has happened to us?

Further proof of Mr. Roosevelt's intentions, if such be needed, is offered by the August 12 extension of the Selective Service Act allowing peacetime conscription. Pulling out all political stops and shamelessly exploiting his party's Congressional majorities, the President rammed the measure through by a single vote in the House, a vote some Representatives certainly now regret…

December 11, 1941—Boston Traveler
AXIS, U.S. DECLARE WAR

December 12, 1941—Los Angeles Times editorial
TWO-FRONT WAR

Having suffered a stinging setback in the Pacific, we now suddenly find ourselves called upon to fight two European enemies as well. FDR's inept foreign-policy team has much to answer for. Mothers whose sons are drafted may well wonder whether the fight is worthwhile and whether the government that orders them into battle has any idea what it is doing...

December 22, 1941—The New Yorker
FIASCO IN THE PACIFIC

War Department officials privately concede that U.S. preparations to defend Hawaii and the Philippines weren't up to snuff. "It's almost criminal, how badly we fouled up," said one prominent officer, speaking on condition of anonymity. "The administration really didn't know what the devil it was doing out there."

He and other sources sketch a picture of incompetence on both the strategic and tactical levels. Ships from the Pacific Fleet were brought into port at Pearl Harbor every Saturday and Sunday, offering the Japanese a perfect chance to schedule their attacks. U.S. patterns became predictable as early as this past February, said a source in the Navy Department who is in a position to know.

Further, U.S. search patterns the morning of the attack were utterly inadequate. Airplanes searched a diamond extending as far as 200 miles west of Pearl Harbor and a long, narrow rectangle reaching as far as 100 miles south of the ravaged base, *and that was all.* There was no search coverage north of the island of Oahu, the direction from which the Japanese launched their devastating attack.

It has also been learned that a highly secret electronic warning system actually detected the incoming Japanese planes half an hour before they struck Pearl Harbor. When an operator at this base in the northern part of Oahu spotted these aircraft, he suggested calling in a warning to Pearl Harbor. His superior told him he was crazy.

The junior enlisted man persisted. He finally persuaded his superior to call the Information Center near Fort Shafter. The man reported "that we had an unusually large flight—in fact, the largest I had ever seen on the equipment—coming in from almost due north at 130-some miles."

"Well, don't worry about it," said the officer in charge there, believing the planes to be B-17s from the U.S. mainland.

A private asked the officer, "What do you think it is?"

"It's nothing," the officer replied. About twenty minutes later, bombs began falling.

In the White House, a tense meeting of Cabinet and Congressional leaders ensued. "The principal defense of the whole country and the whole West Coast of the Americas has been very seriously damaged today," Roosevelt admitted.

Senator Tom Connally angrily questioned Navy Secretary Knox: "Didn't you say last month that we could lick the Japs in two weeks? Didn't you say that our navy was so well prepared and located that the Japanese couldn't hope to hurt us at all?"

According to those present, Knox had trouble coming up with any answer.

Connally pressed him further: "Why did you have all the ships at Pearl Harbor crowded in the way you did? You weren't thinking of an air attack?"

"No," was all Knox said. Roosevelt offered no further comment, either.

"Well, they were supposed to be on the alert," Connally thundered. "I am amazed by the attack by Japan, but I am still more astounded at what happened to our navy. They were all asleep. Where were our patrols?"

Again, the Secretary of the Navy did not reply.

In the Philippines, the picture of U.S. ineptitude is no better. It may be worse. Another of these secret, specialized electronic range-finding stations was in place in the northern regions of the island of Luzon. It detected Japanese planes approaching from Formosa, but failed to communicate with airfields there to warn them. Some sources blame radio interference. Others point to downed land lines. Whatever the reason, the warning never went through.

And U.S. bombers and fighters were caught on the ground. Although General MacArthur knew Hawaii had been attacked, our planes were caught on the ground. They suffered catastrophic losses from Japanese bombing and strafing attacks. With a third of our fighters and more than half of our heavy bombers—again, the B-17, the apparently misnamed Fighting Fortress—lost, any hope for air defense of the Philippines has also been destroyed. Reinforcement also appears improbable. Our forces there, then, are plainly doomed to defeat...

December 23, 1941—Washington Post
FDR DECRIES LEAKS
Claims They Harm National Security

President Roosevelt used a so-called fireside chat last night to condemn the publication in *The New Yorker* and elsewhere of information about U.S. military failings. "We are in a war now," he said, "so the rules change. We have to be careful about balancing the people's need to know against the damage these stories can cause our Army and Navy."

He particularly cited the electronic rangefinder mentioned in the *New Yorker* article. Roosevelt claims the Japanese were ignorant of this device and its potential. (The *Post* has learned that the apparatus is commonly called *radar*—an acronym for RAdio Detecting And Ranging.)

A Republican spokesman was quick to challenge the President. "I yield to no one in my support of our troops," he said. "But this administration's record of incompetence in military preparation and in the conduct of the war to date must be exposed. The American people are entitled to the facts—*all* the facts—from which, and from which alone, they can make a proper judgment."

December 29, 1941—The New Yorker
DID WAKE HAVE TO FALL?

More fumbling by officials in Honolulu and Washington led to the surrender of Wake Island to the Japanese last Tuesday. Wake, west of the Hawaiian chain, was an important position. Even disgraced Admiral Husband E. Kimmel, who so recently mismanaged the defense of Hawaii, could see this. In a letter dated this past April which a Navy Department source has made available to me, Kimmel wrote:

"To deny Wake to the enemy, without occupying it, would be difficult; to recapture it, if the Japanese should seize it in the early period of hostilities, would require operations of some magnitude. Since the Japanese Fourth Fleet includes transports and troops with equipment especially suited for land operations, it appears not unlikely that one of the initial operations of the Japanese may be directed against Wake."

He was right about that—he could be right about some things. He also recommended that Wake be fortified. But work there did not begin until August 19, more than three months after his letter. Guns were not emplaced until mid-October. Obsolescent aircraft were flown in to try to help defend the island.

After the first Japanese attack on Wake failed, Kimmel proposed a three-pronged countermove, based on our fast carrier forces. Why he thought they might succeed in the face of already established Japanese superiority may be questioned, but he did. The plan did not succeed.

Bad weather kept one carrier from refueling at sea. Bad intelligence data led to a raid on the Japanese base at Jaluit, which proved not to need raiding. Then sizable Japanese air and submarine forces were anticipated in the area. They turned out not to be there, but it was too late.

The relief force, centered on the *Saratoga*, was within 600 miles of Wake Island when the Japanese launched their second attack. They were able to move quickly and think on their feet; we seemed capable of nothing of the kind. They destroyed our last two fighters with continuing heavy air raids, and landed 2,000 men to oppose 500 U.S. Marines.

At this point, Admiral Pye, who replaced Admiral Kimmel before Admiral Nimitz arrived—another illustration of our scrambled command structure—issued and then countermanded several orders. The result was that the relieving force was recalled, and Wake was lost. The recall order provoke a near-mutiny aboard some U.S. ships, but in the end was obeyed.

In another document obtained from Navy Department sources, Admiral Pye wrote, "When the enemy had once landed on the island, the general strategic situation took precedence, and conservation of our naval forces became the first consideration. I ordered the retirement with extreme regret."

How many more retirements will we have to regret—extremely—in days to come?

January 1, 1942—New York Times editorial
FREEDOM AND LICENSE

President Roosevelt believes news coverage of the war hampers U.S. foreign policy. Neither Mr. Roosevelt nor any lesser figure in his administration has denied the truth of stories recently appearing in this newspaper and elsewhere. On the contrary. The administration's attitude seems to be, Even though this is true, the people must not hear of it.

Some in the administration have questioned the press's patriotism. They have pointed to their own by contrast. Quoting Samuel Johnson—"Patriotism is the last refuge of a scoundrel"—in this context is almost too easy, but we shall not deny ourselves the small pleasure. By wrapping themselves in the American flag, administration officials appear to believe that they become immune to criticism of their failures, which are many and serious.

We are not for or against anybody. We are for the truth, and for publishing the truth. Once the people have the whole truth in front of them, they can decide for themselves. If our government claims it has the right to suppress any part of the truth, how does it differ from the regimes it opposes?

One truth in need of remembering at the moment is that, just over a year ago, Mr. Roosevelt was running for an unprecedented third term. On October 30, 1940, a week before the election, he categorically stated, "I have said this before, but I shall say it again and again and again: your boys are not going to be sent into any foreign wars."

Did Mr. Roosevelt believe even then that he was telling the truth? Given the disasters and the constant missteps that have bedeviled us since we found ourselves in this unfortunate conflict, would it not be better if he had been?

January 3, 1942—Los Angeles Times
FDR'S POLL NUMBERS PLUMMET

Since the outbreak of war last month, Franklin D. Roosevelt's personal popularity with American voters has dramatically faded. So has public confidence in his ability to lead the United States to victory. Newest figures from the George Gallup organization make the slide unmistakably clear.

Last December 15, 63% of Americans polled had a favorable impression of FDR, while 59% thought he was an effective war leader. In a survey conducted on December 29, only 49% of respondents had a favorable impression of the President. Faith in his leadership fell even more steeply. Only 38% of those responding believed him "effective" or "very effective" as commander-in-chief.

These figures are based on a survey of 1,127 Americans of voting age who described themselves as "likely" or "very likely" to cast ballots in the next election. The margin for error is ±3%.

January 5, 1942—Chicago Tribune
CAN'T FIGHT WAR WITH POLLS, WHITE HOUSE ALLEGES

A White House spokesman called the latest Gallup Poll figures "irrelevant" and "unimportant." In a heated exchange with reporters, the press secretary said, "It's ridiculous to think you can run a war by Gallup Poll."

This is only the latest in a series of evasions from an administration longer on excuses than results. If Roosevelt and his clique keep ignoring public opinion, they will be punished in a poll that matters even to them: the upcoming November elections.

Reporters also asked why Roosevelt is so sensitive about being photographed in a wheelchair. "Everybody knows he uses one," a scribe said.

"Is he afraid of being perceived as weak?" another added.

The press secretary, a former advertising copywriter, termed these queries "shameless" and "impertinent." He offered no explanation for his remarks. Since the war began, the administration has had few explanations to offer, and fewer that can be believed...

January 8, 1942—Philadelphia Inquirer
DEMONSTRATORS CLASH—COPS WADE IN
Accusations of Police Brutality

Pro- and antiwar demonstrators threw rocks and bottles at one another in an incident in front of city hall yesterday. Shouting "Nazis!" and "Fascists!" and "Jap-lovers!", the prowar demonstrators attacked people peacefully protesting Roosevelt's ill-advised foreign adventures.

Police were supposed to keep the two groups separate. The antiwar demonstrators, who carried placards *READING SEND JAPAN OIL, NOT BLOOD* and *U.S. TROOPS OUT OF AUSTRALIA* and *FDR LIED*, did not respond to the provocation for some time. When they began to defend themselves, the cops weighed in—on their opponents' side.

"They were swinging their nightsticks, beating on people—it was terrible," said Mildred Andersen, 27. She had come down from Scranton to take part in the protest. "Is this what America's supposed to be about?"

"The cops rioted—nothing else but," agreed Dennis Pulaski, 22, of Philadelphia. He had a gash above his left eyebrow inflicted by a police billy club. "They're supposed to keep the peace, aren't they? They only made things worse."

Police officials declined comment.

January 15, 1942—Variety
ANTIWAR PICS PLANNED
MGM, Fox Race to Hit Theaters First

Major Hollywood talent is getting behind the building antiwar buzz. Two big stars and a gorgeous gal will crank out *The Road to Nowhere*—shooting begins tomorrow. Expect it in theaters this spring.

NEWS FROM THE FRONT

A new radio program, *Boy, Do You Bet Your Life,* airs Wednesday at 8 on the Mutual Network. Its shlemiel of a hero soon discovers Army life ain't what it's cracked up to be. Yeah, so you didn't know that already.

And a New Jersey heartthrob crooner is putting out a platter called "Ain't Gonna Study War No More." The B side will be "Swing for Peace." Think maybe he's out to make a point? Us, too.

———

February 5, 1942—newsreel narration

What you are about to see has been banned by the Navy Department. The Navy has imposed military censorship about what's going on at sea on the entire East Coast of the United States. That's one more thing it doesn't want you to know. Our cameraman had to smuggle this film out under the noses of Navy authorities to get it to you so you can see the facts.

On the thirty-first of last month, that cameraman and his crew were on the shore by Norfolk, Virginia, when a rescue ship brought thirty survivors from the 6,000-ton tanker *Rochester* into port. You can see their dreadful condition. Our intrepid interviewer managed to speak to one of them before they were hustled away.

"What happened to you?"

"We got torpedoed. Broad daylight. [Bleep] sub attacked on the surface. We never had a chance. We started going down fast. Next thing I knew, I was in the drink. That's how I got this [bleep] oil all over me."

"Did you lose any shipmates?"

"Better believe it, buddy."

"I'm sorry. I—"

At that point, we had to withdraw, because naval officers were coming up. They would have confiscated this film if they'd been able to get their hands on it. They have confiscated other film, and blocked newspaper reporting, too. The *Rochester* is the seventeenth ship known to be attacked in Atlantic waters since the war began. How many had you heard about? How many more will their be?

And how many U-boats has the Navy sunk? Any at all?

February 9, 1942—The New Yorker
DOWN THE TUBES

The Mark XIV torpedo is the U.S. Navy's answer to Jane Russell: an expensive bust. Too often, it doesn't go where our submariners aim it. When it does, it doesn't sink what they aim it at. Why not? The answer breaks into three parts—poor design, poor testing, and poor production.

Some Mark XIVs dive down to the bottom of the sea shortly after launch. Some run wild. A few have even reversed course and attacked the subs that turned them loose. Despite this, on the record Navy Department officials continue to insist that there is no problem. Off the record—but only off the record—they are trying to figure out what all is wrong and how to fix it.

The magnetic exploder is an idea whose time may not have come. It was considered and rejected by the German U-boat service, which has more experience with submarine warfare than anyone else on earth. Still, in its infinite wisdom, FDR's Navy Department chose to use this unproved system.

And, in its infinite wisdom, FDR's Navy Department conducted no live-firing tests before the war broke out. None. Officials were sure the magnetic exploder would perform as advertised. If you're sure, why bother to test?

Combat experience has shown why. Our Mark XIVs run silent and run deep. More often than not, they run *too* deep: under the keeps of the ships at which they're aimed and on their merry way. Or, sometimes, the magnetic exploder—which is a fragile and highly temperamental gadget—will blow up before the torpedo gets to its target. Manufacturing quality is not where it ought to be—not even close.

Despite this, Navy Department brass is making submariners scrimp with their "fish." They are strongly urged to shoot only one or two torpedoes at each ship, not a large spread. The brass is sure one hit from a torpedo with a magnetic exploder will sink anything afloat. Getting the hit seems to be the sticking point.

Japan builds torpedoes that work even when dropped from airplanes. Why don't we? The answer looks obvious. We want to save money. Japan wants to win the war. When fighting a foe who shows such fanatical determination, how can we hope to prevail?

———

February 13, 1942—Washington Post
ADMINISTRATION RIPS NAYSAYERS
"We Can Gain Victory," FDR Insists

President Roosevelt used the excuse of Lincoln's Birthday to allege that the United States and its coalition partners might still win the war despite the swelling tide of opposition to his ill-planned adventure.

In a national radio address, Roosevelt said, "Those who point out our weaknesses and emphasize our disagreements only aid the enemy. We were taken by surprise on December 7. We need time to get rolling. But we *can* do the job."

The President seemed ill at ease—almost desperate—as he went on, "These leaks that torment us have got to stop. They help no one but the foes of freedom. It is much harder to go forward if Germany and Japan know what we are going to do before we do it."

In the Congressional response to his speech, a ranking member of the Foreign Affairs Committee said, "The President's speech highlights the bankruptcy of his policies. After promising to keep us out of war, he got us into one we are not ready to fight. Our weapons don't work, and we can't begin to keep our shipping safe. We don't have enough men to do half of what the President and the Secretary of War are trying to do. And even if we did, what they want to do doesn't look like a good idea anyhow."

Peaceful pickets outside the White House demanded that the President bring our troops back to the United States and keep them out of harm's way. The presence of photographers and reporters helped ensure that White House police did not rough up the demonstrators.

February 23, 1942—Washington Post
HOUSE REJECTS RATIONING BILL

In an embarrassing defeat for the administration, the House of Representatives voted 241–183 to reject a bill that would have rationed fuel, food, and materials deemed "essential to wartime industries."

"Why should the American people have to suffer for Roosevelt's mistakes?" demanded a Congressman who opposed the bill. "If we rationed these commodities, you could just wait and see. Gas would jump past thirty cents a gallon, and there wouldn't be enough of it even at that price."

A War Department official, speaking off the record, called the House's action "deplorable." The only public comment from the executive branch was that it was "studying the situation." Had it done that in 1940 and 1941…

March 17, 1942—San Francisco Chronicle
MACARTHUR BAILS OUT OF PHILIPPINES!
Leaves Besieged Garrison to Fate

General Douglas MacArthur fled the Philippines one jump ahead of the Japanese. PT boats and a B-17 brought him to Darwin, Australia. (Incidentally, Japanese bombers leveled Darwin last month and forced its abandonment.)

"I shall return," pledged MacArthur. But the promise rings hollow for the men he left behind. Trapped on the Bataan Peninsula in a war they do not understand, they soldier on as best they can. Since Japanese forces surround them, the only question is how long they can hold out.

Roosevelt hopes MacArthur can lead counterattacks later in the war. Given the disasters thus far, this seems only another sample of his blind and foolish optimism...

March 23, 1942—The New Yorker
CAN WE HUNT THE SEA WOLVES?

German U-boats are taking a disastrous toll on military goods bound for England. In the first three months of the war, subs sank ships carrying 400 tanks, 60 8-inch howitzers, 880 25-pounder guns, 400 2-pounder guns, 240 armored cars, 500 machine-gun carriers, 52,100 tons of ammo, 6,000 rifles, 4,280 tons of tank supplies, 20,000 tons of miscellaneous supplies, and 10,000 tanks of gasoline. A secret War Department estimate calls this the equivalent of 30,000 bombing runs.

And the administration cannot stop the bleeding. Blackout orders are routinely ignored. Ships silhouetted at night against illuminated East

Coast cities make easy targets. Businessmen say dimming their lights at night would hurt their bottom line.

Although the Navy Department claims to have sunk several U-boats and damaged more, there is no hard evidence it has harmed even one German sailor.

Britain urges the United States to begin convoying, as she has done. U.S. Navy big shots continue to believe this is unnecessary. How they can maintain this in the face of losses so staggering is strange and troubling, but they do.

The issue is causing a rift between the United States and one of her two most important allies. Last Wednesday, Roosevelt wrote to Churchill, "My navy has definitely been slack in preparing for this submarine war off our coast... By May 1 I expect to get a pretty good coastal patrol working."

Churchill fears May 1 will be much too late.

"Those of us who are directly concerned with combatting the Atlantic submarine menace are not at all sure that the British are applying sufficient effort to bombing German submarine bases," said U.S. Admiral Ernest J. King.

As the allies bicker, innocent sailors lose their lives for no good purpose.

March 24, 1942—New York Times
NEW YORKER OFFICES RAIDED
Magazine's Publication Suspended

A raid by FBI and military agents shuttered the offices of *The New Yorker* yesterday. The raid came on the heels of yet another article critical of the war and of the present administration's conduct of it.

"We are going to close this treason down," said FBI spokesman Thomas O'Banion. Mr. O'Banion added, "These individuals are spreading stories nobody's got a right to know. We have to put a stop to it, and we will."

He did not dispute the truth of the stories articles published in *The New Yorker.*

ACLU attorneys are seeking the release of jailed editors and writers. "These are important freedom-of-speech and freedom-of-the-press issues," one of them said. "We're confident we'll prevail in court."

———

March 26, 1942—Philadelphia Inquirer
PEACE SHIPS SAIL
Reaching out to Germany and Japan

More than fifty American actors, musicians, and authors sailed from Philadelphia today aboard the *Gustavus Vasa,* a Swedish ship. Sweden is neutral in Roosevelt's war. Their eventual destination is Germany, where they will confer with their counterparts and seek ways to lower tensions between the two countries.

Another similar party also sailed today from San Francisco aboard the Argentine ship *Rio Negro.* Like Sweden, Argentina has sensibly stayed out of this destructive fight. After stopping in Honolulu to pick up another antiwar delegation there, the *Rio Negro* will continue on to Yokohama, Japan.

"We have to build peace one person at a time," explained Robert Noble of the Friends of Progress. His Los Angeles-based organization, along with the National Legion of Mothers and Women of America, sponsored the peace initiative. Noble added, "The Japanese did the proper thing under the exigencies of the time when they bombed Pearl Harbor. Now it is all over in the Pacific, and we might as well come home."

Noble has been arrested twice recently, once on a charge of sedition and once on one of malicious libel. The government did not bring either case to trial, perhaps fearing the result.

Some of the travelers bound for Germany and Japan have volunteered as human shields against U.S. and British bombing. There is no response yet from the governments under attack to their brave commitment.

Bureaucrats in the Roosevelt administration have threatened not to allow the peaceful performers and intellectuals to return to the United States. Travel to their destinations is technically illegal, though a challenge to the ban is under way in the courts. This vindictiveness against critics is typical of administration henchmen.

———————

April 3, 1942—transcript of radio broadcast
THIS IS LONDON

People in the States ask me how the morale situation is over here. They ask whether the English have as many doubts about which way their leaders are taking them as we do back home.

The answer is, of course they do. If anything, they have more. They've been hit hard, and it shows. Nearly two years ago, Germany offered a fair and generous peace. A sensible government would have accepted in a flash.

But Churchill had seized power a few months earlier in what almost amounted to a right-wing coup. He refused a hand extended in friendship, and his country has taken a right to the chin. London and other industrial cities have been bombed flat. Tens of thousands are dead, more wounded and often crippled for life.

"Look at France," a cab driver said to me the other day. "They went out early, and they have it easy now. We just keep getting pounded on. I'm tired of it, I am."

Calls for British withdrawal from Malta and North Africa grow stronger by the day. Sooner or later—my guess is sooner—even Churchill will have to face the plain fact that he has led his country into a losing war...

———

April 5, 1942—AP story
THE PHILIPPINE FRONT

Sergeant Leland Calvert is a regular guy. He was born in Hondo, Texas, and grew up in San Antonio. He is 29 years old, with blond hair, blue eyes, and an aw-shucks grin. He is a skilled metalworker, and plays a mean trumpet. He's a big fellow—six feet two, maybe six feet three. Right now, Leland Calvert weighs 127 pounds.

That is how it is for the Americans stuck on the Bataan Peninsula. That is also how it is for the Philippine troops and civilians crammed in with them. There are far more people than there are supplies, which is at the heart of the problem.

"I don't know who planned this," Calvert said in an engaging drawl. "I don't reckon anybody did. Sure doesn't seem much point to it. Hell, we're licked. Anybody with eyes in his head can see that."

Way back in January, rations for 5,600 men in the 91st Division were 19 sacks of rice, 12 cases of salmon, 3-1/2 sacks of sugar, and four carabao quarters. A carabao is a small, scrawny ox. Well, everybody and everything on the peninsula is scrawny now. Feeding 5,600 people with those supplies makes the miracle of the loaves and fishes look easy as pie.

And that was January. Things are much worse now. Sergeant Calvert has eaten snake and frog—not frog's legs, but frog. "Snake's not half bad," he said. "I drew the line at monkey, though. I saw a little hand cooking in a pot, and I didn't think I could keep it down." I asked him about the monkey's paw story, but he has never heard of it.

Disease? That's another story. Leland has dysentery. He has had dengue fever, but he is mostly over it now. He is starting to get beriberi, which comes from lack of vitamins. Beriberi takes the gas right out of your motor. I ought to know—I have it, too. Leland does not think he has got scurvy, but he knows men who do.

He has got malaria. Most people here have got it. Again, I am one of them. The doctors are out of quinine. They are also out of atabrine, which is a fancy new synthetic drug. And they are plumb out of mosquito nets. Something like 1,000 people are going into the hospital with malaria every day now. Without the medicines, there is not much anyone can do for them.

"If I knew why we were here, I would feel better about things," Leland said. "This all seems like such a waste, though. We're fighting for a little stretch of jungle nobody in his right mind would want. What's the point?"

Seems like a good question to me, too. It doesn't look like anyone here has a good answer. I don't know when I'll see that Girl again. I don't know if she'll ever see me again. I wish I could say the effort here is worth the candle. But I'm afraid I'm with Leland Calvert. This all seems like such a waste.

———

April 14, 1942—Honolulu Star-Bulletin
ADMINISTRATION PURSUES VENGEANCE POLICY

According to a Navy Department source, two aircraft carriers and several other warships sailed from Midway yesterday, bound for the Japanese home islands. Aboard one of the carriers, the *Hornet,* are U.S.

Army B-25s. Pilots have secretly trained in Florida, learning to take off from a runway as short as a flight deck.

The theory is that the B-25s will be able to strike Japan from farther out to sea than normal carrier-based aircraft could. Most of Roosevelt's theories about the war up till now have been wrong, though. Maybe the planes will go into the drink. Maybe the Japanese will be waiting for them. Maybe some other foul-up will torment us. But who will believe this force can succeed until it actually does?

Given the administration's record to date, in fact, many people will have their doubts even then. As a wise man once said, "Trust everybody—but cut the cards."

April 21, 1942—Washington Post editorial
BLAMING THE TOOLS

Everyone knows what sort of workman blames his tools. Franklin Roosevelt claims that, if a Hawaiian newspaper had not publicized the plan of attack against the Japanese islands, it might have succeeded. He also claims we would not have lost a carrier and a cruiser and had another carrier damaged had secrecy not been compromised.

This is nonsense of the purest ray serene. The Navy tried a crack-brained scheme, it didn't work, and now the men with lots of gold braid on their sleeves are using the press as a whipping boy. This effort, if we may dignify it with such a name, was doomed to fail from the beginning.

Reliable sources inform us that the Army pilots involved were not even told they would attempt to fly off a carrier deck till they boarded the *Hornet.* The Japanese have twice our carrier force in the Pacific. Why were we wasting so much of our strength on what was at best a propaganda stunt? Are we so desperate that we need to throw men's lives away for the sake of looking good on the home front?

Evidently we are. If that is so, we should never have got involved in this war in the first place. Our best course now, plainly, is to get out of it as soon as we can, to minimize casualties and damage to our prestige. We have already paid too much for Roosevelt's obsessive opposition to Japan and Germany.

April 25, 1942—New York Times
READING THE OTHER GENTLEMAN'S MAIL
U.S., British Codebreakers Monitor Germany, Japan

"Gentlemen do not read each other's mail." So goes an ancient precept of diplomacy. But for some time now, the United States and Britain have been monitoring Germany and Japan's most secret codes.

War Department and Navy Department sources confirm that the U.S. and the U.K., with help from Polish experts, have defeated the German Enigma machine and the Japanese Type B diplomatic cipher machine.

The most important codebreaking center is at Bletchley Park, a manor 50 miles north of London. Other cryptographers work in the British capital, in Ceylon, and in Australia. American efforts are based in Washington, D.C., and in Hawaii.

Purple is the name of the device that deciphers the Type B code. It is not prepossessing. It looks like two typewriters and a spaghetti bowl's worth of fancy wiring. But the people who use it say it does the job.

Getting an Enigma machine to Britain was pure cloak-and-dagger. One was found by the Poles aboard a U-boat sunk in shallow water (not, obviously, anywhere near our own ravaged East Coast) and spirited out of Poland one jump ahead of the Germans at the beginning of the war.

Why better use has not been made of these broken codes is a pressing question. No administration official will speak on the record. No administration official will even admit on the record that we are engaged in codebreaking activity.

Only one thing makes administration claims tempting to believe. If the United States and Britain are reading Germany and Japan's codes, they have little to show for it. Roosevelt dragged this country into war by a series of misconceptions, deceptions, and outright lies. Now we are in serious danger of losing it.

April 26, 1942—Chicago Tribune
WHITE HOUSE WHINES AT REVELATIONS

In a news conference yesterday afternoon, Franklin D. Roosevelt lashed out at critics in the press and on the radio. "Every time sensitive intelligence is leaked, it hurts our ability to defeat the enemy," Roosevelt claimed.

As he has before, he seeks to hide his own failings behind the veil of censorship. If the press cannot tell the American people the truth, who can? The administration? FDR sure wants you to think so. But the press and radio newscasters have exposed so many falsehoods and so much bungling that no one in his right mind is likely to trust this White House as far as he can throw it.

May 1, 1942—Los Angeles Times
FDR'S POLL NUMBERS CONTINUE TO SINK

Franklin D. Roosevelt's popularity is sinking faster than freighters off the East Coast. In the latest Gallup survey, his overall approval rating is at 29%, while only 32% approve of his handling of the war. The poll, conducted yesterday, was of 1,191 "likely" or "very likely" voters, and has an error margin of ±5%.

Polltakers also recorded several significant comments. "He doesn't know what he's doing," said one 58-year-old man.

"Why doesn't he bring the troops home? Who wants to die for England?" remarked a 31-year-old woman.

"We can't win this stupid war, so why fight it?" said another woman, who declined to give her age.

Roosevelt's approval ratings are as low as those of President Hoover shortly before he was turned out of office in a landslide. Even Warren G. Harding retained more personal popularity than the embattled current President.

May 3, 1942—Washington Post
VEEP BREAKS RANKS WITH WHITE HOUSE
Demands Timetable for War

In the first public rift in the Roosevelt administration, Vice President Henry Wallace called on FDR to establish a timetable for victory. "If we can't win this war within 18 months, we should pack it in," Wallace said, speaking in Des Moines yesterday. "It is causing too many casualties and disrupting the civilian economy."

Wallace, an agricultural expert, also said, "Even if by some chance we should win, we would probably have to try to feed the whole world afterwards. No country can do that."

Support for Wallace's statement came quickly from both sides of the partisan aisle. Even Senators and Representatives who supported Roosevelt's war initiative seemed glad of the chance to distance themselves from it. "If I'd known things would go this badly, I never would have voted for [the declaration of war]," said a prominent Senator.

White House reaction was surprisingly restrained. "We will not set a timetable," said an administration spokesman. "That would be the same as admitting defeat."

Another official, speaking anonymously, said FDR had known Wallace was "off the reservation" for some time. He added, "When the ship sinks, the rats jump off." Then he tried to retract the remark, denying that the ship was sinking. But the evidence speaks for itself.

May 9, 1942—Miami Herald
MORE SINKINGS IN BROAD DAYLIGHT
U-Boats Prowl Florida Coast at Will

The toll of ships torpedoed in Florida waters in recent days has only grown worse. On May 6, a U-boat sank the freighter *Amazon* near Jupiter Inlet. She sank in 80 feet of water.

That same day, also under the smiling sun, the tanker *Halsey* went to the bottom not far away. Then, yesterday, the freighter *Ohioan* was sunk. So was the tanker *Esquire*. That ship broke apart, spilling out 92,000 barrels of oil close to shore. No environmental-impact statement has yet been released.

There is still no proof that the U.S. Navy has sunk even a single German submarine, despite increasingly strident claims to the contrary.

May 11, 1942—Washington Post

MOTHER'S DAY MARCH

War Protesters Picket White House

Mothers of war victims killed in the Pacific and Atlantic marched in front of the White House to protest the continued fighting. "What does Roosevelt think he's doing?" asked Louise Heffernan, 47, of Altoona, Pennsylvania. Her son Richard was slain in a tanker sinking three weeks ago. "How many more have to die before we admit his policy isn't working?"

A mother who refused to give her name—"Who knows what the FBI would do to me?"—said she lost two sons at Pearl Harbor. "It's a heartache no one who hasn't gone through it can ever understand," she said. "I don't think anyone else should have to suffer the way I have."

Placards *READ END THE WAR NOW!, NO BLOOD FOR BRITAIN!,* and *ANOTHER MOTHER FOR PEACE.* Passersby whistled and cheered for the demonstrators.

March 12, 1942—Los Angeles Times

JAPAN BATTERS U.S. CARRIERS IN CORAL SEA

The Navy Department has clamped a tight lid of secrecy over the battle in the Coral Sea (see map) last week. Correspondents in Hawaii and Australia have had to work hard to piece together an accurate picture of what happened. The Navy's reluctance to talk shows that it considers the engagement yet another defeat.

One U.S. fleet carrier, the *Lexington,* was sunk. Another, the *Yorktown,* was severely damaged, and is limping toward Hawaii for repair. American casualties in the battle were heavy: 543 dead and a number of wounded the Navy still refuses to admit.

In addition to the carriers, the U.S. lost a destroyer, a fleet oiler, and 66 planes. Japanese aircraft hit American ships with 58% of the bombs and torpedoes they dropped. Prewar predictions of bombing accuracy were as low as 3%.

Navy sources claim to have sunk a Japanese light carrier, and to have damaged a fleet carrier—possibly two. They assert that 77 Japanese airplanes were downed, and say Japanese casualties "had to have been" heavier than ours. Given how much the Navy exaggerates what it has done in the Atlantic, these Pacific figures also need to be taken with an ocean of salt.

May 15, 1942—St. Louis Post-Dispatch
WALLACE SAYS FDR LIED
President Expected War, VP Insists

Vice President Henry Wallace broke ranks with Roosevelt again in a speech in Little Rock, Arkansas. "Roosevelt looked for us to get sucked into this war," Wallace said. "He was getting ready for it at the same time as he was telling America we could stay out.

"I see that now," the Vice President added. "If I'd seen it then, I never would have agreed to be his running mate. The USA deserves better. How many women—and men—are grieving today because the President of the United States flat-out lied? And how much more grief do we have to look forward to?"

Stormy applause greeted Wallace's remarks. Arkansas is a longtime Democratic stronghold, but FDR's popularity is plummeting there, as it has across the country. After Wallace finished speaking, shouts of "Impeach Roosevelt!" rang out from the crowd. They were also cheered.

Asked whether he thought Roosevelt should be impeached, Wallace said, "I can't comment. If I say no, people will think I agree with his policies, and I don't. But if I say yes, they will think I am angling for the White House myself. The people you need to talk to are the Speaker of the House and the chairman of the Judiciary Committee."

A reported also asked Wallace if he would seek peace if he did become President. "A negotiated settlement has to be better than the series of catastrophes we've suffered," he replied. "Why should our boys die to uphold the British Empire and Communist Russia?"

May 16, 1942—Washington Post
IMPEACHMENT "RIDICULOUS," FDR SAYS

Beleaguered Franklin Roosevelt called talk of impeachment "ridiculous" in a written statement released this morning. "I am doing the best job of running this country I can," the statement said. "That is what the American people elected me to do, and I aim to do it. We can win this war—and we will, unless the ingrates who stand up and cheer whenever anything goes wrong have their way."

Roosevelt's statement also lambasted his breakaway Vice President, Henry Wallace. "He is doing more for the other side than a division of panzer troops," it said.

Wallace replied, "I am trying to tell America the truth. Isn't it about time somebody did? We deserve it."

House Speaker Sam Rayburn declined comment. A source close to the Speaker said he is "waiting to see what happens next."

May 26, 1942—Honolulu Star-Bulletin
YORKTOWN TORPEDOED, SUNK
Loss of Life Feared Heavy

A day before she was to put in at Pearl Harbor for emergency repairs, the carrier *Yorktown* was sunk by a Japanese sub southwest of Oahu. The ship sank quickly in shark-infested waters. Only about 120 survivors have been rescued.

The *Yorktown*'s complement is about 1,900 men. She also carried air crew from the *Lexington*, which went down almost three weeks ago in the Coral Sea. Nearly as many men died with her as did at Pearl Harbor, in other words.

The plan was to quickly fix up the *Yorktown* and send her to defend Midway Island along with the *Hornet* and the *Saratoga*. Midway is believed to be the target of an advancing fleet considerably stronger than the forces available to hold the island. Now the two surviving carriers—one damaged itself—and their support vessels will have to go it alone.

If the Japanese occupy Midway, Honolulu and Pearl Harbor will come within reach of their deadly long-range bombers.

May 28, 1942—Honolulu Advertiser editorial
STAR-BULLETIN SHUT DOWN
Censors' Reign of Error

Because bullying Navy and War Department censors unconstitutionally closed down our rival newspaper yesterday, it is up to us to carry on in the *Star-Bulletin*'s footsteps. We aim to tell the truth to the people of Honolulu and to the people of America. If the maniacs with the blue pencils try to silence us, we will go underground to carry on the fight for justice and the First Amendment.

From where we sit, the fat cats in the Roosevelt administration who think they ought to have a monopoly on the facts are worse enemies of freedom than Tojo and Hitler put together. In dragging us into this pointless war in the first place, they pulled the wool over the country's eyes. They thought they had the right to do that, because they were doing it for our own good. They knew better than we did, you see.

Only they didn't. One disastrous failure after another has proved that. Up till now, the USA has never lost a war. Unless we can wheel FDR out of the White House soon, that record won't last more than another few weeks.

———

May 29, 1942—Cleveland Plain Dealer
DEMONSTRATORS CLASH DOWNTOWN
Pro- and Antiwar Factions, Police Battle in Streets

Thousands of protesters squared off yesterday in downtown Cleveland. Police were supposed to keep the passionately opposed sides separate. Instead, they joined the pro-FDR forces in pummeling the peaceful demonstrators who condemn the war and, in increasing numbers, call for Roosevelt's impeachment and removal from office.

Antiwar demonstrators far outnumbered the President's supporters. Those who still blindly back Roosevelt, however, came prepared for violence. They were armed with clubs, rocks, and bottles, and were ready to use them.

"War! War! FDR! Now the President's gone too far!" chanted the peaceful antiwar forces. Another chant soon swelled and grew: "Impeach Roosevelt!"

FDR's supporters attacked the antiwar picketers then. Vicious cops were also seen beating protesters with billy clubs and kicking them on the ground (see photo above this story). Some protesters withdrew from the demonstration. Others fought back, refusing to be intimidated by Roosevelt's thuggish followers or by the out-of-control police.

"This can only help our cause," said a man bleeding from a scalp laceration and carrying a *NO MORE YEARS!* sign. "When the country sees how brutal that man in the White House really is, it will know what to do. I'm sure of it."

May 31, 1942—Honolulu Advertiser

HORNET, SARATOGA SAIL FOR MIDWAY

America's two surviving fleet carriers in the Pacific left Pearl Harbor yesterday. Sources say they are bound for strategic Midway Island, about 1,000 miles to the northwest.

With the carriers sailed the usual accompaniment of cruisers and destroyers. The ships made a brave show. But how much can they hope to accomplish against the disciplined nationalism of Japan and the determined bravery of her soldiers and pilots and sailors?

This strike force seems to be Roosevelt's last desperate effort to salvage something from the war he blundered into. The odds look grim. Japan may be low on scrap metal and oil thanks to FDR, but she is long on guts and stubbornness. If the Navy fails here, as it has failed so often, the outlook for Hawaii and for the west coast of the mainland looks bleak indeed.

June 1, 1942—Official proclamation
HONOLULU ADVERTISER NO LONGER TO BE PUBLISHED

WHEREAS, it is provided by Section 67 of the Organic Act of the Territory of Hawaii, approved April 30, 1900, that the Governor of that territory may call upon the commander of the military forces of the United States in that territory to prevent invasion; and

WHEREAS, it is further provided by the said section that the Governor may, in case of invasion or imminent danger thereof, suspend the privilege of habeas corpus and place the territory under martial law; and

WHEREAS, the *Honolulu Advertiser* has egregiously violated the terms of censorship imposed on the territory following December 7, 1941;

NOW, THEREFORE, I order the said *Honolulu Advertiser* to suspend publication indefinitely and its staff to face military tribunals to judge and punish their disloyalty.

DONE at Honolulu, Territory of Hawaii, this 1st day of June, 1942.

(SEAL OF THE TERRITORY OF HAWAII)

—Lt. Col. Neal D. Franklin

Army Provost Marshal

June 7, 1942—San Francisco Chronicle
DISASTER AT MIDWAY!
Carriers Sunk—Island Invaded

The Imperial Japanese Navy dealt the U.S. Pacific Fleet a devastating blow off Midway Island three days ago. Though Navy officials are maintaining a tight-lipped silence, reliable sources say both the *Saratoga* and the *Hornet* were sunk by Japanese dive bombers. Several support vessels were also sunk or damaged.

Japanese troops have landed on Midway. The *Yamato,* the mightiest battleship in the world, is bombarding the island with what are reported to be 18-inch guns. Japanese planes rule the skies. Resistance is said to be fading.

When the Japanese succeed in occupying Midway, Hawaii will be vulnerable to their bombers. So will convoys coming from the mainland to supply Hawaii—and so will convoys leaving Hawaii for Australia and New Zealand.

Japanese submarines sailing out of Midway will have an easier time reaching the West Coast. They could even threaten the Panama Canal.

This war has seemed to be an uphill fight from the beginning. For all practical purposes, it is unwinnable now. The only person in the country who fails to realize that, unfortunately, lives at 1600 Pennsylvania Avenue in Washington.

———————

June 8, 1942—Baltimore News-Post
ROOSEVELT TEARS INTO PRESS
Blames Leaks for U.S. Defeats

Trying to shore up flagging public support for his war, FDR lashed out at American newspapers in a speech before midshipmen at the Naval Academy in Annapolis yesterday. "How can we fight with any hope of success when they trumpet our doings to the foe?" he complained.

The midshipmen applauded warmly. Whether Roosevelt could have found such a friendly reception from civilians is a different question.

"Reporters seem proud when they find a new secret and print it," he said, shaking his fist from his wheelchair. "If printing that secret means our brave sailors and soldiers die, they don't care. They have their scoop."

According to FDR, the staggering loss at Midway can be laid at the feet of newsmen. Our own military incompetence and Japanese skill and courage apparently had nothing to do with it. However loudly the young, naive midshipmen may cheer, the rest of the nation is drawing other conclusions.

June 9, 1942—Washington Post editorial
RESPONSIBILITY

Nothing is ever Franklin D. Roosevelt's fault. If you don't believe us, just ask him. German U-boats are sinking ships up and down the Atlantic coast? It's all the newspapers' fault. The Navy and the Army have suffered a string of humiliating defeats in the Pacific? The papers are to blame there, too.

Throwing rocks at the press may make FDR feel better, but that is all it does. What he really blames the newspapers for is pointing out his mistakes. Now the whole country can take a good look at them. Roosevelt does not care for that at all.

With him, image is everything; substance, nothing. Have you ever noticed how seldom he is allowed to be photographed in his wheelchair? If people aren't reminded of it, they won't think about it. That is how his mind works.

But when it comes to the acid test of war, image is not enough. You need real victories on the battlefield, and the United States has not been able to win any. Why not? No matter what Roosevelt and his stooges say, it is not because the press has blabbed our precious secrets.

The fact of the matter is, whether we read codes from Germany and Japan hardly matters. Even when we have good intelligence, we don't know what to do with it. Example? The Japanese tried out their Zero fighter in China in 1940. General Claire Chennault, who led the volunteer Flying Tigers, warned Washington what it was like. It came as a complete surprise to the Navy anyhow.

Most of our intelligence, though, was incredibly bad. We were sure France could give Germany a good fight. We were just as sure our navy could whip Japan's with ease. We fatally underestimated German technology and resourcefulness, to say nothing of Japanese drive and élan. Japan and Germany are fighting for their homelands. What are *we* fighting for? Anything at all?

FDR is too sunk in pride to get out of the war he stumbled into while the country still has any chestnuts worth pulling from the fire. He will not—he seems unable to—admit that the many mistakes we have made are his and his henchmen's.

And since he will not, we must put someone in the White House who will. Impeachment may be an extreme step, but the United States is in extreme danger. With this war gone so calamitously wrong, we need peace as soon as we can get it, and at almost any price.

———

June 11, 1942—Boston Globe
WALLACE PLEDGES PEACE, IF...

Vice President Henry Wallace said American foreign policy needs to change course. "I'm not the President. I can't make policy," he said last night at a Longshoremen's Union banquet. "Right now, the President doesn't even want to listen to me. But I can see it's time for a change. Only peace will put our beloved country back on track."

Wallace did not speak of the growing sentiment for impeachment. After all, he stands to take over the White House after Roosevelt is ousted. But he left no doubt that he would do everything in his power to pull American troops back to this country. He also condemned the huge deficits our massive military adventure is causing us to run.

With his common-sense approach, he seemed much more Presidential than the man still clinging to power in Washington.

———

June 16, 1942—Washington Post
RAYBURN, SUMNERS CONFER
Articles of Impeachment Likely

House Speaker Sam Rayburn and Judiciary Committee Chairman Hatton Sumners met today to discuss procedures for impeaching President Roosevelt. Both Texas Democrats were tight-lipped as they emerged from their conference.

Sumners offered no comment of any kind. Rayburn said only, "I am sorry to be in this position. The good of the country may demand something I would otherwise much rather not do."

Only one President has ever been impeached: Andrew Johnson in 1868. The Senate failed by one vote to convict him.

Sumners has experience with impeachment. He was the House manager in the proceedings against Judges George English and Halsted Ritter. English resigned; Ritter was convicted and removed from office.

Sumners has also clashed with FDR before. He was the chief opponent of Roosevelt's 1937 scheme to pack the Supreme Court.

Roosevelt's time in office must be seen as limited now. And that is a consummation devoutly to be wished. With a new leader, one we can respect, will surely come what Abraham Lincoln called "a new birth of freedom." It cannot come soon enough.

THE MALTESE
ELEPHANT

Miles Bowman was a man built of rectangular blocks. His head was one, squared off with short-cut graying hair at the top and a sharp jaw at the bottom. His chest and shoulders made a thick brick, his belly below them a slightly smaller one. His arms and legs were thick, muscular pillars. He trimmed his nails straight across at the ends of his fingers.

His partner Tom Trencher, that smiling devil, was dead. In the hallway outside the office, a sign painter was using a razor blade to scrape BOWMAN & TRENCHER off the frosted glass. When he was done, he would paint Bowman's name there by itself in gilt. Centered.

The phone rang. His secretary answered it. Hester Prine was a tall, skinny, brown-haired girl. She wore good clothes as if they were sacks. But when she talked, any man who heard her had hungry dreams for days.

She covered the mouthpiece with her hand. "It's your wife."

Bowman shook his head. "I don't want to talk to Eva."

"She wants to talk to you about Tom."

"I figured she did. What else would she call me about here? I don't want to talk to her, I told you. Tell her I'm out on a case. I'll see her tonight. She can talk to me then."

His secretary's mouth twisted, but she took her hand away and said what Bowman had told her to say. She had to say it three times before she could hang up. Then she rose and walked over to Bowman's desk in the inner office. She looked down at him. "You're a louse, Miles."

"Yeah, I know," he said comfortably. His arm slid around her waist. He pulled her closer to him.

"Louse," she said again, in a different tone of voice. She hesitated. "Miles, she wants to talk to you because—" She ran down like a phonograph that needs winding.

"Because she thinks I killed Tom." His hand tightened on her hip. He smiled. His teeth were not very good. "Why would she think a thing like that?"

"Because you know she and—" Hester Prine ran down again. "You're hurting me."

"Am I?" He did not let go. "I know lots of things. But I didn't kill Tom. Eva won't pin that one on me. The cops won't, either."

Soft footsteps came down the hall. They paused in front of the office. The sign painter stopped scraping. Hester Prine twisted away from Bowman. This time he did not try to stop her.

The door opened. By then Bowman's secretary was back at her desk. A woman walked into the office. The sign painter stared at her until the door closed and cut off his view. Then, with reluctant razor, he went back to work.

The woman was small and swarthy and perfect, with a heart-shaped face and enormous black eyes that could smile or sob or blaze or do all three at once in the space of a couple of heartbeats. Her crow's-wing hair fell almost to her shoulders in a straight bob. It was not what they were wearing this year, but on her it was right. So was her orange crêpe silk frock with a flared peplum skirt.

She strode past Hester Prine as if the secretary did not exist and went into Bowman's inner office. He got up from in back of his desk. "Miss Lenoir," he said. He shut the door behind her.

"Your partner," Claire Lenoir said in a broken voice. "It's my fault." Tears glistened in her eyes, but did not fall.

"Not all of it," he answered. "Tom knew what he was doing, and you told him the guy he was tailing—the guy who's been tailing you—was one rough customer. You don't get into this business if you think everything is going to be easy all the time. Or you better not."

Her hands fluttered. She wore two rings, of gold and emeralds. They glowed against her dark skin. "But—" she said.

Bowman waved dismissively. "You mean that story you told us before? That didn't have anything to do with anything. If Tom and I had believed it, it might have, but we didn't. So don't worry about that. But you're going to have to level sooner or later, if you want me to do whatever you really want me to do."

The outer door opened. Hester Prine talked with someone—a man—for a few seconds. The phone on Bowman's desk jangled. He picked it up. "A Mr. Nicholas Alexandria wants to see you right now," his secretary said. "He says it's worth two hundred dollars."

"Have you seen the money?" Bowman asked.

"He's got it," she answered.

Bowman mouthed the name "Nicholas Alexandria" to Claire Lenoir. She started violently. The blood drained from her face, leaving her skin the color of old newspaper. She shook her head so her hair for a moment flew across her face. One strand stuck at the corner of her red-painted mouth. She brushed it away with an angry gesture.

"Send him in, sweetheart," Bowman said placidly. He hung up the telephone.

The man who came through the door might have been born in the city that gave him his name. He was darker than Claire Lenoir. His nose curved like a saber blade. His mouth, a Cupid's bow, was red but not painted. He stank of patchouli.

His eyes, hard and shiny and black as obsidian, flicked to Claire Lenoir and widened slightly. Then they returned to Bowman. "Your secretary did not say you had—this woman here," he said in a fussy, precise voice.

"Did you ask her?" Bowman asked. Nicholas Alexandria's eyes widened again. He shook his head, a single, tightly controlled gesture. Bowman said, "Then you've got no cause for complaint. I hear you're two hundred dollars interested in talking to me." He held out his hand, palm up.

Nicholas Alexandria's finely manicured hand drew from the pocket of his velvet jacket a wallet of tanned snakeskin. He removed from it four bills bearing the image of Ulysses S. Grant, held them out to Miles Bowman.

Bowman took them, studied them, put them into his own wallet, and stuck it back in his hip pocket. "All right," he said. He waved to a chair. "Sit. Talk."

Alexandria sat. His red mouth contracted petulantly. "I might have known Miss Tellini would be here, when I wished to discuss with you matters pertaining to the Maltese Elephant."

Bowman's head turned on its thick neck. "Miss Tellini?" he asked Claire Lenoir.

"Gina Tellini," Nicholas Alexandria said with a certain cold relish. "Why? Under what name do you know her?"

"It's not important," Bowman answered. He smiled at the girl. "Got any others?"

Her skin darkened. She looked away from him. Nicholas Alexandria said, "That is the appellation with which she was born in the district of New York known as, I believe, Hell's Kitchen, any representations to the contrary notwithstanding." Gina Tellini spat something in Italian. Nicholas Alexandria answered in the same language, his diction precise.

Her mouth fell open. His smile was frigid. In English, he said, "You see, I can get down in the gutter, too."

Miles Bowman held up a meaty hand. "Enough, already," he said. He waved to Alexandria. "You wanted to talk about the Maltese Elephant. Go ahead and talk."

"You are already familiar with this famous and fabulous creature?" Nicholas Alexandria inquired.

"Never heard of it," Bowman said politely.

Nicholas Alexandria gave another of his tightly machined head-shakes. "I am afraid I cannot believe you, Mr. Bowman," he said. He reached inside his jacket once more. His hand returned to sight with a snub-nosed chromed automatic. He pointed it at Miles Bowman's chest. "Place both your hands wide apart on the desk immediately."

"You stinking little pansy," Bowman said.

Nicholas Alexandria's red, full lips narrowed into a thin pink slash. His tongue darted out like a snake's. The hand holding the automatic did not waver.

Bowman lowered a shoulder, twisted his body a little to one side. Then he spoke with savage satisfaction: "All right, Alexandria, now you've got a gun and I've got a gun. But you've got that cheap .22 and I'm holding a .45. You shoot me, I spend some time in the hospital getting patched up. I shoot you, pal, you're not just history, you're archaeology." He laughed loudly at his own wit. "Now put your little toy away and we'll talk."

"I do not believe you have a weapon," Nicholas Alexandria said.

"The more fool you," Bowman answered. "My partner didn't believe in packing a gun, and now the fool is dead. I'm a lot of things, but I'm no fool."

"He has it," Gina Tellini said. "I can see his hand on it."

"You would say the same in any case." Nicholas Alexandria's eyes did not move toward her. To Bowman, he said: "Shooting through the front of your desk does not strike me as like to produce the results you would desire."

Bowman leaned back in his chair. One of his feet left the nubby, mustard-colored wool rug for a moment. It slammed against the inside of the center panel of the desk. The panel bowed outward. At the sudden crash, Nicholas Alexandria's finger tightened on the trigger. Then it eased again. Bowman's voice was complacent: "Cheap plywood, varnished to look like mahogany. A slug won't even know it's there."

Alexandria's mouth screwed tight, as if he were about to kiss someone he did not like. He slid the revolver back into the inner pocket of his jacket. As if he had never taken it out, he said, "Perhaps Miss Tellini did not see fit to tell you the Maltese Elephant—*a* Maltese elephant, I should say—is in San Francisco now."

"No, she didn't tell me that," Miles Bowman said. He looked Gina Tellini up and down. Now her eyes were as flat and opaque as Nicholas Alexandria's. Bowman turned back to the man in the velvet jacket. "So what do you want me to do about it? Find this elephant and sell it to the circus?"

Nicholas Alexandria rose and bowed. "I see I am being mocked. I shall return another time, in the hope of finding you alone and serious."

"Sorry you feel that way." Bowman also got up. He came around the desk and stood towering over Nicholas Alexandria as he opened the door to let the slighter man out of the inner office.

Alexandria raised one finger. "A moment. Did you truly have a pistol?"

Bowman reached under his jacket. The motion exposed a battered leather holster on his right hip. He pulled out the Colt Model 1911A and let it lie, heavy and ugly and black, in his palm. It bore no frill, no ornament, no chromium. It was a killing machine, nothing else. Nicholas Alexandria stared at it. He let out a small, gasping sigh.

"I never bluff," Bowman said. "No percentage to it." He shifted the pistol in his hand. His fingers closed on the checkered grip. With a motion astonishingly fast from such a heavyset man, he slammed the Colt's hard steel barrel against the side of Alexandria's face. "Remember that."

The blow knocked Alexandria back two paces. He staggered but did not fall. The raised foresight had cut his cheek. Blood dripped onto his jacket. Slowly he removed the silk handkerchief from his breast pocket. He dabbed at the jacket, then raised the handkerchief to his face. "I shall remember, Mr. Bowman," he whispered hoarsely. "Rely on it."

He walked past Hester Prine without looking at her, and out of the office.

Gina Tellini brought her hands together several times, clapping without sound. "Now I know you will be able to protect me—Miles." She lingered half a heartbeat over his Christian name.

He shrugged. "All in a day's work. You have anything you want to tell me about this Maltese Elephant?"

Those quicksilver eyes betrayed an instant's alarm. Then they were her servants again. She shook her head. "I can't, not yet," she said huskily.

"Have it your way." Bowman's thick shoulders moved up and down once more. "You're going to, or Alexandria will, or somebody." He watched her. She stood very still, like a small, hunted animal. He shrugged a third time, motioned for her to precede him out of the inner office. "See you later."

When her footsteps could no longer be heard in the hall, he turned to Hester Prine. "I'm going home." He checked his wristwatch. "Quarter past seven already. Jesus, where does the time get to?" He set his hand on her shoulder. "Go on back to your place, too. To hell with all this."

She did not look at him. "I have some more typing to do," she said tonelessly.

"Have it your way," Bowman said, as he had to Gina Tellini. He closed the outer door—now it read BOWMAN, in letters bigger than BOWMAN & TRENCHER had been painted—and strolled down the hall to the elevator.

As he walked, he whistled "Look for the Silver Lining." He whistled out of tune, and flat. The elevator boy looked at him as he got into the cage. He looked back. The elevator boy suddenly got busy with the buttons and took him to the ground floor.

He walked across the street to the garage where he kept his Chevrolet. He threw the kid on the corner a nickel. The kid handed him a copy of the *San Francisco News*. He tossed it into the front seat of the car. The starter whined when he turned the key. Coughing, the motor finally caught. He put the Chevrolet in gear and drove home.

———————

The house on Thirty-third Avenue in the Sunset district needed a coat of paint. The houses to which it was joined on either side had been painted recently, one blue, the other a sort of rose pink. That made the faded, blotchy yellow surface look all the shabbier.

Bowman bounded up the steps two at a time. He turned the key in the Yale lock, mashed his thumb down on the latch. With a click like a bad knee, the door opened.

The interior was all plush and cheap velvet and curlicued wood and overstuffed furniture. "Is that you, honey?" Eva's voice wafted out of the kitchen with the smell of pot roast and onions. She sounded nervous.

"Who else do you know with a key?" Bowman asked. He scaled his hat toward the couch. It fell short and landed on the fringe of the throw rug under the coffee table. He dropped the *News* onto the table.

Eva came out and stood in the kitchen doorway. He walked over, kissed her perfunctorily. They had been married thirteen years. She was ten years the younger. She was about the age Tom Trencher had been. Trencher wouldn't get any older.

Eva's short red curls got their color from a bottle. They'd been the same color when he married her, and from the same source. They went well with her green eyes. She was twenty pounds heavier now than when they'd walked down the aisle, but big-boned enough to wear the pounds well. She wore a ruffled apron over a middie blouse and a cotton skirt striped brightly in gold and blue.

Her smile was a little too wide. It showed too many teeth. "Do the police know anything more about—who killed Tom?" She looked at the point of his chin, not his eyes.

"If they do, they haven't told me. I didn't talk with 'em today." He shrugged. "Get me a drink."

"Sure, honey." She hurried away. She opened the pantry, then the icebox, and came back with a tumbler of bourbon on the rocks. "Here." That too-ingratiating smile still masked her face.

Bowman drank half the tumbler with two long swallows. He exhaled, long and reverently, and held up the glass to scrutinize its deep amber contents against the light bulb in the kitchen ceiling lamp. "This is the medicine," he announced, and finished the bourbon. He handed Eva the glass. "Fix me another one of these with supper."

"Sure, Miles," she said. "We ought to be just about ready." The pot lid clanked as she lifted it off to check the roast. She set it back on the big iron pot. The oven door hinge squeaked. "The meat is done, and so are the potatoes. I'll set the table and get you your drink."

Bowman buttered his baked potato, spread salt and pepper lavishly over the thick slab of red-brown beef Eva set before him. He ate steadily, methodically, without waste motion, like a man shoveling coal into a locomotive firebox. Every so often, he sipped from the tall glass of bourbon next to the chipped china plate that held his supper.

Eva dropped her knife on the flowered linoleum floor. Bowman looked up for the first time since he'd seated himself at the table. Eva flushed. She flung the knife into the sink. Then she got up and took a clean one from the silverware drawer.

Before Bowman could resume his assault on the pot roast, she said, "Miles, honey, who do you think murdered Tom?"

"Had to be that guy he was shadowing," he answered. He speared another piece of meat with his fork, but did not raise it to his lips. "Thursday, that was his name. Evan Thursday." He ate the piece of meat. With his mouth full, he went on, "Couldn't have been anybody else." He swallowed, and smiled at Eva. "Could it?"

"No, I don't imagine it could," she said quickly. She bent her head over her plate. A moment later, her fork clattered to the floor. Her lips twisted. "I'm as twitchy as a cat tonight."

"Can't imagine why," Bowman said. He drank from the tumbler. Two ice cubes clinked against its side.

When supper was done, Bowman went out to the living room. He set what was left of his drink on the coffee table, then sat down on the sofa. The springs creaked under his weight. He bent over, grunting a little, untied his shoes, and tossed them under the table.

"Eva, get me my slippers," he said.

"What?" she called over the noise of running water in the kitchen. He repeated himself, louder. The water stopped running. Drying her hands on a dish towel, Eva bustled past him into the bedroom. She came back with the towel draped over her arm and the slippers in her hands. "Here they are." He slid them onto his feet. She returned to the dishes.

He smoked three cigarettes waiting for her to finish washing and drying them. When she came out, he handed her the tumbler. She washed it and dried it and put it away. He had opened the *News* by then, and was going through it front to back, as systematically as he ate.

Eva sighed softly and went over to a bookcase. She pulled out a sentimental novel and carried it into the bedroom. Bowman went on reading. When he came to the *Ships in Port* listing, he chewed thoughtfully on his underlip. He got up. In the clutter of papers and matchbooks in the top drawer of the hutch, he found a pencil. He underlined the names of four ships:

Daisy Miller from London

La Tórtola from Gozo

Admiral Byng from Minorca

Golden Wind from Bombay

After he read the advertisements on the other side of the page that held *Ships in Port,* he tore out the three-inch length of agate type and stuck it in his trouser pocket. Then he worked his way through the rest of the newspaper.

"Miles?"

Bowman looked up. Eva stood in the doorway that led to the bedroom. She was wearing a thin, clinging silk crêpe de chine peignoir. Bowman had given it to her for their anniversary a few years before. She did not wear it very often.

"It's getting late," she said. "Aren't you coming to bed?" She had not washed off her makeup and smeared her face with cold cream, the way she usually did at bedtime.

Bowman folded up the paper and tossed it on the floor. His fingers were stained with ink from the cheap newsprint. He rubbed them on the thighs of his pants, rose from the couch. "Don't mind if I do," he said.

———

A hard fist pounded on the front door. Bowman sat up in bed. The pounding went on. "Who's that?" Eva asked, her voice half drunk with sleep.

"Damned if I know, but I'm going to find out." Bowman groped for the switch on the lamp by the bed. He flicked it, and screwed up his eyes against the sudden flare of light. He peered at the alarm clock on the nightstand by the lamp. Midnight. Scowling, he got out of bed. He had hung his holster on a chair. He pulled out his pistol, clicked off the safety.

"What are you going to do?" Eva asked. The cold cream made her round cheeks glisten like the rump of a greased pig.

"See who it is," Bowman answered reasonably. "You stare here." He slid into his pajama bottoms and padded out toward the door. For a bulky man, he was surprisingly light on his feet. He closed the bedroom door after him.

The pounding had slowed when the light went on. Bowman yanked the door open. He pointed the pistol at the two men on the front porch. A moment later, he lowered it. "Jesus Christ," he said. "You boys trying to get yourselves killed? I knew cops were dumb, but this dumb?" He shook his head.

"We've got to talk to you, Miles," one of the policemen said. "Can we come in?"

"You got a warrant, Rollie?" Bowman asked.

"Not that kind of talk, I swear." Detective Roland Dwyer crossed himself to show he was serious.

Bowman considered. He nodded gruffly. "All right, come in, then," he said, and turned on the imitation Tiffany lamp on the table by the door. "But if you and the Captain here are playing games with me—" He did not say what would happen then, but left the implication it would not be pretty.

"Thanks, Miles," Dwyer said with an air of sincerity. He was a tall Irishman heading toward middle age. His hair had naturally the color to which Eva's aspired. His face was long and ruddy and triangular, with a wide forehead and a narrow chin. He wore a frayed shirt collar and pants shiny with wear at the knees: he was, on the whole, an honest cop.

Bowman waved him toward the sofa. The Captain followed him in. Bowman quickly closed the door. The night was chilly, and had the clammy dankness of fog. Bowman sat down in the rocking chair next to the table that held the lamp with the colored glass shade. His voice turned hard: "All right, what won't keep till morning?"

Dwyer and the Captain looked at each other. The latter was a short, pudgy man, a few years older than Bowman. He had a fringe of silver hair futilely clinging to the slopes of his pate, skin as fine and pink as a baby's, and innocent blue eyes. His suit was new, and tailored in the English fashion. He smelled of expensive Bay Rum after-shave lotion.

After a brief hesitation, the Captain said: "Evan Thursday's dead, Miles, One slug, right between the eyes."

"So?" Bowman said. "Good riddance to him is all I have to say, Bock."

Captain Henry Bock steepled his fingers. He pressed them so tight together, the blood was forced from their tips, leaving them pale as boiled veal. "Where have you been tonight, Miles?" he asked delicately.

Bowman heaved himself out of the rocker. He took two steps toward the Captain before he checked himself. "Get out of here," he snarled. "Rollie tells me everything's going to be jake, and you start with that—" He expressed his opinion with vehemence, variety, and detail.

Roland Dwyer spread his hands placatingly. "Come on, take it easy," he said. "This guy gets iced, we have to talk with you. We think he shot Tom, after all, and Tom was your partner."

"Yeah? Is that what you think?" Bowman made a slashing gesture of disgust with his left hand. "Looked like you were trying to pin Tom on me. Or do you figure I took care of both of 'em now?"

"Where have you been tonight?" Captain Bock repeated.

"At the office and here, dammit, nowhere else but," Bowman said. "Ask my secretary when I left, ask Eva when I got here. You want me to get her out so you can ask her?" He glanced over to the closed bedroom door. "Only take a minute."

"It's all right, Miles," Detective Dwyer said. "We believe you." He looked over at Henry Bock again. "Don't we, Captain?"

Bock shrugged. "Neither of those women is likely to tell us anything different from what Bowman says, anyhow."

The Captain had spoken quietly. Bowman glanced at the bedroom door again. When he answered, he too held his voice down, but anger blazed in it: "And what the hell is that supposed to mean? You come round here with one load of rubbish, and now you start throwing around more? I ought to—"

"Shut up, Bowman," Captain Bock said flatly. "What the women say doesn't matter, not this time. Thursday caught his right outside Kezar Stadium, in Golden Gate Park. If you'd arranged to meet him there, it wouldn't have been five minutes out of your way."

"And if pigs had wings—" Bowman stood up, opened the front door. "Get out," he growled. "Next time you come here, you bring a warrant, like I said. My lawyer'll be here with me, too."

"I'm sorry, Miles," Dwyer said. "We're doing our job, too, remember. You aren't making it any easier for us, either."

"Go do it somewhere else," Bowman said.

The two policemen got up and walked into the building fog. They got into their car, which they had parked behind Bowman's. The heavy, wet air muffled the sound of the motor starting. In the fog, the beams the headlamps cast seemed thick and yellow as butter.

Bowman shut the door and locked it. He went back into the bedroom, replaced the pistol in its holster. Eva was sitting up, reading the novel she'd abandoned earlier. "What—did they want?" she asked hesitantly.

"Somebody punched that Evan Thursday's ticket for him," Bowman answered.

"And they think it was you?" Eva's eyes widened. "That's terrible!"

"It's nothing to worry about," Bowman said, shrugging. "I didn't do it, so they can't pin it on me, right?" He lay down beside her, clicked off the lamp on his side of the bed. He yawned. "You going to look at that thing all night?"

"No, dear." Eva put down the book and turned off her lamp. Although she stretched out next to Bowman, she wiggled and fidgeted the way she did when she was having trouble going to sleep. Bowman shrugged once more, breathed heavily, then soon began to snore.

———————

The telephone rang, loud in the night as a fire alarm. Bowman thrashed, twisted, sat up, and turned on the bedside lamp. The alarm clock said it was almost three. He shook his head. "I don't believe this."

The phone kept ringing. "Answer it," Eva told him. She pulled the pale blue wool blanket up over her head.

Muttering, he walked into the leaving room. He snatched the earpiece off the hook, picked up the rest of the instrument, and barked his name into the mouthpiece: "Bowman." The voice on the other end of the line spoke. "Now?" Bowman asked. "Are you sure?... Jesus Christ, it's three in the morning... All right, if that's the way it's got to be... Room 481, right? See you there... Yeah, fifteen minutes if the fog's not too thick."

He slammed the mouthpiece down on his goodbye, stalked back into the bedroom. Eva had turned off the light. He turned it on again. He unbuttoned the shirt to his pajamas and walked naked to the dresser.

"What's wrong?" Eva asked as he pulled a clean pair of white cotton boxer shorts out of a dresser drawer. "Why are you getting dressed?" She sounded frightened.

"I'm going down to the station." He got into the same trousers he had worn the day before. "Bock and Dwyer, they have some more questions for me." He put on socks and shoes, got a fresh shirt from the closet, knotted a tie with a jungle pattern of hot blues and oranges and greens, shrugged a jacket over his wide shoulders. He ran a comb through his hair, then planted a curled-brim fedora on his head.

"Shouldn't you call your lawyer?" Eva said.

"Nah, it'll be all right." He started out. At the bedroom door, he stopped and blew her a kiss.

The fog was there, but not too thick. He had the roads all to himself. Once his Chevrolet and a police car passed each other on opposite sides of the street. He waved to the men inside. One of them recognized him and waved back.

He turned right off Market onto New Montgomery. During business hours, no one could have hoped to find a parking space there. Now the curb was his to command. He walked over to the eight-story Beaux Arts building of tan brick and terra cotta at the corner of Market and New Montgomery. A man in uniform held the door open for him. He strode across the lobby to the bank of elevators.

"Fourth floor," he told the operator as he got into one.

"Fourth floor, yes, sir," the man answered. "Welcome to the Palace Hotel."

Bowman stood with his feet slightly spread, as if at parade rest. He looked straight ahead. The elevator purred upward. When it got to the fourth floor, the operator opened the cage. Bowman stepped out while the fellow was telling him the floor.

A sign on the wall opposite the elevator announced:

401-450   451-499

< >

Bowman went >. The carpet in the hall was so thick that the pile swallowed the welt of his shoe each time his weight came down on it. He paused a moment in front of room 481, then folded his thick hand into a fist and rapped on the door just below the polished brass numbers.

It opened. "Come in," Gina Tellini said. She looked as fresh as she had the afternoon before, but at some time between then and now had changed into a dark green velvet lounging robe of Oriental cut. The front of a Chinese dragon, embroidered in deep golds and reds, coiled across her breast.

Bowman stepped into the hotel room. Gina Tellini closed the door after him. As she started back past him, he said, "Thursday's dead."

She stopped in her tracks. A hand started to fly up to her mouth, but checked itself. "How do you know that?" she asked in a shaken voice.

"Cops—how else?" He barked mirthless laughter. "They want to put that one on my bar tab, too, along with Tom." His lips thinned, stretching his mouth into a speculative line. "You could have done it. You would have had time, after you left the office."

"No, not me." She dismissed the idea in three casual words. "Here, sit down, make yourself comfortable." She waved Bowman to a chair upholstered in velvet two shades lighter than her gown. She sat down on the edge of the bed facing him. The bed had not been slept in since the maid last prepared it.

"All right, not you," Bowman said agreeably, crossing his legs. "Who, then?"

"It could have been Nicholas Alexandria," Gina Tellini said. "He carries a gun. You saw that."

"Yeah, I saw that. It could have been. But a lot of people carry guns. I carry one myself. 'Could have been' doesn't cut much ice."

"I know." Gina Tellini nodded. The motion made the robe come open, very slightly, at the neckline. "But somebody besides Alexandria wants the Maltese Elephant."

"Somebody besides Alexandria and you." Bowman's gaze focused on the point, a few inches below her chin, where velvet had retreated. "Thursday's dead. Who else is there?"

"A man named Gideon Schlechtman," she answered promptly. "Sometimes he and Alexandria work together, sometimes Alexandria is on his own, or thinks he is. But if he gets the elephant, Schlechtman will try to take it from him."

"I bet he will," Bowman said. "And what about you and Alexandria and what's-his-name, Schlechtman? I bet the three of you are one big happy family, right?"

"It's not funny, Miles," Gina Tellini insisted. "Schlechtman is— dangerous. If Evan Thursday is dead, that's all the more reason to believe he's come to San Francisco."

"Is that so?" Bowman said. "All I have is your word, and your word hasn't been any too real good, you know what I mean? And if this here Schlechtman is real and is in town, whose side are you on?"

"That's a terrible question to ask." Gina Tellini's eyes blazed for a moment. Then sudden tears put out the fire. "You don't believe a word I've told you. It's so—hard when you don't trust me. I'm here in your city all alone and—" The rest was muffled when she buried her face in her hands.

Bowman rose from the chair, sat down beside her on the bed. "Don't get upset, sweetheart," he said. "One way or another, I'll take care of things."

She looked up at him. Lamplight sparkled on the tracks two tears had traced on her cheeks. "I'm so damned tired of always being alone," she whispered.

"You're not alone now," he said. She nodded, slowly, her eyes never leaving his. He slipped his left arm around her shoulder, drew her to him. Her lips parted. They kissed fiercely. When they fell back to the mattress together, his weight pinned her against its firm resilience.

———

The rumble of a cable car and the clang of its bell outside the window woke Miles Bowman. The gray light of approaching dawn seeped through the thick brocaded curtains of Gina Tellini's room.

Moving carefully, Bowman slid out from under her arm. She stirred and murmured but did not wake. Bowman dressed with practiced haste. The door clicked when he closed it. He paused outside in the hall. No sound came from within. Satisfied, he walked back to the elevator.

More automobiles were on the street now, but not too many to keep Bowman from making a U-turn on New Montgomery. He turned right onto Market Street and took it all the way to the Embarcadero.

The Ferry Building was quiet. Its siren would not wail for another two hours, not until eight o'clock. Through the thinning fog, its high clock tower loomed, brooding and sinister. Man-o'-War Row and berths for passenger liners stretched south of the Ferry Building, commercial piers for foreign lines north and west around the curve of the shore. Bowman turned left, toward them, onto the Embarcadero. Between gear changes, his right hand grubbed in his trouser pocket. He pulled out the piece of newsprint he had torn from the *San Francisco News*.

He parked the car and got out. His nostrils dilated. The air was thick with the smells of rotting piles and roasting coffee, mud and fish and salt water. Sea gulls mewed like flying cats. He padded along, burly as the longshoremen all around but standing out from them by virtue of jacket and collar and tie.

The *News* listed ships in order of the piers at which they were docked. The *Daisy Miller* was tied up by Pier 7. Shouting dock workers loaded wooden crates onto her. Stenciled letters on the sides of the crates declared they held sewing machines. They were the right size for rifles. Bowman shrugged and walked on to Pier 15, where *La Tórtola* was berthed.

A handful of sailors worked on deck, swabbing and painting under the watchful eye of a skinny blond man in a black-brimmed white officer's cap and a dark blue jacket with four gold rings circling each cuff. He saw Bowman looking at him. "What do you want, you?" he called. He had a German accent, or maybe Dutch.

Bowman put hands on hips. "Who wants to know?"

"I am Captain Wellnhofer, and I have the right to ask these questions. But you—" The captain's face had been pale. Now it was red and angry.

"Keep your shirt on, buddy," Bowman said. He looked down at the scrap of newspaper in his hand. "This here the boat that's supposed to get another load of fodder today?"

Captain Wellnhofer's face got redder. "Do you not know in your own language the difference between a boat and a ship? And we have no need for fodder now. You are mistaken. Go away."

The *Admiral Byng* was docked at Pier 23. Nobody aboard her admitted any need for fodder, either. Bowman grimaced and hiked on to Pier 35, which held the *Golden Wind*. "Halfway to Fisherman's damn Wharf," he muttered. The only men visible aboard her were little brown lascars in dungarees. None of them seemed to speak any English. Bowman held a couple of silver dollars in the palm of his hand. A lascar hurried to the rail with a sudden white smile. Bowman tossed him one of the coins. He asked the same question he had before. The lascar didn't understand fodder. "Hay, straw, grain—you know what I mean," Bowman said.

"You crazy?" the lascar said. "We got tea, we got cotton, we got copra. We take away steam engines, petrol engines. You think maybe we feed them this grain?" He spoke in his own singsong language. The other lascars laughed.

"Yeah, well, just for that, funny guy—" Bowman jammed the other silver dollar back into his trouser pocket. The lascar's Hindustani oaths followed him as he strode down the pier toward the Embarcadero. He paused at the base of the bier to scribble a note: EXPENSES— INFORMATION—$2. Then he walked back along the curb of the harbor to his automobile.

He parked it in the garage across the street from his office. Lounging against the brick wall not far from the entrance was a burly middle-aged man with the cold, hard, angular features of a Roman centurion. With its wide, pointed lapels, padded shoulders, and pinstripes, his suit stood on one side or the other of the line between fashion and parody. Bowman looked him over, then started up the steps.

The lounger spoke: "You don't want to go in there. You want to come with me."

"Yeah? Says who?" Bowman dropped his right hand from the doorknob. It came to rest at his side, near waist level.

"Says my boss—he's got a business proposition to put to you," the fellow answered. He stood straighter. One of his hands rested in the front pocket of his jacket. "And says me. And says—" The hand, and whatever it held, moved a little, suggestively.

Bowman came down the steps. "All right, take me to your boss. I'll talk business with anybody. As for you, pal, you can get stuffed." He spoke the words lightly, negligently, as if he didn't care whether the hard-faced man followed through on them or not.

The hard-faced man took a step toward him. "You watch your mouth, or—"

Bowman hit him in the pit of the stomach. His belly was hard as oak. Against a precisely placed blow to the solar plexus, that proved irrelevant. He doubled over with a loud, whistling grunt. His suddenly exhaled breath smelled of gin. While he gasped for air, Bowman plucked a revolver from his pocket and put it in his own. He hauled the burly man back to his feet. "I told you—take me to your boss."

The man glared at him. Hatred smoldered in his eyes. He started to say something. Bowman shook his head and raised a warning forefinger. The burly man visibly reconsidered. "Come on," he said, and Bowman nodded.

The seventeen-story white brick and stone Clift Hotel on Geary Street was five blocks west of the Palace. The hard-faced man said nothing more on the way there, nor through the lobby, which was decorated in the style of the Italian Renaissance. He and Bowman took the elevator to the fourteenth floor in silence. He rapped at the door to suite 1453.

Nicholas Alexandria opened it. His chrome-plated pistol was in his hand. "Ah, Mr. Bowman, so good to see you again," he said in a tone that belied the words. His left hand rose to a sticking plaster on his cheek. The plaster did not cover all the bruise there. "Won't you come in?"

"Don't mind if I do," Bowman said, and stepped past him. The suite was furnished in spare and modern style. Gina Tellini sat on a chair that looked as if it might pitch her off at any moment. She sent Bowman a quick, nervous glance, but did not speak. Nicholas Alexandria closed the door, sat on a similar chair beside her.

The couch opposite them was low and poorly padded enough to have come from ancient Greece. On it, hunched forward as if not to miss anything, sat a thin, pale, long-faced man with a lantern jaw and gold-rimmed spectacles. He wore a suit of creamy linen, a Sea Island cotton shirt, and a burgundy silk tie whose bar was adorned with a small silver coin, irregularly round, that displayed a large-eyed owl.

"Schlechtman?" Bowman said. The pale man nodded. Bowman took the revolver out of his pocket. He handed it to him. "You shouldn't let your little chums play with toys like this. They're liable to get hurt."

The hard-featured man who had unwillingly brought Bowman to the Clift Hotel flushed. Before he could speak, Gideon Schlechtman held up a hand. His fingers were long and white, like stalks of asparagus. "Hugo, that was exceedingly clumsy of you," he said, his voice dry, meticulous, scholarly.

He glanced a question at Bowman. Bowman nodded. Schlechtman returned the revolver to Hugo. The burly man growled wordlessly as he received it.

Bowman said: "Your bully boy tells me you want to talk business."

Schlechtman shifted so he could draw a billfold from his left hip pocket. From the billfold he took a banknote with a portrait of Grover Cleveland. He set it on the black lacquered table in front of him. Four more with the same portrait went on top of it. "Do you care for the tone of the conversation thus far?" he enquired.

"Who wouldn't like five grand?" Bowman asked hoarsely. His eyes never left the bills. "What do I have to do?"

"You have to deliver to me, alive and in good condition, the Maltese Elephant currently in this fair city of yours," Gideon Schlechtman replied.

"If you'll pay me five thousand for it, it's worth plenty more than that to you," Bowman said. Schlechtman smiled. He had small white even teeth. Gina Tellini caught her breath. Bowman went on: "I ought to have something to work from. Give me two grand now."

Gideon Schlechtman pursed his lips. He took one bill from the top of the stack, held it out to Bowman between thumb and forefinger. Bowman seized it, crumpled it, stuffed it into the trouser pocket where he kept his keys. Schlechtman neatly replaced the rest of the banknotes in his wallet. The wallet returned to the pocket from which it had come. Nicholas Alexandria sighed.

"All right," Bowman said. "Next thing is, everybody here knows more about this damned elephant that I do. Even Hugo does, if Hugo knows anything about anything."

"Why, you lousy—" Hugo began.

Again Schlechtman held up his hand. Again Hugo subsided into growls. Schlechtman said, "Your request is a fair one, Mr. Bowman. If you are to assist us with your unmatchable knowledge of San Francisco, you must also have some knowledge of the remarkable beast we seek.

"Though the Maltese Elephant has of course been known since haziest antiquity to the human inhabitants with whom it shares its island, it was first memorialized in literature in the *Periplus* of Hanno the Carthaginian, which was translated from Punic to Greek in the fourth century B.C. Hanno's is a bald note: *Thêridion ho elephas Melitês estin.*"

"It's Greek to me, by God," Bowman said.

Schlechtman continued his lecture as if Bowman had not spoken: "Aristotle, in the *Historia Animalium*, 610a15, says of the Maltese Elephant, *Ho elephas ho Melitaios megethei homoios tê nêsô en hê oikei.* And Strabo, in the sixth book of his geography, notes Maltese dogs shared a similar trait: *Prokeitai de tou Pakhynou Melitê, hothen ta kynidia te kai elephantidia, ha kalousi Melitaia, kai Gaudos,* Gaudos being the ancient name for Malta's island neighbor.

"The Maltese Elephant retained its reputation in Roman days as well. In the first century B.C., Cicero, in his first oration against Verres, claims, *Et etiam ex insulolae Melitae elephantisculos tres rapiebat.* More than a century later, Petronius, in the one hundred thirty-second chapter of the *Satyricon,* has his character Encolpius put the curled and preserved ear of a Maltese Elephant to a use which, out of deference to the presence here of Miss Tellini, I shall not quote even in the original. And in the fifth century of our era, as St. Augustine sadly recorded in the *Civitas dei, Res publica romanorum in statu elephantis Melitae nunc deminuitur.* So you see, Mr. Bowman, the beast whose trail we follow has a history extending back toward the dawn of time. I could provide you with many more citations—"

"I just bet you could," Bowman interrupted. "But what does any of 'em have to do with the price of beer?"

"I am coming to that, never fear," Gideon Schlechtman said. "You were the one who complained of lack of background. Now I have provided it to you. In the foreground is the presence on Malta since 1530 of the Knights of St. John of Jerusalem. During the great siege by the Ottoman Turks in 1565, a Maltese Elephant warned of an attack with its trumpeting. Since that time, it has come to be revered as a good-luck totem not only by the Knights but also by the great merchants who, under the British crown, are the dominant force on Malta today. The return of one of these beasts to its proper home would be...suitably appreciated by these men."

"Yeah? If they're so much in love with these elephants of theirs, how'd one of 'em go missing in the first place?" Bowman demanded.

"Evan Thursday knew the answer to that question, I believe," Schlechtman answered. "He is, unfortunately, in no position to furnish us with it. Unless, that is, he conveyed it to Miss Tellini. Her involvement in this affair has been, shall we say with the charity Scripture commends, ambiguous."

"He didn't," Gina Tellini said quickly. "I have a cousin on Malta—in Valetta—who—hears things. That's how I found out."

Bowman shrugged. "It's a story. I've heard a lot of stories from her." His voice was cool, indifferent.

Her flashing eyes registered anger, with hurt hard on its heels. "It's true, Miles. I swear it is."

"Her word is not to be trusted under any circumstances," Nicholas Alexandria said.

"As if yours is," Gina Tellini retorted hotly.

Bowman turned back to Gideon Schlechtman. "The five grand is mine provided I find this Maltese Elephant for you, right?"

"Provided we do not find it first through our unaided efforts, yes," Schlechtman said.

"Yeah, sure, I knew you were going to tell me that," Bowman said, indifferent again. "But if you thought you could do it on your own, you never would've dragged me into it." He started for the door. Passing Hugo, he patted him on the hip. "See you around, sweetheart."

Hugo slapped his hand away, cocked a fist. Beefy face expressionless, Bowman hit him in the belly again, in the exact spot his fist had found before. Hugo fell against an end table of copper tubing and glass. It went over with a crash.

At the door, Bowman looked back to Gideon Schlechtman. "A smart man like you should get better help."

He closed the door on whatever answer Schlechtman might have made. Waiting for the elevator, he peered back toward suite 1453. No one came out after him. The elevator door opened. "Ground floor, sir?" the operator asked.

"Yeah."

Bowman stepped into his office. Hester Prine stared up from her typing. Relief, anger, and worry warred on her face. "Where have you been?" she demanded. "Your wife has called three times already. She asked me if you were under arrest. Are you?"

"No." Bowman hung his hat on the tree. "I'd better talk to her this morning. Anybody else call?"

"Yes," she said in her lascivious voice. She looked down at the pad by her telephone. "He said his name was Wellnhofer." She spelled it. "He said he'd already talked to you once today, and he wanted to see you by ten. I was sure you'd be in—I was sure then, anyhow."

"What did he sound like?" Bowman asked.

"He had an accent, if that's what you mean."

Bowman did not answer. He went into his inner office, closed the door. He sat down in the swivel chair, lit a cigarette, and sucked in harsh smoke with quick, savage puffs. After he stubbed it out, he picked up the phone and called. "Eva?… Yeah, it's me. Who else would it be?… No, I'm not in jail, for God's sake… What do you mean, you called them up and they said they didn't have me?… What time was that?… I was gone by then… No, I didn't see any point to coming home when I had to go in to the office anyway. I ate breakfast and did some looking around. Now I'm here. All right?"

He hung up, smoked another cigarette, and went back out of his private office. From his pocket he took the silver dollar he had not given to the lascar sailor. He dropped it on his secretary's desk. It rang sweetly. "Go around the corner and get me some coffee and doughnuts. Get some for yourself, too, if you want."

"I thought you already ate breakfast," she said. She picked up the cartwheel and started for the door.

Bowman swatted her on the posterior, hard enough to make her squeak. "I'm going to have to soundproof that door," he said gruffly. "Go on, get out of here."

He returned to his office, pulled the telephone directory off its shelf, pawed through it. "Operator, give me McPherson's Agricultural Supplies." He drummed his fingers on the desk. "McPherson's? Yeah, can you tell me if you've filled any big, unusual orders for hay the last couple days?... No? All right, thanks." He went through the book again. "Let me have The Manger." He asked the same question there. He received the same answer, and slammed the earpiece back onto its hook.

The outer door opened. Hester Prine came in with two cardboard cups and a white paper sack. Grease already made the white paper dark and shiny in several places.

"I thought maybe you were Wellnhofer," Bowman said.

"No such luck." Hester Prine took a half dollar, a dime, and a nickel from her purse and gave them to Bowman. He dropped them into his pocket. She opened the bag and handed him a doughnut whose sugar glaze glistened like ice on a bad road. He devoured it, drained his coffee. She pointed to the bag and said, "There's another one in there, if you want it."

"Don't mind if I do." Bowman was reaching for it when several sharp pops, like firecrackers on Chinese New Year, sounded outside the office building. Down on the street, a woman screamed. A man cried out. Bowman snatched the doughnut from the bag. "That's a gun," he said, and ran for the stairs.

He gulped down the last of the doughnut as he burst out into the fresh air. The man who lay crumpled on the sidewalk wore a navy blue jacket with four gold rings at each cuff. His cap had fallen from his head. It lay several feet away, upside down. The brown leather sweatband inside was stained and frayed.

"I called the cops," a man exclaimed. "A guy in a car shot him. He drove off that way." The man pointed west.

Bowman squatted beside Captain Wellnhofer. The seaman had taken two slugs in the chest. Blood soaked his shirt and jacket. It puddled on the pavement. He stared up at Bowman. His eyes still held reason. "Warehouse," he said, and exhaled. Blood ran from his nose and mouth. With great effort, he spoke through it: "Warehouse near Eddy and Fillm—" He exhaled again, but did not breathe in. He looked blindly up at the pale blue morning sky.

Bowman was getting to his feet when a car pulled to a screeching stop in front of him. Out sprang Detective Dwyer and Captain Bock. Bock looked from Bowman to the corpse and back again. "People have a way of dying around you," he remarked coldly.

"Go to hell, Bock," Bowman said. "You can't pin this on me. Don't waste your time trying. I was upstairs with Hester when the shooting started." He pointed to the man who had said he had called the police. "This guy here saw me come out."

"What were you doing up there with Hester?" Dwyer asked, amusement in his voice.

"Eating a doughnut. What about it?"

"You've got sugar on your chin," Dwyer said.

Bowman wiped his mouth on his sleeve. Bock asked several questions of the man who had called the police. His mouth curling down in disappointment, he turned back to Bowman. "Do you know the victim?" he asked.

"His name's Wellnhofer," Bowman answered unwillingly. "He was coming to see me. He had a ten o'clock appointment." He looked at his watch. "He was early. Now he's late."

"You were down there by him when we drove up," Dwyer said. "Did he say anything to you before he died?"

"Not a word," Bowman assured him. "He must have been gone the second he went down."

"Two in the chest? Yeah, maybe," Dwyer said.

"Are you going to take a formal statement from me, or what?" Bowman asked. "If you are, then do it. If you aren't, I'm going back upstairs." He jerked a thumb in the direction of Wellnhofer's body. "A hole just opened up in my schedule."

"You're a cold-blooded so-and-so," Dwyer said. He and Captain Bock walked over to their car and put their heads together. When they were done, Dwyer came back to Bowman. "Go on up, Miles. We've got enough from you for now. If we need more later, we know where to find you."

"Yeah, I know," Bowman said bitterly.

———

Hugo pushed the room-service cart to the door of Gideon Schlechtman's suite in the Clift Hotel. He opened the door, pulled the cart through, left it in the hall. Then he closed the door and returned to the others in the ever so modern living room.

To Schlechtman, Bowman said: "Much obliged. Lobster and drawn butter, baked potato. I usually like my liquor hard, but that wine was tasty, too."

"That was a Pouilly-Fumé from the valley of the Loire, Mr. Bowman, and a prime year, too," Gideon Schlechtman replied, steepling his long, thin, pale fingers.

"Didn't I say it was good?" Bowman asked equably. "Now, before we go any further, we have to figure out who gets thrown to the wolves. There's three bodies with holes in 'em lying on slabs in the morgue. That kind of business gets the cops all up in arms. They're going to be looking for somebody to blame. If we give 'em somebody, they won't do any real digging on their own. Cops, they're like that."

"Whom do you suggest, Mr. Bowman?" Schlechtman enquired.

"Hugo's just hired muscle," Bowman answered. "Turn up a flat rock and you'll find a dozen like him. Dwyer and Bock'll see it the same way."

The hard-faced man snarled a vile oath. He yanked out his revolver and pointed it at Bowman's chest. Schlechtman raised his hand.

"Patience, Hugo. I have not said I agree to this. What other possibilities have we?"

Bowman shrugged. "Alexandria there's a squiff. With three strapping men dead, that might do. Rollie Dwyer, he's got seven kids."

"You are an insane, wicked man," Nicholas Alexandria cried shrilly. His hand darted inside his coat. Lamplight glittered from his chromed automatic. He aimed the little gun at Bowman's face. Hugo still held his pistol steady.

"Nicholas, please." Schlechtman held up his hand again. "We do have a problem here which merits discussion. Everything is hypothetical." He turned back to Bowman. "Why not Miss Tellini?"

"We could work the frame that way, for Tom and Thursday, anyhow," Bowman said. "A guy plugged Wellnhofer, though. We'd have to drag in Hugo or Alexandria any which way."

Gina Tellini sent Bowman a Bunsen burner glance. "Why not Schlechtman?" she demanded.

"Don't be stupid, darling," Bowman answered. "He's paying the bills."

"Whoever finds the Maltese Elephant can pay the bills," she said.

"If we find the elephant, we shall be able to pay the attorneys' fees to keep us from the clutches of the intrepid San Francisco police, as well," Gideon Schlechtman said. He pointed to Hugo and to Nicholas Alexandria in turn. "Put up your weapons. We are all colleagues in this matter. And, as the saying has it, if we do not hang together, we shall hang separately."

"You're the boss," Hugo said. He put the gun back in his pocket. His muddy eyes raked Bowman once more. Nicholas Alexandria bit his lip. Purple and yellow bruises still discolored his cheek. He had taken off the sticking plaster that covered the dried-blood scab on the cut Bowman's pistol had made there. At last, the little chromed automatic disappeared.

Schlechtman smiled. The stretch of lips was broader and more fulsome than his rather pinched features could comfortably support. "Shall we be off, Mr. Bowman?" he said.

Bowman got to his feet, went to the window, pulled aside the curtain. He looked at the night, then at his watch. "Give it another half hour," he said. "I want it good and dark, and the fog's starting to roll in, too."

"How fitting," Schlechtman remarked. "This whole business of the elephant has been dark and foggy."

At the hour Bowman had chosen, they left suite 1453 and rode down to the Clift's elegant lobby. Outside, the fog had thickened. It left the taste of the ocean on the lips. Defeated streetlamps cast small reddish-yellow puddles of light at the feet of their standards. Automobile headlamps appeared out of the mist, then were swallowed up once more. Walking in the fog was like pushing through soaked cotton gauze.

Hugo looked around nervously. His hand went to the pocket where the revolver nestled. "I don't like this," he muttered.

"We've got three guns with us—at least three," Bowman amended, glancing from Schlechtman to Gina Tellini. "You don't like those odds, go home and play with dolls."

"You're pushing it, Bowman. Shut your stinking mouth or—"

"After the elephant is in our hands, these quarrels will seem trivial," Gideon Schlechtman said. "Let us consider them so now."

They walked four blocks down Taylor to Eddy, then turned right onto Eddy. "It's a mile from here, maybe a little more," Bowman said. He lit a cigarette. Fog swallowed the smoke he blew out.

As they passed Gough, shops and hotels and apartments fell away on their left. The mist swirled thickly, as if it sprang from the grass in the open area there. A few trees grew near enough streetlamps to be seen. "What is this place?" Hugo said.

Bowman rested a hand on his pistol. "It's Jefferson Square," he answered. "In the daytime, people get up on soapboxes and make speeches here. Nights like this, the punks come out." He peered warily into the fog until they left the square behind. Then, more happily, he said, "All right, three-four blocks to go."

He turned right on Fillmore, then left into an alley in back of the buildings that fronted on Eddy. The alley had no lights. Gravel scrunched under the soles of his shoes.

"I don't trust him," Nicholas Alexandria said suddenly. "This is a place for treachery."

"Shut up, dammit," Bowman said. "You make me mess up and you'll get all the treachery you ever wanted." He walked with his left hand extended. Like a blind man, he brushed the bricks of the buildings with his fingertips to guide himself. "Stinking fog. Hell of a lot easier to find this place this afternoon," he muttered, but grunted a moment later. "Here we are. These are stairs. Come on, everybody up."

The stairway and handrail were made of wood. They led to a second-floor landing. The door there wore a stout lock. Gideon Schlechtman felt of it. "I presume you have some way to surmount this difficulty?" he asked Bowman.

"Nah, we're all going to stand around here and wait for the sun to come up." Bowman pulled a small leather case from his inside jacket pocket. "Move. I've got picks." He worked for a few minutes, whistling softly and tunelessly between his teeth. The lock clicked. He pulled it from the hasp and laid it on the boards of the landing. He opened the door. "Let's go."

Bowman waited for his comrades to enter first. When he went in, he closed the door. It was no darker inside than out. The air was different, though: drier, warmer, charged with a thick odor not far from that of horse droppings. Again, he ran his hand along the wall. His fingers found a light switch. He flicked it.

Several bare bulbs strung on a wire across the warehouse ceiling sprang to life. He pointed from the walkway on which he and the others stood down to the immense gray-brown beast occupying the floor of the warehouse proper. Its huge ears twitched at the light. Its trunk curled. It made a complaining noise: the sound of a trumpet whose spit valve has not worked for years. "There it is, right off *La Tórtola*." Bowman stood tall. "The Maltese Elephant."

Gina Tellini, Schlechtman, Nicholas Alexandria, and Hugo stared down at the elephant. Then their eyes swung to Bowman. The same expression filled all their faces. Hugo drew his pistol. He pointed it at the detective. "He's mine now," he said happily.

"No, mine." The chromium-plated automatic was in Nicholas Alexandria's right hand.

Gina Tellini fumbled in her handbag. "No, he's mine." She too proved to carry a small automatic, though hers was not chromed.

"I am sorry, but I must insist on the privilege." Gideon Schlechtman had worn a .357 magnum in a shoulder holster. His stance was like a Marine gunnery sergeant's, left hand supporting right wrist. The pistol was pointed at a spot an inch and a half above the bridge of Bowman's nose.

Bowman stared down the barrel of the gun. His eyes crossed slightly. His right hand stayed well away from the gun at his belt. "What the hell is the matter with you people?" he demanded. "I find your damned elephant, and this is the thanks I get?"

"Let's all fill him full of holes, boss," Hugo said. His finger tightened on the trigger.

"No, wait," Schlechtman said. "I want him to die knowing what an ignorant idiot he is. Otherwise he would not understand how richly he deserves it."

"This stupid ox? It is a waste of time," Nicholas Alexandria said.

"Possibly, but we have time to waste," Gideon Schlechtman replied. "Mr. Bowman, that great lumpish creature down there—in that it bears a remarkable resemblance to you, eh?—is an elephant, but not a Maltese elephant, not *the* Maltese Elephant we have sought so long and hard."

"How do you know?" Bowman said. "An elephant is an elephant, right?"

"An elephant is an elephant—wrong," Schlechtman answered. "A Maltese Elephant is easily distinguished from that gross specimen by the simple fact that a grown bull is slightly smaller than a Shetland pony."

"Yeah, and rain makes applesauce," Bowman said with a scornful laugh. "Go peddle your papers."

"The old saw about he who laughs last would seem not to apply in your case, Mr. Bowman," Schlechtman said. "I spoke nothing but the truth. For time immemorial, Malta has been the home of a rare race of dwarf elephants. And why not? Before man came, the island knew no large predators. An elephant there had no need to be huge to protect itself. Natural selection would also have favored small size because the forage on Malta has always been less than abundant; smaller beasts need smaller amounts of food. The Maltese and their later conquerors preserved the race down to the present as an emblem of their uniqueness—and you tried to fob off this great, ugly creature on us? Fool!"

The elephant trumpeted. The noise was deafening. The beast took a couple of steps. The walkway trembled, as if at an earthquake. Nicholas Alexandria nearly lost his balance. Almost involuntarily, Gina Tellini and Hugo glanced toward the elephant for an instant. Even Gideon Schlechtman's expression of supreme concentration wavered for a moment.

Bowman jerked out his .45 in a motion quicker than conscious thought. "Come on," he snarled. "Who's first? By God, I'll nail the first one who plugs me—and if you don't shoot straight, I'll take out two or three of you before I go."

The tableau held for perhaps three heartbeats. The elephant trumpeted again. The door to the warehouse opened. "Drop the guns!" Detective Roland Dwyer shouted. His own pistol covered the group impartially. Behind him came Henry Bock, and behind him two men in uniform. All were armed. "Drop 'em!" Dwyer repeated. "Hands high!"

Nicholas Alexandria let his little automatic fall. It clattered on the walkway. Then Hugo threw down his gun. So did Gina Tellini. At last, with a shrug, Gideon Schlechtman surrendered.

Bowman stepped back against the wall, the heavy pistol still in his hand. Captain Henry Bock might have had something to say about that. Before he could speak, Dwyer asked Bowman, "Just what the hell is going on here, Miles?"

Bowman pointed to Gina Tellini and said: "She's the one who fingered Wellnhofer. Had to be: I visited the docks right after I saw her, and I had the list of ships I was going to check in my trouser pocket then."

"How'd she have a chance to find out what was in your trouser pocket without you knowing it?" Bock demanded, leering.

"You said you loved me," Gina Tellini hissed.

"Loved you?" Bowman shook his head. "You must have heard wrong, sweetheart. I'm a married man." He went on talking to Detective Dwyer: "She may have fingered Tom for that Evan Thursday item, too. I don't know that for a fact, but you knew Tom. He wouldn't have been easy to take down, not unless somebody recognized him who wasn't supposed to. Or she may have shot him herself. Tom would go after anything in a skirt."

"Yeah," Dwyer said. One of the uniformed policemen behind him nodded.

"I figure laughing boy here probably canceled Wellnhofer's stamp." Bowman jerked a thumb at Hugo. "Gina and Schlechtman knew each other pretty well, and Hugo's Schlechtman's hired gun."

"So who did Thursday?" Roland Dwyer asked.

"Could have been Hugo again," Bowman answered, shrugging. "Or it could have been sweetheart here"—he grinned at Nicholas Alexandria, who returned a hate-filled glare—"on account of I'm not sure if Hugo was in town yet."

Dwyer pointed to Gideon Schlechtman. "What about him?"

"The hell with it," Captain Bock said. "He's in it some kind of way. We'll take 'em all in and sort it out later." He gestured to the uniformed policemen. They advanced with their handcuffs. The one who cuffed Gina Tellini shoved her lightly in the middle of the back. She stumbled out of the warehouse. The others glumly followed.

"You almost got too cute for your own good, Miles," Detective Dwyer said. "If that witness hadn't heard Wellnhofer spill to you—and if he hadn't decided to tell us about it—you wouldn't have had yourself a whole lot of fun, didn't look like." He stared down at the elephant. It pulled hay from a bale with its trunk and stuffed it into its mouth. "What the devil were you doing here, anyway?"

"Who, me?" Bowman replaced his Colt in its holster. "I was just on a wild elephant chase, Rollie, that's all."

"Yeah?" Dwyer's eyes swung to the door through which Gina Tellini had just gone. "You going to tell Eva all about it?"

"I'll tell her what she needs to know: I got paid."

Dwyer shook his head. "You're a louse, Miles."

"That's what everybody tells me." Miles Bowman laughed. "Thanks," he said.

MUST AND
SHALL

12 July 1864—Fort Stevens, north of Washington, D.C.

General Horatio Wright *stood up on the earthen parapet to watch the men of the Sixth Corps, hastily recalled from Petersburg, drive Jubal Early's Confederates away from the capital of the United States. Down below the parapet, a tall, thin man in black frock coat and stovepipe hat asked, "How do we fare, General?"*

"Splendidly." Wright's voice was full of relief. Had Early chosen to attack the line of forts around Washington the day before, he'd have faced only militiamen and clerks with muskets, and might well have broken through to the city. But Early had been late, and now the veterans from the Sixth Corps were pushing his troopers back. Washington City was surely saved. Perhaps because he was so relieved, Wright said, "Would you care to come up with me and see how we drive them?"

"I should like that very much, thank you," Abraham Lincoln said, and climbed the ladder to stand beside him.

Never in his wildest nightmares had Wright imagined the President accepting. Lincoln had peered over the parapet several times already, and drawn fire from the Confederates. They were surely too far from Fort Stevens to recognize him, but with his height and the hat he made a fine target.

Not far away, a man was wounded and fell back with a cry. General Wright interposed his body between President Lincoln and the Confederates. Lincoln spoiled that by stepping away from him. "Mr. President, I really must insist that you retire to a position of safety," Wright said. "This is no place for you; you must step down at once!"

Lincoln took no notice of him, but continued to watch the fighting north of the fort. A captain behind the parapet, perhaps not recognizing his commander-in-chief, shouted, "Get down, you damn fool, before you get shot!"

When Lincoln did not move, Wright said, "If you do not get down, sir, I shall summon a body of soldiers to remove you by force." He gulped at his own temerity in threatening the President of the United States.

Lincoln seemed more amused than anything else. He started to turn away, to walk back toward the ladder. Instead, after half a step, he crumpled bonelessly. Wright had thought of nightmares before. Now one came to life in front of his horrified eyes. Careless of his own safety, he crouched by the President, whose blood poured from a massive head wound into the muddy dirt atop the parapet. Lincoln's face wore an expression of mild surprise. His chest hitched a couple of times, then was still.

The captain who'd shouted at Lincoln to get down mounted to the parapet. His eyes widened. "Dear God," he groaned. "It is the President."

Wright thought he recognized him. "You're Holmes, aren't you?" he said. Somehow it was comforting to know the man you were addressing when the world seemed to crumble around you.

"Yes, sir, Oliver W. Holmes, 20th Massachusetts," the young captain answered.

"Well, Captain Holmes, fetch a physician here at once," Wright said. Holmes nodded and hurried away. Wright wondered at his industry—surely *he could see Lincoln was dead. Who, then, was the more foolish, himself for sending Holmes away, or the captain for going?*

———

21 July 1864—Washington, D.C.

From the hastily erected wooden rostrum on the East Portico of the Capitol, Hannibal Hamlin stared out at the crowd waiting for him to deliver his inaugural address. The rostrum was draped with black, as was the Capitol, as had been the route his carriage took to reach it. Many of the faces in the crowd were still stunned, disbelieving. The United States had never lost a President to a bullet, not in the eighty-eight years since the nation freed itself from British rule.

In the front row of dignitaries, Senator Andrew Johnson of Tennessee glared up at Hamlin. He had displaced the man from Maine on Lincoln's reelection ticket; had this dreadful event taken place a year later (assuming Lincoln's triumph), he now would be President. But no time for might-have-beens.

Hamlin had been polishing his speech since the telegram announcing Lincoln's death reached him up in Bangor, where, feeling useless and rejected, he had withdrawn after failing of renomination for the Vice Presidency. Now, though, his country needed him once more. He squared his broad shoulders, ready to bear up under the great burden so suddenly thrust upon him.

"Stand fast!" he cried. "That has ever been my watchword, and at no time in all the history of our great and glorious republic has our heeding it been more urgent. Abraham Lincoln's body may lie in the grave, but we shall go marching on—to victory!"

Applause rose from the crowd at the allusion to "John Brown's Body"— and not just from the crowd, but also from the soldiers posted on the roof of the Capitol and at intervals around the building to keep the accursed rebels from murdering two Presidents, not just one. Hamlin went on, "The responsibility for this great war, in which our leader gave his last full measure of devotion, lies solely at the feet of the Southern slaveocrats who conspired to take their states out of our grand Union for their own evil ends. I promise you, my friends—Abraham Lincoln shall be avenged, and those who caused his death punished in full."

More applause, not least from the Republican Senators who proudly called themselves Radical: from Thaddeus Stevens of Pennsylvania, Benjamin Wade of Ohio, Zachariah Chandler of Michigan, and bespectacled John Andrew of Massachusetts. Hamlin had been counted among their number when he sat in the Senate before assuming the duties, such as they were, of the Vice President.

"Henceforward," Hamlin declared, "I say this: let us use every means recognized by the Laws of War which God has put in our hands to crush out the wickedest rebellion the world has ever witnessed. This conflict is become a radical revolution—yes, gentlemen, I openly employ the word, and, what is more, I revel in it—involving the desolation of the South as well as the emancipation of the bondsmen it vilely keeps in chains."

The cheers grew louder still. Lincoln had been more conciliatory, but what had conciliation got him? Only a coffin and a funeral and a grieving nation ready, no, eager for harsher measures.

"They have sowed the wind; let them reap the whirlwind. We are in earnest now, and have awakened to the stern duty upon us. Let that duty be disregarded or haltingly or halfway performed, and God only in His wisdom can know what will be the end. This lawless monster of a Political Slave Power shall forevermore be shorn of its power to ruin a government it no longer has the strength to rule.

"The rebels proudly proclaim they have left the Union. Very well: we shall take them at their word and, once having gained the victory Providence will surely grant us, we shall treat their lands as they deserve: not as the states they no longer desire to be, but as conquered provinces, won by our sword.

I say we shall hang Jefferson Davis, and hang Robert E. Lee, and hang Joe Johnston, yes, hang them higher than Haman, and the other rebel generals and colonels and governors and members of their false Congress. The living God is merciful, true, but He is also just and vengeful, and we, the people of the United States, we shall be His instrument in advancing the right."

Now great waves of cheering, led by grim Thaddeus Stevens himself, washed over Hamlin. The fierce sound reminded him of wolves baying in the backwoods of Maine. He stood tall atop the rostrum. He would lead these wolves, and with them pull the rebel Confederacy down in ruin.

---

11 August 1942—New Orleans, Louisiana

Air brakes chuffing, the Illinois Central train pulled to a stop at Union Station on Rampart Street. "New Orleans!" the conductor bawled unnecessarily. "All out for New Orleans!"

Along with the rest of the people in the car, Neil Michaels filed toward the exit. He was a middle-sized man in his late thirties, most of his dark blond hair covered by a snap-brim fedora. The round, thick, gold-framed spectacles he wore helped give him the mild appearance of an accountant.

As soon as he stepped from the air-conditioned comfort of the railroad car out into the steamy heat of New Orleans summer, those glasses steamed up. Shaking his head in bemusement, Michaels drew a handkerchief from his trouser pocket and wiped away the moisture.

He got his bags and headed for the cab stand, passing on the way a horde of men and boys hawking newspapers and rank upon rank of shoeshine stands. A fat Negro man sat on one of those, gold watch chain running from one pocket of his vest to the other. At his feet, an Irish-looking fellow plied the rag until his customer's black oxfords gleamed.

"There y'are, sir," the shoeshine man said, his half-Brooklyn, half-Southern accent testifying he was a New Orleans native. The Negro looked down at his shoes, nodded, and, with an air of great magnanimity, flipped the shoeshine man a dime. "Oh, thank you very much, sir," the fellow exclaimed. The insincere servility in his voice grated on Michaels's ears.

More paperboys cried their trade outside the station. Michaels bought a *Times-Picayune* to read while he waited in line for a taxi. The war news wasn't good. The Germans were still pushing east in Russia and sinking ship after ship off the American coast. In the South Pacific, Americans and Japanese were slugging away at each other, and God only knew how that would turn out.

Across the street from Union Station, somebody had painted a message: YANKS OUT! Michaels sighed. He'd seen that slogan painted on barns and bridges and embankments ever since his train crossed into Tennessee—and, now that he thought about it, in Kentucky as well, though Kentucky had stayed with the Union during the Great Rebellion.

When he got to the front of the line at the cab stand, a hack man heaved his bags into the trunk of an Oldsmobile and said, "Where to, sir?"

"The New Orleans Hotel, on Canal Street," Michaels answered.

The cabbie touched the brim of his cap. "Yes, sir," he said, his voice suddenly empty. He opened the back door for Michaels, slammed it shut after him, then climbed into the cab himself. It took off with a grinding of gears that said the transmission had seen better days.

On the short ride to the hotel, Michaels counted five more scrawls of YANKS OUT, along with a couple of patches of whitewash that probably masked others. Servicemen on the street walked along in groups of at least four; several corners sported squads of soldiers in full combat gear, including, in one case, a machine-gun nest built of sandbags. "Nice quiet little town," Michaels remarked.

"Isn't it?" the cabbie answered, deadpan. He hesitated, his jaw working as if he were chewing his cud. After a moment, he decided to go on:

"Mister, with an accent like yours, you want to be careful where you let people hear it. For a damnyankee, you don't seem like a bad fellow, an' I wouldn't want nothin' to happen to you."

"Thanks. I'll bear that in mind," Michaels said. He wished the Bureau had sent somebody who could put on a convincing drawl. Of course the last man the FBS had sent ended up floating in the Mississippi, so evidently his drawl hadn't been convincing enough.

The cab wheezed to a stop in front of the New Orleans Hotel. "That'll be forty cents, sir," the driver said.

Michaels reached into his trouser pocket, pulled out a half dollar. "Here you go. I don't need any change."

"That's right kind of you, sir, but—you wouldn't happen to have two quarters instead?" the cabbie said. He handed the big silver coin back to his passenger.

"What's wrong with it?" Michaels demanded, though he thought he knew the answer. "It's legal tender of the United States of America."

"Yes, sir, reckon it is, but there's no place hereabouts I'd care to try and spend it even so," the driver answered, "not with *his* picture on it." The obverse of the fifty-cent piece bore an image of the martyred Lincoln, the reverse a Negro with his manacles broken and the legend SIC SEMPER TYRANNIS. Michaels had known it was an unpopular coin with white men in the South, but he hadn't realized how unpopular it was.

He got out of the cab, rummaged in his pocket, and came up with a quarter and a couple of dimes. The cabbie didn't object to Washington's profile, or to that of the god Mercury. He also didn't object to seeing his tip cut in half. That told Michaels all he needed to know about how much the half-dollar was hated.

Lazily spinning ceiling fans inside the hotel lobby stirred the air without doing much to cool it. The colored clerk behind the front desk smiled to hear Michaels's accent. "Yes, sir, we do have your reservation," she said after shuffling through papers. By the way she talked, she'd been educated up in the Loyal States herself. She handed him a brass key. "That's room 429, sir. Three dollars and twenty-five cents a night."

"Very good," Michaels said. The clerk clanged the bell on the front desk. A white bellboy in a pillbox hat and uniform that made him look like a Philip Morris advertisement picked up Michaels's bags and carried them to the elevator.

When they got to room 429, Michaels opened the door. The bellboy put down the bags inside the room and stood waiting for his tip. By way of experiment, Michaels gave him the fifty-cent piece the cabbie had rejected. The bellboy took the coin and put it in his pocket. His lips shaped a silent word. Michaels thought it was *damnyankee,* but he wasn't quite sure. The bellboy left in a hurry.

A couple of hours later, Michaels went downstairs to supper. Something shiny was lying on the carpet in the hall. He looked down at the half-dollar he'd given the bellboy. It had lain here in plain sight while people walked back and forth; he'd heard them. Nobody had taken it. Thoughtfully, he picked it up and stuck it in his pocket.

———————

A walk through the French Quarter made fears about New Orleans seem foolish. Jazz blasted out of every other doorway. Neon signs pulsed above ginmills. Spasm bands, some white, some Negro, played on streetcorners. No one paid attention to blackout regulations—that held true North and South. Clog-dancers shuffled, overturned caps beside them inviting coins. Streetwalkers in tawdry finery swung their hips and flashed knowing smiles.

Neil Michaels moved through the crowds of soldiers and sailors and gawking civilians like a halfback evading tacklers and heading downfield. He glanced at his watch, partly to check the time and partly to make sure nobody had stolen it. Half past eleven. Didn't this place ever slow down? Maybe not.

He turned right off Royal Street onto St. Peter and walked southeast toward the Mississippi and Jackson Square. The din of the Vieux Carré faded behind him. He strode past the Cabildo, the old Spanish building of stuccoed brick that now housed the Louisiana State Museum, including a fine collection of artifacts and documents on the career of the first military governor of New Orleans, Benjamin Butler. Johnny Rebs kept threatening to dynamite the Cabildo, but it hadn't happened yet.

Two great bronze statues dominated Jackson Square. One showed the square's namesake on horseback. The other, even taller, faced that equestrian statue. Michaels thought Ben Butler's bald head and rotund, sagging physique less than ideal for being immortalized in bronze, but no one had asked his opinion.

He strolled down the paved lane in the formal garden toward the statue of Jackson. Lights were dimmer here in the square, but not to dim to keep Michaels from reading the words Butler had had carved into the pedestal of the statue: *The Union Must and Shall Be Preserved,* an adaptation of Jackson's famous toast, "Our Federal Union, it must be preserved."

Michaels's mouth stretched out in a thin hard line that was not a smile. By force and fear, with cannon and noose, bayonet and prison term, the United States Army had preserved the Union. And now, more than three quarters of a century after the collapse of the Great Rebellion, U.S. forces still occupied the states of the rebel Confederacy, still skirmished in hills and forests and sometimes city streets against men who put on gray shirts and yowled like catamounts when they fought. Hatred bred hatred, reprisal bred reprisal, and so it went on and on. He sometimes wondered if the Union wouldn't have done better to let the Johnny Rebs get the hell out, if that was what they'd wanted so badly.

He'd never spoken that thought aloud; it wasn't one he could share. Too late to worry about such things anyhow, generations too late. He had to deal with the consequences of what vengeful Hamlin and his like-minded successors had done.

The man he was supposed to meet would be waiting behind Butler's statue. Michaels was slightly surprised the statue had no guards around it; the Johnny Rebs had blown it up in the 1880s and again in the 1920s. If New Orleans today was reconciled to rule from Washington, it concealed the fact very well.

Michaels ducked around into the darkness behind the statue. "Four-score and seven," he whispered, the recognition signal he'd been given.

Someone should have answered, "New birth of freedom." No one said anything. As his eyes adapted to the darkness, he made out a body sprawled in the narrow space between the base of the statue and the shrubbery that bordered Jackson Square. He stooped beside it. If this was the man he was supposed to meet, the fellow would never give him a recognition signal, not till Judgment Day. His throat had been cut.

Running feet on the walkways of the square, flashlight beams probing like spears. One of them found Michaels. He threw up an arm against the blinding glare. A hard Northern voice shouted, "Come out of there right now, you damned murdering Reb, or you'll never get a second chance!"

Michaels raised his hands high in surrender and came out.

Outside Antoine's, the rain came down in buckets. Inside, with oysters Rockefeller and a whiskey and soda in front of him and the prospect of an excellent lunch ahead, Neil Michaels was willing to forgive the weather.

He was less inclined to forgive the soldiers from the night before. Stubbing out his Camel, he said in a low but furious voice, "Those great thundering galoots couldn't have done a better job of blowing my cover if they'd rehearsed for six weeks, God damn them."

His companion, a dark, lanky man named Morrie Harris, sipped his own drink and said, "It may even work out for the best. Anybody the MPs arrest is going to look good to the Johnny Rebs around here." His New York accent seemed less out of place in New Orleans than Michaels's flat, Midwestern tones.

Michaels started to answer, then shut up as the waiter came over and asked, "You gentlemen are ready to order?"

"Let me have the *pompano en papillote*," Harris said. "You can't get it any better than here."

The waiter wrote down the order, looked a question at Michaels. He said, "I'll take the *poulet chanteclair*." The waiter nodded, scribbled, and went away.

Glancing around to make sure no one else was paying undue attention to him or his conversation, Michaels resumed: "Yeah, that may be true now. But Ducange is dead now. What if those stupid dogfaces had busted in on us while we were dickering? That would have queered the deal for sure, and it might have got me shot." As it hadn't the night before, his smile did not reach his eyes. "I'm fond of my neck. It's the only one I've got."

"Even without Ducange, we've still got to get a line on the underground," Harris said. "Those weapons are somewhere. We'd better find 'em before the whole city goes up." He rolled his eyes. "The whole city, hell! If what we've been hearing is true, the Nazis have shipped enough guns and God knows what all else into New Orleans to touch off four or five states. And wouldn't that do wonders for the war effort?" He slapped on irony with a heavy trowel.

"God damn the Germans," Michaels said, still quietly but with savage venom. "They played this game during the last war, too. But you're right. If what we've heard is the straight goods, the blowup they have in mind will make the Thanksgiving Revolt look like a kiss on the cheek."

"It shouldn't be this way," Harris said, scowling. "We've got more GIs and swabbies in New Orleans than you can shake a stick at, and none of 'em worth a damn when it comes to tracking this crap down. Nope, for that they need the FBS, no matter how understaffed we are."

The waiter came then. Michaels dug into the chicken marinated in red wine. It was as good as it was supposed to be. Morrie Harris made ecstatic noises about the sauce on his pompano.

After a while, Michaels said, "The longer we try, the harder it gets for us to keep things under control down here. One of these days—"

"It'll all go up," Harris said matter-of-factly. "Yeah, but not now. Now is what we gotta worry about. We're fighting a civil war here, we ain't gonna have much luck with the Germans and the Japs. That's what Hitler has in mind."

"Maybe Hamlin and Stevens should have done something different—God knows what—back then. It might have kept us out of—this," Michaels said. He knew that was heresy for an FBS man, but everything that had happened to him since he got to New Orleans left him depressed with the state of things as they were.

"What were they supposed to do?" Harris snapped.

"I already said I didn't know," Michaels answered, wishing he'd kept his mouth shut. What did the posters say?—LOOSE LIPS SINK SHIPS. His loose lips were liable to sink him.

Sure enough, Morrie Harris went on as if he hadn't spoken: "The Johnnies rebelled, killed a few hundred thousand American boys, and shot a President dead. What should we do, give 'em a nice pat on the back? We beat 'em and we made 'em pay. Far as I can see, they deserved it."

"Yeah, and they've been making us pay ever since." Michaels raised a weary hand. "The hell with it. Like you said, now is what we've got to worry about. But with Ducange dead, what sort of channels do we have into the rebel underground?"

Morrie Harris's mouth twisted, as if he'd bitten down on something rotten. "No good ones that I know of. We've relied too much on the Negroes down here over the years. It's made the whites trust us even less than they would have otherwise. Maybe, though, just maybe, Ducange talked to somebody before he got killed, and that somebody will try to get hold of you."

"So what do you want me to do, then? Hang around my hotel room hoping the phone rings, like a girl waiting to see if a boy will call? Hell of a way to spend my time in romantic New Orleans."

"Listen, the kind of romance you can get here, you'll flunk a short-arm inspection three days later," Harris answered, chasing the last bits of pompano around his plate. "They'll take a damnyankee's money, but they'll skin you every chance they get. They must be laughing their asses off at the fortune they're making off our boys in uniform."

"Sometimes they won't even take your money." Michaels told of the trouble he'd had unloading the Lincoln half-dollar.

"Yeah, I've seen that," Harris said. "If they want to cut off their nose to spite their face, by me it's all right." He set a five and a couple of singles on the table. "This one's on me. Whatever else you say about this damn town, the food is hellacious, no two ways about it."

"No arguments." Michaels got up with Harris. They went out of Antoine's separately, a couple of minutes apart. As he walked back to the New Orleans Hotel, Michaels kept checking to make sure nobody was following him. He didn't spot anyone, but he didn't know how much that proved. If anybody wanted to put multiple tails on him, he wouldn't twig, not in crowded streets like these.

The crowds got worse when a funeral procession tied up traffic on Rampart Street. Two black horses pulled the hearse; their driver was a skinny, sleepy-looking white man who looked grotesquely out of place in top hat and tails. More coaches and buggies followed, and a couple of cars as well. "All right, let's get it moving!" an MP shouted when the procession finally passed.

"They keep us here any longer, we all go in the ovens from old age," a local said, and several other people laughed as they crossed the street. Michaels wanted to ask what the ovens were, but kept quiet since he exposed himself as one of the hated occupiers every time he opened his mouth.

When he got back to the hotel, he stopped at the front desk to ask if he had any messages. The clerk there today was a Negro man in a sharp suit and tie, with a brass name badge on his right lapel that read THADDEUS JENKINS. He checked and came back shaking his head. "Rest assured, sir, we shall make sure you receive any that do come in," he said—a Northern accent bothered him not in the least.

"Thank you very much, Mr. Jenkins," Michaels said.

"Our pleasure to serve you, sir," the clerk replied. "Anything we can do to make your stay more pleasant, you have but to ask."

"You're very kind," Michaels said. Jenkins had reason to be kind to Northerners. The power of the federal government maintained Negroes at the top of the heap in the old Confederacy. With the Sixteenth Amendment disenfranchising most Rebel soldiers and their descendants, blacks had a comfortable majority among those eligible to vote—and used it, unsurprisingly, in their own interest.

Michaels mused on that as he walked to the elevator. The operator, a white man, tipped his cap with more of the insincere obsequiousness Michaels had already noted. He wondered how the fellow liked taking orders from a man whose ancestors his great-grandfather might have owned. Actually, he didn't need to wonder. The voting South was as reliably Republican as could be, for the blacks had no illusions about how long their power would last if the Sixteenth were ever to be discarded.

Suddenly curious, he asked the elevator man, "Why don't I see 'Repeal the Sixteenth' written on walls along with 'Yanks Out'?"

The man measured him with his eyes—measured him for a coffin, if his expression meant anything. At last, as if speaking to a moron, he answered, "You don't see that on account of askin' you to repeal it'd mean you damnyankees got some kind o' business bein' down here and lordin' it over us in the first place. And you *ain't.*"

So there, Michaels thought. The rest of the ride passed in silence.

With a soft whir, the ceiling fan stirred the air in his room. That improved things, but only slightly. He looked out the window. Ferns had sprouted from the mortar between bricks of the building across the street. Even without the rain—which had now let up—it was plenty humid enough for the plants to flourish.

———

Sitting around waiting for the phone to ring gave Michaels plenty of time to watch the ferns. As Morrie Harris had instructed, he spent most of his time in his room. He sallied forth mostly to eat. Not even the resolute hostility of most of white New Orleans put a damper on the food.

He ate boiled beef at Maylié's, crab meat *au gratin* at Galatoire's, crayfish bisque at La Louisiane, *langouste* Sarah Bernhardt at Arnaud's, and, for variety, pig knuckles and sauerkraut at Kolb's. When he didn't feel like traveling, he ate at the hotel's own excellent restaurant. He began to fancy his trousers and collars getting tighter than they had been before he came South.

One night, he woke to the sound of rifle fire not far away. Panic shot through him, panic and shame. Had the uprising he'd come here to check broken out? How would that look on his FBS personnel record? Then he realized that, if the uprising had broken out, any damnyankee the Johnnies caught was likely to end up too dead to worry about what his personnel record looked like.

After about fifteen minutes, the gunfire petered out. Michaels took a couple of hours falling asleep again, though. He went from one radio station to another the next morning, and checked the afternoon newspapers, too. No one said a word about the firefight. Had anybody tried, prosecutors armed with the Sedition Act would have landed on him like a ton of bricks.

Back in the Loyal States, they smugly said the Sedition Act kept the lid on things down South. Michaels had believed it, too. Now he was getting a feeling for how much pressure pushed against that lid. When it blew, if it blew…

A little past eleven the next night, the phone rang. He jumped, then ran to it. "Hello?" he said sharply.

The voice on the other end was so muffled, he wasn't sure whether it belonged to a man or a woman. It said, "Be at the Original Absinthe House for the three a.m. show." The line went dead.

Michaels let out a martyred sigh. "The three a.m. show," he muttered, wondering why conspirators couldn't keep civilized hours like anyone else. He went down to the restaurant and had a couple of cups of strong coffee laced with brandy. Thus fortified, he headed out into the steaming night.

He soon concluded New Orleans's idea of civilized hours had nothing to do with those kept by the rest of the world, or possibly that New Orleans defined civilization as unending revelry. The French Quarter was as packed as it had been when he went through it toward Jackson Square, though that had been in the relatively early evening, close to civilized even by Midwestern standards.

The Original Absinthe House, a shabby two-story building with an iron railing around the balcony to the second floor, stood on the corner of Bourbon and Bienville. Each of the four doors leading in had a semicircular window above it. Alongside one of the doors, someone had scrawled, *Absinthe makes the heart grow fonder*. Michaels thought that a distinct improvement on *Yanks Out!* You weren't supposed to be able to get real absinthe any more, but in the Vieux Carré nothing would have surprised him.

He didn't want absinthe, anyway. He didn't particularly want the whiskey and soda he ordered, either, but you couldn't go into a place like this without doing some drinking. The booze was overpriced and not very good. The mysterious voice on the telephone hadn't told him there was a five-buck charge to go up to the second story and watch the floor show. Assuming he got out of here alive, he'd have a devil of a time justifying that on his expense account. And if the call had been a Johnny Reb setup, were they trying to kill him or just to bilk him out of money for the cause?

Michaels felt he was treading in history's footsteps as he went up the stairs. If the plaque on the wall didn't lie for the benefit of tourists, that stairway had been there since the Original Absinthe House was built in the early nineteenth century. Andrew Jackson and Jean Lafitte had gone up it to plan the defense of New Orleans against the British in 1814, and Ben Butler for carefully undescribed purposes half a century later. It was made with wooden pegs: not a nail anywhere. If the stairs weren't as old as the plaque claimed, they sure as hell were a long way from new.

A jazz band blared away in the big upstairs room. Michaels went in, found a chair, ordered a drink from a waitress whose costume would have been too skimpy for a burly queen most places up North, and leaned back to enjoy the music. The band was about half black, half white. Jazz was one of the few things the two races shared in the South. Not all Negroes had made it to the top of the heap after the North crushed the Great Rebellion; many still lived in the shadow of the fear and degradation of the days of slavery and keenly felt the resentment of the white majority. That came out in the way they played. And the whites, as conquered people will, found liberation in their music that they could not have in life.

Michaels looked at his watch. It was a quarter to three. The jazz men were just keeping loose between shows, then. As he sipped his whiskey, the room began filling up in spite of the five-dollar cover charge. He didn't know what the show would be, but he figured it had to be pretty hot to pack 'em in at those prices.

The lights went out. For a moment, only a few glowing cigarette coals showed in the blackness. The band didn't miss a beat. From right behind Michaels's head, a spotlight came on, bathing the stage in harsh white light.

Saxophone and trumpets wailed lasciviously. When the girls paraded onto the stage, Michaels felt his jaw drop. A vice cop in Cleveland, say, might have put the cuffs on his waitress because she wasn't wearing enough. The girls up there had on high-heeled shoes, headdresses with dyed ostrich plumes and glittering rhinestones, and nothing between the one and the other but big, wide smiles.

He wondered how they got themselves case-hardened enough to go on display like that night after night, show after show. They were all young and pretty and built, no doubt about that. Was it enough? His sister was young and pretty and built, too. He wouldn't have wanted her up there, flaunting it for horny soldiers on leave.

He wondered how much the owners had to pay to keep the local vice squad off their backs. Then he wondered if New Orleans bothered with a vice squad. He hadn't seen any signs of one.

He also wondered who the devil had called him over here and how that person would make contact. Sitting around gaping at naked women was not something he could put in his report unless it had some sort of connection with the business for which he'd come down here.

Soldiers and sailors whooped at the girls, whose skins soon grew slick and shiny with sweat. Waitresses moved back and forth, getting in the way as little as possible while they took drink orders. To fit in, Michaels ordered another whiskey-and-soda, and discovered it cost more than twice as much here as it had downstairs. He didn't figure the Original Absinthe House would go out of business any time soon.

The music got even hotter than it had been. The dancers stepped off the edge of the stage and started prancing among the tables. Michaels's jaw dropped all over again. This wasn't just a floor show. This was a— He didn't quite know what it was, and found himself too flustered to grope for *le mot juste.*

Then a very pretty naked brunette sat down in his lap and twined her arms around his neck.

"Is that a gun in your pocket, dearie, or are you just glad to see me?" she said loudly. Men at the nearest table guffawed. Since it was a gun in his pocket, Michaels kept his mouth shut. The girl smelled of sweat and whiskey and makeup. What her clammy hide was doing to his shirt and trousers did not bear thinking about. He wanted to drop her on the floor and get the hell out of there.

She was holding him too tight for that, though. She lowered her head to nuzzle his neck; the plumes from her headdress got in his eyes and tickled his nose. But under the cover of that frantic scene, her voice went low and urgent: "You got to talk with Colquit the hearse driver, Mister. Tell him Lucy says Pierre says he can talk, an' maybe he will."

Before he could ask her any questions, she kissed him on the lips. The kiss wasn't faked; her tongue slid into his mouth. He'd had enough whiskey and enough shocks by then that he didn't care what he did. His hand closed over her breast—and she sprang to her feet and twisted away, all in perfect time to the music. A moment later, she was in somebody else's lap.

Michaels discovered he'd spilled most of his overpriced drink. He downed what was left with one big swig. When he wiped his mouth with a napkin, it came away red from the girl's—Lucy's—lipstick.

Some of the naked dancers had more trouble than Lucy disentangling themselves from the men they'd chosen. Some of them didn't even try to disentangle. Michaels found himself staring, bug-eyed. You couldn't do *that* in public...could you? Hell and breakfast, it was illegal in private, most places.

Eventually, all the girls were back on stage. They gave it all they had for the finale. Then they trooped off and the lights came back up. Only after they were gone did Michaels understand the knowing look most of them had had all through the performance: they knew more about men than men, most often, cared to know about themselves.

In the palm of his hand, he could still feel the memory of the soft, firm flesh of Lucy's breast. Unlike the others in the room, he'd had to be here. He hadn't had to grab her, though. Sometimes, facetiously, you called a place like this educational. He'd learned something, all right, and rather wished he hadn't.

———

Morrie Harris pursed his lips. "Lucy says Pierre says Colquit can talk? That's not much to go on. For all we know, it could be a trap."

"Yeah, it could be," Michaels said. He and the other FBS man walked along in front of the St. Louis Cathedral, across the street from Jackson Square. They might have been businessmen, they might have been sightseers—though neither businessmen nor sightseers were particularly common in the states that had tried to throw off the Union's yoke. Michaels went on, "I don't think it's a trap, though. Ducange's first name is—was—Pierre, and we've found out he did go to the Original Absinthe House. He could have got to know Lucy there."

He could have done anything with Lucy there. The feel of her would not leave Michaels's mind. He knew going back to the upstairs room would be dangerous, for him and for her, but the temptation lingered like a bit of food between the teeth that keeps tempting back the tongue.

Harris said, "Maybe we ought to just haul her in and grill her till she cracks."

"We risk alerting the Rebs if we do that," Michaels said.

"Yeah, I know." Harris slammed his fist into his palm. "I hate sitting around doing nothing, though. If they get everything they need before we find out where they're squirreling it away, they start their damn uprising and the war effort goes straight out the window." He scowled, a man in deep and knowing it. "And Colquit the hearse driver? You don't know his last name? You don't know which mortuary he works for? Naked little Lucy didn't whisper those into your pink and shell-like ear?"

"I told you what she told me." Michaels stared down at the pavement in dull embarrassment. He could feel his dubiously shell-like ears turning red, not pink.

"All right, all right." Harris threw his hands in the air. Most FBS men made a point of not showing what they were thinking—Gary Cooper might have been the Bureau's ideal. Not Morrie Harris. He wore his feelings on his sleeve. *New York City*, Michaels thought, with scorn he nearly didn't notice himself. Harris went on, "We try and find him, that's all. How many guys are there named Colquit, even in New Orleans? And yeah, you don't have to tell me we got to be careful. If he knows anything, we don't want him riding in a hearse instead of driving one."

A bit of investigation—if checking the phone book and getting somebody with the proper accent to call the Chamber of Commerce could be dignified as such—soon proved funerals were big business in New Orleans, bigger than most other places, maybe. There were mortuaries and cemeteries for Jews, for Negroes, for French-speakers, for Protestants, for this group, for that one, and for the other. Because New Orleans was mostly below sea level (Michaels heartily wished the town were underwater, too), burying people was more complicated than digging a hole and putting a coffin down in it, too. Some intrepid sightseers made special pilgrimages just to see the funeral vaults, which struck Michaels as downright macabre.

Once they had a complete list of funeral establishments, Morrie Harris started calling them one by one. His New York accent was close enough to the local one for him to ask, "Is Colquit there?" without giving himself away as a damnyankee. Time after time, people denied ever hearing of Colquit. At one establishment, though, the receptionist asked whether he meant Colquit the embalmer or Colquit the bookkeeper. He hung up in a hurry.

Repeated failure left Michaels frustrated. He was about to suggest knocking off for the day when Harris suddenly jerked in his chair as if he'd sat on a tack. He put his hand over the receiver and mouthed, "Said he just got back from a funeral. She's going out to get him." He handed the telephone to Michaels.

After just over a minute, a man's voice said, "Hello? Who's this?"

"Colquit?" Michaels asked.

"Yeah," the hearse driver said.

Maybe it was Michaels's imagination, but he thought he heard suspicion even in one slurred word. Sounding like someone from the Loyal States got you nowhere around here (of course, a Johnny Reb who managed to get permission to travel to Wisconsin also raised eyebrows up there, but Michaels wasn't in Wisconsin now). He spoke quickly: "Lucy told me Pierre told her that I should tell you it was okay for you to talk with me."

He waited for Colquit to ask what the hell he was talking about, or else to hang up. It would figure if the only steer he'd got was a bum one. But the hearse driver, after a long pause, said, "Yeah?" again.

Michaels waited for more, but there wasn't any more. It was up to him, then. "You do know what I'm talking about?" he asked, rather desperately.

"Yeah," Colquit repeated: a man of few words.

"You can't talk where you are?"

"Nope," Colquit said—variety.

"Will you meet me for supper outside Galatoire's tonight at seven, then?" Michaels said. With a good meal and some booze in him, Colquit was more likely to spill his guts.

"Make it tomorrow," Colquit said.

"All right, tomorrow," Michaels said unhappily. More delay was the last thing he wanted. No, not quite: he didn't want to spook Colquit, either. He stared to say something more, but the hearse driver did hang up on him then.

"What does he know?" Morrie Harris demanded after Michaels hung up, too.

"I'll find out tomorrow," Michaels answered. "The way things have gone since I got down here, that's progress." Harris nodded solemnly.

———

The wail of police sirens woke Neil Michaels from a sound sleep. The portable alarm clock he'd brought with him was ticking away on the table by his bed. Its radium dial announced the hour: 3:05. He groaned and sat up.

Along with the sirens came the clanging bells and roaring motors of fire engines. Michaels bounced out of bed, ice running down his back. Had the Rebs started their revolt? In that kind of chaos, the pistol he'd brought down from the North felt very small and useless.

He cocked his head. He didn't hear any gunfire. If the Southern men were using whatever the Nazis had shipped them, that would be the biggest part of the racket outside. Okay, it wasn't the big revolt. That meant walking to the window and looking out was likely to be safe. What the devil *was* going on?

Michaels pushed aside the thick curtain shielding the inside of his room from the neon glare that was New Orleans by night. Even as he watched, a couple of fire engines tore down Canal Street toward the Vieux Carré. Their flashing red lights warned the few cars and many pedestrians to get the hell out of the way.

Raising his head, Michaels spotted the fire. Whatever was burning was burning to beat the band. Flames leaped into the night sky, seeming to dance as they flung themselves high above the building that fueled them. A column of thick black smoke marked that building's funeral pyre.

"Might as well find out what it is," Michaels said out loud. He turned on the lamp by the bed and then the radio. The little light behind the dial came on. He waited impatiently for the tubes to get warm enough to bring in a signal.

The first station he got was playing one of Benny Goodman's records. Michaels wondered if playing a damnyankee's music was enough to get you in trouble with some of the fire-eating Johnny Rebs. But he didn't want to hear jazz, not now. He spun the dial.

"—Terrible fire on Bourbon Street," an announcer was saying. That had to be the blaze Michaels had seen. The fellow went on, "One of New Orleans's longstanding landmarks, the Original Absinthe House, is going up in flames even as I speak. The Absinthe House presents shows all through the night, and many are feared dead inside. The building was erected well over a hundred years ago, and has seen—"

Michaels turned off the radio, almost hard enough to break the knob. He didn't believe in coincidence, not even a little bit. Somewhere in the wreckage of the Original Absinthe House would lie whatever mortal fragments remained of Lucy the dancer, and that was just how someone wanted it to be.

He shivered like a man with the grippe. He'd thought about asking Colquit to meet him there instead of at Galatoire's, so Lucy could help persuade the hearse driver to tell whatever he knew—and so he could get another look at her. But going to a place twice running let the opposition get a line on you. Training had saved his life and, he hoped, Colquit's. It hadn't done poor Lucy one damn bit of good.

He called down to room service and asked for a bottle of whiskey. If the man to whom he gave the order found anything unusual about such a request at twenty past three, he didn't show it. The booze arrived in short order. After three or four good belts, Michaels was able to get back to sleep.

Colquit didn't show up for dinner at Galatoire's that night.

When Morrie Harris phoned the mortuary the next day, the reception-ist said Colquit had called in sick. "That's a relief," Michaels said when Harries reported the news. "I was afraid he'd call in dead."

"Yeah." Harris ran a hand through his curly hair. "I didn't want to try and get a phone number and address out of the gal. I didn't even like making the phone call. The less attention we draw to the guy, the better."

"You said it." Michaels took off his glasses, blew a speck from the left lens, set them back on his nose. "Now we know where he works. We can find out where he lives. Just a matter of digging through the papers."

"A lot of papers to dig through," Harris said with a grimace, "but yeah, that ought to do the job. Shall we head on over to the Hall of Records?"

Machine-gun nests surrounded the big marble building on Thalia Street. If the Johnny Rebs ever got their revolt off the ground, it would be one of the first places to burn. The Federal army and bureaucrats who controlled the conquered provinces of the old Confederacy ruled not only by force but also by keeping tabs on their resentful, rebellious subjects. Every white man who worked had to fill out a card each year listing his place of employment. Every firm had to list its employees. Most of the clerks who checked one set of forms against the other were Negroes. They had a vested interest in making sure nobody put one over on the government.

Tough, unsmiling guards meticulously checked Harris and Michaels's identification papers, comparing photographs to faces and making them give samples of their signatures, before admitting them to the hall. They feared sabotage as well as out-and-out assault. The records stored here helped helped down all of Louisiana.

Hannibal Dupuy was a large, round black man with some of the thickest glasses Michaels had ever seen. "Mortuary establishments," he said, holding up one finger as he thought. "Yes, those would be in the Wade Room, in the cases against the east wall." Michaels got the feeling that, had they asked him about anything from taverns to taxidermists, he would have known exactly where the files hid. Such men were indispensable in navigating the sea of papers before them.

Going through the papers stored in the cases against the east wall of the Wade Room took a couple of hours. Michaels finally found the requisite record. "Colquit D. Reynolds, hearse driver—yeah, he works for LeBlanc and Peters," he said. "Okay, here's address and phone number and a notation that they've been verified as correct. People are on the ball here, no two ways about it."

"People have to be on the ball here," Morrie Harris answered. "How'd you like to be a Negro in the South if the whites you've been sitting on for years grab hold of the reins? Especially if they grab hold of the reins with help from the Nazis? The first thing they'd do after they threw us damnyankees out is to start hanging Negroes from lampposts."

"You're right. Let's go track down Mr. Reynolds, so we don't have to find out just how right you are."

Colquit Reynolds's documents said he lived on Carondelet, out past St. Joseph: west and south of the French Quarter. Harris had a car, a wheezy Blasingame that delivered him and Michaels to the requisite address. Michaels knocked on the door of the house, which, like the rest of the neighborhood, was only a small step up from the shotgun shack level.

No one answered. Michaels glanced over at Morrie Harris. FBS men didn't need a warrant, not to search a house in Johnny Reb country. That wasn't the issue. Both of them, though, feared they'd find nothing but a corpse when they got inside.

Just as Michaels was about to break down the front door, an old woman stuck her head out a side window of the house next door and said, "If you lookin' for Colquit, gents, you ain't gonna find him in there."

Morrie Harris swept off his hat and gave a nod that was almost a bow. "Where's he at, then, ma'm?" he asked, doing his best to sound like a local and speaking to the old woman as if she were the military governor's wife.

She cackled like a laying hen; she must have liked that. "Same place you always find him when he wants to drink 'stead of workin': the Old Days Saloon round the co'ner." She jerked a gnarled thumb to show which way.

The Old Days Saloon was painted in gaudy stripes of red, white, and blue. Those were the national colors, and so unexceptionable, but, when taken with the name of the place, were probably meant to suggest the days of the Great Rebellion and the traitors who had used them on a different flag. Michaels would have bet a good deal that the owner of the place had a thick FBS dossier.

He and Harris walked in. The place was dim and quiet. Ceiling fans created the illusion of coolness. The bruiser behind the bar gave the newcomers the dubious stare he obviously hauled out for any stranger: certainly the four or five men in the place had the look of longtime regulars. Asking which one was Colquit was liable to be asking for trouble.

One of the regulars, though, looked somehow familiar. After a moment, Michaels realized why: that old man soaking up a beer off in a corner had driven the horse-drawn hearse that had slowed him up on his way back to the hotel a few days before. He nudged Morrie Harris, nodded toward the old fellow. Together, they went over to him. "How you doin' today, Colquit?" Harris asked in friendly tones. The bartender relaxed.

Colquit looked up at them with eyes that didn't quite focus. "Don't think I know you folks," he said, "but I could be wrong."

"Sure you do," Harris said, expansive still. "We're friends of Pierre and Lucy."

"Oh, Lord help me." Colquit started to get up. Michaels didn't want a scene. Anything at all could make New Orleans go off—hauling a man out of a bar very much included. But Colquit Reynolds slumped back onto his chair, as if his legs didn't want to hold him. "Wish I never told Pierre about none o' that stuff," he muttered, and finished his beer with a convulsive gulp.

Michaels raised a forefinger and called out to the bartender: "Three more High Lifes here." He tried to slur his words into a Southern pattern. Maybe he succeeded, or maybe the dollar bill he tossed down on the table was enough to take the edge off suspicions. The Rebs had revered George Washington even during the Great Rebellion, misguided though they were in other ways.

Colquit Reynolds took a long pull at the new beer. Michaels and Harris drank more moderately. If they were going to get anything out of the hearse driver, they needed to be able to remember it once they had it. Besides, Michaels didn't much like beer. Quietly, so the bartender and the other locals wouldn't hear, he asked, "What do you wish you hadn't told Pierre, Mr. Reynolds?"

Reynolds looked up at the ceiling, as if the answer were written there. Michaels wondered if he was able to remember; he'd been drinking for a while. Finally, he said, "Wish I hadn't told him 'bout this here coffin I took for layin' to rest."

"Oh? Why's that?" Michaels asked casually. He lit a Camel, offered the pack to Colquit Reynolds. When Reynolds took one, he used his Zippo to give the hearse driver a light.

Reynolds sucked in smoke. He held it longer than Michaels thought humanly possible, then exhaled a foggy cloud. After he knocked the coal into an ash tray, he drained his Miller's High Life and looked expectantly at the FBS men. Michaels ordered him another one. Only after he'd drunk part of that did he answer, "On account of they needed a block and tackle to get it onto my hearse an' another one to get it off again. Ain't no six men in the world could have lifted that there coffin, not if they was Samson an' five o' his brothers. An' it *clanked*, too."

"Weapons," Morrie Harris whispered, "or maybe ammunition." He looked joyous, transfigured, likely even more so than he would have if a naked dancing girl had plopped herself down in his lap. *Poor Lucy,* Michaels thought.

He said, "Even in a coffin, even greased, I wouldn't want to bury anything in this ground—not for long, that's for damn sure. Water's liable to seep in and ruin things."

Colquit Reynolds sent him a withering, scornful look. "Damnyankees," he muttered under his breath—and he was helping Michaels. "Lot of the times here, you don't bury your dead, you put 'em in a tomb up above ground, just so as coffins don't get flooded out o' the ground come the big rains."

"Jesus," Morrie Harris said hoarsely, wiping his forehead with a sleeve, and then again: "Jesus." Now he was the one to drain his beer and signal for another. Once the bartender had come and gone, he went on, "All the above-ground tombs New Orleans has, you could hide enough guns and ammo to fight a big war. Goddamn sneaky Rebs." He made himself step. "What cemetery was this at, Mr. Reynolds?"

"Old Girod, out on South Liberty Street," Colquit Reynolds replied. "Don' know how much is there, but one coffinload, anyways."

"Thank God some Southern men don't want to see the Great Rebellion start up again," Michaels said.

"Yeah." Harris drank from his second High Life. "But a hell of a lot of 'em *do.*"

———

Girod Cemetery was hidden away in the railroad yards. A plaque on the stone fence surrounding it proclaimed it to be the oldest Protestant cemetery in New Orleans. Neil Michaels was willing to believe that. The place didn't seem to have received much in the way of legitimate business in recent years, and had a haunted look to it. It was overgrown with vines and shrubs. Gray-barked fig trees pushed up through the sides of some of the old tombs. Moss was everywhere, on trees and tombs alike. Maidenhair ferns sprouted from the sides of the above-ground vaults; as Michaels had seen, anything would grow anywhere around here.

That included conspiracies. If Colquit Reynolds was right, the ghost of the Great Rebellion haunted this cemetery, too, and the Johnnies were trying to bring it back to unwholesome life.

"He'd better be right," Michaels muttered as the jeep he was riding pulled to a stop before the front entrance to the cemetery.

Morrie Harris understood him without trouble. "Who, that damn hearse driver? You bet he'd better be right. We bring all this stuff here" —he waved behind him—"and start tearin' up a graveyard, then don't find anything…hell, that could touch off a revolt all by itself."

Michaels shivered, though the day was hot and muggy. "Couldn't it just?" Had Reynolds been leading them down the path, setting them up to create an incident that would make the South rise up in righteous fury? They'd have to respond to a story like the one he'd told; for the sake of the Union, they didn't dare not respond.

They'd find out. Behind the jeep, Harris's *all this stuff* rattled and clanked: not just bulldozers, but also light M3 Stoneman tanks and heavy M3 Grants with a small gun in a rotating turret and a big one in a sponson at the right front of the hull. Soldiers—all of them men from the Loyal States—scrambled down from Chevy trucks and set up a perimeter around the wall. If anybody was going to try to interfere with this operation, he'd regret it.

Against the assembled might of the Federal Union (*it must and shall be preserved,* Michaels thought), Girod Cemetery mustered a stout metal gate and one elderly watchman. "Who the devil are y'all, and what d'you want?" he demanded, though the *who* part, at least, should have been pretty obvious.

Michaels displayed his FBS badge. "We are on the business of the federal government of the United States of America," he said. "Open the gate and let us in." Again, no talk of warrants, not in Reb country, not on FBS business.

"Fuck the federal government of the United States of America, and the horse it rode in on," the watchman said. "You ain't got no call to come to no cemetery with tanks."

Michaels didn't waste time arguing with him. He tapped the jeep driver on the shoulder. The fellow backed the jeep out of the way. Michaels waved to the driver of the nearest Grant tank. The tank man had his head out of the hatch. He grinned and nodded. The tank clattered forward, chewing up the pavement and spewing noxious exhaust into the air. The wrought-iron gate was sturdy, but not sturdy enough to withstand thirty-one tons of insistent armor. It flew open with a scream of metal; one side ripped loose from the stone to which it was fixed. The Grant ran over it, and would have run over the watchman, too, had he not skipped aside with a shouted curse.

Outside the cemetery, people began gathering. Most of the people were white men of military age or a bit younger. To Michaels, they had the look of men who'd paint slogans on walls or shoot at a truck or from behind a fence under cover of darkness. He was glad he'd brought overwhelming force. Against bayonets, guns, and armor, the crowd couldn't do much but stare sullenly.

If the cemetery was empty of contraband, what this crowd did wouldn't matter. There's be similar angry crowds all over the South, and at one of them...

The watchman let out an anguished howl as tanks and bulldozers clanked toward the walls of above-ground vaults that ran up and down the length of the cemetery. "You can't go smashin' up the ovens!" he screamed.

"Last warning, Johnny Reb," Michaels said coldly: "don't you try telling officers of the United States what we can and can't do. We have places to put people whose mouths get out in front of their brains."

"Yeah, I just bet you do," the watchman muttered, but after that he kept his mouth shut.

A dozer blade bit into the side of one of the mortuary vaults— an oven, the old man had called it. Concrete and stone flew. So did chunks of a wooden coffin and the bones it had held. The watchman shot Michaels a look of unadulterated hatred and scorn. He didn't say a word, but he might as well have screamed, *See? I told you so.* A lot of times, that look alone would have been plenty to get him on the inside of a prison camp, but Michaels had bigger things to worry about today.

He and Harris hadn't ordered enough bulldozers to take on all the rows of ovens at once. The tanks joined in the job, too, knocking them down as the first big snorting Grant had wrecked the gate into Girod. Their treads ground more coffins and bones into dust.

"That goddamn hearse driver better not have been lying to us," Morrie Harris said, his voice clogged with worry. "If he was, he'll never see a camp or a jail. We'll give the son of a bitch a blindfold; I wouldn't waste a cigarette on him."

Then, from somewhere near the center of Girod Cemetery, a tank crew let out a shout of triumph. Michaels had never heard sweeter music, not from Benny Goodman or Tommy Dorsey. He sprinted toward the Grant. Sweat poured off him, but it wasn't the sweat of fear, not any more.

The tank driver pointed to wooden boxes inside a funeral vault he'd just broken into. They weren't coffins. Each had *1 Maschinengewehr 34* stenciled on its side in neat black-letter script, with the Nazi eagle-and-swastika emblem right next to the legend.

Michaels stared at the machine-gun crates as if one of them held the Holy Grail. "He wasn't lying," he breathed. "Thank you, God."

"*Omayn*," Morrie Harris agreed. "Now let's find out how much truth he was telling."

———

The final haul, by the time the last oven was cracked the next day, astonished even Michaels and Harris. Michaels read from the list he'd been keeping: "Machine guns, submachine guns, mortars, rifles—including antitank rifles—ammo for all of them, grenades... Jesus, what a close call."

"I talked with one of the radio men," Harris said. "He's sent out a call for more trucks to haul all this stuff away." He wiped his forehead with the back of his hand, a gesture that had little to do with heat or humidity. "If they'd managed to smuggle all of this out of New Orleans, spread it around through the South...well, hell, I don't have to draw you a picture."

"You sure don't. We'd have been so busy down here, the Germans and the Japs would have had a field day over the rest of the world." Michaels let out a heartfelt sigh of relief, then went on, "Next thing we've got to do is try and find out who was caching weapons. If we can do that, then maybe, just maybe, we can keep the Rebs leaderless for a generation or so and get ahead of the game."

"Maybe." But Harris didn't sound convinced. "We can't afford to think in terms of a generation from now, anyhow. It's what we were talking about when you first got into town: as long as we can hold the lid on the South till we've won the damn war, that'll do the trick. If we catch the guys running guns with the Nazis, great. If we don't, I don't give a damn about them sneaking around painting YANKS OUT on every blank wall they find. We can deal with that. We've been dealing with it since 1865. As long as they don't have the toys they need to really hurt us, we'll get by."

"Yeah, that's true—if no other subs drop off loads of goodies some-place else." Michaels sighed again. "No rest for the weary. If that happens, we'll just have to try and track 'em down."

A growing rumble of diesel engines made Morrie Harris grin. "Here come the trucks," he said, and trotted out toward the ruined entryway to Girod Cemetery. Michaels followed him. Harris pointed. "Ah, good, they're smart enough to have jeeps riding shotgun for 'em. We don't want any trouble around here till we get the weapons away safe."

There were still a lot of people outside the cemetery walls. They booed and hissed the newly arrived vehicles, but didn't try anything more than booing and hissing. They might hate the damnyankees—they *did* hate the damnyankees—but it was the damnyankees who had the firepower here. Close to eighty years of bitter experience had taught that they weren't shy about using it, either.

Captured German weapons and ammunition filled all the new trucks to overflowing. Some of the ones that had brought in troops also got loaded with lethal hardware. The displaced soldiers either piled into jeeps or clambered up on top of tanks for the ride back to barracks, where the captured arms would be as safe as they could be anywhere in the endlessly rebellious South.

Michaels and Harris had led the convoy to the cemetery; now they'd lead it away. When their jeep driver started up the engine, a few young Rebs bolder than the rest made as if to block the road.

The corporal in charge of the pintle-mounted .50-caliber machine gun in the jeep turned to Michaels and asked, "Shall I mow 'em down, sir?" He sounded quiveringly eager to do just that.

"We'll give 'em one chance first," Michaels said, feeling gener-ous. He stood up in the jeep and shouted to the Johnnies obstructing his path: "You are interfering with the lawful business of the Federal Bureau of Suppression. Disperse at once or you will be shot. First, last, and only warning, people." He sat back down, telling the driver,

"Put it in gear, but go slow. If they don't move—" He made hand-washing gestures.

Sullenly, the young men gave way as the jeep moved forward. The gunner swung the muzzle of his weapon back and forth, back and forth, encouraging them to fall back further. The expression on his face, which frightened even Michaels, might have been an even stronger persuader.

The convoy rattled away from the cemetery. The Johnnies hooted and jeered, but did no more than that, not here, not now. Had they got Nazi guns in their hands...but they hadn't.

"We won this one," Morrie Harris said.

"We sure did," Michaels agreed. "Now we can get on with the business of getting rid of tyrants around the world." He spoke altogether without irony.

ISLANDS IN THE SEA

A.H. 152 (A.D. 769)

The Bulgar border guards had arrows nocked and ready as the Arab horsemen rode up from the south. Jalal ad-Din as-Stambuli, the leader of the Arab delegation, raised his right hand to show it was empty. "In the name of Allah, the Compassionate, the Merciful, I and my men come in peace," he called in Arabic. To be sure the guards understood, he repeated himself in Greek.

The precaution paid off. The guards lowered their bows. In Greek much worse than Jalal ad-Din's, one of them asked, "Why for you come in peace, whitebeard?"

Jalal ad-Din stroked his whiskers. Even without the Bulgar's mockery, he knew they were white. Not many men who had the right to style themselves *as-Stambuli*, the Constantinopolitan, still lived. More than fifty years had passed since the army of Suleiman and Maslama had taken Constantinople and put an end to the Roman Empire. Then Jalal ad-Din's beard had not been white. Then he could hardly raise a beard at all.

He spoke in Greek again: "My master the caliph Abd ar-Rahman asked last year if your khan Telerikh would care to learn more of Islam, of submission to the one God. This past spring Telerikh sent word that he would. We are the embassy sent to instruct him."

The Bulgar who had talked with him now used his own hissing language, Jalal ad-Din supposed to translate for this comrades. They answered back, some of them anything but happily. Content in their paganism, Jalal ad-Din guessed—content to burn in hell forever. He did not wish that fate on anyone, even a Bulgar.

The guard who knew Greek confirmed his thought, saying, "Why for we want your god? Gods, spirits, ghosts good to us now."

Jalal ad-Din shrugged. "Your khan asked to hear more of Allah and Islam. That is why we are here." He could have said much more, but deliberately spoke in terms a soldier would understand.

"Telerikh want, Telerikh get," the guard agreed. He spoke again with his countrymen, at length pointed at two of them. "This Iskur. This Omurtag. They take you to Pliska, to where Telerikh is. Iskur, him know Greek a little, not so good like me."

"Know little your tongue too," Iskur said in halting Arabic, which surprised Jalal ad-Din and, evidently, the Bulgar who had been doing all the talking till now. The prospective guide glanced at the sun, which was a couple of hours from setting. "We ride," he declared, and started off with no more fanfare than that. The Bulgar called Omurtag followed.

So, more slowly, did Jalal ad-Din and his companions. By the time Iskur called a halt in deepening twilight, the mountains that made the northern horizon jagged were visibly closer.

"Those little ponies the Bulgars ride are ugly as mules, but they go and go and go," said Da'ud ibn Zubayr, who was a veteran of many skirmishes on the border between the caliph's land and Bulgaria. He stroked the mane of his elegant, Arab-bred mare.

"Sadly, my old bones do not." Jalal ad-Din groaned with relief as he slid off his own horse, a soft-gaited gelding. Once he had delighted in fiery stallions, but he knew that if he took a fall now he would shatter like glass.

The Bulgars stalked into the brush to hunt. Da'ud bent to the laborious business of getting a fire going. The other two Arabs, Malik ibn Anas and Salman al-Tabari, stood guard, one with a bow, the other with a spear. Iskur and Omurtag emerged into firelight carrying partridges and rabbits. Jalal ad-Din took hard unleavened bread from a saddlebag: no feast tonight, he thought, but not the worst of fare either.

Iskur also had a skin of wine. He offered it to the Arabs, grinned when they declined. "More for me, Omurtag," he said. The two Bulgars drank the skin dry, and soon lay snoring by the fire.

Da'ud ibn Zubayr scowled at them. "The only use they have for wits is losing them," he sneered. "How can such folk ever come to acknowledge Allah and his Prophet?"

"We Arabs were wine-bibbers too, before Muhammad forbad it to us," Jalal ad-Din said. "My worry is that the Bulgars' passion for such drink will make khan Telerikh less inclined to accept our faith."

Da'ud dipped his head to the older man. "Truly it is just that you lead us, sir. Like a falcon, you keep your eye ever on our quarry."

"Like a falcon, I sleep in the evening," Jalal ad-Din said, yawning. "And like an old falcon, I need more sleep than I once did."

"Your years have brought you wisdom." Da'ud ibn Zubayr hesitated, as if wondering whether to go on. Finally he plunged: "Is it true, sir, that you once met a man who had known the Prophet?"

"It is true," Jalal ad-Din said proudly. "It was at Antioch, when Suleiman's army was marching to fight the Greeks at Constantinople. The grandfather of the innkeeper with whom I was quartered lived with him still: he was a Medinan, far older then than I am now, for he had soldiered with Khalid ibn al-Walid when the city fell to us. And before that, as a youth, he accompanied Muhammad when the Prophet returned in triumph from Medina to Mecca."

"*Allahu akbar,*" Da'ud breathed: "God is great. I am further honored to be in your presence. Tell me, did—did the old man grant you any *hadith,* any tradition, of the Prophet that you might pass on to me for the sake of my enlightenment?"

"Yes," Jalal ad-Din said. "I recall it as if it were yesterday, just as the old man did when speaking of the journey to the Holy City. Abu Bakr, who was not yet caliph, of course, for Muhammad was still alive, started beating a man for letting a camel get loose. The Prophet began to smile, and said, 'See what this pilgrim is doing.' Abu Bakr was abashed, though the Prophet did not actually tell him to stop."

Da'ud bowed low. "I am in your debt." He repeated the story several times; Jalal ad-Din nodded to show him he had learned it perfectly. In the time-honored way, Da'ud went on, "I have this *hadith* from Jalal ad-Din as-Stambuli, who had it from—what was the old man's name, sir?"

"He was called Abd al-Qadir."

"—who had it from Abd al-Qadir, who had it from the Prophet. Think of it—only two men between Muhammad and me." Da'ud bowed again.

Jalal ad-Din returned the bow, then embarrassed himself by yawning once more. "Your pardon, I pray. Truly I must sleep."

"Sleep, then, and Allah keep you safe till the morning comes."

Jalal ad-Din rolled himself in his blanket. "And you, son of Zubayr."

———

"Those are no mean works," Da'ud said a week later, pointing ahead to the earthen rampart, tall as six men, that ringed Pliska, Telerikh's capital.

"That is a child's toy, next to the walls of Constantinople," Jalal ad-Din said. "A double wall, each one twice that height, all steep stone,

398

well-ditched in front and between, with all the Greeks in the world, it seemed, battling from atop them." Across half a century, recalling the terror of the day of the assault, he wondered still how he had survived.

"I was born in Constantinople," Da'ud reminded him gently.

"Of course you were." Jalal ad-Din shook his head, angry at himself for letting past obscure present that way. It was something old men did, but who cares to remember he is old?

Da'ud glanced around to make sure Iskur was out of earshot, lowered his voice. "For pagan savages, those are no mean works. And see how much land they enclose—Pliska must be a city of greater size than I had supposed."

"No." Jalal ad-Din remembered a talk with a previous envoy to Telerikh. "The town itself is tiny. This earthwork serves chiefly to mark off the grazing lands of the khan's flocks."

"His flocks? Is that all?" Da'ud threw back his head and laughed. "I feel as I though I am transported to some strange new world, where nothing is as it seems."

"I have had that feeling ever since we came through the mountain passes," Jalal ad-Din said seriously. Da'ud gave him a curious look. He tried to explain: "You are from Constantinople. I was born not far from Damascus, where I dwell yet. A long journey from one to the other, much longer than from Constantinople to Pliska."

Da'ud nodded.

"And yet it is a journey through sameness," Jalal ad-Din went on. "Not much difference in weather, in crops, in people. Aye, more Greeks, more Christians in Constantinople still, for we have ruled there so much less time than in Damascus, but the difference is of degree, not of kind."

"That is all true," Da'ud said, nodding again. "Whereas here—"

"Aye, here," Jalal ad-Din said with heavy irony. "The olive will not grow here, the sun fights its way through mists that swaddle it as if it were a newborn babe, and even a Greek would be welcome, for the sake of having someone civilized to talk to. This is a different world from ours, and not one much to my liking."

"Still, we hope to wed it to ours through Islam," Da'ud said.

"So we do, so we do. Submission to the will of God makes all men one." Now Jalal ad-Din made sure Iskur was paying no attention. The nomad had ridden ahead. Jalal ad-Din went on, "Even Bulgars." Da'ud chuckled.

Iskur yelled something at the guards lounging in front of a wooden gate in Pliska's earthen outwall. The guards yelled back. Iskur shouted again, louder this time. With poor grace, the guards got up and opened the gate. They stared as they saw what sort of companions Iskur led.

Jalal ad-Din gave them a grave salute as he passed through the gate, as much to discomfit them as for any other reason. He pointed ahead to the stone wall of Pliska proper. "You see?"

"I see," Da'ud said. The rectangular wall was less than half a mile on a side. "In our lands, that would be a fortress, not a capital."

The gates of the stone wall were open. Jalal ad-Din coughed as he followed Iskur and Omurtag into the town: Pliska stank like—stank worse than—a big city. Jalal ad-Din shrugged. Sooner or later, he knew, he would stop noticing the stench.

Not far inside the gates stood a large building of intricately carven wood. "This Telerikh's palace," Iskur announced.

Tethered in front of the palace were any number of steppe ponies like the ones Iskur and Omurtag rode and also, Jalal ad-Din saw with interest, several real horses and a mule whose trappings did not look like Arab gear. "To whom do those belong?" he asked, pointing.

"Not know," Iskur said. He cupped his hands and yelled toward the palace—yelling, Jalal ad-Din thought wryly, seemed the usual Bulgar approach towards any problem. After a little while, a door opened. The Arab had not even noticed it till then, so lost was its outline among carvings.

As soon as they saw someone come out of the palace, Iskur and Omurtag wheeled their horses and rode away without a backwards glance at the ambassadors they had guided to Pliska. The man who had emerged took a moment to study the new arrivals. He bowed. "How may I help you, my masters?" he asked in Arabic fluent enough to make Jalal ad-Din sit up and take notice.

"We are envoys of the caliph Abd ar-Rahman, come to your fine city"—Jalal ad-Din knew when to stretch a point—"at the bidding of your khan to explain to him the glories of Islam. I have the honor of addressing—?" He let the words hang.

"I am Draogmir, steward to the mighty khan Telerikh. Dismount; be welcome here." Dragomir bowed again. He was, Jalal ad-Din guessed, in his late thirties, stocky and well-made, with fair skin, a full brown beard framing rather a wide face, and gray eyes that revealed nothing whatever—a useful attribute in a steward.

Jalal ad-Din and his companions slid gratefully from their horses. As if by magic, boys appeared to hitch the Arabs' beasts to the rails in front of the palace and carry their saddlebags into it. Jalal ad-Din nodded at the other full-sized horses and the mule. "To whom do those belong, pray?" he asked Dragomir.

The steward's pale but hooded eyes swung toward the hitching rail, returned to Jalal ad-Din. "Those," he explained, "are the animals of the delegation of priests from the pope of Rome at the bidding of my khan to expound to him the glories of Christianity. They arrived earlier today."

———

Late that night, Da'ud slammed a fist against a wall of the chamber the four Arabs shared. "Better they should stay pagan than turn Christian!" he shouted. Not only was he angry that Telerikh had also invited Christians to Pliska as if intending to auction his land to the faith that bid highest, he was also short-tempered from hunger. The evening's

401

banquet had featured pork. (It had *not* featured Telerikh; some heathen Bulgar law required the khan always to eat alone.)

"That is not so," Jalal ad-Din said mildly.

"And why not?" Da'ud glared at the older man.

"As Christians they would be *dhimmis*—people of the Book—and thus granted a hope of heaven. Should they cling to their pagan practices, their souls will surely belong to Satan till the end of time."

"Satan is welcome to their souls, whether pagan or Christian," Da'ud said. "But a Christian Bulgaria, allied to Rome, maybe even allied to the Franks, would block the true faith's progress northwards and could be the spearpoint of a thrust back toward Constantinople."

Jalal ad-Din sighed. "What you say is true. Still, the true faith is also true, and the truth surely will prevail against Christian falsehoods."

"May it be so," Da'ud said heavily. "But was this land not once a Christian country, back in the days before the Bulgars seized it from Constantinople? All the lands the Greeks held followed their usages. Some folk hereabouts must be Christian still, I'd wager, which might incline Telerikh toward their beliefs."

A knock on the door interrupted the argument. Da'ud kept one hand on his knife as he opened the door with the other. But no enemies stood outside, only four girls. Two were colored like Dragomir—to Jalal ad-Din's eyes, exotically fair. The other two were dark, darker than Arabs, in fact; one had eyes that seemed set at a slant. All four were pretty. They smiled and swayed their way in.

"Telerikh is no Christian," Jalal ad-Din said as he smiled back at one of the light-skinned girls. "Christians are not allowed concubines."

"The more fools they," Da'ud said. "Shall I blow out the lamps, or leave them burning?"

"Leave them," Jalal ad-Din answered. "I want to see what I am doing..."

Jalal ad-Din bowed low to khan Telerikh. A pace behind him, Da'ud did the same. Another pace back, Malik ibn Anas and Salman al-Tabari went to one knee, as suited their lower rank.

"Rise, all of you," Telerikh said in passable Arabic. The khan of the Bulgars was about fifty, swarthy, broad-faced, wide-nosed, with a thin beard going from black to gray. His eyes were narrow, hard, and shrewd. He looked like a man well able to rule a nation whose strength came entirely from the ferocity of its soldiers.

"Most magnificent khan, we bring the greetings of our master the caliph Abd ar-Rahman ibn Marwan, his prayers for your health and prosperity, and gifts to show that you stand high in his esteem," Jalal ad-Din said.

He waved Salman and Malik forward to present the gifts: silver plates from Persia, Damascus-work swords, fine enamelware from Constantinople, a robe of glistening Chinese silk, and, last but not least, a *Qu'ran* bound in leather and gold, its calligraphy the finest the scribes of Alexandria could provide.

Telerikh, though, seemed most interested in the robe. He rose from his wooden throne, undid the broad bronze belt he wore, shrugged out of his knee-length fur caftan. Under it he had on a linen tunic and trousers and low boots. Dragomir came up to help him put on the robe. He smiled with pleasure as he ran a hand over the watery-smooth fabric.

"Very pretty," he crooned. For a moment, Jalal ad-Din hoped he was so taken by the presents as to be easily swayed. But Telerikh, as the Arab had guessed from his appearance, was not so simple. He went on, "The caliph gives lovely gifts. With his riches, he can afford to. Now please take your places while the envoys of the pope of Rome present themselves."

Dragomir waved the Arab delegation off to the right of the throne, close by the turbaned boyars—the great nobles—who made up Telerikh's court. Most were of the same stock as their khan; a few looked more like Dragomir and the fair girl Jalal ad-Din had so enjoyed the night before. Fair or dark, they smelled of hard-run horses and ancient sweat.

As he had with the caliph's embassy, Dragomir announced the papal legates in the throaty Bulgarian tongue. There were three of them, as Jalal ad-Din had seen at the banquet. Two were gorgeous in robes that reminded him of the ones the Constantinopolitan grandees had worn so long ago as they vainly tried to rally their troops against the Arabs. The third wore a simple brown woolen habit. Amid the Bulgar chatter, meaningless to him, Jalal ad-Din picked out three names: Niketas, Theodore, and Paul.

The Christians scowled at the Arabs as they walked past them to approach Telerikh. They bowed as Jalal ad-Din had. "Stand," Telerikh said in Greek. Jalal ad-Din was not surprised he knew that language; the Bulgars had dealt with Constantinople before the Arabs took it, and many refugees had fled to Pliska. Others had escaped to Italy, which no doubt explained why two of the papal legates bore Greek names.

"Excellent khan," said one of the envoys (Theodore, Jalal ad-Din thought it was), also in Greek, "we are saddened to see you decked in raiment given you by our foes as you greet us. Does this mean you hold us in contempt, and will give us no fair hearing? Surely you did not invite us to travel so far merely for that?"

Telerikh blinked, glanced down at the silk robe he had just put on. "No," he said. "It only means I like this present. What presents have you for me?"

Da'ud leaned forward, whispered into Jalal ad-Din's ear: "More avarice in that one than fear of hell." Jalal ad-Din nodded. That made his task harder, not easier. He would have to play politics along with expounding the truth of Islam. He sighed. Ever since he learned Telerikh had also bid the men from Rome hither, he'd expected no less.

The Christians were presenting their gifts, and making a great show of it to try to disguise their not being so fine as the ones their rivals had given—Jalal ad-Din's offerings still lay in a glittering heap beside Telerikh's throne. "Here," Theodore intoned, "is a copy of the Holy Scriptures, with a personal prayer for you inscribed therein by his holiness the pope Constantine."

Jalal ad-Din let out a quiet but scornful snort. "The words of Allah are the ones that count," he whispered to Da'ud ibn Zubayr, "not those of any man." It was Da'ud's turn to nod.

As he had with the *Qu'ran,* Telerikh idly paged through the Bible. Perhaps halfway through, he paused, glanced up at the Christians. "You have pictures in your book." It sounded almost like an accusation; had Jalal ad-Din said it, it would have been.

But the Christian in the plain brown robe, the one called Paul, answered calmly, "Yes, excellent khan, we do, the better to instruct the many who cannot read the words beside them." He was no longer young—he might have been close to Jalal ad-Din's age—but his voice was light and clear and strong, the voice of a man sure in the path he has chosen.

"Beware of that one," Da'ud murmured. "He has more holiness in him than the other two put together." Jalal ad-Din had already reached the same conclusion, and did not like it. Enemies, he thought, ought by rights to be rogues.

He got only a moment to mull on that, for Telerikh suddenly shifted to Arabic and called to him, "Why are there no pictures in your book, to show me what you believe?"

"Because Allah the one God is infinite, far too mighty for our tiny senses to comprehend, and so cannot be depicted," he said, "and man must not be depicted, for Allah created him in his image from a clot of blood. The Christians' own scriptures say as much, but they ignore any law which does not suit them."

"Liar! Misbeliever!" Theodore shouted. Torchlight gleamed off his tonsured pate as he whirled to confront Jalal ad-Din.

"No liar I," Jalal ad-Din said; not for nothing had he studied with men once Christian before they saw the truth of Muhammad's teaching. "The verse you deny is in the book called Exodus."

"Is this true?" Telerikh rumbled, scowling at the Christians.

Theodore started to reply; Paul cut him off. "Excellent khan, the verse is as the Arab states. My colleague did not wish to deny it." Theodore looked ready to argue. Paul did not let him, continuing, "But that law was given to Moses long ago. Since then, Christ the Son of God has appeared on earth; belief in him assures one of heaven, regardless of the observance of the outdated rules of the Jews."

Telerikh grunted. "A new law may replace an old, if circumstances change. What say you to that, envoy of the caliph?"

"I will quote two verses from the *Qur'an,* from the *sura* called The Cow," Jalal ad-Din said, smiling at the opening Paul had left him. "Allah says, 'The Jews say the Christians are astray, and the Christians say it is the Jews who are astray. Yet they both read the Scriptures.' Which is to say, magnificent khan, that they have both corrupted God's word. And again, 'They say: "Allah has begotten a son." Allah forbid!'"

When reciting from the *Qur'an,* he had naturally fallen into Arabic. He was not surprised to see the Christians following his words without difficulty. They too would have prepared for any eventuality on this mission.

One of Telerikh's boyars called something to the khan in his own language. Malik ibn Anas, who was with Jalal ad-Din precisely because he knew a little of the Bulgar speech, translated for him: "He says that the sacred stones of their forefathers, even the pagan gods of the Slavs they rule, have served them well enough for years upon years, and calls on Telerikh not to change their usages now."

Looking around, Jalal ad-Din saw more than a few boyars nodding. "Great khan, may I speak?" he called. Telerikh nodded. Jalal ad-Din went on, "Great khan, you need but look about you to see proof of Allah's might. Is it not true that my lord the caliph Abd ar-Rahman, peace be unto him, rules from the Western Sea to India, from your borders to beyond the deserts of Egypt? Even the Christians, who know the one God imperfectly, still control many lands. Yet only you here in this small country follow your idols. Does this not show you their strength is a paltry thing?"

"There is more, excellent khan." Niketas, who had been quiet till then, unexpectedly spoke up. "Your false gods isolate Bulgaria. How, in dealing with Christians or even Muslims, can your folk swear an oath that will be trusted? How can you put the power of God behind a treaty, to ensure it will be enforced? In what way can one of you lawfully marry a Christian? Other questions like these will surely have occurred to you, else you would not have bid us come."

"He speaks the truth, khan Telerikh," Jalal ad-Din said. He had not thought a priest would have so good a grasp of matters largely secular, but Niketas did. Since his words could not be denied, supporting them seemed better than ignoring.

Telerikh gnawed on his mustaches. He looked from one delegation to the other, back again. "Tell me," he said slowly, "is it the same god both groups of you worship, or do you follow different ones?"

"That is an excellent question," Jalal ad-Din said; no, Telerikh was no fool. "It is the same god: there is no God but God. But the Christians worship him incorrectly, saying he is Three, not One."

"It is the same God," Paul agreed, once more apparently overriding Theodore. "Muhammad is not a true prophet and many of his preachings are lies, but it is the same God, who gave His only begotten Son to save mankind."

"Stop!" Telerikh held up a hand. "If it is the same God, what difference does it make how I and my people worship him? No matter what the prayers we send up to him, surely he will know what we mean."

Jalal ad-Din glanced toward Paul. The Christian was also looking at him. Paul smiled. Jalal ad-Din found himself smiling back. He too felt the irony of the situation: he and Paul had more in common with each other than either of them did with the naïve Bulgar khan. Paul raised an eyebrow. Jalal ad-Din dipped his head, granting the Christian permission to answer Telerikh's question.

"Sadly, excellent khan, it is not so simple," Paul said. "Just as there is only one true God, so there can be only one true way to worship him, for while he is merciful, he is also just, and will not tolerate errors in the reverence paid him. To use a homely example, sir, would it please you if we called you 'khan of the Avars'?"

"It would please me right well, were it true," Telerikh said with a grim chuckle. "Worse luck for me, though, the Avars have a khan of their own. Very well, priest, I see what you are saying."

The Bulgar ruler rubbed his chin. "This needs more thought. We will all gather here again in three days' time, to speak of it further. Go now in peace, and remember"—he looked sternly from Christians to Muslims—"you are all my guests here. No fighting between you, or you will regret it."

Thus warned, the rival embassies bowed their way out.

———

Jalal ad-Din spent more time before his next encounter with the priests exploring Pliska than he had hoped to. No matter how delightful he found his fair-skinned pleasure girl, he was not a young man: for him, between rounds meant between days.

After the barbarous richness of Telerikh's wooden palace, the Arab found the rest of the town surprisingly familiar. He wondered why until he realized that Pliska, like Damascus, like Constantinople, like countless other settlements through which he had passed at one time or another, had been a Roman town once. Layout and architecture lingered long after overlords changed.

Jalal ad-Din felt like shouting when he found a bath house not only still standing but still used; from what his nose had told him in the palace, he'd doubted the Bulgars even suspected cleanliness existed. When he went in, he found most of the bathers were of the lighter-colored folk from whom Dragomir and his mistress had sprung. They were, he'd gathered, peasant Slavs over whom the Bulgars proper ruled.

He also found that, being mostly unacquainted with either Christianity or Islam, they let in women along with the men. It was scandalous; it was shocking; in Damascus it would have raised riots. Jalal ad-Din wished his eyes were as sharp as they'd been when he was forty, or even fifty.

He was happily soaking in a warm pool when the three Christian envoys came in. Theodore hissed in horror when he saw the naked women, spun on his heel, and stalked out. Niketas started to follow, but Paul took hold of his arm and stopped him. The older man shrugged out of his brown robe, sank with a sigh of pleasure into the same pool Jalal ad-Din was using. Sergios, by his expression still dubious, joined him a moment later.

"Flesh is flesh," Paul said calmly. "By pledging yourself to Christ, you have acknowledged that its pleasures are not for you. No point in fleeing, then."

Jalal ad-Din nodded to the Christians. "You have better sense, sir, than I would have looked for in a priest," he told Paul.

"I thank you." If Paul heard the undercurrent of irony in the Arab's voice, he did not let it affect his own tone, which briefly shamed Jalal ad-Din. Paul went on, "I am no priest in any case, only a humble monk, here to advise my superiors if they care to listen to me.

"'Only!'" Jalal ad-Din scoffed. But, he had to admit to himself, the monk sounded completely sincere. He sighed; hating his opponents would have been much easier were they evil. "They would be wise to listen to you," he said. "I think you are a holy man."

"You give me too much credit," Paul said.

"No, he does not," Niketas told his older colleague. "Not just by words do you instruct the barbarians hereabouts, but also through the life you live, which by its virtues illuminates your teachings."

Paul bowed. From a man squatting naked in waist-deep water, the gesture should have seemed ludicrous. Somehow it did not.

Niketas turned to Jalal ad-Din. "Did I hear correctly that you are styled as-Stambuli?"

"You did," the Arab answered proudly.

"How strange," Niketas murmured. "Perhaps here God grants me the chance to avenge the fall of the Queen of Cities."

He spoke as if the caliph's armies had taken Constantinople only yesterday, not long before he was born. Seeing Jalal ad-Din's confusion, Paul said, "Niketas's mother is Anna, the daughter of Leo."

"Yes?" Jalal ad-Din was polite, but that meant nothing to him. "And my mother was Zinawb, the daughter of Mu'in ibn Abd al-Wahhab. What of it?"

"Ah, but your grandfather, however illustrious he may have been (I do not slight him, I assure you) was never *Basileus ton Rhomaion*— Emperor of the Romans."

"*That* Leo!" Jalal ad-Din thumped his forehead with the heel of his hand. He nodded to Niketas. "Your grandfather, sir, was a very devil. He fought us with all he had, and sent too many brave lads to paradise before their time."

Niketas raised a dark eyebrow. His tonsured skull went oddly with those bushy brows and the thick beard that covered his cheeks almost to the eyes. "Too many, you say. I would say, not enough."

"So you would," Jalal ad-Din agreed. "Had Leo beaten us, you might be Roman Emperor yourself now. But Abd ar-Rahman the commander of the faithful rules Constantinople, and you are a priest in a foreign land. It is as Allah wills."

"So I must believe," Niketas said. "But just as Leo fought you with every weapon he had, I shall oppose you with all my means. The Bulgars must not fall victim to your false belief. It would be too great a blow for Christendom to suffer, removing from us all hope of greater growth."

Niketas's mind worked like an emperor's, Jalal ad-Din thought—unlike many of his Christian colleagues, he understood the long view. He'd shown that in debate, too, when he pointed out the problems attendant on the Bulgars' staying pagan. A dangerous foe—pope Constantine had sent to Pliska the best the Christians had.

Whether that would be enough… Jalal ad-Din shrugged. "It is as Allah wills," he repeated.

"And Telerikh," Paul said. When Jalal ad-Din looked at him in surprise, the monk went on, "Of course, Telerikh is in God's hands too. But God will not be influenced by what we do. Telerikh may."

"There is that," Jalal ad-Din admitted.

———

"No telling how long all this arguing will go on," Telerikh said when the Christian and Muslim embassies appeared before him once more. He spoke to Dragomir in his own language. The steward nodded, hurried away. A moment later, lesser servants brought in benches, which they set before Telerikh's throne. "Sit," the khan urged. "You may as well be comfortable."

"How would you have us argue?" Jalal ad-Din asked, wishing the bench had a back but too proud to ask for a chair to ease his old bones.

"Tell me of your one god," Telerikh said. "You say you and the Christians follow him. Tell me what you believe differently about him, so I may choose between your beliefs."

Jalal ad-Din carefully did not smile. He had asked his question to seize the chance to speak first. Let the Christians respond to him. He began where any Muslim would, with the *shahada,* the profession of faith: *"La illaha ill'Allah; Muhammadun rasulu'llah*—'There is no God but Allah; Muhammad is the prophet of Allah.' Believe that, magnificent khan, and you are a Muslim. There is more, of course, but that is of the essence."

"It is also a lie," Theodore broke in harshly. "Excellent khan, the books of the Old Testament, written hundreds of years before God's Son became flesh, foretold His coming. Neither Old nor New Testament speaks one word of the Arab charlatan who invented this false creed because he had failed as a camel-driver."

"There is no prophecy pertaining to Muhammad in the Christians' holy books because it was deliberately suppressed," Jalal ad-Din shot back. "That is why God gave the Prophet his gifts, as the seal of prophecy."

"The seal of trickery is nearer the truth," Theodore said. "God's only begotten Son Jesus Christ said prophecy ended with John the Baptist, but that false prophets would continue to come. Muhammad lived centuries after John and Jesus, so he must be false, a trick of the devil to send men to hell."

"Jesus is no son of God. God is one, not three, as the Christians would have it," Jalal ad-Din said. "Hear God's own words in the *Qur'an:* 'Say, God is one.' The Christians give the one God partners in the so-called Son and Holy Spirit. If He has two partners, why not three, or four, or more? Foolishness! And how could God fit into a woman's womb and be born like a man? More foolishness!"

Again it was Theodore who took up the challenge; he was a bad-tempered man, but capable all the same. "God is omnipotent. To deny the possibility of the Incarnation is to deny that omnipotence."

"That priest is twisty as a serpent," Da'ud ibn Zubayr whispered to Jalal ad-Din. The older man nodded, frowning. He was not quite sure how to respond to Theodore's latest sally. Who was he to say what Allah could or could not do?

Telerikh roused him from his unprofitable reverie by asking, "So you Arabs deny Jesus is the son of your one god, eh?"

"We do," Jalal ad-Din said firmly.

"What do you make of him, then?" the khan said.

"Allah commands us to worship none but himself, so how can he have a son? Jesus was a holy man and a prophet, but nothing more. Since the Christians corrupted his words, Allah inspired Muhammad to recite the truth once more."

"Could a prophet rise from the dead on the third day, as God's Son did?" Theodore snorted, clapping a dramatic hand to his forehead. "Christ's miracles are witnessed and attested in writing. What miracles did Muhammad work? None, the reason being that he could not."

"He flew to Jerusalem in the course of a night," Jalal ad-Din returned, "as the *Qur'an* records—in writing," he added pointedly. "And the crucifixion and resurrection are fables. No man can rise from the dead, and another was set on the cross in place of Jesus."

"Satan waits for you in hell, blasphemer," Theodore hissed. "Christ healed the sick, raised the dead, stopped wind and rain in their tracks. Anyone who denies Him loses all hope of heaven, and may garner for his sin only eternal torment."

"No, that is the fate reserved for those who make One into Three," Jalal ad-Din said. "You—"

"Wait, both of you." Telerikh held up a hand. The Bulgar khan, Jalal ad-Din thought, seemed more stunned than edified by the arguments he had heard. The Arab realized he had been quarreling with Theodore rather than instructing the khan. Telerikh went on, "I cannot find the truth in what you are saying, for each of you and each of your books makes the other a liar. That helps me not at all. Tell me instead what I and my people must do, if we follow one faith or the other."

"If you choose the Arabs' false creed, you will have to abandon both wine-drinking and eating pork," Theodore said before Jalal ad-Din could reply. "Let him deny it if he may." The priest shot the Arab a triumphant look.

"It is true," Jalal ad-Din said stoutly. "Allah has ordained it."

He tried to put a bold face on it, but knew Theodore had landed a telling blow. The mutter that went up from Telerikh's boyars confirmed it. A passion for wine inflamed most non-believers, Jalal ad-Din thought; sadly, despite the good counsel of the *Qur'an,* it could capture Muslims as well. And as for pork—judging from the meals they served at Pliska, the Bulgars found it their favorite flesh.

"That is not good," Telerikh said, and the Arab's heart sank.

A passion for wine...passion! "Magnificent khan, may I ask without offense how many wives you enjoy?"

Telerikh frowned. "I am not quite sure. How many is it now, Dragomir?"

"Forty-seven, mighty khan," the steward replied at once, competent as usual.

"And your boyars?" Jalal ad-Din went on. "Surely they also have more than one apiece."

"Well, what of it?" the khan said, sounding puzzled.

Now Jalal ad-Din grinned an unpleasant grin at Theodore. "If you become a Christian, magnificent khan, you will have to give up all your wives save one. You will not even be able to keep the others as concubines, for the Christians also forbid that practice."

"What?" If Telerikh had frowned before, the scowl he turned on the Christians now was thunderous. "Can this be true?"

"Of course it is true," Theodore said, scowling back. "Bigamy is a monstrous sin."

"Gently, my brother in Christ, gently," Paul said. "We do not wish to press too hard upon our Bulgar friends, who after all will be newly come to our observances."

"That one is truly a nuisance," Da'ud whispered.

"You are too right," Jalal ad-Din whispered back.

"Still, excellent khan," Paul went on, "you must not doubt that Theodore is correct. When you and your people accept Christianity, all those with more than one wife—or women with more than one husband, if any there be—will be required to repudiate all but their first marriages, and to undergo penance under the supervision of a priest."

His easy, matter-of-fact manner seemed to calm Telerikh. "I see you believe this to be necessary," the khan said. "It is so strange, though, that I do not see why. Explain further, if you will."

Jalal ad-Din made a fist. He had expected Christian ideas of marriage to appall Telerikh, not to intrigue him with their very alienness. Was a potential monk lurking under those fur robes, under that turban?

Paul said, "Celibacy, excellent khan, is the highest ideal. For those who cannot achieve it, marriage to a single partner is an acceptable alternative. Surely you must know, excellent khan, how lust can inflame men. And no sin is so intolerable to prophets and other holy men as depravity and sexual license, for the Holy Spirit will not touch the heart of a prophet while he is engaged in an erotic act. The life of the mind is nobler than that of the body; on this Holy Scripture and the wise ancient Aristotle agree."

"I never heard of this, ah, Aristotle. Was he a shaman?" Telerikh asked.

"You might say so," Paul replied, which impressed Jalal ad-Din. The Arab knew little of Aristotle, hardly more than that he had been a sage before even Roman times. He was certain, however, that Aristotle had been a civilized man, not a barbarous pagan priest. But that was surely the closest equivalent to sage within Telerikh's mental horizon, and Paul deserved credit for recognizing it.

The Bulgar khan turned to Jalal ad-Din. "What have you to say about this?"

"The *Qur'an* permits a man four lawful wives, for those able to treat them equally well," Jalal ad-Din said. "For those who cannot, it enjoins only one. But it does not prohibit concubines."

"That is better," the khan said. "A man would get bored, bedding the same woman night after night. But this business of no pork and no wine is almost as gloomy." He gave his attention back to the priests. "You Christians allow these things,"

"Yes, excellent khan, we do," Paul said.

"Hmm." Telerikh rubbed his chin. Jalal ad-Din did his best to hide his worry. The matter still stood balanced, and he had used his strongest weapon to incline the khan to Islam. If the Christians had any good arguments left, he—and the fate of the true faith in Bulgaria—were in trouble.

Paul said, "Excellent khan, these matters of practice may seem important to you, but in fact they are superficial. Here is the key difference between the Arabs' faith and ours: the religion Muhammad preached is one that loves violence, not peace. Such teaching can only come from Satan, I fear."

"That is a foul, stinking lie!" Da'ud ibn Zubayr cried. The other two Arabs behind Jalal ad-Din also shouted angrily.

"Silence!" Telerikh said, glaring at them. "Do not interrupt. I shall give you a chance to answer in due course."

"Yes, let the Christian go on," Jalal ad-Din agreed. "I am sure the khan will be fascinated by what he has to say."

Glancing back, he thought Da'ud about to burst with fury. The younger man finally forced out a strangled whisper: "Have you gone made, to stand by while this infidel slanders the Prophet (may blessings be upon his head)?"

"I think not. Now be still, as Telerikh said. My ears are not what they once were; I cannot listen to you and Paul at once."

The monk was saying, "Muhammad's creed urges conversion by the sword, not by reason. Does not his holy book, if one may dignify it by that title, preach the holy war, the *jihad*"—he dropped the Arabic word into his polished Greek—"against all those who do not share his faith? And those who are slain in their murderous work, says the false prophet, attain to heaven straightaway." He turned to Jalal ad-Din. "Do you deny this?"

"I do not," Jalal ad-Din replied. "You paraphrase the third *sura* of the *Qur'an*."

"There, you see?" Paul said to Telerikh. "Even the Arab himself admits the ferocity of his faith. Think also on the nature of the paradise Muhammad in his ignorance promises his followers—"

"Why do you not speak?" Da'ud ibn Zubayr demanded. "You let this man slander and distort everything in which we believe."

"Hush," Jalal ad-Din said again.

"—rivers of water and milk, honey and wine, and men reclining on silken couches and being served—served in all ways, including pandering to their fleshly lusts (as if souls could have such concerns!)—by females created especially for the purpose." Paul paused, needing a moment to draw in another indignant breath. "Such carnal indulgences—nay, excesses—have no place in heaven, excellent khan."

"No? What does, then?" Telerikh asked.

Awe transfigured the monk's thin, ascetic face as he looked within himself at the afterlife he envisioned. "Heaven, excellent khan, does not consist of banquets and wenches: those are for gluttons and sinners in this life, and lead to hell in the next. No: paradise is spiritual in nature, with the soul knowing the eternal joy of closeness and unity with God, peace of spirit and absence of all care. That is the true meaning of heaven."

"Amen," Theodore intoned piously. All three Christians made the sign of the cross over their breasts.

"That is the true meaning of heaven, you say?" Telerikh's blunt-featured face was impassive as his gaze swung toward Jalal ad-Din. "Now you may speak as you will, man of the caliph. Has this Christian told accurately of the world to come in his faith and in yours?"

"He has, magnificent khan." Jalal ad-Din spread his hands and smiled at the Bulgar lord. "I leave it to you, sir, to pick the paradise you would sooner inhabit."

Telerikh looked thoughtful. The Christian clerics' expressions went from confident to concerned to horrified as they gradually began to wonder, as Jalal ad-Din had already, just what sort of heaven a barbarian prince might enjoy.

Da'ud ibn Zubayr gently thumped Jalal ad-Din on the back. "I abase myself before you, sir," he said, flowery in apology as Arabs so often were. "You saw further than I." Jalal ad-Din bowed on his bench, warmed by the praise.

His voice urgent, the priest Niketas spoke up: "Excellent khan, you need to consider one thing more before you make your choice."

"Eh? And what might that be?" Telerikh sounded distracted. Jalal ad-Din hoped he was; the delights of the Muslim paradise were worth being distracted about. Paul's version, on the other hand, struck him as a boring way to spend eternity. But the khan, worse luck, was not altogether ready to abandon Christianity on account of that. Jalal ad-Din saw him focus his attention on Niketas. "Go on, priest."

"Thank you, excellent khan." Niketas bowed low. "Think on this, then: in Christendom the most holy pope is the leader of all things spiritual, true, but there are many secular rulers, each to his own state: the Lombard dukes, the king of the Franks, the Saxon and Angle kings in Britain, the various Irish princes, every one a free man. But Islam knows only once prince, the caliph, who reigns over all Muslims. If you decide to worship Muhammad, where is there room for you as ruler of your own Bulgaria?"

"No one worships Muhammad," Jalal ad-Din said tartly. "He is a prophet, not a god. Worship Allah, Who alone deserves it."

His correction of the minor point did not distract Telerikh from the major one. "Is what the Christian says true?" the khan demanded. "Do you expect me to bend the knee to your khan as well as your god? Why should I freely give Abd ar-Rahman what he has never won in battle?"

Jalal ad-Din thought furiously, all the while damning Niketas. Priest, celibate the man might be, but he still thought like a Greek, like a Roman Emperor of Constantinople, sowing distrust among his foes so they defeated themselves when his own strength did not suffice to beat them.

"Well, Arab, what have you to say?" Telerikh asked again.

Jalal ad-Din felt sweat trickle into his beard. He knew he had let silence stretch too long. At last, picking his words carefully, he answered, "Magnificent khan, what Niketas says is not true. Aye, the caliph Abd ar-Rahman, peace be unto him, rules all the land of Islam. But he does so by right of conquest and right of descent, just as you rule the Bulgars. Were you, were your people, to become Muslim without warfare, he would have no more claim on you than any brother in Islam has on another."

He hoped he was right, and that the jurists would not make a liar of him once he got back to Damascus. All the ground here was uncharted: no nation had ever accepted Islam without first coming under the control of the caliphate. Well, he thought, if Telerikh and the Bulgars did convert, that success in itself would ratify anything he did to accomplish it.

If... Telerikh showed no signs of having made up his mind. "I will meet with all of you in four days," the khan said. He rose, signifying the end of the audience. The rival embassies rose too, and bowed deeply as he stumped between them out of the hall of audience.

"If only it were easy," Jalal ad-Din sighed.

———

The leather purse was small but heavy. It hardly clinked as Jalal ad-Din pressed it into Dragomir's hand. The steward made it disappear. "Tell me, if you would," Jalal ad-Din said, as casually as if the purse had never existed at all, "how your master is inclined toward the two faiths about which he has been learning."

"You are not the first person to ask me that question," Dragomir remarked. He sounded the tiniest bit smug: *I've been bribed twice,* Jalal ad-Din translated mentally.

"Was the other person who inquired by any chance Niketas?" the Arab asked.

Telerikh's steward dipped his head. "Why, yes, now that you mention it." His ice-blue eyes gave Jalal ad-Din a careful once-over: men who could see past their noses deserved watching.

Smiling, Jalal ad-Din said, "And did you give him the same answer you will give me?"

"Why, certainly, noble sir." Dragomir sounded as though the idea of doing anything else had never entered his mind. Perhaps it had not: "I told him, as I tell you now, that the mighty khan keeps his own counsel well, and has not revealed to me which faith—if either—he will choose."

"You are an honest man." Jalal ad-Din sighed. "Not as helpful as I would have hoped, but honest nonetheless."

Dragomir bowed. "And you, noble sir, are most generous. Be assured that if I knew more, I would pass it on to you." Jalal ad-Din nodded, thinking it would be a sorry spectacle indeed if one who served the caliph, the richest, mightiest lord in the world, could not afford a more lavish bribe than a miserable Christian priest.

However lavish the payment, though, it had not bought him what he wanted. He bowed his way out of Telerikh's palace and spent the morning wandering through Pliska in search of trinkets for his fair-skinned bedmate. Here too he was spending Abd ar-Rahman's money, so only the finest goldwork interested him.

He went from shop to shop, sometimes pausing to dicker, sometimes not. The rings and necklaces the Bulgar craftsmen displayed were less intricate, less ornate than those that would have fetched highest prices in

Damascus, but had a rough vigor of their own. Jalal ad-Din finally chose a thick chain studded with fat garnets and pieces of polished jet.

He tucked the necklace into his robe, sat down to rest outside the jeweler's shop. The sun blazed down. It was not as high in the sky, not as hot, really, as it would have been in Damascus at the same season, but this was muggy heat, not dry, and seemed worse. Jalal ad-Din felt like a boiled fish. He started to doze.

"*Assalamu aleykum*—peace to you," someone said. Jalal ad-Din jerked awake, looked up. Niketas stood in front of him. Well, he'd long since gathered that the priest spoke Arabic, though they'd only used Greek between themselves till now.

"*Aleykum assalamu*—and to you, peace," he replied. He yawned and stretched and started to get to his feet. Niketas took him by the elbow, helped him rise. "Ah, thank you. You are generous to an old man, and one who is no friend of yours."

"Christ teaches us to love our enemies," Niketas shrugged. "I try to obey his teachings, as best I can."

Jalal ad-Din thought that teaching a stupid one—the thing to do with an enemy was to get rid of him. The Christians did not really believe what they said, either; he remembered how they'd fought at Constantinople, even after the walls were breached. But the priest had just been kind—no point in churlishly arguing with him.

Instead, the Arab said, "Allah be praised, day after tomorrow the khan will make his choice known." He cocked an eyebrow at Niketas. "Dragomir tells me you tried to learn his answer in advance."

"Which can only mean you did the same." Niketas laughed dryly. "I suspect you learned no more than I did."

"Only that Dragomir is fond of gold," Jalal ad-Din admitted.

Niketas laughed again, then grew serious. "How strange, is it not, that the souls of a nation ride on the whim of a man both ignorant and barbarous. God grant that he choose wisely."

"From God come all things," Jalal ad-Din said. The Christian nodded; that much they believed in common. Jalal ad-Din went on, "That shows, I believe, why Telerikh will decide for Islam."

"No, you are wrong there," Niketas answered. "He must choose Christ. Surely God will not allow those who worship him correctly to be penned up in one far corner of the world, and bar them forever from access to whatever folk may lie north and east of Bulgaria."

Jalal ad-Din started to answer, then stopped and gave his rival a respectful look. As he had already noticed, Niketas's thought had formidable depth to it. However clever he was, though, the priest who might have been Emperor had to deal with his weakness in the real world. Jalal ad-Din drove that weakness home: "If God loves you so well, why has he permitted us Muslims dominion over so many of you, and why has he let us drive you back and back, even giving over Constantinople, your imperial city, into our hands?"

"Not for your own sake, I'm certain," Niketas snapped.

"No? Why then?" Jalal ad-Din refused to be nettled by the priest's tone.

"Because of the multitude of our own sins, I'm certain. Not only was—is—Christendom sadly riddled with heresies and false beliefs, even those who believe what is true all too often lead sinful lives. Thus your eruption from the desert, to serve as God's flail and as punishment for our errors."

"You have answers to everything—everything but God's true will. He will show that day after tomorrow, through Telerikh."

"That he will." With a stiff little bow, Niketas took his leave. Jalal ad-Din watched him go, wondering if hiring a knifeman would be worthwhile in spite of Telerikh's warnings. Reluctantly, he decided against it; not here in Pliska, he thought. In Damascus he could have arranged it and never been traced, but he lacked those sorts of connections here. Too bad.

Only when he was almost back to the khan's palace to give the pleasure girl the trinket did he stop to wonder whether Niketas was thinking about sticking a knife in *him*. Christian priests were supposed to be above such things, but Niketas himself had pointed out what sinners Christians were these days.

———

Telerikh's servants summoned Jalal ad-Din and the other Arabs to the audience chamber just before the time for mid-afternoon prayers. Jalal ad-Din did not like having to put off the ritual; it struck him as a bad omen. He tried to stay serene. Voicing the inauspicious thought aloud would only give it power.

The Christians were already in the chamber when the Arabs entered. Jalal ad-Din did not like that either. Catching his eye, Niketas sent him a chilly nod. Theodore only scowled, as he did whenever he had anything to do with Muslims. The monk Paul, though, smiled at Jalal ad-Din as if at a dear friend. That just made him worry more.

Telerikh waited until both delegations stood before him. "I have decided," he said abruptly. Jalal ad-Din drew in a sudden, sharp breath. From the number of boyars who echoed him, he guessed that not even the khan's nobles knew his will. Dragomir had not lied, then.

The khan rose from his carven throne, stepped down between the rival embassies. The boyars muttered among themselves; this was not common procedure. Jalal ad-Din's nails bit into his palms. His heart pounded in his chest till he wondered how long it could endure.

Telerikh turned to face southeast. For a moment, Jalal ad-Din was too keyed up to notice or care. Then the khan sank to his knees, his face turned toward Mecca, toward the Holy City. Again Jalal ad-Din's heart threatened to burst, this time with joy.

"La illaha ill'Allah; Muhammadun rasulu'llah," Telerikh said in a loud, firm voice. "There is no God but Allah; Muhammad is the prophet

423

of Allah." He repeated the *shahada* twice more, then rose to his feet and bowed to Jalal ad-Din.

"It is accomplished," the Arab said, fighting back tears. "You are a Muslim now, a fellow in submission to the will of God."

"Not I alone. We shall all worship the one God and his prophet." Telerikh turned to his boyars, shouted in the Bulgar tongue. A couple of nobles shouted back. Telerikh jerked his arm toward the doorway, a peremptory gesture of dismissal. The stubborn boyars glumly tramped out. The rest turned toward Mecca and knelt. Telerikh led them in the *shahada*, once, twice, three times. The khan faced Jalal ad-Din once more. "Now we are all Muslims here."

"God is most great," the Arab breathed. "Soon, magnificent khan, I vow, many teachers will come from Damascus to instruct you and your people fully in all details of the faith, though what you and your nobles have proclaimed will suffice for your souls until such time as the *ulama*—those learned in religion—may arrive."

"It is very well," Telerikh said. Then he seemed to remember that Theodore, Niketas, and Paul were still standing close by him, suddenly alone in a chamber full of the enemies of their faith. He turned to them. "Go back to your pope in peace, Christian priests. I could not choose your religion, not with heaven as you say it is—and not with the caliph's armies all along my southern border. Perhaps if Constantinople had not fallen so long ago, my folk would in the end have become Christian. Who can say? But in this world, as it is now, Muslims we must be, and Muslims we shall be."

"I will pray for you, excellent khan, and for God's forgiveness of the mistake you make this day," Paul said gently. Theodore, on the other hand, looked as if he was consigning Telerikh to the hottest pits of hell.

Niketas caught Jalal ad-Din's eye. The Arab nodded slightly to his defeated foe. More than anyone else in the chamber, the two of them understood how much bigger than Bulgaria was the issue decided here today. Islam would grow and grow, Christendom continue to shrink. Jalal ad-Din had heard that Ethiopia, far to the south of Egypt, had Christian rulers yet. What of it? Ethiopia was so far from the center of affairs as hardly to matter. And the same fate would now befall the isolated Christian countries in the far northwest of the world.

Let them be islands in the Muslim sea, he thought, if that was what their stubbornness dictated. One day, *inshallah,* that sea would wash over every island, and they would read the *Qur'an* in Rome itself.

He had done his share and more to make that dream real, as a youth helping to capture Constantinople and now in his old age by bringing Bulgaria the true faith. He could return once more to his peaceful retirement in Damascus.

He wondered if Telerikh would let him take along that fair-skinned pleasure girl. He turned to the khan. It couldn't hurt to ask.

DECONSTRUCTION GANG

You have your degree. You are, as the piece of thick, creamy paper they handed you attests, a doctor of philosophy in English with all the rights and privileges thereto pertaining.

You need not have spent years studying literary theory to get to the outside of the text printed on that creamy paper, to understand what those rights and privileges thereto pertaining are: nothing.

You have other pieces of paper, not so thick, not so creamy as your diploma, but textually similar in what they offer: nothing. You know the polite phrases so well: *Thank you for your interest in the assistant professorship at the University, but…; pleased to be in the position of choosing from among such a large number of highly qualified applicants; confident that with your outstanding record you will soon be able to find an appointment elsewhere; due to financial constraints, the Department will not be hiring this year.*

Critical theory makes continuity and meaning suspect, but you have trouble interpreting these polite letters as implying anything save *fuck you very much* and *up yours truly.*

No one wants you.

Along with your degree, you have an apartment, a car, a fiancée whose father suspects academics on general principles, unemployed academics in particular, and most especially the one unemployed academic who happens to be engaged to his one daughter. You also have no health insurance, which seems increasingly insane each day older than thirty you become. You know every possible way to make macaroni and cheese taste like something else. You know none of them works.

You never wanted to be anything but a scholar, to teach other budding scholars the ineffable difference between *différence* and *différance,* to show them that which appears in no text but lurks between the words of all texts. But too many have the same ambition. Too many of them have jobs; none is left for you.

You can't remember when you first thought about looking for work outside the university. That first time, you shook your head in indignation; such an indignity could never befall you. Your checking account was fuller then, your credit cards less overdrawn. Your landlord made no pointed remarks when you walked past her on the way to the laundry room.

After a while, you see your choice clearly: you can go forth and confront the Other, or you can sit tight, watch your savings slip through your fingers until nothing is left...and then go forth and confront the Other.

Put that way, it should be obvious. As a matter of fact, it is obvious. You wait a last week even so, hoping a miracle will happen. God must be busy somewhere else. The five dollars you waste on the lottery is just that, waste, and one more rejection letter adds insult to injury.

Tomorrow, you tell yourself, but you put it off again till the day after.

The last time you looked for work away from a campus was after your senior year of high school. That's a long time ago now. You wonder how much things have changed—you wonder how much you've changed—since then. You'll find out soon.

When the morning comes, you put on slacks, shirt, tie, the herringbone tweed jacket which irrevocably brands you an academic, the shiny black shoes that always start squeezing your toes after you wear them for fifteen minutes. You throw half a dozen copies of your vita into a manila folder, go downstairs to your car. You hope it starts. It does.

You have your list with you: addresses for three banks, an insurance company, a software outfit that needs someone who can write documentation, and a God-knows-what called Humanoid Systems, Inc., that needs a technical editor. None of them is what you had in mind when you decided to go into the graduate program. Were it happening to someone else, it might be funny in an existential way.

You soon see you won't get to any of your possibilities very soon. Traffic is a mess; the main street into downtown has one only lane open in each direction. You start, stop, go forward a few more feet, stop again. You watch the temperature needle creep upward and remember the garage man telling you your water pump won't last forever. Neon-orange diamond-shaped signs seem to hang from every street light and telephone pole: RIGHT 2 LANES CLOSED AHEAD alternates with ROAD DECONSTRUCTION IN PROGRESS. You have plenty of time to read them.

You creep forward another couple of blocks. Then, under a DECONSTRUCTION IN PROGRESS sign, you see a different one, a small black-and-white rectangle: ROAD CREW HIRING OFFICE, 2 BLOCKS EAST, complete with an arrow for the directionally challenged.

A nihilistic wind blows through you. If you're out to confront the Other, why not at its most Otherly? Besides, you'll break out of this godawful traffic jam. When you get to the corner, you turn right.

A line snakes toward a house with its front door open. You almost make a U-turn in the middle of the street when you see the people who are standing in that line: pick-and-shovel types, every one of them. You're not desperate enough to want calluses on your hands, not yet. But you've come this far. You may as well find out just who's getting hired. You park your car and walk over to the tail of the line.

With your jacket and tie, you are the Other here. A couple of work-booted musclemen elbow each other in the ribs and point your way. You pretend you don't notice them. They don't hassle you, though, for which you thank the God you can't quite believe in. They need work as badly as you do, and they've been in these lines before: they know they'll get thrown out if they give you a bad time.

The line slithers forward. Men fall into place behind you. Most of the people who come out the front door look glum. A few wear ear-to-ear grins. They've found jobs, so they'll be able to make the next payment on the Harley after all.

You work your slow way up the stairs, across the porch, and into the house. It's as tacky inside as you expected, maybe worse. Till this minute, you never believed anybody would actually frame a print of those poker-playing dogs and hang it in the living room. Again, you almost turn around and leave.

But by now you're only three men away from the hiring boss behind the office-style folding table sitting in the middle of the floor. You watch him, listen to him while he questions the guys ahead of you. He is the Other, all right: hard hat, cigar, beer belly with a black T-shirt stretched obscenely tight across it. On the T-shirt is a skeleton in a football helmet. The legend reads, KICK ASS AND TAKE NAMES.

The hiring boss talks as if he's been chewing rocks for the past couple of hundred years. "Sorry, bud, can't use you," he growls to the man in front of you. The fellow's longshoreman shoulders sag. He turns and shambles out of the house. Now it's your turn.

The hiring boss looks you over. The way he takes in everything at once makes you realize for the first time that, while he might not be educated, he's a long way from stupid. The cigar waggles in his mouth. "Well, well," he says. "What have we here?"

He hasn't seen anything like you in a while, that's for certain. If he sounded scornful, you'd walk away. But he doesn't; he's just honestly curious. Trying to make your voice somewhere near as deep as his, you answer, "I'm looking for work on your deconstruction crew."

"Are you?" He looks you over again, in a different kind of way. "Just so you know, kid, we call it a gang, not a crew." You want to glare; nobody's called you *kid* since you were once. But this fellow holds that greatest of all plums, a job, in the palm of his hand. Besides, if you annoy him, you have no doubt he'll kick your ass around the block now and worry about lawsuits later.

He holds out his hand. You give him a copy of your vita, meanwhile trying to decide which of your original targets you'll save for another day. The bank that's been having trouble with the FDIC over too many bad loans, probably. You say, "I'm a recent Ph.D. from—"

He grunts. It's not a *go on* grunt; it's a *shut up* grunt. He goes through your vita so fast you know he's not really reading it, then tosses it carelessly onto the table in front of him. "I see more bullshit on this job," he remarks to no one in particular. When he looks up at you again, cunning lights his narrow eyes. Around the fat cigar, he says, "Awright, kid, you're so damn smart, tell me something—*quick,* now—about Paul de Man."

For a second you just gape, astounded a dinosaur like this ever heard of de Man. Then you remember he bosses deconstruction crews (no, gangs; you'd like to trace the evolution of that text one day). He'd better have some idea of what his hired help is up to.

He's still watching you; you feel the same almost paralyzing attack of nerves you did in front of the committee for your doctoral exams. As you did then, you fight it down: "One of the things de Man talks about is the figurality that alters the way we perceive what a text means, the mechanism through which any text asserts the opposite of what it appears to say."

The hiring boss's heavy features light up in the sort of smile he'd give if he drew four nines to an ace kicker. "Goddamn! You know what you're talking about!" His handshake crushes your fingers, but you don't dare wince any more than you dared glare before. Then he says the magic words: "When do you want to start?"

You haven't asked about pay yet, or benefits. This was just supposed to be a nihilistic lark. Now all of a sudden it's serious, so you ask. The answers make you blink: better money than any assistant professor's job you've seen advertised, and *much* better bennies. You hear yourself say, "If you really need me, I can be here tomorrow morning."

The hiring boss squashes your hand again. "Kid, you're okay." He turns around, grabs a white hard hat from a pile behind him, reaches up and sticks it on your head. You feel as if you've just been knighted. He says, "Be right here at half past seven. We'll do your paperwork then, and I'll assign you to a gang. See you tomorrow."

Reality starts to set in as you head back to your car. What have you just done to yourself? When you get in, the first thing you do after you fasten your seat belt is take off the hard hat and throw it onto the mat under the glove compartment. Even if you can't find an academic job right now, do you want to work the *roads*?

You look at the manila folder still almost full of vitas, then at your watch. If you hustle, you can still spread your name around today. Then you look at the plastic hard hat. You have a job right there if you want it. What a funny feeling that is!

In the end, you drive back to your apartment instead of downtown. You call up your fiancée. She squeals in your ear when you tell her you found work, then says absolutely nothing after you explain what kind of work it is. You picture her by the phone with her mouth hanging open.

After a long, long pause, she asks, "Are you sure this is what you want to do with your life?" She sounds wary, as if she's wondering what else the you she thinks she knows has managed to hide for the past three and a half years.

"Of course it's not what I want to do with my life. But it's money, and we need that." When you tell her how much money it is, she inhales sharply: she's at least as surprised as you were. You say, "And you know what else?"

"No, what?"

"They gave me my very own hard hat, too."

That does it. You both start cracking up over the phone. She says. "I can't wait to see you in it. Are you going to start hanging out in cowboy bars, too?"

"Jesus, I hope not." If that isn't a fate worse than death, you can't think of one offhand. "Look, honey, if this turns out to be awful, I'll quit, that's all. But the pay is good enough that I ought to see what it's like."

"Okay. Dad'll be glad to hear you've gotten hired." She hesitates a split second too long, then says, "Do you want me to tell him what the job is?"

You can hear she doesn't want to. You can't really blame her, either. "No, you don't need to, not right away. We'll see how it goes."

"Okay," she says again, and yes, she is relieved. But before you can decide whether you're irked about it, she adds, "I love you, honey." In the face of that, irk can wait.

You microwave your favorite frozen entree to celebrate, and wash down the herbed chicken with a glass of cheap white wine. You contemplate a second glass, but virtue triumphs. You're going to have to be sharp tomorrow. No David Letterman tonight, either.

At half past six, the alarm clock goes off right beside your head, like a car bomb when the timer reaches the hour of doom. You shower in a hurry, put on jeans and a T-shirt with the tweed jacket over it, throw a pop tart into the toaster. You gulp a cup of muddy instant coffee, then head down to your car.

When you pull up in front of the hiring house, you start to get out, then remember the hard hat and plant it on your head. It's not light like a baseball cap. You wonder how your neck will like wearing it all day.

The hiring boss grins when you walk in. "Ha! You did come back. When I take on a guy out of college, I always wonder if he'll show up the next morning. Come here. I'm gonna need your signature about sixty thousand times."

You come. He's just barely kidding—you sign and you sign and you sign. It's a government job, after all. Your formal job title, you learn, is deconstructive analyst. You like it. It won't look half bad on your vita, so long as you're vague about exactly what it entails.

By the time you write your name for the last time, it doesn't look like yours any more. You might as well be signing travelers' checks. "All right," the hiring boss says when you're done. "I'm gonna put you on Crew 4; they've been a man short for a coupla weeks now. Here—" He points to one of the maps spread out on the table. "They're at 27th and Durant. You hustle, you'll be there by 8:45. Ask for Tony. I'll call him, let him know you're on your way. He'll show you where you need to go." He slaps you on the back. "Good to have you aboard."

You're still a long way from sure it's good to be aboard, but you go back to your car and head for 27th and Durant. The hiring boss knows how traffic works, all right; you get there at 8:43. Fellows in hard hats check you out as you head toward them. You're wearing yours, too, so you may be one of them, but they've never seen you before. You say, "I'm looking for Tony."

"I'm Tony." He's a big black guy, looks like he played defensive end at a medium-good college maybe twenty years ago. His handshake has the gentleness of controlled strength; his smile shows a mouthful of gold. "Hiring boss told me you were coming. Good to have you with us, man. We've been understrength too long. Come on, I'll take you over to the deconstruction gang. Watch where you step."

434

It's no idle warning. You step over boards and small pieces of pipe and tools, walk around other pieces of pipe almost big enough for you to go through them without stooping. Tony negotiates the chaos as effortlessly as a chamois bouncing up an Alp. He leads you to four men in hard hats sitting on dirt-strewn grass beside a trench that looks as if it escaped from World War I.

"Here's the new fish," Tony says.

They get up, shake your hand, give you their names: Brian, Louis, Pete, and Jerome. You all talk for a few minutes, getting to know one another. It turns out Brian, Louis, and Jerome are refugee academics like you; Brian, whose hair is gray, has been doing this for fifteen years now. You still find that a chilling thought, even if you're part of the gang now, too. Pete, who's almost the size of Tony, picked up deconstruction after he joined the road crew. He's not as smooth as the other three, but listening to him you can tell he knows enough to do the job.

Names flash back and forth through the chitchat: Derrida and de Man, Levinas and Bataille, Hegel and Heidegger, Melville and Taylor. You never thought you'd have to raise your voice to make them heard over the pounding roar of jackhammers and the diesel snarl of skiploaders. The world has done a lot of things to you that you never thought of till they happened.

Finally Brian, who's the gang leader, says, "Enough chatter. Time for us to get busy and earn our day's pay."

You sit on the grass with the rest of the deconstruction gang. Everyone is quiet for a while, peering down into the trench. You begin to get a handle on the problem: traffic here has gotten heavier than the roadbed was designed to handle. You can see how things have shifted, how pipes are bent, how this stretch of Durant is going to be nothing but potholes and cracked asphalt unless you do something about it now. A proper deconstruction job when they first built the road would have saved a lot of trouble, but back then they'd never heard of deconstruction. Now you have to worry about fixing the old blunders.

Brian starts out by getting everybody into the proper frame of mind to do what needs doing. He says, "We are the instruments that change the world. Since we are here, we have to understand what's in front of us and act to transform the world and ourselves."

You look admiringly at him: it's good Hegel, translated into language anybody can understand. Listening to Brian, you start to see how someone like Pete can pick up an abstruse skill like deconstruction just by keeping his ears open and thinking about what he hears.

And it's Pete, in fact, who supports Brian and provides the framework for the heavy deconstruction that will follow: "Error isn't fatal, so long as it keeps a grasp on the problem at hand. Even when you say the opposite of what you should be saying, you're still addressing the proper issue."

The proper issue here, of course, is the roadbed, and the error its weakness. Back when it was built, Durant was a residential street. Now it leads to a big shopping district and an industrial park. There are generally more cars around these days, too.

Brian looks at you next. Your stomach knots; it's like the first time you're called on in class. Outside the spoken text, evasive but pervading as Derrida's *différance,* a single thought hangs in the air: *let's see what the new guy can do.*

You're ready, too. You've been thinking about this ever since you impressed the hiring boss yesterday. Even so, you take a deep breath before you say, "As far as I can see, the best approach to deconstructing this roadbed is to bear in mind that nothing, whether idea or test or roadway, truly happens *in relation to* anything else, before, after, or contemporary. Things *do not* relate to one another; they just *are.* We have to reintegrate the things that are to suit our purposes, not those of the original road builders."

Silence for a few seconds. Then Brian reaches out with a closed fist and lightly taps you on your denim-covered knee. You grin. You've passed the test. Better—you've aced it.

From then on, the work flows smoothly. You English professors always insisted deconstruction is a universally valid technique. In your undergrad days, you found historians using deconstructive concepts like demystification and privileged ideas. Now you truly involve yourself in the broader application of the technology.

From the framework Brian, Peter, and you have set up, the gang goes on as you thought it would, analyzing the textuality of the roadbed, considering all the implications of the opposition roadway/traveler.

In the old days, they would have been inextricably linked. Travelers went where and how the roadway allowed, and that was that. It's different now; deconstruction has established that the roadway possesses its own existence, independent of travelers and their purposes. Because events are just events, not related, deconstruction lets the gang reach back through the false connections of time and make the roadway into what it always should have been, regardless of the builders' original intentions.

It's the hardest work you've ever done. Sweat trickles down from under your hard hat, drips off your chin. You take off your jacket and lay it on the ground. But in the trench, you can see the progress you're making. Jerome pushes against the referential being of the roadbed. Just as the new figurality, the one you've been grinding toward, begins to take shape, the lunch whistle blows.

"We've got to keep at it," Brian says quickly, before anyone can get up and head for the catering truck that's just parked down the block. "If we knock off now, we'll get a regression to the opposite and we'll have to do most of the work all over again."

So on you go, though the savor of hot grease from the truck makes your stomach growl like an angry beast. Tony walks by, sees you're all too busy to go to lunch. He doesn't say anything; he knows deconstruction is delicate work and doesn't want to distract you. But when you get to a place where you can stop for a while, he comes back with a gray cardboard carton full of hamburgers, fries, and Cokes.

"Tony, you're a lifesaver," Brian says. Everybody else nods.

Tony just grins. "Keeping you folks doing your job is part of my job." He won't even let any of you pay for the food. He has other things to see to. With people like him in this business, you begin to understand why the rest of the academics in your gang aren't busting a gut trying to escape.

Then you unwrap your hamburger from its yellow waxed paper and sink your teeth in. It's burnt on the outside, raw and soggy in the middle, and it hasn't been hot, or even warm, for quite a while. "Dewishush," you say with your mouth full.

You eat fast. So does everyone else; the deconstruction you've established up to now is only metastable. If it regresses before you can establish and validate your new and strong synthesis, you'll be in deep kimchi, worse off than if you never started.

It tries to snap, too, not five minutes after you go back to work. It's Louis who saves the bacon with a beautiful adaptation from Derrida. Together, you force the road back toward the pattern unperceived by its designers, toward strength and away from weakness, a signifying structure of the sort only deconstructive analysis can produce.

"De la Grammatologie," you say when you have a moment to catch your breath.

"Bet your ass." Louis sounds even more exhausted than you are. If he is, he has a right to be; he carried the ball when things were toughest. After that, you're going downhill. Deconstruction by its nature subverts what was authoritative and revises what has been accepted. The road will be, and indeed always *will have been,* as it should exist by your analysis, not as it was made—with good intentions, no doubt, but also with ultimate ignorance—by the authors of its design.

You keep close watch on the roadbed, tracking the progress your figurality makes in replacing its inadequate predecessor. For a long, tense moment, the deconstructive operation allows both versions of the roadbed to exist together. Then, as if in consummation, the veil is torn and the new figurality displaces the old for good.

Tony, naturally, is there when it happens. "Way to go," he says to Brian. "The night crew'll have to check out what you've done, of course, but it looks real good to me."

"Thanks." Brian points at you. "He pulls his weight. Glad you found him."

Tony nods. "I thought he looked good when I met him." You just stare down at your dirty Reeboks, but you feel nine feet tall, maybe ten. These guys are all right.

Brian glances at his watch. "My God, is it five o'clock already? We wouldn't have come close to finishing this stretch today without a whole gang." He turns to you. "Want to have a beer before you head home? I'll buy."

You're not much of a beer drinker, but you say, "Sounds wonderful. Thanks." Camaraderie counts.

Your joints creak as you stand up and stretch. All over the work site, men are putting away tools, heading for their cars or for the bus stop. *Quitting time,* you think. Fair enough—you've earned your day's pay, as Brian said when you started out what feels like a week ago.

A pretty redhead in *tight* jeans walks by across the street. Along with everyone else who notices her, you whistle like a steam engine. She just walks faster. A couple of guys laugh. You feel sheepish; you'd never have done that back on campus. But what the hell? You have to fit in where you work.

THE GENETICS
LECTURE

It was lovely outside, too lovely for the student to want to stay cooped up in here listening to a lecture on genetics. The sun shone brightly. Bees buzzed from flower to flower. Butterflies flitted here and there. The air smelled sweet with spring.

And the professor droned on. The student made himself take notes. This stuff would be on the midterm—he was sure of that. Even so, staying interested enough to keep writing wasn't easy.

If only the prof weren't so...old-fashioned. Oh, he was impressive enough in a way: tall and straight, with big blue eyes. But his suit wouldn't have been stylish in his father's day, and those glasses clamped to the bridge of his beak... *Nobody* wore those any more. Except he did.

"This complex of Hox genes, as they're called, regulates early bodily development," he said. The student scribbled. However old-fashioned the prof was, he was talking about stuff on the cutting edge. "Like all insects, the fruit fly has eight Hox genes. The amphioxus, a primitive chordate, has ten."

He picked up a piece of chalk and drew on the blackboard. "The amphioxus is sometimes called a lancelet from its scalpel-like shape, which you see here," he said. "In reality, the animal is quite small. Now where was I? Oh, yes. Hox genes.

"All animals seem to share them from a long-extinct Proterozoic ancestor. There is a correspondence between the orientation of the gene complex and that of the animal. The first Hox gene in both the fruit fly and the amphioxus is responsible for the head end of each animal, the last for the abdomen and tail, respectively.

"And let me tell you something still more remarkable. We have created, for example, mutant fruit flies that are eyeless. If we transfer this *eyeless* gene to an amphioxus, its progeny will be born without their usual eye spots. Note that the normal *expression* of the gene, as we say, is vastly different in the two animals. The amphioxus has only light-sensitive pigment patches at the head end, where the fruit fly has highly evolved compound eyes."

"What about us, Professor?" another student asked. "Why are we so much more complex than fruit flies and the waddayacallit?"

"The amphioxus?" The professor beamed at her. "I was just coming to that. We're more complex because our Hox genes are more complex. It's that simple, really. Instead of a single set of eight or ten Hox genes, we have four separate sets, each with up to thirteen genes in it. The mutations that give rise to this duplication and reduplication took place in Cambrian and Ordovician times, on the order of 400,000,000 years ago. We are what we are today because our ancient ancestors suddenly found themselves with more genes than they knew what to do with." He beamed again. "Animal life as we know it today, and especially the development of our own phylum, would have been impossible without these mutations."

That intrigued the student almost in spite of himself. When the lecture was over, he went up to the front of the classroom. "Ask you something, Professor?"

"Of course, of course." Even with those silly glasses, the prof wasn't such a bad guy.

"Mutations are random, right? They can happen any old place, any old time?"

"On the whole, yes." The prof was also cautious, as a good academic should be.

"Okay." That *on the whole* was all the student needed. "What if, a long time ago, these Hox genes got doubled and redoubled in arthropods instead of us? Or even in, uh, chordates instead of us?" He was damned if he'd try to say *amphioxus*.

"Instead of in us mollusks? I think the idea is ridiculous—ridiculous, I tell you. We were preadapted for success in ways this sorry little creature's ancestors never could have been." As if to show what he meant, the professor reached out with one of the eight tentacles that grew around the base of his head, snatched up the eraser, and wiped the picture of the lancelet off the board with three quick strokes.

The student flushed a deep green with embarrassment. "I'm sorry, Professor Cthulhu. I'll try not to be so silly again."

"It's all right, Nyarlathotep," the professor said gently—he did calm down in a hurry. "Go on now, though. Have a nice day."

AND SO TO BED

May 4, 1661. A fine bright morning. Small beer and radishes for to break my fast, then into London for this day. The shambles on Newgate Street stinking unto heaven, as is usual, but close to it my destination, the sim marketplace. Our servant Jane with too much for one body to do, and whilst I may not afford the hire of another man or maid, two sims shall go far to ease her burthen.

Success also sure to gladden Elizabeth's heart, my wife being ever one to follow the dame Fashion, and sims all the go of late, though monstrous ugly. Them formerly not much seen here, but since the success of our Virginia and Plymouth colonies are much more often fetched to these shores from the wildernesses the said colonies front upon. They are also commenced to be bred on English soil, but no hope there for me, as I do require workers full-grown, not cubs or babes in arms or whatsoever the proper term may be.

The sim-seller a vicious lout, near unhandsome as his wares. No, the truth for the diary: such were a slander on any man, as I saw on his conveying me to the creatures.

445

Have seen these sims before, surely, but briefly, and in their masters' livery, the which by concealing their nakedness conceals as well much of their brutishness. The males are most of them well made, though lean as rakes from the ocean passage and, I warrant, poor victualing after. But all are so hairy as more to resemble rugs than men, and the same true for the females, hiding such dubious charms as they may possess nigh as well as a smock of linen: nought here, God knows, for Elizabeth's jealousy to light on.

This so were the said females lovely of feature as so many Aphrodites. They are not, nor do the males recall to mind Adonis. In both sexes the brow projects with a shelf of bone, and above it, where men do enjoy a forehead proud in its erectitude, is but an apish slope. The nose broad and low, the mouth wide, the teeth nigh as big as a horse's (though shaped, it is not to be denied, like a man's), the jaw long, deep, and devoid of chin. They stink.

The sim-seller fell of compliments on my coming hard on the arrival of the *Gloucester* from Plymouth, he having thereby replenished his stock in trade. Then the price should also be not so dear, says I, and by God it did do my heart good to see the ferret-faced rogue discomfited.

Rogue as he was, though, he dickered with the best, for I paid fell a guinea more for the pair of sims than I had looked to, spending in all £11.6s.4d. The coin once passed over (and bitten, for to ensure its verity), the sim-seller signed to those of his chattels I had bought that they were to go with me.

His gestures marvelous quick and clever, and those the sims answered with too. Again, I have seen somewhat of the like before. Whilst coming to understand in time the speech of men, sims are without language of their own, having but a great variety of howls, grunts, and moans. Yet this gesture-speech, which I am told is come from the signs of the deaf, they do readily learn, and often their masters answer back so, to ensure commands being properly grasped.

Am wild to learn it my own self, and shall. Meseems it is in its way a style of tachygraphy or short-hand such as I use to set down these pages. Having devised varying tachygraphic hands for friends and acquaintances, 'twill be amusing taking to a *hand* that is exactly what its name declares.

As I was leaving with my new charges, the sim-seller did bid me lead them by the gibbets on Shooter's Hill, there to see the bodies and members of felons and of sims as have run off from their masters. It wondered me they should have the wit to take fee meaning of such display, but he assured me they should. And so, reckoning it good advice if true and no harm if a lie, I chivvied them thither.

A filthy sight I found it, with the miscreants' flesh all shrunk to the bones. But *hoo!* quoth my sims, and looked close upon the corpses of their own kind, which by their hairiness and flat-skulled heads do seem even more bestial dead than when animated with life.

Home then, and Elizabeth as delighted in my success as am I. An excellent dinner of a calf's head boiled with dumplings, and an abundance of buttered ale with sugar and cinnamon, of which in celebration we invited Jane to partake, and she grew right giddy. Bread and leeks for the sims, and water, it being reported they grow undocile on stronger drink.

After much debate, though good-natured, it was decided to style the male Will and the female Peg. Showed them to their pallets down cellar, and they took to them readily enough, as finer than what they were accustomed to.

So to bed, right pleased with myself despite the expense.

May 7. An advantage of having sims present appears that I had not thought on. Both Will and Peg quite excellent ratters, finer than any puss-cat. No need, either, to fling the rats on the dungheap, for they devour them with as much gusto as I should a neat's tongue. They having subsisted on such small deer in the forests of America, I shall not try to break them of the habit, though training them not to bring in their prey when we are at table with guests. The Reverend Mr. Milles quite shocked, but recovering nicely on being plied with wine.

———

May 8. Peg and Will the both of them enthralled with fire. When the work of them is done of the day, or at evening ere they take their rest, they may be found before the hearth observing the sport of the flames. Now and again one will to the other say *hoo!*—this noise, I find, they utter on seeing that which does interest them, whatsoever it may be.

Now as I thought on it, I minded me reading or hearing, I recall not which, that in their wild unpeopled haunts the sims know the use of fire as they find it set from lightning or other such mischance, but not the art of its making. No wonder then they are Vulcanolaters, reckoning flame more precious than do we gold.

Considering such reflections, I resolved this morning on an experiment, to see what they might do. Rising early for to void my bladder in the pot, I put out the hearthfire, which in any case was gone low through want of fuel. Retired then to put on my dressing gown and, once clad, returned to await developments.

First up from the cellar was Will, and his cry on seeing the flames extinguished heartrending as Romeo's over the body of fair Juliet when I did see that play acted this December past. In a trice comes Peg, whose moaning with Will did rouse my wife, and she much upset at being so rudely wakened.

When the calm in some small measure restored, I bade by signs, in the learning of which I proceed apace, for the sims to sit quietly before the hearth, and with flint and steel restored that which I had earlier destroyed. They both made such outcry as if they had heard sounded die Last Trump.

Then doused I that second fire too, again to much distress from Peg and Will. Elizabeth by this time out of the house in some dudgeon, no doubt to spend money we lack on stuffs of which we have no want.

Set up in the hearth thereupon several small fires of sticks, each with much tinder so as to make it an easy matter to kindle. A brisk striking of flint and steel dropping sparks onto one such produced a merry little blaze, to the accompaniment of much *hoo*ing out of the sims.

And so the nub of it. Shewing Will the steel and flint, I clashed them once more the one upon the other so he might see the sparks engendered thereby. Then pointed to one of the aforementioned piles of sticks I had made up, bidding him watch close, as indeed he did. Having made sure of't, I did set that second pile alight.

Again put the fires out, the wailing accompanying the act less than heretofore, for which I was not sorry. Pointed now to a third assemblage of wood and timber, but instead of myself lighting it, I did convey flint and steel to Will, and with signs essayed to bid him play Prometheus.

His hands much scarred and callused, and under their hair knobby-knuckled as an Irishman's. He held at first the implements as if not taking in their purpose, yet the sims making tools of stone, as is widely reported, he could not wholly fail to grasp their utility.

And indeed ere long he did try parroting me. When his first clumsy attempt yielded no result, I thought he would abandon such efforts as beyond his capacity and reserved for men of my sort. But persist he did, and at length was reward with scintillae like unto those I had made. His grin so wide and gleeful I thought it would stretch clear round his head.

Then without need of my further demonstration he set the instruments of fire production over the materials for the blaze.

Him in such excitement as the sparks fell upon the waiting tinder that beneath his breeches rose his member, indeed to such degree as would have made me proud to be its possessor. And Peg was, I think, in such mood as to couple with him on the spot, had I not been present and had not his faculties been directed elsewhere than toward the lectual.

For at his success he cut such capers as had not been out of place upon the stage, were they but a trifle more rhythmical and less unconstrained. Yet of the making of fire, even if by such expedient as the friction of two sticks (which once I was forced by circumstance to attempt, and would try the patience of Job), as of every other salutary art, his race is as utterly ignorant as of the moons of Jupiter but lately found by some Italian with an optic glass.

No brute beast of the field could learn to begin a fire on the technique being shown it, which did Will nigh readily as a man. But despite most diligent instruction, no sim yet has mastered such subtler arts as reading and writing, nor ever will, meseems. Falling in capacity thus between man and animal, the sims do raise a host of conundrums vexing and perplexing. I should pay a pound, or at the least ten shillings, merely to know how such strange fusions came to be.

So to the Admiralty full of such musings, which did occupy my mind, I fear, to the detriment of my proper duties.

———

May 10. Supper this evening at the Turk's Head, with the other members of the Rota Club. The fare not of the finest, being boiled venison and some few pigeons, all meanly done up. The lamb's wool seemed nought but poor ale, the sugar, nutmeg and meat of roasted apples hardly to be tasted. Miles the landlord down with a quartan fever, but ill served by his staff if such be the result of his absence.

The subject of the Club's discussions for the evening much in accord with my own recent curiosity, to wit, the sims. Cyriack Skinner did maintain them creatures of the Devil, whereupon was he roundly rated by Dr. Croon as having in this contention returned to the pernicious heresy of the Manichees, the learned doctor reserving the power of creation of the Lord alone. Much flinging back and forth to Biblical texts, the which all struck me as being more the exercise of ingenuity of the debaters than bearing on the problem, for in plain fact the Scriptures nowhere mention sims.

When at length the talk did turn to matters more ascertainable, spoke somewhat of my recent investigation, and right well-received my remarks were, or so I thought. Others with experience of sims with like tales, finding them quick enough on things practic but sadly lacking in any higher faculties. Much jollity at my account of the visible manifestation of Will's excitement, and whispers that his lady or that (the names, to my vexation, I failed to catch) owned her sims for naught but their prowess in matters of the mattress.

Just then came the maid by with coffee for the Club, not of the best, but better, I grant, than the earlier wretched lamb's wool. She a pretty yellow-haired lass called I believe Kate, a wench of perhaps sixteen years, a good-bodied woman not over thick or thin in any place, with a lovely bosom she did display most charmingly as she bent to fill the gentlemen's cups.

Having ever an eye for beauty, such that I reckon little else beside it, I own I did turn my head for to follow this Kate as she went about her duties. Noticing which, Sir William Henry called out, much to the merriment of the Club and to my chagrin, "See how Samuel peeps!" Him no mean droll, and loosed a pretty pun, if at my expense. Good enough, but then at the far end of the table someone, I saw not who, worse luck, thought to cap it by braying like the donkey he must be, "Not half the peeping, I warrant, as at his sims of nights!"

Such mockery clings to a man like pitch, regardless of the truth in't, which in this case is none. Oh, the thing could be done, but the sims so homely 'twould yield no titillation, of that I am practically certain.

May 12. The household being more infected this past week with nits than ever before, resolved to bathe Peg and Will, which also I hoped would curb somewhat their stench. And so it proved, albeit not without more alarums than I had looked for. The sims most loth to enter the tub, which must to them have seemed some instrument of torment. The resulting shrieks and outcry so deafening a neighbor did call out to be assured all was well.

Having done so, I saw no help for it but to go into the tub my own self, notwithstanding my having bathed but two weeks before. I felt, I think more hesitation stripping down before Peg than I should in front of Jane, whom I would simply dismiss from consideration but in how she performed her duties. But I did wonder what Peg made of my body, reckoning it against the hairy forms of her own kind. Hath she the wit to deem mankind superior, or is our smoothness to her as gross and repellent as the peltries of the sims to us? I cannot as yet make shift to enquire.

As may be, my example showing them they should not be harmed, they bathed themselves. A trouble arose I had not foreseen, for the sims being nearly as thickly haired over all their bodies as I upon my head, the rinsing of the soap from their hides less easy than for us, and requiring much water. Lucky I am the well is within fifty paces of my home. And so from admiral of the bath to the Admiralty, hoping henceforward to scratch myself less.

May 13. A pleasant afternoon this day, carried in a coach to see the lions and other beasts in the menagerie. I grant the lions pride of place through custom immemorial, but in truth am more taken with the abnormous creatures fetched back from the New World than those our forefathers have known since the time of Arthur. Nor am I alone in this conceit, for the cages of lion, bear, camel had but few spectators, whilst round those of the American beasts I did find myself compelled to use hands and elbows to make shift to pass through the crowds.

This last not altogether unpleasant, as I chanced to brush against a handsome lass, but when I did enquire if she would take tea with me she said me nay, which did irk me no little, for as I say she was fair to see.

More time for the animals, then, and wondrous strange ever they strike me. The spear-fanged cat is surely the most horridest murderer this shuddering world hath seen, yet there is for him prey worthy of his mettle, what with beavers near big as our bears, wild oxen whose horns are to those of our familiar kine as the spear-fanged cat's teeth to the lion's, and the great hairy elephants which do roam the forests.

Why such prodigies of nature manifest themselves on those distant shores does perplex me most exceedingly, as they are unlike any beasts even in the bestiaries, which as all men know are more flights of fancy than sober fact. Amongst them the sims appear no more than one piece of some great jigsaw, yet no pattern therein is to me apparent; would it were.

Also another new creature in the menagerie, which I had not seen before. At first I thought it a caged sim, but on inspection it did prove an ape, brought back by the Portuguese from Afric lands and styled there, the keeper made so good as to inform me, shimpanse. It flourishes not in England's clime, he did continue, being subject to sickness in the lungs from the cool and damp, but is so interesting as to be displayed whilst living, howsoever long that may prove.

The shimpanse a baser brute than even the sim. It goes on all fours, and its hinder feet more like unto monkeys' than men's, having thereon great toes that grip like thumbs. Also, where a sim's teeth, as I have observed from Will and Peg, are uncommon large, in shape they are like unto a man's, but the shimpanse hath tushes of some savagery, though of course paling alongside those of the spear-fanged cat.

Seeing the keeper a garrulous fellow, I enquired of him further anent this shimpanse. He owned he had himself thought it a sort of sim on its arrival, but sees now more distinguishing points than likenesses: gait and dentition, such as I have herein remarked upon, but also in its habits. From his experience, he has seen it to be ignorant of fire, repeatedly allowing to die a blaze though fuel close at hand. Nor has it the knack of shaping stones to its ends, though it will, he told me, cast them betimes against those who annoy it, once striking one such with force enough to render him some time senseless. Hearing the villain had essayed tormenting the creature with a stick, my sympathies lay all for the shimpanse, wherein its keeper concurred.

And so homewards, thinking on the shimpanse as I rode. Whereas in the lands wherewith men are most familiar it were easy distinguishing men from beasts, the strange places to which our vessels have but lately fetched themselves reveal a stairway ascending the chasm, and climbers on the stairs, some higher, some lower. A pretty image, but why it should be so there and not here does I confess escape me.

———

May 16. A savage row with Jane today, her having forgotten a change of clothes for my bed. Her defense that I had not so instructed her, the lying minx, for I did plainly make my wishes known the evening previous, which I recollect most distinctly. Yet she did deny it again and again, finally raising my temper to such a pitch that I cursed her right roundly, slapping her face and pulling her nose smartly.

Whereupon did the ungrateful trull lay down her service on the spot. She decamped in a fury of her own, crying that I treated the sims, those very sims which I had bought for to ease her labors, with more kindlier consideration than I had for her own self.

So now we are without a serving-maid, and her a dab hand in the kitchen, her swan pie especially being toothsome. Dined tonight at the Bell, and expect to tomorrow at the Swan on the Hoop, in Fish Street. For Elizabeth no artist over the hearth, nor am I myself. And as for the sims, I should sooner open my veins than indulge of their cuisine, the good Lord only knowing what manner of creatures they in their ignorance should add to a pot.

Now as my blood has somewhat cooled, I must admit a germ of truth in Jane's scolds. I do not beat Will and Peg as a man would servitors of more ordinary stripe. They, being but new come from the wilds, are not inured to't as are our servants, and might well turn on me their master. And being in part of brute kind, their strength does exceed mine, Will's most assuredly and that of Peg perhaps. And so, say I, better safe. No satisfaction to me for the sims on Shooter's Hill gallows, were I not there to see't.

———

May 20. Today to my lord Sandwich's for supper. This doubly pleasant, in enjoying his fine companionship and saving the cost of a meal, the house being still without maid. The food and drink in excellent style, as to suit my lord. The broiled lobsters very sweet, and the lamprey pie (which for its rarity I but seldom eat of) the best ever I had. Many other fine victuals as well (the tanzy in especial), and the wine all sugared.

Afterwards backgammon, at which I won £5 ere my luck turned. Ended 15s. in my lord's debt, which he did graciously excuse me afterwards, a generosity not looked for but which I did not refuse. Then to crambo, wherein by tagging *and rich* to *Sandwich* I was adjudged winner, the more so for playing on his earlier munificence.

Thereafter nigh a surfeit of good talk, as is custom at my lord's. He mentioning sims, I did relate my own dealings with Peg and Will, to which he listened with much interest. He thinks on buying some for his own household, and unaware I had done so.

Perhaps it was the wine let loose my tongue, for I broached somewhat my disjoint musings on the sims and their place in nature, on the strangeness of die American fauna and much else besides. Lord Sandwich did acquaintance me with a New World beast found in their southerly holdings by the Spaniards, of strange outlandish sort: big as an ox, or nearly, and all covered over with armor of bone like a man wearing chain. I should pay out a shilling or even more for to see't, were one conveyed to London.

Then coffee, and it not watered as so often at an inn, but full and strong. As I and Elizabeth making our departures, Lord Sandwich did bid me join him tomorrow night to hear speak a savant of the Royal Society. It bore, said he, on my prior ramblings, and would say no more, but looked uncommon sly. Even did it not, I should have leaped at the chance.

This written at one of the clock, for so the watchman just now cried out. Too wound up for bed, what with coffee and the morrow's prospect. Elizabeth aslumber, but the sims also awake, and at frolic meseems, from the noises up the stairway.

If they be of human kind, is their fornication *sans* clergy sinful? Another vexing question. By their existence, they do engender naught but disquietude. Nay, strike that. They may in sooth more sims engender, a pun good enough to sleep on, and so to bed.

May 21. All this evening worrying at my thoughts as a dog at a bone. My lord Sandwich knows not what commotion internal he did by his invitation, all kindly meant, set off in me. The speaker this night a spare man, dry as dust, of the very sort I learned so well to loathe when at Cambridge.

Dry as dust! Happy words, which did spring all unbidden from my pen. For of dust the fellow did discourse, if thereby is meant, as commonly, things long dead. He had some men bear in bones but lately found by Swanscombe at a grave-digging. And such bones they were, and teeth (or rather tusks), as to make it all I could do to hold me in my seat. For surely they once graced no less a beast than the hairy elephant whose prototype I saw in menagerie so short a while ago. The double-curving tusks admit of no error, for those of all elephants with which we are anciently familiar form but a single segment of arc.

When, his discourse concluded, he gave leave for questions, I made bold to ask to what he imputed the hairy elephant's being so long vanished from our shores yet thriving in the western lands. To this he confessed himself baffled, as am I, and admiring of his honesty as well.

Before the hairy elephant was known to live, such monstrous bones surely had been reckoned as from beasts perishing in the Flood whereof Scripture speaks. Yet how may that be so, them surviving across a sea wider than any Noah sailed?

Meseems the answer lieth within my grasp, but am balked from setting finger to't. The thwarting fair to drive me mad, worse even, I think, than with a lass who will snatch out a hatpin for to defend her charms against my importuning.

———————

May 22. Grand oaks from tiny acorns grow! This morning came a great commotion from the kitchen. I rushing in found Will at struggle with a cur dog which had entered, the door being open on account of fine weather, to steal half a flitch of salt bacon. It dodging most nimbly round the sim, snatched up the gammon and fled out again, him pursuing but in vain.

Myself passing vexed, having intended to sup thereon. But Will all downcast on returning, so had not the heart further to punish him. Told him instead, him understanding I fear but little, it were well men not sims dwelt in England, else would wolves prowl the London streets still.

Stood stock still some time thereafter, hearing the greater import behind my jesting speech. Is not the answer to the riddle of the hairy elephant and other exotic beasts existing in the New World but being hereabouts long vanished their having there but sims to hunt them? The sims in their wild haunts wield club and sharpened stone, no more. They are ignorant even of the bow, which from time out of mind has equipt the hunter's armory.

Just as not two centuries past we Englishmen slew on this island the last wolf, so may we not imagine our most remotest grandsires serving likewise the hairy elephant, the spear-fanged cat? They being more cunning than sims and better accoutered, this should not have surpassed their powers. Such beasts would survive in America, then, not through virtue inherent of their own, but by reason of lesser danger to them in the sims than would from mankind come.

Put this budding thought at luncheon today to my lord Sandwich. Him back at me with Marvell to his coy mistress (the most annoyingest sort!), viz., had we but world enough and time, who could reckon the changes as might come to pass? And going on, laughing, to say next will be found dead sims at Swanscombe.

Though meant but as a pleasantry, quoth I, why not? Against true men they could not long have stood, but needs must have given way as round Plymouth and Virginia. Even without battle they must soon have failed, as being less able than mankind to provide for their wants.

There we let it lay, but as I think more on't, the notion admits of broader application. Is't not the same for trout as for men, or for lilacs? Those best suited living reproduce their kind, whilst the trout with twisted tail or bloom without sweet scent die all unmourned leaving no descendants. And each succeeding generation being of the previous survivors constituted, will by such reasoning show some little difference from the one as went before.

Seeing no flaw in this logic, resolve tomorrow to do this from its tachygraphic state, bereft of course of maunderings and privacies, for prospectus to the Royal Society, and mightily wondering whatever they shall make of it.

May 23. Closeted all this day at the Admiralty. Yet did it depend on my diligence alone, I fear me the Fleet should drown. Still, a deal of business finished, as happens when one stays by it. Three quills worn quite out, and my hands all over ink. Also my fine camlet cloak with the gold buttons, which shall mightily vex my wife, poor wretch, unless it may be cleaned. I pray God to make it so, for I do mislike strife at home.

The burning work at last complete, homeward in the twilight. It being washing-day, dined on cold meat. I do confess, felt no small strange stir in my breast on seeing Will taking down the washing before the house. A vision it was, almost, of his kind roaming England long ago, till perishing from want of substance or vying therefor with men. And now they are through the agency of men returned here again, after some great interval of years. Would I knew how many.

The writing of my notions engrossing the whole of the day, had no occasion to air them to Lord Brouncker of the Society, as was my hope. Yet expound I must, or burst. Elizabeth, then, at dinner made audience for me, whether she would or no. My spate at last exhausted, asked for her thoughts on't.

She said only that Holy Writ sufficed on the matter for her, whereat I could but make a sour face. To bed in some anger, and in fear lest the

Royal Society prove as close-minded, which God prevent. Did He not purpose man to reason on the world around him, He should have left him witless as the sim.

———

May 24. To Gresham College this morning, to call on Lord Brouncker. He examined with great care the papers I had done up, his face revealing nought. Felt myself at recitation once more before a professor, a condition whose lack these last years I have not missed. Feared also he might not be able to take in the writing, it being done in such haste some short-hand characters may have replaced the common ones.

Then to my delight he declared he reckoned it deserving of a hearing at the Society's weekly meeting next. Having said so much, he made to dismiss me, himself being much occupied with devising a means whereby to calculate the relation of a circle's circumference to its diameter. I wish him joy of't. I do resolve one day soon, however, to learn the multiplication table, which meseems should be of value at the Admiralty. Repaired there from the college, to do the work I had set by yesterday.

———

May 26. Watch these days Will and Peg with new eyes. I note for instance them using between themselves our deaf-man's signs, as well as to me and my wife. As well they might, them conveying far more subtler meanings than the bestial howlings and gruntings that are theirs in nature. Thus though they may not devise any such, they own the wit to see its utility.

I wonder would the shimpanse likewise?

A girl came today asking after the vacant maidservant's post, a pretty bit with red hair, white teeth, and fine strong haunches. Thought myself she would serve, but Elizabeth did send her away. Were her looks liker to Peg's, she had I think been hired on the spot. But a quarrel on it not worth the candle, the more so as I have seen fairer.

———————

May 28. This writ near cockcrow, in hot haste, lest any detail of the evening escape my recollection. Myself being a late addition, spoke last, having settled the title "A Proposed Explication of the Survival of Certain Beasts in America and Their Disappearance Hereabouts" on the essay.

The prior speakers addressed one the organs internal of bees and the other the appearance of Saturn in the optic glass, both topics which interest me but little. Then called to the podium by Lord Brouncker, all aquiver as a virgin bride. Much wished myself in the company of some old soakers over roast pigeons and dumplings and sack. But a brave front amends for much, and so plunged in straightaway.

Used the remains of the hairy elephant presented here a sennight past as example of a beast vanished from these shores yet across the sea much in evidence. Then on to the deficiencies of sims as hunters, when set beside even the most savagest of men.

Thus far well-received, and even when noting the struggle to live and leave progeny that does go on among each kind and between the several kinds. But the storm broke, as I feared it should and more, on my drawing out the implications therefrom: that of each generation only so many may flourish and breed; and that each succeeding generation, being descended of these survivors alone, differs from that which went before.

My worst and fearfullest nightmare then came true, for up rose shouts of blasphemy. Gave them back what I had told Elizabeth on the use of reason, adding in some heat I had expected such squallings of my wife who is a woman and ignorant, but better from men styling themselves natural philosophers. Did they aim to prove me wrong, let them so by the reason they do profess to cherish. This drew further catcalling but also approbation, which at length prevailed.

Got up then a pompous little manikin, who asked how I dared set myself against God's word insofar as how beasts came to be. On my denying this, he did commence reciting at me from Genesis. When he paused for to draw breath, I asked most mildly of him on which day the Lord did create the sims. Thereupon he stood discomfited, his foolish mouth hanging open, at which I was quite heartened.

Would the next inquisitor had been so easily downed! A Puritan he was, by his somber cloak and somberer bearing. His questions took the same tack as the previous, but not so stupidly. After first enquiring if I believed in God, whereat I truthfully told him aye, he asked did I think Scripture to be the word of God. Again said aye, by now getting and dreading the drift of his argument. And as I feared, he bade me next point him out some place where Scripture was mistaken, ere supplanting it with fancies of mine own.

I knew not how to make answer, and should have in the next moment fled. But up spake to my great surprise Lord Brouncker, reciting from Second Chronicles, the second verse of the fourth chapter, wherein is said of Solomon and his Temple, *Also he made the molten sea of ten cubits from brim to brim, round in compass, and the height thereof was five cubits, and a line of thirty cubits did compass it round about.*

This much perplexed the Puritan and me as well, though I essayed not to show it. Lord Brouncker then proceeded to his explication, to wit that the true compass of a ten-cubit round vessel was not thirty cubits, but above one and thirty, I misremember the exact figure he gave. Those of the Royal Society learned in mathematics did agree he had reason, and urged the Puritan make the experiment for his self with cup, cord, and rule, which were enough for to demonstrate the truth.

I asked if he was answered. Like a gentleman he owned he was, and bowed, and sat, his face full of troubles. Felt with him no small sympathy, for once one error in Scripture is admitted, where shall it end?

The next query was of different sort, a man in periwig enquiring if I did reckon humankind to have arisen by the means I described. Had to reply I did. Our forefathers might be excused for thinking otherwise, them being so widely separate from all other creatures they knew.

But we moderns in our travels round the globe have found the shimpanse, which standeth nigh the flame of reasoned thought; and more important still the sim, in whom the flame does burn, but more feebly than in ourselves. These bridging the gap twixt man and beast meseems do show mankind to be in sooth a part of nature, whose engenderment in some past distant age is to be explained through natural law.

Someone rose to doubt the variation in each sort of living thing being sufficient eventually to permit the rise of new kinds. Pointed out to him the mastiffe, the terrier, and the bloodhound, all of the dog kind, but become distinct through man's choice of mates in each generation. Surely the same might occur in nature, said I. The fellow admitted it was conceivable, and sat.

Then up stood a certain Wilberforce, with whom I have some small acquaintance. He likes me not, nor I him. We know it on both sides, though for civility's sake feigning otherwise. Now he spoke with smirking air, as one sure of the mortal thrust. He did grant my willingness to have a sim as great-grandfather, said he, but was I so willing to claim one as great-grandmother? A deal of laughter rose, which was his purpose, and to make me out a fool.

Had I carried steel, I should have drawn on him. As was, rage sharpened my wit to serve for the smallsword I left at home. Told him it were no shame to have one's great-grandfather a sim, as that sim did use to best advantage the intellect he had. Better that, quoth I, than dissipating the mind on such digressive and misleading quibbles as he raised. If I be in error, then I am; let him shew it by logic and example, not as it were playing to the gallery.

Came clapping from all sides, to my delight and the round dejection of Wilberforce. On seeking further questions, found none. Took my own seat whilst the Fellows of the Society did congratulate me and cry up my essay louder, I thought, than either of the other two. Lord Brouncker acclaimed it as a unifying principle for the whole of the study of life, which made me as proud a man as any in the world, for all the world seemed to smile upon me.

And so to bed.

THE WEATHER'S
FINE

Tom Crowell goes into the little kitchen of his apartment, pulls a Bud out of the refrigerator. To save money, the place is conditioned to only the mid-seventies. He pulls off the ring tab and tosses it into the trash. Then he goes into the living room and turns on the TV news. The couch squeaks as he flops down onto it. Even in the mid-seventies, it isn't new.

As always, the weather is big news, especially in other parts of the country: "The old front sweeping down out of Canada continues to ravage our northern tier of states. It has caused widespread communications breakdowns. Authorities are doing their best to combat them, but problems remain far too widespread for portable generators to be adequate. This film footage, some of the little coming out of the area, is from Milwaukee."

The weatherman disappears from the screen, to be replaced by jerky, grainy black-and-white footage. The streets are tree-lined; horse carts and boxy cars compete for space. The men wear hats, and the women's skirts reach to the ground.

Not for the first time, Tom is glad he lives in southern California, where the weather rarely gets below the fifties. No wonder so many people move here, he thinks.

The weatherman comes back with the local forecast. The weather will be about standard for Los Angeles in April: mostly in the late sixties. Tom decides he won't bother with the conditioner in the car tomorrow. He looks good in long sideburns.

After the news, he stays in front of the TV. No matter where he sets the year conditioner, TV is pretty bad, he thinks. That doesn't stop him from watching it. Finally, he gives up and goes to bed.

He leaves the window down as he drives to work. The Doors, the Stones when they're really the Stones, the Airplane, Creedence—the music coming out of the car radio is better than it will be. The speaker, though, sounds tinny as hell. Trade-offs, Tom thinks.

He feels more businesslike when he gets into the buying office. The boss keeps the conditioner really cranked up. Eighties computer technology makes the expense worthwhile, he claims. Tom doesn't complain, but he does wonder, What price computers when the only links to the upper Midwest are telegraphs and operator-assisted telephones?

He sighs and buckles down to his terminal. It's not his problem. Besides, things could be worse. He remembers the horrible winter when Europe was stuck in the early forties for weeks. He hopes that won't happen again any time soon.

His pants start flapping at the ankles as he trots for his car at quitting time. He grins. He likes bell-bottoms. He remembers he has a cousin with a birthday coming up and decides to go to the mall before he heads home.

Everyone else in the world, it seems, has a cousin with a birthday coming up, too. Tom has to drive around for ten minutes before he can find a parking space. He hikes toward the nearest entrance. "Which isn't any too damn near," he says out loud. Living alone, he has picked up the habit of talking to himself.

Some people are getting up to the entrance, turning around and heading back toward their cars. Tom wonders why until he sees the sign taped to the glass door: SORRY, OUR YEAR CONDITIONER HAS FAILED. PLEASE COME IN ANYHOW. Maybe the people who are leaving really don't have cousins with birthdays coming up. Tom sighs. He does. He pulls the door open and goes in.

Sure enough, the conditioner is down. He doesn't feel the blast of air it ought to be putting out, doesn't hear its almost subliminal hum. The inside of the mall is stuck in the late sixties, same as outside.

Tom smells incense and scented candles. He hasn't been in a shopping center this downyear for a long while. He wonders what he can find for his cousin here-and-now. He smiles a little as he walks past a Jeans West, with its striped pants and Day-Glo turtlenecks. He doesn't go in. His cousin's taste runs more to cutoffs and T-shirts.

He climbs the stairs. The Pier 1 Imports is a better bet. No matter what the weather is like, they always have all kinds of strange things. The longhair behind the counter nods at him. "Help you find something, man?"

"Just looking now, thanks."

"No problem. Holler if you need me."

The sitar music coming out of the stereo goes with the rugs from India that are hanging on the walls and the rickety rattan furniture in the center of the store. It's not as good an accompaniment for the shelves of German beer steins or for the silver-and-turquoise jewelry "imported from the Navaho nation." Wrong kind of Indians, Tom thinks.

He picks up a liter stein, hefts it thoughtfully, puts it down. It will do if he can't find anything better. He turns a corner, goes past some cheap flatware from Taiwan, turns another corner and finds himself in front of a display of Greek pottery: modern copies of ancient pieces.

He's seen this kind of thing before, but most of it is crude. This has the unmistakable feel of authenticity to it. The lines of the pots are spare and perfect, the painting elegantly simple. He picks up a pot, turns it over. His cousin doesn't have anything like it, but it goes with everything he does have.

Tom is just turning to thread his way through the maze toward the cash register when a girl comes round the corner. She sees him, rocks back on her heels, then cries. "Tom!" and throws herself into his arms.

"Donna!" he exclaims in surprise. She is a big armful, every bit as tall as his own 5'8", with not a thing missing—she's good to hug.

She tosses her head, a characteristic Donna gesture, to get her long, straight black hair out of her face. Then she kisses him on the mouth. When Tom finally comes up for air, he looks at the familiar gray eyes a couple of inches from his, asks, "Are you here for anything special?"

She grins. "Just to spend money." Very much her kind of answer, he thinks.

"Let me pay for this; then do you want to come home with me?"

Her grin gets wider. "I thought you'd never ask." They link arms and head for the front of the store. She whistles *Side by Side.* Now he is grinning, too.

When he sets the pot on the counter so the clerk can ring it up, Donna exclaims over it. "I didn't even notice it before," she says. "I was too busy looking at you." That makes Tom feel ten feet tall as the longhair gives him his change.

When they get to the glass door with the sign on it, he holds it open so she can go through. The only thing he can think when he sees what dark, patterned hose and a short skirt do for her legs is, Gilding the lily. Or lilies, he amends—she definitely has two of them. He admires them both.

He opened the passenger door to let her in, then goes around to his own side. He doesn't bother with the year conditioner. He likes the weather fine the way it is. He does keep having to remind himself to pay attention to his driving. Her skirt is even shorter when she's sitting down.

———————

There is a parking space right in front of his building. He slides the car into it. "Sometimes you'd rather be lucky than good," he says.

Donna looks at him. "I think you're pretty good."

His right arm slips around her waist as they climb the stairs to his apartment. When he takes it away so he can get out his keys, she is pressed so tightly against him that he can hardly put his hand in his pocket. He enjoys trying, though. She doesn't seem unhappy, either. If anything, she moves closer to him.

She turns her head and nibbles his ear while he is undoing the dead-bolt. After that, he has to try more than once before he can work the regular lock. Finally, the key goes in, turns. He opens the door.

The conditioned air inside blows on him and Donna. He can feel his memories shift forward. Because he stands outside instead of going straight in, it happens slowly. It's probably worse that way.

Now he looks at Donna with new eyes. She can't stand the seventies, even when she's in them. He always just goes on with his life, or tries to. And because of that, they always fight.

He remembers a glass shattering against a wall—not on his head, but only by luck and because she can't throw worth a damn. Her hand jumps up to her cheek. He knows she is remembering a slap. He feels his face go hot with mingled shame and rage. With a sound like a strangled sob, she turns away and starts, half stumbling, down the steps.

He takes a reflexive step after her. It moves him far enough from his apartment for the bad times to fade a bit in his mind.

She stops, too. She looks at him from the stairs. She shakes her head. "That was a bad one," she says. "No wonder we don't hang out together all the times."

"No wonder," he says tonelessly. He feels beat up, hung over; too much has happened too fast. He is horny and angry and emotionally bruised, all at once. He walks down the stairs to Donna. She doesn't run or swing on him, which is something. Standing by her, he feels better. In the sixties, he usually feels better standing by her.

He takes a deep breath. "Let me go inside and turn the conditioner off."

"Are you sure you want to? I don't want you to mess up your place just for me."

"It won't be bad," he says, and hopes he isn't lying.

She squeezes his hand. "You're sweet. I'll try to make you glad you did."

The promise in that is enough to send him up the stairs two at a time. A couple of half-trotting steps to the walkway and he is in the apartment.

He was right. Doing it all at once is better than a little bit at a time, the way diving into a cold swimming pool gets you used to it faster than going in by easy stages. The memories come rushing back, of course. They always do. But in the fully conditioned mid-seventies of his apartment, they are older, mostly healed; they don't have the hurt they did before, when they were fresher.

He puts his hand on the chronostat, turns it off with a decisive twist of his wrist. Its hum dies. He's used to the background noise. He goes into the bedroom, opens the window to let outside air in faster. The mingling makes memories jump into focus again, but only for a moment: now they are going rather than coming.

When he walks back into the living room, the little calculator is gone from his coffee table. That's a good sign, he thinks. He glances at the chronostat needle. It's already down around seventy. He opens and closes the front door several times to bring in fresh air. The swirl is confusing, but only for a little while.

He looks at the needle again. Sixty-eight, he sees. That should be plenty good. Donna is still waiting on the stairs. "Come on in," he says.

"All right," she says. Now she takes the steps two at a time. She shows a lot of leg doing it.

"Wine?"

"Sure. Whatever you've got."

He opens the refrigerator. A half-gallon of Spañada is in there. He pours a couple of glasses, takes them into the living room.

"I like the poster," she says. It's a black-light KEEP ON TRUCKIN' poster, about the size of a baby billboard. When the conditioner is running, it isn't there. That doesn't matter to Tom if Donna likes it. He won't even miss the Chinese print that will replace it.

And then, as they have done a lot of times before, they head for the bedroom. Afterward, still naked, Tom wheels the TV in from out front. He plugs it in, spins the dial till he finds some news, then flops back onto the bed with Donna.

For a while, he doesn't pay much attention to the TV. Watching the flush fade from between Donna's breasts is much more interesting. He does hear that Minnesota is finally up into the thirties. "Not good, but better," he says, to show he has been following what's going on.

Donna nods; she really is watching. "Remember last winter, when it got below double zero and stayed there, and they had to try to get food to the markets with horses and buggies? People starved. In the United States, starved. I couldn't believe it."

"Terrible," Tom agrees. Then he has to start watching, too, because the weatherman is coming on.

As usual, the fellow is insanely cheerful. "The early seventies tomorrow through most of the metropolitan area," he says, whacking the map with his pointer, "rising into the mid- or late seventies in the valleys and the desert. Have a *fine* day, Los Angeles!" He whacks the map again.

Donna sucks in air between her teeth. "I'd better go," she says, catching Tom by surprise. She swings her feet onto the floor, turns her panties right side out, slides them up her legs.

"I'd hoped you'd spend the night," he says. He is trying to sound hurt but fears that the words have come out petulant instead.

Evidently not. Donna replies gently, "Tom, right now, I love you very much. But if I sleep with you tonight—and I mean sleep—and we wake up in the early seventies, what's going to happen?"

His scowl says he knows the answer to that. Donna's nod is sad, but she stands up and starts pulling on her pantyhose. Tom aches at the thought of having her go, and not just because he wants her again. Right now, he really loves her, too.

He says, "Tell you what. Suppose I set the conditioner for sixty-eight. Will you stay then?"

He has startled her. "Do you really want to?" she says. She doesn't sound as if she believes it, but she does get back onto the bed.

He wonders if he believes it himself. The place won't be the same in the late sixties. He'll miss that little calculator. There should be a slide rule around somewhere now, he thinks, but a slide rule won't help him keep his checkbook straight. And that's just the tip of the iceberg. The frozen pizza will taste more like cardboard and less like pizza in the sixties. But—

"Let's try it," he says. Better cardboard with Donna, he thinks, than mozzarella without.

He shuts the bedroom window, goes out front to adjust the chronostat. It doesn't kick in right away, since the place is already around sixty-eight, but moving the needle makes him think again about what he's doing. A bookcase is gone, he sees. He'll miss some of those books.

"Hell with it," he says out loud and heads for the bathroom. While he is brushing his teeth, he starts rummaging frantically through the drawers by the sink. The toothbrush is still in his mouth; fluoridated foam dribbles down his chin, so that he looks like a mad dog. He stops as suddenly as he started. He does have a spare toothbrush, rather to his surprise. Donna giggles when, with a flourish, he hands it to her.

"When are you working these days?" she asks when she comes back to bed. "If it's close to when you had this place before—"

"No," he says quickly. He understands what she means. If he spends his office time reliving fights that are fresh to him, this will never fly, no matter how well they get on when they are home together. "How about you?" he asks.

She laughs. "I probably wouldn't have gone into the mall if I hadn't heard the year conditioner had broken down. I like the sixties. I work in a little record store called Barefoot Sounds. It suits me."

"I can see that," he says, nodding. Donna will never be a pragmatist. The more she stays out of the eighties, the better off she'll be. He yawns, lies down beside her. "Let's go to bed."

She smiles a broad's smile at him—there's no other word for it. "We've already done that."

He picks up a pillow, makes as if to hit her with it. "To sleep, I mean."

"Okay." She sprawls across him, warm and soft, to turn off the light. She has, he knows, a gift for falling asleep right away. Sure enough, only a couple of minutes later, her voice is blurry as she asks, "Drive me to work in the morning?"

"Sure." He hesitates. With a name like Barefoot Sounds, her record store sounds like a thoroughly sixties place. "If the weather changes, will I be able to find it?"

The mattress shifts to her nod. "It's year-conditioned. No matter what the weather's like outside, there are always sixties refugees popping in. We do a pretty good business, as a matter of fact."

"Okay," he says again. A couple of minutes later, he can tell that she has dropped off. He takes longer to go to sleep himself. He hasn't shared a bed with a woman for a while. He is very conscious of her weight pressing down the bed, of the small noises her breathing makes, of her smell. To trust someone enough to sleep with him, he thinks, takes more faith in some ways than just to go to bed with him. Suddenly, he wants her even more than he did before.

He lies still in the darkness. He has never yet met a woman who is eager just after she wakes up. Besides, he thinks, she'll be here tomorrow.

He hopes… Weather in the early seventies tomorrow. Nasty weather for him and Donna.

He falls asleep worrying about it. Sometime around two in the morning, the year conditioner kicks in. He wakes with a start. Donna never stirs. He reaches over, softly puts his hand on the curve of her hip. She mutters something, rolls onto her stomach. He jerks his hand away. She doesn't wake up. He takes a long time to go back to sleep.

The alarm clock's buzz might as well be a bomb going off by his ear. He needs a loud one. The adrenaline rush keeps him going till his first cup of coffee. The only thing that wakes Donna is his bouncing out of bed. He has forgotten what a dedicated sleeper she is.

But she has two plates of eggs scrambled, toast buttered, and the coffee perking by the time his tie is knotted. "Now I know why I asked you to stay," he says. "I just eat corn flakes when I'm here by myself."

"Poor baby," she croons. He makes a face at her.

While he is stacking the dishes in the sink, he asks, "So where is this Barefoot Sounds of yours?"

"Down in Gardena, on Crenshaw. I hope I'm not going to make you late."

He looks at his watch, calculates in his head. "I ought to make it. I won't bother washing up now, though. I'll get 'em tonight. Shall I pick you up? What time do you get off?"

"Four-thirty."

He grunts. "I probably can't get up that way till maybe half past five."

"I'll stay inside," she promises. "That way, I'll be sure to be glad to see you."

She does have sense, he knows, no matter how she sometimes hides it. "Sounds like a good idea to me," he says.

Just how good it is he discovers the minute they walk out the door. It's in the seventies, all right: the weatherman had it right on the button. By the time Tom and Donna get to the bottom of the stairs, they aren't holding hands any more.

He strides ahead of her, turns back to snap, "I don't have all day to get you where you're going, you know."

"Don't do me any favors." She puts her hands on her hips. "If you're in such a hurry, just tell me where the nearest bus stop is and take off. I'll manage fine."

"It's—" All that saves things is that he has no idea where the nearest bus stop is. Like a lot of people in L.A., he's helpless without a car. "Just come on," he says. In the seventies, she really does drive him crazy. The angry click of her heels on the walk tells him it's mutual.

He unlocks her door, goes around to unlock his, slides behind the wheel; he's not opening doors for her, not right now. He doesn't even look at her as she gets in. The engine roars to life when he turns the key, floors the gas pedal. He doesn't wait for it to warm up before he reaches for the year-conditioner switch. He has to change the setting; usually he keeps it in the eighties, to help him gear up for work.

The conditioner takes a while to make a difference; but little by little, the tense silence between Tom and Donna becomes friendlier. "My last car didn't have a year conditioner," he says.

She shakes her head. "I couldn't live like that."

He finds Barefoot Sounds without much trouble. It's at the back of a little shopping center where most of the stores are kept a lot newer. He shrugs. From what Donna says, the place pays the rent, and that's what counts. Besides, he likes sixties music. "Maybe I'll stop in when I pick you up," he says.

"Sure, why not? I'll introduce you to Rick, the guy who runs the place." She leans over to kiss him, then gets out. He drives right off; he's left the motor running while he stops in the parking lot—he doesn't want the year conditioner to die.

But he doesn't like the look on Donna's face that he sees in the rear-view mirror. The seventies are hard on them, and that's all there is to it. He hopes she does remember to wait for him in the store. If she stays outside, she'll be ready to spit in his eye by the time he gets there.

More likely, he thinks, she'll just up and leave.

If she does, she does; there's nothing he can do about it. He chews on that unsatisfying bit of philosophy all the way down the San Diego Freeway into Orange County.

———————

When he gets out of the car, in the company lot, he hopes she *won't* be there in the afternoon. He hurries across the asphalt to the mirror-fronted office building, which is firmly in the eighties. A little more of this whipsawing and he won't be good for anything the rest of the day.

But he gains detachment even before he gets his computer booted up. As soon as he gets on line, he is too busy to worry about anything but his job. Now that the old front in the upper Midwest is finally breaking up, new orders come flooding in, and he has to integrate them into everything the system thinks it already knows.

He doesn't begin to get his head above water till lunchtime. Even then, he is too rushed to go out; he grabs a cheeseburger and a diet cola at the little in-house cafeteria. As he wolfs them down, Donna returns to the surface of his mind.

Being so far upyear gives him perspective on things. He knows that whenever the weather is in the early seventies, it'll be a dash from one year-conditioned place to another. Can he handle that? With eighties practicality, he realizes he'd better if he wants to keep her. He wonders what going from this long-distance indifference to a hot affair every night will do to him.

He also wonders what Donna is like in the eighties. He doubts he'll find out. She has made her choice, and this isn't it.

He has second thoughts again as he goes back out into the seventies at quitting time. But he has to go to his car anyhow, and as soon as it starts, he's all right again—he's left the year conditioner on. It's tough on his timing belt but good for his peace of mind.

Traffic is appalling. He's stoic about that. When the weather is in the eighties, things are even worse, with more cars on the road. When it drops into the fifties, the San Diego Freeway isn't there. Getting into town from Orange County on surface streets is a different kind of thrill.

He pulls into a parking space in front of Barefoot Sounds around 5:15. Not bad. Again he lets the year conditioner die with the engine without turning it off. He's trotting to the record store before the hum has altogether faded.

He's hardly out in the seventies long enough to remember to get hostile toward Donna. Then he's inside Barefoot Sounds and in the late sixties with a vengeance.

The place is wall-to-wall posters: a KEEP ON TRUCKIN' even gaudier than his, Peter Fonda on a motorcycle, Nixon so stoned his face is dribbling out between his fingers, Mickey and Minnie Mouse doing something obscene. Patchouli fills the air, thick enough to slice. And blasting out of the big speakers is "Love One Another," not the Youngbloods singing but a cover version: slower, more haunting, not one he hears much on the radio, no matter when he is…

"My God!" Tom says. "That's H. P. Lovecraft!"

The fellow behind the cash register raises an eyebrow. He has frizzy brown hair and a Fu Manchu mustache. "I'm impressed," he says. "Half my regulars wouldn't know that one, and you're new here. Can I help you find something?"

"Only in a manner of speaking. I'm here to pick up Donna." Tom looks around. He doesn't see her. He starts worrying. There aren't many places to hide.

But the fellow—he must be the Rick she mentioned, Tom realizes—sticks his head behind a curtain, says, "Hon, your ride's here." *Hon?* Tom scowls until he notices that the guy is wearing a wedding ring. Then he relaxes—a little.

Donna comes out. The way her face lights up when she sees him makes him put his silly fears in the trash, where they belong. In the late sixties, he and Donna are good together. He whistles a couple of bars from the Doors song.

Rick cocks that eyebrow again. "You know your stuff. You should be coming in here all the time."

"Maybe I should. This is quite a place." Tom takes another look around. He rubs his chin, considering. "Who does your buying for you?"

"You're looking at him, my man," Rick says, laughing. He jabs himself in the chest with a thumb. "Why?"

"Nothing, really. Just a thought." Tom turns to Donna. "Are you ready to go?"

"And then some."

She's been waiting for him, Tom realizes. She can't be happy standing around while he chews the fat with her boss. "Sorry," he says. He nods at Rick. "Good to meet you."

"You, too." Rick pulls his wallet out of the hip pocket of his striped bell-bottoms. He extends a card, hands it to Tom. He may be a freak, but he's not running Barefoot Sounds to starve. "You ever get anywhere on that thought of yours, let me know, you hear?"

"I will." Tom sticks the card in his own wallet. Donna is at the door, tapping her foot. No matter how good he and she are, she is going to be one unhappy lady any second now. Maybe gallantry will help. With an extravagant bow, Tom holds the door open for her.

She steps through. "Took you long enough," she says. Her voice has an edge to it—she's outside, back in the early seventies. As he joins her, Tom feels his stomach start to churn.

This time, the tension breaks before it builds to a full-scale fight, thanks to Tom's car's being just a couple of steps away. They are inside and the year conditioner is going before they can do much more than start to glare at each other.

They both relax as it goes to work. Tom heads for his apartment. After a while, Donna asks, "What were you thinking about back there in the store?"

But Tom says, "Let it keep for now. It isn't ripe yet. Let's see how things go with us, then maybe I'll bring it up again."

"The curiosity will kill me." Donna doesn't push, though. In the seventies, she'd be all over him, which would only make him clam up harder. Luckily, she's thinking of something else when he pulls up in front of his building. The silence is guarded as they go up the stairs, but at least it is silence, and things are fine again once they're inside his place.

———

Come the weekend, Donna moves her stuff into his apartment. Without ever much talking about it, they fall into a routine that gets firmer day by day. Tom likes it. The only fly in the ointment, in fact, is his job. It's not the commute that bothers him. But he doesn't like not caring about Donna eight hours a day. He can deal with it, but he doesn't like it.

Finally, he digs out Rick's card and calls him.

"You sure?" Rick says when he's done talking. "The pay would be peanuts next to what you're pulling down in your eighties job."

"Get serious," Tom says. "Every twenty-dollar bill I have in my wallet there turns into a five here."

Rick is silent awhile, thinking it over. At last, he says, "I'd say I've got myself a new buyer." He hesitates. "You love her a lot, don't you? You'd have to, to do something like this."

"In the sixties, I love her a lot, and she's a sixties person. If I want to stay with her, I'd better be one, too. Hell—" Tom laughs, "I'm getting good on my slide rule again."

Donna's smile stretches across her entire face the first day they go into Barefoot Sounds together to work. This time, she holds the door open for him. "Come on in," she says. "The weather's fine."

"Yes," he says. "It is." She follows him in. The door closes after them.

THE CASTLE OF THE
SPARROWHAWK

Sir John Mandeville heard the tale of the castle of the sparrowhawk, but only from afar, and imperfectly. If a man could keep that sparrowhawk, which dwelt in the topmost tower of the castle, awake for seven days and nights, he would win whatever earthly thing might be his heart's desire. So much Mandeville knew.

But he lied when he put that castle in Armenia. Armenia, surely, was a strange and exotic land to his readers in England or France or Italy, but the castle of the sparrowhawk lay beyond the fields we know. How could it be otherwise, when even Mandeville tells us a lady of Faerie kept that sparrowhawk?

Perhaps we may excuse him after all, though, for the tale as he learned it did involve an Armenian prince—Mandeville calls him a king, to make the story grander, but only the truth here. Natural enough, then, for him to set that castle there. Natural, but wrong.

You might think Prince Rupen of Etchmiadzin had no need to go searching for the castle of the sparrowhawk. He was young. He was strong, in principality and in person. He was brave, and even beginning to be wise. His face, a handsome face in the half-eagle, half-lion way so many Armenians have, was more apt to be seen in a smile than a scowl.

Yet despite his smiles, he was not happy, not lastingly so. He felt that nothing he owned was his by right. His principality he had from his father, and his face and form as well. Even his bravery and the beginnings of wisdom had been inculcated in him.

"What would I have been had I been born an ugly, palsied pig-farmer?" he cried one day in a fit of self-doubt.

"Someone other than yourself," his vizier answered sensibly.

But that did not satisfy him. He was, after all, only *beginning* to be wise.

In the east, the line between the fields we know and those beyond is not drawn so firmly as in our mundane corner of the world. Too, in the tortuous mountains of Armenia, who knows what fields lie three valleys over? And so, when Rupen, armed with no more than determination—and a crossbow, in case of dragons—set out to seek the castle of the sparrowhawk, he was not surprised that one day he found it.

But for a certain feline grace, the grooms and servants of the castle were hardly different from those he had left behind at Etchmiadzin. They tended his horse, fed him ground lamb and pine nuts, and gave him wine spiced with cinnamon. He drank deeply and flung himself on the featherbed to which they led him. To hold the sparrowhawk wakeful seven days and nights, he would have to go without sleep himself. He stored it away now, like a woodchuck fattening itself for winter.

No one disturbed his rest; he was allowed to emerge from his chamber when he would. After he had eaten again, the seneschal of the castle asked leave to have speech with him. The mark of Faerie lay more heavily on that man than on his underlings. In the fields we know, his mien and bearing would have suited a sovereign, not a bailiff. So would his robes, of sea-green samite shot through with silver threads and decked with pearls.

Said he to Rupen, "Is it your will to essay the ordeal of the sparrowhawk?"

"It is," the prince replied.

The seneschal bowed. "You have come, no doubt, seeking the reward success will bring. My duty is to inform you of the cost of failure; word thereof somehow does not travel so widely. If the bird sleep, you forfeit more than your life. Your soul is lost as well. The prayers of your priests do not reach here to save it."

Rupen believed him absolutely. The churches of Armenia with their conical domes had never seemed more distant. For all that, he said, "I will go on."

The seneschal bowed again. "Be it so, then. Honor to your courage. I will take you to the lady Olissa. Come."

There were one hundred and forty-four steps on the spiral stair that led to the sparrowhawk's eyrie. Prince Rupen counted them one by one as he climbed behind the seneschal. His heart pounded and his breath came short by the time they reached the top. The seneschal was unchanged; he might have been a falcon himself, by the ease with which he took the stairs.

The door at the head of the stairway was of some golden wood Rupen did not know. Light streamed into the gloomy stairwell when the seneschal opened it, briefly dazzling Rupen. As his eyes took its measure, he saw a broad expanse of enameled blue sky, a single perch, and standing beside it one who had to be Olissa.

"Are you of a sudden afraid, then?" the seneschal asked when Rupen hung back. "You may yet withdraw, the only penalty being that never again shall you find your way hither."

"Afraid?" Rupen murmured, as from far away. "No, I am not afraid." But still he stayed in the antechamber; to take a step might have meant pulling his eyes away from Olissa for an instant, and he could not have borne it.

Her hair stormed in bright waves to her waist, the color of the new-risen sun. Her skin was like snow faintly tinged with ripe apples. The curves of her body bade fair to bring tears to his eyes. So, for another reason, did the sculpted lines of her chin, her cheeks, the tiny curve of her ear where it peeped from among fiery ringlets. He thought how the pagan Greeks would have slain themselves in despair of capturing her in stone.

Her eyes? Like the sea, they were never the same shade twice.

He stood until she extended a slim hand his way. Then indeed he moved forward, as iron will toward a lodestone. When she spoke, he learned what the sound was that silver bells sought. "Knowing the danger," she asked, "you still wish to undertake the ordeal?"

He could only nod.

"Honor to your courage." Olissa echoed the seneschal; it was the first thing that recalled him to Rupen's mind since he set eyes on her. Then the man of Faerie was again forgotten as she went on, "I will have provender fetched here; you must undertake the test alone with the sparrowhawk."

The thought that she would leave filled him with despair. But when she asked him, "Will you drink wine at meat?" he had to think of a reply, if only not to appear a fool before her.

"No, bring me water or milk, if you would," he said. He would not have chosen them in Armenia, but he feared no flux here. He felt bound to explain, "Come the seventh day, I shall be drowsy enough without the grape."

"A man of sense as well as bravery. It shall be as you wish, or even better."

Already Rupen heard servants on the stairs, though no sign he could detect had summoned them. Along with the flaky loaves and smoked meats, they set down ewers the fragrance of whose contents made his nose twitch.

"Fruit nectars," Olissa said. "Does it please you?"

He bowed his thanks. Against the liquid elegance of the seneschal, his courtesy seemed a miserable clumsy thing, but he gave it as a man will give a copper when he has no gold to spend.

She nodded to him, and he felt as if the Emperor of Byzantium and the Great Khan had prostrated themselves at his feet. Saying, "Perhaps we shall meet again in seven days, you and I," she stepped past him to join the seneschal in the antechamber at the head of the stairs.

The door of the golden wood was swinging shut when Rupen blurted out a final thought: "If no one is here to watch me, how will you know if I fail?"

He had hoped for a last word from Olissa, but it was the seneschal who answered him. "We shall know, never fear," he said, and the iron promise in his voice sent a snake of dread slithering through Rupen's bowels. Soundlessly, the door closed.

With the glory of Olissa gone, Rupen turned to the sparrowhawk for the first time. It stared back at him with fierce topaz eyes, and screeched shrilly. He had flown hawks, and knew what that cry meant. "Hungry, are you? I was not sure the birds of Faerie had to eat."

Among the supplies the castle servants had brought was a large, low, earthen pot with a lid of openweave wickerwork. Small scuttling sounds came from it. When Rupen lifted the lid, he found mice, brown, white, and gray, scrambling about inside. He reached in, caught one and killed it, and offered it to the sparrowhawk. The bird ate greedily. It called for more, though the tip of the mouse's tail still dangled from its beak.

Rupen shook his head. "A stuffed belly makes for restfulness. We'll both stay a bit empty through this week." The sparrowhawk glared as if it understood. Perhaps, he thought, it did.

As dusk fell, it tucked its head under a wing. He clapped his hands. The sparrowhawk hissed at him. He lit a torch and set it in its sconce. It burned with the clean, sweet smell of sandalwood.

That night, drowsiness did not trouble Rupen, who was sustained by imaginings of Olissa. He felt fresh as just-fallen snow when dawn streaked the eastern sky with carmine and gold. The sparrowhawk, by then, was too furious with him to think of sleep.

Noon was not long past when he fed it another mouse. Soon after, the first yawn crept out of hiding and stretched itself in his throat. He strangled it, but felt others stirring to take its place. Presently they would thrive.

To hold them back, he began to sing. He sang every song he knew, and sang them all once again when he was through. The din sufficed to keep the sparrowhawk awake through most of the night. Eventually, though, it grew used to the sound of his voice, and began to close its eyes. Seeing that, he fell silent, which served as well as a thunderclap. The bird started up wildly; its bright stare had hatred in it.

That was how the second day passed.

Prince Rupen stumbled through the third and fourth days as if drunk. He laughed hoarsely at nothing, and kept dropping the chunks of bread he cut for supper. He was too tired to notice they had not gone stale, as they would have in the fields we know. The sparrowhawk began to sway on its perch. Some of the luster was gone from its bright plumage.

On the fifth day, it took Rupen a very long time to catch the bird its mouse. The mice were wide awake. When at last he had the furry little creature, he started to pop it into his own mouth. Only the sparrowhawk's shriek of protest recalled him to himself, for a little while.

He remembered nothing whatsoever of the sixth day.

Sometime in the middle of the last night, he decided he wanted to die. He lurched over to the edge of the eyrie's floor and looked longingly at the castle courtyard far below. The thought of forfeiting his soul for failing the ordeal did not check him, nor did the certainty that suicides suffered the same fate. But he lacked the energy to take the step that would have sent him tumbling down.

He did not remember why he kept snapping his fingers in the sparrowhawk's face. The bird, by then, lacked the spirit even to bite at him. Its eyes might have been dull yellow glass now, not topaz. Both of them had forgotten the mice.

The sun came up. Rupen stared at it until the pain penetrated the fog between his eyes and his brain. Tears streamed down his cheeks, and continued to flow long after the pain was past. He had no idea why he wept, or how to stop.

Nor did the sound of footsteps on the stairs convey to him a meaning. Yet when the door swung open, he somehow contrived a bow to the lady Olissa.

She curtseyed in return, as lovely as she had been a week before. "Rest now, bold prince," she murmured. "You have won."

The seneschal sprang out from behind her to ease Rupen to the slates of the floor, his first snores already begun. Olissa paid the man no attention, but crooned to the sparrowhawk, "And thou, little warrior, rest thyself as well." The bird gave what would have been a chirp had its voice been sweeter, and pushed its head into the white palm of her hand like a lovesick cat. Then it too slept.

The seneschal said, "To look at him lying there, this mortal now has in his possession his heart's desire."

"Ah, but he will not reckon it so when he wakes," Olissa replied.

———

The sun sliding fingers under his eyelids roused Rupen. He sprang up in horror, certain he was doomed. Ice formed round his heart to see the perch he had so long guarded empty.

Olissa's laugh, a sound like springtime, made him whirl. "Fear not," she said. "You have slept the day around. The ordeal is behind you, and you have only to claim your reward."

"You did come to me, then," Rupen said, amazed. "I thought surely it was a dream."

"No dream," she said. "What would you?"

He was not yet ready for that question. "The sparrowhawk—?" he asked.

His concern won a smile from her. "It is a bird of Faerie, and recovers itself more quickly than those you may have known. Already it is on the wing, hunting mice it does not have to scream for."

Rupen flushed to be reminded of his vagaries during the trial. That reminded him of his present sadly draggled state. "As part of my reward, may I ask for a great hot tub and the loan of fresh clothing?"

"It shall be as you desire; you are not the first to make that request. While you bathe, think on what else you would have. I shall come to your bedchamber in an hour's time, to hear you." The soaps and scents of Faerie, finer and more delicate than the ones we know, washed the last lingering exhaustion from his bones. His borrowed silks clung to him like a second skin. As he combed his hair and thick curly beard, he noticed the mirror on the wall above the tub was not befogged by steam. He wished he could take that secret back with him to Etchmiadzin.

He started when the soft knock came at the bedchamber door. At the first touch of the latch, the door opened as silently as all the others in the castle of the sparrowhawk. The lady Olissa stepped in. As if it were a well-trained dog, the door swung shut behind her.

She watched him a moment with her sea-colored eyes. "Ask for any earthly thing you may desire, for you have nobly acquitted yourself in the task set you."

Had it been the seneschal granting him that boon, Rupen would have answered differently. But he was a young man, and quite refreshed, so he said, "Of earthly things, Etchmiadzin fills all my wants. Therefore—" His resolve faltered, and he hesitated, but at last he did go on, all in a rush: "—I ask of you no more than that you share this bed with me here for a night and a day. I could desire nothing more."

Still her eyes reminded him of the sea, the sea at storm. Almost he quailed before her anger, and was steadied only by the thought that she would despise him for his fear.

She said, "Beware, mortal. I am no earthly thing, but of the Faerie realm. Choose you another benison, one suited to your station."

"Am I not a prince?" Rupen cried. He was only beginning to be wise. "In truth, I would ask for nothing else."

"For the last time, can I not dissuade you from this folly?"

"No," he said.

"Be it so, then," she said with a wintry sigh, "but with this gift you demand of me I shall give you another, such as you deserve for your presumption. Etchmiadzin will not so delight you on your return; you will come to know war and need and loss. And ten years hence I charge you to think upon this day and what you have earned here now."

Her words fell on deaf ears, for as she spoke she was loosing the stays of her gown and letting it fall to the floor. Rupen had imagined how she might be. Now he saw what a poor, paltry, niggling thing his imagination was. Then he touched her, and that was past all imagining.

———

Afterward, riding back to Etchmiadzin, he wished he had asked for a year. On the other hand, half an hour might have served as well, or as poorly. Anything less than forever was not enough.

He returned by the road he had taken into Faerie, but somehow he did not enter the fields we know where he had left them. Yet he was still in Armenia, only a few days' journey from his principality. He had half looked for a greater vengeance.

Then he found his border closed against him, and his onetime vizier holding the throne of his ancestors. "If a prince go haring into Faerie rather than look after his own land, he does not deserve to rule," the usurper had told the nobles, and most said aye and swore him allegiance.

But not all. Prince Rupen soon mustered a band of warriors and undertook to regain by force what had once been his by right. Fighting and siege and murder engulfed the land of Etchmiadzin that had been so fair. By his own hand Rupen slew a cousin who had been a dear friend. He watched comrades of old die in his service, or live on maimed.

And in the end it did not avail. Etchmiadzin remained lost. By the time he admitted that in his heart, Rupen had lived the soldier's life so long that he found any other savorless. From a nest high in the hills—to its sorrow, Armenia has many of them—he and his swooped down into the valleys to seize what they might.

Sometimes Rupen was nearly as rich as a bandit chief as he had been in the castle of Etchmiadzin. More often he went hungry. There were white scars on his arms, and along his ribs, and a great gash on his cheek and forehead that was only partly hidden by the leather patch covering the ruin of his left eyesocket.

He seldom thought of Faerie. Few even of the hard-bitten crew who rode with him had the nerve to bring up his journey to the castle of the sparrowhawk. After a while, most of those who had known of it were dead.

Then one day, as the lady Olissa had decreed, full memory came flooding back, and he knew in astonishment that a decade had passed. He thought of the tiny space of time he had spent in her arms, of his life as a prince before, and the long years of misfortune that came after. He thought of what he had become: ladder-ribbed, huddled close to a tiny fire in a drafty hut, drinking sour wine.

He thought of Olissa again. Not even the folk of Faerie see all the future, exactly as it will be. "I'd do it over again, just the same way," he said out loud.

One or two of his men looked up. The rest kept on with what they were doing.

THE LAST
ARTICLE

Nonviolence is the first article of my faith. It is also the last article of my creed.
—Mohandas Gandhi
The one means that wins the easiest victory over reason: terror and force.
—Adolf Hitler, *Mein Kampf*

The tank rumbled down the rajpath, past the ruins of the Memorial Arch, toward the India Gate. The gateway arch was still standing, although it had taken a couple of shell hits in the fighting before New Delhi fell. The Union Jack fluttered above it.

British troops lined both sides of the Rajpath, watching silently as the tank rolled past them. Their khaki uniforms were filthy and torn; many wore bandages. They had the weary, past-caring stares of beaten men, though the Army of India had fought until flesh and munitions gave out.

The India Gate drew near. A military band, smartened up for the occasion, began to play as the tank went past. The bagpipes sounded thin and lost in the hot, humid air.

A single man stood waiting in the shadow of the gate. Field Marshal Walther Model leaned down into the cupola of the Panzer IV. "No one can match the British at ceremonies of this sort," he said to his aide.

Major Dieter Lasch laughed, a bit unkindly. "They've had enough practice, sir," he answered, raising his voice to be heard over the flatulent roar of the tank's engine.

"What is that tune?" the field marshal asked. "Does it have a meaning?"

"It's called 'The World Turned Upside Down,' " said Lasch, who had been involved with his British opposite number in planning the formal surrender. "Lord Cornwallis's army musicians played it when he yielded to the Americans at Yorktown."

"Ah, the Americans." Model was for a moment so lost in his own thoughts that his monocle threatened to slip from his right eye. He screwed it back in. The single lens was the only thing he shared with the clichéd image of a high German officer. He was no lean, hawk-faced Prussian. But his rounded features were unyielding, and his stocky body sustained the energy of his will better than the thin, dyspeptic frames of so many aristocrats. "The Americans," he repeated. "Well, that will be the next step, won't it? But enough. One thing at a time."

The Panzer stopped. The driver switched off the engine. The sudden quiet was startling. Model leaped nimbly down. He had been leaping down from tanks for eight years now, since his days as a staff officer for the IV Corps in the Polish campaign.

The man in the shadows stepped forward, saluted. Flashbulbs lit his long, tired face as German photographers recorded the moment for history. The Englishman ignored cameras and cameramen alike. "Field Marshal Model," he said politely. He might have been about to discuss the weather.

Model admired his sangfroid. "Field Marshal Auchinleck," he replied, returning the salute and giving Auchinleck a last few seconds to remain his equal. Then he came back to the matter at hand. "Field

Marshal, have you signed the instrument of surrender of the British Army of India to the forces of the Reich?"

"I have," Auchinleck replied. He reached into the left blouse pocket of his battledress, removed a folded sheet of paper. Before handing it to Model, though, he said, "I should like to request your permission to make a brief statement at this time."

"Of course, sir. You may say what you like, at whatever length you like." In victory, Model could afford to be magnanimous. He had even granted Marshal Zhukov leave to speak in the Soviet capitulation at Kuibishev, before the marshal was taken out and shot.

"I thank you." Auchinleck stiffly dipped his head. "I will say, then, that I find the terms I have been forced to accept to be cruelly hard on the brave men who have served under my command."

"That is your privilege, sir." But Model's round face was no longer kindly, and his voice had iron in it as he replied, "I must remind you, however, that my treating with you at all under the rules of war is an act of mercy for which Berlin may yet reprimand me. When Britain surrendered in 1941, all Imperial forces were also ordered to lay down their arms. I daresay you did not expect us to come so far, but I would be within my rights in reckoning you no more than so many bandits."

A slow flush darkened Auchinleck's cheeks. "We gave you a bloody good run, for bandits."

"So you did." Model remained polite. He did not say he would ten times rather fight straight-up battles than deal with the partisans who to this day harassed the Germans and their allies in occupied Russia. "Have you anything further to add?"

"No, sir, I do not." Auchinleck gave the German the signed surrender, handed him his sidearm. Model put the pistol in the empty holster he wore for the occasion. It did not fit well; the holster was made for a Walther P38, not this man-killing brute of a Webley and Scott. That mattered little, though—the ceremony was almost over.

Auchinleck and Model exchanged salutes for the last time. The British field marshal stepped away. A German lieutenant came up to lead him into captivity.

Major Lasch waved his left hand. The Union Jack came down from the flagpole on the India Gate. The swastika rose to replace it.

Lasch tapped discreetly on the door, stuck his head into the field marshal's office. "That Indian politician is here for his appointment with you, sir."

"Oh, yes. Very well. Dieter, send him in." Model had been dealing with Indian politicians even before the British surrender, and with hordes of them now that resistance was over. He had no more liking for the breed than for Russian politicians, or even German ones. No matter what pious principles they spouted, his experience was that they were all out for their own good first.

The small, frail brown man the aide showed in made him wonder. The Indian's emaciated frame and the plain white cotton loincloth that was his only garment contrasted starkly with the Victorian splendor of the Viceregal Palace from which Model was administering the Reich's new conquest. "Sit down, *Herr* Gandhi," the field marshal urged.

"I thank you very much, sir." As he took his seat, Gandhi seemed a child in an adult's chair: it was much too wide for him, and its soft, overstuffed cushions hardly sagged under his meager weight. But his eyes. Model saw, were not a child's eyes. They peered with disconcerting keenness through his wire-framed spectacles as he said, "I have come to enquire when we may expect German troops to depart from our country."

Model leaned forward, frowning. For a moment he thought he had misunderstood Gandhi's Gujarati-flavored English. When he was sure he had not, he said, "Do you think perhaps we have come all this way as tourists?"

"Indeed I do not." Gandhi's voice was sharp with disapproval. "Tourists do not leave so many dead behind them."

Model's temper kindled. "No, tourists do not pay such a high price for the journey. Having come regardless of that cost, I assure you we shall stay."

"I am very sorry, sir; I cannot permit it."

"*You* cannot?" Again, Model had to concentrate to keep his monocle from falling out. He had heard arrogance from politicians before, but this scrawny old devil surpassed belief. "Do you forget I can call my aide and have you shot behind this building? You would not be the first, I assure you."

"Yes, I know that," Gandhi said sadly. "If you have that fate in mind for me, I am an old man. I will not run."

Combat had taught Model a hard indifference to the prospect of injury or death. He saw the older man possessed something of the same sort, however he had acquired it. A moment later, he realized his threat had not only failed to frighten Gandhi, but had actually amused him. Disconcerted, the field marshal said, "Have you any serious issues to address?"

"Only the one I named just now. We are a nation of more than three hundred million; it is no more just for Germany to rule us than for the British."

Model shrugged. "If we are able to, we will. We have the strength to hold what we have conquered, I assure you."

"Where there is no right, there can be no strength," Gandhi said. "We will not permit you to hold us in bondage."

"Do you think to threaten me?" Model growled. In fact, though, the Indian's audacity surprised him. Most of the locals had fallen over themselves, fawning on their new masters. Here, at least, was a man out of the ordinary.

Gandhi was still shaking his head, although Model saw he had still not frightened him—a man out of the ordinary indeed, thought the field marshal, who respected courage when he found it. "I make no threats, sir, but I will do what I believe to be right."

"Most noble," Model said, but to his annoyance the words came out sincere rather than with the sardonic edge he had intended. He had heard such canting phrases before, from Englishmen, from Russians, yes, and from Germans as well. Somehow, though, this Gandhi struck him as one who always meant exactly what he said. He rubbed his chin, considering how to handle such an intransigent.

A large green fly came buzzing into the office. Model's air of detachment vanished the moment he heard that malignant whine. He sprang from his seat, swatted at the fly. He missed. The insect flew around a while longer, then settled on the arm of Gandhi's chair. "Kill it," Model told him. "Last week one of those accursed things bit me on the neck, and I still have the lump to prove it."

Gandhi brought his hand down, but several inches from the fly. Frightened, it took off. Gandhi rose. He was surprisingly nimble for a man nearing eighty. He chivvied the fly out of the office, ignoring Model, who watched his performance in open-mouthed wonder.

"I hope it will not trouble you again," Gandhi said, returning as calmly as if he had done nothing out of the ordinary. "I am one of those who practice ahimsa: I will do no injury to any living thing."

Model remembered the fall of Moscow, and the smell of burning bodies filling the chilly autumn air. He remembered machine guns knocking down Cossack cavalry before they could close, and the screams of the wounded horses, more heartrending than any woman's. He knew of other things too, things he had not seen for himself and of which he had no desire to leann more.

"*Herr* Gandhi," he said, "how do you propose to bend to your will someone who opposes you, if you will not use force for the purpose?"

"I have never said I will not use force, sir." Gandhi's smile invited the field marshal to enjoy with him the distinction he was making. "I will not use violence. If my people refuse to cooperate in any way with yours, how can you compel them? What choice will you have but to grant us leave to do as we will?"

Without the intelligence estimates he had read, Model would have dismissed the Indian as a madman. No madman, though, could have caused the British so much trouble. But perhaps the decadent Raj simply had not made him afraid. Model tried again. "You understand that what you have said is treason against the Reich," he said harshly.

Gandhi bowed in his seat. "You may, of course, do what you will with me. My spirit will in any case survive among my people."

Model felt his face heat. Few men were immune to fear. Just his luck, he thought sourly, to have run into one of them. "I warn you, *Herr* Gandhi, to obey the authority of the officials of the Reich, or it will be the worse for you."

"I will do what I believe to be right, and nothing else. If you Germans exert yourselves toward the freeing of India, joyfully will I work with you. If not, then I regret we must be foes."

The field marshal gave him one last chance to see reason. "Were it you and I alone, there might be some doubt as to what would happen." Not much, he thought, not when Gandhi was twenty-odd years older and thin enough to break like a stick. He fought down the irrelevance, went on, "But where, *Herr* Gandhi, is your *Wehrmacht?*"

Of all things, he had least expected to amuse the Indian again. Yet Gandhi's eyes unmistakably twinkled behind the lenses of his spectacles. "Field Marshal, I have an army too."

Model's patience, never of the most enduring sort, wore thin all at once. "Get out!" he snapped.

Gandhi stood, bowed, and departed. Major Lasch stuck his head into the office. The field marshal's glare drove him out again in a hurry.

"Well?" Jawaharlal Nehru paced back and forth. Tall, slim, and saturnine, he towered over Gandhi without dominating him. "Dare we use the same policies against the Germans that we employed against the English?"

"If we wish our land free, dare we do otherwise?" Gandhi replied. "They will not grant our wish of their own volition. Model struck me as a man not much different from various British leaders whom we have succeeded in vexing in the past." He smiled at the memory of what passive resistance had done to officials charged with combating it.

"Very well, *Satyagraha* it is." But Nehru was not smiling. He had less humor than his older colleague.

Gandhi teased him gently: "Do you fear another spell in prison, then?" Both men had spent time behind bars during the war, until the British released them in a last, vain effort to rally the support of the Indian people to the Raj.

"You know better." Nehru refused to be drawn, and persisted, "The rumors that come out of Europe frighten me."

"Do you tell me you take them seriously?" Gandhi shook his head in surprise and a little reproof. "Each side in any war will always paint its opponents as blackly as it can."

"I hope you are right, and that that is all. Still, I confess I would feel more at ease with what we plan to do if you found me one Jew, officer or other rank, in the army now occupying us."

"You would be hard-pressed to find any among the forces they defeated. The British have little love for Jews either."

"Yes, but I daresay it could be done. With the Germans, they are banned by law. The English would never make such a rule. And while the laws are vile enough, I think of the tales that man Wiesenthal told, the one who came here, the gods know how, across Russia and Persia from Poland."

"Those I do not believe," Gandhi said firmly. "No nation could act in that way and hope to survive. Where could men be found to carry out such horrors?"

"Azad Hind," Nehru said, quoting the "Free India" motto of the locals who had fought on the German side.

But Gandhi shook his head. "They are only soldiers, doing as soldiers have always done. Wiesenthal's claims are for an entirely different order of bestiality, one which could not exist without destroying the fabric of the state that gave it birth."

"I hope very much you are right," Nehru said.

———

Walther Model slammed the door behind him hard enough to make his aide, whose desk faced away from the field marshal's office, jump in alarm. "Enough of this twaddle for one day," Model said. "I need schnapps, to get the taste of these Indians out of my mouth. Come along if you care to, Dieter."

"Thank you, sir." Major Lasch threw down his pen, eagerly got to his feet. "I sometimes think conquering India was easier than ruling it will be."

Model rolled his eyes. "I *know* it was. I would ten times rather be planning a new campaign than sitting here bogged down in pettifogging details. The sooner Berlin sends me people trained in colonial administration, the happier I will be."

The bar might have been taken from an English pub. It was dark, quiet, and paneled in walnut; a dartboard still hung on the wall. But a German sergeant in field-gray stood behind the bar and, despite the lazily turning ceiling fan, the temperature was close to thirty-five Celsius. The one might have been possible in occupied London, the other not.

Model knocked back his first shot at a gulp. He sipped his second more slowly, savoring it. Warmth spread through him, warmth that had nothing to do with the heat of the evening. He leaned back in his chair, steepled his fingers. "A long day," he said.

"Yes, sir," Lasch agreed. "After the effrontery of that Gandhi, any day would seem a long one. I've rarely seen you so angry." Considering Model's temper, that was no small statement.

"Ah, yes, Gandhi." Model's tone was reflective rather than irate; Lasch looked at him curiously. The field marshal said, "For my money, he's worth a dozen of the ordinary sort."

"Sir?" The aide no longer tried to hide his surprise.

"He is an honest man. He tells me what he thinks, and he will stick by that. I may kill him—I may have to kill him—but he and I will both know why, and I will not change his mind." Model took another sip of schnapps. He hesitated, as if unsure whether to go on. At last he did. "Do you know, Dieter, after he left I had a vision."

"Sir?" Now Lasch sounded alarmed.

The field marshal might have read his aide's thoughts. He chuckled wryly. "No, no, I am not about to swear off eating beefsteak and wear sandals instead of my boots, that I promise. But I saw myself as a Roman procurator, listening to the rantings of some early Christian priest."

Lasch raised an eyebrow. Such musings were unlike Model, who was usually direct to the point of bluntness and altogether materialistic—assets in the makeup of a general officer. The major cautiously sounded these unexpected depths: "How do you suppose the Roman felt, facing that kind of man?"

"Bloody confused, I suspect," Model said, which sounded more like him. "And because he and his comrades did not know how to handle such fanatics, you and I are Christians today, Dieter."

"So we are." The major rubbed his chin. "Is that a bad thing?"

Model laughed and finished his drink. "From your point of view or mine, no. But I doubt that old Roman would agree with us, any more than Gandhi agrees with me over what will happen next here. But then,

I have two advantages over the dead procurator." He raised his finger; the sergeant hurried over to fill his glass.

At Lasch's nod, the young man also poured more schnapps for him. The major drank, then said, "I should hope so. We are more civilized, more sophisticated, than the Romans ever dreamed of being."

But Model was still in that fey mood. "Are we? My procurator was such a sophisticate that he tolerated anything, and never saw the danger in a foe who would not do the same. Our Christian God, though, is a jealous god, who puts up with no rivals. And one who is a National Socialist serves also the *Volk,* to whom he owes sole loyalty. I am immune to Gandhi's virus in a way the Roman was not to the Christian's."

"Yes, that makes sense," Lasch agreed after a moment. "I had not thought of it in that way, but I see it is so. And what is our other advantage over the Roman procurator?"

Suddenly the field marshal looked hard and cold, much the way he had looked leading the tanks of Third Panzer against the Kremlin compound. "The machine gun," he said.

The rising sun's rays made the sandstone of the Red Fort seem even more the color of blood. Gandhi frowned and turned his back on the fortress, not caring for that thought. Even at dawn, the air was warm and muggy.

"I wish you were not here," Nehru told him. The younger man lifted his trademark fore-and-aft cap, scratched his graying hair, and glanced at the crowd growing around them. "The Germans' orders forbid assemblies, and they will hold you responsible for this gathering."

"I am, am I not?" Gandhi replied. "Would you have me send my followers into a danger I do not care to face myself? How would I presume to lead them afterward?"

"A general does not fight in the front ranks," Nehru came back. "If you are lost to our cause, will we be able to go on?"

"If not, then surely the cause is not worthy, yes? Now let us be going."

Nehru threw his hands in the air. Gandhi nodded, satisfied, and worked his way toward the head of the crowd. Men and women stepped aside to let him through. Still shaking his head, Nehru followed.

The crowd slowly began to march east up Chandni Chauk, the Street of Silversmiths. Some of the fancy shops had been wrecked in the fighting, more looted afterward. But others were opening up, their owners as happy to take German money as they had been to serve the British before.

One of the proprietors, a man who had managed to stay plump even through the past year of hardship, came rushing out of his shop when he saw the procession go by. He ran to the head of the march and spotted Nehru, whose height and elegant dress singled him out.

"Are you out of your mind?" the silversmith shouted. "The Germans have banned assemblies. If they see you, something dreadful will happen."

"Is it not dreadful that they take away the liberty which properly belongs to us?" Gandhi asked. The silversmith spun round. His eyes grew wide when he recognized the man who was speaking to him. Gandhi went on, "Not only is it dreadful, it is wrong. And so we do not recognize the Germans' right to ban anything we may choose to do. Join us, will you?"

"Great-souled one, I—I—" the silversmith spluttered. Then his glance slid past Gandhi. "The Germans!" he squeaked. He turned and ran.

Gandhi led the procession toward the approaching squad. The Germans stamped down Chandni Chauk as if they expected the people in front of them to melt from their path. Their gear, Gandhi thought, was not that much different from what British soldiers wore: ankle boots, shorts, and open-necked tunics. But their coal-scuttle helmets gave them a look of sullen, beetle-browed ferocity the British tin hat did not convey.

Even for a man of Gandhi's equanimity it was daunting, as no doubt it was intended to be.

"Hello, my friends," he said. "Do any of you speak English?"

"I speak it, a little," one of them replied. His shoulder straps had the twin pips of a sergeant-major; he was the squad-leader, then. He hefted his rifle, not menacingly, Gandhi thought, but to emphasize what he was saying. "Go to your homes back. This coming together is *verboten.*"

"I am sorry, but I must refuse to obey your order," Gandhi said. "We are walking peacefully on our own street in our own city. We will harm no one, no matter what; this I promise you. But walk we will, as we wish." He repeated himself until he was sure the sergeant-major understood.

The German spoke to his comrades in his own language. One of the soldiers raised his gun and with a nasty smile pointed it at Gandhi. He nodded politely. The German blinked to see him unafraid. The sergeant-major slapped the rifle down. One of his men had a field telephone on his back. The sergeant-major cranked it, waited for a reply, spoke urgently into it.

Nehru caught Gandhi's eye. His dark, tired gaze was full of worry. Somehow that nettled Gandhi more than the Germans' arrogance in ordering about his people. He began to walk forward again. The marchers followed him, flowing around the German squad like water flowing round a boulder.

The soldier who had pointed his rifle at Gandhi shouted in alarm. He brought up the weapon again. The sergeant-major barked at him. Reluctantly, he lowered it.

"A sensible man," Gandhi said to Nehru. "He sees we do no injury to him or his, and so does none to us. "

"Sadly, though, not everyone is so sensible," the younger man replied, "as witness his lance-corporal there. And even a sensible man may not be well-inclined to us. You notice he is still on the telephone."

———————

The phone on Field Marshal Model's desk jangled. He jumped and swore; he had left orders he was to be disturbed only for an emergency. He had to find time to work. He picked up the phone. "This had better be good," he growled without preamble.

He listened, swore again, slammed the receiver down. "Lasch!" he shouted.

It was his aide's turn to jump. "Sir?"

"Don't just sit there on your fat arse," the field marshal said unfairly. "Call out my car and driver, and quickly. Then belt on your sidearm and come along. The Indians are doing something stupid. Oh, yes, order out a platoon and have them come after us. Up on Chandni Chauk, the trouble is."

Lasch called for the car and the troops, then hurried after Model. "A riot?" he asked as he caught up.

"No, no." Model moved his stumpy frame along so fast that the taller Lasch had to trot beside him. "Some of Gandhi's tricks, damn him."

The field marshal's Mercedes was waiting when he and his aide hurried out of the viceregal palace. "Chandni Chauk," Model snapped as the driver held the door open for him. After that he sat in furious silence as the powerful car roared up Irwin Road, round a third of Connaught Circle, and north on Chelmsford Road past the bombed-out railway station until, for no reason Model could see, the street's name changed to Qutb Road.

A little later, the driver said, "Some kind of disturbance up ahead, sir."

"Disturbance?" Lasch echoed, leaning forward to peer through the windscreen. "It's a whole damned regiment's worth of Indians coming at us. Don't they know better than that? And what the devil," he added, his voice rising, "are so many of our men doing ambling along beside them?

Don't they know they're supposed to break up this sort of thing?" In his indignation, he did not notice he was repeating himself.

"I suspect they don't," Model said dryly. "Gandhi, I gather, can have that effect on people who aren't ready for his peculiar brand of stubbornness. That, however, does not include me." He tapped the driver on the shoulder. "Pull up about two hundred meters in front of the first rank of them, Joachim."

"Yes, sir."

Even before the car had stopped moving, Model jumped out of it. Lasch, hand on his pistol, was close behind, protesting, "What if one of those fanatics has a gun?"

"Then Colonel-General Weidling assumes command, and a lot of Indians end up dead." Model strode toward Gandhi, ignoring the German troops who were drawing themselves to stiff, horrified attention at the sight of his field marshal's uniform. He would deal with them later. For the moment, Gandhi was more important.

He had stopped—which meant the rest of the marchers did too—and was waiting politely for Model to approach. The German commandant was not impressed. He thought Gandhi sincere and could not doubt his courage, but none of that mattered at all. He said harshly, "You were warned against this sort of behavior."

Gandhi looked him in the eye. They were very much of a height. "And I told you, I do not recognize your right to give such orders. This is our country, not yours, and if some of us choose to walk on our streets, we will do so."

From behind Gandhi, Nehru's glance flicked worriedly from one of the antagonists to the other. Model noticed him only peripherally; if he was already afraid, he could be handled whenever necessary. Gandhi was a tougher nut. The field marshal waved at the crowd behind the old man. "You are responsible for all these people. If harm comes to them, you will be to blame."

"Why should harm come to them? They are not soldiers. They do not attack your men. I told that to one of your sergeants, and he understood it, and refrained from hindering us. Surely you, sir, an educated, cultured man, can see that what I say is self-evident truth."

Model turned his head to speak to his aide in German: "If we did not have Goebbels, this would be the one for his job." He shuddered to think of the propaganda victory Gandhi would win if he got away with flouting German ordinances. The whole countryside would be boiling with partisans in a week. And he had already managed to hoodwink some Germans into letting him do it!

Then Gandhi surprised him again. *Ich danke Ihnen, Herr Generalfeldmarschall, aber das glaube ich kein Kompliment zu sein,"* he said in slow but clear German: "I thank you, field marshal, but I believe that to be no compliment."

Having to hold his monocle in place helped Model keep his face straight. "Take it however you like," he said. "Get these people off the street, or they and you will face the consequences. We will do what you force us to."

"I force you to nothing. As for these people who follow, each does so of his or her own free will. We are free, and will show it, not by violence, but through firmness in truth."

Now Model listened with only half an ear. He had kept Gandhi talking long enough for the platoon he had ordered out to arrive. Half a dozen Sd.Kfz. 251 armored personnel carriers came clanking up. The men piled out of them. "Give me a firing line, three ranks deep," Model shouted. As the troopers scrambled to obey, he waved the halftracks into position behind them, all but blocking Qutb Road. The halftracks' commanders swiveled the machine guns at the front of the vehicles' troop compartments so they bore on the Indians.

Gandhi watched these preparations as calmly as if they had nothing to do with him. Again Model had to admire his calm. His followers were less able to keep fear from their faces. Very few, though, used the pause to slip away. Gandhi's discipline was a long way from the military sort, but effective all the same.

"Tell them to disperse now, and we can still get away without bloodshed," the field marshal said.

"We will shed no one's blood, sir. But we will continue on our pleasant journey. Moving carefully, we will, I think, be able to get between your large lorries there." Gandhi turned to wave his people forward once more.

"You insolent—" Rage choked Model, which was as well, for it kept him from cursing Gandhi like a fishwife. To give him time to master his temper, he plucked his monocle from his eye and began polishing the lens with a silk handkerchief. He replaced the monocle, started to jam the handkerchief back into his trouser pocket, then suddenly had a better idea.

"Come, Lasch," he said, and started toward the waiting German troops. About halfway to them, he dropped the handkerchief on the ground. He spoke in loud, simple German so his men and Gandhi could both follow: "If any Indians come past this spot, I wash my hands of them."

He might have known Gandhi would have a comeback ready. "That is what Pilate said also, you will recall, sir."

"Pilate washed his hands to evade responsibility," the field marshal answered steadily; he was in control of himself again. "I accept it: I am responsible to my Führer and to the *Oberkommando-Wehrmacht* for maintaining the Reich's control over India, and will do what I see fit to carry out that obligation."

For the first time since they had come to know each other, Gandhi looked sad. "I too, sir, have my responsibilities." He bowed slightly to Model.

Lasch chose that moment to whisper in his commander's ear: "Sir, what of our men over there? Had you planned to leave them in the line of fire?"

The field marshal frowned. He had planned to do just that; the wretches deserved no better, for being taken in by Gandhi. But Lasch had a point. The platoon might balk at shooting countrymen, if it came to that. "You men," Model said sourly, jabbing his marshal's baton at them, "fall in behind the armored personnel carriers, at once."

The Germans' boots pounded on the macadam as they dashed to obey. They were still all right, then, with a clear order in front of them. Something, Model thought, but not much.

He had also worried that the Indians would take advantage of the moment of confusion to press forward, but they did not. Gandhi and Nehru and a couple of other men were arguing among themselves. Model nodded once. Some of them knew he was in earnest, then. And Gandhi's followers' discipline, as the field marshal had thought a few minutes ago, was not of the military sort. He could not simply issue an order and know his will would be done.

───────────

"I issue no orders," Gandhi said. "Let each man follow his conscience as he will—what else is freedom?"

"They will follow *you* if you go forward, great-souled one," Nehru replied, "and that German, I fear, means to carry out his threat. Will you throw your life away, and those of your countrymen?"

"I will not throw my life away," Gandhi said, but before the men around him could relax he went on, "I will gladly give it, if freedom requires that. I am but one man. If I fall, others will surely carry on; perhaps the memory of me will serve to make them more steadfast."

He stepped forward.

"Oh, damnation," Nehru said softly, and followed.

For all his vigor, Gandhi was far from young. Nehru did not need to nod to the marchers close by him; of their own accord, they hurried ahead of the man who had led them for so long, forming with their bodies a barrier between him and the German guns.

He tried to go faster. "Stop! Leave me my place! What are you doing?" he cried, though in his heart he understood only too well.

"This once, they will not listen to you," Nehru said.

"But they must!" Gandhi peered through eyes dimmed now by tears as well as age. "Where is that stupid handkerchief? We must be almost to it!"

———

"For the last time, I warn you to halt!" Model shouted. The Indians still came on. The sound of their feet, sandal-clad or bare, was like a growing murmur on the pavement, very different from the clatter of German boots. "Fools!" the field marshal muttered under his breath. He turned to his men. "Take your aim!"

The advance slowed when the rifles came up; of that Model was certain. For a moment he thought that ultimate threat would be enough to bring the marchers to their senses. But then they advanced again. The Polish cavalry had shown that same reckless bravery, charging with lances and sabers and carbines against the German tanks. Model wondered whether the inhabitants of the *Reichsgeneralgouvernement* of Poland thought the gallantry worthwhile.

A man stepped on the field marshal's handkerchief. "Fire!" Model said.

A second passed, two. Nothing happened. Model scowled at his men. Gandhi's deviltry had got into them; sneaky as a Jew, he was turning the appearance of weakness into a strange kind of strength. But then trained discipline paid its dividend. One finger tightened on a Mauser trigger. A single shot rang out. As if it were a signal that recalled the other men to their duty, they too began to fire. From the armored personnel carriers, the machine guns started their deadly chatter. Model heard screams above the gunfire.

The volley smashed into the front ranks of marchers at close range. Men fell. Others ran, or tried to, only to be held by the power of the stream still advancing behind them. Once begun, the Germans methodically poured fire into the column of Indians. The march dissolved into a panic-stricken mob.

Gandhi still tried to press forward. A fleeing wounded man smashed into him, splashing him with blood and knocking him to the ground. Nehru and another man immediately lay down on top of him.

"Let me up! Let me up!" he shouted.

"No," Nehru screamed in his ear. "With shooting like this, you are in the safest spot you can be. We need you, and need you alive. Now we have martyrs around whom to rally our cause."

"Now we have dead husbands and wives, fathers and mothers. Who will tend to their loved ones?"

Gandhi had no time for more protest. Nehru and the other man hauled him to his feet and dragged him away. Soon they were among their people, all running now from the German guns. A bullet struck the back of the unknown man who was helping Gandhi escape. Gandhi heard the slap of the impact, felt the man jerk. Then the strong grip on him loosened as the man fell.

He tried to tear free from Nehru. Before he could, another Indian laid hold of him. Even at that horrid moment, he felt the irony of his predicament. All his life he had championed individual liberty, and here his own followers were robbing him of his. In other circumstances, it might have been funny.

"In here!" Nehru shouted. Several people had already broken down the door to a shop and, Gandhi saw a moment later, the rear exit as well.

Then he was hustled into the alley behind the shop, and through a maze of lanes which reminded him that old Delhi, unlike its British-designed sister city, was an Indian town through and through.

At last the nameless man with Gandhi and Nehru knocked on the back door of a tearoom. The woman who opened it gasped to recognize her unexpected guests, then pressed her hands together in front of her and stepped aside to let them in. "You will be safe here," the man said, "at least for a while. Now I must see to my own family."

"From the bottom of our hearts, we thank you," Nehru replied as the fellow hurried away. Gandhi said nothing. He was winded, battered, and filled with anguish at the failure of the march and at the suffering it had brought to so many marchers and to their kinsfolk.

The woman sat the two fugitive leaders at a small table in the kitchen, served them tea and cakes. "I will leave you now, best ones," she said quietly, "lest those out front wonder why I neglect them for so long."

Gandhi left the cake on his plate. He sipped the tea. Its warmth began to restore him physically, but the wound in his spirit would never heal. "The Armritsar massacre pales beside this," he said, setting down the empty cup. "There the British panicked and opened fire. This had nothing of panic about it. Model told me what he would do, and he did it." He shook his head, still hardly believing what he had just been through.

"So he did." Nehru had gobbled his cake like a starving wolf, and ate his companion's when he saw Gandhi did not want it. His once-immaculate white jacket and pants were torn, filthy, and blood-spattered; his cap sat awry on his head. But his eyes, usually so somber, were lit with a fierce glow. "And by his brutality, he has delivered himself into our hands. No one now can imagine the Germans have anything but their own interests at heart. We will gain followers all over the country. After this, not a wheel will turn in India."

"Yes, I will declare the *Satyagraha* campaign," Gandhi said. "Noncooperation will show how we reject foreign rule, and will cost the Germans dear because they will not be able to exploit us. The combination of nonviolence and determined spirit will surely shame them into granting us our liberty."

"There—you see." Encouraged by his mentor's rally, Nehru rose and came round the table to embrace the older man. "We will triumph yet."

"So we will," Gandhi said, and sighed heavily. He had pursued India's freedom for half his long life, and this change of masters was a setback he had not truly planned for, even after England and Russia fell. The British were finally beginning to listen to him when the Germans swept them aside. Now he had to begin anew. He sighed again. "It will cost our poor people dear, though."

———

"Cease firing," Model said. Few good targets were left on Qutb Road; almost all the Indians in the procession were down or had run from the guns.

Even after the bullets stopped, the street was far from silent. Most of the people the German platoon had shot were alive and shrieking: as if he needed more proof, the Russian campaign had taught the field marshal how hard human beings were to kill outright.

Still, the din distressed him, and evidently Lasch as well. "We ought to put them out of their misery," the major said.

"So we should." Model had a happy inspiration. "And I know just how. Come with me."

The two men turned their backs on the carnage and walked around the row of armored personnel carriers. As they passed the lieutenant commanding the platoon, Model nodded to him and said, "Well done."

The lieutenant saluted. "Thank you, sir." The soldiers in earshot nodded at one another: nothing bucked up the odds of getting promoted like performing under the commander's eye.

The Germans behind the armored vehicles were not so proud of themselves. They were the ones who had let the march get this big and come this far in the first place. Model slapped his boot with his field marshal's baton. "You all deserve courts-martial," he said coldly, glaring at them. "You know the orders concerning native assemblies, you there you were tagging along, more like sheepdogs than soldiers." He spat in disgust.

"But, sir—" began one of them—a sergeant-major. Model saw. He subsided in a hurry when Model's gaze swung his way.

"Speak," the field marshal urged. "Enlighten me—tell me what possessed you to act in the disgraceful way you did. Was it some evil spirit, perhaps? This country abounds with them, if you listen to the natives— as you all too obviously have been."

The sergeant-major flushed under Model's sarcasm, but finally burst out, "Sir, it didn't look to me as if they were up to any harm, that's all. The old man heading them up swore they were peaceful, and he looked too feeble to be anything but, if you take my meaning."

Model's smile had all the warmth of a Moscow December night. "And so in your wisdom you set aside the commands you had received. The results of that wisdom you hear now." The field marshal briefly let himself listen to the cries of the wounded, a sound the war had taught him to screen out. "Now then, come with me, yes, you, sergeant-major, and the rest of your shirkers too, or those of you who wish to avoid a court." As he had known they would, they all trooped after him. "There is your handiwork," he said, pointing to the shambles in the street. His voice hardened. "You are responsible for those people lying there—had you acted as you should, you would have broken up that march long before it ever got so far or so large. Now the least you can do is give those people their release." He set hands on hips, waited.

No one moved. "Sir?" the sergeant-major said faintly. He seemed to have become the group's spokesman.

Model made an impatient gesture. "Go on, finish them. A bullet in the back of the head will quiet them once and for all."

"In cold blood, sir?" The sergeant-major had not wanted to understand him before. Now he had no choice.

The field marshal was inexorable. "They—and you—disobeyed the Reich's commands. They made themselves liable to capital punishment the moment they gathered. You at least have the chance to atone, by carrying out this just sentence."

"I don't think I can," the sergeant-major muttered.

He was probably just talking to himself, but Model gave him no chance to change his mind. He turned to the lieutenant of the platoon that had broken the march. "Place this man under arrest." After the sergeant-major had been seized, Model turned his chill, monocled stare at the rest of the reluctant soldiers. "Any others?"

Two more men let themselves be arrested rather than draw their weapons. The field marshal nodded to the others. "Carry out your orders." He had an afterthought. "If you find Gandhi or Nehru out there, bring them to me alive."

The Germans moved out hesitantly. They were no *Einsatzkommandos*, and not used to this kind of work. Some looked away as they administered the first *coup de grace*; one missed as a result, and had his bullet ricochet off the pavement and almost hit a comrade. But as the soldiers worked their way up Qutb Road they became quicker, more confident, and more competent. War was like that. Model thought. So soon one became used to what had been unimaginable.

After a while the flat cracks died away, but from lack of targets rather than reluctance. A few at a time, the soldiers returned to Model. "No sign of the two leaders?" he asked. They all shook their heads.

"Very well—dismissed. And obey your orders like good Germans henceforward."

"No further reprisals?" Lasch asked as the relieved troopers hurried away.

"No, let them go. They carried out their part of the bargain, and I will meet mine. I am a fair man, after all, Dieter."

"Very well, sir."

———

Gandhi listened with undisguised dismay as the shopkeeper babbled out his tale of horror. "This is madness!" he cried.

"I doubt Field Marshal Model, for his part, understands the principle of *ahimsa*," Nehru put in. Neither Gandhi nor he knew exactly where they were: a safe house somewhere not far from the center of Delhi was the best guess he could make. The men who brought the shopkeeper were masked. What one did not know, one could not tell the Germans if captured.

"Neither do you," the older man replied, which was true; Nehru had a more pragmatic nature than Gandhi. Gandhi went on, "Rather more to the point, neither do the British. And Model, to speak to, seemed no different from any high-ranking British military man. His specialty has made him harsh and rigid, but he is not stupid and does not appear unusually cruel."

"Just a simple soldier, doing his job." Nehru's irony was palpable.

"He must have gone insane," Gandhi said; it was the only explanation that made even the slightest sense of the massacre of the wounded.

"Undoubtedly he will be censured when news of this atrocity reaches Berlin, as General Dyer was by the British after Armritsar."

"Such is to be hoped." But again Nehru did not sound hopeful.

"How could it be otherwise, after such an appalling action? What government, what leaders could fail to be filled with humiliation and remorse at it?"

———

Model strode into the mess. The officers stood and raised their glasses in salute. "Sit, sit," the field marshal growled, using gruffness to hide his pleasure.

An Indian servant brought him a fair imitation of roast beef and Yorkshire pudding: better than they were eating in London these days, he thought. The servant was silent and unsmiling, but Model would only have noticed more about him had he been otherwise. Servants were supposed to assume a cloak of invisibility.

When the meal was done. Model took out his cigar-case. The *Waffen-SS* officer on his left produced a lighter. Model leaned forward, puffed a cigar into life. "My thanks, *Brigadeführer*," the field marshal said. He had little use for SS titles of rank, but brigade-commander was at least recognizably close to brigadier.

"Sir, it is my great pleasure," Jürgen Stroop declared. "You could not have handled things better. A lesson for the Indians—less than they deserve, too" (he also took no notice of the servant) "and a good one for your men as well. We train ours harshly too."

Model nodded. He knew about SS training methods. No one denied the daring of the *Waffen-SS* divisions. No one (except the SS) denied that the *Wehrmacht* had better officers.

Stroop drank. "A lesson," he repeated in a pedantic tone that went oddly with the SS's reputation for aggressiveness. "Force is the only thing the racially inferior can understand. Why, when I was in Warsaw—"

That had been four or five years ago, Model suddenly recalled. Stroop had been a *Brigadeführer* then too, if memory served; no wonder he was still one now, even after all the hard fighting since. He was lucky not to be a buck private. Imagine letting a pack of desperate, starving Jews chew up the finest troops in the world.

And imagine, afterward, submitting a 75-page operations report bound in leather and grandiosely called *The Warsaw Ghetto Is No More.* And imagine, with all that, having the crust to boast about it afterward. No wonder the man sounded like a pompous ass. He *was* a pompous ass, and an inept butcher to boot. Model had done enough butchery before today's work—anyone who fought in Russia learned all about butchery—but he had never botched it.

He did not revel in it, either. He wished Stroop would shut up. He thought about telling the *Brigadeführer* he would sooner have been listening to Gandhi. The look on the fellow's face, he thought, would be worth it. But no. One could never be sure who was listening. Better safe.

———

The shortwave set crackled to life. It was in a secret cellar, a tiny dark hot room lit only by the glow of its dial and by the red end of the cigarette in its owner's mouth. The Germans had made not turning in a radio a capital crime. Of course, Gandhi thought, harboring him was also a capital crime. That weighed on his conscience. But the man knew the risk he was taking.

The fellow (Gandhi knew him only as Lai) fiddled with the controls. "Usually we listen to the Americans," he said. "There is some hope of truth from them. But tonight you want to hear Berlin."

"Yes," Gandhi said. "I must learn what action is to be taken against Model."

"If any," Nehru added. He was once again impeccably attired in white, which made him the most easily visible object in the cellar.

"We have argued this before," Gandhi said tiredly. "No government can uphold the author of a cold-blooded slaughter of wounded men and women. The world would cry out in abhorrence."

Lai said, "That government controls too much of the world already." He adjusted the tuning knob again. After a burst of static, the strains of a Strauss waltz filled the little room. Lai grunted in satisfaction. "We are a little early yet."

After a few minutes, the incongruously sweet music died away. "This is Radio Berlin's English-language channel," an announcer declared. "In a moment, the news program." Another German tune rang out: the Horst Wessel Song. Gandhi's nostrils flared with distaste.

A new voice came over the air. "Good day. This is William Joyce." The nasal Oxonian accent was that of the archetypical British aristocrat, now vanished from India as well as England. It was the accent that flavored Gandhi's own English, and Nehru's as well. In fact, Gandhi had heard, Joyce was a New York-born rabblerouser of Irish blood who also happened to be a passionately sincere Nazi. The combination struck the Indian as distressing.

"What did the English used to call him?" Nehru murmured. "Lord Haw-Haw?"

Gandhi waved his friend to silence. Joyce was reading the news, or what the Propaganda Ministry in Berlin wanted to present to English-speakers as the news.

Most of it was on the dull side: a trade agreement between Manchukuo, Japanese-dominated China, and Japanese-dominated Siberia; advances by German-supported French troops against American-supported French troops in a war by proxy in the African jungles. Slightly more interesting was the German warning about American interference in the East Asia Co-Prosperity Sphere.

One day soon, Gandhi thought sadly, the two mighty powers of the Old World would turn on the one great nation that stood between them. He feared the outcome. Thinking herself secure behind ocean barriers, the United States had stayed out of the European war. Now the war was bigger than Europe, and the oceans barriers no longer, but highways for her foes.

Lord Haw-Haw droned on and on. He gloated over the fate of rebels hunted down in Scotland: they were publicly hanged. Nehru leaned forward. "Now," he guessed. Gandhi nodded.

But the commentator passed on to unlikely sounding boasts about the prosperity of Europe under the New Order. Against his will, Gandhi felt anger rise in him. Were Indians too insignificant to the Reich even to be mentioned?

More music came from the radio: the first bars of the other German anthem, "Deutschland über Alles." William Joyce said solemnly, "And now, a special announcement from the Ministry for Administration of Acquired Territories. *Reichsminister* Reinhard Heydrich commends Field Marshal Walther Model's heroic suppression of insurrection in India, and warns that his leniency will not be repeated."

"Leniency!" Nehru and Gandhi burst out together, the latter making it into as much of a curse as he allowed himself.

As if explaining to them, the voice on the radio went on, "Henceforward, hostages will be taken at the slightest sound of disorder, and will be executed forthwith if it continues. Field Marshal Model has also placed a reward of 50,000 rupees on the capture of the criminal revolutionary Gandhi, and 25,000 on the capture of his henchman Nehru. "

"Deutschland über Alles" rang out again, to signal the end of the announcement. Joyce went on to the next piece of news. "Turn that off," Nehru said after a moment. Lai obeyed, plunging the cellar into complete darkness. Nehru surprised Gandhi by laughing. "I have never before been the henchman of a criminal revolutionary."

The older man might as well not have heard him. "They commended him," he said. "Commended!" Disbelief put the full tally of his years in his voice, which usually sounded much stronger and younger.

"What will you do?" Lai asked quietly. A match flared, dazzling in the dark, as he lit another cigarette.

"They shall not govern India in this fashion," Gandhi snapped. "Not a soul will cooperate with them from now on. We outnumber them a thousand to one; what can they accomplish without us? We shall use that to full advantage."

"I hope the price is not more than the people can pay," Nehru said.

"The British shot us down too, and we were on our way toward prevailing," Gandhi said stoutly. As he would not have a few days before, though, he added, "So do I."

———

Field Marshal Model scowled and yawned at the same time. The pot of tea that should have been on his desk was nowhere to be found. His stomach growled. A plate of rolls should have been beside the teapot.

"How am I supposed to get anything done without breakfast?" he asked rhetorically (no one was in the office to hear him complain). Rhetorical complaint was not enough to satisfy him. "Lasch!" he shouted.

"Sir?" The aide came rushing in.

Model jerked his chin at the empty space on his desk where the silver tray full of good things should have been. "What's become of what's-his-name? Naoroji, that's it. If he's home with a hangover, he could have had the courtesy to let us know."

"I will enquire with the liaison officer for native personnel, sir, and also have the kitchen staff send you up something to eat." Lasch picked up a telephone, spoke into it. The longer he talked, the less happy he looked. When he turned back to the field marshal, his expression was a good match for the stony one Model often wore. He said, "None of the locals has shown up for work today, sir."

"What? None?" Model's frown made his monocle dig into his cheek. He hesitated. "I will feel better if you tell me some new hideous malady has broken out among them."

Lasch spoke with the liaison officer again. He shook his head. "Nothing like that, sir, or at least," he corrected himself with the caution that made him a good aide, "nothing Captain Wechsler knows about."

Model's phone rang again. It startled him; he jumped. *"Bitte?"* he growled into the mouthpiece, embarrassed at starting even though only Lasch had seen. He listened. Then he growled again, in good earnest this time. He slammed the phone down. "That was our railway officer. Hardly any natives are coming in to the station."

The phone rang again. *"Bitte?"* This time it was a swearword. Model snarled, cutting off whatever the man on the other end was saying, and hung up. "The damned clerks are staying out too," he shouted at Lasch, as if it were the major's fault. "I know what's wrong with the blasted locals, by God—an overdose of Gandhi, that's what."

"We should have shot him down in that riot he led," Lasch said angrily.

"Not for lack of effort that we didn't," Model said. Now that he saw where his trouble was coming from, he began thinking like a General Staff-trained officer again. That discipline went deep in him. His voice was cool and musing as he corrected his aide: "It was no riot, Dieter. That man is a skilled agitator. Armed with no more than words, he gave the British fits. Remember that the Führer started out as an agitator too."

"Ah, but the Führer wasn't above breaking heads to back up what he said." Lasch smiled reminiscently, and raised a fist. He was a Munich man, and wore on his sleeve the hashmark that showed Party membership before 1933.

But the field marshal said, "You think Gandhi doesn't? His way is to break them from the inside out, to make his foes doubt themselves. Those soldiers who took courts rather than obey their commanding officer had their heads broken, wouldn't you say? Think of him as a Russian tank commander, say, rather than as a political agitator. He is fighting us every bit as much as much as the Russians did."

Lasch thought about it. Plainly, he did not like it. "A coward's way of fighting."

"The weak cannot use the weapons of the strong." Model shrugged. "He does what he can, and skillfully. But I can make his backers doubt themselves, too; see if I don't."

"Sir?"

"We'll start with the railway workers. They are the most essential to have back on the job, yes? Get a list of names. Cross off every twentieth one. Send a squad to each of those homes, haul the slackers out, and shoot them in the street. If the survivors don't report tomorrow, do it again. Keep at it every day until they go back to work or no workers are left."

"Yes, sir." Lasch hesitated. At last he asked, "Are you sure, sir?"

"Have you a better idea, Dieter? We have a dozen divisions here; Gandhi has the whole subcontinent. I have to convince them in a hurry that obeying me is a better idea than obeying him. Obeying is what counts. I don't care a *pfennig* as to whether they love me. *Oderint, dum metuant.*"

"Sir?" The major had no Latin.

"'Let them hate, so long as they fear.'"

"Ah," Lasch said. "Yes, I like that." He fingered his chin as he thought. "In aid of which, the Muslims hereabouts like the Hindus none too well. I daresay we could use them to help hunt Gandhi down."

"Now that *I* like," Model said. "Most of our Indian Legion lads are Muslims. They will know people, or know people who know people. And"—the field marshal chuckled cynically—"the reward will do no harm, either. Now get those orders out, and ring up Legion-Colonel Sadar. We'll get those feelers in motion—and if they pay off, you'll probably have earned yourself a new pip on your shoulderboards."

"Thank you very much, sir!"

"My pleasure. As I say, you'll have earned it. So long as things go as they should, I am a very easy man to get along with. Even Gandhi could, if he wanted to. He will end up having caused a lot of people to be killed because he does not."

"Yes, sir," Lasch agreed. "If only he would see that, since we have won India from the British, we will not turn around and tamely yield it to those who could not claim it for themselves."

"You're turning into a political philosopher now, Dieter?"

"Ha! Not likely." But the major looked pleased as he picked up the phone.

———

"My dear friend, my ally, my teacher, we are losing," Nehru said as the messenger scuttled away from this latest in a series of what were hopefully called safe houses. "Day by day, more people return to their jobs."

Gandhi shook his head, slowly, as if the motion caused him physical pain. "But they must not. Each one who cooperates with the Germans sets back the day of his own freedom."

"Each one who fails to ends up dead," Nehru said dryly. "Most men lack your courage, great-souled one. To them, that carries more weight than the other. Some are willing to resist, but would rather take up arms than the restraint of *Satyagraha*."

"If they take up arms, they will be defeated. The British could not beat the Germans with guns and tanks and planes; how shall we? Besides, if we shoot a German here and there, we give them the excuse they need to strike at us. When one of their lieutenants was waylaid last month, their bombers leveled a village in reprisal. Against those who fight through nonviolence, they have no such justification."

"They do not seem to need one, either," Nehru pointed out. Before Gandhi could reply to that, a man burst into the hovel where they were hiding. "You must flee!" he cried. "The Germans have found this place! They are coming. Out with me, quick! I have a cart waiting."

Nehru snatched up the canvas bag in which he carried his few belongings. For a man used to being something of a dandy, the haggard life of a fugitive came hard. Gandhi had never wanted much. Now that he had nothing, that did not disturb him. He rose calmly, followed the man who had come to warn them.

"Hurry!" the fellow shouted as they scrambled into his oxcart while the hump-backed cattle watched indifferently with their liquid brown eyes. When Gandhi and Nehru were lying in the cart, the man piled blankets and straw mats over them. He scrambled up to take the reins, saying, *"Inshallah,* we shall be safely away from here before the platoon arrives." He flicked a switch over the backs of the cattle. They lowed indignantly. The cart rattled away.

Lying in the sweltering semi-darkness under the concealment the man had draped on him, Gandhi peered through chinks, trying to figure out where in Delhi he was going next. He had played the game more than once these last few weeks, though he knew doctrine said he should not. The less he knew, the less he could reveal. Unlike most men, though, he was confident he could not be made to talk against his will.

"We are using the technique the American Poe called the 'purloined letter,' I see," he remarked to Nehru. "We will be close by the German barracks. They will not think to look for us there."

The younger man frowned. "I did not know we had safe houses there," he said. Then he relaxed, as well as he could when folded into too small a space. "Of course, I do not pretend to know everything there is to know about such matters. It would be dangerous if I did."

"I was thinking much the same myself, though with me as subject of the sentence." Gandhi laughed quietly. "Try as we will, we always have ourselves at the center of things, don't we?"

He had to raise his voice to finish. An armored personnel carrier came rumbling and rattling toward them, getting louder as it approached. The silence when the driver suddenly killed the engine was a startling contrast to the previous racket. Then there was noise again, as soldiers shouted in German.

"What are they saying?" Nehru asked.

"Hush," Gandhi said absently, not from ill manners, but out of the concentration he needed to follow German at all. After a moment he resumed, "They are swearing at a black-bearded man, asking why he flagged them down."

"Why would anyone flag down German sol—" Nehru began, then stopped in abrupt dismay. The fellow who had burst into their hiding-place wore a bushy black beard. "We had better get out of—" Again Nehru broke off in midsentence, this time because the oxcart driver was throwing off the coverings that concealed his two passengers.

Nehru started to get to his feet so he could try to scramble out and run. Too late—a rifle barrel that looked wide as a tunnel was shoved in his face as a German came dashing up to the cart. The big curved magazine said the gun was one of the automatic assault rifles that had wreaked such havoc among the British infantry. A burst would turn a man into bloody hash. Nehru sank back in despair.

Gandhi, less spry than his friend, had only sat up in the bottom of the cart. "Good day, gentlemen," he said to the Germans peering down at him. His tone took no notice of their weapons.

"Down." The word was in such gutturally accented Hindi that Gandhi hardly understood it, but the accompanying gesture with a rifle was unmistakable.

Face a mask of misery, Nehru got out of the cart. A German helped Gandhi descend. *"Danke,"* he said. The soldier nodded gruffly. He pointed the barrel of his rifle—toward the armored personnel carrier.

"My rupees!" the black-bearded man shouted.

Nehru turned on him, so quickly he almost got shot for it. "Your thirty pieces of silver, you mean," he cried.

"Ah, a British education," Gandhi murmured. No one was listening to him.

"My rupees," the man repeated. He did not understand Nehru; so often, Gandhi thought sadly, that was at the root of everything.

"You'll get them," promised the sergeant leading the German squad. Gandhi wondered if he was telling the truth. Probably so, he decided. The British had had centuries to build a network of Indian clients. Here but a matter of months, the Germans would need all they could find.

"In." The soldier with a few words of Hindi nodded to the back of the armored personnel carrier. Up close, the vehicle took on a war-battered individuality its kind had lacked when they were just big, intimidating shapes rumbling down the highway. It was bullet-scarred and patched in a couple of places, with sheets of steel crudely welded on.

Inside, the jagged lips of the bullet holes had been hammered down so they did not gouge a man's back. The carrier smelled of leather, sweat, tobacco, smokeless powder, and exhaust fumes. It was crowded, all the more so with the two Indians added to its usual contingent. The motor's roar when it started up challenged even Gandhi's equanimity.

Not, he thought with uncharacteristic bitterness, that that equanimity had done him much good.

━━━━━━━━━

"They are here, sir," Lasch told Model, then, at the field marshal's blank look, amplified: "Gandhi and Nehru."

Model's eyebrow came down toward his monocle. "I won't bother with Nehru. Now that we have him, take him out and give him a noodle"—army slang for a bullet in the back of the neck—"but don't waste my time over him. Gandhi, now, is interesting. Fetch him in."

"Yes, sir." The major sighed. Model smiled. Lasch did not find Gandhi interesting. Lasch would never carry a field marshal's baton, not if he lived to be ninety.

Model waved away the soldiers who escorted Gandhi into his office. Either of them could have broken the little Indian like a stick. "Have a care," Gandhi said. "If I am the desperate criminal bandit you have styled me, I may overpower you and escape."

"If you do, you will have earned it," Model retorted. "Sit, if you care to."

"Thank you." Gandhi sat. "They took Jawaharlal away. Why have you summoned me instead?"

"To talk for a while, before you join him." Model saw that Gandhi knew what he meant, and that the old man remained unafraid. Not that that would change anything, Model thought, although he respected his opponent's courage the more for his keeping it in the last extremity.

"I will talk, in the hope of persuading you to have mercy on my people. For myself I ask nothing."

Model shrugged. "I was as merciful as the circumstances of war allowed, until you began your campaign against us. Since then, I have done what I needed to restore order. When it returns, I may be milder again."

"You seem a decent man," Gandhi said, puzzlement in his voice. "How can you so callously massacre people who have done you no harm?"

"I never would have, had you not urged them to folly."

"Seeking freedom is not folly."

"It is when you cannot gain it—and you cannot. Already your people are losing their stomach for—what do you call it? Passive resistance?

A silly notion. A passive resister simply ends up dead, with no chance to hit back at his foe. "

That hit a nerve, Model thought. Gandhi's voice was less detached as he answered, *"Satyagraha* strikes the oppressor's soul, not his body. You must be without honor or conscience, to fail to feel your victim's anguish."

Nettled in turn, the field marshal snapped, "I have honor. I follow the oath of obedience I swore with the army to the Führer and through him to the Reich. I need consider nothing past that."

Now Gandhi's calm was gone. "But he is a madman! What has he done to the Jews of Europe?"

"Removed them," Model said matter-of-factly; *Einsatzgruppe* B had followed Army Group Central to Moscow and beyond. "They were capitalists or Bolsheviks, and either way enemies of the Reich. When an enemy falls into a man's hands, what else is there to do but destroy him, lest he revive to turn the tables one day?"

Gandhi had buried his face in his hands. Without looking at Model, he said, "Make him a friend."

"Even the British knew better than that, or they would not have held India as long as they did," the field marshal snorted. "They must have begun to forget, though, or your movement would have got what it deserves long ago. You first made the mistake of confusing us with them long ago, by the way." He touched a fat dossier on his desk.

"When was that?" Gandhi asked indifferently. The man was beaten now. Model thought with a touch of pride: he had succeeded where a generation of degenerate, decadent Englishmen had failed. Of course, the field marshal told himself, he had beaten the British too.

He opened the dossier, riffled through it. "Here we are," he said, nodding in satisfaction. "It was after *Kristallnacht,* eh, in 1938, when you urged the German Jews to play at the same game of passive resistance you were using here. Had they been fools enough to try it, we would have thanked you, you know: it would have let us bag the enemies of the Reich all the more easily."

"Yes, I made a mistake," Gandhi said. Now he was looking at the field marshal, looking at him with such fierceness that for a moment Model thought he would attack him despite advanced age and effete philosophy. But Gandhi only continued sorrowfully, "I made the mistake of thinking I faced a regime ruled by conscience, one that could at the very least be shamed into doing that which is right."

Model refused to be baited. "We do what is right for our *Volk,* for our Reich. We are meant to rule, and rule we do—as you see." The field marshal tapped the dossier again. "You could be sentenced to death for this earlier meddling in the affairs of the Fatherland, you know, even without these later acts of insane defiance you have caused."

"History will judge us," Gandhi warned as the field marshal rose to have him taken away.

Model smiled then. "Winners write history." He watched the two strapping German guards lead the old man off. "A very good morning's work," the field marshal told Lasch when Gandhi was gone. "What's on the menu for lunch?"

"Blood sausage and sauerkraut, I believe."

"Ah, good. Something to look forward to." Model sat down. He went back to work.

THE GIRL WHO TOOK
LESSONS

Karen Vaughan looked at her watch. "Oh my goodness, I'm late," she exclaimed, for all the world like the White Rabbit. Her fork clattered on her plate as she got up from the table. Two quick strides took her to her husband. She pecked him on the cheek. "I've got to run, Mike. Have fun with the dishes. See you a little past ten."

He was still eating. By the time he'd swallowed the bite of chicken breast he'd been chewing, Karen was almost out the door. "What is it tonight?" he called after her. "The cake decorating class?"

She frowned at him for forgetting. "No, that's Tuesdays. Tonight it's law for non-lawyers."

"Oh, that's right. Sorry." The apology, he feared, went for naught; Karen's heels were already clicking on the stairs as she headed for the garage. Sighing, he finished dinner. He didn't feel especially guilty about not being able to keep track of all his wife's classes. He wondered how she managed herself.

He squirted Ivory Liquid on a sponge, attacked the dishes in the sink. When they were done, he settled into the rocking chair with the latest Tom Clancy thriller. His hobbies were books and tropical fish, both of which kept him close to the condo. After spending the first couple of years of their marriage wondering just what Karen's hobbies were, he'd decided her main one was taking lessons. Nothing that had happened since made him want to change his mind.

Horseback riding, French cuisine, spreadsheets—what it was didn't matter, Mike thought in the couple of minutes before the novel completely engrossed him. If UCLA Extension or a local junior college or anybody else offered a course that piqued her interest, Karen would sign up for it. Once in a while, she'd sign him up too. He'd learned to waltz that way. He didn't suppose it had done him any lasting harm.

Tonight's chicken breasts, sautéed in a white wine sauce with fresh basil, garlic, and onions, were a legacy of the French cooking class. That was one that had left behind some lasting good. So had the spreadsheet course, which helped Karen get a promotion at the accounting firm she worked for. But she hadn't even looked at the epee in the hall closet for at least three years.

Mike shrugged. If taking lessons was what she enjoyed, that was all right with him. They could afford it, and he'd come to look forward to his frequent early evening privacy. Then he started turning pages in his page-turner, and the barking thunder of assault rifles made him stop worrying about his wife's classes.

He jumped at the noise of her key in the deadbolt. By the time she got in, though, he was back to the real world. He got up and gave her a hug. "How'd it go?"

"All right, I guess. We're going to get a quiz next week, he said. God knows when I'll have time to study." She said that whenever she had any kind of test coming up. She always did fine.

While she was talking, she hung her suit jacket in the hall closet. Then she walked down the hall to the bathroom, shedding more clothes as she went. By the time she got to the shower door, she was naked.

As he always did, Mike followed appreciatively, picking up after her. He liked to look at her. She was a natural blonde, and not a pound— well, not five pounds—heavier than the day they got married. He wished he could say the same.

He took off his own clothes while she was getting clean, scratched at the thick black hair on his chest and stomach. He sighed. Yes, he was an increasingly well-fed bear these days.

"Your turn," Karen said, emerging pink and glowing.

She was wearing a teddy instead of pajamas when he came back into the bedroom. "Hi, there," he said, grinning. After a decade of living together, a lot of their communication went on without words. She turned off the light as he hurried toward the bed.

Afterward, drifting toward sleep, he had a thought that had occurred to him before: she made love like an accountant. He'd never said that to her, for fear of hurting her feelings, but he meant it as a compliment. She was competent and orderly in bed as out, and if there were few surprises there were also few disappointments. "No, indeed," he muttered.

"What?" Karen asked. Only a long, slow breath answered her.

Their days went on in that regular fashion, except for the occasional Tuesday when Karen came home with bits of icing in her hair. But the magnificent chocolate cake she did up for Mike's birthday showed she had really got something out of that class.

Then, out of the blue, her firm decided to send her back to Chicago for three weeks. "We just got a big multinational for a client," she explained to Mike, "and fighting off a takeover bid has left their taxes screwed up like you wouldn't believe."

"And your people want *you* to go help straighten things out?" he said. "That's a feather in your cap."

"I'll just be part of a team, you know."

"All the same."

"I know," she said, "but three weeks! All my classes will go to hell. And," she added, as if suddenly remembering, "I'll miss you."

Typical, thought Mike, to get mentioned after the precious classes. But he wasn't too annoyed. He knew Karen was like that. "I'll miss you too," he said, and meant it; they hadn't been apart for more than a couple of days at a time since they'd been married.

Next Monday morning, he made one of love's ultimate sacrifices— he took a half-day off from his engineering job to drive her to LAX through rush-hour traffic. They kissed in the unloading zone till the fellow in the car in back of them leaned on his horn. Then Karen scooped her bags out of the trunk and dashed into the terminal.

While she was away, Mike did a lot of the clichéd things men do when apart from their wives. He worked late several times; going home seemed less attractive without anyone to go home to. He rediscovered all the reasons why he didn't like fast food or frozen entrees. He got horny and rented *Behind the Green Door,* only to find out few things were lonelier than watching a dirty movie by himself.

He talked with Karen every two or three days. Sometimes he'd call, sometimes she would. She called one of the nights he stayed late at the office and, when he called her the next day, accused him of having been out with a floozie. "'Bimbo' is the eighties word," he told her. They both laughed.

Just when he was eagerly looking forward to having her home, she let him know she'd have to stay another two weeks. "I'm sorry," she said, "but the situation here is so complicated that if we don't straighten it out now once and for all, we'll have to keep messing with it for the next five years."

"What am I supposed to do, pitch a fit?" He felt like it. "I'll see you in two weeks." From his tone of voice, she might have been talking about the twenty-first century—and the late twenty-first century, at that.

However much they tried not to, the days crawled by. Another clichéd thing for a man to do is hug his wife silly when she finally gets off her plane. Mike did it.

"Well," Karen said, once she had her breath back. "Hello."

He looked at his watch. "Come on," he said, herding her toward the baggage claim. "I made reservations at the Szechuan place we go to, assuming your flight would be an hour late. And since you were only forty minutes late—"

"—we have a chance to get stuck on the freeway instead," Karen finished for him. "Sounds good. Let's do it."

"No, I told you, we'll have dinner first," he said. She snorted. The world—even traffic—was a lot easier to handle after spicy pork and a couple of cold Tsingtao beers. Mike said so, adding, "The good company doesn't hurt, either." Karen was looking out the window. She didn't seem to have heard him.

When they got back to the condo, she frowned for a few seconds. Then her face cleared. She pointed to Mike's fish tanks. "I've been gone too long. I hear all the pumps and filters and things bubbling away. I'll have to get used to screening them out again."

"You've been gone too long." Mike set down her suitcases. He hugged her again. "That says it all." His right hand cupped her left buttock. "Almost all, anyway."

She drew away from him. "Let me get cleaned up first. I've been in cars and a plane and airports all day long, and I feel really grubby."

"Sure." They walked to the bedroom together. He took off his clothes while she was getting out of hers. He flopped down on the bed. "After five weeks, I can probably just about stand waiting another fifteen minutes."

"Okay," she said. She went into the bathroom. He listened to the shower running, then to the blow dryer's electric whine. When she came back, one of her eyebrows quirked. "From the look of you, I'd say you could just barely wait."

She got down on the bed beside him. After a while, Mike noticed long abstinence wasn't the only thing cranking his excitement to a pitch he hadn't felt since their honeymoon and maybe not then. Every time, every place she touched him, her caress seemed a sugared flame. And he had all he could do not to explode the instant she took him in her mouth. Snakes wished for tongues like that, he thought dizzily.

When at last he entered her, it was like sliding into heated honey. Again he thought he would come at once. But her smooth yet irresistible motion urged him on and on and on to a peak of pleasure he had never imagined, and then to a place past that. Like a thunderclap, his climax left him stunned.

"My God," he gasped, stunned still, "you've been taking lessons!"

From only a few inches away, he watched her face change. For a moment, he did not know what the change meant. Of all the expressions she might put on, calculation was the last he expected right now. Then she answered him. "Yes," she said, "I have…"

The law for non-lawyers course did not go to waste. A couple of months later, she did their divorce herself.

BUT IT DOES MOVE

Spring in Rome. Mild, mostly sunny days. Pretty women's smiles, as bright as the sun. Plants putting forth new leaves—a green almost painfully beautiful. A torrent of birdsong. Music in the air along with the birdsong, after it fell silent as well. Monuments of mellowed marble, some close to 2,000 years old.

What heart could know such marvels without rejoicing?

Galileo Galilei's heart had no trouble at all.

With all that heart, Galileo wished he were back in Florence, where he belonged. Was the sun less brilliant there? Were the pretty women's smiles? Did the birds not sing there? Had they no musicians, no monuments? Of course not!

Had they no Holy Inquisition in Florence? They did—they did indeed. But Pope Urban VIII was not convinced it had done all it should concerning Galileo. And so the astronomer had been summoned to Rome for interrogation, like any common criminal.

Muttering to himself, Galileo shook his head. Summoned like a criminal? Yes. Like a common criminal? No. The Inquisition didn't bother with common criminals. He wished with all his heart that it hadn't bothered with him.

When the summons came, he pleaded age. Was he not sixty-eight? Travel truly wasn't easy for him any more. He'd pleaded ill health. He was not a well man; who approaching his threescore and ten was what he had been earlier in life? Three learned Florentine physicians attested to his infirmities. There was plague in Florence. He would have had to spend time in quarantine before being suffered to enter the Papal States.

Did the Inquisition care about any of that? Galileo did some more muttering. As well expect Michelangelo's David to weep as the Inquisition to care!

And bending Galileo to its will—showing that it had both the power and the right to bend him to its will—was part of his punishment. Worse would have befallen him had he refused the summons. He'd really thought he could get away with the *Dialogue Concerning the Two Chief World Systems*. He'd published it to much acclaim the summer before. But the Inquisition's summons to Rome was acclaim he would gladly have done without.

Here he was, though, like it or not. He'd lodged with Francesco Niccolini, the Tuscan ambassador, from the middle of February to the second week of April. That wasn't...so bad. But then the Inquisition decided he'd cooled his heels long enough. It ordered him to the palace that served as its headquarters and began to question him.

Even now, things could have been worse. He understood that, and thanked God they weren't. The Inquisition housed him in the quarters usually used by a prosecutor, not in the cells where they kept most prisoners. He could stroll around the courtyard if he liked. When the inquisitors questioned him, they used only words—they didn't put him to *the* question. All the same, they had the authority to torture him if they chose to, and the threat that they might hung in the air.

So yes, things could have been worse. But they also could have been better. He could have been free, for instance. This was what he got for trying to understand how the natural world worked?

Yes. This was what he got.

––––––––––

Sparrows hopped and fluttered in the courtyard. They hopped up to Galileo instead of fluttering away. People here fed them. They didn't net them and pluck them and bake them in pies. Galileo was fond of songbirds in pies, but he was also fond of the living birds. He ground a chunk of stale bread between his palms and scattered crumbs on the grass.

Chirping excitedly, the sparrows fell on the feast. More little birds hurried toward Galileo. He smiled thinly. Beggars were all the same, whether they wore feathers or ragged cloaks. If you gave to a few, they expected you to give to everyone.

He spread his hands, empty now. "Sorry, *amici*. That was all I had."

The birds flew away. But that wasn't because they understood what he said. Another man was approaching, and his red, flapping cardinal's robes had to be what made the birds take flight.

Nodding to Galileo, the newcomer said, "You are *Signor* Galilei, is it not so?"

"Yes, your Eminence." Galileo bent to kiss the cleric's ring. "Please forgive me, sir, but I fear you have the advantage of me." Whoever this fellow was, he wasn't one of the ten cardinals who'd been grilling him.

"No reason for you to know me." The churchman smiled. He was about Galileo's age. He had a long face and clever, melancholy eyes; he wore a neat white mustache and chin beard. His Italian, while accurate, was slow and gutturally accented. When he went on, he explained that: "My name is Sigismondo Gioioso—I translate the surname into your tongue. His Holiness the Pope summoned me from Vienna to help in the investigation of your case and in determining what should result from it."

"He did?" Galileo could have done without the honor, if that was what it was. "You have come a long way, your Eminence. Certainly my insignificant self is not worth such a journey." Galileo was anything but the most modest of men. But he did not want this scholarly cleric from beyond the Alps focusing attention on him like a convex lens focusing sunlight.

"Oh, but I believe you are, *Signor* Galilei," Cardinal Gioioso said. "Not only for the beliefs you hold, but also for the reasons you have for holding them."

"I hold no beliefs contrary to those accepted as true by the holy Catholic Church," Galileo said quickly. He had to say such things. He might be an old man, but he didn't want to die just yet, or to spend the rest of his days in some bleak and sordid prison cell, locked away not only from life but also from all possibilities of further research. No, he didn't want that one bit!

Sigismondo Gioioso smiled at him. "I have read the *Dialogue Concerning the Two Chief World Systems* with great interest and attentiveness. You are a fine writer, *Signor*—a fine writer indeed."

"You do me too much honor, your Eminence," Galileo mumbled.

"Do I? I think not," Gioioso replied. "And your support for the Copernican hypothesis therein is eloquent, truly eloquent. Salviati has much the better of the argument with Simplicio, who follows the long-accepted Ptolemaic view. Even the name you gave Simplicio suggests that you are unlikely to agree with the ideas he expresses."

Not for the first time lately, Galileo wished he'd called Simplicio something—anything—else. "I fear I was trying to be too clever when I wrote," he said. "Now that I look back on the book, I see I should have done a better job of balancing the arguments on both sides. I took a contrarian view, trying to make the worse case appear the better."

"That is what Aristophanes accused Socrates of doing," Cardinal Gioioso said. "But Socrates did not accuse himself of the same thing."

"No doubt you are right," said Galileo, who cared much less about Aristophanes' views than about those of Aristotle—which, along with Ptolemy's, had become part of the Church's doctrinal underpinnings. The astronomer hurried on: "I hope you also noted that I clearly stated in the dialogue's conclusion that it was impossible, based on what we currently know, to choose between the two competing world systems."

"I most assuredly did note that, yes," Sigismondo Gioioso said. Galileo winced in spite of himself. He'd never heard such devastating agreement in all his born days. The cardinal from Vienna continued, "An attentive reader might at that point be forgiven for doubting your complete sincerity."

"Do you think so, your Eminence?" Galileo exclaimed, as if the idea had never before occurred to him. As if? If only!

"Well, yes, I am afraid I do, actually," Gioioso answered. He didn't quite sound like a judge passing sentence—no, not quite. But then, instead of leaping on Galileo like a fierce dog, he shifted his ground: "What truly interests me, though, is how and why you have come to hold your, ah, interesting beliefs."

"Please, sir, these are the beliefs set forth in the *Dialogue*," Galileo said. "They are not mine. Of necessity, they cannot be mine, for they contradict those held by the Church, of which I am, and am proud to be, a loyal son."

"Of course," Cardinal Gioioso said—another agreement that undermined everything it claimed to agree with. "Would you be willing to talk with me about how you came to espouse these beliefs so strongly, even though you do not hold to them? As I say, that is what truly intrigues me."

"Talk with you?" Galileo asked cautiously. Sometimes the word meant what it said, no more and no less. Sometimes it was a euphemism for all the ingenuities the Inquisition could inflict on a man. Galileo didn't *think* Gioioso meant it that way…but it wouldn't do to find himself mistaken.

"Talk. That's all." By the cardinal's reassuring tone—and by his slightly crooked smile—he knew what Galileo feared. Well, how could he not? These were nervous times for the Catholic Church. Copernicanism wasn't the only threat it faced. Lutheranism and Calvinism also tore at its vitals. Threatened by such a vast radical conspiracy, how could the Church be anything but vigilant in its struggle against misbelievers of all stripes?

It couldn't—not if you asked any good and pious churchman.

"Talk?" Galileo asked again.

"Talk," Sigismondo Gioioso said firmly. "May God be my witness, *Signor*—nothing more." He crossed himself to seal the vow.

"Well, then, your Eminence, I am at your service." Galileo would have been at the cardinal's service in any case. But sometimes even the illusion of free will was pleasant.

Cardinal Gioioso's room was no larger, no finer, than the one the Inquisition had granted to Galileo. The astronomer reminded himself once more how lucky he was to have the quarters he enjoyed, not the dark, dank ones so many prisoners of the Inquisition failed to enjoy. Luck, of course, was relative; he could have been back in Florence, doing what he wanted.

"So good of you to join me, *Signor*," the cardinal said, as if Galileo's arrival were altogether unconstrained. "Will you take some wine with me? And these little cakes are very tasty. They tempt me into the sin of gluttony—indeed they do."

"*Grazie,* your Eminence," Galileo said. The cakes, rich with almond paste and honey, were as good as Cardinal Gioioso claimed. And the wine was sweet and strong. Galileo wagged a finger at the prelate. "I think you are trying to make me drunk."

"*In vino veritas?* Is that what you think I am after?" Gioioso asked.

"Truthfully, sir, I do not know what you are after," Galileo replied. Not knowing worried him. With the ten cardinals of the Inquisition who had interrogated him before, he knew exactly what they wanted: an abjuration from him. He was willing to give them one. A man had to live. And, abjuration or not, thanks to the printing press too many copies of the *Dialogue* were out there for the Church to hope to suppress it. His ideas would live, even if his work ended up in the Index of Prohibited Books.

"It is as I told you before," Sigismondo Gioioso said. "I wish to discuss with you, not so much your beliefs, but your reasons for holding them."

"I am in your hands," Galileo said. "What you want strikes me as curious, but I find myself in no position to complain."

"Which is to say, if the Holy Inquisition had not summoned you to Rome, you would sooner see me damned than give me the time of day," Gioioso observed. In a different tone of voice, words like those might have meant torture or death or torture and then death. The cardinal from Vienna sounded world-weary and amused, not hot to suppress heresy. He sounded like that, yes. Whether how he sounded had anything to do with how he felt, Galileo did not know him well enough to guess.

That being so, the astronomer hastened to point out the obvious: "You said this, your Eminence, not I."

"As Matthew tells us our Lord responded to Pontius Pilate," Cardinal Gioioso said.

"I am not our Lord, sir. Neither are you a Roman governor," Galileo said earnestly. "And so I entreat you—please do not twist my words or my meaning."

"I am not trying to put you in fear, *Signor*," Gioioso said. Trying or not, he was doing a good job. Maybe he wouldn't have, had Galileo and he met as man and man. Meeting as man and servant of the Inquisition… The cardinal, plainly a clever man, must have realized the difficulty. Doing his best to put Galileo at ease, he waved to a couch against the far wall of his room. "As I promised before, no harm will come to you from this. Sit down, please. Make yourself comfortable. Lie down, if you would rather."

Galileo did lie down—the couch had no back, and he didn't feel like leaning against the painted plaster of the wall. Cardinal Gioioso dragged a chair over alongside the couch so they could talk conveniently. Then, instead of sitting down, he poured himself another cup of wine. When he raised a questioning eyebrow, Galileo nodded.

"I thank you," Galileo said after Gioioso gave him the fresh cup. "How many ordinary men can boast they have had a cardinal pour wine for them with his own hands?"

"Whatever else you may be, you are not an ordinary man," Sigismondo Gioioso said.

Galileo waved that aside. "You know what I mean. How many secular men, I should say, can make that boast?"

"*Not* an ordinary man," Gioioso repeated, as if the astronomer hadn't spoken. "And part of what interests me is how you became so *extra*ordinary. Tell me of your parents. Tell me of the family in which you grew up." He steepled his fingertips, visibly composing himself to listen and to absorb whatever Galileo said.

"I am the eldest of seven—I had two brothers and four sisters, though not all, sadly, remain among the living," Galileo answered. "My father, God rest his soul, was among the best lutanists of his generation. He wrote on both the theory and the practice of music, and also on mathematics."

"So you sought to follow in his footsteps? To outdo him if you could?" Gioioso asked.

"Actually, your Eminence, when I was young I thought of joining the priesthood, but my father had other plans for me. He hoped I would become a doctor. I was something of a musician in those days myself, but my father made it plain to me keeping afloat at that trade was far from easy," Galileo said.

"You would have ornamented the field of medicine. And you would assuredly have ornamented our holy Catholic Church," Cardinal Gioioso said.

"I also thought of becoming a painter," Galileo remarked.

"You were a butterfly," Gioioso remarked.

"I was," Galileo agreed, "until I chanced to light on mathematics myself. I had just begun at the University of Pisa, and after that I knew what I wanted to do with my life. No—I knew what I had to do."

"Your father had written on mathematics."

"*Sì.*"

"But he did not want you following in his footsteps?"

"Not one bit, your Eminence."

"Why not? Did you not resent him for trying to keep you away from something you proved to love?"

"He told me a musician would always have trouble getting enough to eat, but a mathematician was sure to starve. How can you be angry at a man who wants you to have more food on your table than he had on his?"

"Believe me, *Signor,* a great many men would find it the easiest thing in the world," Sigismondo Gioioso said.

"I hope I am not so dead to honor and respect as to become one of them," Galileo said.

"Yes—one always hopes," Gioioso said enigmatically.

"What do you mean, your Eminence?"

Instead of answering, the cardinal said, "I notice you have told me next to nothing of your mother."

Galileo scratched his head. "What is there to say? She bore me. She raised me. She loved me. She put up with me—and I have always been a man who is not so easy to put up with." He smiled; a sort of somber pride filled his voice. "I wish it were not so—it will cost me time in Purgatory if it does not send me to a warmer place yet. And you may be sure that I pray for her soul as I pray for my father's. May they both have found places in heaven." He crossed himself.

"Yes. May it be so," Gioioso said—more for politeness' sake, Galileo judged, than from any great sincerity. The prelate stroked his beard. "Now tell me, *Signor,* if you would be so kind...did you ever have moments in your childhood when you wished your mother gave you a larger share of her affection?"

"Did I what?" This time, Galileo laughed out loud. "How could I not? I told you, I had two brothers and four sisters. My mother was a busy woman—too busy, sometimes, for me."

"Indeed." Galileo thought his words ordinary and commonplace, but Sigismondo Gioioso seemed to invest them with a special significance. "And your father—did you ever wish he were out of the way so your mother would be able to give you more love, more affection?"

"We banged heads every so often, my father and I," Galileo admitted. "What boy coming to manhood does not bang heads with his father? When you are young, you are sure you already know it all. And when you are a father, you know better, and you are sure your son is a stupid blockhead who will never learn anything. Was it not so with you, your Eminence?"

Cardinal Gioioso's mouth bent—barely—into a thin smile. "Oh, it might have been," he said. "But we were speaking of you. And I was not thinking so much of the time when your beard sprouted. I had in mind your younger days—much younger. Was there not a time when you wished your father would disappear so you could have your mother all to yourself?"

Galileo scratched his cheek as he frowned in thought. "If there ever was, your Eminence, I must confess that I do not recall it."

"Don't worry about that," the cardinal said in reassuring tones. "I have questioned a large number of men about these matters. Very few remember them...at first. If you permit it, we shall have more discussions in times to come."

"If *I* permit it?" Galileo raised a grizzled eyebrow. "I am in the hands of the Holy Inquisition. How can I say no?" He knew what happened to people who resisted the Inquisition and its ministrations. He didn't want anything like that happening to him.

But Gioioso answered, "If we are to go forward, I require cooperation that springs from your own free will. Force and coercion have no place here. I meant it when I said no harm would come to you. You may converse with me or not, as you please."

He sounded sincere. Galileo, like any man who'd lived as long as he had, had met plenty of people who seemed sincere and proved to be anything but. Was this cardinal from beyond the Alps another one? Even if he was, the Inquisition couldn't do anything else to Galileo while the prelate talked with him.

The calculation required no more than a heartbeat. "Of course I am at your service, your Eminence," Galileo said.

"Excellent!" Cardinal Gioioso's smile could be surprisingly warm. "We shall continue, then—at your convenience, of course."

"Of course," Galileo said. He understood full well that *at your convenience,* here as so often, meant *at my convenience.* Life might have grown difficult had he not grasped that. Since he did, it wouldn't—not that way, anyhow.

———

He soon found that the cardinal was an indefatigable questioner. Under such patient, persistent prodding, he dredged up more recollections of his very early life than he'd ever imagined he could. "May I ask you a question for a change, your Eminence?" he said after a while.

"Certainly." Gioioso's manner was placid.

"Why do you want to know so much about the time before I lost my milk teeth?"

"When you look at a building, at how it is made, at how the upper stories rise up, what do you do first?" Gioioso said. "You look at the foundations. From what is below, you can see how what is above has arisen."

"But many different buildings may be raised from the same kind of foundation," Galileo objected.

"True. But when we see a building of such-and-such a type, we may deduce that it should have had this kind of foundation, and could not possibly have been built up from that one," the cardinal said. "Your early dealings with your mother and father helped put you on the course you took to manhood. Had they been different, you would be different today. Or does it seem otherwise to you?"

Galileo wagged a finger at him. "I may have written a dialogue, but you have also read your Plato, your Eminence. And here I think you enjoy playing Socrates yourself."

"If I do, then I suffer from the sin of pride, and I shall have to do penance for it when I make my next confession," Gioioso said. "Any man who dares compare himself to Socrates surely labors under a delusion."

"I think so, too," Galileo said. "Time and again I would notice how much windier than Plato's my characters seemed. But I did not see what else I could do, if I was to put across the ideas I wanted the world to see."

"Since you mention your clever dialogue—and it is very clever indeed, *Signor,* as I have said before—let me ask you something not so firmly rooted in your early years," Sigismondo Gioioso said.

"I am your servant," Galileo said, hope and apprehension warring within him.

"You—you of all people—are no man's servant," Cardinal Gioioso said.

Galileo only shrugged, which was awkward and uncomfortable on the couch. "I am vehemently suspected of heresy," he said. Suspicion of heresy was in itself a crime; vehement suspicion was a higher grade of the same offense. That being so... "I am of course a servant of the Holy Inquisition, and of the holy Catholic Church."

"Every man is, or ought to be, a servant of the Church," Gioioso said. "But the Church is not a man, nor is the Inquisition. The Church is a building put together over centuries, and the Inquisition its fire-watch."

"I cannot quarrel with you, your Eminence, nor would I if I could." Galileo was already in plenty of trouble. He didn't need or want more.

"I quite understand," Gioioso said, which meant...what, exactly? Before Galileo could decide, the cardinal asked, "How is it that you became such a strong supporter of the Copernican hypothesis?"

That was a question Galileo would rather not have heard. It had a number of possible answers, all of them dangerous. Some, though, were more dangerous than others. Galileo chose the safest one he could, the one he'd used all along to defend himself from the charges against him: "In 1616, Cardinal Bellarmine notified me that the Copernican doctrine was contrary to the Bible and could not be defended or held. I accepted that then, and I accept it still."

"Your dialogue gives me cause to wonder at the truth of that," Gioioso said.

"I am sorry that it should," Galileo said, which was true, even if perhaps not altogether in the sense in which he wanted Gioioso to take it. "Nothing in the holy cardinal's injunction ordered me not to discuss the Copernican doctrine hypothetically, which is all I was doing in the book. And I do not claim it is true. In the end, I declare that it is impossible to know whether the Copernican or the Ptolemaic doctrine is true."

"So you do. Yet you show a greater zeal for the former," Cardinal Gioioso said, as he had when they first met.

"I am sorry for that, too," Galileo exclaimed, and, again, he meant it in more than one way.

The cardinal steepled his fingers again. "May we say that you hold a…hypothetical affection for Copernicanism?"

"As much as the Church permits," Galileo said. "Not a feather's weight more."

"All right." He won another of the prelate's small but warm smiles. "Splendid. Very well. Shall we stipulate that for the purposes of discussion?"

"Meaning what, your Eminence?" Galileo asked cautiously. A vulgar phrase occurred to him—he wasn't about to buy a pig in a poke.

Nor did Sigismondo Gioioso seem interested in selling him one. "Meaning that I will take whatever you say in defense of the Copernican heresy to be hypothetical only. I will not claim that you espouse it."

"If you will be gracious enough to put your promise in writing, so that in case of need I may show it to another gentleman from the Holy Inquisition, I am your man," Galileo said. If that didn't show him whether Gioioso was serious, nothing ever would.

The cardinal didn't bat an eye. "Just as you please, *Signor*. Please wait a moment while I get paper and pen." Gioioso was gone no longer than he'd said he would be. "My written Italian, I fear, is not all it might be. Do you mind if the pledge is in Latin?"

"Not at all. Anyone in the civilized world will be able to read it then," Galileo said. After a moment, he politely added, "You speak my language well."

"*Grazie.* I manage, but you give me too much credit." Cardinal Gioioso signed his name with a flourish, then waited for the ink to dry before handing Galileo the paper. "I trust this will prove satisfactory?"

Galileo put on spectacles to read it, as Gioioso had used them to write it. Age had lengthened both men's sight. Grinding good spectacle lenses was a long step toward grinding good spyglass lenses. But that thought slipped from Galileo's mind as he read the churchman's promise. Gioioso might not trust his written Italian, but his Latin was elegant—almost Ciceronian. That surprised Galileo not at all. The astronomer nodded. "Oh, yes. Everything you said it would be. May I keep it?"

"Why else would I have written it? It is your shield—nothing you say here today will be used against you." Cardinal Gioioso leaned forward a little in his chair—he reminded Galileo of a hunting hound taking a scent. The image worried Galileo, but no help for it now. The cardinal said, "Let us begin, then. Why *do* you find yourself so attracted to Copernicanism...in a hypothetical way, naturally?"

"Naturally," Galileo agreed, his voice dry. "Because—in a hypothetical way, again—it does a better job of predicting the phenomena we actually observe in the sky than the Ptolemaic hypothesis does."

"I see," Gioioso said. "And why is this so important to you?"

"Because it gives me a better, a deeper, understanding of the way the universe works." Galileo hesitated, then recast that so even a cleric could not fail to grasp it: "Of the way God's creation works."

"Is this not the sin of pride—presuming to understand how God does what he does?" Gioioso asked.

Galileo muttered to himself. He might have known a priest—and a priest who belonged to the Holy Inquisition, at that—would see things so. He tried again: "The more I learn, the better I can praise and glorify Him."

"So you believe that accurate knowledge is required for God to hear and accept one's prayers?" the cardinal said.

There was a snare! Galileo was canny enough to spot it. Was he canny enough to evade it? Picking his words with great care, he replied, "Why would God have arranged things as He did, and why would He have made men as He did, if He did not expect them to try to learn all they could of His creation?"

"Why? I have no idea why," Sigismondo Gioioso said calmly. "Will you tell me you know *why* God chose the Copernican world system—if He did so choose—and not the Ptolemaic? Will you say He could not as easily have chosen the other one?"

That was a trap, too, but a less dangerous one. "God might have done anything He chose to do. Not even a Protestant heretic would claim otherwise," Galileo said. *So there,* he thought. "I do not know why the evidence seems to me to show He chose the Copernican way of shaping the universe. I only know that it seems to show He did."

"Can you give me some examples of how this seems to be so?" Gioioso asked.

"Well, your Eminence, to begin with, the Copernican hypothesis more accurately predicts the positions of the planets against the starry backdrop of the heavens," Galileo said.

"By how much?" the cardinal enquired.

"Oh, by a very large margin!" Galileo said. "Sometimes by as much as half a degree."

"Which is how much in layman's terms?" Gioioso asked, adding, "I have tried to learn what I could of your art, but I am no astronomer."

How much more than he admitted did he really know? A lot, or Galileo missed his guess. He answered with the truth: "Why, the diameter of the sun, or of the full moon."

"I see." By the way Cardinal Gioioso nodded, Galileo judged he wasn't hearing this for the first time. He asked, "And how much earlier or later does this make the heavenly bodies rise and set than they would have under the old calculations? Half an hour? An hour? More?"

"No, your Eminence," Galileo said. "It is not such a large error as that, or the Ptolemaic world system would never have become part of the doctrine of the Catholic Church to begin with. As I noted in my own copy of the *Dialogue,* the Church endangers itself when it declares heretical a view that may one day be proved true by logic or by physical means."

"Well, how large an error *are* we speaking of, *Signor*? You have yet to tell me," Gioioso said.

"It is a matter of up to two minutes," Galileo replied, again giving information he was pretty sure the other man already had.

If Sigismondo Gioioso did have it, he concealed that most artfully. "Two minutes?" he exclaimed, making the sign of the cross. "By the blessed Virgin Mother of God, is that all?"

"It may not seem like much, your Eminence, but it is an error easily detected by good instruments and good clocks, both of which grow ever easier to come by these days," Galileo said stubbornly.

The cardinal might as well not have heard him. "Two minutes!" Gioioso repeated. "For the sake of two minutes—for the sake of two minutes *at the most,* you said—you and Copernicus propose setting Christendom on its ear?"

"All Copernicus tried to do was find a better way to conceive of the workings of the heavens," Galileo said. "All I tried to do in my *Dialogue* was to give the evidence for and against his views. We never wished to oppose the holy Catholic Church. Rather, the Church has chosen to oppose us."

"When Giordano Bruno chose to cling to Copernicanism despite having every chance to renounce his views, he was burned at the stake," Gioioso said. "Are two minutes—at most two minutes—worth a man's life?"

"I have done my best to make it plain that I do not personally hold to the Copernican world system," Galileo said. "I will make whatever abjurations the Holy Inquisition requires of me. But, even if it is a false hypothesis, Copernicanism is also a useful one."

"Useful in what way?" Gioioso asked.

"In making more exact astronomical calculations," Galileo answered.

"But if, in saving up to two minutes, you cast the Church into disrepute, you throw the whole world into confusion and argument and strife where before everything had seemed certain and clear, if you cast doubt on the Holy Scriptures and on God Himself, is that a useful thing to do?" Seldom had Galileo heard such scorn as that with which Cardinal Gioioso laced the word *useful*.

The astronomer hesitated, however much he didn't care to. Consequences were less easily calculated than planetary motions. At last, he said, "I never intended any such things to happen."

"Eve and Adam also sinned unwittingly," Gioioso pointed out. "Would the world not be a better place had they abstained from doing so?"

"How can I possibly deny that?" Galileo said.

"If you can deny one part of Holy Scripture, why not deny another? Why not deny every line?" Sigismondo Gioioso stood and stretched. His joints creaked—sure enough, he was as old as Galileo. "Perhaps we would do better to continue our conversation tomorrow."

"Perhaps we would," Galileo agreed. Stretching out on the cardinal's couch helped him forget his own painful arthritis. All the same, he'd rarely been so glad to get out of a room as he was to escape that one.

———

"Good morning, *Signor*. A pleasure to see you," Cardinal Gioioso said when Galileo unwillingly returned the next morning. To Galileo's surprise, the cardinal sounded as if he meant it. They might never have clashed verbal swords the day before.

"Good morning, your Eminence." Galileo kissed Gioioso's ring.

Gioioso waved to a table. "By all means, refresh yourself before we begin. Here are wine and bread and olive oil. I am told the oil is quite good. Myself, I like butter more. But butter is easier to keep fresh in Vienna than it is here."

"No doubt." Galileo ate. He drank. What else could he do? It gave him an excuse to wait before reclining on that comfortable but dangerous couch.

So he stretched things as long as he could, and then a little longer. At last, though, Cardinal Gioioso asked, "Shall we begin?"

"I am your servant," Galileo said once more.

Once more, Gioioso denied it: "By no means, not when I am a servant of the Pope and his Holiness is the servant of the servants of Christ."

He waited for Galileo's response, but Galileo made none. The cardinal could phrase things as prettily as he pleased. All the same, Galileo knew which one of them had ordered the other to be here. He knew which of them asked questions, and which had to answer. And he knew what he thought about that.

Or he thought he knew. He couldn't deny that some of the questions Cardinal Gioioso asked were...interesting. As much as Copernicanism did, they made Galileo look at the world from a different perspective.

Something else occurred to the astronomer. When dealing with someone as savvy as Gioioso, it was better to get everything out in the open. "I presume, your Eminence, that the agreement we made yesterday in regard to the Copernican, ah, hypothesis remains in force?" Galileo asked.

"Assolutamente," Gioioso affirmed. In his slow, ponderous Italian, the word sounded especially impressive. He went on, "I will give you another written pledge if you so desire, or amend the earlier one to clarify that it extends throughout our, ah, analysis here."

That willingness to agree might mean he was inherently trustworthy. On the other hand, it might not. In Galileo's present situation, he was not inclined to take chances. Producing the pledge Sigismondo Gioioso had written the day before, he said, "If you would be so kind..."

The cardinal made the change and initialed it without batting an eye. He handed the paper back to Galileo. It was exactly what he had promised. When Galileo nodded, Gioioso picked up the thread where they had left it the day before: "You maintain that there are many reasons for accepting the Copernican world system in place of the Ptolemaic, not one alone."

"Speaking hypothetically, that is what the evidence suggests—yes, your Eminence," Galileo said.

"Of course we are speaking hypothetically!" Cardinal Gioioso exclaimed. "Were we not, would you have that sheet I just gave back to you?"

"By no means," Galileo admitted, as he had to.

"Well, then," Gioioso said, "perhaps you will be good enough to expound upon another. So it is not only refined calculations of planetary positions, then?"

"By no means!" Galileo said again, this time more enthusiastically. "Another very strong argument in favor of the Copernican system is that, when viewed through a spyglass, Venus appears to show phases like those of the moon. She appears now as a crescent, now as if at first or third quarter, now gibbous, depending on her position relative to sun and earth."

"You do not speak of seeing Venus when she is full," Gioioso noted.

"True. I do not, for I have not seen her so," Galileo replied. "Nor has anyone, nor will anyone. By the geometry inherent in the Copernican world system, Venus when she is full lies beyond the sun: the earth, the sun, and Venus then form a straight line. Thus she would be in the sky when the sun is also, and his much greater light would obscure hers."

"Anyone observing her through a spyglass would see the same thing?" Gioioso asked. "Two people observing through different spyglasses would see the same thing as well?"

"So long as they did so at the same time, yes," Galileo said. The questions were reasonable. More than twenty years earlier, when he'd first started examining the heavens through his spyglasses, many people had wondered whether something inherent in the instrument caused it to yield the results it did. How trustworthy could those results be, if they were invisible to the naked eye?

Cardinal Gioioso hit on that very point: "Without the spyglass, no one will see these things?"

"No, your Eminence," Galileo said. "Otherwise, astronomers would have observed them long ago. I will point out, however, that there are a great many spyglasses in Europe these days, in lands both Catholic and Protestant. A large number of people have observed these phenomena."

"Which would not occur under the Ptolemaic world system?" the cardinal asked.

"Just so. The Ptolemaic system is centered on the earth, not the sun. The path Venus necessarily takes in that system forbids these apparitions," Galileo said. "If you give me leave to sketch for you, I can demonstrate why this needs must be so."

"I believe I can visualize the differing paths," Gioioso said. By the way he said it, Galileo saw at once that it was so. No astronomer, Gioioso claimed? Galileo didn't believe that for a moment. The cardinal continued, "These effects you describe are invisible without the spyglass?"

"Not precisely, your Eminence," Galileo said.

"Wait." For the first time, he surprised Sigismondo Gioioso. "A moment ago, you said no one could see them. If someone could, why did nobody notice them before you perfected the instrument?"

That made Galileo smile. He had indeed greatly improved the device. Learning that Dutch spectacle makers had devised spyglasses that would magnify three or four or five times, he'd delved into the theory of optics and improved their results tenfold. He'd had to become a lens-maker himself to bring it off, and he had.

None of which, however, much as it salved Galileo's pride, had much to do with the cardinal's question. "No one could notice it with the eyes in his head," Galileo said. "But, as early as December in the year 1610, my former student, Benedetto Castelli, wrote to me asking if Venus' appearance was as I described to you, and as the Copernican world system predicts. Even if you decline to see the diagrams, I must remind you that, as the Ptolemaic system arranges the heavens, Venus, lying between us and the sun, can be only a crescent if the sun's light illuminates her."

"*Sì, sì,*" Cardinal Gioioso said impatiently. "So Castelli deduced this more than twenty years ago, and from the Copernican hypothesis alone?"

"He did," Galileo answered, and a new kind of pride filled him. "Any capable geometer could do the same, your Eminence. Most cities will have one such man; many will have several. And books, these days, are printed in editions of hundreds, sometimes even thousands. New discoveries spread more quickly than they did in years gone by."

"The man who first devised the printing press was a German like me," Gioioso said morosely. "He has much to answer for—and I do not mean simply the lying Calvinist and Lutheran pamphlets that come out in editions far larger than the ones you mention."

"I fear the world is as it is, your Eminence, not as we wish it were," Galileo answered. "That is why I said yesterday that the Church should not nail itself to doctrines liable to be proved false."

"To nail itself?" Sigismondo Gioioso's voice held an ominous purr, like that of a cat seeing a mouse's tail sticking out from under a pile of clothes.

Even with the pledge about discussing the Copernican hypothesis in hand, Galileo realized, he could go too far. He'd just gone too far, in fact. "Forgive me," he said quickly. "I should have phrased that better."

"Yes. You should have." But Gioioso seemed inclined to accept the apology. Galileo hoped so, anyhow. The cardinal was devilishly hard to read. He sent Galileo a hooded stare. "You were saying...?"

"Only that the Church might sail a safer course if she did not make pronouncements on how the physical world is framed," Galileo answered.

"The Church has been refining its doctrines since our Lord's time," Cardinal Gioioso said, "and has had the aid of the Holy Spirit in so doing. His Holiness the Pope is the direct successor to St. Peter, the rock on whom Jesus Christ founded the Church. Do you deny this?"

"Not at all, your Eminence. How could I possibly?" *How could I possibly, when you would roast me like a leg of veal if I dared?*

"Then how can you deny that its doctrines are correct?" Gioioso demanded.

Sadly, Galileo spread his hands. "It is not I, your Eminence. If the evidence contradicts the doctrine, which is to change?"

Cardinal Gioioso sighed. "The Church never objected when a few astronomers used the Copernican hypothesis to improve their calculations. Who could care about something so small as that? We were always sure a hypothesis was simply a hypothesis. Whether it had anything to do with the real world...well, who could say? Come to that, who cared?"

"I understand this. It is also how I was trained. But the spyglass... The spyglass changes things," Galileo said. "Now we can test the different world systems against the evidence, and see which is stronger."

"Now you can shout from the housetops: 'Ptolemy is wrong! Aristotle is wrong! The holy Catholic Church believed them right, so the Church is wrong as well! And behold! The Book of Joshua says that the sun stood still in the sky. But it is not the sun that moves! No, it is the earth! And so Joshua is wrong as well!' And what is left of the holy Catholic Church after that, *Signor* Galilei? What is left of any religion?"

"As a matter of fact, your Eminence, the Copernican world system can explain the events described in Joshua better than the Ptolemaic system can," Galileo said eagerly. "I have written on this very topic, and I would be delighted to expound on it for you. When properly construed, the Copernican hypothesis is altogether compatible with the words of the Holy Scriptures."

But Sigismondo Gioioso disappointed him by holding up a hand. "Spare me," the prelate said. "Seldom do laymen find their way into deep water faster than when they try to tell clerics what the Bible means."

He was not the first churchman to tell Galileo something along those lines. In a way, the astronomer could see the clerics' point. In another way... When Galileo looked at things another way, rage ripped through him. "Why should I not interfere in your business, your Eminence?" he ground out. "You enjoy interfering in mine enough, by God!"

As soon as the words were out of his mouth, he wished he had them back. Too late, of course. Wishes like that always came too late. He waited apprehensively. Cardinal Gioioso had pledged to let him defend the Copernican world system in a hypothetical way. The cardinal hadn't said a thing about letting him attack the Catholic Church. Maybe, at least, they would strangle him before they burned him, as the Spaniards had done for that savage king in the New World a hundred years before.

But Gioioso merely sat there studying him. Yes, the cardinal was doing just that. Slowly, Galileo realized he himself was as interesting to Gioioso as the Medicean stars going around Jupiter or the convoluted landscape of the moon was to him. "You are angry," Gioioso said, and nothing more.

"If I have disturbed your Eminence's tranquility, I humbly beg pardon." Galileo would eat crow if he had to. If he had to, he would eat raven.

Cardinal Gioioso waved this apology aside. "Explain to me, *Signor,* if you would be so kind, *why* you are angry."

"Why?" Galileo growled. "Can't you see that for yourself?"

"If I could, would I be inquiring of you?" Nothing but tranquility and interest was in Gioioso's voice, not that Galileo could hear. The astronomer might have sounded like that himself, when he first turned his spyglass on the Pleiades and saw a host of tiny stars his unaided eye could not discern. *Perhaps I did sound like that,* Galileo thought, bemused.

And Gioioso sat waiting, patient as a pillar saint. Galileo had to look inside himself to find an answer. "*Because* the Church is meddling in affairs that are not its proper concern," he said at last.

"Does the way the Church is acting in this matter remind you of how your father would behave?" Gioioso asked.

"I had not thought of that before, but it does—it does!" Galileo said. "Stubborn, wrongheaded, always trying to have his own way…"

"I see," Gioioso said, with an air of now-we're-getting-somewhere. "And your reaction to this unpleasant stimulus is…?"

"How could any man help getting angry?" Galileo asked rhetorically.

"But when you do, *Signor,* do you not also show your own stubbornness? Do you not seek to have your own way in every respect?" Unfailingly courteous, the cardinal said nothing about Galileo's being wrongheaded. He didn't have to. Galileo could—and did—supply that for himself.

He did not believe he was wrongheaded—or wrong. But Gioioso's questions made him examine himself in a way he never had before. "I am a proud man, your Eminence, and I think I have earned my pride," he said. "When I am pushed, what can I do but push back?"

"You might wonder *why* you are being pushed," Cardinal Gioioso said. "You might wonder whether you did not push first, maybe without even noticing, and so unwittingly gave offense. Or you might wonder if, having been pushed in this way when you were young, you now believe yourself pushed even when no one intended to push you, perhaps even when no one pushed you at all?"

"Do you say I imagine that I am being pushed?" Galileo demanded—pushily.

"I said no such thing," Gioioso replied. "You did."

"Yes, I did," Galileo agreed. "I was pushed to Rome. I was pushed to the palace of the Inquisition. I was pushed to these sessions with you. I was pushed onto your *couch,* your Eminence!"

"Say rather, *Signor,* that you pushed yourself here by your deeds and writings," Sigismondo Gioioso said. "For is not the holy Catholic Church the spiritual father of all believers? And do you not push against it because your own father pushed against you in days gone by?"

"He did not want to let me do with my life as I would, as I must." All these years later, the memory still stung. He'd denied that before to

Gioioso, but he found that with further reflection he'd changed his mind about it. And he added, "Nor does the Church today."

"Could it not be that you are throwing your views of your father forward onto the Church?" the cardinal said.

"Throwing my views forward?" Galileo frowned. "Please excuse me, your Eminence, but I fail to follow you."

"My Italian must be imperfect. I know what I wish to say, but how to say it…?" Sigismondo Gioioso thought for a moment, then smiled and held up a forefinger, exactly as one of Galileo's countrymen might have done. "I have it! I wanted to suggest that you might be *projecting* your views."

"Ah. Now I understand! *Grazie.*" It was Galileo's turn to do some more thinking. As he did it, he eyed Gioioso with respect no less real for being reluctant. "There may indeed be some truth in this, and you are a most astute man"—*a dangerously astute man*, he thought—"for pointing it out."

"This is the purpose of the kind of analysis I have devised: to help a man see that which lies within himself but which he would not find without someone to help show him the way to it," Cardinal Gioioso replied.

"Well, your Eminence, you have considerable skill in this art, as you must know without needing me to tell you." Galileo paused again. Then he raised his forefinger, too, but not in the same way as the churchman had. "When I said there was some truth in your remarks, I meant there was only some. As I've told you again and again, it is not my projection that the Holy Inquisition summoned me—a sick old man—from Florence to Rome, imprisoned me, and is now interrogating me. I am not imagining these things, and they are not happening because I want them to. So do I not possess veritable reasons, altogether apart from anything that may have passed between my father and me, for being unhappy with the way the Church has treated me?"

Gioioso considered. Their conversations seemed filled with hesitations on both sides. "Did you not know, when you published the *Dialogue Concerning the Two Chief World Systems*, that it would lead to this?"

"I knew there would be fireworks," Galileo admitted. He couldn't help smiling; he'd hoped for, craved, fireworks. But he went on, "I didn't think it would come to *this*. After all, I had the Church's *imprimatur*, allowing the work to be printed, and, by so doing, acknowledging it contained nothing contrary to doctrine or to the Scriptures."

"Yes. You did." Gioioso let the words hang in the air. Galileo wished he hadn't thought of hanging. Better than burning, but still... The cardinal continued, "As I have told *you*, no one would have objected to your quietly using Copernican calculations to reclaim your precious two minutes of rising and setting. Quietly, I say. But when you parade through the center of town with horns and lutes and viols and drums, all played loud as may be, you must expect the magistrates to notice. I have to wonder whether, at some level below that of conscious thought, you did not *want* them to notice."

"How can one want something without being conscious of wanting it?" Galileo said. "If one is not conscious, one is not alive."

"So it might seem at first, but the mind has depth, just as the heavens do," Gioioso answered. "What man does not wish to be loved, to be admired, to be noticed? Most of the time, he is not aware of those desires. He does not go around constantly thinking *I must be loved, I must be admired, I must be noticed!* By no means! But, whether he knows of them or not, these urges push him on regardless. Or do you believe differently? You may, and freely—the Church has not pronounced on these opinions of mine."

"The Church would have done better not to pronounce on matters astronomical. Much better, since those matters have nothing to do with the human spirit, while your interesting ideas do." Galileo didn't want to show how interesting he found Gioioso's notions. Depth in the mind...

The idea would have been better with some mathematics behind it, but was interesting enough and to spare even without. *Had* he wanted to be noticed so badly that he prodded the Church into noticing him too much? Maybe he had. All the same, though... "You cannot make true heavenly phenomena disappear, you know."

"Maybe the phenomena are true. Which hypothesis best explains them..." Gioioso's shrug was less expressive than an Italian's would have been, but it got his meaning across. "And when you measure that against the disservice you do the Church and the world by screeching about what you say they mean—"

"Screeching?" That affronted Galileo. "The *Dialogue* only presents the facts and the evidence. It does not even reach any sure conclusion."

"Not at the end, but your belief is plain all through it," Gioioso said.

"Then how did it gain the *imprimatur,* your Eminence?"

"An interesting question. Probably because the churchmen who gave it were...naïve." Sigismondo Gioioso might have said something else, something stronger, but he refrained. "It has plenty in it to make people no longer credit the holy Catholic Church's teachings."

"For a long time," Galileo said slowly, "all the people who believed in the Ptolemaic world system would laugh at the ones who thought Copernicus was right. Until I started making good spyglasses, there wasn't much to choose from between the two systems. Calculations a little more precise...but so what? After that, though... People should have seen."

"They should have, but they didn't?" Gioioso suggested, his voice quiet and gentle.

"They didn't." Galileo, by contrast, sounded sad. "I published the *Sidereus Nuncius,* with word of the mountains and valleys of the moon, with word of all the stars the spyglass showed that the eye could not, and with word of the Medicean stars circling Jupiter as the planets circle—as Copernicus *says* the planets circle—the sun. And what did I get? I got a miserable little manikin named Martin Horky, who wrote a tract that said I was a crackpot, like the fools who claim they can square the circle or double the cube or make the Philosopher's Stone. *That* is what I got."

"And you wanted to pay this Horky back with the *Dialogue*? Sigismondo Gioioso asked. "You wanted to pay back all the doubters?"

"All the scoffers," Galileo said.

"But do you not see how you wound the Church when you do this?" the cardinal asked. "Do you not see how you make people doubt not only the Ptolemaic world system but all the Church's teachings? Do you not see how destructive that is? And why have you done it? To pay back the scoffers—and, could it not be, to pay back your father with them."

"To see what lies behind the everyday is not for ordinary souls," Galileo said. "So your worries, your Eminence, seem to me misplaced."

"They are not, and the reason they are not is what you said at first," Gioioso said. "Most souls *cannot* see what lies behind the everyday—not by themselves. That is why the holy Catholic Church does not mind astronomers using the Copernican hypothesis, so long as they are discreet about it. But when you wrote your book, *Signor*...and in Italian this time, not even in scholars' Latin! And it is being translated into other vulgar tongues. That part of you below conscious thought, the part that wanted to be noticed, got more than it bargained for this time. Do you see?"

"Well, perhaps I do," Galileo said, and it was much less of a lie than it would have been before he started talking with Cardinal Gioioso. "You have given me a great many fascinating things to think about: no doubt of that. And may I beg your indulgence to give me leave to think about them till tomorrow? As my years grow heavier, I tire ever more easily."

Everyone tired. The Inquisition used that as a weapon. Torture included being deprived of sleep, so a man grew as if drunk and hardly knew what he was saying. It included water in the face till the victim feared drowning. It included all kinds of other ingenious torments that left not a mark on the body, no matter what they did to the spirit.

But Gioioso didn't say a word about any of that. All he said was, "Of course, *Signor*. Please forgive me for overtaxing you in my zeal. Let us resume in the morning." But whether he mentioned them or not, he held those weapons in his arsenal, and both he and Galileo knew it.

———

"Buon giorno, Signor," the cardinal said when Galileo returned to his quarters the next day. "I hope you slept well. Are you refreshed?"

"I *am* refreshed, your Eminence, even if I slept less than I might have," Galileo replied. "I spent considerable time after leaving your honored presence contemplating the many fascinating notions you propounded concerning the mind and its workings."

Gioioso graciously inclined his head. "No man could hope for higher praise. And what conclusions did you reach, if any?" He waved toward the couch. "Why not make yourself comfortable before you tell me?"

"Thank you." Galileo stretched out. "This is an agreeable way to converse, sure enough… Conclusions? No, not really. But sometimes new questions are as interesting, and as important, as answers."

A servant came in with wine and bread and anchovies and olives and other snacks. After the man withdrew, Gioioso remarked, "You are devoted to the new."

"No, your Eminence. Say rather that I am devoted to the true, wherever I find it."

"We mentioned Pontius Pilate earlier in our discussions. Pilate was not altogether a fool when he asked what truth was and then washed his hands," Gioioso replied. "Often, deciding what is true means no more than deciding on the proper point of view, and on how much weight to give this, that, or the other factor, eh?"

"Often, but not always," Galileo said. "Mathematics is true regardless."

"As are the teachings and doctrines of the Church—yes," Gioioso said.

"Of course, your Eminence." Galileo did believe that. He always had. But he would have agreed even if he hadn't. He was in the worst possible position to disagree.

Thoughtfully, but also casually, almost as if the answer didn't matter, the cardinal asked, "Could God make it so the truths of mathematics were different?"

Denying God's omnipotence would be deadly dangerous here, in the most literal sense of the words. But, again, Galileo didn't want to. "I believe He could, your Eminence. To us mere mortals, that different truth would seem as genuine, as perfect, as the actual dispensation does now." He could have said that the Copernican world system would one day replace the Ptolemaic in just that way. He could have, but he didn't. He could tell when not saying something seemed the best idea. Sometimes he could, anyhow. The *Dialogue*... No, he hadn't been able to resist the *Dialogue*.

If Sigismondo Gioioso had expected him to risk a heretical statement or an outright blasphemy, the prelate gave no sign. He ate a couple of olives, then said, "Have you given me all your reasons for—hypothetically—preferring the Copernican world system?"

"I have not." With Gioioso's pledge in hand, Galileo was on safe ground here—or ground as safe as any in quicksand-laden Rome. "Yesterday, in fact, I briefly alluded to that which may be the most important: the motion of the four Medicean stars around Jupiter."

"Yes, you did mention them yesterday," Gioioso said. "Will you do me the honor of explaining why you find them so significant?"

"Certainly," Galileo said. "First, the Ptolemaic world system is founded on the view that there can be only one center of motion—that is, the earth. By moving around Jupiter, the Medicean stars contradict this."

"But they cannot be seen without your spyglass," Gioioso said.

"That does not mean they are not there," Galileo replied. "Clerics and laymen have observed them for twenty years now, and unanimously attest that they do exist. And we must presume they existed for all the ages before the spyglass first rendered them visible. Surely God would not have popped them into place the day before I first turned the instrument toward Jupiter."

"Had He so desired, He could have," Cardinal Gioioso said. When Galileo failed to rise to that, the prelate added, "I must admit, it seems unlikely. You said that was your first reason. This means you have more?"

"Sì. Here you have these stars, performing their evolutions in periods ranging from forty-two hours to sixteen days, all on the sphere of Jupiter, which in the Ptolemaic world system takes twelve years to revolve around the earth. And beyond that is the sphere of Saturn, which takes thirty years. And beyond that is the sphere of the fixed stars. And it revolves in what? Only a day! Where is the logic in that? Whereas if the earth rotates, as the Copernican world system postulates—"

"You falsify Holy Scripture," Cardinal Gioioso broke in.

"Not necessarily, as I have tried to show in my writings on the Book of Joshua," Galileo said.

"Those writings have been weighed in the balance and found wanting," Sigismondo Gioioso said. "You are an admirable astronomer, but you make a less than admirable theologian. I have spoken of this before."

"Yes, your Eminence," Galileo said resignedly. "As *I* have said before, I might be less inclined to meddle in theology if the Church were less inclined to meddle in astronomy."

"But astronomy and its truths connect to the Scriptures," Gioioso said. "How can the holy Catholic Church not concern itself with the heavens as well as the earth?"

"If the Church does, then its learned theologians risk being called less than admirable astronomers," Galileo said.

"How does this follow?" Gioioso asked.

"How?" Galileo yelped. "Surely it must be obvious—"

"No." The cardinal held up a hand. "What is *obvious, Signor,* is that the world stands still and the heavens revolve around it. Otherwise this would not have been believed by everyone since the days of the Old Testament. It would not have been set down in writing in the unerring Holy Scriptures. What your spyglass shows may be there, but it is not *obvious.*"

"It is true," Galileo maintained.

"In a sense, perhaps," Gioioso said. "But it is also disruptive of good order all over Europe. Is that not true as well?"

"In a sense, perhaps," Galileo echoed slyly.

He won a small smile from Gioioso. "So the question is, does your loud, aggressive espousal of the truths your spyglass has shown about Venus and the Medicean stars—places to which we can never hope to go, even in dreams—justify the chaos you unleash on this world? Why do you imagine that these magnified images are more important than wars and uprisings and rebellions against longstanding authority?"

"I intend no such thing, your Eminence," Galileo protested.

"Nor do I claim you intend it," the cardinal said. "If I did, the matter would be far more serious. An evil will, a malicious will…" He shook his head. "But I claim no such thing. Neither does any other cleric, to my knowledge. Still, do you not see that the result of an unintended act can be as dreadful as that which springs from an intended one?"

"What am I do do, then? I truly believed I was but speaking hypothetically when I wrote the *Dialogue,* as the way I ended it shows." That was Galileo's story, and he was sticking to it. If he'd let what he actually believed show through to excess as he wrote…well, how surprising was it?

Sigismondo Gioioso's left eyebrow couldn't have risen more than an eighth of an inch. That was all he needed to show he didn't believe a word of it. Had Galileo entered the priesthood, were he now interrogating some enthusiastic Copernican, he wouldn't have believed a word of it, either. Perspective *did* have something to do with deciding what truth was—at least some truths. Gioioso hid all sorts of interesting notions under his crimson cassock.

He didn't come right out and call Galileo a liar, as some of the other inquisitors had done. Instead, he said, "And so, in scandalizing your father, you aim not merely to turn the world upside down but to set it spinning as well?"

"Imagining that it does spin does the best job of explaining the phenomena we observe," Galileo said.

"The phenomena you observe with a fancy spyglass." Cardinal Gioioso's snort was a distillation of scorn. "You say many people have seen these things. How many is *many*? Hundreds? A few thousand at most?"

"Something on that order, yes," Galileo agreed. "For matters of this import, that is a great many."

"It could be. But what is it when set against the number of souls in Christendom?" Gioioso asked. "How many millions dwell in Italy? In Germany? In France? In Spain? In Portugal? In their new lands beyond the sea? In Poland, out of which your precious Copernicus came? Against all those souls, these hundreds have not even the weight of a mustard seed. Is this so, or is it not?"

"It is, your Eminence. But—"

"No, *Signor*. But me no buts here. When the farmer goes home after a day in the fields, what does he see? When the miller leaves off grinding grain at day's end, what does he see? When the monk finishes his evening prayer, what does he see? The sun going down. Not the earth spinning, but the sun setting. He sees no hills and valleys on the moon, no phases on Venus, no new stars attending Jupiter. He sees what the Bible says he sees, what the God-inspired men who wrote the Bible saw, what our Lord saw during the Incarnation, and what Ptolemy saw not long after. Is *this* so, or is it not?"

"They saw incompletely," Galileo said. "They saw inaccurately. They saw, if you will, through a glass, darkly."

"You are the one seeing darkly through your glass, *Signor,*" Gioioso answered. "For you do not see the chaos and confusion you cause here on earth with your phases of Venus and your Jovian stars. Truly I wonder if it is not Satan's work associating these marvels with the planets named for two of the most licentious pagan gods."

"Sometimes a planet is only a planet, your Eminence!" Galileo exclaimed.

"You think so, do you?" But a twinkle in Cardinal Gioioso's gray eyes betrayed him. "Well, possibly not, not about that. Nevertheless, though, I am altogether in earnest when I say you forget about this earth when you keep your eyes ever to the heavens. For what is the effect when your hundreds start shouting about what their spyglasses show?"

"They spread the truth?" the astronomer suggested.

"What they spread is doubt," Sigismondo Gioioso said in a voice as hard and cold as stone. "And doubt corrodes faith as surely as salt water corrodes iron. The farmer, the miller, the monk—they hear of these marvels they cannot see. They hear these men who imagine themselves to be clever defaming the Scriptures and the holy Catholic Church. So many people, sadly, are like magpies, like jackdaws: they imitate everything they see, everything they hear. And faith, and faith's community, and peace itself, are torn to bits. Is *this* so, or is it not?"

"It…could be," Galileo said. "But you cannot blame me for the rise of Protestantism, which began before I was born, nor for the war now raging in Germany."

"The Protestants sowed the seed of disbelief in the mother Church's authority," Gioioso said. "They have yet to reap the thorny harvest, for disbelief, once sown, will grow and eat them up, too. You mark my words, *Signor*—that day will come. I do not blame you for Luther or Calvin, no, nor for the accursed German war, which seems to go on forever. Still, is it better to spread more disorder through a world that already has too much, or to work toward restoring peace and unity of purpose?"

"Surely working for peace is better," Galileo said. The cardinal's questions took the discussion to a level he had never considered when he grinned and cackled as his pen made Salviati flay Simplicio—made Copernicanism flay Ptolemy's outmoded views. That astronomy could concern the ordinary world as well as the rarefied atmosphere of the heavens and of scholarship hadn't crossed his mind…till now.

Gioioso found one more mild-sounding question: "Will you say now from your heart that you were working toward peace and unity when you composed the *Dialogue Concerning the Two Chief World Systems?*"

"Your Eminence, looking into my heart, I find I cannot say that and mean it," Galileo answered. Not for the first time, he wondered if the prelate from Vienna was some sort of he-witch. Gioioso certainly had a knack for making anyone he talked to feel as if his head were as transparent as glass.

"Are you sure of what you tell me?" Sigismondo Gioioso asked.

"Before God, I am. That I am surprises me, but it is so. You have done what I would have thought to be impossible: you have made me look at myself, look within myself, in a whole new way," Galileo said.

"That is the goal of analysis of this kind, *Signor.*" Was the smallest hint of smugness in Gioioso's voice? Did he himself exhibit once more, if only for a moment, the sin of pride? If he did, Galileo didn't call him on it.

———

Proud or not, Cardinal Gioioso was not the man who pronounced sentence on Galileo. Cardinal Guido Bentivoglio, with the title of Santa Maria del Popolo, read out the Inquisition's decree on the day after the summer solstice.

Galileo listened to the words wash over him. He was convicted of vehement suspicion of heresy. He had held and promoted a false belief—that the sun, not the earth, was at the center of things and that the earth, not the sun, moved. The *Dialogue* was to be prohibited. He was sentenced to formal imprisonment at the Inquisition's pleasure, and would be required to recite penitential hymns weekly for the next three years. And he had to abjure all his heretical beliefs, there in public before Cardinal Bentivoglio and his inquisitorial colleagues.

He had to make the abjuration on his knees, which pained him physically as well as spiritually. Still, he said what they required of him, reading from a statement he'd drafted in advance. When he looked up from the words, he tried to look at Cardinal Gioioso rather than any of the others. He would have abjured whether he'd spoken with Gioioso or not. Whether he would have abjured so sincerely and with such authentic faith, as the Inquisition's decree required of him, might have been a different story.

At last, it was done. He struggled back to his feet, which also hurt. Some of the inquisitors came forward to congratulate him. He could have done without that. Gioioso, who had helped shape his thoughts, had the sense to leave him alone with them.

"But it does move," Galileo muttered under his breath. It was one last protest, which he answered with the insight he'd gained from the Viennese cardinal: "But so what?"

COPYRIGHT
INFORMATION